ICARUS

Also by Roger Levy:

Reckless Sleep
Dark Heavens

ICARUS

Roger Levy

GOLLANCZ

LONDON

First published in Great Britain in 2006 by
Gollancz
An imprint of the Orion Publishing Group
Orion House, 5 Upper St Martin's Lane,
London WC2H 9EA

A CIP catalogue record for this book is
available from the British Library

ISBN 0 57507 859 6 (cased)
ISBN 9 780 57507 859 8 (cased)
ISBN 0 57507 860 X (trade paperback)
ISBN 9 780 57507 860 4 (trade paperback)

1 3 5 7 9 10 8 6 4 2

Typeset by Deltatype Ltd,
Birkenhead, Merseyside

Printed in Great Britain by
Clays Ltd, St Ives plc

The Orion Publishing Group's policy is to use papers that
are natural, renewable and recyclable products and made
from wood grown in sustainable forests. The logging and
manufacturing processes are expected to conform to the
environmental regulations of the country of origin.

www.orionbooks.co.uk

For Tina, Alex and Georgia

HAVEN

'Here we are,' Quill said, for something to say. Scheck glanced across at him and raised his eyebrows. The two men from Fact didn't react much. The taller factotem – Quill thought he'd said his name was Java – let a sour fizz of air through his lips.

'Here we are indeed,' the other one, Rheo, said cheerily. He rubbed his hands together and then clapped them hard. The noise was effortlessly swallowed by the geometrically puckered walls of the monitoring chamber. A few of the destruct team looked briefly away from their screens, one of them blinking as if unpleasantly woken.

'You ever get claustrophobic in here?' Scheck clapped a hand down hard on the shoulder of one of the team. The man didn't even look up at him, his eyes never leaving the arc of screens with their ticking lines and soothing gel colours. Scheck looked around the chamber and eyed Rheo and Java. 'You?'

Rheo didn't respond at all, but Java grinned widely. 'Don't fret it. We're screened for all that. We're neck-deep in tests. Just like you two.'

'Just like us, huh?' Scheck glanced at Quill, who gave him back a quick frown, but Scheck ignored it, going on to Java, 'You trust the screenings? Really?' He ran his eyes from Java's head to his boots, and said, 'And you're a bit tall, aren't you? Anyone mention that to you? They screened you for this, maybe, but did they measure you for the coredors?'

'Not just the coredors,' Java said, and then stopped at a sharp look from his partner.

'Leave him be, Scheck,' Tanner said uncomfortably. 'Let's go down.'

Quill flexed his fists and closed his eyes, wishing himself in rock now. He thought how typical it was of Tanner to try and smooth Scheck's abrasiveness. Tanner, the between-man, their hinge. He wondered what Fact was doing, sending men to survey Survey. But no one on Haven questioned Fact. To ask was to imply distrust.

One of the destruct team glanced fractionally at Tanner, then

1

twitched a finger and one of the puckered walls gently slid up, as if floating, and came to rest at head height.

'Don't make any unnecessary movements, will you?' Scheck said, moving towards the revealed darkness. They went through the far door, leaving the monitoring chamber in single file, Scheck first, as he always liked to be, then Quill and Tanner, and finally Java and Rheo. The door closed at their rear, and dim amber lighting came up around them.

The bolt chamber was circular and huge, with a single small opening in the far wall. The ceiling, though, barely cleared their scalps.

'Hear it?' Scheck said, and stopped, making everyone else halt. 'You two still not claustrophobic?' He brushed his hand across the ceiling, his elbows not extending beyond a box angle. Java was stooped already and looking awkward. Scheck whispered, 'Wait . . . there. Hear that?'

The hiss was hardly perceptible. Quill always wondered whether he was imagining it.

'That's the bolt readying.' Scheck stamped a boot on the solid metal plate of the floor. 'You're standing on the head of the bolt. Look up. See that? That gleam? That shine's the bolt's action. Every time, soon as we pass—' He clapped his hands, the sound pounding like thunder, holding them still, fists in their ears. 'Wham!'

Hearing the factotems grunt in the eventual hollowed silence, Quill remembered the first time he'd stood in the metal slot and been told what Scheck now was telling the men from Fact.

'Look at your feet. What you're standing on is the last line of safety for the monitoring team back in that room. The bolt weighs fifty thousand kigs, and it's timed from the door closing on us. Rams up home into this slot—' Scheck thumped the ceiling again, '—in a fingerclick. Hell of a bang. They say it's so quick you actually hear it as your boots kick through your brain.'

'Yeah?' Rheo said.

Quill thought, oddly, that Rheo's so-what wasn't just make-up, that Rheo actually wasn't impressed. But maybe Quill had been overimpressed by Scheck all those years back, his first time through the door.

Scheck hadn't noticed Rheo's attitude, so perhaps Quill was just oversensitive. They had no imagination in Fact, anyway. It was trained out of them, everyone knew.

'That's right,' Scheck said. 'Bolthead's got a fifty em span. That door's fifty em away.' He turned on the balls of his feet, then pointed up and ahead at the far end of the slot, dimly lit by fluorescents. 'Oh, and they're running an exercise today, did anyone tell you?' Scheck tapped the glass on his chrono and grinned. 'Ready, now? You've got eight seconds.'

He half-crouched and started to run across the chamber, Quill keeping up with him easily, Tanner hard behind him. Quill could hear Java and Rheo stumbling and head-bumping as they came, not used to a low run. Making ground, Quill was thinking, Why do this, Scheck?

When they were past the metal and onto rock, filing one by one into the shoulderwide coredor beyond the bolt chamber, Scheck kept going, running and running, Quill and Tanner smoothly with him. Only when one of the factotems tripped face down behind them, swearing, did Scheck slow and stop, and hug his knees to laugh.

'Did I say eight seconds? My mistake. I meant thirty.'

Whatever anyone might have said was drowned by the deafening sound of the bolt. Rheo and Java cradled their heads as the slug of air drove past them. Scheck and Tanner and Quill had already dropped flat to let it pass. As the bolt locked down, the wind roared down from uptop through the long, baffled runoff at the bolt's heel, and then it kept coming, seething and groaning at their ears.

No one said anything else as they walked in the wind down the tiny coredor with its calculated undulations, its baffles and curves, to the final descent shaft.

'We go down one at a time,' Tanner told Rheo and Java, apologetically. Quill wasn't sure if he was excusing Scheck or this indignity. 'This isn't just a drop-shaft. It's part of the escape valve. If Scheck and Quill blow magma or anything during the survey, the idea is, it finds its way up here and sidetracks, takes an easy route uptop.' He pointed to the shaft's roof. 'It's weakened up there, packed with loose rubble. It might do enough to divert the flow. This is the first line. There's another one a kil back, and then there's the runoff at the bolt. And then of course there's the destruct team.'

Scheck stepped into the shaft, twisting awkwardly to face the rest of them. His arms were above his head, wrists crossed. He looked at the factotems and said, 'What I was saying about claustrophobia? It wasn't about back there, and it isn't about this, either,' and dropped away, leaving the small echo of a laugh in the shaft. It took a minute for the line to stop humming and two more for the platform to return. Rheo shouldered past Quill with difficulty and went next, and then Java.

'Why does he do it?' asked Tanner, as the platform came up. 'Scheck.'

'Ask him,' Quill said. 'Why's Fact here? They tell you?'

'Monitoring procedures. Routine.' And then Tanner gave a shrug, and Quill had a feeling about the gesture, rather like Rheo's so-what, standing on the bolt.

Tanner went down next, hunching quickly into the shaft and dropping away.

Going down, watching the rock slide past, smoothed, uncoloured, turned to grey glass by speed and the shivering of his eyeballs, Quill thought, Something isn't right here.

At the bottom of the shaft, he began to elbow his way through the crawl tube to the go station. The air was thin in the tube, and stank of sweat and oil. Even Quill sometimes felt claustrophobic in the crawl tube, as his lungs opened to pull in every last scrap of oxygen. He imagined his chest swelling so much that it would jam him in the tube as it fought for breath.

At go, Scheck was already in their coffin, system-checking, and Tanner was sitting wired in his slot. Lensed as he was, it was impossible to tell whether he was staring at the monitors or they were staring at him. Quill wondered what it was like for him once the coffin had slid away, left here alone between it and destruct.

At least Quill and Scheck had each other. There was no one else in the support room with Tanner. He was absolutely alone. Once Scheck and Quill's coffin was in rock, there was no one even close to Tanner. No one down the crawl tube, no one in the drop-shaft, no one at all this side of the bolt that shut off the destruct station that was the true, safe border of Haven. Uptop, where the winds and storms raged, was a border beyond exploration. On Haven, there was only down.

Quill usually tried not to think of the destruct team, whose sole purpose, nearly a kilometre above and over two kilometres east of the go station where Tanner sat, was to make a decision in less than two seconds to collapse the intervening shafts and coredors and gorge them irretrievably with rock.

The go station was already beyond the edge of the known, and it was Quill and Scheck's dive point. This was where Quill came alive, and Scheck too.

Though today there were also the men from Fact.

'Where are they?' Quill asked Tanner.

'They said they wanted to look at the other coffins,' Tanner said. 'Checking the new one in the dock.'

'They get to see it before we do, huh?' Quill glanced at the door through to the hangar where the backup coffins were kept. No one from Survey had seen the new one yet, which was crazy, as only Survey would be using it. It had been over a year in construction, everything broken down small enough to bring here for assembly and dock-testing by Fact-supervised engineers.

'They locked the door behind them,' Tanner said absently, without looking away from his screens. 'Scheck already tried.'

Quill spread his shoulders and made the last full stretches of his arms

4

and legs that he'd be able to do for three weeks, then he inched into the coffin and sat at his console to start his own system checks, and forgot about the factotems.

'You clear in there, Quill?'

'Yeah, Tanner. Set.'

'Scheck? You clear?' Tanner waited. 'Scheck? You hear me?'

Quill looked across at Scheck, who was running his comms frequency tests. He wasn't too involved in it all to answer Tanner, Quill knew; he just wasn't going to. Tanner knew that, which was why he kept it up.

'I said, you clear?'

'We're clear,' Quill said, at the fourth time.

'I asked you already. I'm asking him.'

'Scheck,' Quill said. 'You want to go or not?'

'Yeah.'

'Okay, Tanner? He just said he's clear. You heard him.'

'He wasn't talking to me.'

Quill gave up. He ducked his head below the forward bulkhead and crawled into the overhead of the small cylinder and then pulled in his elbows to roll into his bunk, pulling up his knees to accommodate himself. Not that he was tall, but any height was too tall in a coffin. He could hear muttering – Tanner still not appeased – and then a sigh and a few unintelligible words from Scheck.

Then Scheck's feet appeared as he swung himself round and rolled into his own bunk across the tiny aisle from Quill, his head to Quill's feet.

'We're go,' Scheck said. Then, 'Quill?'

'Yes?'

'Wasn't it my turn, feet to stern, this trip?'

'No. Anyway, the pan doesn't stink as bad as your feet. You haven't got it so terrible.'

'Is that right?' Scheck pulled up his knees until they touched the curve of the roof, and wriggled his cotton-sleeved feet at Quill.

'Yes. Oath's sake, Scheck, take them away.'

'In which case let's swap and you can have the pan as a freshener for my feet. Perfect solution.'

'You know what, Scheck?'

'What?'

Quill contorted his head until he got a foreshortened view of Scheck's face, Scheck looking back at him the same way and grinning. 'I wouldn't be partnering anyone else.'

'Nor me. Set?'

'Set.'

'Then say goodbye to the world.'

'Goodbye world.'

Quill took a last glance at Tanner through the open hatch. As it closed, he saw Tanner turn his head sharply and make some gesture, but not towards the coffin. There was an unfathomable expression on his face as he turned.

The coffin hatch closed, bolted and sealed itself. Quill belched along with Scheck as the coffin air engaged. Then the motors kicked in, and the dampers with them.

And now, muffled silence and a disorientating, apparent stillness. Quill felt his nausea come on and waited for it to pass.

'Okay if I sit?'

'Fine by me,' Quill said. Scheck was usually desperate to get going, and then instantly restless in the coffin. Quill knew he'd never fully understand his partner, but he supposed he didn't understand himself too deeply either.

Scheck had inched himself up the tube and swung the seatbar out from beneath the bunk, and now he was sitting hunched over the tiny screen console beside Quill's head.

'Call me when,' Quill said, and slipped his shades on and went into headspace. He made himself a complex dream in which the coffin was not inching through rock, grinding forward, funnelling and packing vitrified grit into its wake, but was floating almost motionless in a clear pool under a clear sky. The coffin was one of the canoes you'd rent by the hour to paddle along the high-roofed stretches of the jade river, over in Red where he'd lived as a child. The stars were zeolites. A silver moon was in holo above, swollen but not yet full, and there was the sound of birds.

And then a bell, a gentle echoing bell far away in the distance, so faint that when he first heard it he realised he'd been conscious of it for some time already. He came out of the headspace and rolled sideways.

'We're just about there,' Scheck told him. He angled the screen for Quill to see. 'First station point.'

Quill revolved his shoulders and rubbed feeling into the whitening tips of his fingers. Raynaud's syndrome. His peripheral circulation was getting worse. It was a side-effect of spending too much time wired. Maybe the coffin as well, the vibration of its movement in spite of the damping. And maybe the low-frequency interstation comms. And genes, and all the rest of it. He flexed his fingers and turned his hands over.

'You okay?'

The coffin stopped moving. Quill sensed it more than he physically felt it. The deceleration from a few centimetres a second to dead still was not great, but Quill was tuned to it.

'Fine,' Quill said. 'You want me to take the probe out yet?'

'There's never a time like now.' Scheck reached forward into the delivery channel and took out the probe, holding it in the palm of his hand as though it might break if he shook it. It was better than diamond-hard, a coffin in miniature except that it was stuffed full of comms and sensors and could grind through rock at ten times the speed of its parent. Scheck patted it, and Quill felt the touch almost physically on his own skin, even though he wasn't wired yet. It was an odd, tender gesture from Scheck that made him more inscrutable than ever.

Scheck replaced the probe in its delivery tube and locked it away. It hummed and set off, embedding itself automatically forward of the tube and depositing a tiny wake of smoking powder in the rocklock cavity. Tanner waited for it to cool, then opened the lock and scooped some of the dust into his hand. He and Quill looked at it. It was a ritual between them, examining the first spoor at the first station.

This was fine, grey, flecked with brown. Scheck spread it over his palm with a finger. Neither of them said anything.

The console chirped. Scheck poured the dust delicately into a bag and sealed it, then hit the comms. 'Yes?'

'Scheck? You there?'

'No, Tanner, I'm here.'

'Don't be funny, Scheck. You hear me clear?'

'Sadly, I do.'

'Yes or no, Scheck, that's all I need.'

'I know what you need, Tanner.'

'Start your arcs. Let me speak to Quill. I—'

'Quill's getting wired. What is this, a social call? You want to ask him back for a visky?'

Scheck looked at Quill, grinning. 'Tanner's gone. I think you insulted him.'

'You should stop needling him. Every time, Scheck, soon as we go, you start on him.' Quill wondered whether Tanner had sounded odd, more tense than usual, but he didn't say anything to Scheck.

'It keeps him awake,' Scheck said. 'Sitting back there at go, you can get crazy. What he does, it's the end of the line. Like holding the rope in case we fall. It's a sleep job unless he has to actually do it. He knows we won't ever need him, but he has to dream it might happen, and if it does and he's not sharp, he never gets to have the last word. He never gets to hear me say, "Thanks, Tanner, you saved my life," and never has the chance to say back, "Well, the pleasure was all yours, Scheck." That's what keeps him awake for us.'

'Are you sure about that? He could just cut us off one day, wander back to the world and tell them we didn't make it. Maybe that'd be enough of a last word for him.'

'No,' Scheck said. 'He's too crazy for that.'

'Crazier than you?'

'Hell, yes. We hit fire or flood, and die, it's been our mistake. If we spike something big enough to spit back—' Scheck shrugged, momentarily serious. 'He's in our hands, Quill. And he tries to needle us! He has to be crazy. Would you put yourself in our hands?'

'When I'm wired out there, you put yourself in mine, Scheck. What about that?'

'Not the same.'

Quill thought again that he'd never understand Scheck. He laid himself back on the bunk and set the wires up, the laceface stiff until it had wormed its way into his nostrils, his ears and the corners of his eyes. He felt it spreading warmly through his body until he was lying steady in stagnant water the colour of the dust in Scheck's hand in the coffin behind him.

'What can you see?' Scheck's voice had a faint reverb.

'Nothing yet. Give me a chance.' He looked over his shoulder, an effortless one-eighty degrees with no crick in his neck, and saw the coffin sitting there like a finless fish, receding into the dark, vanes and ridges for scales, a mantle of pulverised and liquefying rock caught about it like a frozen eddy. 'Okay, I'm starting my first circuit.'

This was Quill's speciality. Quill was the face worker of the team. Scheck wouldn't do it, but Quill wouldn't do what Scheck did, the calculations and evaluations. Being wired to a probe was easy work, once you swallowed the edge of risk. It was like swimming, though not like swimming in any river Quill had ever plunged into. It was like being underwater but breathing, with no current, no surface or riverbed. Just a view in every direction for a few metres, a few centimetres, sometimes a millimetre or two, depending on the type of rock. For Quill, it was the most perfect form of freedom.

This was Haven, and Haven was an excavated world. It was tunnelled and refined. But farout and deepdown, beyond the endwall of the last-dug coredor, was forever the unknown. Without Survey, every strike of a pick, each strum of a drillhead, held the potential for world-ending catastrophe. And Survey itself held that potential to a perfect degree.

There was provisional stability, and that was all. Beyond any depth of dependable, cavitatable rock lay unstable shelves of magnetic scree, or intrusions of permeable rock being progressively cavitated by pressurised gases, toxic and inert. Huge, reliable folds and sheets of dense and intrinsically stable rock were poised over porous rubble and voids that could crumble at a touch and collapse everything.

'Good so far,' Quill said. 'Stay with me. I'm going straight. Good visibility. I can't hear anything. No creaks.'

It was possible to carry out communication and structure-analysis through the rock to varying distances, depending on the type of rock, but actually to drill, to penetrate, risked weakening the periphery of a major problem. It had to be done, though. To extend the world, to build anything under Haven, you didn't need to construct foundations, but you had to test them.

'Quill?'

'Nothing yet. Granite as far as I can see.' It was in greens, subtly shaded, rippling away from him as he slowly swam through it. Beautiful and calm. He kept on moving at what felt like speed. 'Temperature stable. Keep coming.'

'Okay. I'm hard-mapping it two ems on your either arm. Go on three ems, then swing four dot two east-east-down and come back.'

'I'm on it. It's a beautiful day out here, Scheck.'

The deeper, further, outer excavation of Haven was slow, carried out delicately by pindrills and probes, the endless work of Survey.

And that was where Scheck and Quill came in. They were first-outers. They were there to redefine the boundaries of Haven. They explored not just the areas where coredors were to be extended, but beyond and beneath, to ensure – as far as was possible under Haven – that the extensions would remain stable. And they were there to search for water and to map rivers, to decide at what point it was safe to tap them.

'This is your fifth run, Quill. You want to stop and eat? You've been out for three hours.'

'I'll keep going. One more run.'

The subgeones, the coffins that carried them, were self-sealing in their wakes, to minimise the possibility of flowback. So were the probes. In theory, as soon as Quill probed close to anything suspicious, he'd border-flag it and withdraw, re-approach it from a different direction, let Scheck map the entire fault, and on his computation recommend total or local area avoidance.

But Quill could also spring the whole thing, weaken a thin rock envelope and let go a firespit. The probes were tiny, but a corefire spit could snap along a probe track with only the faintest of temperature rises in warning before the coffin fried. And then magma would open the crack further, backtracking it along the weakness of the coffin's wake, and sensors at the go station would bypass Tanner and give the destruct team their few moments of consideration to throw the bolt and cross their fingers that Survey's engineers had designed the runoffs well enough.

'Okay, Scheck. We're over the edge and in hard lava. One kil down and we're still above the lake floor. Should we go deeper?'

'Not yet. We'll check the lake's solidstate and stable at this depth all the way across, like planned. Then we'll drop a few ems and swing back, see if we can find the floor. Keep going for now. Temperature's still fine. Looks like it self-plugged from deep, the whole lake got isolated, cooled and set. Crise, Quill, they've given us a sleep exercise. We're supposed to be first choice. You think they don't trust us any more?'

Quill didn't answer. An hour passed. Then he said, 'I've got something here, Scheck.'

'Hold it a moment. We're starting to lose Tanner's signal. I'm just seeding a link . . . Done. We're in comms again.' Scheck chuckled. 'He's not talking to me. What is it, Quill?'

Quill didn't reply.

'Quill? Quill?'

'Half an em ahead. I don't think it's anything. Stay back, though.'

'What is it? I'm getting nothing on my readers here.'

'Some kind of metal, not an ore I recognise, an odd shade. I'm sure it's not on the charts. And silicon. And . . . Oath! It's greyed out. I've got impenetrability ahead.'

'Stop there. Come back, Quill. We'll go round.'

'No. Wait. I don't understand this. It's clear to either side, and temperature's stable. It's an isolate of some sort. I'm going on, at dead slow.'

'Quill—'

'Wait. I'm within two milliems and I still can't see into it or go through it. It's not magma, can't be. I'm going to withdraw and use the heatlance.'

'Quill, I—'

And suddenly, when the lance was within half a milliem of the impenetrability, the grey area became a brilliant red and the probe slid straight into it. And then, just as he'd penetrated it, the swirl of colour fluctuated crazily, as if it were not exactly melting, but somehow changing. It almost seemed to retract from the probe. He'd stopped dead but the colours kept shifting, red to scarlet to crimson.

'Scheck, something weird's happening here. I've hit some sort of odd concretion. It feels like its molecular structure's shifting in reaction to the lance. Heat-sensitivity at extreme temperature.'

'Some new element, maybe, pushed up from the core with the flow. Maybe this lake's not so dull after all.'

Quill could almost hear him grin.

'Be a pat on our backs. Go round it. All the way, full-frame grid, and I'll model it,' Scheck said. 'Better do this right. Then dock the probe and we'll look at it.'

It took Quill two more hours. Then he slept a few hours and had something to eat while Scheck worked the screen.

Eventually Scheck sat back and said, 'Look at it. That shape. It's not a concretion, Quill. Not a geode either. You know what? I think you've found a fossil. I think there's only ever been three or four, all the time we've been here. This is a good find. But look. If I go to himag at the edges—'

Quill watched the screen as Scheck moved the image around. There were more than twenty tendrils extending from the central core of the thing into the encasing rock. Then he said, 'I need some more sleep, Scheck. We'd better move on. Map it, if you like. They can send someone else after it if they want. Not our job.'

But when he woke up again, Scheck had the thing inside the coffin, sitting on the small foldout table in the tiny aisle.

'Crise, Scheck. What did you do that for?'

'It wasn't easy. I had to sever most of its extremities with the lance to get it through the sample port.'

'Well, jettison it. There's no room.'

'No. Look at the scan,' Scheck said. 'It's interesting.' He twisted the screen to show Quill.

On the screen, the sheathing rock was like frosted jelly. The fossil was outlined in red and whorled with pink and purple. 'It's totally soft, as far as I can make out. No exoskeleton. Or else it's totally hard.' He rotated the image. 'No flattening, no compression. It looks—' He stopped, not finding the word.

'It looks comfortable,' Quill said.

'Yes. Except,' he touched the screen. 'Except where we cut through the tendrils. According to the sample, we didn't. There's a clear margin of rock around the whole thing. We've got the whole thing here.'

'No,' Quill said. 'We haven't got it all. Look at the tapering of the tendrils. Go in on that. See? They *are* cut off. Where the heatlance cut through the rock, the melt flowed to cover the site of the cut.'

Scheck looked from the screen to the rock to Quill. He didn't need to say anything. He didn't need to point out what was also apparent. That the tendril, tapering away from the body and approaching the cut, bulged minutely at the cut end. It had actively withdrawn from the cutting tool, and the meltrock had flowed into the void and set.

It wasn't a fossil. It had just been alive.

On the table, the rock didn't move. Scheck rotated the image again, reassessing it. 'Look at the rock,' he said, quietly. 'Those faint lines around the body. That's rippling. Like when you're swimming. All around it, those broad ripples.' He pulled the image in at one of the cut tendrils. 'You're right. Here, where you thought you'd severed the limbs, these tiny, tighter ripples.'

They looked at the lump of rock on the table, in the coffin with them. 'I'll jettison it. Like you said, Quill, no room in here, and not our job. And anyway, it's dead now, that's for sure.'

Scheck picked it up and tossed it cautiously in his hands, and then he voided it into the rock behind. As they started to move forward again, with the thing jettisoned into the superheated, vitrifying rock to their rear, for a moment Quill was sure the coffin shivered, as if shaken and then let go.

'Well, that was a time waste,' Scheck said, forcing a smile.

'Yeah,' Quill said. 'Any more of those, we'll go round. You told Tanner about it?'

'Yes. No. That last link we dropped, it must have been faulty. Or one of them along the line. Seems to be transmitting, but I'm getting nothing back. It'll clear.'

'Crise! Aren't they clustered?'

'It happens. I've dropped some more, ultrawide frequency, lower wavelength. One of them'll cut through to the next link.'

'Or Tanner's getting his slice of us. I told you to leave him be.'

'It's not Tanner. It's a fault. And don't worry.'

They mapped eight more days of cold lava and found no more fossils, and stopped talking about it. Tanner still wasn't responding, but there was nothing to be done about that. Apart from the occasional boulder of foreign rock suspended in the lava, it was an increasingly tedious survey. By the ninth day, they had settled into a pattern of sleeping and mapping. The confines of the coffin didn't matter to Quill any longer. When he was awake, he was in the probe, and otherwise, in the coffin, he was either too tired to notice Scheck, or asleep.

Some time during the tenth day, a sea of green all around him, Quill wanted to scratch his nose. He knew the urge was just a program fault, that he didn't actually have a nose to scratch or a finger to relieve it with, but that made no difference.

'I want to scratch my nose,' he said. 'Can you fix that?'

A moment's silence. Then a tinny, distant voice, 'Any better?' and Quill said, 'Aah, yes, that's it.'

'Anywhere else I can rub for you?'

'I don't think so.' Quill wasn't always sure how to take Scheck's humour. He hesitated and went on, suddenly needing some form of company, 'The itch. What was it?'

'Magnetic flare, twenty-three centimetres back. I've compensated for it.'

'Is that anything to do with the comms fault? Are we still unstrung from go?'

'No and yes, and don't worry about it. It's Tanner's problem. How are you doing? Want to call it a day?'

'How long have we been going?'

'All our lives and then some, Quill.' In Scheck's pause, the comms crackled like metal foil on glass.

'Philosophy, Scheck? You okay?'

'Fine. These screens, that's all. So, you want to call it? I've got enough data for a few hours.'

Quill thought about it, and realised he didn't want to return yet. He closed his eyes and let the senses take control, imagining himself hanging weightless and motionless in an endless sea of gel.

'Quill? You're humming. Are you okay?'

'Fine, Scheck. In my element. Give me this, will you?'

He felt Scheck retreat, and was alone and alive.

This was Quill's reason for being in Survey. The chance of one of these occasional perfect moments made everything else tolerable. They made it all, the risk and the fear and the boredom and the cramp and all of it, tolerable. This, here, now, was the purest joy he could imagine. He had an infinite sense of his body, but couldn't feel or see any part of it. It was invisible but like blinding colour, it was hollow but like bursting fullness. It was like emptiness but all knowledge, all knowing, all feeling.

He tried to fix this fleeting state now, as he had each time it had happened, which was three times including this one, in over three thousand hours of probe time. He held it in his mind, feeling it already start to leave him.

He moved, and it was still there. With infinite delicacy, Quill pulled himself in and somersaulted joyously in the brilliant, colloidal void, and it was as if he were forcing the entire universe, star by star, through every pore of his body. Brilliantly he turned, and turned, and . . .

The sensation was gone, and with it the universe, and he was empty. Around him was rock.

He took a long, forlorn breath, then murmured, 'I'm done, Scheck. What have we got left?'

The memory of it was fading already, and all he had was the aching knowledge of an experience beyond capture.

Scheck waited a moment longer than he needed to, and Quill said, 'I'm okay.' Aware of his breathing, like a slow, regathering tide, he added, 'Thanks, Scheck.' And that awareness fading and gone, too, and he was only alive.

Firmly, this time, he said, 'I'm okay.' He could almost see Scheck crouched over the console in the coffin, eleven metres behind him.

'Fine. We're short an arc of three degrees, and this is the last section on the schedule. Maybe a metre of travel. The rate you're cutting, it should take you no more than a couple of days.'

'Very funny, Scheck. Okay, I'm coming back.'

In the coffin Quill unwired, stretched cautiously until his fingertips and heels scraped the metal, and opened his eyes. Under the low green light he saw what seemed a shadow at the end of his nose, and he felt something itching there. Startled, he jerked and flicked it away, swearing, his forehead crunching on the bulkhead. He swore again, then squinted at the floor and carefully picked the thing up.

A piece of wire delicately folded to hook over the bridge of his nose. Typical, he thought. He rolled heavily out of his bunk, on to the narrow strip of floor between it and Scheck's, and tossed the wire over his head to drop on Scheck's lap. 'Funny.'

But Scheck didn't react. He was hunched tight to his console, and Quill had to lean over his shoulder to see what he was staring at. Scheck immediately raised his shoulder to nudge Quill's chin away, and muttered, 'Personal space, Quill.'

Quill backed off the half metre that the coffin permitted, and voided into his division of the pan. Scheck still wasn't speaking, so Quill squeezed some myco into his mouth and chewed it as quietly as he could, sitting on the edge of his bunk.

'Look at this.' Scheck raised his knees to swing round so that he could face Quill. He handed the console over to him.

'You know it means nothing to me, Scheck.' Quill looked at it anyway, the 3diagram with the go station on its extreme right, and stretching out from it the webbing of vitrified trails, and themselves, and beyond them the almost completed arc of their survey. At Scheck's nod Quill went into the orb, running the screen through it, watching the colours bleed, the representations of the molecular, electromagnetic, thermal and all the other parameters that he only ever saw or felt,

14

pushing forward, wired to the probe, as variations of colour, physical resistance and granularity.

'What am I looking at?' But as he said it he could see something at the furthermost point in the sphere, immediately beyond where he had been probing. Quill ran the cursor back to cover the area.

'That's it. Resonance suggests we're approaching a cavity, Quill. Rather like ours, in fact. Like this coffin. Only a great deal bigger.'

'Maybe—'

'No, I just checked that. This is definitely virgin rock, no crossover probes, no other trails. It was never mapped. If it had been, you and I wouldn't be here, would we? They'd just be sending in a check team.' He leant over Quill and oscillated the image across the anomaly. 'Look. It has some sort of skin, like it's encysted. And up from it there's the edge of what I'm guessing is a tube, maybe a tunnel of some type, hardly visible, like it's been plugged somehow, like our wakes, only not vitrified, or maybe blocked access tunnels.'

'What do you think?'

'Thermal readouts are negative, it's the same temperature as the rock. Nothing alive. But I don't think it's natural. Not a geode. And there's nothing like it on record. You know what I think? Maybe something came down out of the sky and into the lake while it was cooling.'

'It must have come down pretty hard to reach this depth.'

'Well, it didn't just slip over the edge and slowly sink.'

Quill looked at the screen, but the colours and curves didn't help him. 'Maybe the other side of it there's something.'

'So. Do we go? Do we wait and tell—'

'No. We can't tell Tanner, can we? Unless we stop and go back far enough to string up again.'

'Anyway, he's probably sitting with those morons from Fact,' Quill said. 'They'd probably stop us. Or maybe tell us to go on. But it'd be their say. What do you think?'

'What do you want to do?'

'Go on,' Quill said.

'That's what I thought.' Scheck switched off the comms back to Tanner at go. 'If it suddenly clears, Tanner'll think we've run into an emag source and he'll wait. As long as we get back to go in a few weeks, we're okay.'

And if we don't, Quill thought, they'll map and flag the area as dangerous, and that'll be the end of it. But we'd deserve it.

They slept a few hours, then Quill started to put on the laceface.

Scheck touched his arm. The feeling was odd for Quill, half-laced already and his head almost in rock. Scheck said, 'You think it's safe?'

Quill squinted at him. It was what Scheck usually said to him as he left, but this time Scheck's grin was a little slow and a little muted.

'Sure it is,' Quill said.

And he was in the sea of green, the rock, the hard, cold lava. Ahead of him was a faint blue haze, becoming clearer and broader as he approached it. But its temperature was constant.

'Scheck? I'm looking at it. It must be okay. What could it be? If it's a reservoir of toxic gas, it can't get to us, and we know it's not magma or melt.'

'Exactly. We don't know. Not till we get closer. Keep going. We'll circumnavigate it, map all around it first. Or anyway get some idea of scale.'

'We haven't got time or supplies for that, Scheck. We could have happened across a tiny anomaly or be at the edge of a vast chamber. It's now or not at all. I'll have to go in.'

And Quill pushed forward, swimming through the rock and packing it back behind him, millimetre by millimetre. It had a texture like wet sand, sliding awkwardly away from his touch.

'Wait.'

Scheck's voice surprised Quill, pulling him out of his thoughts. Ahead of him was a wall of luminous blue.

'What?'

'You're very close. Do you hear anything?'

'No.' Quill didn't have to think about it. He went a millimetre further. 'It feels thin.'

'. . . ing—'

'What? What was that, Scheck?'

'Th . . . s . . . ck.'

Another electromagnetic source, it had to be. Quill reversed a couple of millimetres down his own track. 'What did you say?'

Silence, and then, 'You're going to have to make a decision here, Quill.' Scheck sounded a long way away, suddenly. Quill wanted to vacate, but that was crazy. He was where he was, even though he felt himself out there, where his senses were.

'It is thin,' Scheck was saying. Quill imagined he could hear Scheck's fingers scratching the console, his sign of nerves. 'It's metal. Then traces of oxygen, nitrogen—' a pause, then, '—the cavity's had breathable air there at some time. The metal's a fabrication, has to be. Regular fault lines, which means manufactured plates sealed together.' He slowed. Then he said, 'Definitely curved, and regularly. No sign of it shifting its angle in any direction. Storage tank maybe, I don't know, though how

16

or why it got there . . . Other than that, it's your guess. You want to find out?'

Scheck's tone had slipped to neutral, and Quill knew exactly why that was. He was thinking of Hether.

Hether had been Scheck's probe before Quill, and she had gone a millimetre too close to a tiny firejet. It had been too small to backtrack down the probe's wake, so the coffin hadn't been breached, and she and Scheck had survived it. But like all probe workers, like Quill, she'd had her senses onefifty-percented, and she'd vacated late. In the tiny coffin she'd sat up screaming, ripping at her eyes before unwiring the laceface, damaging her optic nerve, screwing up her olfactories and a lot of other stuff Quill wasn't sure whether to believe. But he'd seen Hether in the small gloomy dugout outdown of blue72 that was her home. He'd seen her crouched on the chair, biowired, in that place that was hardly bigger than a coffin, seen her looking like she was more a machine than anything else.

'What do you think?' Scheck repeated.

'What's your guess? What is it?'

The rock around Quill was still pale green in every direction except directly ahead, where it pulled to deep blue. The consistency was uneven and the expanse of blue seemed as he came a few hundred nanometres closer to become faintly translucent, which appearance Quill perceived as a thinness. He withdrew again. None of the manuals contained a transliteration of this hue and shade and chroma, he was sure. But translucency meant cavity. What in Crise was in the cavity, though? That was the thunderdollar question.

'Vacate, Quill. Unwire and let's talk.'

In the coffin Scheck passed Quill a watersac and sucked from his own, the emptying skin fusing to itself, a contact reaction crumbling the sac to a leaf that Scheck powdered in a palm and chased down his throat. No waste, but no taste either. He belched. 'It isn't natural. It's an artefact, no question. Like I said, maybe a storage tank. Or maybe there's a vast chamber and we've hit its edge and the edge of an escape tunnel. Maybe it's not a wake but a runoff.'

'Why's it filled?'

'Good question. Good one.'

'Can't be a runoff, otherwise we'd know about it,' Quill said.

Scheck ran his tongue over his chapped and fissured lips. 'It could be they had some slow penetration event, gas maybe. The metal was an attempt to hold it together while they evacuated, the tunnel was their escape route, and they plugged it behind them.'

'Same problem. Any made chamber would be mapped.'

'And this isn't. Why would they need first-outers? They'd just need anyone. Not us.'

'No. In which case we should back off and report it.'

'In which case we should.'

'So?'

Scheck ran his fingers over the console keys. Quill waited.

'It could be it's something buried. Something no one knows anything about any longer. Buried away at the bottom of a hot lake, way back, maybe for safety. Something worth finding. It could be.'

'Why bury anything worth finding that well? There's nothing above it. It's all this way down. That distance, it's not a safe burial, it's paranoid disposal. It could be toxic waste. What about that?'

Scheck shrugged. 'Okay, what about this? Maybe they do know about it, that it's somewhere around here, and they sent us out, knowing we'd eventually find it, you and me. And it's valuable but they don't want it known it's been found. We get back, we report it, they kill us and come down our mapped road to get it.'

Quill looked at Scheck. 'When I just used the word paranoid—'

'I'm putting it out, Quill. We've got to look at all the possibilities, that's all. Why are those factotems sitting back there keeping Tanner company?'

'Okay. Well? What are you saying we should do?'

'One. We go back and report it. In the paranoid option, we get dead. Even if we don't, this route gets closed off permanently and we never get to know what it was. We never know, Quill. You want to turn round and never know what we're sitting outside?'

'Go on.'

'Two, we don't go back, we investigate. If it's toxic, you vacate, we go back, give our report, it gets closed off. But at least we know why. Pats on our backs.' Scheck licked his lips. 'But if it isn't toxic, Quill, you and I get to be the first people ever to see it. Some stuff. Maybe some history. And then if the paranoid option's the right one and it's weird stuff, we clam up, come back, tell them we just found radiation and backed off, and they don't kill us. What do you think?'

Quill thought about Hether, sitting there like a junkpit machine. Scheck was persuasive. Quill wasn't sure whether he had really thought this through or just wanted to know, wanted to push on. Quill thought of their route back, re-excavating to the go station. Weeks of backtracking, knowing they were leaving this behind them, knowing they would never know. He asked, 'How much time is there?'

'Oxygen for twenty-six days, food and water for the same. Take us twenty-three days straight back from here. Meantime, a day on to get to the void, another day back to here. Gives us a day there.'

'What do you mean, a day back to here? The probe takes us to the void . . .' And we can vacate, abandon the probe, save time, he was going to say. But he trailed off, slow to get what Scheck was meaning.

Scheck said it, patient and steady, like he was just going over an agreed plan. 'I'll dig through there. You carry ahead with the probe, but I'll be right behind you, catching up. Not waiting. We'll have a proper access tunnel, not just a probe. We'll go right into the cavity, physically. We'll go in, head, hands and feet. We'll make a breach and take the whole coffin up to it, make an airlock and enter it. There's no time to do it the slow way.'

'Suppose it's toxic after all.'

'You'll still be getting there a little before me with the probe and I'll know. We can still come back. We already know it isn't fire or water or radiation. No raised pressure, so we're not risking a penetration blow. No added risk at all, this way. See? It's fine, Quill.'

Quill looked at Scheck's eager face and wondered exactly what he had told Hether just before it had happened. Not for the first time he wondered what it was that Hether kept muttering to herself in that tiny niche that was quivering with wires and ticking with screenery. But this was the first time the thought made him worry more than fleetingly.

'I mean it, Quill. It's fine. There's more risk turning round. I've thought it through all the way. Believe me.'

Quill didn't believe a word of what Scheck ever said about risk, but the thing was that he wanted it too. Scheck was a first-outer exactly because of this type of opportunity, but so was Quill. Quill hadn't been dealt Scheck as a partner after what had happened to Hether; he'd listed himself for it. He'd known Scheck's reputation and hitched himself to it.

'Let me think a moment, Scheck.'

'Every second's a second down—'

'Personal space, Scheck.'

Scheck turned round immediately, and Quill sighed. There was no doubt about it. The pause was just for self-respect. 'Okay, Scheck,' he said. 'Let's go.'

Scheck crawled to the far end of the flattened cylinder of the station and swung the drill across and centred it at the pindrill's exit site. He closed the curtain and checked the seal, and grinned at Quill. 'Beyond!' he said, raising an imaginary glass to his lips. And then the drill engaged, and there was nothing else to be heard. There was just the partially damped vibration of the coffin as it started to move in the drill's wake.

Quill laid himself back on his bunk and picked up the laceface. Out

19

there, the probe was where he had left it, as it always was. The colours, everything exactly the same. Going back was like re-entering a frozen time. He could see it clearly now, the green thinness. He made straight for it, a sluggish colloidal flow swirling away from him as he approached, matt jade in glittering amber.

'Keep going, Quill. I'm right up your ass.'

Quill didn't answer. It took him three cautious hours to reach the metal, which appeared as a sheen of fluorescent blue emerging from a blinding emerald green that fragmented and then dissolved as Quill approached it. He could hear and feel the drill closing on him.

'You'd better stop while I go in, Scheck,' he said.

'No need. I'm two ems back. You've got at least an hour before I get to you.'

Scheck had to have the drill at full drive for that. It was too fast, Quill thought. 'No. I don't know how long it'll take me. Stop, Scheck. Wait.'

'It's going to part for you like cloud for a kite, Quill. I've got the readout. You'll go through it in seconds. Get on with it.'

Quill hesitated. It was that thin? Why put something so fragile down here? What was it protecting?

'Quill—'

'I'm moving.' Scheck wasn't going to wait. The last thing they needed was for Scheck to bring the whole rig in before Quill had checked it was safe. Not that Scheck would really do that. Probably.

Quill pushed, and here it was. A curved wall of gleaming blue, regularly beaded with crimson at five-centimetre intervals along parallel lines twenty centimetres apart, for as far as he could see – spotsealed and riveted, Quill guessed. The wall curled away from him above and below, to left and to right. Around it was a swirl of green.

Quill tracked forward again until he contacted the blue at the edge of a crimson bead. It felt cold. Absolute confirmation of metal. And Scheck was right, it gave almost effortlessly, the crimson splintering and then the blue blooming away from him in seemingly soft petals that grew yellow tips and folded away, and he was in emptiness.

He had the sensation of falling – one of the few wired perceptions that was an accurate transensation – and then the probe's pinjets stabilised him.

Scheck's voice came through. 'Okay, Quill, like I told you. Readouts are fine, no air worth sucking up, but nothing toxic either. No, wait. I'm getting air, now. Must be auto, on sensors. The breach triggered it. It's breathable in there.'

Quill spun round and felt dazed by the speed of it. He wasn't used to working the probe out of rock, on the jets. 'The breach I made is already sealed. You're right. It's self-securing.'

'What do you see?'

Quill didn't know what he was seeing. The probe wasn't set for natural optics. Everything was at the same temperature, except for the seal, which was already cooling. No help there.

Slightly nauseous, he peered around, adjusting his optics. 'It's a small chamber. I can see a far wall, ten ems away.' He wasn't used to having this sort of range. It was dizzying. Usually the probe gave him a metre at max through the most porous rock. He felt almost agoraphobic. 'I'm moving forward—' queasily, without the support of a rock medium, '— and there's the shapes of consoles, a door,' he tried to pull shapes from the depthless patterns of lines by moving to and fro, hoping for a sense of perspective, but that made the nausea worse. 'I'm guessing it's some sort of command cell, by the arrangement of—' he swayed uncomfortably, not fully in control of the floating probe, '—of fixed chairs, I think they are. Oh. There's something—'

'Crise, Quill, you've vomited. What's going on there? You'd better vacate. I'm not clearing this up.'

He came out, heaving. The coffin was vibrating with the drill's movement, and Quill could feel the ruptured rock churning past the station's skin as it pulsed forward.

Scheck said, 'What was that?'

'There's a corpse. In a chair at a command console. Must have been preserved or something. I guess the sudden air . . .' He took a breath. 'The head dropped forward, gave me a shock.' He wiped his face and neck with a wadded shirt and voided the shirt into the wake.

'Some day that'll be an archaeological find,' Scheck said without looking up from his screen. Quill looked over his shoulder at the pulsing representation of the chamber. He checked the scale. They were a metre away from the pindrill's entry site.

Scheck's voice changed. 'Quill, I need to show you something. On the screen, here.'

Quill looked, the screen not making sense to him for a moment, and then he said, 'What is it? That isn't the chamber, is it? That's the rock behind us.'

'Yes. I'm getting a reading. Our comms are still down, back to Tanner; every comms seed I've dropped stays up for a while and then just fails. But here, I'm getting a faint wake-reading. See? Only found it because I was looking.'

'Why were you looking? And why didn't you tell me?'

'Because I was curious, and it's my job, not yours. And I said, I only just found it.'

Quill watched the screen. He wasn't as good at this as Scheck. 'Tell me.'

'Something's there. Something's following us. Unstringing our comms. Probably by accident.'

'Following us?'

'Or a fault on my screen. Most likely that. I just thought I'd tell you.' He shrugged. 'Nothing we can do. I'm carrying on. You've got one hour, Quill. You want to sleep?'

But Quill could never sleep while the coffin was moving, and certainly not now, with what Scheck had half said. He laid himself down on his bunk and closed his eyes. His eyeballs shivered in his skull like dice in a throwing cup.

'Wake up, Quill,' Scheck said quietly, and Quill opened his eyes.

'You were out cold. Wish I could sleep like that. We're nearly there.'

Quill swung round as Scheck muttered. 'Brace yourself. Another mil—'

The coffin's bow juddered and scraped, and came to a halt. The deceleration was hardly a tic of movement, but to Quill it felt like the ground at the end of a suicide leap.

'We're docked,' Scheck said, staring at his screen.

There wasn't the same enthusiasm in his voice, suddenly, and Quill looked at the image. It was a rear view, with the edge of colour that had given away the ship behind them transformed into an oval blister that was almost visibly in motion across the screen.

Quill said, 'Now what?'

'We send out another probe. Mark me an entry point. Your turn, Quill.' He flipped screens to show the chamber wall, and Quill said, 'How far are they?'

Scheck didn't look at him, just saying, 'Not far. They aren't in a coffin like ours. I've reviewed the whole route, my screens. I should have seen them before, but there was no reason to look back. They're moving faster than we can, and they must have better comms. But they don't have a probe, I'm guessing.'

'We're their probe. If they have good comms, maybe they can read us when we're talking between probe and coffin.' Quill stopped abruptly, then said, 'You think they can hear us in here, talking?'

Scheck's face drained, and Quill saw him as if from the probe, changing colour, as if he were turning to granite. And then Scheck said, firmly, 'No. No way.'

He took a scribe from his chest pocket and scribbled a word on the back of his hand, and showed it to Quill.

Maybe.

'No,' Quill said, trying to put some certainty into it. 'That's what I thought.' He took a sheaf of paper from under the bunk, and another scribe.

What we do? Who they?

Fact? Those two? But no choice, we carry on. No suspicion. Scheck held the scribe in his fist and said aloud, 'They're probably doing some sort of training run in a new machine. Must be that one in the hangar, the one we'll get when it's ready. They're just trying to impress us. Their sense of humour.'

'Yeah,' Quill said. Neither of them went for the paper.

'Okay,' Scheck said. 'You may as well go.' He put a hand on Quill's shoulder, and Quill covered it with his own. He wanted to say something more to Scheck, but didn't know what, and he was afraid that his voice was going to fail.

He laced himself and went through. The colours were as brilliant, but they meant nothing to him now. He found a point between lines of rivets, so that Scheck wouldn't risk breaking a long seal, and stopped there. He said, 'Scheck?'

'Yes?'

'Scheck, can you hear me?'

'Sharp and clear. Go—'

'I can't hear you. I'm exiting.' Quill exited. The laceface was still withdrawing as he started writing. *It's marked. Push the coffin through. Get it wedged so we can get out and into the ship. There's oxygen. If they're on our side, they'll rescue us. If they're not, we've had it anyway.*

Scheck nodded. He was grinding the coffin forward.

'Something's wrong with the motors,' he said. 'I can't hit reverse.'

Quill swore loudly, grinning at Scheck, feeling close to him, that everything was going to be fine. The coffin moved, then stopped again.

'We're stuck,' Scheck said. 'Shit and Crise.'

'Is that other machine still there?'

'Let's hope so. Let's hope they can hear us. I'm sending out a Helpus,' Scheck said, his head bent over the screen. He looked up. 'All we can do is wait.'

Quill took the scribe. *Now what?*

We're in place, chamber wall breached and locked against it. We open probe maintenance cavity. Should be able squeeze thro'.

Then?

Scheck shrugged, jotting, *??*

Quill said, 'I'm just going to see if I can retrieve the other probe.'

Telling them you're going in?

They'll hear'n'guess anyway.

Scheck shrugged. 'I'll give you a hand.'

The coffin's nose was triple-sheeted with staggered seals. Moving fast, it still took the two of them an hour to expose the maintenance bay and then detach the nose. They only knew they were through when the beam cutter suddenly grew an extra three metres and then jerked off.

'Somehow I was expecting it to be light in there,' Quill said in the silence. Scheck ducked back and returned with the emergency torch to throw a spot into the chamber. He crawled the beam across the matt green, faintly curved far wall. The spot jumped abruptly towards them, hitting the chair Quill had seen, and Scheck took it over the slumped skull.

Quill rolled through the hole and tipped into the cabin, then stood up carefully and stretched. The vertical wasn't quite true, and he staggered a little on the tilted floor before making his way up to the console in front of the corpse. He touched a few buttons at random, and the chamber's lights came up.

He looked around properly at the walls, the readouts and tubes and fat bulkheads and gas cylinders. It wasn't a storage chamber at all. It was a ship. Not a coffin, this big, and not a planetside ship. It was some kind of space rig. On the walls someone had scrawled, over and again, the words *I was betrayed.*

'Quill?' There was an echo to Scheck's voice, and Quill looked back at the breach in the hull. Scheck had crawled back into the coffin.

'Yes?'

'They're coming.'

Quill went back to the breach in the ship's hull and peered inside at Scheck. He raised his voice to say, 'Great. We'll be okay now. We just wait for them. May as well wait in the big ship as in there, huh? How long do you think we've got?'

The coffin seemed suddenly small and fragile to Quill. Maybe it was just that he'd never seen it from this perspective. Scheck looked cowed and anxious, hunched over his screen inside.

'I said, how much time have we got?'

'Couple of hours.' Scheck crawled out into the ship again.

Quill said, 'Hell, this is big. How long do you think it's been here?' He was at the console beside the corpse. The skull's jaw was down, resting on its chest. There were threads of mummified flesh on its cheeks, and an expression of glee. The corpse's clothing was a plain grey overall.

Quill touched it without thinking, and a hunk of cloth fell away to roll down the slope of the metal floor and dissolve to dust.

'Long time,' Scheck said, glancing over Quill's shoulder. 'I don't recognise any of these board configurations.'

Quill guessed at a comms icon and keyed it. The screen ahead lit up, grey-green, and a message came on.

NO OTHER SHIPS CURRENTLY ACCESSIBLE. CHECKING. CHECK-ING. CHECKING. CONFIRMED. NO OTHER SHIPS CURRENTLY ACCES-SIBLE.

Quill offed it.

'This is an escape pod,' Scheck said, wandering off to explore. 'Look, there's a hatch over here. See the seal on it? It's a hatch/detach unit. This guy was trying to land. He did that all right. Probably heading for Haze, or coming back, got into trouble. Came down hard, anyway, to bury himself this deep. Good thing the pod was heat-hard.'

Quill was still at the console, keying. He muttered, 'Didn't do him much good.' The body was leaning over his shoulder.

'What are you doing, Quill?'

'This.' The screen grew tightly patterned. 'These are his last sequence of commands. Or hers.' He moved them up and down the screen, squinting.

'Anything interesting?'

'He wasn't using his comms at all. Not sending or receiving.'

'Maybe they weren't working.'

'They're working. They're working now. They just told us that.' He looked at the corpse. 'No other ships,' he murmured. 'The onboard comms weren't even set to search outside ship ranges. Is that odd?'

'Only if there was anything other than another ship to receive you. Or you didn't want to be received by anything else but a ship.' Scheck walked awkwardly up the tilted deck, back to the console. He stroked the corpse's jaw, then pointed at the screen and said, 'Well, the clock's not right. And why the writing on the wall? Who betrayed him? What's that about?'

Neither of them said anything for a while. Scheck returned to the breach and crawled back through into the coffin. Quill carried on playing with the console. There was nothing else in the cabin to look at. It was an escape pod. Quill wanted more but there was no more. Just an engine and a pod and a computer and a corpse. Even the clothes had virtually gone now in the new flux of air, crumbled away with the flesh. There were no clues. No clues at all. He scrolled through the command history. The guy must have been some time falling into the atmosphere and through it, desperately adjusting his trajectory. Judging by this, his engines had been mis-set. Maybe they'd been tampered with.

There was a repeated text, Quill noticed. He drew it up.

CARGO INTACT.

Quill tried to explore the term cargo, but couldn't. It was pass-protected.

He called out, 'Scheck, come here. I need your help with this.'

Scheck squeezed himself back through into the ship. 'You found something?' He looked at the screen, then tried some keys. 'Interesting. I doubt I can crack this. I don't even know what the keys are. We'll do it later, if they let us. Won't be long. They're closing fast, Quill.' His hands flashed over the keys, but nothing happened on the screen. 'We haven't got anything like their speed. Wonder how they're powered. They're really close. Maybe ten minutes.' He stopped. 'Hear that?'

'Yes.'

A hum, and rising, throbbing now. He wasn't sure whether he was hearing it or feeling it.

'It has to be a nuclear drive. That's how it's so fast. And that's why it can't use an external probe.'

'But that's crazy, bringing a nuke into unmapped rock.'

'Not if you've got us up ahead.'

'I still don't see the point of it.'

'Nor do I. But in a minute you can ask them that, Quill.' Scheck sighed and shook his head at the screen. 'I can't read this, Quill. It'll have to wait.' He went back to the coffin.

Quill stared at the console. Did the pilot know he was going to die, a long time ahead of it? *I was betrayed.* How long had he been in this pod? The cargo was clearly important to him, and was here, but the pod had no cargo bay.

At a thought, Quill ran his fingers under the console and found a slot, and beside it an indented, edged thumb key. Holding his palm against the slot, he keyed RELEASE CARGO and then thumbed what had to be the eject key.

A flat silver case levered itself firmly into his hand. He took it up and looked at it, knowing he was holding the only thing the corpse had taken with him on the final journey from his ship to his death. It nestled in his palm, small and oval and set with three raised glass blisters, each the size of the ball of his thumb. Beneath each blister was a swirl of gas. The blisters reminded Quill of the observation turrets uptop, and he wondered for a moment whether he'd ever see uptop again.

He slipped the case into his pocket and was aware of the hum in the ship reducing.

Scheck started to crawl back out of the coffin.

'They've switched off the nuke. Docked it. They're about to—'

He looked behind, then turned and disappeared back into the coffin. His voice was muffled. Quill heard him say, his voice rising slightly, 'Hey, careful—'

And then the breach and the coffin behind it were full of light and silence.

Quill froze. Then he whispered, 'Scheck? Scheck?'

There was still silence from the coffin. The light dimmed and became a beam that roved around, and there were noises, grunts.

Then, a flat voice echoing. 'He's dead.'

Quill felt sharply sick and cold. That wasn't Scheck's voice, which meant maybe it was Scheck who was dead. And the voice wasn't regretting it. Quill looked around the cabin, his heart slamming at his ribs so hard he couldn't breathe for a moment. It must be Scheck. Scheck would have said something.

There was nowhere to hide, and even if there was, there was nowhere to run. He stumbled around the console in panic, ducking behind the chair, and saw among the last threads of the corpse's clothing a small holstered palm-sized device. He slid it into his hand as the first man came out of the coffin. The less cheerful one, Java, unfolding himself like a pupa assuming its adult form.

His heart still cracking his chest, Quill stood up. There was no point in doing anything else. The weapon was in his pocket. He didn't even know if it was a weapon. He explored it with his fingers, trying to make sense of it by touch. It was a bar with an offset ridged handle, and a pair of buttons, side by side. Maybe it was just a comms device. Transmit, receive. More likely than a weapon, in an escape pod. Why would you have a weapon? Crise, Quill thought.

Casually inspecting Quill, Java slid his hands into his own pockets. 'Your partner,' he said. 'I'm sorry. I didn't expect him to be in the ...' he made an apologetic face. 'Unfortunate word. The coffin. Survey humour, eh.' He looked round. 'Well, well. Well, well, well. What have we here? Would you step away from the console, please? And take your hands out of your pockets?'

Quill moved back, lifting his empty hands for Java, who craned his head and looked at the idle screen. 'Been playing around, have you? Found anything? Moved anything?'

'No. Just looking.' Quill tried to be calm. To seem he might believe it was all a mistake, Scheck's death. An accident.

'Good.' Java took his hands from his pockets. In his right was a hand weapon. The dark zero at the end of its barrel was fixed on Quill. 'We'll take over from here. This isn't really your field, is it?' He gestured for Quill to move towards the far side of the pod. 'Sit there a moment, would you? On your haunches, squatting.' He waved the gun. 'Feet further forward, leaning back against the wall. That's it. Good man. Hands on your knees, now, hold them tight, like they're the last tits you'll ever feel. Uncomfortable? Good.'

For a moment Quill thought of asking why they had killed Scheck, but there was no point. He tried to adjust his weight a little. The metal was cold against his back. A muscle in his thigh began to quiver and he moved a hand to rub the cramp out of his leg. Java frowned, then chuckled at him, and took a step towards the console, calling out, 'Okay, Rheo. It's covered here. Survey teams don't get enough exercise.'

Java was turned around for a moment, and Quill thought of going for the device in his pocket, but if Rheo stayed out of sight, Quill would never get him, and Rheo could pull back in his vessel and simply leave him here to die. Quill didn't want to die.

Rheo stuck his head through the breach and came through, straightening his back and staggering briefly on the sloping floor. He glanced around and said, 'Is this it?'

Java shrugged. Rheo looked across at Quill, and if Quill had had any uncertainty about his situation, the expression in Rheo's eyes cleared it up.

'Now?' Rheo asked Java.

'Wait. Let's check he and his friend haven't done anything stupid.' Java shook out a piece of paper from a pocket and started to sequence keys on the console. His weapon was sitting on the console, in easy reach.

Rheo went across the deck to join Java. The screen came up, lighting their faces. Java smiled and carried on keying.

Slowly, bracing himself against the cold hull of the ship, Quill brought the device from his pocket and onto his lap. He turned it in his hand. There were no clues there. And there was no point in bluffing with it, not with Java and Rheo. Two buttons. One red, one green. On/off? Transmit/receive?

They were still keying. Java had his hand under the console, searching for the eject slot. Rheo was clacking the skeleton's jaw, squealing in a high voice, 'I'm *so* hungry. I haven't eaten in *years*.'

'I'm not accessing it,' Java muttered.

Quill had no idea what the device in his hand was. There was no hole in its barrel, if it even was a barrel, just a tiny rectangular grille at one end. If it was a weapon at all, it was a beam weapon. He'd never seen anything like it. He moved his fingertip across the buttons. Red, green. Kill/stun?

He looked up and saw Java staring straight at him.

'Where is it?' Java said, tense. 'Where's the case?'

And then Rheo said, 'What's that in his hand?' and was reaching for his belt as Java swore and grabbed his weapon from the console.

Quill pointed the device at Java and hit the red button, and braced himself against the wall. Java's gun barrel was still rising but he froze as Quill's hand jerked with the force of his finger on the device.

A small squeak came from Java's mouth, but nothing else at all happened. Whatever it was, the thing was dead. All this time, what had Quill expected?

Java snorted and dropped his hand.

'I'll kill him now, shall I?' Rheo said.

'No. He's got the case. Or he's hidden it somewhere here. Get it off him, then you can kill him. And take that other thing too, whatever it is. He might try to hit you over the head with it.' He pocketed his gun. Almost idly, Rheo drew its twin from his belt, holding the weapon loosely in his fist.

Rheo grinned. 'Okay, drop it on the floor,' he told Quill.

Quill pointed the device at Rheo and hit the green button. The device whined, the whine rising. Nothing else happened. But Quill saw the understanding hit Rheo at the same time it struck him.

Charge/operate.

Quill maintained his aim as Rheo took a step towards him and fired his own weapon, but in his urgency he overlooked the tilt of the deck and stumbled. His shot went wide, burning a thin curl on the hull's skin. The whine of Quill's device levelled and then receded and he went for the abruptly flashing red button, and this time a neat hole appeared in Rheo's chest and his lungs sprayed a mist of blood as he sighed and dropped, rolling once down the tilt of the deck and settling against the wall.

Java was looking from Rheo's body to Quill as Quill tried to shoot him, but the device wasn't recharged. He hit green again and rolled down the deck as the weapon started its slow keen, the slight slope giving him speed. Java was fast, his weapon whipping a slick of pain across Quill's back. Quill came up again as Java went to steady himself against the chair for a better shot, but the chair swung round sharply and the corpse's arm flailed, striking the factotem on the shoulder. The dried flesh of its hand flaked into the air and Java coughed, breathing it in.

The whine of Quill's weapon receded again and he fired. Java's surprised expression seemed to fix, and then it slackened as he slumped over the console.

Quill waited until the shaking in his body stopped. He spent some more time in the ship, trying to make decisions, to make his brain and body do what he thought he needed them to do, and knowing that what he was really doing was avoiding seeing Scheck dead.

And then he went through the breach and into his and Scheck's coffin.

Except for the hole in his gut, Scheck looked hardly more than badly arranged where he lay, pooled in his own blood.

Quill crawled awkwardly over Scheck's body and through into the other coffin. The factotems had docked against the Survey pod, which was now useless.

This coffin was no bigger than the other, but there was only Quill left, now, and he felt as if he were wallowing in the space. He looked around and checked the screenery and knew he could work it alone. It was set up for Java and Rheo to use, and they'd had no Survey training.

Without thinking, he went back and started to drag Scheck's corpse through into the coffin with him, and had to force himself to let the body drop. He had to leave Scheck behind.

He knelt down. Scheck's corpse was still leaking blood into the darkening pool on the coffin floor, but his face was intact, as if he were waiting patiently to be fixed up again. Unable to look at him, Quill draped a thin sleep sheet over the body, but its edges instantly began to absorb the blood, dragging and moulding the sheet tight down on Scheck.

Quill pulled himself away and returned to Java and Rheo's coffin. He sat down, took the blistered oval case out of his pocket and looked at it. It meant nothing, looked like nothing he'd ever seen. Either it was obsolete technology or it was too new for him to recognise.

He tried to concentrate, to think, wanting to discuss it. 'Okay, Scheck,' he said aloud. 'Now what do we do?' The acoustics in this coffin were different, he noticed. Of course, being alone changed the characteristics of voice anyway, but his own unanswered voice sounded pitiful. 'Now what?' he whispered hopelessly. 'What on Oath do we do?'

He went back again, stepping over Scheck, whose shroud was moulded horribly to his face. He took all the food and drink through into the other coffin and sat down for a moment, feeling exhausted.

Stand up, he told himself, sitting there. But his legs wouldn't do it. They started quivering, just like his thigh had quivered in the ship. Then his arms started shaking too, and he started crying.

He cried for a while, then laid himself down and slept. He woke up talking to Scheck, who told him what to do.

Go back to the pod and see what else there is. There might be something else. Search it thoroughly. Step over me. Don't look at me.

Quill did it. He checked the ship's walls, the ceiling, the deck, the almost empty storage bays. There were some food containers, unopened. Quill twisted the top off one, and bore the stench just long enough to screw it back tight. It was foul, but it was probably edible. He counted the cans. There was enough food and drink for four people for a year. The pilot hadn't lasted long enough to get hungry a first time.

The vessel had a sealed docking ring. The ring had a maintenance counter reading 1/ONE USE COMPLETED. RECONSTITUTE SEAL NOW!

So it was definitely a landing pod or an escape pod, and this had been its first and last journey. Quill moved on through the pod. There was a small sleep section with four bays, all sealed. The pilot hadn't had the time to sleep. Scheck told him not to bother with the sleep bays. I know, Quill replied, tetchily.

The drive engines and environmental support equipment he didn't mess with, either. The pilot was alone in the ship, so he wouldn't have needed to conceal anything. If there was anything else, it would be in plain view.

The factotems were still sprawled where they had dropped, their blood beginning to pool at the lowest corner of the pod, starting patchily to dull and congeal. He searched their pockets, but there was nothing to find.

He ended up back at the console again. The pilot's body had been tipped partly off his seat by Java, and was only restrained awkwardly by a seat harness. Quill used a knife to free the corpse, and lifted it gently to the floor. It was stiff and seemingly leathery, though the flesh crumbled at his touch. The clothing fell easily to rags and then dust. A few hard objects dropped free. A pen, some coins that meant nothing to him, a set of simple keys on a ring. Quill left them all there and went back towards the coffin, suddenly furious with Scheck.

'Now what?' he yelled. 'Now what?'

But Scheck didn't have an opinion on that. Quill went to the breach and screamed down at him, 'Now what? WHAT?'

And then he felt the puke shooting up his throat and he emptied his guts all over Scheck. He stood, doubled over, shivering and dribbling puke from his mouth and nose, and sat down on the seat of the coffin he had shared with Scheck for so long.

31

'You're dead,' he muttered. He wiped the back of his hand across his mouth. 'You're dead. So don't talk to me any more.'

Now what? He tried to think through it. He couldn't just go back, say there had been a terrible accident. He and Scheck had been intended to find the ship. Whoever had sent Java and Rheo after them had known the ship was at least approximately there. Quill and Scheck were meant to locate it and be killed. If Quill went back, alone, with the oval case . . .

No.

Tanner was dead. Quill was sure of it. There was no going back.

Okay. Next question. What were Rheo and Java going to do once they'd got the case and killed Quill and Scheck. Just go back? That wasn't likely. If the whole thing was so sensitive, they'd want to destroy everything. And then when Quill and Scheck didn't return, it could be announced as an accident or geological fault, and the area would be closed. And that would be the end of it.

Except that without an actual geo-event, someone might suggest a search party or reSurvey.

So Rheo and Java would have made sure there was an event.

Quill went through into the other coffin, and eventually located the small sac of compression explosive and the timer, and then he sat with it in his hands, moulding it like mycodough while he worked the situation through in his head. He was starting to feel clearer.

It wouldn't be hard to fake an event with this explosive. Set the timer, start tunnelling clear of the area, and that would be it.

That was what Java and Rheo must have intended, but that wouldn't be enough for Quill's safety. He needed more than that. Whoever had sent the factotems would have to believe the ship was beyond reach and everyone was dead. They'd have to believe they could forget the whole thing, that the only things gone wrong were the additional loss of their own men and the failure to recover the case.

But it needed to be big, and it needed to be definite.

He squeezed the explosives sac some more, then put it down and went to the coffin's nuclear drive and disabled it, then unshipped its core. He lugged the core through the coffin, over Scheck's body, and hauled the Survey drive unit back to the factotems' coffin and connected it up. Then he fixed the explosive to the nuclear core and rigged it to go. It wouldn't make a huge explosion, not nuclear, but it should reach the release tunnel with enough force and radiation to make them believe there had been an accident involving the nuclear-driven coffin, and to dissuade them from investigating any further. The escape pod would go up too – there must still be fuel in it.

Quill felt curiously charged. Moving around between the coffins and inside the escape pod with its corpses and the pilot's bones, he felt separated from the situation, and almost buoyant. The sight of Scheck's corpse didn't trouble him at all now, any more than what was left of the pilot's skeleton. He felt light-headed and oddly cheerful now that he was leaving. He took all the food and drink from his and Scheck's coffin, stacked it on what must have been Java's cot, and checked that there was no machine security on the coffin's screen, no passcode or identity check, and that his new coffin was maploaded and the exchanged motor operational.

And he was ready to set off. There was enough food for months, if necessary. And with the fuel transferred from his old coffin, he could tunnel for just as long.

As he was about to leave, he had a final thought, and went back into the escape pod. There was a smell there for the first time, of blood, perhaps, or something else organic. He went to the pilot's corpse, and centred the skull firmly in the palms of his hands.

It took more effort than he expected to rupture the mummified ligaments and free the head from the spine. The released body slid to the deck.

With the skull safely stowed in the new coffin, Quill went back to his old one for the last time. He set the timer in the explosive, then knelt by Scheck's side. He touched a kiss to his finger, then touched the palm of that hand to the sheet over Scheck's face, and whispered, 'Goodbye. Goodbye, Scheck.'

And without looking back, he sealed himself into the new coffin and sat down, staring at the coffin's far wall, an arm's length away. Some time passed before he moved again, but he moved decisively.

He called the map onto the screen and examined the currently surveyed and documented area of Haven. He looked at it for a long while. The map in this coffin seemed to have more parameters and indices, more detail than any he'd seen before, and Quill thought he'd seen every map and survey of Haven that had been made in the last ten years.

He put that aside for the moment to program an initial course away from the ship. He'd need to refine it later, but he didn't want to think about that immediately. Scheck was the one who did that. It was his job, not Quill's, to get them in and out. Quill was the probe, Scheck was the screen and the drive. And while Quill could cover for Scheck, and vice versa, it was rough cover and no more.

Forget that for now. Time to go, he told himself.

The motor's distant grind was the same as it ever was, but this time the initial thump of engagement startled him as much as it had his first time out.

'It sounds like the world's shitting us,' he said, aloud, just as he had said it to Scheck then, that first time, all those years ago.

And then he laid himself down on the bed and closed his eyes.

'Yes,' Scheck said, 'It does.'

Had said, Quill thought, exhausted and confused, but Scheck was talking to him now, as if remembering with him. 'That's what I sometimes think. Other times it's like we're maggots in a colossal Haze-apple.'

Quill felt himself smile, his eyes still tight shut, as centimetre by centimetre, the coffin wormed away from the ship, from Scheck, and from Rheo and Java. Maybe he was asleep, he couldn't tell.

The grind of the motor fell away again to become a comforting hum, developing long, almost imperceptible rhythms as the coffin traced the meandering series of arcs of Quill's course.

Quill fed himself into the rhythm, murmuring the old sleep-rhyme to himself.

'Ironstone,' he began, in a voice that was too loud. He cleared his throat and started again. 'Ironstone, stinkstone, starstone, hairstone, smokestone, snakestone, serpentine, slate . . .' And with each word he watched the structure crystallise in his mind, inspected it as if he were turning a mined fragment of it in his hand, or pushing his forward probe gently through it. Haven, this world of rock. '. . . proustite, tantalite, stilbite, witherite, hiddenite, lazurite, mica, jet . . .'

The mantra eventually settled him, and Scheck's presence receded. Every few hours the stabilisers corrected the inner capsule for gravity, of which Quill was aware only from a brief sense of headiness.

He ate, he slept. And most of the rest of the time he chanted himself into some kind of a trance. He saw magma and mantlerock in his mind, watched the yearning heave of the planet around him. He was in the coffin dreaming he was in the coffin, dreaming.

Time stopped passing. Waking and dreaming became the same thing. Scheck came back, muttering craziness to him.

'You can't be comfortable like that,' Quill said. 'Did it hurt? Dying?'

'I didn't realise I was dying at the time. I was just thinking something, I can't remember what. I was irritated. There was pain for a moment.' He frowned. 'Longer than a moment. I'm a bit numb, now, and I've got cramp in my arm. Apart from that, I'm dead. I can't complain.'

'Can you take your fist out of your stomach? It makes me feel sick.'

'Believe me, Quill, if I do that, you'll feel a lot sicker.' He withdrew his hand a fraction, and blood swelled around it and something else swelled out.

'Okay, put it back,' Quill said quickly. 'But shouldn't the bleeding stop if you're dead?'

'I shouldn't be here. Don't look for logic in your unconscious. At least not that kind of logic. You have to ask me things.'

Quill couldn't think of anything to ask Scheck, unless it was 'Am I going crazy?'

'That's right, you can't ask me that.'

'I need you, Scheck. Why did you get yourself killed? I need you. And I'll miss you.'

'I know.' Scheck waited.

'How am I going to get back to downbelow without being read? And if I make it, what do I do then?'

'Those are good questions. You'll get the answers.'

Quill swore exhaustedly at him. This was insane, this conversation, even the idea of it. But he couldn't think of anything better to do than to bicker with the ghost of his partner. 'Why did you ever want to do this, Scheck?' he asked. 'Look where it got you. Why did you want to join Survey?'

He knew the answer to that, though. He'd never forgotten what Scheck had told him the night before his first trip into rock, before their first survey as a team.

Scheck had taken him to Maskin's bar, deep down in the rough tunnels of indigo54, where Survey crews went to drink on their last and first nights, and talked of rock and death, as if you could talk the connection away. Scheck had sat him down and lined up two short rows of thick-stemmed glasses, then thrown his head back and downed the first of his own in two swift jerks of his adam's apple.

Jeb and Anny, they'd been there, a few metres down the bar, lining up their own drinks. Quill hadn't known them, then, but he could see it was enough for them that he was with Scheck, and they'd quietly raised their glasses and saluted him.

'Should we go over?' Quill had asked Scheck.

'No. They're just back from rock. If they want to talk, they'll come to us.' Sheck returned their salute, then drank his second glass. 'It's for them to choose, for us to respect.'

And that had been Quill's first lesson of the rites and companionship of Survey teams. Quill had picked up his glass and sank the spirit until he could stare right through the lensed base.

They had talked of the Survey, and as they had walked back from the bar, up from Indigo to Lilac and on up to the broad, well-lit, high-roofed Primaries, Quill had asked Scheck why he had volunteered for the coffins.

He couldn't remember much of what Scheck had said, but he had seen that for Scheck, the rock was more real than anything else. Solidity, mass, density – '*Substance*,' Scheck had yelled in one of the dim, tortuous passages of Indigo – the rock was more substantial, and therefore it was more real. For Scheck, it was as simple as that. He had no philosophy, there was nothing fancy about it at all. He could scratch his hands on the rock, bang his fist against it. It was simply *there*.

Quill smiled at the memory of Scheck swishing his hands crazily through the air as they ascended, stumbling through Lilac's coredors. 'What's this, Quill? Air! You can fall through it. It's nothing.' He grunted to himself, drunk, staggering. 'What's the point in that? Breathe it in, flush it out.' He stopped abruptly and did so, harshly, forcing a groan up through his throat. The sound echoed briefly and faded. 'See? No resistance. No—' He smacked a fist into a palm.

'It keeps you alive,' Quill had said.

Scheck shrugged that off and seemed to be sober. 'Alive is natural. The real is what that comes up against. *That's* what's interesting. And anyway, that's the difference, the whole point. There's alive-breathing, and there's alive-alive.' He punched his fist against the rock and showed his knuckles to Quill, made Quill watch the blood prickle up through the bristled skin. 'That's alive,' Scheck said. 'The rest is just insomnia.'

Now, in the coffin, Scheck sat back, breathing hard, adjusting the fist in his gut, which was oozing a little. 'Resistance is what makes you live, Quill. That's what the rock has. That's what we have to do. Resist everything there is, whatever there is. Life. Death. Otherwise you're just *being*. Just flapping about, breathing uselessly.'

He grinned at Quill, and swallowed a mouthful of red spit. 'This is where I'm alive. Surrounded by rock.' He pounded the wall again. 'Resisting.'

'Not any more, though,' Quill pointed out.

'But I died doing it.' Scheck sighed. 'What about you, though, Quill? Why are you here? Why do you do this? It isn't just the pretty colours. Don't tell me that.'

Quill had never told Scheck what had first drawn him to Survey. It had sounded so flat in his mind after what Scheck had said. He'd just muttered something about curiosity, and at the time Scheck had let it go.

'Don't you think I deserve an answer? Now I'm dead?'

'It wouldn't do you any good.'

'It might do you some.'

'You don't ever give up, Scheck, do you?'

'You don't let me. Anyway, like they say, all flesh is farce.' Scheck took his fist from his gut. Blood welled out and carried on coming until it was up to his ankles in the coffin and rising. Clots formed and jellied around the metal spars. In sudden fury, Quill threw himself across the aisle at Scheck, who disappeared, along with all his blood.

Quill's mouth was dry and his eyeballs itched. He drank water, a litre of it, then washed his face and ate something. Then he got the screen up and checked his location.

What he saw first was the time. Two weeks. He'd been two weeks out from the ship. Scheck had been dead for two weeks. He was out of the lake, now, and back in complex rock.

The explosive would blow in thirty-seven hours, and if the map was right, he was still more than a hundred metres the wrong side of the shaft.

'Now I need you, Scheck,' he said to the empty coffin, and for the first time he felt alone there. Scheck was data, Quill was probe. They were a team. Like a nervous system, split into the sensory and the motor. The see and the do.

'Crise, Scheck. What do I do?'

He tried to remember. He laid the geology over the positional data, and input the coffin's capabilities through all the intervening strata. He gave the computer a safety range and a deadline of thirty five hours to be within it.

And then he sat back, wondering if he'd done enough to save his life.

The screen worked. Swirls of Haven's senseless core flowed and gusted across it as it did its work, tracing courses, retracing them, starting again and again.

ESTIMATE THIRTY SIX HOURS TWO MINUTES. ROUTE ABORTED. ESTIMATE FORTY FIVE HOURS ELEVEN MINUTES. ROUTE ABORTED. ESTIMATE THIRTY THREE HOURS TWENTY EIGHT MINUTES. ROUTE LOGGED. ACTION? ESTIMATE THIRTY FOUR HOURS FIFTY ONE MINUTES. ROUTE LOGGED. ACTION?

Quill ended up with five workable options. Into these he inserted an extra parameter, telling the screen to leave enough shielding material between himself and the outer ring of Survey comms at all times to keep the coffin undetected. It meant remaining a few metres beyond the Surveyed world, and coming in below it. And it was a risk.

And having programmed that risk, he sat back to watch the screen struggle with it, expecting minutes to pass.

The screen cleared to jade after about ten seconds. A message crystallised, blue and sharp.

ESTIMATE THIRTY FOUR HOURS TWENTY EIGHT MINUTES. ROUTE LOGGED. ACTION?

He sat forward. Shit and Crise. The computer was underloaded. It didn't have all the data it needed. The computation was incomplete. The route had come through much too fast for the calculation to possibly be thorough.

'Scheck, I need you now. I really need you. What's it missing? What on Oath's it missing? I should have known this was too good.'

He called up the screen's geo-materials database, not knowing what to look for in it, but it seemed complete enough. There were pages of it. Everything he could think of was catalogued. If anything, this was longer than the Survey coffin's database. All the properties were there, too, as far as he could tell. Structural, electrical . . . what else?

'What else, Scheck? You're data, here. All I know is a few of the commands. All I know is what everything looks like on the probe. What it feels like. Oath!'

But there was no choice. He couldn't calculate a route manually, as Scheck might have. All he could do was hope that whatever was missing didn't matter.

He disabled the coffin's comms facilities now, to continue along his route blind and deaf, not taking risks, relying entirely on the mapping program.

He set two timers on the screen. One was the remaining time until the ship blew. The other was the estimated time until the coffin reached the point of safety beyond the shaft. The first clock leaked time steadily, evenly. The second stuttered. It slowed, accelerated again, accelerated faster as the coffin finely adjusted its course and recalculated. It was keeping the coffin beyond the mapped, and so it was guessing at rock.

After the first hour, he had a margin of one point six hours between security and bang. After three hours, he had almost two hours, and was starting to relax. After five hours, after skirting an unanticipated firespit and a fissure pressurised with pore fluid, he only had just over an hour.

After that, he cancelled the safety clock, just leaving the detonation timer on.

He tried to sleep, but sleep wouldn't come, so he sat up and tried to work the whole thing through. Why Scheck was dead.

He laid the things he had taken from the pod in front of him and stared at them. The weapon and the case. 'Crise, Scheck,' he murmured. 'Shit and Crise.' He picked up the shining case. In the dim coffin light, he realised there was lettering on its side.

And below it a sequence of symbols. A stylised, square-shouldered man, an arrow pointing to his skull, the brain shaded grey. Then a number of men, but in a circle, their heads solidly greyed, and bubbles rising from each skull to merge into one larger bubble.

What did it mean? What was in the case? Quill ran his hand gently over the smooth blisters and put the case away, abruptly nervous of it.

Why had Fact sent Rheo and Java? They had obviously known the ship was there all along, so why let Quill and Scheck find it? Why not tell Survey there was something there, something Fact wanted for itself?

He was chewing a mycobar as the answer hit him, and when it did, he almost choked.

Fact didn't want it known that the ship was there. That was clear, but this was something beyond Fact. Someone had waited patiently for a routine survey to be sent in the ship's direction, and arranged for a natural disaster. Even Rheo and Java probably hadn't know exactly the meaning of what they had been sent to get. They probably would have been killed too, on their return.

So. So someone knew of the ship's existence, and presumably they also knew exactly what the ship was, since they knew about the case. Which left them still ahead of Quill

But Quill was alive, and they didn't know that.

He was starting to feel a little better, now. He took another bite out of the mycobar.

'Good,' Scheck said. 'Life's just a vale of cherries, huh?'

The timer was glowing black on the screen. There was less than an hour to go. Quill wanted to check the other clock, but he forced himself away from the screen, retreating again to the comfort of the catalogue of stones singing inside his head. 'Jasper, moonstone, cat's eye, bloodstone, hawk's eye, helidor, chrysolite, quartz . . .'

On the screen, the minute count went to zero and vanished.

Nothing happened. Quill exhaled. He felt like yelling aloud. He was safe.

In green, the number 59 appeared. It went to 58, 57, 56 . . .

Quill stopped breathing.

34, 33 . . .

He leaned forward to reactivate the other clock and to check his position, but he wasn't able to take his eyes from the numbers.

10, 9 . . .

The screen went to zero and cleared again. This time Quill held his breath.

Nothing happened, again. Nothing at all.

Then it came. An initial approaching rumble that lasted a fraction of a second, and then a long, gathering, shuddering pulse that started to rattle the coffin.

CAP

'Darling, how are you this morning?'

I close the door behind me and the room swallows my voice. I've never got used to bad acoustics. After a moment, the atmosphere in here reconfigures itself to my presence with a brief hum that quickly recedes into the background of muted clicks and beeps. In her sleep, my still beautiful wife turns her head effortfully towards me, and her pupils dilate slightly in their deep wells of jade green flecked with blue. Such eyes she has. Tubes and wires shift gently beneath the bedclothes, up and away to her liver, her gut, her heart and of course, her spine. She doesn't answer me.

It was her eyes that first drew me towards her. I remember it so well. On the screen I saw her in the line outside the arena, and then a few hours later there she was in the flesh, in the front row of the vast auditorium, in the very middle. A quadriplegic. Her head was straight and upright, pinioned against some kind of strut, yet not at all awkwardly, but rather as if it were her strength or her strength of will that held it there, instead of the harness. Her hair was blonde, cut and styled perfectly around the strut. She was wearing a short-sleeved pale blue shirt, and her arms were draped as if casually on the armrests of the chair. She had the long painted nails of the indolent. Crimson nails. Her legs were resting quietly beneath a long, modest skirt.

She was astonishingly, breathtakingly beautiful, her body held proudly upright and firmly in place. She was in a chair and not standing, and certainly not pinned to any cross, but otherwise she was, I thought immediately, just like Our Lord.

It's a memory of her that sustains me.

To the record, then. Where was I? Yes.

I'd been in my room, backstage, preparing myself for the long day ahead. The make-up girl was fussing around me, plucking and primping and painting until I was tired of her. When she was done I went through my hand and head exercises – the stretch out, the draw down, the wordless beseech. Then my voice exercises – 'Meeee. Mememememe.' Then my face exercises – stretch the lips, bare those teeth, those teeth bleached white as angel wings, then open the eyes, open them wider. A drop of belladonna from the make-up girl helped there.

This was what I was doing when John came in quietly and closed the door behind him. 'I've given the journalists their packs,' he said. 'And I've chosen two of the most sympathetic for interviews later.'

'Good. Please sit down, John,' I told him. 'Now. Who have you got for me?' I sipped my water, offered him a glass poured from my own jug. The time display above the mirror told me there were just two hours and forty-three minutes before the doors would be opened.

He bent and lit up the screens.

There they were, out there in a long line stretching away from the big oak doors and around the great building, standing and sitting, waiting patiently to come into the auditorium. Old, young, diseased and infirm, the hopeful and the hopeless, the despairing and the desperate. The blood sang in my veins to see my people waiting for me.

'I've picked out ten, Cap. This one—' John pulled the view tight on an old woman about twenty metres from the head of the line, which meant she'd arrived three days ago. She looked like an Alzheimer's sufferer to me, with her nowhere stare, her clothes neither neat nor untidy and beside her the carer who had to be a daughter caught uncertainly between doing something that would make no difference at all to her mother and appearing heartless by just standing there doing nothing. '. . occasional lucid periods,' John was reading from the data scrolling along the base of the image, 'medication having a diminishing effect . . .'

I nodded. 'She'll be fine. Keep on your toes, though. I'll take her towards the end, before sing and pledge, but if you spot lucidity at any time, alert me and I'll transfer and use her immediately.' I checked my sleeves for the tiny nasal spray pouches of smelling salts that I could pull down and squeeze between finger and thumb. 'What's her name?'

'Uh, Marsha Rhodes.'

'Fine.' I touched my forehead carefully, not to bring away the make-up, and experimented with voice. 'Uh, you're out there but you're stuck, stuck, in a quicksand, a quagmire, a, a marsh—' I pushed out a hand, made a fist, tugged the air and twisted it, '—yes, a marsh—' wait a beat, lock the fist hard and yank it down, '—*Marsha*, Marsha, and it's a hard road you're travelling inside, a road that's so very hard and dark but the Lord's with you on that hard, dark road, on the roads—' and now, *oof*, the other fist, '—*Rhodes*, yes! Is there a, is there a Marsha Rhodes here?

42

Marsha? The Lord's with you, Marsha Rhodes? Will you *answer* the Lord?'

'Good,' John said, writing a note. 'We'll put her at about two o'clock, say row K, stalls.'

'Not too near the centre. Near the aisle is best, but not an aisle seat. Maybe four in. So there's a little effort, but not enough to make her a nuisance.'

'Captain, how many years have I been doing this for you?' He smiled at me, a good, relaxed smile.

'I know.' I touched his arm. He liked to think I was a little insecure, I depended on him.

He gave me a few other candidates, most of them in chairs and who, with the adrenaline of the arena and maybe a little extra help from me, could be made to totter a few paces; and for variety a selection of the not quite blind, the not entirely this, the almost that, but not the stomach-churningly other. They'd been hours in the line out there, waiting for the doors to open, all of them registered and documented weeks ago, so John had their names, their medical histories, personality profiles, drug tolerances, everything we needed for the show. For some I had sprays of specific, fast but brief-acting medications in finger-blisters and a subdermal infuser at the tip of each thumb. In the thrill of the arena, no one ever noticed the tiny scratch and sting as I touched them with the Lord's caress.

Every little helped, and preparation was everything.

You're judging me on this, aren't you? You out there in the future. I know I'm not immortal – that's why I'm making this record. So be careful who you judge. Listen, and be very careful.

'Did you sleep well, Mary?' Perhaps she nods, faintly.

This is her room and her universe. The tubes that sustain her, the drugs that control her, the replacement organs. Her heart pumps for me alone now. If not for my love, she wouldn't be alive.

I check the monitors. The beeps of her heart. She's awake. Her eyes follow me. I bend to kiss her lips, and I can smell the clean cotton of her nightdress. Her breasts rise and fall evenly. What would it be, if we made love now? She can't consent or decline. Our love now is wordless. All we can do is stare at each other with that love.

Your judgement of me in that room, backstage; shallow, manipulative, cynical. A stage healer, a charlatan, a fraud.

I'll give you a little more information. My people all paid a great deal of money to come here and see miracles, or, if they were actually chosen, to have miracles committed upon them. They left even more money with me when they departed.

But when they left, they were always heartened. They departed with joy and hope.

That's not enough for you? Listen.

They were more than simply heartened. Those ten or fifteen who were restored miraculously on the stage – I never use the word cured – after the show, they were cared for by my Foundation for as long as necessary. A number of them were subsequently cured in my hospitals, by my doctors and my nurses. Not just the ones that John and I selected to come on stage, but many others too. All the money that came to me on that day and every other day, funded my hospitals, my doctors and my nurses. It funded all my research. The shows? That was just part of how I fundraised.

Are you quite so sure about me?

Let me tell you some more about my Mary Trulove.

I fell in love with Mary the moment I saw her on the screen for the first time. She was staring straight ahead, patiently waiting for the doors of the auditorium to open. John wanted to move the cam on down the line, but I held his arm.

He examined his notes. 'She'd be a drain, Captain,' he said quietly. 'Bad candidate. She has a long life ahead of her, and there's no certainty we can do anything at all to improve it. On stage she'd be a dud. We can't stimulate her at all. You'd lose everyone. You'd stand there with her and the whole show would die on the spot. Even you couldn't turn it around after something as flat as that.'

I stared at her. Two hours eleven minutes to go. 'Check again with the medical director, will you, John?'

He went to do that, and while he was gone, I homed in on her. I examined John's dossier on her and discovered her name. How could that not be a sign? Mary Trulove. The medical notes meant nothing to me. She was blonde, and she was the most beautiful woman I had ever seen. Her arms were pale and slender, her hands lean and long-fingered, and she had a stillness to her that I had never observed before in any but the dead. You may laugh.

Her eyes, though. Even though she could not move her head, could not even have faced the cam if she had been aware it was there on the wall above her, Mary Trulove's eyes burned through the lenses of the cam, through the wires, through this screen and into my heart.

The clock ticked down. I nibbled at a sandwich. The medical director came in with John.

'Peter,' I said, pointing at the screen. 'What can we do for Mary Trulove?'

He'd brought detailed notes, and he consulted them slowly, flipping pages forward and back. There were a lot of pages there. Mary Trulove had certainly been fully investigated.

'Biosurgically,' Peter eventually, reluctantly, said, 'a little, perhaps. With gene therapy, maybe more. Stem cells promise a lot, but there's been little in the way of result. There's some research – not our own, but we can access it – that suggests NNI, I'm sorry, neuronanoimplant procedures, might make some contribution to mobility in cases like hers.' He ducked and squinted at Mary, motionless in her chair. 'But it's just research.'

I looked from him to Mary Trulove and pretended that it was at that moment I made my decision, instead of the very first moment I saw her. 'John, you choose the rest of them. I'll leave it to you. But I'll finish the show with Mary. Can she vocalise?'

'I'm not sure,' John said. He looked at Peter, who ran his fingers up a page and down another and said, 'Yes. Primitive software, so she'll sound a little jerky.' Peter and John exchanged a small glance, but I knew they wouldn't say anything.

'Then give her some modulation, some depth. Some heart. Override her software and channel it through my throat mike.'

'Fine. I'll arrange a proximity switch,' Peter said. 'One metre be okay?'

'Yes. I'll get her to speak when I'm out of range first, so she changes as I close in. That'll give it some impact.'

Peter left. I checked the clock. Under an hour and a half. 'John, give her the best seat. I don't care how it looks or who you move. Got it?'

He made a note. At the door he said, 'Do you want to meet her first, Captain? Just to be sure about this?'

The idea of it made my heart jump. 'No. Just get her ready for me.'

I left the rest of my food untouched. All I could think of was Mary Trulove. I watched the clock run down, half-listening over the speakers to the sounds of the auditorium filling up, the drum of seats and the chatter of strangers greeting. Then the full, almost bursting silence of the place as it began.

I never switched my dressing room monitor on, and I didn't then, though I was desperate to see Mary in her seat. I repeated my exercises and checked my earpiece was working, ran through the names of the people I would be calling out and roughly where they would be sitting – I had used to memorise the exact seat numbers, but that worked less well – and then I listened to John's rise-up sermon and the prayers and songs. John and I had been doing this for years together. He was perfect, as always, heartening me as much as he heartened my people out there before him. And this time I was somehow almost nervous, in a way quite different from the usual irritable tenseness that I have in the last few moments before a show.

I checked and rechecked my finger-blisters and aerosols as John built them up once more and calmed them a fraction and said, 'And now—'

And I put on my jacket and my shoes and did my breathing and walked the hundred metres of grimy corridors and gloomy stairs from my dressing room to the wings of the stage. My stage.

And then, still in the wings, I smiled, and with the smile I walked on and spread my arms. All my tension disappeared.

That day, I was on fire. Our Lord was in my voice and hands. Our Lord had directed John too, and the comms teams, and everyone. Everyone believed. Everyone in that building was heartened.

And that was even before I closed my eyes three hours later and swung my arm around and let it dart at Mary Trulove's seat and yelled, 'Is there a, a Mary down here? A Mary who bursts with love?'

The vids of that day alone sold more than all my other shows put together. The Foundation made millions, and continued to until – well, I'm leaping ahead. But on the back of that day we opened a new hospital, a centre for the investigation of neurological disease, and it was called the Trulove Centre.

On the stage, I didn't try to make her walk. I could have easily given her a few paces, could have supported her without seeming to – I'm strong, physically, and walking the lame across the stage is a matter of strength and balance – but I had no intention of doing that. There would be no puppetry with Mary Trulove. What happened with her had to be real.

I knelt at the edge of the stage, judging my distance from her carefully. The footlights at my shoulders were almost burning my white suit. I glanced up at the high monitor and saw myself gleaming there. That's the image we used on the face of the vid, but I wasn't thinking of that at the time. I leaned forward and talked to her from just over a metre.

That was the first time I heard her voice. The poor synth of a voice gulped and croaked.

'My name is Mary Trulove,' she said.

'And how are you, Mary Trulove?' I asked her. I came closer now, less than an arm's length from her. It was perfect. Peter had chosen the perfect voice for her, and she was wonderful.

'I'm tired,' she said softly. 'I'm tired of this,' and she was crying.

And then, with her permission, I took her up in my arms and

presented her to my people. They also saw in her what I had seen. I know that. The sales of the vids, the response to that show, all that happened afterwards confirms it.

I promised her that she would walk. 'As all of you are my witness, I promise that through my—' I was crying too, and real tears, '—through my Foundation, and through all of your contributions to the Foundation, the Lord will make Mary Trulove walk again.'

I have never heard such a noise as we heard then, crashing and tumbling over the stage like an avalanche of love. The boards shook. On the vid, at this point the sound becomes unmanageable. It sounds false at this point, doctored, but the truth is that the recording machinery simply could not cope with the level of love.

'You will walk,' I whispered to her. On the vid, you can't hear it above the clapping and the cheers and the sound of seats banging as people rose to their feet. You can see my lips move, but you can't hear the words. We had to caption it.

In the midst of this thundering tumult, Mary stared at me with those eyes. The tears were still flowing in mine, too, real tears. John closed the cams in on us and framed our faces. It was just perfect.

I sit down beside her bed. 'Do you remember when we first met? I'll never forget the way you looked, your voice. You were so light as I raised you up.'

She's like a doll still, so immensely fragile. I stroke her hair, straighten her nightdress. The lights are bright and hum faintly in the background. I go back to the door and tune them down a touch, and the monitors appear to brighten against the dusk light. I opaque the outlooking windows for our privacy, though there's no one out in the courtyard, and the room generates a vista of mountains and lakes instead. I think it's based on Scotland, though that will mean nothing to you.

So beautiful she is. If we make love, what would it be? Only she and I know. The monitors would lie – after all, what is passion, and what's its opposite? Who's to say?

'Darling, you feel cold. Let me warm you a little.'

The numbers on the screens are distracting and they won't be dimmed, so I switch them off for the moment. It's more intimate now. There are clouds over the mountains, shadows scratching across the hazy slopes. On the monitors above us, just treadmill spikes endlessly renewing.

'What's this, eh? Are you teasing me?' With my other hand, I stroke her cheek. I stare into her eyes, breathing a little more heavily and faster. My hand moves. I have to do everything, but I don't mind. I can't

47

concentrate with those lines scribbling away, though, so I turn off the monitors altogether for a while. I know her peaks and waves better than anyone else, now. She's safe with me. She knows that.

And then I straighten her nightdress and recompose her, and switch the monitors on again and turn the room lights back up. I sit down again beside her. There's a look in her eyes again.

She's the only one I really confide in. The only one I can trust. So I talk to her.

This is my life. I look back on it – not that it's ending, or ended. Far from it. But I look back, as we all do, all the time; and as we all do, I compare my life with those of the people around me. I judge myself, but I judge others, too.

And that, I believe, is ultimately what we all want from the people who surround us. We don't really want to know them at all. We want to feel – to be – better than they are. We don't want to be judged by them, but to judge them. More than this, we want to judge them and to find them wanting.

And that, you must admit, is why you're interested in me.

It's like this. If they're richer, you want to say, 'Ah, but I'm more secure.' Or vice versa, it doesn't matter. If they're richer and more secure, and other things against which you can't compete, then you say, 'Ah, but I'm happier.' You can't truly believe they're happier than you are, though, not without hating them.

So, what you want of me is to make judgement. Was I good, was I evil. Was I happy.

And all you have to judge me on is what I tell you.

So I shall tell you. But first, give me a moment to rest.

That's better. Dreamless rest is Our Lord's reward, and one day, one day I shall have it. But not yet, not while there's work to be done.

So, there we were, in my dressing room after that show, just Mary and me. My head and heart were ablaze with emotion. I stayed with Mary Trulove in that room and we talked and talked. In the distance I could still hear the applause from the arena. John was with them, carrying on the work as ably as he always did. My right-hand man, John. My first brother, as I always called him, since I had no true, no real brother. Though I try never to use that that word, *real*, since – as I said so often, only Our Lord is real, and what is in our hearts and in our minds. What is in our eyes is not the real. What our senses tell us is not the real.

48

Although I would have denied that, at that moment, staring at Mary Trulove. She was more real than anything I had ever known.

I stood behind her to peel away my clothes, and then I showered, acutely conscious in her presence of the sweat and grime of the evening that was upon me.

After a delivery, my shower was something of a ritual. I had to rinse away the vast burden that I had assumed, the pain and the hope and of course the disappointment of thousands (and later, hundreds of thousands) of people. I had to flood it away and empty myself of it all, and then I had to let the power of the pure water pound down on my skull and fill me with energy again. After a hard night, I could stand in the shower for an hour or more.

That night, I didn't need more than five minutes. Through the shower screen, ablur with foam and water, I could make out the shape of Mary Trulove in her chair, her profile unmoving against the downwash of water, and it was if she were rising, rising like an angel.

I came out and dried myself in front of her. I knew she wouldn't mind, and I was right. I made myself some coffee, and I sat down with her.

And then I told her about my family, about my father. She listened quietly, of course.

Hours passed. Normally I would have been silent and let her talk, and just listened to her unburdening, but I knew instinctively that I could talk freely to her.

I told her how my father had died of a cancer that would have been curable had it been diagnosed in time, and had we been able to afford the treatment for it. I told her how he died at home, neither peacefully nor quietly, after going through the classic phases of suffering. I wasn't talking about the pain of it, but the mental state.

Mary didn't move a muscle, but I felt her winged heart coming out to me.

'Afterwards, I read about the progression of mental states cancer sufferers pass through,' I told her. 'It's the same for everyone. You'd think we'd all be different, but we're not.' I ticked my fingers. 'Denial first, then shock, anger, depression and at last, acceptance. That's the sequence. Always happens. Except sometimes it's depression and then anger.'

Talking about it like that, I remembered the anger, particularly. The rage upon him. It was hard to say it, but I had to tell her. 'This was while he still had his strength, and oh, how he used it, beating my mother and beating me. He'd be spitting blood, quite literally, spraying his cancerous blood over us.'

I'd never told anyone about this before, about the beatings. I don't actually know why I began to tell her. It's not usually the sort of thing you tell someone you've just fallen in love with, I imagine. It was a shock to me that I was telling her, and it was also a shock because as I told her, I remembered more of it. It was like each sentence I said triggered the memory of the next sentence. Like as I was telling it, I was pulling it out. Like some sort of strange prayer meeting that was getting out of control. But I couldn't stop, because I wanted to know it, and I did know that if I stopped, the line would be cut and whipped away for ever.

'He had cancer of the tongue and the throat,' I told her. 'He'd smoked and drank since he was a child. They'd done some botched surgery on him, taken most of his jaws and tongue away, and given him a voice—' I was suddenly acutely aware of Mary's voice. My father had had a synth-assisted voice, and I suddenly realised that hers was faintly reminiscent of his. It was odd that I hadn't been struck by this until now, '—but the voice was poor. He could hardly eat, but he wouldn't use a tube. We had to boil everything to mush for him, and he'd paste it into his mouth and flush it down with whisky.'

I could remember it. I could smell the stink of whiskied food so precisely that I gagged to speak of it. Mary asked me if I was all right. I wiped my mouth with the towel and went on, quickly, not wanting to cut the thread.

'After he'd eaten what he could and was drunk with it, he'd catch my mother and start kissing her, and take her into their bedroom. I could hear them—'

For a minute I couldn't go on. The memories had suddenly leaped far ahead of the words, and I had to wait a while. Mary was patient. It was only her presence that made me able to go on at all.

'He wasn't strong, but he was stronger than her. She was small and thin. She'd grown weaker with his disease, and she was drinking too. But she hadn't ever really drunk alcohol before the cancer, and she couldn't hold him away. Without the drink, she probably could have kept clear of him, but I don't think she saw that. Or maybe she did, I don't know. I—'

I was crying. Mary rolled her chair towards me until her knee touched mine. That gave me the strength to carry on.

'Then one day I went in the room and dragged him off her. I threw him away, to the floor. My mother was there on the bed, her eyes squeezed tight, her face smeared with my father's blood and spit. And then my mother opened her eyes and stared at me.'

I was conscious of silence. The silence was in the dressing room, the distant arena now empty and the two of us alone, but also it was silent in my head, in my parents' bedroom as my father and mother both stared at me, bloody-mouthed and naked.

'My father tried to get up on his feet,' I whispered.

She was on the floor with him, holding him to her. My hand was on his arm, tugging him up, but she was still clutching him tightly. It made me think of trips to the beach, me trying to pull a hank of seaweed from a rock and ripping it clear, the rock left marked and the seaweed useless in my fist.

'Cap—' my mother said to me. 'Cap, don't—'

I didn't know what I was doing. My father pushed himself from both of us, then took my arm and pulled me out of the room. There was an astonishing strength in him, but the way he looked at me, I couldn't have resisted him anyway.

He closed the door, shutting my mother inside. He looked at me, straight in the eyes.

I almost told Mary Trulove what he did to me then. I almost freed the words, but in the end I couldn't say them and they stayed locked in my skull. I did tell her what he did to me after it, my own father leaning carefully over me and opening his ruined one-lipped mouth, slopping his blood and his cancerous whisky spit in long beady strings from his mouth into mine. 'Blood and blood,' he murmured. 'What's mine is yours. That's how it works, eh? Blood and blood.'

Someone knocked on the door of the dressing room. I yelled at them to go away, and apologised to Mary for the interruption. I was shaking like an earthquake was inside me, out of control. And Mary was as still as a rock.

I took some breaths and after a while I managed to go on. 'That's how it was after that. He never went near my mother again. Just me. Every day, blood and blood. I was drinking his blood, his cancer. I thought I'd catch it from him, but of course I didn't. And sometimes I imagined I'd be taking it away from him, but of course I wasn't.'

The speaker in the dressing room crackled alive. 'Captain,' John said quietly, 'They want to close the doors and lock up. It's four a.m.'

'Tell them . . . tell them I'll take the building for another day.'

'Captain, that's—'

'John, this is important to me. Deal with it, will you, please?'

And he dealt with it. My true brother, he was then. I had John, and I had Mary. I was blessed, and I knew it. Later, of course . . . But I'll get to that.

So I carried on talking to her. 'Eventually, things changed, of course. I grew stronger and he grew weaker.' I was crying again. 'I could always have resisted him if I had really tried, I think, but he was my father. He was that, and I loved him. My mother loved him too, I'm sure. That's why she let him do that to her.'

'He loved you,' Mary said. 'And he loved your mother.'

'Do you think so?'

I believed her. I never would have believed such a thing before, but now, from the mouth of Mary Trulove, it was so. I could believe that he loved us.

'Shortly after he stopped raping her, my mother left us.' I was unable to hide the anger, now. I remembered her going out shopping, and waiting for her until it was dark. And my father laughing at me for waiting. Laughing and spitting blood. He knew she wasn't coming back. 'She just left me.'

'Yes. I know. But not like that.'

I looked at Mary, astonished. It was clear to me that she understood everything. I waited for her to go on.

'You must see how she felt. She'd been letting him do that to her in order to protect you. You had started to protect her, though, and she couldn't cope with that.' Mary gulped air. Her voice clicked and continued. 'She was your mother but there was nothing left for her. She couldn't protect you any more. All she could do was leave, so that you didn't have to submit yourself to him for her any longer. She left because she loved you, Cap.'

I can't remember if she called me Cap just then. But I do remember that night so well. I knelt at her feet. She had beautiful shoes, simple leather, pointed toes, the soles of her shoes quite unworn. I looked at her and gently took her shoes off. Mary Trulove had beautiful ankles, and feet without a callus or any evidence of having touched this world at all. I put my hands around her ankles and said to this beautiful, peaceful person who knew everything, 'I feel as though I should wash your feet, Mary.'

I imagine a chuckle from her. She understood what I meant. 'No, Cap. I'm not that. And nor are you. We're human. But all our faults are forgiven, yours as well as the rest of ours. You can't heal others without releasing yourself for healing too. What happened after she left you?'

I was talking and crying at the same time, blubbering like a child. I released it all to her. 'When he had grown too weak to, to beat me, he started to read books and pamphlets about politics and law and medicine and God. He'd had something of an education, but I don't know what happened, he'd never had a good job and never kept a bad one.' Before the cancer, I remembered now the times between jobs, wishing he had one, and the times when he had one, waiting in fear for his anger to take it from him. Fear was my childhood. Fear and lies.

'So he'd call me to his room and discuss them with me. He'd say there was no truth in any of them. It was the first time my father and I had ever talked. He'd crack the backs of the books, wheezing, coughing, and he'd spit at me about how the world worked. And then, when he had lost the power to do anything for himself, I would read his broken-backed books to him. There was no money. The rent was unpaid, there was no food except what I could beg from neighbours, and they soon tired of giving, since my father seemed to have reached a plateau of illness, intermittently conscious, neither quite living nor dying. He was not an attractive patient.'

'But he was your father.'

'Yes. And we were talking to each other.' And as I was talking to Mary Trulove, I was feeling stronger and stronger. 'I was doing my best to take care of him. I discovered, as I travelled further afield to beg, that I was a good beggar. I would describe in an appropriate amount of detail how my father had treated my mother and me, and his illness, and I would tell them that my father had found Our Lord, but too late to save his marriage, and that he had only me, and that I had been saved from a life on the streets by my dying father's penitence. Thus we were both saved, and by helping us, you were contributing directly to the Lord's work.'

Mary Trulove had tears in her eyes, by then. All of this was the truth that I had told her, and as I told her it, and looked into her shining eyes, I felt for the first time in my life absolved.

And then I held up the ring that I keep on the chain around my neck to show her closely. The gold ring that I had never told even John about.

'This was my father's ring,' I said. I leant forward towards her so that she could see it better. My face was close to hers. The gold of the ring was worn a little in two places; on the inside, from my father's finger, and also on one side where it had rubbed on my chest over the years. 'I keep it to remind myself of him.'

'And now it reminds you of your father in a different way,' she said.

'I wish you could hold it,' I told her.

'I will,' she said. 'One day.'

I cannot begin to describe that feeling of connection, that perfect moment.

'Mary Trulove, may I kiss you?'

'Please. Please kiss me.'

She closed her eyes. Her lips were soft and melting. They were as innocent of the world as the soles of her feet. I was in turmoil, in love.

'Tell me something about yourself,' I said, gathering myself again. I was in heaven.

'Not here.'

Outside, it should have been around dawn, but the dawn was past. John was waiting for me in the foyer, drinking coffee with the security guards, and I introduced him to Mary.

'John, this is Mary,' I said.

John put the coffee down sloppily on the guard's desk and looked at me. I had said it the wrong way round for him. She should have been introduced to him, not the other way round. He was jealous of her, and there was no way back from that. I had unset my past, but I had set my future.

'And Mary, this is John.' I turned to her. 'This is my true brother and best friend. Without John, I would not be here with you.'

But it was too late.

'Without the Lord,' John said, 'None of us would be here, would we, Cap?' His eyes slid away. 'Mary, it's heartening to meet you.'

John wasn't like me. He could never hide his feelings.

'John, I'm taking the morning off,' I told him. 'I'm going with Mary for some breakfast. Can you deal with yesterday's—?'

'Yes, Cap. Will Mary be on the list?'

'She will. I'll get—'

'That's fine. We have her details from before the show, remember? When you picked her out of the line and told me to check on her.'

He was looking straight at Mary as he said this, but she answered him evenly. 'I understand how these things work, John. Look at me. I have no illusions.'

John had the grace to redden, but not enough to apologise to her. He turned and left.

Out of that, would you have imagined that I had anything to worry about?

We went for breakfast. I was already too well known to be able to eat in a public place with the chance of peace, and my vehicle and driver were waiting, so we used the car. It was already adapted for wheelchairs, so taking Mary was no problem. We went to a small private club and I took a room for us to eat and talk. The kitchen arranged for Mary's food to be provided under the instructions of my own staff.

I discovered that I was famished. I devoured eggs, toast, pancakes, mug after mug of coffee. Mary talked while I ate.

It turned out that Mary Trulove's father was a working man, just like my own father.

'My father,' she said. I tried to read emotion, but it was hard to tell how she meant it to sound. The gulping of air, the synthesising of her voice, made it hard at first to tell. Much later, we'd link a sophisticated

54

speech synthesiser to her emotional centres and the machine would modulate her tone according to precisely how she felt. It wasn't foolproof. It had trouble with contempt. Very much later, during one of our bad patches, I discovered how to adjust the device to make her communicate with me in a more loving way, but I'm jumping ahead.

'My dad was a kind man, but he was always at work.' This came out as evenly as everything that followed. You have to imagine odd climaxes of tone in her speech, like a music radio announcer trying to deal with a tragedy. No, that won't mean anything to you, will it? I hadn't really noticed her speech patterns up to then, but of course up to then I'd been doing most of the talking.

'There wasn't much money but enough. We weren't unhappy, no unhappier than most, anyway. My dad worked days, my mother worked nights, both of them in the same company. We had company shares, company pension, company benefits, and all of it going back years.'

Most of the time you can tell where a story's going by the teller's tone, but this wasn't the same. All I had to go on was what I remembered of her file, and what she was now, a quadriplegic.

Clicks of the synthesiser, gulps of air. Tears. I wiped her tears with a napkin.

'For about an hour, my dad was a hero. I still think he was.'

Clicks, gulps. I wondered how often she told this.

'You've heard of the company, but I don't ever say the name. There was fraud. We lost everything. Someone bought the company for a cent and sacked fifty per cent of the workers. They did it off a list on the big screen on the canteen wall, just after my mother got home and as my dad arrived. My mother hadn't known a thing. She'd kissed my dad on the cheek and started cleaning the house.

'So, my father got to work and was told to go to the canteen along with everyone else. A man he'd never seen stood there on a box in a suit and tie and holding a little screen command board, with the list on the wall behind him. Ten names at a time. Five hundred people to get through, and he kept checking his watch. After a while it was apparent that he was working down the list from the letter A with a strike-through button until he'd sacked enough people. He slowed down around the Ns, hesitated at Georgio Starke before striking him out, and then he stopped, muttered something into a small comms device.

'My dad was standing near Georgio Starke. Georgio pushed past him and out of the hall, talking to himself. Georgio had guns at home, everyone knew that. He had lots of them, and he was a bit crazy. All he had at home was an old mother and guns. He lived just down the street from us. We knew him pretty well, and he'd always seemed harmless.

'No one was really thinking about Georgio, though. They were watching the man in the suit as he counted names and struck out a few more. Never once looking up at the people whose names they were.

'He crossed through eight more. The last two names he crossed through were Addy and Greg Trulove, my parents. Bob Truman kept his job. My parents were left with nothing. They had no pension rights and no chance of anything again.'

I leant forward to wipe the water from her eyes as she went on.

'I didn't know any of this. All I knew was when my dad walked in the door and said nothing at all and shot my mother and my sister and me, and then left. Like target practice. Of course I wasn't dead, but the others were. My sister was lying beside me, staring at me as I was staring at her, only she was dead and I couldn't look away. The police who found us two hours later thought at first that Georgio must for some reason have come to us and done it before going back to the canteen.

'It seemed what had happened was Georgio had returned to the canteen with an armful of automatic guns and shot the guy in the suit, and then tossed a coin and shot everyone on the right hand side of the hall. The only word he said was, "Tails." '

I wiped her eyes again. And mine.

'My dad came through the door there just as this was happening, and he shot Georgio as he was tossing his coin again, and then he shot himself. Shooting himself was what made the police wonder about us and come looking.

'It took a while to sort out the truth of it. A few people wanted to let it stay like it seemed, my dad a desperate, tragic hero, but the company didn't want that at all, so it came out what had happened. The new company acted like we were all psychos there anyway, and sacking us had made no difference to that.

'But you know what I think out of all that?' she said, gulping air. 'Some people don't even get the toss of a coin.'

I nodded. It was all I could do.

'So I had nothing. Until then, there was Medicare, but that was from the company, so it was gone. My mom and dad had a little insurance, but I was sued out of it by lawyers for the families of the dead. They got a bit, the lawyers took the rest. You're the first person who's taken a second look at me.'

'My father,' I found myself saying, 'my father developed a view of the world.'

I had never told this to anyone before, and here I was telling it to someone I had known for hardly an hour.

'What my father said was that money behaves in accordance with the trickle-down principle. He said that no matter how hard you work, the money filters through your fingers and drops into the pockets of bankers and accountants, and from there it trickles away altogether and disappears into the pockets of lawyers.'

Mary Trulove laughed. I didn't realise it at first. I thought she was having some sort of seizure, gulping desperately for air and croaking terribly. Then as I came to my feet, not knowing what to do, she said in the same lilt she had used to describe the deaths of all her family, 'I haven't laughed, haven't laughed like that for years.'

I picked up her hand. It was warm and soft. I held her hand in both mine and vowed to myself that I would restore her.

'How long have you believed in God?' she asked me.

I didn't mind her saying that. We understood each other. We both knew that we had found our soulmate, and that we had to share everything.

'I believe passionately in the importance of God,' I told her. 'All I have learnt, I have learnt from my father. I believe in the importance of democracy above all things. I believe that there is a pyramid of opportunity in this world, and I believe that it is only by starting at the bottom and climbing that pyramid to its summit that we can begin to level it to the ground.'

We talked and talked. I explained the credo that I had developed with my father. The morning passed, and most of the afternoon.

And then I called John.

'John,' I said, 'I want you to go with Mary to the Foundation, and I want you to speak to the neurological team.'

HAZE

'Come in.'

Petey pushed the door of the hut open. The small, bright sun was tethered to the high ceiling and droning like an insect. It was always in the same place whenever Jemus summoned her, regardless of the time of day. The cord was to stop it drifting across the room. She'd worried over this with Loren, but he wasn't interested. For the husband, the worry of being there at all crowded thought away. He concentrated purely in saying the right thing to the lord. For Petey it was more than that. It started with maintaining control of herself in that hut.

Jemus pulled at the cuffs of his sleeves, hitching them to his elbows. His arms were hairless and skinny but corded with muscle. He said, 'Sit, sit. Which one are you?'

She swung her eyes down, careful to keep her gaze away from the table. 'I'm Petey.'

As he scanned the list on the square of paper, she leaned forward cautiously. For a lord, he was a bad reader, using a finger to remind himself where he was. Petey wished she could read. At least she could recognise her name, now, as the pattern that he made a mark against each time.

'The husband is Loren and the son is Marten,' she said.

He touched them with his finger, Loren first and then Marten, just where Petey thought they were.

'And there was another child,' she said. 'I had a girl.' The daughter had no symbol any more on Jemus's list, but Petey had scribbled what she remembered of it on a piece of scraped bark that she kept hidden even from Loren.

The lord looked up at her, almost catching her staring at the list. 'Nothing is yours, Petey,' he reminded her sharply. 'Nothing but the parts of your body. And even those at my decision.'

She glanced away, knowing she shouldn't have said that. Nothing in the hut was natural. It was all shine and flatness and perfect straightness.

It had an odd sound. Whatever wood or stone it was, the lords brought it with them, and they kept the tools that worked it hidden too.

'I meant that I carried her,' she said quietly. 'I meant that I gave birth to her.' She pushed back the memory of farewell.

'Did you mean that?' He set his shoulders and flattened his palms on the paper. His voice changed. 'You were seen committing crime, Petey.'

Loren was better at this than she was. What did he say? 'If it's his lie, he'll be quite still and stare directly at you. If it's someone else's lie and he knows it, he'll stare and play with the dead beetle on his table. If he suspects it's truth, he'll tap the beetle on the table, gently. If he's certain it's truth . . .' She forgot the rest.

Jemus stared at her. 'Well?' He moved a finger towards the beetle, stopped and instead made a ripple of sound on the table with his fingernails.

Petey wasn't sure what she should do. 'Nothing,' she said firmly. 'It's a lie, whatever it is.'

'You won't tell me?'

Petey felt the room suddenly become hot. She wanted to stand up, to do something, but knotted her fingers in her lap and made herself be still. 'Is it food?' she asked, and knew she'd made a mistake with the question.

'Is it? Is that it, Petey? Tell me.'

'There is enough food. I meant, is that what someone told you? It's a lie.'

'You say a lot of things you don't mean, Petey.' He stared evenly at her. 'If you don't confess, you'll be punished. And you remember punishment, Petey. Yes?' He waited, watching her remember the last punishment, the lash and then the week wearing the shirt of ants. 'How long ago was it?'

'Two months.'

'Yes. Not even healed, then. And you commit another crime.'

'No crime.'

'Can you imagine another week wearing that shirt over the sores? Take off the shirt, Petey. Let me see your back.'

She stood up and made herself steady, holding the table's sharp, cold edge. Then she turned round and carefully peeled off the shirt. She felt his warm breath on her neck.

'Have you been dressing it? Has anything been put on it to salve it?'

'No. I haven't done anything to ease it.' There was a tremble in her voice now. This wasn't a routine summons at all. Maybe there was an accusation against her. The closed door was in front of her, and she closed her eyes and imagined the clearing beyond it, the twilight coming down through the high, quiet trees and the few scrawny chickens in their cage at the clearing's edge. Loren would be returning soon, or even be back already from the forest with the bow and maybe for once an animal slung across his shoulders. She imagined food. A full belly. Usually the thought of food was to be avoided, but right now she tried to use that against whatever was about to happen to her.

She almost heard the smile in the lord's voice behind her. She heard him scrape his chair on the unnatural floor and his footsteps as he came round the table to stop behind her.

He prodded the back of her head. 'I'll say that again, Petey, so we know that what we say is what we mean.'

His breath was on her back. Even his breath stung the healing skin. 'Has someone else dressed it? You know that isn't permitted.'

He touched a sore on her shoulderblade with a fingertip and held the faint pressure. She gasped at the pain.

'I wonder if this is hurting you as much as I'd expect, Petey? Hmm?'

'It hurts.' She set her teeth tight and let nothing else out. Loren would tell her to show the lord how much it hurt, but something inside Petey made her fight it, made her fight Loren and the lord.

'So I'll give you a chance again. Will you tell me your crime?' His voice was mild. It was as if what he was doing to her was calming him.

'There is no crime.' She slowed and steadied her voice. 'There was no crime.'

'The salve you *khuks* use—'

'No salve. I told you.'

'Listen to me, Petey. The salve is toxic internally. I know what you *khuks* use. You have no secrets. Taken internally, it's what we call a metabolic poison. A very unpleasant one. On flayed skin, it disinfects and promotes healing, but if you rub it into your eye, touch it to your mouth or any other—'

'I said—'

'But did you mean it, Petey? Did you *mean* it?'

She felt his finger tilt and push. His nail worked into the soft, healing skin of her shoulders. He made a further small gouging movement and began to draw the finger down her back, crossing from left to right as he went down to the small of her back, and increasing the pressure so that she had to press back into him to avoid losing balance and taking a pace away. She would not yield. To yield was to be guilty.

'No . . . crime,' she said.

'Really?' His finger was at the belt of her trousers now. 'If I've picked up a trace of salve on my finger, Petey, do you know what it could do to you, inside you?'

'Yes.' She knew. She'd seen it, she remembered Falarien, pale and stumbling from Jemus's hut, and then waking screaming that night, and the screaming not stopping, not letting anyone in the village sleep, until her death a week later. The husband and others had wanted to end it for her earlier, just for their own rest, but they were too scared of what Jemus might do. You could say that – *her* death. Death was the one thing you were allowed to possess.

Jemus scratched at the base of her spine. 'Should I stop, then? Tell me, Petey.'

'No, Jemus. Lord.'

'Good.'

She was crying as he ripped at the trousers and slid his gouging finger down to her buttocks and between them, forcing it hard, twice. He held her there for a moment, pushing and scratching, and then sharply released her.

'Good, Petey. I believe you. You *khuks* can learn, after all, then.' He wiped himself on her trousers and sat down behind his table as she began to dress herself. 'Quickly, quickly.'

She was weeping into the shirt. The pain was more than routine, but not a great deal more. Eventually controlling herself, she dried her eyes and looked at Jemus. He was faintly flushed. She wondered how old he was. He could be no more than twenty.

'What was your village?' she said, needing to hurt him back. 'Do you remember your parents?'

He stood up and slapped the table with his hands. His face was swollen and furious, and Petey felt truly frightened.

Jemus yelled, 'I have nothing! I have nothing! No parents, no village, and ... You *khuk*!' He was almost spitting at her. 'You are a *khuk* amongst *khuks*!'

'I'm sorry, lord. Please, I'm sorry. I didn't mean—' She raised her hands. They were shaking. She was showing him the fear now. Stupid thing to do, baiting him.

'Don't *mean* anything. Be quiet!'

So stupid. She had survived the foulness and pain and then done this. Loren was right, as he always was. 'Be nothing to him. Be no one and nothing, Petey. It's the only way.'

Jemus leant towards her, hissing. 'I will kill you. I think I will kill you all. I—'

Then his eye seemed to catch on the shine of the beetle and he collected himself. 'No. No.' He exhaled slowly and seemed to shrink. 'Better. I'll teach you properly about having nothing.' He picked the beetle up and stroked it. 'The child, Petey.'

The heart faltered, and she had to lean on the table against faintness. 'No. Please, no.'

'What did you say?'

She bit her lip, forcing herself, too late, to silence.

'There was a girl, too, wasn't there? I know what happened to her. What happened was your fault for not submitting.'

'She was not mine,' Petey whispered. 'Nothing is ours, lord. I know that.' The daughter had not been hers, but the loss had been and it still was. The tears and the memory were unalterably hers. Petey was desperate to ask Jemus what had happened to her after she had been taken away, but she knew he wanted her to do that, and it would make things even worse if she did.

'Shall I tell you how she died?'

Petey said nothing. The daughter was dead, then. It should be a relief. She told herself it was a good thing.

Jemus pouted.

He's barely an adult, Petey thought. She closed her eyes momentarily and saw the daughter turn and leave, crossing the stone bridge to the AngWat in the bright afternoon, flanked by lords. A flick of brown hair in the brilliant light. The image faded. Then Petey seemed to drift into the air and be looking down on herself and the lord from beside the small tethered sun.

We are in the hands of our own children, she thought. How can this have happened? How can it carry on happening?

'Marten. The boy. Bring him here, with the husband, tomorrow. Marten will go to the AngWat.'

She could strike at him, call for help. Others would come to her aid. Between them, they could kill Jemus.

They could fight. It could happen. Everything could be different.

'Did you hear me, Petey? Tomorrow morning you and Loren will be ready to take him. The conveners will be here at sunrise.'

'Marten? No, oh, no. Not Marten too. Please, Jemus, please. Please . . .'

Loren said, 'You didn't do anything, Petey. Jemus doesn't decide who's to be summoned or taken. He hasn't the power. He treated you as he treats everyone, and he gave you the orders he'd been given. You didn't provoke it. Maybe if he hadn't those orders to carry out, he would have killed you. Maybe he'll kill you or punish you more when we get back from the AngWat. But what you did changed nothing about Marten.'

'I won't take him. They'll make him like Jemus. Or he'll be killed.' She thought of the daughter, but didn't tell Loren.

'Maybe. Maybe not.' He held her shoulders gently and said, 'He isn't ours, Petey.'

'How can you be like that? How—'

'Quiet, Petey. It's the only way. Anyway, what would we do without the lords' protection? There would be more massacres. More villages destroyed for their food stocks and the area's hunting. Is that better, Petey? They protect us from that. They protect both us and the forest.'

She couldn't stop herself. 'There's never enough, though! We're always hungry. They give us quotas that aren't enough to sustain us. They know we have to break them.'

'We'd destroy the forest if we hunted at will. As it is, we're killing to extinction. So they take children away to where there's more food.'

'And what happens to them then, Loren?'

'It doesn't matter, Petey. It doesn't matter to us. Calm down. If they become lords, they have a good life. Food, safety. Not like us.'

'But the lords, Loren—'

'Are *good*. They are *good*.' He took her shoulders in his hands and shook her and made eyes at the hut's walls, and then touched his lips firmly. 'Petey!'

She shrugged him off, but lowered her voice. 'They play us against each other. Inform, confess. Children are taken forever, or else returned soured and sly, to spy on the parents. And then they become parents, and it goes on.'

'It's how they can survive, Petey. They survive better than us.' He put a hand across his forehead and brought it away damp with sweat. 'Petey, you need to be strong. You need to be patient. And you need to be silent. It's hard to lose Marten, but anything we do will make it worse for him.'

Petey slumped back on the bed. 'You're a good man, Loren. You know, I've never informed on you.'

'I know, Petey.' He looked away.

'And I know you've informed on me,' she told him gently.

'Petey—'

'It's all right, Loren. That's what I'm telling you. I know you're careful what you say to Jemus. You have to give him something, but I know you don't give him anything important.' She took his hand, though he tried to remove it. 'I know I make it hard for you. But you make it easy for me. I – I appreciate it.'

'Maybe I should tell you more,' he said. 'I find it hard, sometimes. Trust. I know you can keep quiet.' He leant over her and stroked her hair. 'Do you want to go and look at Marten?'

'Yes. Together?' She felt the bond between them, immensely strong, as if their talking had reworked it.

The lords saw talk as weakness, and Loren was nervous about it, but for Petey it was vital.

He pulled her up, and they went out of the hut and into the moonlit clearing. The children's hut was close to Jemus's. Light knifed out from beneath the door of the lord's, but the children's hut was dark. It took Petey a few moments for her eyes to accustom to the gloom when they opened the door, but then she easily made Marten out in the line of beds. At eleven years old, he was one of the tallest. The sheet on him barely stretched from his chin to his knees.

Our son, she thought, and as the thought was there, her hand was in Loren's. *Our* son. He squeezed it, and she knew the thought was shared with him, even if he wouldn't say it.

'Come on,' she whispered. 'We need to sleep.'

Somewhere in the night she pushed the husband on to his back and hardened him with her hands before rolling on to his stomach and bringing him inside her.

There was pain from what Jemus had done to her, but denying him her abstinence was part of her reason for doing this tonight.

For much of it, Loren pretended to be asleep, but then he opened his eyes and stared straight at her and said, mock-frowning, 'Petey?'

She hushed him with a palm on his mouth and made him come with her in silence. And when they were done, before she fell asleep, still lying on him, she said softly, 'This is *ours*, Loren.'

It was a three-day walk from the village to the AngWat. Marten was too excited to sleep the first night and exhausted most of the next day. Loren carried him on his back for the first part of the morning, letting him sleep, then he transferred him carefully to Petey. Loren would have carried him all day, but Petey insisted on taking him – not to relieve Loren, but for the pure sake of carrying Marten for almost the last time. She committed to memory the feel of him shifting in his sleep, his knees scoring her back, his chin sharp at her shoulder.

He slept so easily in the broad loop of cloth, his considerable weight slack and comfortable. She relished the solid way her feet hit the ground with his extra weight, and the different way she moved. It made her remember being full with him all those years ago. She had loved being full with child. It had made her feel more substantial. More real.

She tried not to think of the daughter, but it was impossible.

'Loren?'

'Yes?'

'Do you remember—?'

He stopped her. 'Yes. Of course I do.' He halted and looked at her, and at Marten.

'He's asleep,' she said. 'We can talk.'

The forest was familiar and not. They were well beyond the boundaries of the village now, and while the trees were recognisable by species, the smells the same and the sounds the same, she and Loren would be lost here without the path.

'No. He could wake up. I don't want him distressed. We'll talk tonight.'

Ahead, the path led straight for almost twenty metres. In front of them the lead escort was clearly visible. He stopped abruptly, and Petey saw another lord join him, and the two start to talk.

'Wait,' Petey told Loren. Loren looked at the two lords, then looked back until their rear escort came into view. The lord halted, keeping his distance behind Petey and Loren.

Their party must have come across another at a linking of paths. More than a day's travel to go, and they were travelling with a family from another village. This should not happen.

The lead convener walked back towards them. He moved smoothly, his robe billowing at his knees, and stopped a few paces from them.

'You'll stop here for the night,' he said. He pulled a beetle from the robe and flicked at it, opening its shiny green carapace and tweaking the antennae. 'Dead,' he said, and raised his voice. 'How about you?'

The rear escort was just a few steps behind. Petey and Loren were foresters, but the conveners were even more silent than foresters.

'No signal. We're in a dead zone.' The rear escort folded his beetle and slid it away. 'Nothing to be done. Bad management. Jemus changing the schedule.' He nodded at Loren and Petey. 'You can make a fire and set camp for the night. We'll start at dawn tomorrow.'

'Why don't *they* stop? Why us?' She felt her control slipping. The lord stepped smoothly back as Petey advanced on him, and there was a thick twig in his hand pointed at her. A firetube. She stopped again and so did he, two metres and the firetube between them. Marten shifted suddenly on her back and cried out. Loren quickly took the boy and sat him down on the ground. The lord's expression hadn't changed.

Petey sat down and began to cry. All this time she hadn't cried, and now she couldn't stop herself.

'Don't cry for the past,' the lord said without feeling.

'You don't know my—' she stopped herself, '—the past.' She took a hank of the shirt and rubbed it over her eyes. Loren had taken Marten a few metres off the path to relieve himself. The two were out of earshot. 'And I'm crying for the future.'

'You don't know the future,' he told her.

'I know what it doesn't hold.' She flattened her hand hard against the ground. Infinitely patiently, the trees to either side were cracking, their trunks crazing as they sloughed their bark in rough tiles. Petey remembered the sour, sappy wood smell from the last time.

'You mustn't cling to the present. Nothing is yours to keep.' And he nodded at the other escort. The pair of them went forward together along the path and stopped at a faint widening. Both of them had firetubes in their hands now, and they sprayed streams of brightness at the trees and bushes until there was a small clearing around them, off the path. The lead convener beckoned Petey over. 'Sleep here. We'll wake you at dawn.'

'We'll be awake,' Loren said.

Usually Marten would have helped Loren and Petey build shelters and hunt food, but it was early and there was enough time for Loren to do it alone. Petey sat with Marten, intending to talk to him.

'What's going to happen, Petey?' The boy was restless and excited.

'I don't know. You have to be brave and strong. The lords will tell you.' She pulled him to her and hugged him, and he didn't make a show of screwing up his face and pushing her away. He nuzzled tight to her cheek.

'Marten? What is it?'

'I don't want to go. Don't let them take me. I'm frightened.'

She turned and knelt to take him up. The crying tumbled out of him like a river. She let it flood her, wash away all her own thoughts. Wash away what he had said.

'Petey? What's wrong with the boy?'

She looked at Loren. 'Nothing. He's anxious. It's natural. He'll be fine in the morning.'

Loren stroked the son's hair. 'He's almost asleep already. Let's lie him down. You should sleep too.'

'What about you, Loren?'

'I'll sit up a while. I'm not sleepy.'

'Nor am I.'

But she was. She started to construct the web of sounds and colours she always used for safety beyond the village, but tonight the concentration it took was too much. She was as tired as the old forest. She let Loren put her on the bed of moss and leaves, and felt his kiss on her lips, and was asleep.

Loren finished binding his jacket round a thick fallen branch that was almost as long as a man, and then took it up with him to the first branching of a gnarltree overhanging the clearing where Petey and Marten were asleep. He parted the leaves gently to look down.

The view from the vantage point was good, down the path in both directions. Loren hauled the dressed branch into place and bound it securely to the one he was balanced on, then dropped to the ground and crossed to the other side of the clearing. There he pulled branches together and made a rough hide of them, and pushed the pack of spare clothes into it. Then he went back and used a length of vine to bow a sapling over fractionally, and tied it to a nearby tree. The sapling returned almost to its natural height.

In the gloom the vine was invisible. Loren looped it round a root and over another branch and down until the end was by his hand. Then he sat cross-legged, at the camp's edge, concealed behind a bush. He remembered what the father had whispered to him. *Don't hide, but be hidden.*

The dusk slowly deepened and the forest darkened around him. He watched the trees close in. The high canopy let down little light even during the day, but at least the cleared path was a line of relieved gloom. Now, the late afternoon and then the evening had smoothed it to darkness.

Somewhere ahead up the path and to their rear were their escorts. Much further ahead should be the other family, also camped by now. But Loren had seen them clearly there, at the turn of the path. He had recognised them, too, the man Semith who was the village leader.

And along the path, at that instant, Loren had caught Semith's eye. It shouldn't have happened. The escorts hadn't noticed the eye contact. They didn't know Semith. He was a leader of raids. Loren had seen him head the attack, more than once.

It was dark now. Loren closed his eyes and tried to see the trees around him as if it were day. He opened his eyes and looked across the dark clearing. The branch with the clothed wood looked odd only if you were staring straight at it, but not otherwise. An unexpected thickness of shadow. The bowed sapling looked entirely normal. Petey and Marten lay in the open, exposed.

Loren listened. This part of the forest was not familiar to him, and he had to make it his own now. A monkey moving quietly off to his right, on the ground, leaping up, up higher, down again. He tipped his head, listening. No, two monkeys together. Insects, and Loren made himself a map of them in his head, their clickings and rubbings, and overlaid a mental grid of rodents scratching away. He was aware of the metre or so of void around himself, but there was nothing he could do about that without mud and slime and a few more hours.

The forest came closer to him with its sounds and shadows, and diamonds of moonlight began to edge away the darkness.

Now, he thought, now would be the time, and as he thought it, the tree across the clearing moved slightly. Loren's impression was that it was one of the monkeys launching onto it, but then the jerkined branch that Loren had set as his first bait slipped heavily and caught again, and there was stillness once more.

Loren waited, hoping Semith would want to check he had killed Loren, and show himself. But Semith did not. He had recognised Loren as Loren had recognised him. He wouldn't be certain it was a lure, but he was being patient.

Shadows moved and were still, and Loren was abruptly, breath-catchingly aware of a hunched shape a few paces from where he sat.

The figure beside him waited. Loren controlled his breathing again. Go, he thought. Show yourself.

He had the knife in his hand. Semith had pierced the dummy with an arrow and must think he'd killed Loren, and all that was left was to kill the boy.

Semith remained half hidden, though.

Across the path, high, something made a noise. Another arrow.

Loren looked at the tree, which was relinquishing its load. The dummy slipped further, holding its shape rigidly. Loren swore to himself. A corpse would slump.

Semith started to withdraw. Loren knew he couldn't let him disappear. Not now. Semith was too dangerous to be out of his sight. Semith was much better at this than Loren.

Loren tugged the vine. Semith turned directly towards him, aware of the tiny movement so close, but then the sound of the sapling being released to his other side caught his attention, and Loren came out of the bush sharply, standing up, meaning to knock the blade from Semith's hand.

Semith was still too fast, though, slashing at his wrist. Loren's hand fell slack and useless, his grip failing. The blade in his loose fist dropped to the ground.

*

Petey woke up at the noise and saw Loren struggling with someone. She yelled and rolled from the bed and was running across the ground between herself and the man driving a knife into the husband's chest. The belt knife was in her hand as she ran and behind her Marten was screaming. The forest was dark and full of sound, and then it was day-bright as a lord's firetube beam shot wildly across the clearing.

She threw herself at the man who was killing Loren, but he pushed the husband into her way and the two of them fell to the ground. The beam had hit no one, sparking and hissing into the trees. The man drew his arm back and threw his knife at the convener, who clutched at the throat-buried hilt and then fell.

Petey stopped, not believing what she had seen. No one touched lords. No one went within arm's length of a lord. And this man – she recognised him, now – this man Semith had killed one. To sleep, the lord had left his robe open at the neck, and he had died for it.

Loren wasn't moving. Marten was screaming and screaming.

Petey looked at Semith, who was heading towards Marten. Semith's face was dead, his mouth slack.

'No,' Petey said, moving between her son and Semith.

Semith raised his hands. They were like blocks of wood. Petey lifted the knife, but Semith chopped a hand across her forearm and pushed her away, heading for Marten.

Marten's screaming stopped before Semith's hands came together around his throat, and the boy didn't let out another sound as Semith pushed his thumbs into the boy's scrawny throat.

Petey was trying to get to her feet as another beam of light came like a rod across the clearing and went right through Semith. It seemed to be holding him up for a second, but then he slid down, toppling right through the lance of light, his upper body falling apart like an opening red flower.

Marten croaked and started to cough, and Petey ran to him and held him tight, hiding his face from the scene. She turned round to see Loren, and saw the convener kneeling beside him.

'Loren?' she called.

In the gloom, she saw the husband's leg twitch, though later she thought she must have imagined it. The lord's head dipped. She could only see his back.

'Is he alive?' she called out.

A small halo of light shone momentarily around the convener, making a silhouette of him. He stood up and turned to her and said, 'No.'

Petey opened her mouth and closed it. What had just happened? Had the lord just killed Loren? Not knowing what to do, not wanting to speak, she picked Marten up and hugged him. He was like a doll of rag and stick, except for the tears that came and came and mixed with hers.

The convener glanced at Semith, then went to the body of the other convener. Petey expected him to behave differently with his companion, but he treated the body almost in the same way as Semith's.

'Come on,' he said, and walked away. Petey followed, carrying Marten. She didn't turn round to look at Loren again.

They walked for an hour. Trudging steadily along the path, Petey cried to herself for a while. In her arms, Marten had his eyes closed and was still and quiet, but she knew he wasn't asleep.

Above them the canopy whispered and the birds chuckled and hooted. Petey murmured their names to herself for comfort or distraction. Once a troop of monkeys crashed through the branches above them, throwing shadows and spears of light across the path.

The other small campsite was just like their own. Semith's wife was cradling the son. Beside her was the body of one of their conveners.

The lord with Petey knelt briefly by the corpse, then said to the other woman, 'Where's the other lord?'

'I don't know. In the forest. I don't know.' She looked at Petey and wailed, 'I told the husband not to. I told him. But he said, it's the son. It's for him.' She started to keen, rocking on her heels and wailing. Petey wanted to say something to her, but she also wanted the noise to stop, and it was almost a relief when the convener took out his beam and put it to the back of her neck and killed her. Then he told the boy to stand, and to walk ahead of them.

It took them a day more to reach the place. Petey found herself walking between the two boys. The other boy said nothing at all, other than, 'Ley. My name is Ley.' Marten held Petey's hand tightly and wouldn't release it.

The lord let them stop at mid-afternoon to drink water, then pushed them on. Petey couldn't think. She thought there must be something she should do, but didn't know what it was.

The light was starting to fail as they reached the AngWat. As they drew near, the birds were silent. There were no monkeys. Petey remembered this from the last time, and she began quietly to cry again. She had lost everything. She had nothing, she knew that, but she had lost it all.

Marten squeezed her hand. She put out her hand to Ley, but he cracked it away with his knuckles.

A snake crossed the path in front of them, a swift slender curl of gold and green, there and gone, and then the path turned once and suddenly the trees were all behind them.

In front of them were more lords, and behind the lords rose the great silhouette of the AngWat.

HAVEN

As soon as the canopy of the turret started to withdraw, the wind screamed through, rattling and almost lifting the huge parting jaws of half-metre glass, and deafening Mexi until her auditory baffles cut in. She held tight to the ringbar and looked at Lulle. The skin of his cheeks was pressed back and his brown hairtail was whipping at his neck. His lips were white. Mexi could see him struggling for breath, and indicated her throat. He nodded again, triggered his mask, and relaxed slightly.

She took a few breaths into her own mask. Despite the security of the harness around her waist, she was holding so fast to the ringbar that her fingers blanched. She checked the windspeed readout on the curved wall again, watched it blur between amber89 and jet115 kmh. The wind direction arrow couldn't get any sort of fix at all, spinning wildly, and she offed it altogether. That was normal enough, uptop, but she'd never come here when the winds had been anywhere over seventy before. She should have told Lulle it was impossible, but of course he would have misread it.

Still, the small bird in the cage beside her sat steady on its perch, letting the thrashing wind raise its feathers. Its head was still as stone as it stared up into the roaring, streaming purples and greys of the sky.

Despite its stillness, Mexi could sense its excitement. She glanced at Lulle, saw the brightness in his eyes. It wasn't just the water stung from them by the wind. He was never so excited just to be with her, she thought. But what excitement could be like this, downbelow? She'd told him about her birdfishing, but she'd never brought him before to see it. That was one of the things on the list of small grievances against her that Lulle carried in his head, she was sure.

Across the turret, he was holding the kite with its steel struts and stiff folds of azure carbon fabric. His knuckles stood out like bleached pebbles. Seeing his fists like that, hard and strong, folded tight around the struts of the kite, Mexi suddenly felt a huge sadness and a lurching sense of loss. She thought of the night before, with its pooling silence, the central words rippling quietly. 'I think this is over.' Now she couldn't remember which of them had said it.

No, that wasn't true. Lulle had said it. Mexi had just thought it. Having the thought was like suddenly being grown up, and even though the decision was ending them, she had felt bonded with Lulle in the sharing of it. It had prompted her to suggest bringing him here today. She hadn't expected him to agree, and now she thought he was regretting the decision to end it.

Even collapsed like a bundle of sticks, the kite shivered and pulled in the thumping wind. She knew she should tell him to go, now. She needed to concentrate.

Instead she told him, 'Not yet, wait a moment,' touching her throatlink for emphasis, and he fingered his and nodded back, whispering in a voice coarsened by the comms system, 'I know.'

The canopy was fully retracted now and the suck of the wind had steadied and even dwindled slightly. She relaxed her grip on the ringbar and turned away to search the air, squinting. The sun was away to the west and low towards the horizon, its orange halo smoking, but she could feel its hot sting at her cheek, despite the thick smear of screen over her face. She settled the goggles over her eyes and carried on scanning the sky.

For a long time there was nothing but the constant roll and surge of colour. Absentmindedly she stroked the wire of the cage, and felt the bird's wings against her fingers as it rose to be petted. Its fine feathers were layered thick and she could feel their tremble like the idling of a motor. The bird was the size of her fist, but within that volume there was barely a solid pinch of skeleton and skull.

Across the well of the turret, Lulle was up on his toes, looking out too, clutching the folded kite. The wax screen on his face smoothed away a faint pitting of sunburn, and the bright light made him seem exotic and alien. No one had ever been up here with her before. It had always been just Mexi and the tiny bird her father had caught and brought downbelow when Mexi was a child.

Not that her father had actually caught it. It had simply been bowled by the wind into his hair as he had sat in the turret guiding agriwheels across the fields. He had brought it downbelow for food. But Mexi's mother had said, looking at the tiny bird and at Mexi cradling it, there was more amusement in it than meat.

Mexi rubbed at her neck, lowered her head to ease the ache, and looked beyond Lulle and across the ridged, hard red ground to the scratchy scattering of bushes that had never quite taken and the grass that been struggling up in failing patches ever since she could remember.

As far as she could see, glass bubbles like this one glittered airily across the land. The viewing turrets of Haven were among the few constants up here, along with the barrenness and the birds and the lichen and the insects.

She looked up again and pursed her lips in a whistle, the wind tearing the sound from her lips and swallowing it utterly. The birds soared up there, invisibly high in the thermals, somewhat lower in the storms, and close to the ground among the dust devils and the winds here.

Only the birds had ever been successful on Haven. According to Fact records, it had been a relatively simple matter to adapt them to the planet's mild radiation, a matter of cell-stabilisation and adjusting their feathering to adapt to the extremes of temperature. The winds they had taken to with abandon – the same winds that had gnawed the ground-based animals to bones and then eroded them to dust within a few months of their release, each time, no matter what the adaptation. Fur, it seemed, was no good. Resistance was no good.

Mexi had first come up here with the tiny bird three years ago, when she was fifteen, to set it free. It had half-tumbled, half-flown away, and taken a few minutes after the still of downbelow to accustom to the frantic air. With an odd melancholy Mexi had watched it ascend, and then she'd caught her breath as she realised that a great eagle had picked it out and was falling in slow loops towards it. She had yelled helplessly, and as the eagle was in its final tight-winged plummet, the tiny bird had started to dart back down to her. The eagle was arrowing directly towards its prey and the cupola and only began to pull up and out of the dive as the tiny bird tumbled back into Mexi's hands. Thwarted, the predator had pulled smoothly away and would have scythed safely across the ground and up into the high winds again if it hadn't been for the whipneedle aerial beside the cupola that intercepted and killed it, and dropped its body into the turret beside Mexi and the small bird.

The eagle was good meat. Mexi's father had grinned at the small bird back in its cage in the corner and said, 'That's your payment for food and lodging,' and toasted it in visky.

Remembering that, she called out to Lulle, 'Get the reel and line.'

He braced himself against the ringbar and began to set the main kite line as she instructed him, while Mexi prepared the secondary line from the kite's tail, with its bait and barb. Then she opened the birdcage, and the bird hopped neatly to the edge of its perch for her to fix the baitline to the ring that glinted beside the tiny claw at its foot. The bird was the core of the bait.

'Done,' she told Lulle, touching the throatlink. The throatlink and the wind made a huge distance between them.

He said, 'Now?'

Mexi nodded. Lulle handed her the folded kite and she held it tightly to the floor of the cupola and started to unfurl the fabric, but the wind edged immediately beneath it and ripped the kite away from her with a crack and pulled it high into the air. The line curled and Mexi saw that Lulle hadn't secured the reel to the bar. She leapt to catch it as the cord streamed away, shrieking in the wind. Her harness caught and held her as she took hold of the reel to snap it over the bar. The line started to tauten, but too late, and the tiny bird was wrenched by its footring from the perch and catapulted away after the kite.

Mexi watched it go, the kite shrinking, the long tail of feathers on its baitline far beneath it like a small, panicky flock of birds. Like easy prey. Mexi stared at it anxiously. The tail's only movement seemed to be the wind's. She looked furiously at Lulle, who mouthed, 'Sorry.'

There was nothing Mexi could say to him, and nothing she wanted to. The bird might have been stunned or even killed by that exit from the turret. If it was alive, it would have no chance up there now. There would be no birdfishing today, and today was the last day anyway.

She took the heavy reel in her hand and thumbed slowback. The main line began to close down, but after retracting a few metres, the motor whined and the cord jammed. She swore and freed it, and began to wind the kite in by hand. It would be a long haul from that height, and laborious against the wind.

She put her head down and worked the reel. A few minutes passed, and then Lulle made a small noise that jerked her attention back to the sky. The kite was barely lower, but above it was a slow wheel of eagles. She began to wind more swiftly, then relaxed as she saw the eagles start to spin away, either uninterested or not having seen the kite's feathered lure.

And then she started winding faster again, realising they weren't uninterested at all. The great wheel of eagles, fifteen or more huge birds in tight formation, had been scared away.

'What is it?' Lulle said, peering.

Unable to point, she nodded. 'See that brown and white speck above the kite?'

A pause. Then, flatly, he said, 'Yes.'

Mexi didn't have to say anything else. Up there was a lone storm eagle, and even Lulle knew that storm eagles were at the summit of the pyramid. They took the other high predators themselves. A storm eagle could have picked off any of that wheel of great birds like a harvester bending to pluck myco.

Her arms aching, Mexi carried on winding in the kite, squinting into the sky, knowing a storm eagle would go for smaller prey if it were hunting for its own fledgling chicks. It would carefully carry small birds back to a nest built high on a bitter mountainside, precisely break their guide feathers in its sharp beak, and loose the birds among the high rocks for its chicks to practise hunting on.

The storm eagle was circling the kite, its wings spread broad. The wind thrummed in its wings. Mexi hesitated, thinking the eagle wouldn't be interested in lifeless prey, but now she saw the baitline pulling as the tiny bird came to life. The decoy feathers stirred to a frenzy.

Mexi groaned. 'Not a storm eagle. We don't want it. It's too big. Just play dead and I'll bring you back.'

Lulle had close-glasses to his eyes now, and Mexi heard him gasp. Through the throatlink it sounded like a machine malfunction.

'It's huge,' he said.

Mexi grunted. The line was heavy, the kite trying to escape as the wind rose. Pulling against it, she felt herself start to lift from the floor until the harness gripped her waist. The storm eagle circled the lure cautiously, using the terrible winds with precision, then pulled up and rounded the kite a few times. Its wings were like full sails. At another time, Mexi would have just stared at it in awe.

'That's right, it's a trap,' Mexi yelled at it, though her voice was lost to the wind. She carried on reeling the kite down with all her strength. 'Get away!'

The storm eagle continued to follow the kite down, circling and examining the baitline as if there were no wind at all.

'What happens?' Lulle said. 'I mean, what's supposed to happen?'

'The eagle dives at the bird, and the bird dodges and the eagle takes the hook in the baitline instead, and we just reel it in.' Her arms were starting to burn. The upline was a vanishing parabola. 'But not a storm eagle. A storm eagle is smart. It can bring its wings in tight or narrow them to blades. It's very strong and very manoeuvrable. Look at it. It can brace itself directly against the wind, and nothing else on Haven can do that.' Her arms seemed as if they were on fire now. 'This line isn't designed to take a storm eagle.'

'You mean it can snap it?'

She stopped for a moment to catch her breath. Her mouth was dry and her teeth felt etched against her tongue. 'If the harness doesn't go first.'

Lulle looked uncertainly at her, and at the line and the harness. His voice shivered. 'It can take you?'

'They've taken men.'

'Oh, Crise,' he moaned. 'Let go, Mexi. Let the reel go.'

'I can't.'

'Don't be stupid . . .' His voice fell away and he looked up into the sky and then down at her again, clearly realising what she meant. Not that she didn't want to, but that she was unable to. And because of him.

His hand went to his mouth and he whispered, loudly and hopelessly, into the throatlink, 'Oh, Mexi.'

The reel was locked onto the ringbar, but also snagged on Mexi's harness. She couldn't release the reel without undoing her harness.

'It's my fault, Mexi.' Lulle took a few steps along the ringbar towards her. She felt the thrum of the metal. 'What can I do?'

'Stay over there, Lulle.' There was nothing he could do that wouldn't risk the two of them. She tried desperately to reel the line in faster, the rhythm of her arms sending ripples up the loop. She could see the small bird clearly now, fluttering among the bait-feathers. 'Don't worry. I'll—'

She didn't finish the sentence. The huge eagle jerked its wings sharply and stalled, abruptly fixed quite motionless in the high, fevered air, then tucked its wings tight and plummeted directly towards the small bird. Mexi dropped to her knees and yanked down on the reel, trying to shift the kite sharply, but the dead weight of the line soaked up her effort.

The storm eagle was arrowing down, its line of attack taking it between the kite and the main line, and for an instant Mexi thought it had misjudged its dive. Then she saw the eagle was diving deliberately for the kite's main line.

'No,' she whispered.

The storm eagle scythed round sharply beneath the kite which, all tension gone the instant its line was severed by the eagle's claws, collapsed and began to lose height. Its fabric clattered and thrummed as the wind took it. It came down like a missile.

Mexi stood frozen. The kite arrowed down, the wind bringing it across the sky and towards the turret at immense speed. It seemed as if the kite would come down into the bowl, but the wind was too powerful, slamming into the fabric and hurling the spar to bury its tip deep in the ground a few metres from the turret's edge.

The baitline was still intact, though, arcing from the spar with its shredding fabric up into the air. In the baitline the small bird was still alive.

Mexi swore. 'Lulle,' she said, 'I'm going out there. The bird's still there.'

'Let it go. You'll never catch it. It's a storm eagle. And you can't go out there. You'll be swept away.'

'I meant the small bird. I'm not letting it die like that.'

'You're crazy,' he told her, his voice flat.

She didn't bother to answer, working on the reel, unsnagging the line. 'There,' she said. 'The reel's clear. That's one good thing. Lulle, come round here.'

She watched him start to step, quivering, along the ringbar. Waiting for him, she tied the main line's snapped end to the harness around her waist and tested whether it would hold. Then she knotted it again, twice. There were two metres of slack line beyond the knots. She'd need that to tie on to the kite spar.

'Hold the reel,' she told Lulle when he got to her. 'It's my anchor. Let the line out as I go. The wind will take me as soon as I get over the edge, so you'll have to hold hard. Very hard. As soon as I've got the kite, wedge the reel under the ringbar and set it to slowback. It'll do the rest. Understand?'

Lulle shook his head. 'You're crazy and this is stupid.'

She felt the rise in her voice. 'Crise, Lulle. I didn't ask if you agreed. I asked if you understood. Do you?'

He nodded.

Mexi pulled up the fullcover airmask from her collar, dragged it tight over her head, and checked the windscals at her cuffs. She'd have a few minutes before the windtight seals began to cut off the circulation to her hands and feet. She knew what she was doing was stupid, but she couldn't stop herself. It was as if she were fighting Lulle, and testing him too, almost wanting him to fail her. Maybe he was right about her.

'Okay.' She put a foot on the ringbar and a hand on the turret's rim, steadied herself, took a breath and stepped high. She had raised herself only halfway up the side of the ringbar when the wind thumped her from behind and shot her out on to the surface of Haven.

She sprawled and flew, and slammed down on the ground as the line held. She pushed her masked cheek flat to the hard earth. The tight mask felt like it was crushing her jaws, and the edges of the glass blisters at her eyes seemed to be scoring her face bone-deep. She spread her arms and legs, clenched her teeth to stop her jaw dislocating and made herself breathe steadily. The wind was a cataract ripping at her and deafening her. She tried to look around but lost her orientation. The horizon quivered, shooting away from her. It felt like she was falling out of space, endlessly accelerating as the wind streamed past her, scratching and pounding at her with dust and debris. Lulle was right. This was stupid. She was crazy.

She looked again. To her left was a blurred dark spike, and she managed to focus on it, realising it was the kite spar driven steeply into the ground like a spear. It was shivering furiously. The wind that had tried to bury it had nearly worked it free again.

Carefully, she stretched out a hand, but couldn't reach it. She was beside it and close, but it was still a handstretch distant. She stretched further but the wind took her arm and she felt her shoulder socket tearing. She pulled back.

Lulle needed to move along the ringbar with the line. She waited for him to see that and do so, but he hadn't realised it. Mexi was getting tired, too. Her hands and face were starting to feel numb. She almost cried in frustration.

Putting her hands under her stomach, she levered herself away from the ground and kicked her feet, and found that by doing this, she could bring herself fractionally closer to the kite. Each small movement off the ground allowed the wind to pull harder at her harness, and her ribs started to tug, limiting her breathing further. She was feeling light-headed. She hoped Lulle was still watching her. Her eyes were sparking, her vision pinpricking.

She carried on moving, agonisingly slowly. The pain was easing at last, though she was vaguely aware that an absence of pain meant she was starting to shut down. She concentrated on carrying on, not looking at the kite. And then, almost at the end of thought, she desperately flung out her arm and caught the spar, and pulled herself towards it.

Her vision was failing, her field of view shrinking to a tunnel's end. She looped the free end of the line twice around the spar and knotted it as well as she could. The spar was shuddering and she was starting to feel dizzy as well as numb and blind. As she pulled the last knot tight, she felt a surge of pressure at her waist, and the spar whipped free of the ground to spin from her grip and away. Inside the mask, she choked and swallowed bile. She wanted to cry. She was lost. She was rising and at the same time being torn apart. The kite was below her feet, the wind trying to rip it from her, but the knots were all holding, and she distantly realised she was being pulled up, no, back against the churning wind and back towards the turret.

And then the wind was gone, and the most of the pain with it, and she was huddled on the floor, the kite spar clattering around her in the buffered, abruptly insignificant wind of the turret's bowl.

On her knees, she unsealed and unmasked herself, wincing against the tingling and then pain of her regathering circulation, then rubbed her eyes and found Lulle staring across the turret at her. Her ribs ached, but she was alive. She had done it.

'I told you it was crazy,' Lulle said.

She didn't answer. The kite was pitching around the floor, its remaining fabric ripped and slapping, but the baitline was still attached to it, a rising curve lifting away into the seething sky.

Mexi gathered the reel up in her arms and squinted into the wind. She felt calm and steady. There was no hurry now, she thought. There was time. The small bird was still there on the end of the line, alive and working hard in the wind, marshalling its train of decoys while the storm eagle attacked and wheeled away, trying to pick it off.

Mexi attached the reel directly to the baitline before cutting the line away from the kite spar, then settled herself against the bar again and began gradually to pull the baitline in. Above, the storm eagle was still attacking, using its claws expertly to rip away and reduce the feathered trail, leaving the small bird more and more exposed. But it was losing altitude as Mexi reeled in the line.

She fixed the reel to the bar for a moment, picked up the kite and stripped the remaining fabric from it, then knotted a length of line to the spar and tied it to the reel, releasing the baitline altogether. The worn-out small bird was now free except for a few remaining tatters of bait. Mexi was unaware of anything but the storm eagle and the small bird and herself. She checked the reel was secure on the ringbar. The storm eagle was flying barely five metres above the ground as it swept round to attack the small bird again.

Mexi picked up the spar of the kite. Her arms ached from the wind, but she needed all her strength now. The small bird was exhausted, hardly able to hold its train of feathers in the wind. It flew awkwardly down towards Mexi in the cupola, struggling in the wind. The storm eagle scythed steadily along the ground to intercept it, half-stalling at the turret's edge and drawing its claws forward.

Mexi pulled her arm back, gasping at the spar's weight. She heard a muted *caw* as the eagle took the small bird. As it started to rise away, she leant hard and hurled the kite spar with all her strength, like a harpoon, the line feeding out from the reel in its wake. The spar shivered but flew true, shuddering as it took the great bird through the chest.

For a moment the storm eagle stalled. Then, astonishingly, with the lance fixed fully through its chest, it carried on rising, beating its wings and still slowly ascending. It cawed again and the small, limp bird dropped from its claws with the remainder of the ragged decoy.

The eagle pulled again, still somehow hauling itself away from the turret and up into the screaming air, until the line fixed to the kite spar shivered and hummed and went taut. The cable whined and the ringbar creaked and started to bow with the immense pull of the bird's wings, but after another moment the bird slowly folded in on itself. Mexi thought it was accepting its death, but it wasn't. Its wings bowed and quivering with the strain, the bird was somehow hanging almost motionless in the savage air, tearing at the spar with its beak and claws.

Mexi pulled on the line, trying to destabilise the eagle, but it was like pulling against rock. The bird gathered itself again, scooping air into its huge wings. Mexi felt her feet start to leave the ground. And suddenly the eagle gave up. It seemed to shrink, tumbling in the air, the reel screeching as the line retracted, and the bird crashed into the cupola in a great cloud of feathers. In the turret's bowl, the wind took the heavy corpse, flailing its wings and tossing it around the floor. Mexi reined the line all the way to the bent ringbar and secured the bird there. She sat against the warm body, exhausted.

There was a movement at her shoulder, a familiar touch. She lifted her hand and the small bird hopped on to her wrist. She cupped it in both hands to run her fingers cautiously down its tiny body and along its wings. After everything, there were no bones broken, no feathers damaged. Such resilience, she thought. Such strength and determination. Mexi stroked its feathers again, this time with her eyes closed to remember and hold forever the feeling of it. Then she raised her two hands and watched the bird slide into the air and away forever. She thought she would cry, but it was impossible to cry, uptop, and the wind took her tears before they could fall.

She sat against the wall and nestled her head into the thick wing feathers of the dead storm eagle.

Somewhere nearby, Lulle whispered, 'Mexi?' but she didn't answer him. The eagle's wing was broad and soft and comforting. Eventually she stood up. She had to use a foot to pull the kite spar from the eagle's ribcage. After that she started to gather up the mess of reel and line, but Lulle took it from her and slid it all into the throat of the turret's burnchute. She didn't try to stop him. She took one of the eagle's legs in each hand, braced herself, and, with a grunt of effort, she swung the great bird up onto her back. The wind hissed and thrummed in its wings, and for an instant she felt herself extraordinarily light, as if she were about to rise from the surface of Haven and take flight. The moment passed, and she staggered against the churning squall within the bowl of the cupola to the downpod and left the turret, not waiting for Lulle.

The quiet of the elevator seemed unnatural. The eagle's wings hissed against its walls. Mexi counted slowly in her head as the pod dropped, and reached ninety before it slowed and let her out.

It was late afternoon downbelow, the daylites starting to dim and the moonlites easing into their soft glow. Lulle caught up with her as she stepped on to Blue's Main Stretch. The eagle had slipped over her left shoulder, bouncing heavily and wearing at her arm. Lulle trudged along on her right. She tried to concentrate on the bird. It smelled slightly of blood but clean. After the hurlybirdy of uptop, the ordered coredor irritated her. The level whining of the cars, the smooth walls and even pace of it all. And Lulle.

'Mexi?'

She shifted the weight of the bird, and a claw like a scalpel blade swept casually across her cheek.

'You're bleeding,' he said, and wiped the end of his sleeve over her face. She caught a jolt of his shavejuice, sugary and synthetic, and pulled away.

'I'm sorry, is it tender?' he said, misinterpreting.

'Yes. Leave it.' She shrugged the bird into a different position, holding the claws in front of her face like a grilled visor. They walked on.

'Look. It's finished, Lulle,' she eventually told him. 'You said so. Don't change your mind.' At the next junction he walked away without looking back. Mexi stopped to catch her breath and adjust the load, but really to watch him go. He didn't look back once. He just shrank and then disappeared. She thought of the small bird somewhere above her, uptop, free.

The night-bell was starting to sound, mournful and sedative, and the lights of Main Stretch were dimming and going to blue. She went on. The eagle over her shoulder was even heavier than it had seemed up in the turret, and a wing swung into her face until she cracked the joint and let it hang down, the tip feathers trailing on the ground.

Along the Stretch the stores were pulling down their shutters and valving off the air. The ambient aircon was notching down and settling to night mode. The screens high on the walls were full of the endless Game. Sometimes Mexi would stop to watch for a few minutes, but not now. After all that time uptop, she was more conscious than usual of the smell of damp and machine oil and masking chemicals. From the roof, water dripped steadily, clicking into puddles like faraway peals of cracked bells. And every few hundred metres the Game screens bore down on the coredors under Haven with their images from deepdeep-down of the arena with its darkness and blood and hopeless struggle.

Mexi was hot. The bird's thickly feathered body against her back was drawing sweat from her, soaking her shirt and chafing her. The wrist-thick leathery legs were hard to grip, too, slipping through her sore palms. After a while she had to rethink her hold, bringing the bird round her back so that its wings crossed over her chest and its head jutted over her shoulder. Its beak clacked at every step and its claws projected at either side of her waist. Like this, wearing it like a cloak, she was almost comfortable, but the enveloping closeness of it made her sweat more and slow down. Her arms were cramping.

She came off the Stretch at blue88 and carried on down it. The single-height avenue had reached full dim already, and the pale yellow nitelites on their high stalks were illuminated. Looking up, exhausted, Mexi could imagine it was a sky and it was endless. Some private avenues had stars up there, or webbed canopies of shadowed trees, or more fashionably the simple illusion that the rock ceiling was higher.

She turned off into Sapphire, close to home now. On sapphire29 the houses had uniform frontages of broad bays and the breaks between houses were deeply recessed. The recesses were lit with false promise of land to the rear, of thick grass and trees and easy life, like on Haze. There was the faint sound of wind. Not wind like uptop, but soothing and quieting.

Every avenue under Haven was different from all the others, but each house was the same as every other. Jarew Sessi came out of his door as Mexi passed and he stopped, caught in the light of his hallway. In the frame of light he looked like his own absence, a dark man-shaped tunnel. He called out, 'Mexi! What have you got there?' and turned to shout, 'Hey, Chach, come and see this.'

Mexi stopped, irritated by Jarew's usual loud nosiness but grateful for the chance to draw breath. She breathed hard, aware of the smell of the bird as she swung it down, soft and pungent. At the same time she smelt her own sweat and winced.

The shout had drawn attention. More house lights were coming on and a few more people were coming out into the avenue to see what Mexi had brought home. She stood back as they crowded round the bird. For the second time, she realised quite how big it was. Uptop, it had had the sky and the vast wastes of Haven to diminish it, and on her back, trekking down the Stretch and coming home, it had simply been an awkward, huge weight to bear. But it was an astonishing size.

Someone murmured, 'I thought you just went to loose the small bird, girl.'

She took a breath that was more of an indrawn sigh. 'I did. This was an accident.'

'There are no accidents,' came another voice, and Mexi almost turned, but resisted it. She knew the voice.

'No accidents,' it repeated.

No one wanted to engage Vinne on the subject of accidents, and the moment passed, becoming a speculation on the bird's wingspan, weight, sex, diet and possible genetic make-up.

And abruptly the conversation faltered and died. Mexi looked up with the rest of them at the dark upper window of the next house. The window was suddenly glimmering with a turquoise light.

'What's that? A storm eagle? Hah! Hold it up!' The small voice was powerful enough to cut clear through the underhum of aircon. Mexi stared at the silhouette of a tiny head just above the sill. On the crest of the head there seemed to be snakes writhing in a tower of hair, but Mexi knew they were just the tubes and cables that maintained Zelda.

'I'm coming down.'

And now the deferential quiet in the avenue deepened to a total silence in which the aircon seemed to become shrill, and the sound of the fake wind issuing from the recesses seemed to grow bleaker.

The door of Zelda's house opened, and Zelda stood there for a moment before stepping out into the avenue. A few people made to go towards her, but stopped at her gesture, exaggerated by the hiss and bristle of tubing that accompanied it. Light from inside the house flooded around her. Zelda raised an arm, twirling her fingers in an ornate movement. Fluids ran down the thin clear canals that might have been veins or arteries. A bag that might have been her heart shivered on a strap at her side. The strap pulsed evenly. 'I don't need help and I don't need an audience. What is this, am I more interesting than a storm eagle?'

Yes, Mexi thought, suppressing a smile. And you know it.

She caught Zelda's eye, and it glittered under the streetlight.

She was up to the bird now, walking faster than she looked able to on those skinny legs. The skin on her arms was failing and there was the shine of sores and of something like metal bursting through. Old technology. Mexi had heard her surgery was so old that no one dared attempt to fix it. They were probably more wary of Zelda than of the technology, though. Mexi wondered whether she was really as old as she looked, as old as everyone said she was.

She was about the size of the bird, stooping over it, threatening to topple, and pulled up sharply and Mexi heard a hiss that might have been Zelda drawing breath and might have been motors in her joints, correcting her attitude.

'Cook it. It'll feed us all. It won't keep a day, they don't. Enzymes. Those oil glands that keep them safe. A spit.' She looked around. 'Get a spit. This isn't a prissy little bird you can put in your prissy little ovens. This isn't fungus. It's meat!'

Her hand was suddenly on Mexi's arm. It was light but it felt hugely warm, as if she were somehow more alive than any of them standing around the carcass of the storm eagle.

'A spit. A spit. A long flattened rod of steel, at least four cents thick and ten broad or it'll bow under the weight. This bird weighs at least eighty kigs. Here, I'll show you how to pluck it. Keep the feathers. We can use them.'

'What about heat?' someone said doubtfully.

'We'll build a fire. Hasn't anyone here any initiative?' She snorted.

'Street fires are illegal.'

'Because the system couldn't cope with them large-scale. It can cope with this. Look at all of you, you milkmice! Initiative! Is anyone getting that spit?'

A few people slunk away, and Mexi wondered if they were scared enough to be fleeing or obeying. Obeying, she guessed. They'd be far too scared of Zelda to try and flee.

Taking control, Zelda was walking Mexi and a small entourage to the avenue's end, to the bright red stability console set flat into the wall. 'Open it, someone. I haven't the strength in me.' Someone did, exposing the panel of wiring and stuff with its warning EMERGENCY USE BY QUALIFIED PERSONNEL ONLY. Zelda glanced at the instrumentation for a moment, then reached in her wrinkled fingers and made a few adjustments to the panel.

'Remind me to fix this again when we're done. My memory isn't what it was.'

As she turned away from the console, Mexi caught that glitter in her eyes again. She told Mexi, 'It can take a fire. Always used to, anyway. I've disabled the alarms and sprays. It'll just strain the aircon a little, test the system out. We used to do this all the time, when I was a kid.' She sighed and then murmured to herself, 'Time was, memory is.' She looked at Mexi again, this time giving her a long, appraising look. 'Never got to cook a bird big as that, though.'

It tasted like nothing Mexi had tasted before. She'd expected it to taste like other birds, thin and sinewy, but this was richer in flavour. And there were two meats on it, two shades of brown.

'Look here,' Zelda said at her side. She had threaded balls of myco onto skewers and pushed them into the periphery of the fire where they blackened and cracked. She seemed to revel in proximity to the heat. Drawing the skewers out, she shook them on to a plate. 'It's still fungus, but taste that.'

It was like mycobread, but immensely crunchy, and in her mouth the taste blossomed. Mexi frowned, chewing and swallowing.

'Like it?'

Mexi nodded.

'One of the lichens, powdered, gives it that flavour. Be better if it was fresh, mind you. This one's been stored eighty-some years.' Zelda touched her arm, and her voice was softer, barely carrying to Mexi. 'Been thinking of your parents? I guessed, you letting the little bird go. They'd be proud of you. Be proud of you tomorrow. You should think of them. Don't ever forget them, Mexi. People die, but they're still there, always there with you.'

Mexi looked at Zelda, small, straight-backed with her weave of wires and tubes, her face glowing in the light of the fire. Around them groups of people were chattering, pulling with their teeth at the flesh of the storm eagle, drinking visky. Everyone else had forgotten about Zelda in the novelty of the fire and the roasted bird.

At some point much later in the evening, Mexi noticed the conversation abruptly faltering. She turned in the direction everyone was looking, and saw a Robe standing close to the fire, arms folded, hands hidden in sleeves. It was the hands that usually told Mexi whether the Robe was a man or a woman. Unusually, the hood of the cloak was back, and there was a look on the Robe's face that Mexi hadn't seen before. Wistfulness, maybe. This one was a man. He looked quite young, too, though there was the usual wariness in his eyes.

As he began to turn away to leave again, Mexi said, unthinking, 'Would you like some?'

The Robe stopped, and so did everyone else. Even Zelda wasn't moving. Robes never engaged.

A hand came out of the gathered sleeve, and there was a nod of the head.

Mexi took a thick pull of wing meat from the bowl at the fire's edge and held it out. The man hesitated, then he took the meat from Mexi. Now his other hand came clear, and he delicately shredded a single piece away from the lump of meat.

He looked at Mexi and waited.

Not sure what to do next, Mexi took a bite of the meat she had in her own hand, and as she did, the Robe followed. Mexi felt a thrill of tremendous excitement. She watched the Robe chew the meat, adjusting the pace of her own eating to his.

The Robe led the next bite, and Mexi followed, hardly aware now of the surrounding silence, and the two of them ate together until the meat in their hands was gone. Taking the initiative, the Robe licked at his fingers, and Mexi did the same, rather than take one of the napkins from the pile on the small table. And then the Robe inclined his head, first to the fire and the turning spit that was the only thing that still

86

moved other than Mexi and Zelda, and then to Mexi herself. And then he opened his mouth again and said, softly but quite clearly, 'Thank you.'

Mexi wanted to shriek with excitement, but made herself bow also, to the bird and then to the Robe, and whispered as evenly as she could, though her voice trembled, 'My honour.'

The Robe's face was blank again. Mexi smiled, trying to stir something more, but he didn't respond, and she felt deflated as he turned and drifted away from the fire, down the avenue, to disappear.

'Well,' said Zelda. 'You've disturbed the balance there.'

A few people were starting to laugh and mime licking their fingers. Someone bowed and giggled. Visky was poured, and the Robe was forgotten.

Mexi said, 'What do you mean, Zelda?'

'Oh, don't worry, it's a small enough thing. A small protocol. It won't come back to you.'

The fire was still crackling outside, puncturing the whine of the overloaded aircon and filters. Mexi couldn't sleep, and she couldn't think. She had stomach ache from the richness of the meat.

Shortly after the Robe had left, Zelda had returned to her house, claiming she was tired. No one had dared knock to ask her to fix the stability console, so the emergency team had been called. They had asked who had corrupted the console, and someone had eventually told them. They had checked back for instructions and obviously been told to take no further action. Everyone was scared of Zelda, it seemed. Mexi wondered why.

Restless, she turned over and switched the window to an uptop view, and watched the dust seethe and the winds rasp across the surface. After a while she rotated the cam to show the nearest closed turret. Lichen was creeping up the pitted metal in green and pink and purple whorls and coils. She turned up the sound and listened to Haven screech and scream and shiver the great glass eye.

She still couldn't sleep, her head tumbling with unfixed thought. She kept thinking about the storm eagle, about the Robe and about tomorrow, her choice-making. The wailing of Haven didn't help her relax. She cleared the window altogether, then rolled out of bed to look down at the avenue. The fire was a ring of ashes, glowing faintly, and the picked carcass of the storm eagle was still on its spit, like an empty cage. Its feathers lay in a fuzzy-edged pile, retained as Zelda had instructed, but no one knowing what to do with them now. There was the ruminative sound of a wind blowing along the avenue, but the feathers lay as still as stones.

Finally Mexi slept, and had a dream of flying. She was up the sky in turbulence, the winds battering her wings. She turned her bird's head and looked at them and saw they were on fire. She wheeled and slipped into a dive towards the ground, accelerating rapidly, drawing her wings in tight, trying by speed to starve the fire. The ground was far away and she could see the multitudinous turrets of Haven below her. They were all open, but as she came down they began to close against her. The fires of her wings were going out, but the ground was coming at her at increasing speed. If she didn't pull out of the dive, she'd smash into Haven and be killed. But if she flattened out, the fires would swell again and devour her.

She drew in her burning wings even more tightly, hoping they would extinguish in time and that somehow she could still pull back and skim along the ground, but instead the fire caught the feathers of her chest. The turbulence was growing too, battering and shaking her.

Metres from the ground, she woke up, and the turbulence was carrying on. She clutched the sheet and then hugged herself, almost surprised to feel warm skin instead of charred feathers.

But it was still turbulent.

It was a tremor, Mexi realised slowly. The bed was creaking and shivering and she couldn't fix the room into focus. She slipped out of bed, put on a shirt and trousers and went to the window. The floor tapped at her heels and the walls trembled. She wasn't fully awake, and it took her a moment to work out that the window's default view had clicked in during her dream, and she was looking out of the back of the house. The yard was there, stretching away in blue shades of distance, solid, unshakeable and quite unreal, with its trees moving gently in the wind.

She cleared the default to look directly at the avenue. The remains of the fire were scattered slightly and the pile of feathers was spread a little. The tremor was still going on and she even heard a faint rumble beneath the keening wind. A few feathers lifted into the air and floated to redistribute themselves. But the wind wasn't there, it couldn't be disturbing the feathers. Not unless turrets had been breached.

Mexi padded downstairs, more curious than anything else. If there had been a turret breach, alarms would be sounding. This was just a seismic event. But it was the biggest she'd ever felt, or else the closest. Her heart was quickening.

As she opened the door, she felt real air brush her cheek, and the sensation made her stand straight and pull in a sharp breath. It was

88

warm, scented, downbelow air. So, definitely no breach. She looked around. A few windows were clear and lighted along the avenue, but no one else had come out. Mexi went to the fire and saw a white skull nestling there among the ashes. She reached her hand out and picked it up. It was almost light enough to have been a simmed thing. The eye sockets seemed somehow as large as the entire skull. She touched the beak, which was faintly orange.

'Careful with that. Death doesn't take everything. The bird can still cut you.'

Mexi turned. 'Zelda. It woke you, too.' She pocketed the skull.

'Wake me? I don't sleep. I don't think anything in me needs it now. Just maintenance and a few parts that don't exist any more.' Zelda put a light hand on Mexi's arm. 'As your time runs out, you'll find you need less sleep. I need none at all.' She took in the avenue. 'They lie in their beds, all of them. Their eyes are open, though. They all feel this.'

Some of the lights in the windows were going out again, now. The tremor was easing, and most of the feathers had settled back to the ground. Only a few of the very finest were still wandering in the air, fronds of lapis and tiger's eye. Mexi knelt for one of them to drift into the palm of her hand. She stroked it. It was hardly there.

'I won't sleep now,' Mexi said, straightening. The feather curled away.

'Thinking about tomorrow?'

'I suppose.'

'Then let's walk. Let's go up. See what there is to see.'

For Zelda to be so curious, this had to be more unusual than Mexi had realised. Mexi couldn't properly remember the last tremor that had shivered Blue. It had been about eight years back, and it had seemed to her that the world was going to tear itself apart. It had worried her immensely that everyone had laughed her fears away.

This, then, which seemed less, was more. Perhaps it was not to worry about, but it was a remarkable thing.

Zelda had started to make her way towards the end of the avenue. Mexi hesitated, then pulled shut the door of her parents' house and followed her.

The tremor had subsided to a low background rumble, barely pinpricking her ears and the soles of her feet as they walked. All the way up Main Stretch, the nitelites were still on. The Game was there, unchanging. Small bird shapes flickered around the high lightrods, chasing each other endlessly. Mexi found the precise, tiny cries of the birds soothing.

They weren't unsettled by the faint tremor because they weren't real. She found herself remembering walking along here one night long past with her own little bird in its cage and wondering why it wouldn't respond to the calls of the night birds of Main Stretch.

It wasn't yet dawn, but Mexi wasn't at all tired. She loved Haven by night. Everything changed at night. Reaching away before her, Main Stretch became like the start of a new dream, fresh and haunting and all her own.

She looked around as she walked, and saw purple in the shadows by the shuttered kiosks, and a scurrying of rodents on the ground there, their fine brown fur becoming dusty grain as their subprograms strained. The real and the unreal slipped at night, and she could pretend each was the other. Cables and pipes unmouthed from high black facility shafts, snaked along the walls, dropped tributaries and tendrils, and vanished into the walls again. Mexi imagined them like worms swallowing the rock, pulsing hungrily through Haven.

There were a few other people making their way to the nearest observation turret, and many of them smiled at each other in recognition of the moment, but not at Mexi and Zelda.

Mexi glanced at the old woman at her side. She'd miss her as much as she already missed her parents. Maybe more so. Zelda had always been there, just as her parents had, but Zelda had never seemed to change. Her parents had grown more slow, had shrunk, had become merely human, but Zelda had always been the same size, it felt to her; doll-like and fine. She had always been disintegrating, but since she was not her mother, that hadn't mattered. She had always been able to tailor herself to Mexi's need, to her level. Or to somewhere a little above that. No wonder her parents had been jealous of Zelda.

That was Zelda's only fault, Mexi thought. Relishing that jealousy. It was her humanity.

'Zelda,' Mexi said.

'Yes?' Zelda carried on walking, her arms swinging slightly jerkily, her cheeks rubbed red, and her hair, Mexi noticed, not quite straight and not quite the usual colour.

'Yes, Mexi?'

'I'll miss you.'

'Don't be so confident, girl.'

Which was typical of Zelda, Mexi thought.

She caught a splash of orange. A couple of Robes were walking too, heading the same way. Mexi had observed a long time ago that they never acknowledged one another any more than they acknowledged anyone else. At the turret there was a long line of people waiting for the elevator. When it was Mexi and Zelda's turn to go up, the rest of the small crowd stood aside to let the Robes through to join them, and the doors closed on just the four of them, even though the capsule could have accommodated several more. Zelda chuckled in the ascending elevator. She said to the Robes, as if expecting a response, 'Don't be offended. They're more distrustful of me than of you.' She ran her scratchy hand through Mexi's hair.

Mexi enjoyed the open gesture of affection from Zelda. It was rare for her to show it so clearly. Usually it was just in the disdain she held for everyone but Mexi.

One of the Robes seemed momentarily to smile, though neither of them made eye contact with Mexi. She wondered whether it could be the same one who had eaten with her last night. The amazing thrill of it ran through her again, now.

She wondered what Zelda had meant about disturbing the balance. What balance?

There was an officer from Seismic standing at the exit from the elevator capsule, waiting for them. As Mexi and Zelda went into the turret's small safety lock, followed by the Robes, a group of exiting spectators moved into the capsule and the doors closed on them.

The Robes stood back against the wall as the officer, staring at the ceiling, began to explain the situation to Mexi and Zelda in a swift, bored voice.

'A few hours ago, during a routine survey, a survey capsule inadvertently triggered a magma penetration event. The usual precautions had of course been taken by Seismic and Survey, and the event was swiftly diverted through runoffs and brought under control. There is no need for concern. Cavitation and Stability are now working to correct and reduce the outflow, but in the meantime the plume can clearly be seen from here.'

He took a breath and dropped his gaze from the ceiling to the floor, and went on. There was no feeling in his voice. 'The plume rises to a height of two kils and the winds will be dispersing the majority of it within a range of several hundred kils. By the time it reaches this area, any airborne material will be cooled to an upper temperature of no more than several hundred degrees. The relative darkness you'll notice above the turret is partly due to solid and gaseous airborne content, and partly to the deployment of the tinted outer shields of the turret at this time.' He picked at his bottom lip with his teeth, keeping his eyes down. 'The louder noises are volcanic bombs striking the shields. They can't penetrate it. There's nothing to be concerned about. You have fifteen minutes. Here are your timetags.'

He held out his palm, looking at it and not at the four people in front of him.

Mexi and Zelda took the small discs and pinned them to their sleeves. The metal was warm and greasy. The Robes were not offered tags. The officer closed his hand and said, 'Now wait for the doors to open and go through.'

As they entered the turret, another group left, the airlock closing behind them.

After the harsh lighting of the airlock, it was almost night-dark in the turret. This was a great deal bigger than the turret Mexi had been in the day before, birdfishing. It took a few moments for her eyes to begin to dark-adapt.

About twenty people were standing motionless in the turret, all of them silently staring up at the sky, in the direction of a faint lightness to the west. There were noises as if of a distant bombardment, brief hums, dopplering screams and short dull cracks. As Mexi's eyes adapted better to the dimness she saw that the illuminated part of the sky possessed an odd, shifting texture. Hard-edged flashes of darkness shot across the background of light and vanished to the canopy's left and right. Occasionally they swelled centrally and disappeared with a thump as they struck the shield.

'Volcanic bombs,' Zelda whispered. 'Beautiful things.' She sighed. 'You know what they are, Mexi?'

'Gouts of magma. They streamline and harden in flight to form perfect aerodynamic missiles.'

'That's just Fact. They are the tears that the world sheds.'

Mexi looked around quickly, but no one else was listening.

'Don't worry, girl. They won't bring me before Fact for that. I won't be sent down to the Game.' Zelda fell silent for a minute, concentrating, and then she suddenly clutched Mexi's arm and said, her voice sharp, 'This is big, Mexi.'

Mexi wasn't sure if it was the vaulted turret changing her tone, but she had never heard Zelda sound so startled before. No, more than startled, almost shocked.

'This is either very big or very, very close, Mexi. It's not a routine event. Not at all.' She was still gripping Mexi's arm.

Zelda didn't say anything else for a while. The turret continued to crack and boom darkly, while the distant flares ranged from blue to orange. Mexi's eyes were fully dark-adapted now, and she could see the hues and shades and chromas quite clearly. Even under the double-thick, tinted canopy the colours were crystal bright as the planet extruded itself savagely into the sky.

'It's close,' Zelda murmured. 'Look how high it goes. That's more than two kils. And the wind's hardly touching it. It's close. They must be shitting their seats in Seismic. Look at it. I'd bet the first line of vents couldn't divert it.'

She was talking to herself, muttering quickly. Mexi had never seen Zelda like this before. The volcanic light was shining down on her face, picking out the metal pinning of her skull and giving it a furnace glow.

'This close, it means the plume's jetting up the second line of runoffs. Not a plume either, he knew it, he was lying, not looking at us. That's true magma and hot, that colour.' Her eyes were bright as fusing glass. 'The first line barely sidetracked it at all, must have hardly clicked it down a few thousand degrees. No wonder we felt it. The first line took a nibble out of it, weakened it a little, but it ate through and came on anyway, hot as deepest hell and hungry too.' She clutched at Mexi's hand.

'Zelda, you're hurting me.'

'I'm sorry, girl.' She let Mexi go, and seemed to relax slightly. Her features lost the faintly aquiline cast they took on when she was being serious. 'This was a close one. Closer than anything I've ever known. Whoever triggered that, at least they wouldn't have known a thing about it.' She sighed.

Mexi was wondering how Zelda knew so much about Seismic matters. Zelda had been in Nutrition, Mexi had always thought. But considering it now, she couldn't actually recall Zelda ever having said so. Mexi had just assumed it from Zelda's knowledge of myco and food. But she'd seemed always to know something about everything. Like she'd known how to bypass the fire alarms last night.

People were silently arriving and leaving the turret, and eventually Zelda's and Mexi's timetags started to pulse red, and they made their way to the airlock. The two Robes left with them. They stood beside the Seismic officer as the elevator doors slid wide, and Mexi saw him wipe sweat from his forehead. It wasn't hot in the airlock. Mexi realised that the officer wasn't bored, either. Zelda was right. He was scared.

They went down in the elevator. The Robes faced the metal walls as the capsule dropped, their faces blank, and as the doors opened, they pushed past Mexi and Zelda and walked quickly away down Main Stretch.

Mexi wanted to talk about something other than the tremor. Zelda's reaction in the turret, and then the Seismic officer's face, and now the Robes urgently walking off, left her edgy.

'I had a dream last night, Zelda,' she said.

Zelda smiled. 'I used to have dreams. What was yours, then?'

She told Zelda her dream of flying and fire.

At the end of it, Zelda stood there, in the middle of Main Stretch, and looked at Mexi. Above, the nitelites were fading and the broader, diffuse daylites were starting to brighten. Day sounds were rising. Day programs were commencing, morning mist smudging the air and aromas of grass and caffé not quite masking the scents of oil and degenerating myco. Zelda put her hands on Mexi's shoulders and held them there. Mexi felt them, light as feathers.

'Icarus,' Zelda said.

Mexi waited for her to continue, but that was all Zelda said. Around them, stores were opening their shutters and storekeepers spreading their goods on their street-front tables. Main Stretch was coming to life.

'What's Icarus?'

'I don't know,' Zelda said. 'Until you told me your dream, I'd even forgotten the word and the story of it. You've just given it back to me.' She smiled. 'Thank you.'

'So, what is the story?'

'It's not really a story at all. When I was a child, I remember I said to my mother, "I wish I could fly like a bird." And she looked at me—' Zelda was gazing away somewhere, at the roof and through it, her eyes deep and fixed, and Mexi knew she was a child again with her mother, and wondered how long ago that had been. '—And she just answered, "Icarus." And I said, "What's Icarus?" And she sat down and put me on her lap and told me that when she was a child, she'd had exactly the same exchange with her own mother, my grandmother. It was a family story.'

Zelda looked very small, now, and frail as a child. She carried on, slowly. 'The story travels back and back, until it starts with Saria, who was the very first of us to be born on Haven. When Saria was a child, she told her Oath-born mother that she wished she could fly like a bird, and her mother kissed her on the cheek and said, "Icarus." And she asked her mother, whose name is lost, what Icarus was, and her mother sighed and said, 'When there's time, my darling, I'll tell you that and so much more. When there's time.' But of course there had never been time. And all Saria could remember was her mother's tone of voice, and the word.'

Zelda said it again. 'Icarus.' The word, or the way Zelda said it, or both together, sounded wonderful and fearful to Mexi.

'By the tone of it, she took it to be a warning,' Zelda said. '*Beware of what you wish for.* That's what I imagine.' She blew air sharply, trying to dispel the mood, and they started walking again. All the daylites were on now. The roof above them was perfect blue, with a few faint wisps of cloud away to the west. Here and there a program fault that had lingered on for a week picked out the crease where the roof met the wall in a line of brilliant vermilion. Dan and Jan talked quietly on the Game screens.

They came to their exit from Main Stretch.

'Of course Icarus could have meant beware of the sky, or of birds.' Zelda said it lightly, but her voice trembled, and Mexi knew she was still thinking of her mother. Mexi took the old woman's hand, its meld of metal and bone spiky in her palm. Zelda had never had children of her own.

'And you've passed the story on to me, Zelda. Thank you.'

'Oh, don't thank me, child. It may be a curse.'

'Not from you, Zelda.'

'Not meant as one, anyway, not anywhere along the line.'

Mexi squeezed her hand. Perhaps more metal than bone, but fiercely alive. 'And the line continues, Zelda. I'll be sure of that.'

Zelda squeezed back weakly. She was fatigued. They'd walked at least three kilometres, and stood in that turret all that time. She glanced at Mexi and murmured, 'Look at you, with your hair sylvine white. Did I just call you a child? You're grown tall now, girl.' She nodded firmly. 'Woman. I'm as proud as a parent of you, Mexi Taro.'

They were turning the corner of blue88 now. Zelda used her free hand to wipe her eye. 'Faulty lachrymal ducts,' she said. 'Been faulty for years. Never fix them now.' Then, sighing, she added, 'But don't stop wishing, Mexi. Especially today.'

Today. Mexi had almost forgotten. Today was her choice-making.

CAP

John was resistant at first. For weeks he was sullen with me. He saw my attitude to Mary as nothing more than an infatuation. He was, I saw later, hugely jealous. But as time passed, things changed. Mary changed them. John mellowed towards her, and then he began to see in her what I had seen. She had a passion for her work, and not merely because of what it might do for her. Growing up in children's homes and other institutions, she had had no treatment and no money for it, but nevertheless she knew as much as any professional about the state of research connected to her situation, who had carried it out, and which directions were currently most promising.

Looking back on those times now, it astonishes me that I was unaware of the changes around me. I ascribed everything to my happiness. I felt that it was all merely my new perception of the world, and not the world itself adjusting around me.

Around me and Mary, that is.

Let me think back for a moment, to another memory.

My memories are strange, coming and going as they do. Sometimes I seem to think like a machine that clicks and frets about its screen. I close one memory and open another, and go hither and thither, opening and closing memories in the present and the past as if they were all quite unconnected.

Before Mary, then.

It's hard to remember how it was back then, almost as hard as it was to remember my father until then. But I'll try to open that box.

Before I met Mary, I had spent ten years building my people up, preaching in small halls across the country. It was in one of those tin-roofed, bench-seated, creaking and echoing halls that I met John. John was, amongst other things, an alcoholic. He never tried to speak to me. I began to notice him when I preached, though. He never put anything in the collection bag, just stood there as so many others did, simply staring at the bag as he passed it along to the next person. But while other seekers disappeared over time, John migrated gradually to the front of the hall. And over time the halls grew larger and I started to use loudhailers and then microphones to be heard from the farthest seats.

John was always there. From silence he began hesitantly to clap, and then to sing. Once he followed me as I carried the collection bag to the local hospital and put it on the desk in Reception. For a long time I thought he was one of the gaggle of distrusters, or else an undercover journalist sniffing a story of corruption.

I was never corrupt. Never once. I knew that to yield once back then was to lose everything later. My father had taught me that. Those lawyers who sniff at your pockets will never give up. Only if you are pure will you succeed.

And I was pure. I let John follow me. The meetings grew bigger and the bag got heavier.

Wait. You're saying I wasn't pure? I promised cures I couldn't give? I counterfeited healing?

I never did that. Listen to the *words*. 'I will help you to rise.' 'Open yourself up so that Our Lord might heal you.' 'Let me try to help you.'

I know about words. My father told me about words. He told me I'd be dealing with lawyers later, so I learnt all about words. I even changed the way I spoke, so no one could ever tell quite where I came from in the first place.

So I promised nothing I couldn't provide, and the money went directly to hospitals and healing. All of the money. Some of my people gave me food and shelter. There was never any actual Church. That was myth, like so much else, and I condemn it. There was just Our Lord.

The bag that I took to hospitals grew bigger and lighter as the coins became bank notes. John kept following me. I tried to speak to him but he wouldn't reply. He was hard to reach. He was tall and scrawny and stank of alcohol. His eyes were sharp and bright behind filthy clouds of beard and hair, and his clothes were always the same, but growing more and more ragged as we went from San Diego to Houston to Nashville to I don't remember where.

Somewhere in the midwest of America came the first significant Change after the death of my father. By that time I was well enough known to be interviewed by the local papers and to be able to rent commercial arenas with pledges from my people. But I still made a point of taking the collection bags of money directly from the arenas to the hospitals myself. It was proof that I was true to my word.

The local hospital was waiting for me. The bag was heavy. A local journalist had taken an image of me reminiscent of Our Lord carrying

97

His crucifix to Golgotha. As always, I emphatically dissociated myself from this comparison, in the accompanying interview.

As I was about to push open the hospital doors, a motorbike thundered up behind me and the passenger ripped the bag from my hands. The bike started to pull away, and the camflashes caught what happened next.

John was there, ready for it to happen. He was actually waiting for it to happen. He knew it would happen one day, with all the publicity, he told me later. He saw it as a test of himself.

He passed it, of course. He was perfect in the subsequent interviews. There were two sets of images, each captioned *Before* and *After*.

Before, 1 – John bearded, clutching a bottle of whisky.

Before, 2 – Me carrying the bag of money, the motorbike a black blur at my shoulder.

After, 1 – John shaved, smiling shyly, open-palmed, my strong arm around him.

After, 2 – The motorbike on its side, and John standing over the unconscious would-be thief, holding the bag of money out towards me.

There were interviews with me and with John, and then with me and John together. Local interviews and then national interviews, and then international interviews.

In the ten years before this, I had gone from small halls in small towns to commercial arenas in large towns. In the next two months I preached at city stadiums, and as America and Europe became Ameuropa, I travelled unceasingly across the new United Republics.

I preached healing and not politics, and I spoke a language that was english, but neither American nor English. Across the free world, I was a uniter of people.

But I never forgot my father's lessons.

John became my right-hand man. Politicians and would-be politicians sought me out. I was investigated, and nothing was found except my mother. John was investigated and what they unearthed was published, and I stood staunchly by him. He and I became symbols of forgiveness and reconciliation.

The time came, as I had both dreamt and feared it would – the time of lawyers. There was now more money than I could give away without our beneficiaries being tempted by it, so I employed accountants and lawyers. But I had their charges minutely itemised and posted on our Screen. The accountants and lawyers I employed knew that my people would also use them. They knew what profits could be drawn from such a deep well of people, and they knew precisely what the consequences of trickery would be. It was worth their while to be honest.

My Foundation was started. Hospitals, research institutes.

The shows remained crucial. I knew that pure preaching would not remain enough. I started to use the aerosols on stage, the fingersacs and the sprays, and I began to pick and choose who I selected.

I knew that one day my new techniques would get out, that a journalist would think they had a *story*, so I called a press briefing. I had the event recorded, my cams confirming the presence of every major news organisation or agency. Those who weren't actually present in body were connected by simulcam, so that no one could later make out they didn't know it from my own lips.

First, I displayed the drugs and all the delivery apparatus. I explained that they were all the products of my research. Then I took them through the work of my Foundation, explained its history and present state, and its projections – the cures, the homes and hospitals, the charitable works. And then I told them with precision how the stage shows worked, and proved to them that no one was ever duped into believing lies, that no one was ever chosen who couldn't be or wasn't later, other than by their choosing, helped in some way. That all of this was designed to help them, and that for them to be made aware of the simple mechanics of it would not help them.

I pointed out how my people benefited also from the attitude of my lawyers and my accountants; that if those lawyers and accountants swindled a single one of my people, my whole Foundation's attitude to them would change. I flicked up a screen above me and watched them all take it in. It read

MUTUAL TRUST, MUTUAL SUPPORT
THE PEOPLE TRUST THOSE WHOM THE FOUNDATION TRUSTS
THE FOUNDATION TRUSTS THOSE WHOM THE PEOPLE TRUST

And then I made it as clear as crystal how exposing the information that I was freely giving all of them would not merely harm the Foundation and its works, but would do their own constituencies no good either. Not when I was being entirely open about it in the first place and nothing was in any way corrupt. And they all knew there was no corruption, despite their best efforts to discover otherwise. They knew that I had never been false or corrupt.

Above my head, the screen was still there with its plain message of mutual trust and support.

And that, more or less, was it.

I always had the best of relationships with the Press.

Only once, much later, did it go badly, and then only very briefly. It was when one of the leading screenpapers ran me, personally, as the wealthiest man in Ameuropa. The Foundation's lawyers communicated with the screenpaper's lawyers, and it was quickly accepted that in Ameuropean law I was the owner of very little, and that while such an allegation was merely distressing to me personally, more importantly it was hugely damaging to the reputation of the Foundation; that its ability to fundraise would be damaged and that its ongoing work would be crippled.

An apology was issued immediately, and the screenpaper's owners sponsored a new research institute controlled by the Foundation.

This, though, came later.

Just as meeting John had fortuitously projected me to a suddenly greater prominence, meeting Mary Trulove and falling in love with her allowed my work suddenly to achieve a vastly greater audience. A screenpaper (the same one that later confused me with my Foundation) discovered that, in terms of name recognition worldwide, in the two years following me taking Mary into my arms for the first time, my recognition percentage rose from the wrong side of a decimal point to being greater than anyone alive or assassinated within the last five years. Mary was fourth on the list.

The Foundation, then, was doing astonishingly well. It was doing so well that I was forced to deal directly with politicians. Plans, statutes, local laws and limitations had to be addressed, and it was over the need to deal with these irritations that I learnt another important lesson; that the more removed a law was from individual control, the more important individuals were in gaining control over that law.

I'm jumping too far, again. Back now to Mary.

Weeks and months passed after our first meeting, and gradually, as I realised how capable she was, I gave her full control over the Foundation's medical research. My own time was spent raising funds, as before, but each evening I relaxed with Mary. If I could fly back to be with her, I did. If not, we talked in holo, although it was unbearable for me not to be able to touch her. I would tell her this, and she told me how she longed to feel my touch on her skin, elsewhere than on her lips and cheeks, even though that alone meant so much to her.

We were in love, so in love with each other. I ache to think of it. Tears squeeze from my eyes. She told me I could make love to her if I wanted to, and she meant it, I knew. But I wanted our making love to be for us both. I wanted to wait. I wanted it to be special.

I knew what it was for making love not to be special, after all. After my father, and what I had seen him do to my mother. And to me.

I was having flashbacks, too. They would wake me up. Until I had told Mary about my childhood, I hadn't had flashbacks at all, but now I did. They were like an old fever resurfacing to burn itself out, except that they didn't seem to be burning out at all. But at least the flashbacks helped me to wait for conjugal union with Mary Trulove. They had to stop, or I had to stop them. They would sully what had to be pure and perfect.

I came to dread sleep for what it brought. I took tablets to keep sleep at bay, and then other tablets to guide me to an empty sleep.

John noticed the change in me before Mary did. He was with me always, and nothing passed him by. 'Captain,' he said to me, 'Before I met you, I was a drinker. A lost alcoholic. I still am an alcoholic, but I don't drink any more. I owe that to you, as I owe everything to you.'

'No, John—' I tried to say. We were in a plane over a sea, somewhere, rising steeply, unbalanced. There were clouds outside, shooting past us.

'Listen to me, Captain,' he said. 'You and I don't talk so much any more. Things change, I know that. There has to be change. You love Mary, and that makes me very happy, but I haven't stopped being here for you too.'

'I know that, John. I'm sorry.' I saw suddenly that he was right, that I had been focused purely on Mary. I saw everything that John had done, quietly, thoroughly, in the background, as if it were detailed on paper as an invoice I had ignored. 'John, I don't deserve you.'

'You deserve love, Cap. We all do. Mary does, too. She deserves your love, and that's what I'm talking about now, so please listen to me.'

The clouds cleared, and we steadied. We were soaring above them and in the realm of blue, heartbreakingly blue sky. The empyrean. The wild blue yonder.

That moment was my moment of realisation of the future, I think, as I search back through these memories.

But John was speaking to me.

'I've noticed the tablets you take. And Mary's noticed a change in you.'

'Mary? She told you this?'

'She trusts me, Captain. As I hope you still do. She's told no one else, and nor have I. She felt she had to tell someone.' He flexed his hand on the seat's armrest, and looked troubled for the first time. 'She was afraid you'd be cross with her. She said she'd mentioned it to you, but you just told her you were a little tired from all the travelling, and you wouldn't discuss it further. Then she told me not to speak to you about it, because she didn't want you to be cross with me.' He smiled.

I smiled back at him, sharing his unspoken observation that such a thing was so like her, to be so considerate of others. 'I'm not cross with you, John, any more than I am with her.'

It was as if, at that moment, Mary was sitting in the plane with John and me, the three of us so close, such true friends. And indeed, how true that was. And how utterly false.

'John,' I said, pulling his unsettled hand into mine to calm it, 'How far we've come together. Do you ever think that?'

'Every day,' he said.

'But my past—' I couldn't go on.

He waited, then he said, 'That isn't the way to rid yourself of the past, Cap. Not with drugs. I tried that. You saved me.'

I shook my head.

'You saved me, Cap. I'm telling you. I'm not like you, I know, but I can talk to you. Let me talk to you. Please.'

I was looking out the window, at the rushing blue, but his reflection was steady there. I couldn't escape him, and I didn't want to.

'There are things that happened to me that I never told you about,' he said quietly. 'That I never told anyone. I'm going to tell you about it.' And he told me about his uncle, and his father. I already knew it all, of course, he had no secrets from me, but this was his confession of it, and I was touched. I was seeing his story in my head, and mine too, and I was remembering other stories I'd heard as well, stories similar and different, and terrible, all of them.

'In our own ways, we can all break through our pasts,' he said. 'You taught me that. People damage us, but people restore us too, Captain. You restored me.'

There and then, I pulled the bottles of tablets from my pockets and watched him go to the toilet and flush them away into the blue, blue of the sky.

After that, I still got the flashbacks, but less frequently, and when I did, I told Mary and John that I'd had a night of my past again. The episode served to recement my bond with John, and it made the love I had for Mary more profound yet. Mary started to use more empathic speech synthesisers, too.

She and I discussed the progress of the research into her own predicament as well as that of the Foundation generally, and my Mission. Mary used the money well.

The Foundation went from small, specialised hospitals and minor research projects to great centres of healing and major research facilities. We set up international medical care policies. We built communities for the chronically sick.

For herself, Mary was in particular supervising the investigation of stem cell treatment. We talked about this in our quiet moments, the two of us. We talked about how we are haunted by our pasts, all of us, and yet here, in the stem cell, it seems that the past remains to help us. That the hand that holds us down might raise us up.

We were excited, so excited. 'Make love to me, please,' Mary would say from her chair, and I would take her limp hands up and answer her, 'Soon, Mary. So very soon. We will make love together, I swear to you.'

Stem cell research was problematic, though. As well as the complexity of the research itself, there were frustrating, pointless legal restrictions. The name of Our Lord was even brandished in the face of our research. I found myself speaking more and more to politicians, begging for their help, leaving the shows in John's hands. He was thriving on the responsibility, though. He discovered he had a talent for it. The funds kept coming.

I had more energy than I could have believed. Thanks to Mary, my Foundation grew a thousand times more effective. Combined, Mary and I were an immensely powerful force. I was raising money, and without at first even realising it, raising influence too, and Mary was focusing everything on research and medicine.

By this time, the Foundation was not merely extraordinarily wealthy, it was organised. I learned how to do everything I needed to, to oil the wheels, as they say, until they rolled noiselessly.

And then, from simply oiling the wheels, I started to buy the vehicles that drove the wheels. From healing in stadiums I went on to television program, and then I bought the television stations. Instead of delivering newsletters, I owned screenpapers. The accusations of scandal that always seemed to dog evangelical movements did not attach to me and Mary, simply because together we were pure. I had no interest in small corruptions, money, the flesh. We were a love story. We were head-lines.

I can't look back now and see the precise point at which it changed. But one day, the Foundation – I – had power. And not merely the power of bankers, or accountants, or even lawyers.

My father would have thrown back his head and spewed with laughter – I found myself with political power.

This sounds as though it happened abruptly, but of course it didn't. To my surprise, I noticed that the politicians I pleaded with were announcing to the media that they had done business with me. Of course they always promised more than they gave, but I knew I had to be patient. They began consulting me about things they had to be aware I had no knowledge of. I was being photographed with them, I thought, but then I suddenly saw that it was the other way round; they were being photographed with me.

That was the next significant Change in my life, then. First my father, then John, then Mary, and now this. Political power.

I decided not to exert my new power directly, though. I was the voice of Medicine For All and of Our Lord, at the same time, and for a while I remained no more than this. Politicians came to me, for my endorsement, and I bartered my endorsement for tax relief for my Foundation.

Slowly, carefully, I started to ask for more. Mary told me precisely what small relaxations were needed in the law at each stage of her stem cell research, and I would arrange her publicity to make it easy for the politicians to adjust the law just enough for the research to proceed along that next stage. In that way the law was changed; by tiny, complex and apparently insignificant fractions, and with the law seeming to be driven by public desire, and the politicians seemingly powerless to resist and grateful for that. The public burned with righteousness, the politicians reacted with compassion. A win-win situation, they would have called it.

My mother reappeared briefly around this time, but she didn't get on with Mary, which I regretted. I dealt with that, I think justly, and we never saw her again.

It was about then that Mary began to improve. She didn't tell me herself. It came from the director at the hospital. I wasn't seeing Mary quite so much at that time. She was busy, travelling a lot internationally, visiting hospitals, following up research, interviewing scientists. On many of these trips John was accompanying her, and each evening one or the other of them would update me. Gradually, it became John more often than Mary. I mentioned this to her, and she brushed me off, laughing unconvincingly. She always used the older voice synthesisers on these long-distance comms links. She said they worked more effectively with the software.

I guessed what was happening, but not for some time. She'd been away for two months. In the evenings we'd talked in holo, but she'd given me no clue, no idea, sitting motionless in her chair, glimmering translucently in the corner of my room. She didn't even tell me she was intending returning home that evening. She simply walked through the door.

I had nothing to say. I actually couldn't believe my eyes. I blinked. I thought she must be someone else. She wasn't walking well, with a slight limp and her upper body and arms shaking a little, but she was walking. I couldn't even stand up, I was so shocked.

And she spoke to me in a voice I didn't identify. 'Cap,' she said in that new, hoarse voice.

No synthesiser. She wasn't using a synthesiser at all. It was her voice. Her own voice that she hadn't used since the day her father had tried to shoot her dead.

I stumbled to my feet, more clumsy than Mary in my joy.

'Mary! It's you! My darling! Oh, why didn't you tell me?' I couldn't help throwing my arms about her and swinging her round, as I'd done so many times, the pair of us flying round and round until we were both dizzy. I was happier at that moment than I had ever been in my life, happier even than when I'd first seen her those three years before.

'Cap,' she said again, pushing herself awkwardly off my lap where she had fallen in our delirious, dizzy collapse. She stumbled away and sat across the room from me as if merely exhausted.

'Don't call me that, Mary,' I said. 'You sound like John.'

She stopped, wheezing breathlessly.

'But don't stop talking, either. Oh, you sound wonderful! Your voice. Your—' I spread my arms. 'Everything. And you kept it such a secret.'

I started to cry. It was too much. I was still wiping my eyes when the knock on the door came, and Mary rose to let John in.

'John,' I said, 'Look!'

That was all I said. John was looking from her to me, and I saw what had happened. I saw that it was all over. Everything was finished. It was all over, all of it.

And then something very curious happened. Mary came quickly across to me and hugged me, almost falling in her haste, and said, 'John, see how happy he is? I told you he would be.'

And John swallowed and said, 'Cap . . .' and stopped. Then, 'Mary, Cap, I just wanted to give you both my, my love. I'll see you in the morning.' And he backed out of the room and pulled the door quietly closed in front of him.

I knew that Mary wondered whether I had seen the truth. But she pitied me. She lifted her head and kissed me. I turned my cheek so that the kiss struck me there. Like Judas, I was thinking.

'Make love to me,' she said.

'Soon,' I told her, controlling myself. 'When you are properly restored. Not yet. But soon.'

I saw the relief in her face. She couldn't hide it. Like John, she couldn't hide her feelings. Not like me.

From then, most of my time was spent with politicians.

This was as my father had predicted I would have to do. I had changed his plan for me, though, having had no choice. He had told me to become a lawyer, to take advantage of the trickle-down effect, but I had had no education and that route had been barred to me. But Our Lord had provided me with the voice to preach His Word, and through it I had at last gained access not merely to lawyers, as my father had dreamed, but to politicians. To those who create the law.

Of course, politicians are usually lawyers. And if they are not lawyers, then they have lawyers. My father said, ask a poor man what he needs more than anything else, he'll tell you it's food and drink. Ask a rich man, he'll tell you it's his lawyer and the money to pay for him.

My father told me this when we were deciding what I was to do with my life. This was before I found Our Lord. We discussed the law, accountancy, banking. He said – and this is the man whose great great grandparents lost everything in the Company, everything lost twice; first to the presidents and vice presidents and vice-vice presidents, and then again to the lawyers defending them and the lawyers attacking them – he said to me, 'Whatever you do, be a lawyer first.'

This was his credo: 'Son, there is this theory and that theory of the economy. You can take them or leave them. They mean squat. Only one thing matters. What you can get for yourself and keep.'

I had thought he was wrong, for a long time. I had forgotten my father in healing, and I had forgotten him in John. I had remembered him and then forgotten him once more in Mary Trulove.

But now I remembered him again. I remembered my father every night, my father hawking into my mouth, blood and blood. Jerking and gasping into me.

I would forget again, though. I had dealt with the past before, and I would deal with it again.

HAZE

Marten lost the comfort of the mother's hand at the exact moment he first saw the AngWat. The trees were suddenly gone and in front of him, beyond the lord who had startled Petey, was what Marten saw as a long, low, uneven wall of stone reflected in a pool of water and ridged against the orange and pink dusk sky. Before the wall, the broad, still mirror of water was centrally divided by a stone path leading to a stubby central pillar set into the wall.

It was the shrinking away from him of the stone path – which he now saw was actually a causeway – that told him the wall was far away, not a wall at all but an unimaginably huge building, and the stubby pillar was a tall tower.

And his hand was empty.

He felt his other hand taken by the lord. This hand was softer than the mother's, but its grip was a great deal firmer. Marten knew he wouldn't shake that hand away if he tried, but instinctively he also knew not to try.

He looked at the mother. She wasn't looking back at him, but at the building straight ahead, and there was the same expression on her face that he'd seen a few hours earlier, when they'd left the father. He didn't know what the expression meant, but he still wished the mother had let him wake the father to tell him goodbye.

Maybe that was why she was looking like that. She wished she'd woken him. She felt bad.

'Don't worry,' Marten told her, catching her attention back. 'Tell him I said goodbye when you go back.'

Petey gave him an empty smile. 'Marten—' she started, but the lord was pulling him forward, him and the other boy, who was leaning back, his heels scudding against the stone cobbles, and sobbing.

They started to walk down the bridge towards the building. The walkway was flanked along its length with scowling, ape-headed figures of stone. Marten glanced back at Petey. There was another lord holding her now, his hand at her elbow.

Seeing Petey like that, Marten twisted away from the man jerking him forward, his heart unaccountably pumping so hard he couldn't hold himself, but as he tried to pull away he felt his hand yanked back so violently that pain shot through his wrist and he tripped. The lord holding him lost his balance too and fell, but without releasing either Marten or the other boy, who also tumbled over. Marten hit his head against a stone bridge guard. He tried dizzily to look back at the mother, but the stone wall flanking the bridge was in the way. In sudden panic he yelled, 'Petey!' and heard her yell back, and then the lord with him stood up and pulled him so hard by the hand that his feet left the ground. Marten screamed with the pain. His wrist felt on fire.

The lord bent to his ear and whispered calmly, 'If you do that again, boy, I'll break your wrist for you, and then this one here will kill you for certain.' He yanked the other boy round so that he was facing Marten. Marten could hear shouting behind him, the yells of men, and his mother's voice screaming. Marten didn't turn round. He was too scared. The other boy's face was grimed with tears and earth dust, and his lips were shivering. But his gaze at Marten was stony.

The lord muttered, 'Do you know what you're here for? Eh?' He showed Marten first and then the other boy his spade-like teeth in a grin. 'Do you? You *khuks*.' He straightened and pulled them both onward, along the bridge.

As they walked, Marten looked out over the water. He flexed his free hand, the one that wasn't spiking pain up his arm, and tried to remember the feel of the mother's comforting hand there. She was gone now.

The water was blotched with weed here and there, and its stillness was pricked by ripples spinning out from the mouths of surfacing fish that rose and sank again, dark gold beneath the great pool's rich blue. Marten knew the father hadn't been left sleeping. The mother had lied to him.

He flexed his free hand. The pain in his other was intense, but the trouble in his head overshadowed it. He wondered how it could be that actual pain could be less hard to bear than this invisible turmoil. Petey would soothe him and say it was just back-thinking, and he had merely to control it, but she was gone. He'd have to do it himself.

That was why he was here, though. He knew he would be leaving Petey and Loren at the AngWat anyway. The way of it didn't matter. It was done. They were gone and he was here.

The stone wall grew quickly in front of him, rising against the sun until the sun was gone and the building was set there like a mountain carved into stairs and windows, pillars and roofs and walls and balustrades. He had to pull his head back to see the top of it. He had never seen anything so big.

Petey had told him it was big. Loren hadn't talked about it at all, but Marten could tell that Loren had seen it too.

They'd both been here before, then. He wondered about the sister.

At the end of the causeway, two more lords were there to meet them, and Marten's throbbing hand was transferred to one of them. The other lord took the other boy and walked off with him along a walkway that led into the building. Marten watched him disappear, and saw with a shock that this immense building was little more than a facade, and beyond a cluster of stone and wooden buildings of no more than two storeys was a wide expanse of forest cleared into cultivated fields. There were more buildings again at the far side of the fields, and a further wall beyond them, as tall as the one they had just passed through.

'What happened?'

Marten looked up, but the question wasn't directed at him. He looked at the lord who had brought him here, astonished at the tone this new lord had used to one of his fellows.

'Laxity, Josefus. The parents with the other one tried to kill this one. The father killed the other three lords.'

Josefus was clearly the superior lord. His eyes were big but hooded and dark, and the skin on his cheeks was veined with age. He glanced briefly at Marten, and said to the other lord, 'And the adult *khuks*?'

'I needed one to help me get the other boy here. I couldn't manage both myself.'

'Yes, the woman. I know. Stupid error.' He sighed lightly. 'The corpses can be useful. Have them appropriately found for their villages. And our own bodies?'

'Two are located. The other's somewhere in the forest. In a dead zone.'

'Ensure it's found quickly. Bring them all back.'

Marten tried not to be listening. He felt himself shaking.

'What is it?'

The new lord was looking at him.

'My hand,' Marten said, staring at the ground. The ground was the only solid thing now.

'He tried to run on the causeway, and fell and twisted his wrist.'

Marten let the pain of his hand wash through him. The throbbing of it pulsed across what they were saying like a tide, but he knew he would never forget what was in their words.

109

'Now, boy. What are you called?'

He looked up into Josefus's face. The lord was smiling gently, and Marten didn't know how to react to that. To say nothing?

Petey and Loren had told him always to obey the lords, as they and everybody else did. Everything that there was, was due to them, and to AngWat. The lords were not rulers, after all, but the AngWat's interpreters. If they were harsh, it wasn't because they wanted to be, but because it was forced on them by the weakness of the people.

'Marten,' he said.

'Good,' said Josefus. 'Now, Marten, let's go and have your wrist looked at. You'll be no use to anyone with a sprained wrist, will you?'

Dawn was the best time in the AngWat. The sun rose slowly over the great tower, bringing the stone, which against the night sky was just a high, starless battlement, into soft pink life. The day gave it mass. At night, it loomed and threatened invisibly, and by full day it was harsh and real.

Marten woke up every morning tired, sore and stiff. He had his tasks done by the time the sun was its own height above the tower. The breadcorn was weeded and the traps emptied. Across the moat he could see the forest rising like a green wall. Somewhere in there was the old home. Somewhere there was the past, the dead life. Occasionally he still thought of that, but not so much, and no longer painfully.

The bell rang and he walked over, through the familiar network of buildings, the dormitories and classrooms and administrative rooms, to his group's canteen. He was the last of them to arrive for his breakfast. The other six boys were already eating.

Baraba beckoned him over. He was the one Marten got on with best, though Baraba was easy enough with everyone. Marten didn't feel so at ease with any of the others. Maybe it was that he felt Ley had minded them all against him, even though the parents to Ley had tried to kill him in the dead life. But it was a dead life, a dead life, and didn't matter. For Ley, too, a dead life.

In the AngWat, no one ever talked about the villages, so there should have been no hatreds. But Ley and Marten knew they were enemies, and Marten already knew that nothing in the AngWat's rules would make him forget that.

Ley was sitting with Kash, his closest friend, the tallest of them all and the most simple, though Josefus called him straightforward, but in a barbed tone. Kash was best at the tasks Marten always seemed to get, the most backbending and tiring. Kash simply got on with them, briskly and untiringly. But that was why Marten was given them, he knew. To teach him not to question, even in his head. To punish him for what he had done in the dead life. To permit him to forget the dead life and whatever he had done in it.

This morning Joridin sat with Kash and Ley, scooping porridge into his mouth. Joridin was either silent or eating. He never talked voluntarily, only answered questions and never asked them. Marten knew nothing about Joridin, but he was sure the boy had done something terrible in the dead life, as they all had. Joridin's green eyes were always moving, shifting across from left to right, as if he were in a constant state of panic.

Emory and Ghet sat together, chattering away. They had made friends as soon as they had arrived at the AngWat and were almost inseparable. It puzzled Marten that the lords had never tried to part them.

Baraba crashed his plate down beside Marten's. 'What did you catch this morning, then?'

Marten swallowed the sweet porridge and said, 'A dozen rats. I handed them in to the kitchen.' He touched Baraba on the arm, making his face serious and lowering his voice. 'I saw you across the fields this morning, you know. By the moat.'

'I saw you, too,' Baraba murmured mildly. 'A long way away, though. Too far to wave, right? Too far to see properly. I wasn't sure it was you, even. Hmm?' Baraba grinned and carried on eating.

Marten wasn't sure what to do, now. He hadn't expected Baraba to be like that about what he had done.

But he couldn't take the matter any further. Josefus came in, and everyone swallowed quickly and put down their spoons and stood until Josefus had taken his seat at the table. He gestured to Kash, who went to fetch water from a jug and give it to the lord. Kash took his seat again, and they all sat along the great table, breakfast forgotten, facing Josefus as he stared at them, along the row of them from face to face.

'Good morning, my boys,' he finally said.

'Good morning, Josefus.' All of them in unison, except for Kash, who was a moment faster than the rest.

The lord sipped at his water and put the glass down quietly. 'Now, my boys. It's time for speaking out and being free. Who wants to tell us the rules today?'

Hewl stood up.

'No, my boy, you gave us them yesterday. Sit down.' Josefus turned his head. 'Kash? Will you?'

Hewl sat. Kash stood.

'Today is the only day,' Kash said, staring at the wall and concentrating on the words. 'The AngWat is the only place. They are the

Now and the Here. The only other thing is Truth, and Truth is only with us if we are true. To be true, we must support those around us.'

'Good, my boy,' Josefus said. 'And how do we support each other?'

'By speaking out.'

'Good. Kash, would you like to start?'

Kash picked up a piece of bread and put it down. He stared at it and murmured, 'I was wet in my bed again last night.'

'I'm sorry, my boy. I didn't hear you.'

Kash raised his head a little and repeated the confession.

'Is that all?'

'And I didn't tell Hara.'

'So you slept in wet sheets?'

'Yes, Josefus.'

'You must tell Hara. If you sleep in wet sheets, you'll get ill and be unable to do your work. After breakfast, go to the block for your punishment.'

'Yes, Josefus. Thank you, Josefus.'

'Thank you, Kash.'

Josefus chose Hewl next, who admitted to laziness, skipping the weeding of a few rows of farl, and was referred to the punishment block too.

'Baraba. Do you have anything to say?'

'Yes, Josefus.' He flicked a glance at Marten and then confessed to not making his bed. Josefus gave him the same referral as the others, although they all knew that their punishments at the block would be different and unpredictable.

Marten didn't hear the next ones, and gave his own small confession of spilling a bowl of milk.

Everyone confessed to something. Not to confess to something was to be accused of arrogance, which was more punishable than almost anything else.

'Now,' said Josefus. 'Does anyone have anything more?'

Josefus waited. Marten looked away from the lord.

Josefus always waited long enough for any uncertainty in the mind of one of his boys about saying a thing to be replaced by a certainty that Josefus already knew about it. Usually the boy remembered it then.

Marten flexed his left hand. He had almost forgotten why he found the gesture comforting, even after all this time. He wanted to speak, but couldn't. He wanted to look at Baraba and make him say it, but did not dare.

'Well?'

'Kash,' Ley said.

The silence became deeper and seemed to fill the room.

Josefus looked at Kash. 'Kash? Do you have something more to say?'

Kash shook his head.

'Are you sure, my boy?'

Kash started quietly to cry.

'Ley?'

'He didn't wet his bed, lord. Not *wet*. He—' Ley glanced at his groin and made a gesture.

'Kash? Is this true?'

'No sir. It was in a dream, sir. I didn't mean it, sir.' Kash's cheeks and neck had reddened.

'But you lied to me. Enough. Go to the block now and ask for a day's punishment in isolation with pain. Ley, thank you. Is there anything else?'

Ley shook his head.

'Very well,' Josefus said. His voice changed entirely, becoming jolly. 'Now, the kitchens need meat.' He turned his back on the boys to open the high cupboard on the wall and take out a wide-bellied yellow glass bottle. Every boy but Marten slid their water mug forward towards Josefus for the lord to pour a dribble of the fluid from the bottle into their water. The other boys looked squarely at Josefus as they drank, but Ley stared at Marten over the top of his mug as he drained it and then slapped it down on the table.

Marten said, 'Josefus, please . . .?' But he knew the lord wouldn't let him taste it, and he didn't want it anyway. Not after the first time he'd been given it along with all the others, and had felt immediately hot and then so itchy all over that he'd wanted to rip his skin away, and then had been unable to breathe. And he hadn't remembered the rest, except a pinprick in his arm. But Josefus had never given it to him again.

Ley and the others were breathing quickly now, their eyes were darting about. Josefus gathered the boys up and shepherded them away, leaving Marten to clear away the remnants of their eating and prepare for the boys' return.

Marten did his work quickly and got out the books and papers ready for Josefus to start his teaching. He practised reading and played with numbers in his head, putting them together and removing some and inventing other number tricks of his own.

Ley was the first of them to be back. His eyes were still wide and slightly twitching. He pulled the door closed behind him.

Marten moved to keep the long table between himself and Ley, who was washed and dressed in clean clothes, his hair still wet, slicked back across his skull.

But there was a thick streak of drying blood on his forearm. Ley held

113

it out towards Marten and grinned at him, then licked a finger and wiped the blood away with it, and leant over the table, brandishing his shining red finger at Marten. Marten swayed back, and Ley laughed at him, then licked the blood away and swallowed it.

The door opened and Josefus came in with the other boys, and told them all to sit. He glanced briefly from Marten to Ley before opening his teaching books.

This was Marten's favourite time. Josefus taught them to read and to write, and to deal with numbers in complicated ways. Marten found himself better at this than the other boys. But it was over too soon, his head unexercised, and they all ate lunch.

Marten asked Baraba about the morning, wanting to know about the pig-killing, but Baraba shrugged and said, 'We killed them. That's it.'

The routine of the afternoon was always the same. The boys were taken to the small walled arena in the centre of the compound and practised fighting. The lord who supervised them in the arena was called Herad. Herad had never made any attempt to learn the boys' names. He just pointed and said, 'You!' He wasn't at all like the other lords either, who, though they were disdainful, showed some awareness of the boys.

Herad didn't seem to care about himself. There was grime etched between his toes, and Marten noticed the way his anklebone jutted awkwardly from an ancient break. There was the fraying of his robe's hem, the fading of the dye at his skinny hips where orange turned to pale yellow. And the shallow scoop of the robe's neck where the man's scrawny throat rose to his wrinkled face.

But Herad was strong and fast, whipping his fighting stick into the boys' ribs and cracking it at their temples. 'You! Not fast enough. Drop your hand when I do that, or you're dead.' A quick gesture with the stick. 'Get up, get up and out of my arena. Now you! Your turn.'

After some time, Herad let them use wooden swords and axes against each other, and after another while he let them have real blades to attack him. They never touched him with the metal, but they learned enough care not to let him knock the blades hard back at them.

Herad muttered to himself or to the boys constantly, when he wasn't shouting, 'You!' Marten couldn't catch much of what he said, but occasionally thought he heard, 'No, no, never remember,' and, 'Never, never, never regret.'

Today, Marten was paired with Kash, who kicked and punched him until he was raw, while Herad shouted instructions. 'Be sharper, Kash. Knock him down as quickly as you can. Always fight to win quickly and move away. Never mercy. Think of winning, not who you're fighting. Think to kill. Don't think anything else.'

Marten couldn't do anything to Kash, who was so much taller and stronger than he was. He let Kash knock him over, and curled into a ball, laying there on the hard ground with his eyes closed, his body folded up tight, until Herad's stick gouged him straight again.

'You!' He nodded his scrawny skull at Marten. 'Never give up. Give up and you're dead. Give up once and you'll give up again. Even if you lose, you don't give up. Hear me? You?' He prodded Marten again, hard, and kept doing so until Marten forced himself painfully to his feet under the rain of blows.

'You!' Herad pointed at Kash again, and then at Hewl. 'Fight. Until the first one's unconscious.'

This was a new instruction. Marten looked at Herad, surprised, and saw him looking up at Josefus, who was sitting high in the seats, silhouetted against the blue sky. Josefus didn't usually come to the arena.

Kash and Hewl stared at each other for a moment, then Kash shrugged and lifted his stick and swung it. Marten watched Kash and Hewl quickly turn each others' faces to blood and weals, and as their eyes clouded with blood, the fight became sluggish

Kash would normally have beaten Hewl easily, but he was tired from fighting Marten, and Hewl had started fresh. But Kash won in the end, collapsing Hewl to his knees with the stick to his ribs, and then kicking his face until Hewl fell flat. Muttering to himself, Herad let Kash carry on kicking Hewl when it was clear he was unconscious. Then he abruptly said, 'You!' to Kash, and when Kash looked exhaustedly up, he brought his stick round savagely to his jaw and felled him to lie at Hewl's side.

Herad looked at the rest of the boys. 'You!' he said, indicating Baraba. 'Why did I do that?'

Baraba didn't answer. Herad swung his stick in a tight arc and knocked him down. Baraba lay twitching.

'You!' Herad said to Ley.

Ley said, 'Win quickly and move away. He didn't move away.'

'Yes. Yes.' He swept the stick in a wide gesture. 'Good. Pick them up and carry them away, now. Enough for today.'

HAVEN

Mexi sat by herself in the great vaulted hall, slouched low in the chair, her head hunched down. Around her everyone carried on chattering and waving to each other. She took the chance to look around.

The Captain's Hall was as ancient as anything under Haven. Mexi had known its story since kindlegarden. This had been the original convening place. When it had first been completed, weeks after Arrival, it could accommodate a tenth of the colony. Now a fraction of a year's offspring scrambled for seats.

Compared to the turrets built in the last few years, the hall was rudimentary. It was a scooped bowl more than anything else, a structure half in the planet, half out. A wart. Its roof struts boomed and keened, and the wind-flexed glastic hummed restlessly. If not for its meaning to the colony, Mexi imagined, the hall would have been thrown back to the wind long ago.

She tipped back her head and stared up at the sky through the thumping, gridded glass. Neither here nor there, she thought. That's what we are.

The procurator strode into the hall, struck a posture at the lectern and waited there patiently, gazing steadily around his audience to establish order and then control. He glanced at Mexi with her wind-burnt face, creased eyes, whipped-back ash-white hair, and held her there briefly, before moving on over the rest of them with their underworld pallor and obsidian-black locks.

The procurator cleared his throat. Behind him on the grey wall the Captain's portrait squatted, defined by that sharp, square jaw and those hooded grey eyes. Mexi wondered if the man had ever looked like that. She thought of Zelda's saying, *Time was, but memory is.*

'Good morning. We'll start.' The procurator composed himself, wiping his palms down his jacket, flexing his hands and flattening them on the lectern. From her position Mexi had an oblique view of the lectern screen, a shimmering lozenge of pale blue. The Captain's face stared over the procurator's shoulder as he began.

'Welcome to adulthood, all of you. You are honoured to be here in the Captain's Hall, and we are very proud of you. You are the elite of Haven. You are the fraction of this graduating year who have chosen to work for the Ministration, and have been accepted. You will not be Haven's shopkeepers and scourers, scurrying through its coredors all your lives.' His lips creased into a thin smile of approval. 'Congratulations.'

He smiled again and clapped three times, the sound flurrying briefly around the hall.

'You will have an opportunity this morning to choose which section of the Ministration to join.' He checked himself. 'Most of you. I'm sure you know that a very small number of you will be directed, but those of you to whom this happens should take it as a special honour.' He tapped the desk sharply with something metal, though no one had reacted, and waited a moment more. His voice tautened. 'I want to say something here. Every year—' he looked slowly round the hall. 'Every year, rumours spread about this process. About direction. I want to make it quite clear that it does *not* mean that quotas have been filled by the time your own choice is made. It means that the tests have shown you to have a particular aptitude. Most of you will choose that direction of your own volition. But a few of you will not.' He waited a few seconds, in a silence that only the wind thumping on the canopy failed to respect.

'Those very few are the ones we direct,' he said.

The audience remained quiet. Mexi looked around. No one else was staring anywhere but at the procurator's face. Mexi knew he always said that. Zelda had told her he did. Zelda had told her that direction wasn't necessarily a sign of aptitude, but she hadn't told her what it might be a sign of.

Get on with it, then, Mexi thought, looking up at the scudding sky. She tried to imagine what it might be like beyond that sky.

'You are a small part of the tenth generation of subhabitants to be raised under Haven,' the procurator said. 'Just by that, you are privileged beyond imagination.' He emphasised the point with a nod. 'You have an easier life than your parents, and the work of your lives will make those of *your* children easier yet.' Mexi could see him settling now, slipping into the routine of the speech.

'You all know this, but it bears repeating, and always will. You all know the importance of telling, of Fact. We were intended as no more than a colony for a discovered world. Your parents' parents' parents'

parents—' he took an ostentatious breath, carefully ticking his fingers off, '—left the Oath to become a self-sustaining community. But while they were en route here, contact was abruptly lost. The journey was a terrible one. During its course, the Captain was forced to abandon many ships.'

Everyone listened as if for the first time. As if there might be something new. Mexi glanced around the hall, seeing them almost mouthing the words, ticking their fingers as the procurator ticked his. All that would change as they grew older would be the number of tickings of their fingers. The story was the story. It was protected so that the truth could not get lost like so much else. It was Fact.

'As we finally descended on Haven, on to this planet of roaring wind, the Archive was lost and the Captain perished. It was a time of great trial. Many died. Our forefathers had to struggle and dig deep, both within their new home and within themselves.'

He allowed a silence. The vault above murmured and complained.

'They had no time for reflection or mourning. They wiped their brows, they dug deep and they built. They developed the beginnings of the technologies that keep us alive. And they had children. They taught their children to dig and to build and to use the technologies they had developed and to develop more. And they, and *they*, and then eventually *we* carried on, as *you* will carry on.'

He paused. Despite herself, Mexi found her lips moving with the words. The hall was humming with the story, the story drowning the wind.

'Generations passed in struggle. There was no time for anything but the struggle to survive. By the time someone at last had a moment to catch their breath, there was no one alive who could remember the past, the Oath, and it had disappeared into the wind.' He arched his head back to look up at the vault and the sky beyond, and held his gaze there. Mexi stared at his adam's apple, watched it jerk as the procurator swallowed but still held his gaze firmly to the heavens.

And then he looked down again, sombre. 'But now we are free. We are free of the Oath, and free too of the history of Oath. For the first generations of subhabitants, there was no time to pass on knowledge of it, or to record memories of it. And now we are free entirely of it.' He spread his arms in a gesture that might have been a dismissal or a celebration, and said, 'Whatever happened to the Oath, it cannot reach or destroy us. If the Oath has simply forgotten us, then so let it be. All that remains of the Oath is its name. We hold to language, though. We protect only that, so that if survivors of the Oath should contact us in the years and centuries to come...'

Mexi looked up. She could see the wind bump at the glass. She wondered how many times the glass vaulting had been replaced over the years. She glanced across at the nearest inductee, a boy with pale skin and a shaving cut on his throat. The boy glanced back at her and attempted a smile, but couldn't carry through with it. Nutrition, she thought. That's what he'll be good for.

'Now,' the procurator said, 'It's time for the presentations.'

There was suddenly a different tone to his voice. The ritual part was over.

Mexi glanced round the hall. Everyone was quiet and expectant. She looked at the presentation program on the seat screen in front of her, and scrolled impatiently through the contents.

Seismic was first to present. It was a woman who came from the back of the hall, walking slowly to the lectern where she stopped and rested her palms and then looked slowly around the hall. With each sweep of her head, the silence deepened.

Mexi felt supremely alert. Her impatience slid away. She felt herself an adult in the presence of adults, in a way she had only ever felt before with Zelda. Before their deaths in the rockfall, her parents had started to talk to her almost as an adult, but they couldn't quite manage it. It always came out as if it was a joke she didn't get.

'Now,' the woman said. 'I'll begin by saying that I know most of you have already made your minds up. If you're like I was, you've known where you want to be for as long as you can remember. I always wanted to be part of Seismic.' She paused. 'What do we do? We're responsible for monitoring the movements and fluctuations of Haven's mantle and core. We carry out predictive work. It isn't easy. Haven is not a natural planet, at least not until you get a number of kils deeper than our deepest physical surveys, and whoever terraformed it, kind though they were, they failed to leave a set of plans behind.'

A smattering of laughter eased through the hall. Maybe a few more volunteers for Seismic, Mexi thought.

'So. We analyse, we examine. You will all be aware of the event-monitoring system that runs along every avenue, every boulevard, every stretch and lane that you will ever walk. That entire system is ours. The opportunities in Seismic are probably wider than in any other branch of the Ministration. Last night, for instance—' She caught herself, her tone changed, '—well, a few hours ago, I wasn't sure I'd be giving this talk today. Without Seismic, we might not all have been here.' She seemed to colour slightly, moving her hands on the lectern. 'Only three men died last night. Surveyors. Brave, brave men. If not for Seismic, it would have been a great many more.'

There was a little applause, which seemed to embarrass her. 'There's been talk of the event last night being due to careless work by Survey. This is not so. If you join Seismic today, you'll be working with Survey, and you will very soon realise that the coffin teams are Haven's most heroic men and women. Without Survey, we'd have carried on trying to survive huddled under turrets like this one, and the colony would quickly have failed. Survey discovered this planet as certainly as the Captain did, and Survey is still discovering it.' She looked abruptly off to the side, and shook her head forcefully. 'We in Seismic just predict. Survey teams test those predictions. If we get it wrong, we're usually still here.' She stopped and glanced off to the side again, nodding to someone out of sight. 'I'm sorry, but I wanted to say that. What happened last night shook us all.'

She made herself smile. 'Seismic. Our work is varied and as eternally fascinating as Haven itself. You can devote yourself to the screens, making calculations of risk; you can become an engineer, designing magma-baffles and runoffs . . .'

Mexi was scrolling down her screen again. She wasn't interested in Seismic. But Zelda had been right about last night, it seemed.

Survey was next up. A man, this time. Almost unnoticeably, the woman from Seismic touched his arm as they passed. He came quickly to the lectern, and stood there for a moment as if trying to remember his purpose. He spoke rapidly and didn't take long with his presentation, and made little attempt to excite the hall. 'Everyone here knows about Survey,' he began. His voice was hardly audible, and the hall seemed to tilt towards him as everyone leaned forward to hear. 'Perhaps you'll be thinking about Survey this morning, particularly. As Galena just told you, we lost two coffin surveyors and a go-station technician last night, trying to extend the boundaries of Haven. Brave lives, brave deaths. Brave . . .'

He was suddenly quiet.

'Well. You'll know if you intend to join us, and you'll know if not. I don't want to try to change anyone's mind. Survey is at best a dedication, at worst a need. It can be quite unimaginably beautiful, out there in the rock, but that is not a thing I can explain. If you're suited to it, you know that now. If you're not certain, you are *not* suited. Do something else.

'There are just two other things I want to say, and I say them every year. First, all of you here should hold those of us – those of you – who work in Survey in great respect. Remember this at the end of today – especially today – and always. If you can't have respect, have understanding. When you see one of us in the coredors and avenues, don't judge us by your standards. We are not at our best there, or usually at our ease. Remember what we do.'

His hand cracked on the lectern. He looked around the hall, and even the wind seemed to relent briefly. 'Remember what we do for you all. If you see anyone abusing a Surveyor – and it is sadly a common thing – remember where we go for you. Where we have been for you. Come to our defence.' He took a breath and examined his hand, turning it over and back. 'Those of us who crawl into our coffins and grind out into the hard dark to feel out the planet for its safe places may be driven by our genes and our imaginations to do so, as we are all driven to our fates. That makes us no less scared for our lives and no less brave. It's a fashion to call us the Dead, to whisper it as we pass. This morning, three more of us are dead. Remember that. Remember that without us, we would all be dead.'

He stopped, stepped back as if he were done, then came forward again. The silence in which he moved was like a solid thing holding everyone else still, clamping everyone but him in place. Mexi's spine felt locked tight, each stacked vertebra fixed and immovable. She realised that she was even holding her breath. She might be fossilising. In the entire hall, it seemed only the man from Survey was able to move.

'Yes,' he said. 'The second thing I have to tell you. I said before that you would know if you were suited to Survey. There are of course exceptions. You are aware that one or two of you will be redirected today, steered away from what you think you have chosen, to Survey. I know that those of you to whom it will happen already suspect it. Please don't be anxious. It is the right thing.' He looked quickly around the hall, and a flurry of faint movement ruffled the auditorium as his gaze passed. 'That's all I have to say.'

As he left the hall, Mexi rubbed her neck. Around her, bones clicked, joints freed themselves. The boy beside her made a fist and massaged it, his knuckles sounding off like snapped rubber. 'What does he mean, don't worry? He just made us all suspect it. Crise, no wonder they get treated like they do. Rockheads.'

'*You* don't suspect it,' Mexi told him angrily. 'Didn't you listen to him? You just fear it. Down there—' she nodded at a boy several tiers down, who hadn't moved at all since the Surveyor had left. 'He suspects it.'

'So why tell him? Why let him sit through the rest of this, frenzying up inside?'

'Maybe he was thinking it anyway. Just like the Surveyor said. Maybe this way he can consider it properly, make it his choice.'

The boy at her side made a dismissive grunt and looked away. Mexi glanced back down at the boy below, whose head was jerking gently. Another boy put an arm around him. Mexi noticed her cheek was cold, and wiped water away with the back of a hand. Survey, she thought.

She rubbed her chin and blinked her eyes hard. This was real, she told herself. This was adulthood.

'Nutrition,' the next man said from the lectern. 'We have a twofold function. One is overriding, one is merely important. We make sure there is enough food for us all, and we make it palatable and varied. You all know what it is that we eat. We eat myco. In other words, fungus. Occasionally we supplement it with birdmeat. We don't eat rats or vermin. Occasionally there's food from Haze, but trade regulations limit this. Our friends—' the man's gaze flicked up, and Mexi knew there had to be a Robe at the back of the hall, quietly observing, '—have little stomach for myco.'

Mexi chuckled, along with everyone else. She knew what everyone was thinking, and what the Nutritionist was tacitly acknowledging – that Nutrition was the least respected branch of the Ministration.

'So myco is our staple food,' he said. 'Surface agriculture is still attempted, research continues, but myco will remain our staple for many more years. Which means we have to keep the caverns fertile, productive and disease-free. We have to find new ways to make our myco look different, taste different, and still provide all our dietary needs. We work with genes as well as pans. We cook in laboratories and in kitchens.' He smiled, then said, 'Every one of today's presentations concerns a vital aspect of our existence on Haven. I know every one of you wants to contribute directly to that existence, and has proved yourself able. Many of you think of us in Nutrition as kitchen cooks and mixers, but you're very wrong. Nutrition is very special. We *add* to existence. What we do is highly visible. We make food, and we make it pleasurable.'

Mexi could see no one was convinced. He continued for a while, though, then left. Mexi sat up straight before the next presenter appeared. The word on her screen seemed vibrant.

CONTACT.

Mexi looked around, expecting everyone to be reacting in the same way she was. How could they all not be waiting for this? This was the Ministration branch she had wanted to be part of since she had been a child. To fly higher than a kite, higher than a bird, higher than the sky. To see Haze! Mexi was almost too excited to hear the woman who was presenting introduce herself.

'Almost since contact was first made with Haze, we've been sending people there, and hosting their people in return. I shan't go into that now, but the function of Contact is to foster and maintain good relations with the people of Haze, to ensure a flow of clear communication and understanding between us, and to facilitate the work carried out by all the other branches of Ministration between planets. We try to understand and be sensitive to their culture. We try to ensure the comprehension of all facts relating to their customs. We try to show understanding and also to enable our visitors to have as much understanding of us as possible. Contact is not a one-way process. For it to be worthwhile, it must be to the benefit of all.' There seemed an edge to her voice, and Mexi felt she was missing something.

The atmosphere in the hall relaxed again for the next presentations, Maintenance, Fabric, and Cavitation, and finally it was the turn of Fact.

Mexi wasn't even looking at General Factotem as he began. 'We are all special. Every one of us, and every branch of the Ministration. Everyone who has spoken to you today has made a point – a special point – of this. Every branch of the Ministration is singular and distinctive. I am not going to tell you that about Fact. I am going to tell you that our branch is unique. Fact. We oversee not only every other branch of the Ministration, but everything within and upon Haven.' He stopped for a long moment. 'Fact. Fact is everything. Fact is *what* you believe. Fact is *who* you believe.

'The procurator told you in his introduction how we are free of our history, free of the Oath from which we came. This is true. It is even Fact.' He smiled, the oddly sly expression somehow contradicting what he had said. Although there had been nothing but a few words, Mexi had a sense of uncertainty and danger.

'We don't *know* that the Oath was destroyed. We know that communication ceased, and we know it was never restored. Now, our only true history is the history of Haven. Despite the Captain's efforts, we have nothing of the original Archive. We possess a few documents. A book, *Rufus and the Jungle Trail.* There were also anecdotes, tales spread by worm of mouth. These anecdotes and rumours have been banned, as of course you know. You should know why, if you don't already. They are unsubstantiated, and as they change at every telling, they change the past, and so they are unFact.

'Let me talk a little about our language. It is part of our history, so it is vital that it be accurately preserved. Language is the very core of Fact. Fact cannot be properly safeguarded if the language that holds it does not itself hold firm. The preservation of our language is one of the things that gave us, and gives us, smooth contact with our friends on Haze, who we know must also have arrived from Oath, in likelihood some generations before we came to Haven. It is one of the tasks of Fact, with the help of Contact, to investigate the true history of us all.

'And what if the Oath survives, and one day contacts us again? Will we have lost our common language? Our commonality? Would we want that?' He shook his head, and Mexi found herself shaking her head too.

'Fact is often thought of as a cult of discipline and rigidity. I'm aware of that. I'd answer that such thinking displays a rigid attitude. I'd reply that discipline is a scientific requirement. And I'd also say that such thoughts, such criticisms of Fact, are private opinions, and as such respectable. But to me, Fact is continuity, safety, security.' He shrugged. 'That doesn't sound harsh or rigid, though it sounds dull. But Fact isn't dull at all. It's enquiring. It's questing. It is, if you like, much like the rock that supports us.'

The General paused. 'For all of us on Haven, the future is unknown and exciting. For those of us in Fact, so is the past. Despite what the procurator told you.'

Mexi leaned forward. The sense of risk emanating from the Factotem was there again. He was challenging the procurator's words. There was division, debate. There was dispute, and it was coming from Fact, and directed at the procurator.

The entire hall had registered it. Mexi could sense the attitude of everyone changing. Fact was suddenly interesting. Everyone else had talked of action, but Fact was only words – and yet it challenged everything else. It was more dangerous than anything.

The Factotem still hadn't finished. No one else had spoken at such length. 'There are many of you here who want to travel, one day, to Haze. This will be in your minds when you make your choice in a very few moments. Hmm? What are you thinking? Nutrition? Do you imagine that will be your passport to Haze?' He shrugged. 'Maybe. One nutritionist in five hundred might have a chance to go. How else, then? Contact, is that what you're thinking? Work in Contact, and you'll get to Haze? You think so?' He waited, then slowly shook his head. 'Less than one person in a hundred in Contact ever goes.'

This wasn't debate, or even dispute. General Factotem was setting himself directly against another branch of Ministration.

'Maybe it will be you, that one in a hundred. After twenty years of shadowing your seniors, of learning how to behave without causing insult in *this* situation, under *those* circumstances . . . If you imagine Fact is rigid, then try Contact.' He adjusted his position at the podium, and a glint of light darted from a medal on his chest.

'If you're interested in Haze, Fact is your best route. Not Contact. Why would that be? Let me tell you. Our own small Vault on Haven is well-investigated. But there just may be papers on Haze of which we are unwary. We know they have no knowledge whatever of their history prior to their existence on Haze, but we have a program of exchange by which we hope in time to search for documentation of Oath there. In Fact, we are not restricted by the regulations of Contact.'

He tapped both palms sharply on the lectern and said, 'Remember this. Fact is freedom.' And then he said, 'I'm done,' and walked away.

The procurator returned. 'Now, it's time to make your decision. If you are undecided, wait in your seat, and you'll be directed to the correct branch of the Ministration at the end.'

The presenters were already arranging themselves on the stage behind the procurator. Mexi noticed the Contact representative standing as far as he could from Factotem. She noticed also that the Factotem was given more space than anyone else, and that the others were talking to each other, while the General had his hands behind his back and was staring up at the dome. She joined the people starting to file down the aisles towards the stage. The boy who had been sobbing during the Survey presentation was in front of her. She watched as he made for Seismic, pushing his way into the heart of the small group there. He looked nervous, but settled after a moment, and relaxed enough to start chattering to the others in the group.

Mexi headed straight for Contact. The man smiled at her, glancing at her hair, and for the first time in months she felt herself responding to the attention. 'I was born with it,' she said. 'That's all.'

The procurator waited until everyone had made their choices. All the groups seemed about the same size. Mexi was already imagining herself on Haze, standing in the open air, trees around her, the wind gently blowing.

No one was seated, undecided. But no one got to this stage in their lives and didn't know what they wanted. And she guessed no one would want to risk being directed to Survey.

And then the procurator took a list from his pocket and inspected it, then beckoned over the representatives, one by one, who then went to other groups.

These are the directions, Mexi realised.

Everyone was watching for the Surveyor to take his instructions. The procurator was whispering to him now, and he was nodding, glancing at other groups. Her attention on him, Mexi hardly noticed the man from Fact as he approached her group, and when he touched Mexi's arm, she thought he was just going to ask about her hair. But he said, 'Miz Taro? Mexi Taro? You've been directed to us. I'm sorry it wasn't your choice, but you'll appreciate it in the end. I know you will.'

As she went with the man to his group, numbly wondering why, wondering what made her suitable for Fact and not for Contact, she noticed the Surveyor making for the Seismic group. It parted for him, and he touched the arm of the sobbing boy. There was a warmth and gentleness in the man's touch that surprised Mexi and stopped her thinking about herself.

'Miz Taro? Mexi?'

She turned back.

'This is going to be a busy day for you, so please be fully with me. Come and join us.' He raised his voice. 'Fact group. My name is Gild. Listen to me carefully. Our schedule today. You'll be taken individually to see the Hub. In the Hub you'll get a small taster of life in Nutrition.'

He waited until someone muttered, 'Nutrition?'

'That's right. Nutrition is where you'll go if you don't make it in Fact. If we reject you, or if you deliberately get yourselves rejected – and I know some of you are already considering this – you don't get to make another choice. You go to Nutrition, and you stay there.'

He waited for that to be taken in by the half circle of people around him.

'Good. I don't need to say that again. You understand me. Let me tell you that it isn't easy to complete an apprenticeship in Fact. There are sixteen of you. Every year, a handful of people actively choose us. This year, seven of you chose us, and the other nine were directed to me. Some of you standing – whether you are here by choice or direction – are better suited than others. Some of you will find it impossible to complete the apprenticeship and will be rejected.'

He was looking slowly from face to face.

'Few people choose Fact, and few choose Nutrition. Nutrition, though, is an easy place to work. As you will shortly see, you need little skill. Indeed, you will almost complete the apprenticeship in your short time in the Hub. In the long term, psychological damage rates in Nutrition are high. They are particularly high in the case of those whom Fact rejects.'

He was looking at Mexi now. She looked straight back, trying to meet his unblinking stare. She blinked, and he moved his head on.

'I would recommend that you work as hard as you can, in order to succeed with us. We are feared but we are respected. The rewards are considerable, and so are the consequences of rejection.'

He had turned so far from her that she was out of his peripheral vision, and she took the chance to glance at the Contact group. Seven of them, a few of whom she knew, had chosen the life and not been directed elsewhere. She imagined a ship taking off from its underground

126

hold, climbing up and away. She imagined the ship like a kite swinging up on a thick golden cord that frayed behind it as it rose, and she knew that she would never be able to fly a kite again now. This couldn't be right for her. Not Fact.

'Mexi Taro. You can go to the Hub first. I can see your attention isn't with us. Go with the Hub guide. I'll speak to you later.'

She shook her head. 'I'm sorry,' and her arm was lightly taken, the touch at her elbow jerking her sharply alert. She looked at the tech. He was staring at her in an entirely neutral way, his eyes assessing her.

'Come on, then,' he told her. 'Let's go.' Leading her from the chamber, he said, 'You seen the Hub before?'

'Just flat pictures. Not holos.'

'I meant been there. We don't do holos of the Hub. Put people off.'

She wasn't sure if he was being deliberately irritating. Maybe it was just her prickled mood, though. 'I know it's big,' she said shortly. 'I know there's a drop. Is that what you mean?'

'Part of it. You'll see.'

He didn't seem to want to tell her any more, and she wasn't inclined to talk either. There was no point in staying touchy, so she tried to rebuild her mood and make herself excited about this. She should be. She was going to see the Hub, Haven's great heart and soul and brain. It was bang central, set straightdown of the primary core, at the precise intersection of Red, Yellow and Blue.

She stood in the drop-pod with the tech and felt the gravity fall and rise again, and the stillness and silence in between. The tech was still clearly irritated with her. She guessed this was his moment of authority, where he impressed the new kids. He was losing his hair, she saw, standing slump-shouldered and knot-handed, frowning at the oily sheen of the pod wall. She felt sorry for him, and in doing so, she felt a little less sorry for herself.

'How long have you been in the Hub?' she asked.

'Fifteen years. Sixteen.' He turned his frown to her. 'Why?'

She couldn't think of anything else, though. 'Long time.'

'Sometimes it is,' he said, and gravity dragged the pod to a stop again. The door opened. 'Here,' he said. His frown ebbed. Now he looked at her, but this time as if for the first time, with true interest.

Mexi stood at the entrance to the chamber and looked up. For some reason she'd expected the pod to bring them to the Hub's apex, but here they were about halfway down.

She could sense the tech at her side appreciating her reaction, although she was suddenly unable to move her head or look away from this. She wished she could appreciate it herself. She'd imagined it, but this was beyond imagination.

'Breathe,' he said, and she realised she wasn't, and feeling faint. She took in a rasp of air, and then another, and more, concentrating on the rhythm of it, until it was even again.

'That's why you don't get holos,' the tech said with satisfaction.

'Yes. I see. It's . . .' But there was nothing else to say. Mexi knew that cavitation was more like building in space than on ground. Floors and levels had no meaning. As long as you were within stable rock, there were virtually no restrictions to what you could do. You could excavate down as far as you wanted, and the deeper you delved, the taller your building. There were no worries about the strength of construction materials. As long as you knew what rock you were cavitating and were careful not to undermine, nothing would collapse.

And downbelow, you could always be surprised by the architecture. Doorways gave no clues. Uptop, most of the time you could see the distant mountains, measure and assess the stretch of the plains. Even if it was death to be there, it was evident and unequivocal, transparent as the air itself.

Underground, though, the rock gave perfect concealment not only from uptop, but from what was around the next corner, at the end of the coredor, through the next doorway. It could be a cupboard as easily as it could be—

Mexi knew all of this. And she knew about this place, too. She'd even see it on vids. But this – she couldn't help the long indrawn gasp – this was the real thing.

'Something of a shock, huh?' Cheered at last, the tech clapped her on the shoulder. Able to move again, Mexi looked up, looked down, looked left and right. She had trouble focusing her eyes. The chamber was unimaginably vast, and the distant walls, plated with dull steel, were as tenuous as sky. She tried to get a sense of it. Struts and joists and girders swung provisionally across the chamber like webbing. Cables gathered themselves, looped and swung. The chamber hissed and hummed, clattered, clicked and scraped, and all of these sounds echoed. It was as dizzying to listen to as to look at. She looked and looked. Framework drop-pods rose and fell and even slid sideways. Everywhere, artificial levels were set suspended apparently at random, nested and bristling with work teams.

Mexi's attention was caught by one of these levels descending bodily. A dozen workers concentrated at their posts, apparently unaware as cables detached, collected in bundles, connected and reconnected. She saw someone step over a low guard rail from one level to another as it drifted past.

Everywhere, slow movement and adjustment. It seemed that there was order on a tiny scale and chaos on a vast scale.

The tech said, 'Welcome to the Hub, Miz Taro.'

A walkway swung across to the end of the pier where they stood, and the gate opened. 'After you,' the tech said, waiting.

Trying to keep her breathing even, Mexi stepped quickly on to the walkway. The tech followed her. 'No hesitation. Good sign,' he said. 'You may want to hold on. I wouldn't look down.'

'What do you mean, good sign?' Mexi said. She was fixing her gaze at a level about a hundred metres away. The walkway's gentle movement was shivering her voice, though the tech's was quite steady.

'You're on the walkway under five seconds, you may last more than a week here. I said don't look down.'

Mexi looked sharply up again. The floor was just a grid. Below—

'What did I say?' He was definitely happy now. 'Puke and you're a base-scourer for a month. And not many new recruits climb back up again after that. He told you back there, Nutrition's the worst of it? He doesn't know. Here we are.'

The walkway docked. Mexi glanced back towards the pod niche but couldn't locate it any more. The wall gleamed back at her, featureless.

'Your floor. Your card.' The tech pressed a rectangle of plastic into Mexi's hand. It felt warm and oily. 'You're here, it'll take you back to your door. You're there, it'll bring you here. In Nutrition, that's all you need.'

She stood and tried to follow his passage as he caught rides back towards the side wall, but lost him in the ebb and flow of the Hub, and looked carefully around the platform for somewhere to sit. She guarded her gaze carefully. The roof was too far away and staring down at the floor was out of the question, so the far wall was the only fixed thing she could try to focus on, and even it seemed to be shifting.

There was a seat by her, though, and she sat down on it heavily, realising she was at the end of a short line of seats. Feeling slightly more settled, she surveyed the small platform – all around its edge a slim, knee-height metal rail, and at her side another four seats – and then, cautiously, she looked at the near beyond where, across twenty metres of void, another rack of five seats hung.

After a while, a woman's head rose into view, and then the rest of her, and it was only when the platform on which the woman stood was a metre above Mexi's and still rising that she jumped down onto Mexi's platform. The shock of her landing was quickly damped, cables humming with the brief strain. The woman glanced at Mexi and made a curious sound to herself, then sat next to Mexi and muttered, 'Well, let's get on, then. I've got a long day of puke and stink, and you're the first. I hope you didn't have breakfast.'

Mexi said, 'Are you in Nutrition?'

'No, I'm General Factotem, can't you tell? Crise!' The woman looked away. She was not much older than Mexi. Under the Hub's even light her skin was so clear and pale that the delicate shadows on her cheeks could have been her bones gleaming through. Her lips were red as bloodflow. Mexi wasn't sure if she should say something else to her, but then the holo of a man drifted into vision at the platform's edge, and a screen swung around the arm of her seat and stilled there. She lifted her hands instinctively, but there was no input board, and the screen was a deep and empty azure. Mexi looked up at the holo, a man in his fourth decayd, with a few days' grey stubble at which he was rubbing gently. He was almost hairless otherwise, his scalp starting to mottle and his eyebrows painted to steep ticks of impatience. The shoulders of his jacket were raised to points. She wondered whether he were real and elsewhere or just a flake. Looking through her, he said, 'Mexi Taro. You confirm?'

Mexi nodded.

'Are you ready?'

She looked at the empty screen and then at the woman at her side, who was looking bored. There was a screen in front of her, too.

'Well?'

'I'm ready,' Mexi told him. She glanced at her companion again and met the flecked green of her eyes, and then her attention was taken by a change in her screen, the coalescing of a hard image. The image firmed to become a myco cavern, low and wide and long.

Mexi sighed.

'Don't worry,' the woman said. 'It's your fright. Everyone gets it. I've got a whole day of this ahead of me, but you'll be out of here in—'

The voice fell away, leaving Mexi thinking, '—no time,' unsure whether it was her thought or the lip end of someone else's.

'Oath, Rainer, don't you ever learn? Do you really want to be here all your life?'

This was the holo's voice. Mexi turned again to meet the woman's green eyes, and received a smile this time, and a sense of fluid brown hair that she hadn't noticed before.

The supervisor tapped the woman's shoulder sharply, his hand becoming momentarily grainy at the flaky contact. 'You'll be wise to stay clear of Rainer, Miz Taro. She's too free with her thoughts. She's here most of the time because of it.'

Mexi concentrated on the image on the screen. It seemed to swell as she watched it, refining and colouring until she was there and the screen's borders had edged away beyond the periphery of her vision. She was there in the cavern, and she was hanging in space.

Good.

This was the supervisor's voice, but it was inside her head now.

Don't screw it up, then. Show me a tour. The woman's voice was internal too, now. Mexi hadn't even noticed the inscreening. But even inside her, Rainer's voice was a caress, where the supervisor's had been acerbic to Mexi and a slap to the woman.

Mexi closed her companion out, holding fast to the cavern, which was so sharply defined that it was dizzying to observe. Mexi flexed her hands in the control field, experimenting for a few minutes with the motion bars. They were familiar; like everyone, she'd learnt them as games, as she'd learnt to write. She'd expected her skills to be taking her to Haze, though, but she banished the sour thought and told herself to get on with it. Better Fact than a life of this.

The bars here had a couple of variant features, but nothing awkward. It was just odd to feel the sticks and not see either them or her hands manipulating them. She swung herself slowly forward over the seemingly endless floor. The ceiling was so low that she could have stretched up to skim her hand against it and scoop away clots of spores from either floor or ceiling, if her hand had been with her. The myco was shining, the spores like stars all around her, and she was inscreened to a skimmer, swift as thought and light as a breath of air.

Becoming more comfortable with the movement tools, Mexi flew on, wheeling across the myco fields. After a while she slowed again, aware of something different. Without any change in her environment she had a sense of claustrophobia and agoraphobia at the same time, a sense of flying and falling, of control and helplessness.

There was no break in it. There was no room. She knew how small the spores really were, and yet they looked huge here, great bright globules.

Mexi continued to scythe through the centimetres of space between the ground and the roof, with nothing ahead or behind but empty space. She felt abruptly nauseous, felt bile rise—

Rainer was there, invisibly. *It's okay. I've got you. But just the once.*

A moment's fracture from the image, a sense of cold, and the nausea was gone.

Carry on now. Harvest, please. This voice the supervisor's.

Mexi flew onward. She became aware of patterns within the spore fields, nuances of brightness and shade, and made herself a small circuit, expanded the circuit, started to spot degrees of maturity. Just like the games. No, not quite.

Good. The supervisor's voice was somewhat softer now.

And instantly the woman, but this time caustic. *Oh yes. He's very impressed. If Fact throw you out, he'd very much like to have you. Almost as good as me. Eh, Voice?*

Oath, Rainer. I told you—

I'm just hard-buddying, Voice. My job.

Mexi felt something brush at her side.

That's right, it's me. You want to play tag? Voice won't mind.

I'm warning you, Rainer—

Mexi felt herself tipped awry, and sloughed down into the myco. She corrected late, coughing spores. They tasted bitter and acrid. She came up and drew hard left after Rainer, then instantly flipped right, as Rainer would have doubled back on herself to throw her off. But Rainer hadn't.

What do you think, Voice? You like her? Want to keep her? Like them soft, suddenly?

Mexi was tipped from the left again, back into the myco. Knowing the taste wasn't really there any more than she was didn't help at all. It was still foul.

She stopped dead and swivelled round. Inertialess motion. She'd forgotten. Rainer's skimmer was sitting right behind her, its underside gleaming faintly in the sporelight. The skimmer tilted fractionally and Rainer came at her again, tipping her over and back into the myco, and this time Mexi puked, and she was still puking as Rainer somehow gathered her up completely and spun her round again, vomiting uncontrollably.

I've had enough, now. I'm bored. She's all yours, Voice.

And Rainer was gone.

Mexi moved on. She was retching constantly, now, uncontrollably.

Use your Harvest and Maintain tools, please. Show me something. Don't worry about Rainer.

Mexi kept increasing the radius of her circuit, stopping at a patch of faint desporing. Her eyes were watering with nausea and she was coughing and retching still, but she forced herself to carry on. She checked her sensors, but they shone indeterminately. She started away, then returned, prowling cautiously over the myco, resensitising the sensors and adjusting their parameters. The nausea started to fade.

Good.

And she had a positive reading. It came up like warmth, a buzz of pleasure, neural tools linked to neurosensory reward. Mexi flagged the site, then waited until the crawler came picking its way over the field to spray the infected area.

That'll do, miz. I'm pulling you.

The cavern pulled back and decoloured, and receded to a screen. Mexi was back in the Hub. She looked into the quivering distance and the retching came back. As she wiped her mouth with the back of her hand, her chair was yanked round, facing her towards Voice.

Swallowing bile, Mexi said, 'Well?'

'You didn't puke too much. You'll get over the nausea in time. Rainer likes her job, whatever she says. If you don't like Fact or they don't like you, you may survive back here.'

'Oh, yeah. Voice's bed of fungus is just waiting for you. My advice, stick with Fact. They only fuck with your head there.' Rainer touched the railhead and the platform jerked slightly, heading towards the wall. As it started to move, Rainer glanced over the rail and abruptly vaulted it. Mexi saw her fall a couple of metres and land smoothly on another platform heading out towards the centre of the Hub. Mexi's platform decelerated gently into the wall and docked there. A door opened to the drop-pod from which she'd entered the Hub. Mexi checked the time. She'd been two hours in the Hub. She knew she didn't want to go back there.

Quill's eyes opened to a ruined cocoon. He sniffed, then winced. The air was foul. He wondered how his reserves were, how long he'd been out, how bad a hit the coffin had taken.

His head burned with words and pictures and music, the fill of it making him nauseous. He waited for it to pass, but instead it welled up more furiously. He thought he was going to vomit, but couldn't. His mind whirled with a babble that he felt he could almost make sense of if only it would stop coming at him for a moment.

It's okay, Quill. I've got you. I'm here.

What in Crise was that? Quill thought, when he could think again. He clutched at his head. It felt fragile, as if the plates of his skull were coming apart at their suture lines, like moving tectonics. An odd thought. Haven had no tectonic plates. He rubbed at his forehead.

You should feel how I do, Quill.

The nausea started to pass.

'You're dead, Scheck. Go away.'

The screen was still on, at least, the green rectangle glowing dully on its stalk, though the stalk was slightly twisted. Quill crawled lethargically across the littered cabin to check the time display.

He'd been out two and a half hours.

He pulled up the map, and swore at what it told him. Everything in a wide arc outward of the coffin, everything he'd left behind, was whitemarked. Which meant either the screen had lost memory in the hit, or else it had integrated the event's consequences into its bank, and was showing Quill only what it could be sure of.

He scrolled the map forward, and allowed himself a faint smile at the ragged jags of whitemark stretching ahead of his coffin and swinging along by his side. 'Okay, Scheck,' he muttered, 'The bad news is we're in restructured matter. But the good news is the screen's computing exactly where that restructuring's likely to be all around us.'

Which meant that he would have to reroute his trajectory, but it also told him that this small coffin screen was somehow capable of calculating and predicting the consequences of the event to an astonishingly fine degree. He'd never had a coffin so accurately maploaded.

Quill wondered what else the screen was capable of. He remembered thinking it was underloaded, before the explosion. It hadn't been underloaded at all. It actually was that fast.

It occurred to him to check the parameters of the map further. Experimenting, he brought up the overview map of Haven. In the coffin he'd shared with Scheck, the screen had been loaded for surveys. This screen had everything Scheck's had had, and Scheck's had brimmed with it. This . . .

Quill took a slow breath, released it steadily as the map appeared. He swept around the coredors at random, focusing down, moving on.

It was big. There was more capacity than a map might need, and far more detail. This map held all of Haven. More even than Quill knew to exist, and Quill thought he knew it all. All its perimeter, at least. He and Scheck were partly responsible for that perimeter, after all.

The map was astonishing. He checked outdown and deepdown. No map of Haven was ever accurate other than in gross terms. Even the Survey maps Scheck and Quill used were provisional. Haven was a place of mutable frontier, where every niche and pit was an expansion. There was never quite enough room, downbelow. Innocently and illicitly, almost everyone in Haven tunnelled out, for security, privacy, storage or illegal enterprise. Quill himself kept a small closed cell, two metres in from a dead store.

Mostly the deepening was a matter of a few cubic metres, but sometimes passages were extended and a few metres turned into a few dozen. And now and then Fact came along and plugged a few at random and sent diggers down to the Game.

Quill scrolled on through the screen's map. Illegal, locally more accurate maps than Survey's official ones – grey maps – could be bought from amateur coredor surveyors. These grey maps were useful to Fact, and so they let the walltappers' work go blind-eyed. Scheck, like the mapper of every Survey team, kept updates, but not on this scale.

The updates on this map were date-tagged. The most recent had been loaded just over a month back. Quill was thinking, faintly relieved, that this was not quite so impressive, when he remembered he'd been in the coffin almost exactly that long.

He noticed the small blister case lying on the floor, picked it up and noticed a slight dent in it.

Must have happened in the explosion.

'Thank you, Scheck, but you're dead, remember? I've said goodbye. You can go, now.'

You're not ready for me to go, Quill. You need me.

'What do I need you for?'

I can't tell you. I don't know. I'm dead. You just have to ask me the questions.

'What can you tell me?'

But Scheck didn't answer. That was obviously not one of the questions.

Checking the case, Quill saw a faint seam in the metal at the base of the dent. He turned the case over, then froze. One of the blisters was cracked, the glass turned blue. The other two were still clear, though.

He ran the ball of a finger along the fracture line. He was still alive. He felt okay. Whatever had been in it must be inactive now. He put the case away again. He had other worries.

He had to decide where to go, where he might be safe. He ran through everyone he knew, dismissing them all. He dismissed Walker the first time, then thought of him again.

Everyone else was no use at all, while Walker was just a crazy idea. But Walker might be his only hope.

Walker lived way out. He lived far from the primaries, down in the deepest shades. Walker lived where the desire for privacy crossed the edge of paranoia. Only the Game was as deep as Walker, and even the Game was in solid rock.

Quill told the screen to take him towards Walker, travelling where possible along the distal margins of the whitemarked zones, and otherwise along lines of cleavage. He used anything he could to conceal his presence and mask his route. He figured that if anyone could put the amount of data and the capability to crunch it into a screen in a coffin, then they probably could do a few other things he wouldn't expect. So it made sense to anticipate they could do anything they felt like doing. Whoever they were.

For more than a week he ground his way onward. Keeping his distance, he travelled deepdeepdown of Blue, ondown beyond Indigo and Azure, past Cobalt, and when he was finally tripledeep, he brought the coffin in close to the coredors of Ultramarine. And when he was there, he kept well to the coredor side of what everyone who knew of it called Walker's Sea.

Hunched in his coffin, Quill found himself breathing lightly and listening for creaks, which was crazy. If the coffin was going to quit on him, he'd be bleached cleaner than by any lightning uptop.

The engine ground on. Whoever might be tracking him, looking for him, they could have the tools, but they'd never expect anyone to be coming in from the rock down here.

Even on this map, Walker's Sea was a mystery. No one knew how far it extended into the night and dark of the planet, and here on Quill's screen, everything beyond Ultramarine was whitemarked and tagged: RISK — DO NOT SURVEY.

It took him almost a day to negotiate the last metres approaching what looked on the chart like a dead and deserted coredor, not to collapse the whole thing around himself. The precision and the accuracy of the map were astonishing. He backed the coffin into place and then switched the comms on for the first time since he'd set off from the buried ship, using them, to check no one was near before cracking himself an opening at the rear of what was marked on the map as a storage niche.

He stopped the engine. In the sudden noise vacuum that made his head feel it was swelling, he pulled the emergency kit from its slot in the coffin wall. The kit had never been used, as no kit ever was, since there was never an emergency that wasn't death in a survey coffin. Most survey crews threw the kit away and used its slot to stow other things. Quill had forgotten what Scheck had used their space for.

'What did you put there, Scheck?'

But Scheck didn't say, and Quill had to go on with it alone. He was grateful again that he'd taken Rheo and Java's coffin, and that they were rule-zealots. He pulled the mask out first. It stank, but he covered his face with it and took a breath from the can. It was like sucking from a third-lick myco cigret, but it was better than the now thin coffin air. Quill coughed and retched, persevered, drew can-air again until he could breathe easily, then sat and creamed his exposed flesh thickly from the flash-and-gas tube. After that he tipped the rest of the kit out and spread what there was across the bench. He drank the water, which was pretty fresh but barely a swallow, and quickly knocked back the drypacked myco. That went down like Scheck had told him it would as he'd thrown theirs away, muttering, 'Why do you think you never get to try it during training, Quill? Because it tastes like your toenails. It's why they call it an emergency kit. You know you're shunted if you're even thinking of opening it.'

'So what does that make me, Scheck?' Quill said as he tidied the coffin as best he could before disembarking. Survey had taught him to be tidy. There was no space in a coffin for mess. He stowed the head on Scheck's bed, along with the small case.

He crawled from the coffin and patched the wall as best he could behind him, then adjusted the mask and looked around. A few proximity torches glowed dimly. There was no permanent lighting here. This was Ultramarine, and as deep as it got unless you'd been consigned to the ballgame.

Ultramarine was the gateway to the vast, largely unsurveyed and effectively endless chamber from whose near point Walker's Sea stretched away. If Survey had been as advanced back when the chamber was accidentally exposed as they were now, the immense cavern would have been bound off at a hundred metres and walled away for ever. If Walker hadn't decided to lodge there and if he hadn't discovered a use for his home, it would be walled away now.

Quill walked quickly out of the niche and glanced around. There was no one but himself down there. He checked the niche showed no sign of disturbance, then headed towards Walker's domain.

Heat flowed along the narrow coredors like a current. The walls were damp and glistening. Topaz and celestine, Quill recognised. Sulphur, here and there. He turned a corner and was there, ten metres from the nearest inlet of the sharp-edged shore.

Quill stood and squinted. The dense heat curled in brilliant green smoke off the surface of the still, dark water, and Quill watched it rise through the gleaming stalactites up into the maze of baffled and treated vents where it would lose its chemical sting and warm the upper areas. Out over the sea, shapes formed and vanished, and voids briefly opened in the green miasma and filled again.

The sea was subject to some distant underground climate. It could be calm and so motionless that at its edge there would be a meniscus against the steeply incised shore. Most of the shore was granite, but there was mica too, and veins of silver snaking into the sea.

Now there was a hard, hot wind coming out of the distance, rippling the water uneasily. His mask felt hard against his cheeks and chin, and his skin itched, despite the larding of cream.

He stood there, staring out. In the sudden sense of distance, after weeks in the coffin and these last metres of diminished visibility, he felt slightly faint and dizzy. He took a sharp breath of the canned air to steady himself, and looked to his left, to see the face of Walker's shelter where it was set flush with the back wall of the cavern.

Walker lived here alone in this cooled, incut space. As Quill drew close to the shelter, he was aware of the wind booming and scraping at the almost solid sheet of frigid air at the door and window.

Quill thumped his fist against the door, then at a yell from inside he stood back as the airjets began to scream across the doorway. The door slid down and away, and Quill had a glimpse of Walker inside, blurred by the screeching airwall, gesturing. Quill pushed himself through, and heard the door slam behind him and the airwall close down.

Inside was the odd silence of buffered noise. Walker stared at him, waiting for him to say something. He couldn't think of the words, of any words. He'd been talking in his head to Scheck so long. Now he tried to speak, but choked. Walker was saying something Quill couldn't make out. The noise buffering was struggling, letting ribbons of sound through the wall. Quill shook his head to clear it, but it wouldn't clear, and then Walker leaned forward and reached with both hands for his face, and unclipped the mask. It fell to the floor, and Quill could hear again.

'I thought you were dead, you and Scheck,' Walker said quietly.

'Scheck is.' Quill turned to the window. Through the slur of wind, all he could see was the sea's wispy surface and its low, twisting fog. He turned back into the small room. 'Can we talk?' he said. 'Not here. Outside?'

Walker frowned, then said, standing up. 'If you want, yes. The boat's ready. Take a suit from the pile.' He sniffed. 'Use my shower first. Crise, Quill, where have you been? You stink like death.'

Quill stripped off and ducked into the skinny metal washtube to let the water sluice everything away, but the dirt on his skin and the outer stink was all it removed, though he turned up the power until he couldn't hear anything but the water and could hardly keep on his feet against its cannoning onto his head and shoulders.

Walker was already suited, holding his mask and checking the coredor screen when Quill came out. 'We had your wake at Maskin's two weeks back,' he said. He looked speculatively at Quill.

'In the boat,' Quill said.

'We should be okay. I haven't got anything booked today. What are you expecting?'

'Everything.' Quill shrugged the suit on and sealed its mask in place. He jerked his head. 'I said not here. The boat.'

Walker masked up and led the way from the hut. The wind had dropped to no more than a low whistle, and Quill could hear the faint constant plopping of condensation from the spiked dome of the cavern down into the sea.

The small boat was tied up to a ring set in the wall off to the left, by a fat metal cable. It was pulled out of the water and lying on the shore. Quill stood by as Walker scanned the hull thoroughly before tipping it into the sea. He held it still for Quill to step in.

Checking the dome's heat vents, ducts and baffles was Walker's main job, but sea trips were his sideline. He was famous for it. He'd dress you in a suit and mask you up and row you out until you were lost and heard only his oars and the plipping and booming all around you. He claimed he navigated by the architecture above, and maybe he did. Even Quill didn't know, and Quill was as close to Walker as anyone.

Walker made his boat money in two ways. From thrill-searchers, and from those wanting guaranteed secrecy. He'd row you out there, you and whoever you wanted privacy with, and then he'd hood up until you'd done your business safe from ears and eyes, bugs and tags – safe even from Robes, if it bothered you and then you'd tap him on the shoulder and he'd unhood and row you back and take your money and go back to his hut, and staring out over the endless sea.

Walker bent his back and started to row them out. Quill watched the shore recede and vanish. The air around the boat was marbled and beautiful. The suit felt tight and he felt quite safe, safe as in rock. The boat rocked gently, reassuringly. Quill thought of Scheck, and then, oddly, his mother.

'We have about fifteen more minutes, Quill. The hull won't take much more without re-treating, and there's a methane wind building.'

'I'm sorry.' He'd been dreaming. His face felt wet under the mask. 'What happened while we were gone, Walker? What's been said?'

'There was a hell of an event, an explosion right where you were surveying, you and Scheck. All they know is something went wrong, a core blow probably, radioactive minerals involved. They think the radioactivity might have damaged your instruments or screwed up your probe's readings, fooled you into a bad course. The valves worked perfectly, though, when it blew. Everything was channelled away uptop, and the whole area was sealed and bounded off. No one dead except you and Scheck and your handler. You're heroes, though.'

'Tanner,' Quill said. So he was dead. 'Did you hear anything before the explosion? Anything from Survey? Any announcement, any rumours?'

'No. Why?'

'Because Survey lost contact with us a long time before the event.'

'So?' Walker shrugged. His black suit gleamed. The eyes of his mask had an obsidian shine. 'That happens. Coffins just go quiet, deepdown and outdown. It's just Survey. You know that. Teams die silently, time and time.'

A lick of mist curled between the two men. 'Sure,' Quill said. 'But there are rumours. No one said, Scheck and Quill, they're late, out of contact?'

Walker hesitated. His voice was different. 'No. No, no one did that.' He looked out, staring into the fog. Quill had no idea which direction he was facing, to shore or out into the sea. Quill wondered what he was thinking.

Eventually Walker said, 'So, what happened? And if you made it, why didn't Scheck?'

'It wasn't a core blow. We were followed. We located a ship, must have crashlanded in a lava lake, got buried as it cooled. They killed Scheck, I killed them. They must have killed Tanner.'

Walker took the oars. 'We have to start heading back.' He started rowing. The water moved thickly around the paddles. Walker was careful not to make a splash. 'Why the explosion, then?'

'I did that.'

Walker's stroke slipped. 'Why? Why not come straight back? Report it to Survey, to Fact.'

For a moment Quill couldn't think why he hadn't. Maybe it was paranoia. Scheck had been killed and he'd been crazy. Then he remembered. 'Survey had to have known about us being followed. And there's Fact involvement too. I don't know. They didn't want the ship found.'

'Who wouldn't want a ship found, and why? What ship was it?'

'It was an escape pod. No name. I thought maybe from one of the freighters to Haze and back.'

'So, secret?' Walker relaxed a moment, letting the oars' blades lie on the water. 'What's to hide?'

'The fact that a freighter's lost? I don't ever remember one lost.'

'Unless they don't want it known it was lost. And if so, finding the pod blows the lid on that.'

'Its cargo, then?' Quill said. He didn't mention the blister case. 'Something coming from Haze?'

The shore was in sight now, in a separating of mist. 'Or going there?'

'That's enough for now,' Quill said. 'What I didn't tell you was that the coffin following us had a screen maploaded better than anything from Survey. As far as you know, I'm dead, that's it.'

'Where will you go?'

'I don't know.'

'Be careful. You and Scheck got the hero treatment, your faces screened for weeks. Still are, in fact. You could be recognised.'

Quill took that in. It made sense. They'd have known something had gone seriously wrong when Rheo and Java didn't show up, so they wanted Scheck and Quill picked up quickly if they did reappear anywhere. He said, 'One more thing, Walker. This screen I've got. You know anyone I might talk to about it? Anyone who knows about that sort of thing?'

They were close to the shore now. Walker said, 'Yes. Woman called Skim, lives out in carmine38. She comes down here, uses the boat a lot. I think she deals in screens and other stuff, buy and sell.'

'Thanks, Walker. I owe you.'

Walker smiled. 'A dead man's debt. That's worth a lot. Don't worry about it, Quill. I'm doing it in memory of you.'

The boat nudged against the shore. As Quill stepped back on the hard shore, Walker said, 'I'm sorry about Scheck. I was sorry about you both.' He jumped ashore after Quill, and shipped the oars, turning and inspecting them. The blades were beginning to pit. 'Be careful,' he said. 'Bad enough to die once.'

CAP

All of that was years ago, now. So many years. The wind has gone and the flags raised by that wind are now for ever furled. I still have the words, though. I still have memories.

Huge changes took place. I can't bear to think of them, much of the time. This world. Look at it in its glory.

I must think. I must tell you.

John and Mary and I lived in a faithless world. A world where cancers ripened invisibly in healthy men, where sane men picked up guns and ran berserk. And the world darkening to night.

I think of my father often. It has long struck me that memories are boxes; most of them, most of the time, shut and buried. But when you root them up and lift the lids, what's inside is as fresh as when it was first shovelled away by the eyes and the flesh and the heart. And yet, when you open the box, you somehow corrupt the memory and the present together, and everything swarms and nothing is the same again. It's like some principle of science. Like entropy, perhaps.

I have scientists. I should ask them.

To go on, then.

At some point I met Augustus Speke. Gus Speke, he was, then.

I was still doing the shows in person, from time to time. I moved John around my enterprises a great deal more, giving him more opportunities to betray himself. He was careful, following my orders thoroughly. He knew I was too powerful for him to challenge me directly, and Mary pitied me enough to pretend she still loved me.

I took more of an interest in the stem cell research. I made sure I understood Mary's treatment. I remember being fascinated by the fact that olfactory nerve cells showed most potential for her condition. These cells were ravaged so frequently by the cold virus that they had developed a limited ability to regenerate. There's an elegance in the idea that such a ridiculously common illness can provide a key to such a complex disability.

Mary was progressing wonderfully. When we talked together, the two of us, my heart ached still, but it was no longer that tender ache of love. It was bitter.

Gus came along to the shows I led myself. Not to John's. By this time we had a database of all our regular attendees, and beyond this, our feature-recognition technology, allied to the Citizens' Anti-Terrorist National Identity Program, allowed us to identify ninety-three per cent of our guests within five seconds as they came through the doors, at two per cent error. I was given a highlight of politicians and criminals of a certain calibre as a matter of course. So when Gus came backstage the first time, I was ready for him.

'Mr Speke, it's a real pleasure,' I said, as if I'd recognised him unaided. 'I didn't know you were here. You should have told my office you wanted to come along. I'd have arranged a good seat in the house.'

I was undressed and rubbing my hair dry with a towel. The apparent intimacy of that activity gave dressing-room visitors a sense of unique privilege, far more than a personal blessing. I gestured him to a chair.

'Actually, Cap – may I call you that?' He brushed his palm over the seat, and adjusted his trousers carefully as he sat, not to bag the knees of the fine Italian cloth.

'Everyone does. Please.'

'Actually, this is my third time here.' He smiled. 'But you know that.'

I towelled my face to mask a grin. Ah, politicians, they so loved their games; 'I know you know I know.' But what *I* knew was that the last 'I know' must always be theirs.

'I do,' I chuckled. 'What can we do for each other, then?'

He made himself more comfortable and said, 'I'm Governor of this State. Next year I'm running for President, and I'm going to win.'

'Really?'

'Yes.' He eyed me. 'It's been suggested that you might run, Cap. If you run, you'll be running against me.'

I looked at him closely. Lean, fit and healthy, he looked ten years younger than he was, as if he were still in his forties. He had short brown hair with just enough grey to suggest experience. I knew he also had a law degree and a teenage daughter with a drink problem, and a wife who would be in jail if the parents of the boy she'd knocked down last year hadn't needed the money so much. He'd avoided soldiering and taxes with equal proficiency. He was a man who surrounded himself with allies, and here he was, wanting me not to be his enemy.

What I wanted was more than that. I wanted to be his closest friend.

'I didn't know you were going to run, Governor.'

He smiled. He didn't fully have the smile yet, but it was coming along. He inspected his nails.

'I've never intended running,' I said, when he was looking at me again.

'Your media say you are. Your papers and your screens.'

I went behind a screen to pull my trousers on, then came out to get my shirt. I worked out every day, and I tanned well. I let him see that. Doing up my shirt, I said, 'Don't be fooled by that. I throw a few stones into the pond from time to time, that's all. Just to see the ripples. I wouldn't run against you.' Which was true. I didn't want political power at all. I just wanted access to it. I needed to use it, not to have it. 'I admire you, Governor.'

He let his hands fall to his lap and said, 'How much do you admire me?'

I was well aware that he'd been making speeches and taking public positions on research, on all the issues in my own interest that he could, to draw my attention to him without actually approaching me. And he'd done it efficiently.

I took my tie from the back of a chair and turned to the mirror to knot it. I smiled at his reflection. 'I admire you a great deal, Mr Speke.'

'Gus.'

What I admired about him was not so much what he'd done, as how he had gone about wooing me. As if I might suddenly think, 'Well, gosh, here's a man running for President, and hey, with exactly the same aims as me!' I liked that he was that little bit more subtly conniving than the rest of them, and at the same time stupid enough to imagine I might not see what he was doing for what it was.

I pulled my jacket on and shot my cuffs. 'I like you a lot, Gus. I really do.'

Gus slapped his knees, stood athletically to his feet and held out his hand to me.

'Cap,' he said, 'I think you and I can do business together.'

'Gus,' I answered, 'I'm sure we can.'

He checked his watch. 'I must go. The future beckons, eh, Cap?'

'It does, it does.'

'How's Mary, by the way?'

That took me by surprise. The way he said it, it was as if he knew something. 'Doing very well indeed,' I told him. Then I pulled myself together. 'Glial cells. They're—

'Good, good. Don't blind me with science. I do what I can, I do what I can.'

I stood there, open-mouthed. I couldn't think of a thing to say. He was grinning at me like a fool and I was gaping back at him in disbelief. I wanted to strike him in the face and smash him down. This man actually saw himself as directly responsible for Mary's cure. He had engineered a small tweak in the law, entirely for his own ends, and he considered himself a healer!

He broke the silence. I couldn't. 'You must come round to the house, you and Mary. And you and I must talk again.'

And Gus, Augustus Speke, turned and was gone.

I took off all my clothes again and had myself another long shower before I left.

It was quite amazing just who came along to hear me and be healed, in some way or another. The criminal population was a great deal more than proportionately represented in the ranks of my people. Those responsible for violent crimes in particular seemed to recognise that the damage they did reflected the damage that had been done to them. They repented, and they sought penitence.

They came to me. My service was to seek out these damaged souls and help them. When my software located them, I had them brought discreetly to one of my more secluded clinics to be helped. Where I could, I rechannelled them into more positive expressions of their character.

Lawyers and criminals alike, I helped them all. Mutual trust, mutual support. My father would have been so proud of me.

My father again. Always intruding, always pushing himself into me, into my head. Even now.

Betrayal hurts more than anything else. More than love. Just like Our Lord was betrayed, I was betrayed by those closest to me. My mother deserted me. And my father – before he died, my father explained to me why he did what he did to me.

I kept thinking – I keep thinking – of the blood spewing into my mouth from his, and what else he did to me. He shouldn't have done that, even though I loved him. What he did was wrong. The blood, the blood and blood. Thanks to him, I couldn't eat food without it turning to ashes in my mouth. It was an effort to swallow. And I couldn't shit like other men, thanks to him. Shit and ashes, that was his legacy to me.

My legacy? That's to be judged.

But I have to thank my father, too. I know that. As a child I begged on the streets for him, and if I hadn't done that, day after day after day, I would never have learned how to preach. I wouldn't have found Our Lord.

My father gave me that. He made me strong. He gave me the need to be what I have become, and he told me how to do it. I was to be his revenge upon the world, and he made sure I would never forget that. But I knew that I would be better than my father. I would be better even than a lawyer. My nightmares were greater than his small dreams ever were, and my vengeance would be greater than his could ever have been.

Where was I?

A whirlwind of backslapping later, and we were intimate friends, Gus and I. More than that. We were close political allies, which was necessarily as close as love – in other words, it was everything and nothing. We ate at each other's houses and, as Gus touchingly informed me, we had no secrets. A weekly Friday evening meal at Gus's sprawl of a house was the cement of our relationship.

Of course, Gus wasn't President yet. Things went slightly wrong for him, as they always do in true life. A few of his little secrets got out, his poll-ratings dipped, his main rival's position strengthened. It became close, and then it became worrying. Gus Speke was two points below Dick Cramer. Cramer was a good speaker and a fine thinker, he was three inches taller than Gus, and his attractive wife had recently died tragically and publicly. It was all going for him.

As I had hoped, Gus asked me for help, as a friend, and I was able to provide it. Both pastorally and practically. Gus said to me once, in his den, that I gave him solution and absolution, which I thought was unusually perceptive of him.

So, Gus and I were very close indeed.

At dinner, around the table, we relaxed, easy in each other's company, two ordinary couples together. Every Friday night.

One evening I remember, the four of us sitting as usual at what Gus called the casual end of the maple dining table that would have seated (but never had) twenty-eight, under the twitchy glare of the halogen candelabra.

'How's the food?' Gus's wife asked.

She was an attractive, pointless woman. Like her husband, Jerrylene Speke was fit and healthy and seemed ten years younger than her age. She had a fine, well-honed body, as you would expect. After all, she committed a great deal of time to the people who kept it honed for her.

'Very good, Jerrylene,' I said. 'Very good indeed.' I rolled a tasteless bolus of something around my cheeks. 'Is there a hint of saffron?'

'I'm not sure. I can check Monday, if you like.'

Jerrylene raised her eyebrows at Mary, who said softly, 'It is good. I'm sorry, I haven't much energy at the moment.'

She'd hardly touched the salmon. She could hardly raise her head. She was using a voice synthesiser again. This would be headline news tomorrow.

'Oh, you poor mite,' Jerrylene said. 'Still, you can't be too thin, can you? Look at me, I just can't keep the weight off.' Keeping her nails clear, she smoothed the creaseless blue silk of her dress with her flattened palms, and eyed me. 'Don't you think, Cap?'

Gus pushed back his chair and got to his feet. 'Cap, let's you and me go off to the den for a jaw and a smoke, eh? Leave the gals to gas about clothes and such.'

Mary didn't say a thing. I went up behind her and rested my hands gently on the back of her neck, massaging her for a moment, pressing the muscle, and put my mouth to her ear to say, 'We won't be long, Mary.'

'Hey, Gus,' Jerrylene shrieked. 'You see that? That's love, that is! Why don't you get that close to me any more except in public, huh?'

Gus chuckled and put his arm around my shoulder to lead me away with him. I put my left hand in my pocket to rub away the membrane of the discharged fingersac.

'Hey, Mary, you look a little pale, there,' Jerrylene was saying.

'I'll be fine. It takes me like this, sometimes. I'm sorry.'

Gus's den was in the precise centre of Speke House. Without the staff, who were sent away once the Friday evening meal was prepared, to give us privacy, it had an atmosphere of being haunted rather than inhabited. Our feet creaked and our voices echoed.

It took us five minutes to walk to the den, through the reception rooms, rumpus rooms, games rooms, formal and informal chambers and past the ring of surveillance suites. Outside of the White House, Gus's den was probably the most perfectly screened and protected thirty-eight point six cubic metres of one-to-one talkspace in the free world. It was, I know, quite unbuggable. When you were in there, you were sealed in. Sealed in as in airtight. There was no ventilation in that room. As you breathed and talked, you used up the air, so you said what you couldn't say anywhere else and you kept it short, because after not very long you were getting hot and breathing hard.

He ushered me in and followed me, and then he thumbed the button on the wall that sealed it, and started talking.

I half-listened.

Gus, I had to admit, was quite perfect. He was definitely presidential material. World leader, even.

Like everyone else, I had long ago recognised that the more powerful the nation, the more anodyne the man they chose to lead them. One person could run a small state, if they were strong and angry enough.

But the USA was too big for that. There were too many lobbies to satisfy, too many powerful and contradicting interests to be apportioned leverage; and anyway, any candidate with clear policies would antagonise as many voters as they would attract. After all, the voters were a factor. So personality was out, as were policies, beliefs, desires, ideals.

When Gus had finished speaking, I started.

'This is what we do, Gus. We don't talk about specifics. Let Cramer do that. You have to be Presidential. Big speeches on big issues, and say nothing. Talk about prosperity, not the economy. You rouse them without informing them. You attack his detail, and you promise that yours is to come.'

'Cap, he'll attack me for my lack of detail.'

'That's right. But his attack will be unfocused, and you'll accuse him of weak thinking. Your attack will be focused and effective.' I smiled, and he relaxed a fraction. I said, 'Okay. Listen to me. Nationally, like I said, specifics are out. But locally, it's another matter. The great thing about this country is its size, and the importance of local politics and local issues. This is what we do. We give detail locally. We do it in a focused manner, and we do it intensively. We have representatives who will interpret our aims locally to each small voting constituency in a way that they will understand, and in a way that they will vote for. If they believe the policy is clearly not in their favour, our representatives will explain to them that you, Gus Speke, are personally on their side, and that regardless of policy, the detail will benefit them.'

He was playing with a paperweight on the table, tilting his head and squinting with concentration, watching the light take the bright glass orb. Was he listening to my words, or was he just being soothed? It didn't actually matter. I was used to this, at all levels. I carried on. 'The local lobbying will be so honed and so locally defined that no one could realise that some other community might be voting for you on the basis of entirely opposite aims.'

'That's crazy,' Gus said, putting the paperweight down to squint at me instead.

'No. If contradictions come out, we explain them away as misunderstanding. We smooth it. It would turn out to be Cramer's people sowing confusion.' I deliberately cracked my knuckles, making him wince. 'Attack and confuse, Gus. That's the secret of success in a democracy. Anyone says anything else, they're fair-and-square losers.'

I waited for him to comment, to react. 'I wish you wouldn't do that thing,' he finally said, nodding at my hands.

Yes, he was the perfect candidate. A flat portrait, bland as God. Gus Speke was surely that. Without stopping to think again, I said, momentarily losing the correct tone, 'Don't worry about the Presidency, Gus. Think about the next step. Always be thinking ahead.'

He gave me a sharp look and said, 'Don't patronise me, Cap. Don't ever do that. You're my friend and my adviser. You're behind me and sometimes beside me. I value you, but I am the candidate and *I* will be the President. Remember that.'

I was thrown by that. I had to swallow my natural reaction. But it was my own fault. He wasn't a stupid man.

'I'm sorry, Governor. I just want you to be able to focus on what you have to, and leave the rest to me.'

'Which is good, and which I appreciate. I'm under a great deal of stress, Cap, as I'm sure you understand.' He sighed theatrically and became conciliatory. 'And Gus. Call me Gus.' I noticed him unconsciously spread his hands, just as I do. 'I only want you to keep me in the loop, Cap. That's all. I know these things are necessary, and I know we only do them because Cramer would if he could, but that doesn't make me like it any more.'

His voice changed. It became as sincere as I've ever heard it. I'd coached him myself, but even so, it surprised me how good he was. He sounded as if he were speaking from the heart.

'I value you, Cap,' he said. 'I value you as my closest friend and my closest adviser. Hell, Cap, I tell you things I don't even tell Jerrylene. So when I want you to tell me these things, it's so we share them. So you have someone to talk to, huh? I always feel with you—' He opened his hands and held them apart, palms parallel with each other, emptiness between them. '—What do you say?'

I said nothing. I didn't know what was the right thing.

'Hey, Cap. You okay? Did I say something?'

He seemed to be closing in on me. I didn't know what it was.

'Here, sit down, Cap. That better?'

Maybe it was the air in there, he suggested. We'd been there a while. Maybe we should leave. I said no. I wasn't done yet.

Eventually Gus became more brusque again and said, 'So, let's look at Europa. Next stage, if I win this one. Rudi Cambi. What have you got on him?'

'He'll win the nomination, for sure. He'll be your opposition for the URA.'

'Is he a worry?'

'Not to you. Don't fret. I can deal with it. You're going to beat him, Gus. Trust me.'

'Will he be killed?'

'I said, don't worry. I know how the system works, and I know how

Rudi Cambi works. He's a politician, that's all. Everywhere he goes, I'm already watching and listening. I see his speeches before he does. I know when he wants to piss before he does.'

'He's got war wounds. He's got medals. They love him.' Gus was still anxious. He paced.

'You've got Our Lord, and you've got me. That's all you need.'

'I don't want to win and then lose. They're saying I fight dirty. Your own screenpapers are saying that, for God's sake. What the hell's going on?'

It was starting to get warm in there, and he was feeling it.

'Please don't swear, Gus. It's called editorial independence. I know exactly what I'm doing. You're clean. That's why we're talking in here, isn't it? So you can stay clean. So if there should be any dirt, you can stick it on me and walk away. But that's not going to be necessary.'

He was contrite. 'I'm sorry, Cap. But I hope you know what you're doing. There's a lot riding on these next weeks, and then . . .' he shook his head. 'Cap, they're already polling people on a race between me and Cambi for the URA.'

'Don't worry about polls, Gus. They're just what people intend to do.'

'Maybe you should stop him now, so someone else gets nominated instead, someone I can beat easily. Huh?'

'No. They'll expect us to try that. We stay clear now. Look, you'll get the presidency over here, Cambi will get it over there. Any tricks over there will be his alone. That way they've got no mud to sling when it's you and him for the big one. We only get dirty when we have to get dirty, Gus. You don't have to get dirty at all.'

I was in control again. Gus was running a finger inside his collar. He'd rolled his sleeves up. I touched his bare arm gently and rubbed it with my fingers. There was no trace left on his skin, and I rubbed away the membrane into my handkerchief. 'Sit down a moment. Here.'

I helped him to the chair at the desk. He rested his head in his hands and murmured exhaustedly, 'I'm sorry, Cap. It's been a long week. You know I trust you.' His eyes were closing. I had about fifteen seconds.

'I know that,' I reassured him while behind his back I was slipping the tiny open-reel tape machine from its lodging under a shelf and replacing it with another from my pocket. They were wonderful retrotech devices; oxygen-activated, metal-free, and with a noiseless mechanism. Virtually technology-void, and quite dead to a bug sweep. Whatever conversations he'd had in that sealed room since I left the device there last Friday, I'd listen to later. I went round the desk to face him and said, 'Mutual trust, Gus.'

He nodded lethargically and blinked at me.

'In a few weeks, Gus,' I told him, 'You'll be President of the US and VP of the URA. I'm sure of it. It's under control. And Cambi will be your joint VP, and then in a year it'll be you at the top. You have my word.'

'I know, Cap,' he told me, summoning a smile. 'You're the one sure thing, eh?'

'That's right, Gus.'

I helped him to his feet, and he pressed the door button to let us back out into the harsh, untrustworthy world again.

HAZE

Watching Marten cross the causeway, Petey knew she had to save herself. The lords had killed Loren in the forest, she was certain of it. And if they had done that, there was no reason at all for them to let her live, now that they had the son.

Her crying was real enough. She didn't need to act it, just to let it flood more easily. There was only one lord holding her by the arm, and he was too busy watching Marten trip on the bridge and take the other boy and the lord down with him to concentrate on a weeping woman.

Petey sobbed more loudly and relaxed her legs as if she were fainting, and the lord pulled her up hard to her feet again. As she stood, he slightly slackened his grip, and Petey used all her strength to rip her arm away from him. He lunged at her and opened his mouth to yell, and she kicked him between the legs as hard as she could, his cry instantly cutting itself off. He crumpled to the earth, struggling to breathe.

Another lord, more interested in what was happening on the bridge than in her, was turning slowly as she started to run back towards the forest path. She was at the edge of the trees and under their shade when the first beam flowed past her cheek. She threw herself off the path to her right and then instantly straightened and went left as the beam scythed an arc where she would have been. She was on the path again, but far enough to be out of the lords' sight, and she kept to it, more certain that she could outrun any lord than that she could hide from the spray of their beams in the thick brush to either side.

She ran hard until her breath grew too fast and her heart threatened to burst, and then she slowed to a steady trot that she knew she could maintain for hours.

Her eyes were good in the dark, and the thin stream of light-ants at the path's edges kept her from crashing into the trees. She stumbled over roots occasionally, but kept going until she reached the camp where the wife to Semith was lying dead.

The forest had already started its work on her. Her eye sockets were empty, crawling with ground-wasps, and the flesh of her face was mottled and in places picked to the bone.

As Petey drew closer to her, the woman's stomach and chest moved in a long, agonised breath, and she tried to roll towards Petey.

Petey had to put her hand to her mouth not to scream. The woman moved again, her chest heaving violently, and she dragged her fleshless head further round towards Petey. Petey stepped back, tripping over a root. Her heart thudded.

A reddened snout pushed out of a long rip in the woman's shirt, and a scavenger dog emerged from under her ribs and glanced briefly at Petey. It was chewing at a cord of bowel. As the dog loped off into the wood, the woman's guts rippled along behind it. The evacuated corpse sagged back, seemingly unravelling. A few small animals began to fight over the rest of the guts.

Petey left them to it and moved away, circling the area, searching for tracks, but there were none she could find in the gloom. It was approaching dawn, though, so Petey sat and waited for more light before continuing.

In the light, it wasn't hard. Semith hadn't been trying to hide his tracks, and he'd been tracking the escort in the dark himself. He'd broken twigs and left prints on the soft earth, and disturbed leaves. Brittle insects' nests had been cracked and the signs were simple to follow.

But then it grew harder, and it took her a while to understand the reason. Semith had killed the lord, but then he had had to conceal the body. Tribal murder was hardly a crime, but there was no crime worse than killing a lord. Killing Marten and the parents would not have concerned him, but he would have spent as much time as he dared to hide the lord's body and make the lord appear to have died accidentally.

By now, it was well into the day, and she knew the lords would soon be here, searching for the same thing she was. She tried to be methodical, thinking as Semith might have thought, but there was nothing to find. She was about to give up when, almost by accident, she found the corpse.

There was just a speck of orange winking at her from the ground, from beneath the boughs of a vast tree crashed recently to the ground. Petey squinted at the colour for a long time before actually believing it. Only one thing could be that colour, and it had no business being there. She moved her head, checking it wasn't a trick of the light. No plant had that colour. It could only be a lord's robe.

It would have taken Semith an astonishing amount of effort to push the corpse so far beneath the trunk. He must have hoped that by the

153

time the body was found, it might have appeared that the tree had toppled on to the lord and killed him. If Semith had dared remove the robe, the body might never have been found, but to have removed it would have labelled the crime.

Approaching the tiny bloom of orange through the tangle of branches, Petey lifted her feet high and dropped them carefully. Insects ticked her off, chittering and scratching, making far more noise than she did. As she drew closer to the body a cackabird, nesting in a fork of twigs close to the scrap of material, screeched and flew off awkwardly, feigning a broken wing, then cawed in attack and dived down at her when it realised she wasn't to be distracted. Petey fended it off and the bird settled nearby, watching and fluttering its wings and screeching anxiously until it was satisfied that Petey wasn't an egg-raider. Then it folded its wings and waited, calm as the forest.

The tree had been struck by lightning. The edges of the strike were blackened and jagged where the tree had been whittled by the sky and thrown down, but it had not been totally uprooted, and enough root remained to keep part of the shattered tree alive. Fresh branches stretched up and pushed new leaves high, but the tree would never make it back to the top of the forest canopy. Sawvine was already starting to strangle it, too, thick and sharp. The forest was already reclaiming the wood, breaking it down and consuming it.

As Petey knelt to move away a branch, the skull was the first thing she saw. It was white and seemingly blurred, as if she were seeing it in one of the sharp-edged windows that the lords occasionally carried in their flat boxes. But the blurring was antshroud, and she took a twig and poked it into the sockets of the eyes, one after the other, until the shroud crumbled like ash and the ants poured out and filtered away into the dank leaf mould. She poked a little more with the twig, and the jawbone fell open. A tongue raised itself, shiny black and swollen, and a deep groan came from the jaw, making her gasp until the tongue sprouted legs and a tiny antlered head, and scuttled off.

Petey stood up and looked around, suddenly nervous. She shouldn't have touched it. She should have just walked away as soon as she had noticed the lordly colour. Maybe she could just flee. She would be discovered here at any moment.

Around her the insects had set up an almost rhythmic barrage of sound, and she felt suddenly flushed and faint. She toppled forward a fraction, nauseous, her vision doubling, and her palm touched the soft wood for support but there was none. Her entire arm sank down, folded away into the lichenous, rotting bark.

A stab of pain across her arm brought her senses back. The sawvine.

She pulled a jerk of air into her lungs and shook her head against the soft, pounding noise. She looked at her arm with its deep score of blood. It separated into two parallel lines, and she squinted at them, forcing them to rejoin. They wouldn't.

'Uhuhuhuhuhuh,' she chanted loudly against the seesawing rhythm, panicking, knowing what it meant even though she had never heard the sound before. She felt almost blindly along the branch for the entrance to the colony, cursing at herself for not realising, not recognising the danger in her excitement over the lord's corpse. A child's error. Always be alert for rhythm. She forced concentration on herself, scrabbling over the trunk with her fingernails.

And at last, here it was, her hand sinking right through the bark and deep into the burrowed wood.

Her heart was thudding. She was alone. She knew she could die here. 'Uhuhuhuhuhuh,' she carried on, feeling further down into the heart of the cavity and then squeezing, squeezing toxin out of the soft workers' bodies. The soldiers were reacting, pricking and cutting at her skin, and she was burning from the toxin, but the intense burning was keeping her awake. She opened her hand and squeezed again and again, feeling around inside the hollowed trunk until she closed her hand on the queen's shivering shell case. She gripped it tightly, bracing herself against the branch, and squeezed the huge insect with all her strength.

It was no good. The shell-case simply bristled against her and clattered on.

Still chanting, Petey searched for something to focus her eyes on, to steady herself. Something external. That's what they said. Find stillness. Force that stillness down your arm. Be the stillness. Be stillness.

The lord's skull was all her eyes found, but no matter how hard she tried, it wouldn't be still. It shivered and blurred. Everything blurred out of focus, out of shape. There was no stillness at all. Petey was in deep trouble. This was a young, newly-established colony of mesmers, its queen muscular and thickly chitined. Even holding it and squeezing with all her strength, Petey could feel the vibration almost up to her shoulder. The queen was nearly as big as Petey's fist. She could hardly close her fingers around the carapace. Squeezing the insect seemed only to reinforce the vibration.

'UHUHUHUHUHUH,' Petey moaned, but she could feel her chant changing, settling into the queen's rhythm, and Petey was seeing stars. Her night was falling, her final night. This would be her stillness.

The queen's shivering was starting to numb her arm. Petey sagged against the trunk, and the undermined wood gave way as she fell on to it. But in the fall, her arm pulled free of the mesmer colony and she saw the queen held there in her fist. A huge nub of red, glossy chitin rattling in her fist, fat mandibles fiddling in the air.

Out in the open, the buzzing was deafening. Petey could neither squeeze any harder nor let the queen go. The muscles of her hand and arm were locked in spasm. The blur of her vision was becoming a broad oscillation as the queen adjusted the frequency, searching for resonance. Petey's stomach was starting to rumble curiously, just like Hart had said it did towards the end.

No one knew how it felt after that. Hart had been lucky. Venda had come across him and hacked off his hand with her machete and then mashed both the hand and the queen with the flat of its blade. No one was going to do that for Petey.

The mesmer queen was waving its thorny palps and scissoring its antennae, and worker mesmers were filing steadily up Petey's arm, pricking as they went and and crawling towards her shoulder and her neck.

In desperation, still yelling her chant, Petey twisted her body and slammed her senseless arm against the trembling ground. A few of the mesmers fell off.

The queen stopped thrumming for a moment, then started again, but in that fraction of time Petey saw something beside the lord's skull. A small, black empty tube, no bigger than a finger. It looked hard, though, like a stone, and she managed to control herself enough to pick it up with her free hand as the queen started shivering again.

Petey's stomach was rolling now. Her legs gave way entirely. She felt herself evacuate, warmth streaming down her legs, and as she vomited, the spasm of shit and piss and vomit momentarily interrupted the resonance that was turning her to jelly, and with nothing left to do she stabbed the blunt end of the tube against the queen's shell.

The silence was immediate, and so total that she first thought she had died. Then there was briefly another sort of physical silence that seemed to expand inside her, filling and setting hard in the space that the resonance had created. This was like a soothing warmth.

And then the warmth went and there was so much pain that she couldn't even scream with it. It was like a ball growing inside her, and then so great that it contained her.

The remaining mesmers seemed to lose interest in her and each other. They fell off or crawled away, and gradually the forest sounds returned in their randomness.

Petey slept.

She woke up hungry and thirsty, shaking uncontrollably, not knowing how much time had passed. Her hands were shivering so much that she couldn't touch her palms together. She managed to dislodge the waterskin from the belt with the heel of her hand, but didn't dare attempt to open it for the risk of spilling it all.

She felt tears in her eyes and thought of Loren and Marten. The warmth and love of them, the husband and son. Then she thought Loren might be dead, and slowly realised, remembered he was, and how. The thought made her ache and brought more tears. The mesmers had killed her after all, even if they didn't get to eat her. She would die here, either a slow death from scavenger ants or a savage one at a predator's claws.

Or the lords would find her lying here beside the corpse of one of them.

Now she remembered it all.

Shakily, she pushed herself to her knees and rested there, trembling hugely. Her teeth clattered together.

She tried to think. Hart had had to be cared for like a baby for the best part of a week before he could feed or even clothe himself. Jemus had called a vote to let him die, but the wife had said it would be for her to take responsibility, no common food would be drawn for him, and that had been accepted.

But now Petey was alone, couldn't eat or drink, couldn't move safe or silent, and couldn't be found here with a lord's body. Especially one she'd disturbed, one she'd robbed.

She had to move, for the sake of Marten. She had to conceal the lord's body again. She had to die elsewhere.

It was impossible. She couldn't even crawl. She couldn't clamber over the branches of the tree. She had no energy at all, and no co-ordination.

The tube she had used to kill the mesmer queen was still in her fist. She looked at it and realised what it was – it was the lord's beam weapon, the firetube she had been searching for. She almost laughed to realise it, now, when it was too late. She could hear them talking, still some distance away, but getting closer. They would have firetubes too, and they could see straight.

She sighed and let herself sag back onto the trunk, and as she did so it gave way entirely and dropped her down. One of the living branches slid over her, and the trunk collapsed again, and the body of the lord fell beside her. She tried to push the corpse away but slipped down further, and was in total darkness.

The voices were close by, though Petey had no sense of their direction. There was talk of mesmers. Someone suggested giving up the search, and then there was a lot of movement very close to her, and she realised someone was pulling at the far end of the branch she was half lying on.

And then a distant stab of light, and Petey gripped the tube as firmly as she could, waiting to be discovered. The stab opened into a lozenge, and then it closed again.

'Nothing here,' she heard.

She slept again. When she woke up she was hungry, and her entire body itched. She wondered why that should be, and then she wondered why she hadn't been attacked by anything. And then she realised the answer was in the questions. She was lying in the heart of the mesmer nest. She was splattered by the blood of the dead queen, and the workers were scurrying around her, protecting Petey as they had protected their queen.

She could feel them all over her, marking her with mild toxin. She opened her hand and waited for a mesmer to crawl onto her palm, and closed it. The insect didn't attempt to free itself as she squeezed it, and even her little strength was enough to kill it. It tasted foul, but there was moisture in it.

Petey slept and ate and slept again in the darkness.

After a time, she became able to move her arm a little, and some time later she could move enough to sit up.

She could see, too, in the gloom, her eyes becoming sufficiently accustomed to it to be able to tell day from night. She counted ten days and nights from then, but had no idea how many had gone before. The mesmers fussed over her, crawling into her hand when she was hungry or thirsty. She knew she was nearly ready to climb out when she had to close her eyes to be able to eat them.

There was little strength in her arms, though, and she used the tube to cut her way out of the nest. Then she pulled the robe away from the lord's bones. Unlike Semith, she was stealing the weapon, so taking the robe was no extra risk. She ran it through her hands.

It was astonishingly thin and light. She pulled experimentally at the weave, but it wouldn't give. She folded it carefully and stowed it under her shirt. After that, she pulled branches over what was left of the corpse and went back to the edge of the path.

She looked up and down the beaten trail. One way led to the village, the other to the AngWat.

She turned her back on the path and headed deeper into the forest.

HAVEN

Quill left the coffin docked in the coredor by Walker's Sea and went on foot, keeping his head down, using only small coredors or the great broad ones, avoiding the busy local passages where he was more likely to be noticed. He walked out and up, then when he reached Green he started to drop down again and deepdown, using solo drop-pods where he could, until they brought him to the Canal that ran like a suture all through deepGreen. He saw his face and Scheck's on screens, flashing up whenever the Game slackened.

The Canal tracked all the way from Jade to Emerald, about twenty kilometres and all of it straightline, the water forced one way and then back again, stopping for refiltration and return at Green's borders with Red and with Yellow. The waterway was about twenty metres edge to edge, with a central barrier to divide the currents. Its molten heart was grey, black, gold, silver. The air that pumped up endlessly through the Canal from wherever in Haven's core it was created, bumped and bubbled, scoured clean enough by the Canal for the fragile lungs of men and women, to be machined away throughout the planet and then disposed of uptop.

Quill took a carrypod to the edge of Jade, sitting in a corner in the busy carriage and keeping his head down, holding the awkward case by his side, feeling it bump against his leg. The heat made him sweat, loosened his grip on the bag. His clothes began to feel gritty against his skin. He was thirsty.

Canal water was not drinkable. It was not water. It was the filter that made Haven's subterranean air. Throw yourself in from the walkway two hundred metres above the Canal, where the heat merely burned your cheeks in an instant if you leaned over the rail, and rumour was that you drew a single breath of perfect air as you dropped. And with that perfect air in your lungs you were flayed, boiled, dead before your corpse touched the water.

The Canal was a hundred metres deep and as thick as magma. At its calmest, it crusted and cracked like a jigsaw puzzle. At its most vigorous, it rumbled and burst and spewed arcs and jets of gold to within a handsreach of the walkway. For Haven, the Canal was life and death.

Quill stepped out of the carrypod and breathed the Canal's exquisite air. For the first time since leaving Walker, he relaxed a fraction and looked around.

Canalside was where Haven's elite, its rich and powerful, lived. The first-breathers had the best of it. Here, the air tasted clean and breathed easy. They had the worst of it, the air's last breathings, who lived furthest from here. Far away uptop and in the heart of Blue.

Quill walked Canalside and stood on the fast-track platform to wait for an Emerald-bound pod. The bag sat between his legs.

Everywhere under Haven was at risk from something. The further down and deepdown in Haven you dropped, the more danger there was of seismic cataclysm, but its crucial importance to life under Haven meant that the Canal was so bracketed and cushioned with stabilisation devices that it was as safe from this as anywhere uptop.

A pod blew cool air from its bow as it hissed to stillness. Quill moved to a door. As it slid open, he saw a man sitting there, frowning at a palmscreen. Quill hesitated. The man lowered his hands and glanced across the shine of the screen at him.

Quill hadn't expected company here. He raised a foot to enter the pod, then paused. The man's glance started to focus, and Quill knew he was more likely to be remembered later if he let the pod go than if he took it. He stepped in as the doors closed. The man blinked and went back to his screen.

The track ran along the Canal, and Quill put the bag at his side and sat back on the cooled seat slats, trying to relax for the few minutes it would take the pod to deliver him at the next down elevator he needed.

The man wasn't looking at him at all. A sit/screen worker, Quill guessed from his neat, clean clothes and manicured fingers. Maybe in Nutrition.

Quill looked out of the window. Across the water, habitation terraces rose, stepped back in tiers that followed the Canal. Enclosed bridges arched over the Canal at regular intervals, and Quill glanced up at the immense hanks of heat-shielded cable looping across the out-of-sight top of the long pipetube cavern of the Canal.

Along the cavern, the long-excavated rock was stained and discoloured, patterned roughly and quilted with mould and lichen. There were scattered outcrops of agate and moonstone. It was probably beautiful, Quill thought.

Above the other man's head, a screen showed the Game. There was no escape from it. In the endless arena, Blue and Red toiled to move the ball. Dan and Jan appeared, but their commentary was swallowed by the thud of the pod on its rails.

Quill lowered his gaze and examined his hands. His palms were rimed with sweat. He tried to wipe them on the seat, but the metal slats were damp with condensation. The pod wasn't moving especially rapidly, but it was unsmooth and the juddering was starting to make him nauseous.

You prefer it in a coffin, huh?

Quill tensed and looked at the other man, who was staring openly at him now. Had he said something to Quill? Was he expecting an answer?

Great work, Quill. Stay inconspicuous. Don't draw attention.

More loudly than he meant, Quill said, 'What?'

The man raised a hand and said, 'I just said, I mean, I wondered if you were okay, that's all. You look a bit, well, like you were about to unswallow.'

Scheck. That had been Scheck talking. Quill showed the man a smile. 'Thanks, I'm okay. You're right. I had some bad myco. And I'm late for work.'

The man closed his screen. Great, Quill thought. Conversation. Something for him to remember.

'What do you do?'

Quill patted the bag. 'My samples. I'm a decorator.' He waved a hand at the habitations across the Canal. 'See? They decorate their balconies with displays of stones and jewel clusters. I install them.' He looked out at the receding tiers, pointing randomly at shining examples of glitter and gleam. 'That sort of thing.'

His companion looked with him, nodding with interest.

'I've heard about it.' He looked pointedly from Quill's bag to Quill.

'I'm sorry. Some of the crystals are very fragile.'

'Oh. Do you have a site I can screen, then?' He flipped his palmscreen open and held a finger ready to work it.

Quill massaged his forehead. 'Actually,' he said, leaning forward and whispering, 'I'm not an installer. I'm a direct supplier. My samples come from a source in Fact. I shouldn't be telling you this, but you won't tell anyone, will you?'

The man shook his head tightly. Quill saw the lightweight screen flex briefly in his hands, the amber shine blueing at its edges. He was wishing he hadn't said anything to Quill in the first place, now. Corrupt factotems were not people to know about.

Quill carried on talking, though the man was looking away, making as if he couldn't hear Quill any more. 'My supplier at Fact confiscates it and passes it on to me,' Quill said. 'I distribute it to decorators, back-pay him most of the fee.'

He sat back. It was fine now. He was safe. The man wouldn't tell a soul about him. Even if he later realised who Quill actually was, he'd keep it to himself, just in case Quill was telling the truth. He wouldn't want to risk bringing himself to the attention of a corrupt factotem.

Just to be certain, Quill said, 'You want to see what's in the bag, then? It's fine stuff.' The skull was cloth-wrapped, and the case was unremarkable to look at. Even if the man did glance inside, there was little risk. Quill crossed the carriage to sit next to the man and opened the bag, bringing it close to his face.

The pod jerked abruptly and the head swung. Quill nearly lost balance, catching the bag sharply as it nearly tipped its contents out. Everything inside thumped and rattled.

Quill caught himself and pulled the wide-mouthed bag upright again. He held it out once more, but the man closed his eyes, took a deep, sharp breath and held it in open distaste, and shook his head until Quill closed the bag again and withdrew to his own seat. The man let out his breath loudly. He was not even acknowledging Quill's presence now. He sniffed and wiped his nose with the back of a hand, then opened his screen again and locked his attention there, the pale oblong trembling unreadably in his hand. He looked scared and dizzy. At the next stop he stumbled from the pod.

No one else disturbed Quill's journey. To dispel his travel nausea he focused on the tiers. He could make out the movement of people across the horizontal seams, and of carrypods up and down the vertical. It was like watching an outdated machine perform a calculation.

Just as the pod arrived at his stop, an extraordinarily huge bird, its brilliant turquoise wings spanning the width of the Canal, flew silently past, travelling straight along the waterway towards Jade. Quill stood at the railing and watched the bird slowly fade into the distance, swooping gloriously under bridges, its downstriking wingtips all but flicking the water. All that distinguished it from the real, except its actual impossibility, was that it was perfectly stable in the heat haze.

Quill tightened his hold on the bag and found a carrypod to take him away from the Canal and deeperdown through Maroon and towards Cobalt. After the stifling warmth of the Canal, it seemed cold. It took him a while to get used to the flawed air again, too.

Where Skim lived, Cobalt became Carmine. Walking towards Carmine was like going against wind and tide. Everyone seemed to be coming the other way, and Quill knew why. The rock of Maroon was still just about solid enough, but in Carmine strain gauges every ten metres announced creep figures, and for a while now the creep here had been fluctuating rhythmically. And what this meant was distant cavitation. It could subside, it could accelerate and it could simply carry on as it was. While Seismic hadn't yet asked for the area to be cut off, it wouldn't be long. People were already migrating back into Cobalt and further, and runoffs were being drilled and event deflectors cast and set.

Quill followed Walker's directions to carmine38. He hadn't been to the stalls here before, but the store was, as it had to be, the same as every other indie store. The place was called *More Than Memory*. Quill went inside.

It was a standard trader's allocation, two metres width, two-five height and cavitated five back from coredor-flush. But in this store the holoshelves were pixelsharp and perfect, vaulting the ceiling and pushing back the walls at least another three metres. Keeping his back to the counter, Quill examined the shelves while Skim dealt with the sole customer. It had to be her. She fitted Walker's description perfectly, with her burnt-brown face, heat-squeezed brown eyes and hair as sharp and black as shadow.

What she sold here was mostly screen and comms gear. The comms stuff was nothing new to Quill; what Survey used was several levels up in capability and down in size from any of this. The screenware he was less familiar with, and it struck him how his life had taken him away from so much. Survey had taken him over, and now he was lost. At the edge of his gaze he caught a glimpse of colour and instinctively glanced in its direction.

Orange. It was just a Robe wandering into the store. Without thought, he looked across at Skim and the man she was serving. Neither of them reacted to the Robe. They saw Robes all the time.

Not like us. She's not like us.

Not like you, Scheck. She's alive.

You're as dead as me, Quill. Don't forget that, if you don't want it to happen. Back in the pod, that was lucky. You might not be lucky again.

The woman was looking straight at him.

He looked away, reached out and picked up the holovid for a rockcommer and turned it over in his hand. Its specifications flowed over the casing, letters and numerals blinking serenely at him. He opened his hand and the holovid melted back to the shelf.

He heard the customer leave, and turned around. The Robe had gone too, leaving just him and the woman, Skim. She had dropped one hand beneath the counter.

Now she brought it into plain view again, folded into a fist. Blue metal showed between her knuckles.

'It's okay, I'm not a thief,' he said.

'Oh, fine. Only the last one said something like that, too. Just to tell you, we're not as alone as you think.' Whatever it was, she shifted it to her other hand.

'You don't know what I think.' That had come out wrong, but he couldn't stop himself saying it. Her eyes hooded over and he tried to retrieve the situation. 'Sorry, I didn't mean that the way it sounded.'

She didn't react at all. Quill felt something lightly contact the back of his neck and hold there. He leaned fractionally forward and it followed him, maintaining its presence evenly.

Skim shook her head a little and murmured, 'Like I said.' Her eyes opened a fraction, brown as the brown of her cheeks.

'I don't mean to seem threatening or anything,' Quill said, 'but I know there's no one there. My hearing's good and no one came in. And the way it moves with me—— he ticked his head sharply from side to side, '—no reaction time. It's just a prickler. I'm sorry. A kid's toy. The activator's in your hand there.'

She smiled at him. 'Well, I don't mean to seem smug or anything, but that prickler's target-linked to a nanotorch up in the ceiling behind you, and if I let this deadswitch in my hand here go, it'll bleach you pure.' She tipped her head to the side, renewing the smile. 'Funny thing, the last thief thought the same as you. I really ought to do something about it. Makes it seem I'm bluffing, doesn't it?'

The prickler was warming the back of Quill's neck. This was all going bad. She was the only thing he had, and here she was ready to drop him. He opened his arms carefully and said, 'How did we get from me coming into the shop to this?'

'It seems to me that you got us here. So you get us out.' She shrugged, her hair drifting like shadow. 'Or else just get out. It's up to you. I don't get much casual trade, less still since we developed this stability problem down here. So?'

'I was given your name. But I don't know if you can help me.'

'Nor do I. You're not interested in the shelves. You don't look like you come from Fact, but I'm not discounting the possibility.' She rolled the blue device slowly around her palms, watching him for a reaction. 'Actually, you don't look like you know where on Oath you came from or aim to get to. Or where you are, come to that. I guess that leaves a two-way choice. Am I in trouble or are you?'

'Walker gave me your name.'

A different smile appeared on her face. 'Ah. Walker! You should have said. You look like something he picked up on that shore of his. Walker sends me all his cleanups, did he tell you that? He thinks I'm a charity.'

She tossed the device on the counter. Quill ducked. Nothing happened. He felt suddenly light-headed.

He could see her eyeing the bag. Maybe it stank. He'd had it too long to know, in the coffin and then bumping against his leg all the way here. He felt the bag was rotting and everyone was looking through. As if he was himself, too. Maybe the man in the carrypod had seen it after all.

He felt odd and slightly faint, his sight lagging and his thoughts slow. Maybe he was hungry. Or maybe he'd been exposed to something in the ship or the explosion. Maybe something radioactive. He couldn't see a medic, though, that was for sure. He had to find someone to ask.

No, Scheck, not you.

He tightened his grip on the bag. Something, probably the nose, nuzzled his thigh.

'Are you okay?' she said, looking at him strangely.

'Lack of sleep,' he managed to say. Which was true.

'So, you want something for that? Is that it?'

'No.' He looked at the door. The nausea was passing. It was quiet anyway, down here in Carmine. Skim's store was very quiet indeed. No one passing. But there had been someone here. The place wasn't dead. 'Is there somewhere we can talk?'

'This is fine. I can hear you just fine.'

'I'm not worried about *you* hearing me.'

She shrugged. 'Too bad.' She pulled her lips tight, nodding. 'Sleeplessness is a terrible thing. Late at night, I just lose my memory. You know? You ever get that? Memory trouble?'

He adjusted his grip on the bag. She looked at it, then at him, but her face was questionless.

'Yes,' he said. 'I get that. About four dark, it happens, most nights. Is that what you mean?'

She nodded again. 'About that time, yeah. Four dark.'

She picked up a screen portal from the counter and played with the terminals. Quill was aware of someone standing beside him. He kept his eyes low as he turned to leave the store.

Walking Mexi away from her home, Gild glanced briefly at Zelda's door. Leaving the street, he said, 'What do you know about Fact, Mexi?'

She looked across at him. He hadn't broken stride, and she was slightly breathless from the pace he was keeping to.

'Well? You're part of it now. This is your best time to think about it.

Soon you'll forget what it was like being outside of it. It's important to know, to remember, don't you think?'

'Yes.'

Now he stopped. They were on blue3, one of the wide, original coredors, with space for twenty people to be able barely to touch hands and stretch from wall to wall, but still people changed their pace and drew towards the coredor's walls rather than come too near to Gild and Mexi. Gild looked sharply at a woman approaching and Mexi watched her flinch and almost trip.

'Why did she do that, Mexi? Come on, I'm not going to send you back to Nutrition.'

'She's scared.'

'Yes. Come on, Mexi, talk. What's she scared of? What scares you?'

Mexi watched the woman recover her composure as she walked on. Being with Gild was like clinging to a loose rock in a swift stream. The current was disturbed and Mexi felt her grip unsure. She didn't trust Gild. He was testing her. 'The laws aren't fair. The punishment isn't just. The Game, rock.' She looked at him directly, knowing she shouldn't have said that.

'Fair and just. Those are good, plain words.' He began to move again, and she breathed hard to keep up. They began to overtake people on the avenue. He carried on talking. 'There's no room here on Haven for disturbance. On Oath, things were different, probably.' She understood that he was hinting at something here, but she couldn't guess at what. 'Haven is a hard place to survive, as you know. People who are dissatisfied can't simply give up and leave, though. There's nowhere under Haven for them to go.'

'What about Haze?'

'Haze excites you. You chose Contact, I know. Perhaps, one day. As you know, we barter with them, we learn. It takes time. But we can't let people go there without being sure they're the right people. We can't let our dissatisfied go, for instance. We can't invade, we can't colonise. It would be wrong.'

'But why are the laws so rigid here?'

'Language is cohesion. If language is plain, there can be no secrets. We share language with Haze, and we hold it in trust, in case Oath contacts us. Of course new words are required, as technology moves, and Fact introduces them and ensures assimilation.'

'But the penalties—'

'No one is penalised without an initial warning. Once they've been warned, what reason have they to repeat the crime? None. UnFact is no different from any other crime. But when you understand the consequences to us all of the introduction of division, you see how vital it is that we keep ourselves strong and close. It's for the same reason that stories are forbidden. When we arrived here, there was no time for the past, and the Archive was lost. There was no time for anything but survival. All that mattered was air and warmth and shelter and food.'

'We have them all, now.'

'Yes. And there's time for more. For flying kites. For, what is it? Birdfishing?'

Gild glanced at her, and she fought the rush of colour to her face. 'Well?' she said.

'I'm just observing that there's freedom for that. You were responsible for damaging a dome, and did Fact even warn you? No.'

'But you knew. There are cams everywhere.'

'How else can we be sure of protecting freedom?'

'And stories? What about stories? There's time for stories, now.'

'True. There is time. Let's think of your birdfishing adventure. You told everyone in your street. Fact prohibits the embellishment of the story. Anyone to whom you told the story will be cautious to be accurate if telling someone else, and quite rightly. If we hear of a false story we will eradicate it aggressively. False tales damage the reputations of people and the stability of Haven. Is this wrong?'

'But the pure facts of the story don't tell what it was like. The fear, the excitement—'

'Of course not. But everyone must have their own experiences. No words can convey fear, excitement, beauty, terror. To attempt to do so can only be unFact. Words, language, are powerful tools, Mexi. Words can incite the most content of people to violent action.'

He slowed down and then came to a halt. They were some way off Blue by now, and the avenue was narrower and streaming with people. Gild and Mexi were being allowed less clearance, though Mexi noticed that no one met their eyes. She wondered if this is what she would have to get used to in future. It was an uncomfortable anonymity.

'I'd have said this to anyone, Mexi. Any one of these—' he waved his arm, the gesture causing a flurry of acceleration in the direction of his hand. Someone tripped, pulled themselves up and hurried on. 'I'd discuss this with anyone at all. Fact doesn't stifle discussion. It welcomes the opportunity for clarification.' He smiled at her. 'There was a movement to rename Fact, a few years ago, to Clarity. But Fact was considered clearer.'

With the small joke he smiled at her, and she felt obliged to smile back. They started to walk again, and Mexi stopped noticing the people around them.

'Good,' Gild said. 'We can talk again, at any time. You can talk to any of us. You'll realise that the rigour of correct thought will free you absolutely. Now, let's move on from this discussion to something rather more exciting, shall we? Do you know where we are?'

The coredor opened up into a tall domed chamber. A pair of doors rose ahead of her, and she simply stared at them. Then she quietly said, the chamber echoing her whisper, 'The Vault. This is the Vault.'

The wood was darker than she had expected, but the doors themselves were smaller than she had imagined. Each was nearly two metres wide. But it was wood! Wood cut from trees, sawn and worked and nailed. There was an unevenness and a patina to it that she hadn't imagined from her reading and the sims. She could make no sense of the carving. The heavily grained doors were a mystery, she remembered. They could only have come from Haze, but no one knew when or under what circumstances, and the motifs of strange beasts had no explanation.

'Shall we?'

Mexi looked at Gild, and nodded. The Vault. Fact. This was it, and Mexi was going in, not in sim but in person. She was going to be walking on the Vault's floor, breathing its filtered air. Not ghosting through the Vault like in an EdSim at school, tumbling along with no time to examine and no opportunity to touch the precious relics. She was going to be actually opening the databanks and reading, *reading* the documents.

The left door opened at Gild's fingertouch on the handplate. Mexi felt briefly disappointed that both doors hadn't parted in unison, but it didn't matter when she saw beyond them. This was nothing like the EdSim. The light was dim and somehow serious. There was immediately a sense of quietness too, a sense of thought overruling speech.

The Vault. She still couldn't quite believe it. She was actually, actually inside the Vault.

As she stepped through the door, Mexi felt lightheaded and dizzy. The walls flew back and the floor was suddenly soft and spongy, tipping her forward, and then a hand was in the small of her back, hard, not pushing her but supporting her as the dim light swerved down and stabilised.

'Are you all right?'

She had nearly fainted. 'I'm fine. No breakfast. That's all.'

Gild grinned. 'Come on, then. I'll show you around first. A grand tour.' The doors closed behind them, and a wall of light shot across the coredor ahead, cutting off her view of the Vault beyond. Gild stepped through it, glittering at the interface and becoming a faint silhouette at the far side.

'Step through slowly,' he told her, his voice disconcertingly close, even though he looked to be far away on a fading screen.

Mexi took a breath and stepped at the lightwall. It felt prickly and soft at the same time, reaching through her clothes as though she were naked. Coredors divided ahead of her.

'Now you're printed. You need to inform security if you have gene therapy, any implant, transplant, there's a list of things. It's all in the pack you'll be given as you leave today. Don't worry about it. Is there anything you're particularly interested in?'

Mexi couldn't think of anything. There was too much. What could she say? The Leaving? The Era of Decay? Year Nul? Or should she ask about the Captain? Or the Ark? Or . . .

'Can't decide. You'll kick yourself later, I'm sure. We'll do an overview.' He gestured towards a coredor to Mexi's left, saying, 'Security here takes precedence over everything and everyone. What's contained and archived here is irreplaceable. As you know, our work is vitally important, and it can't be carried out if anything primal is ever damaged. Original sources are protected utterly. Not simply in the sense of environmental damage, but in terms of damage by users. Both accidental and malicious.' He caught Mexi's glance. 'Yes. In the past there have been people who have gained access and attempted to destroy data. Crazy people, rehistorians, all sorts of unFactors. You were chosen, Mexi, by a number of criteria beyond the obvious. You have the intellect we need, but you're stable, too. Not obsessive, and not too imaginative.' They were moving always through branching coredors, and none of them at all was marked or had any distinguishing factors. The lighting was the same everywhere, and the branching angles were regular.

'How do you find your way around?'

'We don't.' Gild put a finger to his ear. 'As you leave today, you'll be given an eartap. It will direct you where you need to be. No more, no less. Right now I don't know where we're going beyond the next junction. If the tap should fail, I'll be as lost as you. You can't work out an exit alone. Many of the coredors you see leading away are dead ends or sims.' He indicated his ear again. 'The taps never fail, or rarely. If they do, they go to alarm, and someone comes to find you. You don't move. In here.'

As he stopped at a door and went in, Mexi realised this was the first door they had seen in about fifteen minutes of walking. Even the doors were simmed away. This was not at all like the EdSims. In them the

Vault was a compact storehouse thriving with workers, all hunched over books and screens and papers, writing and magnifying and simply reading. This room was not like that. This was a single person – a woman – leaning on a desk, her head haloed by the huge screen that filled the wall beyond her. On the screen was a document rendered so perfectly that for a moment Mexi thought it must be pinned there against a transilluminating light.

The woman turned round. She blinked and removed a pair of glasses, folding them flat and tucking them into her palm so that the earloops stuck out like the legs of a tiny crushed bird. The woman looked surprised.

'Excuse us,' Gild said. 'I'm bringing this first-dayer on her tour. I wondered whether we might overlook you for a moment, and perhaps use your station?'

'Certainly,' the woman said. Her glasses seemed to wriggle in her hand. Mexi smiled at her, but she didn't respond. Maybe without her glasses she couldn't see.

'What are you working on?'

The woman opened her glasses and put them on. 'This is a document from the immediate post-contact period. It's about two hundred years old.'

'In fact it's a copy,' Gild interrupted. 'But indistinguishable from the original, except that Miz Harverd has enhanced it. The original is barely legible. The task of researchers is to carry out clarifications as perfectly as possible. They work on precise copies of the original documents, but never the originals, which are never under any circumstances removed from the protection of the deep Archive. Go on, Miz Harverd.'

'Thank you. This paper is from a document referring to a meeting between a spokeswoman from Haze and an envoy from Haven, regarding an initial exchange of steel for a consignment of wood. A barter. This was about the time of first contact. Very early. Observer exchange had just been agreed, and we were very tentative, as you can imagine. Here was a planet where they spoke our language and were human, but at the same time primitive and suspicious. There was a ruling caste – we know them as Robes, but on Haze they're called lords – with whom we dealt, who had some degree of education and rudimentary scientific knowledge. We wanted to trade with them, but couldn't offer them much that they could use without far greater technological skills than they possessed at the time.'

Mexi nodded, staring at the documents on the screen. For the first time, she saw the immense complexity of the situation. She tried to imagine what it must have been like, to discover a planet inhabited by your own people, but reverted to a primitive state, ruled by an unelected elite.

Gild said, 'Miz Taro? Comment?'

'That was the basis of observer exchange, wasn't it? They were wary and distrustful. Our arrival disturbed them. Their culture was secretive and barbaric. They had an idea of what they called reciprovocation. For every visitor to Haze, they sent a Robe back here. Not to learn, but to prove we had no secrets, no intentions to go to war. We allowed their Robes complete freedom to go wherever they wanted. Even though they didn't allow us the same freedom on Haze.'

Ms Harverd said, without turning her eyes from the screen, 'We were desperate to trade with them, so we accepted. Just as we accept it now. Nothing has changed.'

'Go on with your work, Miz Harverd,' Gild said. 'We'll observe.'

This was not a grand tour at all. Gild was not just her guide. This was some sort of initiation into the Vault and its complexities. Mexi felt more lost here than she had in the maze of coredors outside.

Ms Harverd said, 'I'll call up the negotiators' notes regarding the barter.' As she spoke, she was scrolling slowly through reams of documents, her lightlance brilliantly illuminating them, words and sentences flickering and vanishing. 'Other documents confirm that we'd decided to offer them steel plates and girders, building frames that they could use with their own techniques. Rivets they could hammer.' She glanced at Mexi and the screen fixed, a wall covered with papers, the records of conversations and discussions hundreds of years in the past, unimaginable distances away. Ms Harverd sat back in her chair and rested the fine lightlance on the table, gesturing for Mexi to come forward. She turned pages on the screen, showing Mexi more. Mexi read, and read, and read.

The colour and texture of the foliage . . .

We were offered a drink, which we accepted. It tasted . . .

Ms Harverd stood up to let Mexi sit. Without taking her eyes from the screen, Mexi leant forward and picked up the lightlance. Pages turned delicately, more of them and more.

Nothing any of us had ever seen before . . .

The sky was above us, blue as lapis and so still . . .

After long consideration, we decided to ask them for something made of wood to begin with, a token perhaps, a symbol of cooperation and trust . . .

Mexi was so deep in the papers that she could almost close her eyes and summon up the conversations.

They imagined our steel must be wood, of course . . .

She could almost see the faces of the negotiators as they tried to hide their excitement at being on Haze, at being the first to commence bartering with the planet.

Ms Harverd cleared her throat, reining Mexi in. 'As you see, there's a lot of paper. Unfortunately, most of it is irrelevant, useless for research. The problem is that by the time Haze was discovered, Fact was well established and there was a mania for documentation.' She looked at Gild, who made a small, neutral sound of agreement and waved her on.

'As you just saw, Miz Taro, everything was noted and archived, all by ink and paper, since we weren't permitted to take other recording devices to Haze. Vast quantities of material were sealed and stuffed away in the excitement of contact and trade. And then, a number of years ago, when it was thought to check the archives for that period, they were found to have failed. There was contamination by myco and lichen from Haven, and short-surviving but nevertheless destructive insects and plants from Haze. Ink was gone, paper was chewed. Of course, huge efforts were made to reconstruct the important documents, but the rest were allowed to deteriorate.'

She stopped, and Gild took over. 'And if the volume of paperwork was an inverted cascade down from first discussions to agreement, the research effort was the opposite. With each step away from the agreement, less effort was expended. Ten stages away from the agreement, the documentation was most recently accessed a year ago. Twenty stages down the trail, five years.'

Ms Harverd said, 'And the very earliest discussions were last examined thirty years ago.' She pointed her lightlance at the screen. 'Until now.'

'And now,' Gild said, 'We're going to leave you for an hour or so to look around the archive alone. See what you can find. Your access is only to the early records, not to the culmination of the negotiations. See if you can work out what that might be.'

Ms Harverd pushed herself to her feet. 'You've used a lightlance before, you know how to work the screens.' She waited until Mexi was looking at her, and added, 'This may not be Contact, but it's closer to it than you think.'

And they left, Gild and Ms Harverd together.

Mexi picked up the lightlance and brought back the earliest documents in this part of the archive. She could see why it had been neglected for so long. Not only the lack of priority, but the vast quantities of papers were hand-scrawled and going to mush. They had been more or less stabilised, but still they were deteriorating. She imagined no one was prepared to attempt anything further for fear of destroying them utterly.

It took her a while to locate the notes Ms Harverd had shown her, and when she did reach them, it took her much longer to be able to use the refinements of the research lightlance to restore them to anything approaching the legibility Ms Harverd had coaxed out of them. She swung the tool across them, the fine illumination floating them in a murky sea.

She flicked the lightlance in her hand. Other than improving her screen skills, this was pointless. It wasn't like Contact at all. It was just Fact.

In irritation, she brushed the lightlance across the screen and accidentally caught a short document that sharpened in the screen's centre, replacing everything else. This was clearly very old, and she pulled her chair forward, squinting at the paper. It was faded and the writing almost impossible to make out until she had spent a few minutes working it with the lightlance.

She read it twice, and then again. Taking in what she was reading made her distrust her eyes. In the scrolling circle of light, part of a phrase jumped out at her. She took the lightlance and pushed brightness over the awkwardly cursive lettering.

... gesture of god ...

Splatters of something brown across the scrap of paper that she recognised now as crushed insects. This then would have been written at night, when the flies came out to fly into the candle flames and to bite for blood. Hence the scrawl was particularly bad. One of the brown smudges ended in a definite partial fingerprint.

... gesture of god ...

Mexi considered it. The Robes on Haze had no gods, any more than Haven. Gods were unFact.

She looked again, this time more closely. No, it was not *god*. The word extended. It was *good*.

The next word, then. Good *attempt*? Was that it? She brought it up, magnified it, slewed it at an angle and brightened her lance, thinking herself onto Haze, into the negotiator's head.

She'd been pressing hard with the nib in the fly-strewn candlelight, scoring the paper deeply. *She*, Mexi thought, and took a breath. A woman's hand, Mexi was sure. She searched the screen for help, and eventually found what she was looking for. She changed the image from CAM to SIM.

The pressure of the writing implement on the paper threw the word into strong relief. The page took on shape and seemed to come away from the screen. It was slightly curled, she now saw, and that had distorted the image. She flattened it, then turned it obliquely and played with the direction of illumination.

Now she ran the lightlance over *attempt* and lifted the word free of the document. The remainder of the text faded away, leaving the single word on the paper. She picked up the scrap and magnified it further, slanted it a few degrees and shone transverse light across the lettering. The shadows sharpened.

. . . good intent . . .

She punched a handwriting search and waited.

One document uplisted. She screened it. It was definitely the same hand. This time written by day, though, the ink clearer than the shadow.

. . . dors . . . dors . . . godwil . . . wod . . . steel . . .

The stretched *o*. Doors, goodwill, wood. Mexi could feel her heart race. She gave the negotiator time to return to Haven, came out of that section of the Vault and went to Haven's foundry records, keyed a search, then rekeyed a few times until she found it.

There it was. A docket. STEEL DOORS, TWO. MIRROR IMAGES. CAST AND COMPLETED ACCORDING TO DRAWINGS (DESTROYED IN ERROR). JOB SIGNED FOR AND REMOVED.

And in an angry hand, *Pointless!! The detail on this job wasted us over a month. If this isn't unFact, what is??*

Mexi stared at the screen, grinning. She was still grinning when Gild returned with Ms Harverd.

Gild glanced with faint interest at the screen.

'Excellent work. You got further than most apprentices get. You discovered . . .?'

'Foundry records for the steel doors specially made here, and bartered for the doors we use for the Vault. What we were looking at were the negotiations with Haze for the doors to the Vault.'

The words on the screen were still flickering. Mexi couldn't take her eyes from them.

Gild said, 'That's right. Before the proper negotiations began, iron and steel for wood, our manufacturing technology and products for their produce, a goodwill gesture was offered by us, and accepted. It was considered insignificant at the time. The notes were kept out of completeness more than anything else.'

Mexi realised she'd discovered nothing, just been nudged to her conclusion.

Gild went on. 'At the time of first contact with Haze, there was little or nothing in the Vault from before Arrival. After that time, everything was kept, regardless of any perceived value, but there was so much of it that it was categorised, and now there's simply insufficient time to go through it all. There's more data to store all the time, and most of our effort's spent filing and checking what we know has value. Searching the oldest part of the Vault is something we have no time for.' He turned and looked at the screen, but nothing had changed. 'This was important, though, which is why we use it for first-dayers. An important part of the agreement between Haven and Haze was the Exchange Law.' He stopped, nodding at Mexi. 'You were talking about it in the outer coredors.'

'Reciprovocation,' she said. 'Just as we exchange goods, we exchange people. They come here, and they wander around, and when our people return, so do theirs. It's pointless.'

'Haze is a primitive planet. We assume there was some disaster, a long time ago in which they lost everything. They don't know, they have no myths or legends we're aware of, no clues. All they have are hunters and farmers and a ruler caste. They have a strong idea of fair exchange. Their society lives by it. Their Law of Exchange, the reciprovocation, is part of it. It isn't pointless. It's crucial. They wander around Haven, the Robes, but their presence holds the agreement together. It binds it.'

Gild has been to Haze, Mexi thought. He's been there!

She wanted to ask him about it, but behind him the screen was shifting.

'The exchange of people is a matter of trust. They trust us with their people as we trust them with ours. It's also a distrust matter. Each holds hostages. Once there was an accident here, a death. You don't know about that, do you?'

Mexi shook her head.

'We explained, we apologised. Nothing was said, but there was a very similar accident on Haze very shortly afterwards and a factotem from Contact died. Their explanation and apology were almost identical to ours. Later, when one of our men died on Haze, unquestionably accidentally, we made it clear that we understood it was not their responsibility. But a Robe was seen throwing himself into the Canal shortly afterwards.'

Mexi thought about that. Logic, its absence, its negation. And then she thought of something Zelda had said, when Mexi had given the Robe some of the great bird to eat. *You've disturbed the balance.* How would Zelda have known about that?

Gild was still talking. 'The statement of good intent would have been exactly the right thing to appeal to them. An exchange of identical doors, ours in steel, theirs in wood.'

Ms Harverd made a gesture, and Mexi stood to let her sit down. She put her hands to the keys and started to move papers around the screen, bringing them up and replacing them so quickly that Mexi couldn't see the commands before they were accepted. She referenced and cross-referenced. Mexi saw some of her own steps duplicated, others bypassed. A few documents came up that she hadn't discovered. On the few occasions when the screen was briefly dark, Mexi thought she saw the reflection of a smile on Gild's face.

'A little luck, but she was logical, mainly,' Ms Harverd said to Gild, finally sitting back. 'And intuitive. Good blend. Yes, very good. She'll do.' She stood up and held out her hand to Mexi. 'I don't think we'll throw you back to the myco caverns. Welcome to Fact, Mexi.'

Gild smiled at her too, and Mexi realised that he was Ms Harverd's assistant, rather than the reverse.

'Now, Mexi. I think you deserve the rest of your tour.'

In the coredors, Gild started talking to her more easily. 'You see, the Vault is a complex place. You'll be working on documents for a long time before you start making decisions about the alterations and judgments you will be carrying out. Now. Let's see some real documents.'

A door opened, but for a moment there was nothing beyond it, and Mexi thought something was wrong. Then, gradually, a delicate orange light came up, like some kind of rising dawn. Mexi glanced at Gild, who nodded and murmured, 'This light is less injurious to the room's contents than any other wavelength.'

The room was smaller than Mexi had imagined. It stretched back, but not so far that the rear wall was out of sight.

'What you're looking at, Mexi, is the entire original paper documentation that remains from the fleet. This is everything we have. It's fairly sparse, as you can see. Manuals from the ships, mainly. *Rufus and the Jungle Trail.* The fleet's electronic archive was entirely lost, as you know. All we know of Oath comes from oral history, anecdote and what we learnt from the inhabitants of Haze, which of course had been corrupted long before we discovered the planet, and which of course can't explain our Leaving. All unFact. Nothing of it passes beyond the Vault. Small things remain which should strictly be UnFact, but we accept them – when we swear, for instance, we say, "Crise!" It comes from crisis, of course, we know that. Kinese whispers, from kincsis, meaning movement and change. We use other words too in expressions, like Laurel and Hyde, or life's a vale of cherries, and though we understand the expressions, we have no idea of their original meaning.'

Half-listening to Gild, Mexi looked at the material. Barely even clues. Just notes. Just details of matters, the matters themselves forgotten. The books lay curled with age and fixed there. The casings of the electronic storage devices were corroded, rusted, dented.

She saw a fresh light in Gild's eyes, now, and she knew something of his excitement here. 'But the immediate post-Arrival period,' he said. 'That's a different matter. A hard time was had of it. So much energy was wasted trying to tame uptop. The colony nearly failed. The diaries of that part of it make rough reading. Without the genengineering of myco, we'd not be here at all.'

He caught himself, slowed down. 'This is the Vault, then. The hard core of Fact. This is where we reconstruct the past. We're not historians so much as archaeologists. Here, history is physical, a solid thing.' He made a fist and reached it out towards the material, making Mexi jump as his hand struck an invisible barrier. 'It exists. It affects our lives. But time destroys the archive. Even examining the material damages it.'

He passed his hand in front of him and and the pale light faded until the room was dark again. 'Even that delicate light is destructive,' Gild said.

As he guided Mexi out of the room, a Robe passed by, drifting down the coredor. Gild turned to follow it with his eyes. Mexi wondered whether Robes had eartaps.

The Robe disappeared around a corner, and Gild said, 'Haze was the bad luck of Haven turned around. We can't imagine how it must have been for that first outbound ship finally leaving Haven, searching for something, somewhere, and coming down through the mists of Haze to see jungle. To find human life.' He shook his head. 'It's that landing that really saved Haven. The Captain saved us the first time, and the discovery of Haze saved us again.'

CAP

Of course, Gus won. Augustus Speke became the President of America, and simultaneously Joint Vice President of the URA with Rudy Cambi, pending the first election of a President of the United Republics of Ameuropa.

The final election was still a year away, though there was much to do in preparation. But at that point my efforts were hardly distracted by such concerns. I was involved in what Gus's new power could do for my Foundation.

Upon Gus's victory, I had taken stock of the situation, both my own and that of my Foundation.

My own personal position was one of tremendous affliction. My love for Mary, and her betrayal of that love with the man I called my brother, was a terrible thing for me to bear.

Mary was improving and then deteriorating, still. Her doctors could not understand it. All that they did for her failed.

We were living together. She had stopped travelling so much. It was too tiring for her. She carried out all her meetings by remote comms. She had her wing of the house set up with all the research facilities she wanted, and seldom left it. I visited her daily, and I made sure that John visited her too. I gave them both every chance. I waited for her to stop him, and for him to cease his visits, but she did not, and he did not, and they continued.

I saw her every single evening, without fail. I came to her door and stood there while she tremulously held out her hand to me, from her chair, but she would not stand up. I had come to her, but she would not walk to me. When I waited patiently for her, she just asked why I was treating her like this, in that croaky, emotionless voice she had chosen to use with me. When I just stared back at her in silent hope, waiting for her to tell me what I had to hear, she fell quiet and looked injured.

But she was not as hurt as I was. How could she have been? I knew

178

what she and John had been doing. I knew it just as surely as if I had seen vids of them tumbling and jerking in bed together.

I could have had those vids. I could have had cams put in her room as easily as I had had them put everywhere else, but I respected her too much to do that, and I knew that if I had actually seen what I knew took place, I would not have been able to control myself. I pride myself on my self-control.

Mary could have told me. She had enough opportunity. I had always personally heard her Confession, and she could have told me then. When she did not, I merely wondered aloud whether her failure to improve might be connected with some withheld guilt.

She cried when I said that. She cried noisily, huge croaking sobs that rocked her head forward and back, but left her body unmoved.

With relief, I watched her cry. I wanted to hug her to me and tell her I still loved her. I thought that at last I had freed her, and I waited for her to tell me about her betrayal, admit her relationship with John. I would forgive her, I knew, and our love would be perfect again.

But she did not Confess. She simply stopped crying, eventually.

It was apparent that her faith was not strong. And her body would not improve until she fully Confessed. I told her that. I gave her that chance, and she did not take it. The responsibility was not mine, I said as I left. I did not let her make her Confession to me again. I was too hurt. I was nearly disheartened.

I still loved her more than anything in the world, but I turned the force of my attention elsewhere. Not just outwardly, but inwardly, too.

Up until then, I had always been conscious that my Ministry had a certain, well, an irony to it. It had concerned me to do good, but I had never been pious.

Now I accepted that I had an anger within me. It's no surprise to you, from what you've heard me say. Piousness may give a person energy and drive, but anger is fuel. It's rocket fuel, and I was burning with it. I knew where I was heading, and if in the process of achieving my aims I could do some good, then that was fine. Or maybe vice versa – I even forget my original order of priority.

But after Gus's first victory, a strange thing, the strangest thing of all, happened to me.

I was saved. *I* was *saved*!

I started to take comfort in Our Lord. I started to think of the world. I thought of my father and his sins, and I thought of my own terrible sins.

I thought of how Our Lord made us in His image, and that nevertheless we sin.

That troubled me. What did it mean? Did it mean that we were after

179

all not entirely, not perfectly in his image, that He failed in His task to duplicate Himself in us? Or did it mean that Our Lord was also a sinner?

If He sinned, then is sin necessary?

I shut myself away for a long time to contemplate this.

What I concluded was that it was choice that made us sin. But Our Lord had had choice when he created us, so did He sin by giving us choice? If so, perhaps choice is part of the sin as well as its cause. Perhaps it is the very root of sin.

So – I thought – if sin is to be removed, choice must be removed.

My head was on fire with thought. I was so close, so achingly close to a solution. How could we do this? How could we willingly remove choice, temptation and sin?

The answer came to me late in the evening of the seventh day of my ponderings. I was weak with hunger but immensely strong with the thought of Our Lord in my head.

One of us must sin, I realised. One of us must commit the ultimate sin for the sake of all others. That single soul must be the agent to eradicate choice on behalf of all others, for their sake, to remove sin. And that one terrible sinner would be punished more than all others. But he would be a martyr to do so.

My father used to taunt me with an old conundrum from some old book – would one murder an innocent, if by doing so, one could spare all others from all suffering, for all eternity? My father would ask me that and then hold his finger against the soft ball of my eye, pressing it hard, and tell me, 'I would have sacrificed you for such a cause when you were born, my son. I would have slit your throat for it, except that I could see you were cast from your mother's stomach impure and already bursting with sin.'

I was a sinner. My father knew that, and he punished me for it as long as he lived, blood and blood. But he had pointed me to my question; could one man punish himself with eternal damnation for the release of all others to eternity?

And then I saw how insane and impossible this was. Instead, I thought of what heaven might be. I looked around me and I saw this world in its terrible fever, and I yearned for more.

It was night, but I could not sleep for these burning thoughts. I had wrestled with them for hours, and the night was dark and moonless outside my window. I switched off the light beside my chair, but the thoughts would not go away. Restlessly, I turned my gaze out to space.

I was without peace. Not knowing what else to do, I spoke to myself as if I were my own forlorn congregant among a great crowd. I preached to this vast assembly and to myself, crying out, 'At night, when you are hungry and without hope, and the depths within you are dark and without end, what do you do?' I was talking and I was listening, my soul split asunder, and I was Our Lord and I was his lamb, and I was the hand reaching out to join them together.

I cried out to myself and the great crowd and I said, 'What do you do? What do you do? *This* is what you do. You turn your face outward, you turn your face to the endless universe and raise your arms and cry out and ask Our Lord for hope!'

In my darkness I thought of my Mary Trulove and I cried out to Our Lord.

And I stared through the window, out into space, and my cry was answered. Here was my salvation! The endless universe was my salvation and solution.

I slept for ten hours in that chair, and when I woke up, drenched in sweat, I ended my isolation and returned to the world with my answer.

There was already a longstanding Administration program to explore space, and I knew that I had to plunge myself into this search. With Gus's blessing, I set up my own project, Ex Unico Plura. Our search was greater in intensity and scope than the Administration's, and it liberated me. I forgot entirely about Mary and John and their treachery, their terrible and unforgivable betrayal.

The cosmos drew me to itself. I left John to run my Foundation, and I threw myself with all my energy into the universe.

Exploration was the first thing to address. Beyond our solar system, little was known. Simple travel was always the limiting factor in further exploration, I quickly discovered. The unthinkable distances, the speeds required, the sheer factor of risk. But I would not be defeated, and Our Lord was with me.

We experimented, we researched. The breakthrough was finally made by the scientist Dr Ciara Pardaisi, so naturally the media called it the Paradise Device. With her invention, we could transfer matter – even huge, complex matter, as long as it contained no DNA – astonishing distances with considerable success. Light-year transmission was almost as swift and straightforward as to the next room. The difference was that we might know the next room to be empty, or have a table here and the floor just there. But space ... so, we were cautious.

We commenced an exploration cascade.

Exploration always used to be a small and crazy and heroic thing. An adventure, usually tragic. I don't fully understand it, but just as I am the way I am, explorers are the way they are. They are locked to their fates, just as I am locked inexorably to mine. So there it was; a few men and women embarking on rafts or rockets to the unknown, along ever darkening, ever narrowing and always more treacherous routes. Our explorers receding from us not just in terms of distance, but in terms of safety and contact with the known world. And if they returned, they returned burdened with madness and myth as much as with knowledge.

But not any more. Not with the Paradise Device and the exploration cascade.

It was a magnificently simple principle. We began by shipping a single telescope to an initial far point with the Device. From that telescope we peered along an arc of further far points, transferred telescopes to those points, and simply carried on. Images funnelled back along the cascade for analysis.

Of course, we quickly had more data than we could analyse. Imagine it – we were accumulating more information about the universe than we could actually process. The further we travelled, the broader became our search, and the more information we derived.

At first, it was so thrilling that we tried to cope with it all, to keep up. There was extraordinary public interest, wild enthusiasm and wilder speculation. For several months, it was maintained. Excitement united the world. It was a pandemic of expectation. Not expectation, even, but certainty. Success was assured. Would aliens consider us gods? Would they play football? With the Paradise Device, we expected to find exotic life, astonishing wonders. But there was no life out there beyond viruses and bacteria – which in any case we couldn't ship back – and as for wonders, the endless solar systems, supernovas and endless planets soon became repetitive. The more information came back, the less it fired us.

We became bored. Ennui set in. The exploration cascade continued, but the Administration reduced its rate of processing of the results.

But I did not lose hope. Amongst my other many projects, of various magnitudes and degrees of publicity, I began the Eden Foundation. My profile was still high, of course. Just as Gus had, for a shake of my hand and a cam flash, helped me to cure Mary – although her condition had stopped improving and she was regressing steadily now – so he allowed me to take over the processing of the Paradise data.

And of course, to process that data most effectively I needed control of the Device. Gus supplied me with that.

At that time, also, I found myself with an extraordinary amount of energy. I hardly needed sleep.

My other projects were progressing too. One of them involved examining behavioural models. I was still seeking Our Lord. Why, I asked myself, do we act as we do, in His image? Was this really His plan for us, to act in His image? Where, if so, had it gone wrong? How could it be mended?

On Earth, I saw, we change. We evolve. I knew we had evolved. In that sense, I was no fundamentalist. But Our Lord? He doesn't procreate, at least not sexually (the thought was probably blasphemous) so how can He evolve? He made us in his image, so He must have the capacity to evolve. But nevertheless, He has not. It's impossible to be sure of anything except that even though we may once have existed in His image, we surely cannot now be.

Although I needed little sleep, when I did sleep I was having worrying dreams. Dreams of my father, and fornication, and blood, and Our Lord. I would wake with blood on the sheets as if I had bled in the night, but I was unmarked. Was I bearing invisible stigmata?

And then I had a strange conversation with John. He came to me after one of our regular meetings to discuss the Foundation, and asked to talk to me privately.

'Cap,' he said.

'Yes, John?'

And he started to cry.

I put my arm around him, just as I imagined Mary doing, and I let him take my hand and hold it tightly. I was waiting for him to tell me what Mary had not.

'Cap,' he said, 'I feel there's a distance between us. When I see you, we discuss what needs to be discussed, but that's all. We don't *talk*. It isn't the same as it used to be.' He frowned at me anxiously. 'You aren't the same, Cap.'

He was right. I wasn't. At that time, spiritually, I was floating ethereally above him. I could see everything clearly – or so I thought. It was a lesson to me. My hubris was about to be exposed.

I said, 'Why should that be, John?'

He looked away from me. 'Mary—'

'Yes?' I fought an urge to take my hand away and make a fist, but he went on.

'Mary says the same. I thought it was just me, and I thought it was because you felt my jealousy of her. You know how I love you with the love of Our Lord.' He gulped. He looked like he used to look, back at the very beginning, and despite what I knew, I felt myself soften towards him.

'She told me she thought you were upset with her for coming between me and you,' he said.

'I see.' I looked away and asked Our Lord to show me the truth. I imagined the two of them plotting this conversation to blind me to the truth, but there was something in John that made him transparent. He had always been transparent. That night when he had come in on Mary and me, it had been his face, not Mary's, that had led me to see their infidelity.

Maybe, after all, I had been mistaken. Maybe he was telling me the truth. Perhaps Mary had not been having an affair with him at all, all this time.

If that were so, I had hurt him, my John, my brother.

I held him, and I forgave him. My hubris had been punished by Our Lord. Yet as with one hand He punished me, so with the other He rewarded me.

After that, we became close again. I knew I could trust John with many things, and the knowledge freed me.

The dreams continued, but thanks to Our Lord I had John again to confide in.

Mary continued her research with the fortitude that was always within her, and I ensured that her condition began to improve again. We saw each other more, though she no longer asked me to make love to her. She was still strained with me and could not conceal it. She looked at me in a different way.

Of course I guessed why, though I said nothing. John had not betrayed me with her, but she loved him. It was plain to see. I knew that if I asked her, she would deny it, but it was quite clear to me.

So, the Foundation continued raising its billions of dollars, its euros and its yen, and the Ameuropean Presidential election came closer. Gus became more nervous, I made my plans, and Dr Pardaisi's Paradise Device continued quietly rippling its way through the universe.

HAZE

After weeks in the forest, doing nothing but survive, Petey came back to its edge, to the AngWat. A few paces within the protecting line of trees, she built herself a small hide out of branches and spent her days and nights concealed there, peering over the moat, watching in vain for a sight of Marten. At first she only came away to lay traps and empty them, and search for berries. But she was careful not to hunt or forage near the hide, and to rotate her food sources, so she spent a lot of time away.

She was sure it wouldn't be long before she saw him. In the meantime, she concentrated on understanding as much as she could about the AngWat's workings and routines.

To its north and south, fields extended all the way to the edge of the moat. Petey spent days staring at the people, mainly children, tending the fields, but she never saw Marten. The children seemed to be kept in small groups, all of the same sex.

Out in the fields there were small compounds for animals. The pigs and chickens were looked after by the younger children, of about five or six years, and Petey thought of the daughter, who had been taken at that age. But there was no longer any emotion in her at the memory.

Staring at the animals, Petey's mouth flooded with saliva. She was living on berries and insects and the small animals she caught in traps. There was plenty of water from forest streams, but she was always hungry.

Every few days she saw the slaughtering of pigs. It was an ordered ritual involving a number of people. She found it curious. First, a pair of lords came to the enclosures and tethered the animals to be killed, and then a small group of children came and were shown how to sever the tendons at the backs of the pigs' legs to stop them running. The pigs' squeals floated eerily over the fields to Petey. The children sang a little song together as they hacked awkwardly at the pigs' legs with their little machetes, and its tune drifted over the moat to her, although she couldn't hear the words.

The homeliness of the singing tugged at her heart. Despite what they were doing, the way the children sang and acted together in the AngWat compound, so unlike the selfishness of the villagers, gave her a feeling of immense warmth.

After the pigs had been immobilised and lay grunting and squealing even more noisily, a group of older children arrived to slit the pigs' throats while the younger ones sat patiently and watched. And then everyone, even the lords, helped haul the carcasses away.

Petey identified the buildings into which the children were herded at meal times, and at night, but she still didn't see Marten. Even so, every night, as she watched the various dormitory doors being closed on the children, she whispered, 'Goodnight, Marten,' and blew a kiss over the water before rolling herself under her blanket of moss and trying to sleep.

It took about a month for her to make a good map in her head of the visible areas of the AngWat. She knew the sleeping quarters for children of different ages, the rooms where they were instructed together, where they were fed, where animals were kept and slaughtered. She knew the kitchens and she knew the areas restricted to lords.

She could also tell most of the lords apart by their heights and gaits. She could see which were most and least popular with the children. She recognised the tall one to whom everyone deferred, and who had greeted her and Marten on their arrival at the AngWat.

The only part of the AngWat that she couldn't work out was its walled heart. Groups of lords and children would form and then troop there, to become hidden. Sometimes sounds would drift over the water to reach her, unidentifiable but unaccountably disturbing. She noticed that occasionally fewer children emerged than had entered the enclosure, and she remembered stories of the AngWat's arena.

But Marten never appeared. Eventually, frustrated and needing to be active, Petey left her hide to try and work her way around the AngWat complex, hoping to find a better vantage point.

Travelling west, she intended to circle round the compound to its rear, but she was slowed and then blocked by a gradual condensing of the foliage and then a sharp transformation from the usual forest bush to prickle and thorn. There was no reason for this transition that she could make out, no change in soil or irrigation to explain it. The wall had to be designed and cultivated.

Petey followed its edge, letting it lead her away from the AngWat compound, thinking she must be able to skirt around it. But instead of coming to an end, the barrier eventually turned west and continued.

She walked on, but there was still no way through and no end to it. With no other plan, Petey carried on following the brush wall. Occasionally she thought she heard noises beyond it, roars and moans that built evenly and fell away. They didn't sound like animals at all.

She carried on for a day, searching for a way through the thorns. She had no idea how deep the barrier was, but she had to find out what was behind it. It was tempting to use the firetube to cut herself a path, but Petey guessed the weapon had a limited life, and she didn't want to waste it. She had hardly used it yet. She was despondent and thinking of giving up when she finally found a low tunnel in the thorns, about knee-high.

She squatted down and looked for spoor at the entrance of the opening, figuring it was either the start of an animal path, or a trap. A trap for man or animal. She sniffed at the marks and checked the cutting of the brush. Judging by the cracking of twigs and the state of the ground, it was a feral cat's route, and one still in use. Petey looked closer and decided there was just one animal using it, and that it had last entered the tunnel rather than leaving it, which meant that she might meet it face to face in there. That wasn't a good prospect in a narrow tunnel, but it was a lot better than having it attack her unprotected rear.

Sitting on her haunches and running her knife blade on its sharpstone, Petey considered her choices. She could wait for the cat to come out and deal with it before using the tunnel safely, or she could take the risk and go.

Petey felt she'd been waiting long enough. She wanted to be doing something. It was just after midday, so the cat would probably be sleeping. The opening here wasn't likely to lead to the cat's lair, so the path should be clear now. With her knife in her fist, Petey dropped to her hands and knees, ducked her head and wriggled into the tunnel.

Thorns instantly scratched at her back. Her movement made too much noise for her to hear anything else. The tiny noises of her knees scraping the ground and the thorns ripping at her clothes, and her own breathing, were magnified to deafening proportions. She could hear nothing else. To herself she sounded like a storm passing. The tunnel was dark and crooked and hot. It twisted hard to left and right, and her long body scratched agonisingly at the sides as she forced herself through. After only a few turns the tunnel became too low for her to continue on hands and knees, and she was forced to snake on her belly. It would be impossible now to turn around or push herself backwards against the thorns.

She was moving more and more slowly, realising how stupid she had been to start this journey. She wished she had Loren to scold her for it, to have warned her against it. She could almost hear him telling her, 'You're crazy, Petey. Always impatient. Why don't you stop to think? This could be a dead end. It probably leads to the animal's food store.'

But with no choice now, she pushed on. And then she stopped and held her breath.

Something was ahead of her. She could hear it spitting and hissing. She lifted her head and squinted. The noise continued, but she still couldn't see anything in the narrow gloom. She could hardly move, but she laid herself flat on the ground and pushed her arms forward to hold the knife in front of her. She realised she couldn't fight here. It was too confined.

There were two tiny lights ahead of her now. Two eyes. The cat, hissing and screeching, was an arm's length away, staring directly at her.

Petey slowly raised the knife, jamming her elbows as best she could into the hard dirt, the blade braced and in line with her forearms. If the cat came at her, it would impale itself. If it did anything else, she had nowhere to manoeuvre and no defence at all.

The eyes did not blink, and the hissing continued. Petey waited. Her arms began to tremble. The cat still waited. Petey started to hiss back at the cat, and then she shouted at it, as loudly as she could. The eyes blinked once and then again, and this time they didn't open. Petey gripped the blade with all her strength and screamed, and when she drew breath she realised the cat had gone.

She let the blade fall loose in her hand, and in the dark, thorny tunnel she cried. This was the first small thing that had not gone wrong since she had set up the hide to watch for Marten. Here she was, in a thorn tunnel barely wide enough to crawl through, and she was crying with relief. 'Oh, Loren,' she cried. 'Oh, Marten!'

And then the tears stopped and she struggled on, knowing that this was a path after all. If it had been a dead end, the cat would not have turned tail. After a few more turns she came out, to be faced by a perfectly smooth grey track running across her from left to right.

There was no one in sight. Instinctively crouching down, she approached the track cautiously and stopped at its edge. A long way to her right was the southern wall of the AngWat, while to her left the track vanished into the distance as a hairline glassy shimmer, flanked as far as she could see by the protective brush through which she had crawled.

She'd never seen such exposed distance before. Her eyes struggled to focus on the narrowing of the track to a shimmering, starlike point. How long would it take to walk that far? She knelt to examine the track.

It was made of tiny compressed stones, formed into an astonishingly perfect mosaic. The stones were different sizes but all exactly the same colour. It would take about ten of them to cover her thumbnail. She wondered how long it must take to piece together each pace of this road. Who had made it? Where did it lead?

While she was worrying over this, a noise began, one of the tumbling roars she'd heard from the other side of the barrier, and she retreated quickly to the tunnel and lay flat in its opening. There was no time to force her way back.

From the AngWat, a huge silver animal ran evenly along the road, roaring. It didn't draw breath once. She took in that it had no legs nor head, just a hunched back and a single eye. It swelled towards her. Not an animal, she realised. It was a cart. It had wheels, but fat black ones instead of spoked, lanky cartwheels, and nothing to pull it along. Before she knew it, it was close to her and gone, still roaring. In the distance it melted until it was one with the road.

Petey pulled herself back through the tunnel, and in the closeness of the forest she sat down to think.

She had to find Marten. That was more important than anything else. But she had to find out about this, too. What was going on here? There had to be sense to it. There had to be structure. There was structure to everything, she was certain, even if it wasn't obvious, and the structure and sense could be worked out, like reading could be worked out.

She took the daughter's name from her neck and read it to herself, wondering just how what it said, said it. Structure, she thought.

There was the forest, with its tribes and at a smaller level its villages, all struggling to survive, competing for what little food there was, killing each other to reduce the demand on sources of food. There was the struggle within villages too, everyone hungry and thirsty, and only the lords forcing order on it and preventing total war and chaos and extinction.

The lords held everything together. By denying possession, everything was shared. It made sense, she knew that. In the village she would steal from the forest to feed Marten, and that was unjust. The lords were just, even if it didn't seem so.

Who were the lords? Petey worried over that. They were the children of villagers. Those selected for the AngWat were educated and made strong. Most were returned to their villages after a year or two with forest skills, but with something removed, too. They were hard and strong, but no longer quite of the village. They were always the first to go to the village lord and confess to the wrongs of others, and although

Petey knew how important for everyone it was that they did this, it troubled her.

But the children who didn't return soon from the AngWat? Some came back later as village lords and some died in the AngWat. And that was as far as she had ever thought it through before, except for imagining that the others must maintain the AngWat. They had probably built that track. What might they have built at the far end of it?

She started back through the trees towards the AngWat. In her mind she could still hear the roar of that astonishing cart on the road and see it distilling itself to a brilliant dot and vanishing. There was no way she could comprehend it. It was like a pot of water and half-fleshed bones on a fire, boiling away to a single tongue-touch of perfect flavour.

It was not just the cart and the road. The distance astounded her. The only distance she had ever known was when she looked up at the sky, and that distance was inaccessible. The forest had no distance, just a constant extending of itself from tree to tree. And then there was the AngWat, which although it was vast, was comprehensible.

Her head was whirling with the idea that there was far more than she was aware of. She would find Marten, and then she would discover what there was.

The lords were all children, she thought as she walked. Jemus was cruel and cunning but he wasn't clever. Where did their knowledge come from? It was possible to imagine the lords as educated villagers, but that road and that cart hadn't come from learning to read. And the road was hidden. Why? Where did it lead? And what else was secret?

She returned to her hide overlooking the AngWat again and tried to be patient as she waited to see Marten.

She didn't see him, but one morning, after she had been back in her hide for a few weeks, she saw a group of eight men congregate by the main causeway. Petey thought they were villagers. They were wearing clothes in the precise green of her own village. Her heart fired for a second, and she realised how lonely she was, and had to control her tears. But after a long squint at the men as they came across the causeway, she saw they were lords.

It made no sense for them to be dressed like this, and Petey decided to leave her vigil for Marten for a while, to follow them.

She expected them to go to her village, but instead they headed through the jungle towards a village of Semith's tribe. Petey didn't understand this at all. Then, as they came to the outskirts of the village, there were no guards, which made no sense at all with the villages at constant war. The village should have guards posted to sound an alarm and attack the lords in such provocative dress. Petey wondered what was going on. This was very strange.

Outside the village, but close enough that Petey could smell firesmoke and hear chatter, the lords stopped and sat down in a small circle among the trees. One of them took his beetle and whispered into it, then closed it and returned it to its pocket in his village shirt.

Her heart thumping, Petey took herself off and cautiously approached the village until she found a concealed vantage point with a good view of the central clearing.

What she saw made no sense at all at first. The village lord was supervising his villagers, dividing them into two groups, then instructing one half to wind cloth gags tightly around the jaws of the other and bind their elbows behind their backs. When this was done, he divided the free group in half and had them repeat the process, and he did this repeatedly until only one man was free.

The process took some time. No one spoke at all. There was no protest or complaint. Some of the bound and silenced villagers stood together, some squatted as best they could on their haunches, but no one tried to run. They made no eye contact with each other. It was as if the process had locked each one of them away within themselves.

The lord threw a long rope to the free man, who caught the heavy weight of it awkwardly. He was trembling, and Petey was close enough to hear him suddenly moan loudly and continue to moan. The abrupt sound was shocking. He seemed more anxious and afraid than anyone else.

Petey felt numb. She understood what she was seeing, now. She knew this punishment well. Every few years without warning it was carried out in her own village.

The man would be the lord's tool, beating and clubbing the rest of the village with heavy branches and vine whips until the lord was content. When the beater untied them all at the end of it, the beaten would use what strength they had left to beat him. His beating would be far worse than theirs. He would be maimed or killed.

She found herself drifting away from the scene in her head, as she did when it was happening to her. She glanced up at the trees, watched the light fall and the shadows slide in the breeze. Birds sang. She could hear the branches brush against each other above her in tranquillity.

Breathing more easily, Petey was able to watch the man knot one end of the rope firmly to the pillar of a house before feeding the other end between the arms of all the acquiescent victims. Under his lord's eyes, he pulled the rope as taut as he could, heaving with all his strength, the captives struggling to their feet if they could, forming themselves without command into a ragged line. He tied the other end of the rope to a tree across the clearing, then dropped his head and waited for the lord's order.

The disguised lords appeared out of the trees. Their sudden appearance gave Petey a shock. She had forgotten about them. What were they doing here? And dressed like that? She moved back fractionally and crouched lower.

Seeing the lords, the free villager screamed and ran a few steps away from them, then collapsed to his knees. He looked at his own lord and shrieked, 'We're being attacked! Help us!' It surprised Petey that he would say this, but of course he didn't know they were lords.

As if he too didn't know they were also lords, the village lord said, 'Help you? Why should I help you? This is *khuk* business.'

The man ran towards the tree where the rope was tied, but one of the disguised lords ran towards him with a yell and a raised machete, and the man turned and fled the clearing. He disappeared into the trees.

The tethered villagers started to move in panic, but the rope caught them and they knocked each other over. Their gags kept them quiet, and the only sound was the thump and scrape of their bodies on the dirt.

Petey couldn't move. This was crazy. After a moment, she thought she could hear faint singing, high-voiced and brittle. Her head was spinning with the incomprehensibility of the scene, and she could barely take this in. But just as she identified the growing noise as the chanting of children, she saw them arriving at the clearing.

It was one of the small groups of children from the AngWat, and, like the lords, they were wearing the clothes of Petey's village. They were carrying their little machetes on their shoulders.

Petey's heart beat faster for a moment as she searched their faces, but Marten wasn't among them. They were too young, and they were girls. She recognised the tune from the pig-killing at the AngWat, and now she heard the words of the song too.

'We will chop you, chop you, chop you, we will chop you till we stop you.'

At first sight of the marching children, the tethered villagers had stopped moving, but now they started to roll around in panic and kick at the children, who had broken ranks and were trotting up to the captives. Marshalled and encouraged by the lords, and still singing, they began hacking at the ankles of the villagers. Some of them were barely strong enough to hold a machete in two small fists, and some of the lords helped by sitting on the legs of the villagers. There were still no sounds other than the ragged singing of the children and the scuffle of limbs in the dirt, and the crisp thwack of the machetes.

At some point the main tethering rope gave way or was severed by a machete, and a couple of villagers whose tendons hadn't yet been clipped managed to get to their feet and broke for the forest. A fleeing woman was hacked down at the knees by a child. Another hobbled all the way into the forest where the free man had vanished, and a man stumbled straight towards Petey, desperate, gagged, arms still bound behind him.

Petey fell back, then instinctively raised a hand in a quick beckoning movement, but as the man saw her, he stopped dead in his tracks. She could see his cheeks shining and puffed out with air, his nostrils flared and his eyes wide with terror.

'Quickly,' she whispered in a hoarse voice that didn't sound like her own, 'Quickly!' but instead the man collapsed quietly, just a gentle grunt pushing into the gag.

Petey put her hand to her mouth in horror and stared at the small girl awkwardly tugging her machete from the man's calf. She waited for the child to come for her, but instead she sang, 'Chop you, chop you,' and smiled slackly at Petey. There was an unblinking, empty gaze in her huge blue eyes. Petey couldn't look away from them. The girl still gazed at her. Her lips were swollen, her mouth open, her chin shining with saliva. A fleshfly landed at the corner of her eye and slowly crawled onto the creamy white, and the girl knuckled it flat and wiped it away, still without blinking. The fly's thorax floated in the wide blue eye.

Petey felt feverish as the little girl turned and drifted away, back to the clearing.

The only sound was the breathless chanting of the children and the rhythmless clucking of their machetes. And then that stopped and a group of older children filtered from the trees. These were boys. They carried thin knives and were not singing.

This time Petey was afraid to seek out Marten, but she had to search their faces. There was no dullness at all to their expressions. Unlike the younger ones, these were not drugged. Petey looked from one to the next.

Marten was not there.

Petey knew her heart was about to give her away, pounding at her ribs, or that she would have to scream. In the dirt, someone did start screaming; a man had dislodged his gag. One of the boys strode up to him and cupped his chin firmly from behind, using the grip to pull his head back, and slit his throat in a single smooth arc of the knife. The man's scream became a watery sound that dribbled to silence.

Petey had seen blood before, men and women fighting and killing. Life was death, she knew that. But she could taste the blood that flushed out of this twitching, quietening man in her own mouth. She swallowed it and it still came, wetting her chin. She touched a finger to her mouth and found that she had almost bitten through her lip without feeling it.

The rest of the boys went about their work. Hardly anyone else moved now. The younger children stood with the lords at the side of the clearing. The majority of those about to die were entirely still until they were throat-slit, which made them move sharply but quite briefly, and then they were still again. One or two resisted, thrashing like stuck animals, but the uselessness of it quietened the rest.

Petey felt as if she were in another place altogether, watching this massacre. The information of her senses seemed muffled, hardly reaching her; it was not at the right speed to be real. The light was too bright, the sound slurred, everything was blurred or distorted.

A sudden cramp in her leg brought her back to reality again. The pain made her jerk suddenly and yelp, and one of the disguised lords twisted his head and stared straight at her. He squinted at her clothes, then beckoned to her.

She was hot with fear. She didn't know what to do. She couldn't reveal herself. He flicked his finger at her once more and stood up, touching the shoulder of another lord at his side to get his attention.

A piercing, incoherent cry from the pile of corpses distracted the two lords for a moment, and Petey stumbled away into the trees and began to run. She tripped over a woman from the massacred village who was trying to cover herself with mud and leaves, shivering and clutching her cracked leg. Petey swerved away from her and fled, the woman screaming hideously, her fading cry pursuing Petey through the trees.

'I know your village. We'll kill you all for this. We'll kill you all!'

HAVEN

Memory?

Quill glanced at the fogged and apparently failing fluorescent lettering that came and went above the long, narrow lintel of the place.

Memory? was a cafe overlooking the shimmering sim of a river. The name was hard to make out, and he stopped to squint at it before pushing the frosted amber door open and going inside. He'd never been there before. He'd heard about it, though.

As the door swung smoothly closed behind him, the word momentarily flickered again in holo before him, and vanished. He went inside. A yellow sandstone counter was set in the granite wall across the small room, almost luminous against the grey, and above it was a lozenge screen tuned to the Game. Half a dozen crystal tables grew from the floor, and a few drinkers sat on the stone stools watching the screen.

Skim hadn't arrived. Quill was early. It was half past three. He bought himself a drink and sat down to wait for her. On the screen, the section of arena in play was dark, with uv-hilites picking out the stalactites and stalagmites like whittled bones. Quill couldn't remember when he'd last paid attention to the Game. The Analysts were splitscreened in a studio box, chattering to each other. He could never tell the two men apart. Below them, rolling across the screen between them and the arena view, were betting percentages for ball-metrages, hour by hour, red-arrowed left and right-arrowed blue.

'Here we are,' said one of the Analysts animatedly – Jan, Quill thought this was. He was broader-cheeked than his partner, and his identically green eyes were marginally more set back. 'We haven't been over in this part of the arena for a long time. Maybe fifty years. The obstacles have undergone accelerated reform, as you see, Dan, and it's in pristine condition again.'

'Yes, Jan. And we have a treat for the viewers today, don't we?'

The view jerked to pick out a group of players making their way through the irregular spikes. They were clothed in skintight red tunics, though the tunics were rusty with dried blood and flecked with glowing slime. The great cavern's stalactites were high in the gloom above them, and the hiliting showed gobbets of phosphorescence raining steadily down like golden fire. The falling glow ghosted the screen, giving the image a strange, drowned perspective and the players a spectral look.

'And there's the ball!'

The vast iron globe was wedged between a pair of stalagmites. A small team of Reds were heaving exhaustedly at it. The shining ball was as tall as they were.

Quill wondered what the players' crimes had been. It was said that Red and Blue were punishments for different categories of offence, but no one knew except the players, and players never seemed to return from the Game, despite the promises of clemency for metrage.

'Yes, we sure have a treat in this spike section. Each team has a nominated sniper, and an hour to use the gun.'

'But there's a catch, isn't there, Jan?'

'That's right. Rule is, Blue team have an hour with the gun, but no direct attack during that time. The rest of the Blue team withdraws entirely. Blue can make as much ground as possible without fear of any other Game weapon being used against them. That means no knives, machetes, handguns—'

'We get the picture, Jan. And while Blue can use the sniper rifle, which is a powerful weapon, they can't shoot a Red player directly.'

'Precisely. How they use it will be interesting. So. They have an hour, and then Red have their hour under the same conditions.'

The lower screen switched to the Blue sniper lying flat on a small bluff of glittering quartz porphyry, about a hundred metres in front of the Red team. He was steadying a long and slender black-barrelled gun. Dan's voice gained a faint echo, and the sniper sat up to flick back the scope and rub his eyes.

'You're upscreened,' Dan said. 'Anything for the folks above?'

The man looked dull and exhausted. Before he could speak, the cam-view shifted abruptly to Jan, who was grinning and nodding, and then it returned to the sniper. This time the man was sitting straight and smiling. He said, in a tight monotone, 'Watch in woe, if you're betting Red.'

Over the other side of the bar, someone cracked a glass on the table and hissed, 'Just do it, Blueboy. I got you a hundred down for ten ems by daysend.'

The sniper turned and steadied his aim. A moment's pause, and the gun thumped and kicked back. One of the stalagmites holding up the ball splintered and cracked away, and the ball wobbled and lurched free.

The Red players bent their backs and pushed it on, across a few metres of clear ground.

'Shit and Crise!' hissed the drinker across the bar.

Red players continued to wrestle the ball along the cavern floor while a forward scout worked out a route, gesticulating. The team used machetes and picks to hack at obstacles where the ball couldn't be forced between or over them.

'Red. That didn't do you any harm at all. Any comment?'

A spokesman wiped his forehead and said, 'We're happy as harry with this.' He examined his palms and then looked briefly up. 'Hell. This . . .' Sweeping a sleeve across his forehead, he forced enthusiasm into his voice. 'It has to be good for us, Jan, with them out of our way, long as they shoot as bad as this. They can't actually shoot us, right?' He was pale, his eyes hooded and anxious, his neck thin and wrinkled. Quill could see the effort it took him to speak. It was common knowledge that players who weren't civil to Jan and Dan didn't last long. 'I don't know what they think they're doing, but we ought to get at least through the spikes and on to the next section before they figure out how to shoot straight. I can tell you, Jan, these spikes are no fun.' The gun whined again and the player winced. The screen closed tight on his fear. A stalagmite cracked across the ball's path, but not well enough to block it, and the ball was clear to move on.

Jan said, 'Let's speak to the sniper again. Talk to me. Red think you've got a bum deal. Not shooting straight. Is that how you see it?'

'Those were sighters. This is a good gun. You want to watch?' He shouldered the long gun, but this time, instead of pointing the barrel along the floor of the cavern, he aimed high. The charge whined briefly off the roof of the cavern. Below, a few Reds glanced up.

'Jan, do you get it?'

'No, Dan. So far, it's a mystery. Let's wait and see.'

The sniper adjusted his aim and fired again, and this time the tip of a stalactite snapped away and spun down to clatter on the ground close to the Red team. It took a long time to fall. Another long stalactite was hit close to its thick base at the cavern's roof, and hit again, clouds of powder puffing into the air.

The third hit sounded heavier, and with it the long spike creaked and detached. It dropped smoothly and soundlessly. There was only a mild thump as the spike struck the shoulder of one of the men pushing the ball. As it entered him, he seemed to swell. The tip broke clear of his tunic at his thigh and its point shattered like glass beside his heel. Shivering briefly, he came to rest against the ball, almost upright. A hand twitched, the red of his tunic began to darken, and he was still.

Bone-white, the thick fractured stalk of the stalactite rose a metre from his shoulder.

Quill looked around the bar for Skim, but there was still no sign of her. He checked his chrono. Still ten minutes. He sipped his drink.

Dan said, 'Wow! Astonishing! Let's see that again!'

The cam showed it slowly, the spike smoothly piercing the man, hardly deviating from its line.

Jan said, 'That is incredible. I've been watching the Game for twenty years now, since I was a kid, and I don't think I've ever—'

'Hold it, Jan, I'm getting a message. Yes. Yes. We'll take a different angle and look at it again.'

The cam showed it from another low angle. 'What do you think, Jan? Does it?'

Quill watched the screen, wondering what he was looking for. Across the bar, the man with the bet was swearing to himself.

'I think it does, Dan. Look.'

This time it was slowed further, and as the spike came down, Quill saw the ball judder faintly as the spike began to penetrate the man's shoulder.

'I'm not sure,' Jan said. 'I think the s'tite hits him just before it touches the ball. See?' The spike withdrew, repenetrated, withdrew and repenetrated. The struck man seemed to be shrugging himself into it and out again, like a tight piece of clothing. Jan said, 'See? The s'tite takes the man *before* the ball. That counts as direct and illegal. The s'tite's the weapon's direct agent, just like a bullet.'

The man with the bet was thumping the table, swearing.

'Hold on, Dan. Let's look at it again.' The spike went through its jig once more. 'Look carefully. You'll see the player was bending enough to hunch out his tunic. See that?' The man shrugged himself into the spike again. 'It wasn't touching his skin there. The s'tite seems to take the man an instant before it contacts the ball, but in fact at this point – see – it hits the fabric, a fraction clear of his skin.'

'You may be right, Jan. This is incredible. This is the Game at its best. If you're watching this live, you're watching history here. Go on, Jan.'

'So if we—' the image adjusted itself, the pierced player's jacket fading to transparency. The tip of the spike now seemed to touch the player at the same time as its slope contacted the ball.

'Do we have a ruling on that, Jan? That's amazing. That's amazing.'

'Hold on, Jan. It may not all be over.' Dan touched his ear, tipped his head. 'Yes, I have the Fact lawchecker here. Now—'

In a sudden new studio box, the lawchecker was shaking his head. 'It's a simultaneous strike. And that being the case, weapon definition must apply.'

'Dan? Explain.'

'Yes. What he's saying, Jan, in a nutshell, is that if the stalactite is a weapon, then its tip overrules its shank.'

'But surely that ignores the indirect strike rule. The *gun* was the weapon, not the stalactite.'

Quill had lost track of who was claiming what. Across the bar, the agitated drinker slammed his glass on the table. 'Crise! I don't believe this. It's a shitfucken fix!'

'Not necessarily, Jan. The lawchecker says the stalactite was nevertheless a weapon, if an indirect one.' He touched his ear. 'Wait. We're going to a further slomo at himag.'

'I don't think that's possible, is it? Teevee were using uv-hilite, which is too slow frame by frame to be slowed enough for proof.'

'Then it's unproven,' said Dan. 'Rules say it's ball *then* man. It counts as illegal interference with the ball. Which gives Red a double penalty, as they lost a player as a result of illegal action.'

'Hah!' said the drinker.

'Jan?'

'Yes, Dan, I know what you're thinking, and I'm thinking it too. We need a second adjudication. This is history indeed, and history at its most tangible.'

The screen went back to the arena. The Red players were sitting around the ball and the transfixed corpse, squatting on the ground and leaning on stalagmites, in their own thoughts.

'Crise!' The betting drinker slammed his glass down again. The table shattered explosively. The barman yelled, 'You're paying for that table, Yenke.'

'Jan, we have the adjudication. And it's—'

'Yes?'

'Inadvertent fault, Red. Single penalty, to be taken by reversal.'

'Well, what do you make of that, Dan?'

'A truly magnificent adjudication. I think both teams will be equally content with that one.'

'Let's go back down, shall we? Here's the penalty set up for reversal.'

Quill watched the Red player with the gun hitch up his sleeve and take careful aim at the stalactite. On the ground, directly below the stalactite, the Blue sniper was strapped to a stake, straining to look up. The neck strap wouldn't let him. He pushed against the stake, but couldn't get any leverage with his shackled ankles. Ten metres away, the

Red team sat, a few of them glancing without interest at the staked player.

'This is a tense moment,' Jan murmured. 'His breathing's even, though. This needs a steady hand and a good aim. If he aims too high, he may not separate the spike at all, but if he aims too low, too close to the tip, it'll have insufficient weight. It'll spin and could miss altogether or even maim. And we know what a maim means, don't we, Dan?'

Dan chuckled. 'Reverse penalty. Last month, huh?'

'That's right. And if any of you don't remember that, or just want to see it again, it's on Game Channel Eight right now and again on the hour until next Tuesday.'

The door of the bar swung open and Skim came in. She hooded her eyes with a hand and searched Quill out, then went to the counter and bought herself a bottle of juice, and brought it to Quill's table. Sitting down, she glanced around the place before looking at him.

'I talked to Walker,' she said.

'What did he tell you?'

'That you're dead. That you might be in more trouble than a dead man deserves.'

'Can you help me?'

'There's not much anyone can do about being dead.' She sipped her drink. 'You were in Survey.'

'That's right.'

'And you're dead. Great. At least you're a hero. What's in the bag?'

He opened its neck and Skim leant across to look down into it. She bent her head closer, drew sharply back, and then reached a hand gently into the bag and touched the skull.

I think she's okay.

'Yeah, I think so,' Quill said.

Skim sat up again. 'Who are you talking to? Oh, Crise, are you talking to this?' She pointed at the bag.

Quill closed it. 'No.'

She squinted at him. 'I wouldn't like to think you're crazy in any way.' She threw the rest of her drink down her throat. 'Let's go. We'll find somewhere to talk properly.' She stood up, touched the bag delicately and said, 'Don't forget your friend.'

Skim watched him get to his feet. Walker had said he was okay, but then he'd also told her what Quill said had happened to him. And that was a crazy story. Although as far as Skim was concerned, anyone who crawled into a Survey coffin and shot themselves into a world of dead rock was crazy to start off with.

But he was sharp enough, pulling the logic on her shop security like that. And he looked lost, too, which was a hook that always buried itself in her soul.

She walked him away from *Memory?*, taking him out and outdown. Coredors narrowed and swelled like throats gulping them down. Sometimes the coredors were silent, sometimes they creaked and whistled. Distant voices whispered and went, but hardly ever another person. Skim thought about Quill. It was hard to rationalise this man screened everywhere as a dead hero of Survey.

He said, 'Where are we going?'

She pulled herself together. 'Where you can tell me the whole story. Start to finish. Head to tail. And where you might get some help.'

And there was the head. Carrying a head around like that.

They walked, mostly in silence. She walked him for hours through long-unused and redundant coredors. There was only the grain and wet gleam of rock around them. Just ten minutes away from *Memory?* they passed the last person but one that they were going to see all night. Skim noticed Quill didn't ask why they weren't taking fastways or carrypods. She was pretty sure that if she'd suggested it, he'd have walked away and she'd never have seen him again.

Granite and ruin marble swallowed their footfalls and the coredors around them glittered and shone. Crystal shine and water shine. Sometimes Skim found the rock beautiful, but not now.

'Do you trust me?' Quill asked her in the middle of a straight, dark coredor so long that the constant on-off tic and flicker of proximity lighting in the few metres around them seemed to be holding them on a treadmill.

She didn't even glance at him. 'You mean not to kill me? You'd never find your way back.'

'This is virtually a circle we're doing,' he said. 'We've doubled back twice. You won't lose me, I'm Survey-trained. I'll know where we are, within a hundred ems, any direction. My sense of direction's like your eyes.'

Now she glanced at him.

He said, 'I mean do you trust me not to be crazy? I know what I look like. I'm carrying a head in a bag.'

She thinned her lips into a smile and said lightly, 'My weak spot. I can never resist a man with a head in a bag.' Losing the smile, she added, 'Do you trust me?'

'Not to grab my head and run off with it?'

She laughed aloud. The sound of it rippled quickly away, and the coredor lights carried them forward. 'I'm not trying to lose you, Quill.

We're going to see someone. This coredor is monitored by him. By the time we get to the end of it, we'll know if he wants to be visited. He's the one who has to trust you, not me. If he doesn't, we can go back to *Memory?* and I'll buy you another drink and we'll think of something else. At least it's a short trip back.'

'Visiting who?'

She shook her head. The coredor dipped and rose fractionally, bore left and then started to go right.

'Stop here,' Skim said. She examined Quill, standing there with the bag in his hand. 'Men from Survey,' her mother had told her. 'They know the rock better than they know anything. But they'll never know themselves, and you'll never know them. Stay clear of them. Find someone easy. Someone with a shop they can lock up and leave every night.'

Skim rested the flat of her hand against the cool wall of the coredor and stared unfocused at the worn ground. Her mother should have known what she was talking about. She'd been in Survey. And Skim's father had been in Survey, too.

So she'd done what her mother had said and found herself someone with a shop he could leave at night. And what he'd left in the end was her, and all it had got her was a key to a shop.

She sighed. All your parents can ever show you is what doesn't work, she thought. No one can tell you what does.

'Don't worry,' Quill said eventually, adjusting his grip on the bag. 'He doesn't want to be visited, I'll think of something else.'

'There is nothing else.'

He touched her shoulder, making her start, and asked, 'Why were you sighing?'

Skim looked at him. A moment came and went, but before she could decide what to say, the wall shifted behind Quill and she stood quickly straight, staring over his shoulder, and said angrily, 'Oath, Naddy, did you have to do that?' She touched Quill's arm to turn him round, then looked from Naddy to Quill. 'Quill, this is Naddy Harke. Naddy, this is—'

'Yes. I heard. I see you have some poor fellow's head there, and another curio that I couldn't quite identify. Come in, come in out of the hot sun.'

Skim caught Quill's eye as Naddy Harke slipped through the dark doorway at the side of the coredor. 'He's opticked,' she said. 'He's not making a joke. This is a jungle shack to him.'

The wall closed behind them.

'So. How are you, Naddy?' Skim said.

'All the better for eyeing you, Skim.' He sat down at a long table bunched across with wires. 'Quill, sit down and put your head on the table here. And that other thing too. And tell me their story.'

But Quill just stood there. 'Naddy Harke?' he said. 'Really?'

'In rock and ruin,' the man said. 'Naddy Harke, that's me. In truth if not in fact.' He stood up, bowed to Quill and sat again, grinning. 'Well, I have an admirer.'

'Don't encourage him,' Skim told Quill.

'When did I need encouraging?' Naddy said. Then to Quill, arching his eyebrows, 'You've heard of me.'

'Everyone's heard of you,' Quill said.

Skim sat back and looked at Naddy. The man lived in light. He was sure of everything except himself. Once in a time she'd found that endearing, like her mother had found men from Survey endearing, but Naddy was acceptably so, since he wasn't in Survey. She'd loved the idea of a claustrophobe, a man who couldn't live in rock, who was opticked to see trees and sky instead of rock, and open paths through emerald forests and brilliant fields instead of husked-out coredors. He could walk anywhere he wanted. All he had to do was keep to the paths.

She looked at his lidless eyes with their cloaking of blue, blue as lapis. The wiring fanned from the corners of his eyes to his ears, slipping inside his ears and on inward, and she wondered how Quill was looking at him.

It was odd. All she thought about him any more was where was he looking. At the wall, at the table, at Skim herself?

'How does it all work?' Quill said to Naddy.

Naddy stroked the blue of his eyes. 'My biowiring accesses a Hub program via any proximal wiring. I just need to be within three air metres of light wiring, comms wiring, anything centrally connected.'

'How do you see the real?'

'It's all real. Long as I keep to the straight and arrow. Keep to the paths.'

Quill opened the bag and put the head on the table. It rocked a moment and then rested on its cheek. Skim was surprised at how big it was.

'How do you see that?' Quill asked Naddy.

'Same as you see it.' He fanned his fingers across his face. 'The program's distance-mediated. I don't have a problem with rock, or reality. Just with distance. I know where I am, Quill. I watched you walk that coredor, surveyed you. I'm not deluded. I just need to feel I could walk off the path into the trees if I wanted to. I just need the *if*.'

'This room—'

'Is big to me, tall, wide windows opening over the great plain. It's composed from the jungle in *Rufus*. Back on Oath. What's in it is the same as what you see.'

'Can I trust you?'

'If you couldn't, Fact would be here now, wouldn't they? Given my past?

Skim interrupted. 'Naddy used to work for Fact.'

Quill said, 'I'd heard that. What made you leave? Why did they let you? They must know what you do now?'

'Of course they do. Up to a point.' Naddy pushed himself into the chair, his head tilting back ruminatively. 'I left Fact because I started to question it all. I was permitted to leave because I set up a number of systems there, and they don't fully understand those systems.' He dropped his head. 'Though they are working on that. And they know what I do now, approximately. The easy stuff, I feed them. The harder stuff that doesn't matter, I hide badly so they can follow it. The interesting stuff, they have no idea.'

'As far as you know.'

'Oh, no. What they know about, they let me have because it doesn't matter or else it's worth it to them to let me think I'm getting away with it. The *real* stuff—' he glanced at the head, then at Quill's pocket where the silver case was, '—if they had any idea of that, we'd already be gone. Don't have any illusions at all about that.'

He smiled. 'So, have you got a story? I like stories. There are too few of them under Haven.'

Then Naddy sat back and was quiet until Quill was done with his story. And after that Naddy picked up the skull. The mummified flesh had fallen away entirely now.

'This is his head,' Quill said.

Naddy turned it in his hands. 'What were you thinking, taking this?'

'I wasn't thinking. I told you. I don't know.' He shrugged. 'I thought it might be identifiable somehow. Fact were keen enough to make sure the ship wasn't found. I figure it's one of theirs, some expedition gone sour.'

Naddy rubbed a thumb across the skull's forehead. 'We could probably do an ident on this in a moment if I connected to the Hub, but if they know who it is, they'd be on us before the screen greyed.'

'Can't you reconstruct it? Like the suicides they take out of the Silver Sea? Use a reconstruction program?'

Naddy smiled. Without the confirmation of his eyes, it was a disconcerting expression. 'And say what? "We were beach-walking by the Silver Sea, we tripped over this head and we're curious?" No. This wasn't found in Silver. We aren't coroners from Fact. And like I said, if Fact do know who this is, as soon as the program works on it, we're flagged and flushed.'

'So what can you do?'

'We'll reconstruct it, yes. But we'll have to do it the dirty way.'

'You know how?'

'Oh, I think so.' He turned the skull on its axis. 'There's no damage here, no bone fractures pre- or post- or peri-mortem.'

Quill felt prompted. He said, 'Meaning?'

Skim said, 'Quill, I told you not to encourage him.'

Naddy laughed. 'They're Laten words. Laten's a dead language from Oath. From the word latent. Rootless and irrelevant, and thus banned by Fact.'

Skim said, 'See what you get for it when you encourage him?'

Quill repeated, 'And meaning?'

'Meaning no clues. No easy information. He wasn't bashed over the head; not before he died, not in the process of killing him and not after he was dead.'

'See? There's no point in asking him anything, Quill. He can be a real pain. Just let him get on with it.'

Naddy grinned at her. He pulled the skull's lower jaw away and peered at the teeth. Quill noticed flashes of pitted, glittering metal.

Quill asked, 'What's that in his teeth?' Then, 'He? You said *He* wasn't bashed.'

'It's a male skull.' Naddy ran his fingers around the orbits of the eyes, across the cheekbones, the jaw. 'See? Low frontal bone, large mastoid process here, rounded supraorbital margin. You want me to go on?'

'I don't think there's any way to stop you, Naddy,' Skim said.

He looked at her, then at Quill. 'When did you think this man died?'

Quill said, 'I don't know.'

'Well, I'd say around the time of first arrival on Haven. A long time. We don't fix teeth with anything like this. Maybe you found one of the first ships. Could be an escape pod from a ship in trouble, or a scout vessel that crashed? Hmm?'

They knew. We were fuck-fodder all along. Fact knew it was there, Quill, or they suspected it.

Quill stopped himself from answering. Scheck shouldn't be there now. Scheck's voice was just Quill's craziness from that time in the pod. He could go, now.

Naddy and Skim were looking at him.

'What?'

'You were talking to yourself,' Skim said.

'Thinking aloud. Sorry.'

Naddy said, 'Okay, we look at the skull a bit closer. This fits with our theory. This isn't like our skulls today.'

'What do you mean?'

'Ours are mixed,' he said patiently. 'On Oath, there used to be races. Different races. It isn't clear. People competed in these so-called races. They had wars. You know any history, Skim? Quill?'

'I'm sure you'll tell us,' Skim said.

'I can't. No one can. All we know is the technology.' Naddy became animated. 'Nobody cares about the past. The real past, the Oath. We can't simply forget it because all that's left is worm of mouth. It's everything. It's our genes, our . . .' He looked around him. 'Our rock.'

'You don't even see the rock, Naddy.'

'I know it's there. And we're trying to forget the past, as if it never was.'

Quill said, 'Please. Will you two stop this.'

Quill didn't understand them at all, the way they worked together. But then maybe they were just as close as he and Scheck had been, with their almost jealous, bickering dependence on each other.

Bicker? You and me, Quill, we don't bicker. And you're dependent on me, remember, not the other way round. Crise, I'm even dead and you won't let me go.

Naddy pushed out a hard breath. 'We're mixed. On Haven, we're out of the race. This skull, though, has features solely from one race. That I know. I've seen Vault texts. It was called caucasoid.'

The word meant nothing to Quill, and he could see Naddy registering that.

'Never mind. I can get a rough age from the teeth. Then I'll do some modelling. You'll have to leave the skull with me.'

'Modelling?'

'Crise, Quill, don't you learn? Just leave him to it.'

Ignoring Skim, Naddy said, 'Yes. The good thing is that there should be tissue landmark data available from the days of Arrival. The bad thing is that the data will be accessible only from the Vault, and I can't access them via the Hub without the risk of being flagged.'

'Landmark data?' Quill looked from Naddy to Skim, watching her sigh, feeling the tension between them. Naddy had to have the feedback of questions, and Skim simply wanted speed.

All Quill needed was answers, though. He could see how vital the tension was, between Skim and Naddy, how it made them both function. He asked, 'What are landmark data?'

'The points on the skull for which we have tissue depth measurements. They'll put the flesh on our skull.'

Quill felt a stirring of excitement. 'And we'll see him?'

'No.'

Skim snorted. 'A straight answer.'

'It might be close, that's all. What we'll have will be data-informed. But the resemblance will be limited. It's a range, that's all. And there could have been cosmetic surgery carried out, and we wouldn't know.'

He cracked his knuckles. 'Bone is fact, if you like. Flesh is surmise. But you don't get flesh without bone.'

Naddy pushed the skull aside. 'So, I'll talk to a friend, and see if I can get the data I need on that. Now, that case in your pocket.'

Quill brought it out, and Naddy turned it over a few times, then inclined his head towards Quill. It was impossible to read those blue-shielded eyes, but Naddy's voice quivered. 'This fits the theory,' he said. 'This has to be Arrival material. Skim? What do you think?'

She took it from Naddy and said, 'Any clues on the ship's main console?'

'There wasn't exactly time to look.'

'There was once everyone was dead.'

'I wasn't exactly thinking clearly.'

Naddy said, 'Give it to me.'

Quill passed it over. Naddy held it in his hand for a moment, then suddenly dropped it on the table, bent close and cautiously picked it up again.

'Hey,' he whispered, then squinted at it once more.

'Was it like this when you found it?'

'It got dented and the blister must have cracked in the coffin, in the explosion.'

Skim put a hand on Naddy's shoulder to lean over the case.

'Well,' Naddy said, 'There's one left, whatever it was.'

'Two left,' said Quill.

'One.' Naddy looked at him and said, his tone changed, 'When did you last look at it?'

'I don't know.' Quill looked from Naddy to Skim. 'I can't remember.'

No one said anything for a while.

'You're not dead,' Naddy said. 'Let's think.'

'I figured whatever was in the case had to be inactive after all this time.'

'Maybe. Maybe our skull here was trying to dispose of something dangerous. Maybe Fact knew something about that and wanted it disposed of at any cost.'

'There's no symbol for danger on the case.'

'No.' Naddy picked it up. 'It's infectious for sure, though, or was at one time. Affects your brain. You noticed anything, Quill?'

'Like what?'

'I don't know. Anything. You talk to yourself, don't you? Always done that?'

You talk to me. It's a dialogue. That's normal enough. Though I think he's right, you're crazy.

'Scheck,' Quill told Naddy with difficulty. 'My partner, the one they killed. I seem to talk to him, he talks to me. Since he's been dead.' He saw Scheck's corpse again and closed his eyes against it. 'I could do without that. But I had that before the case got cracked, even the first time. Definitely. He just isn't going away. But I know he's dead. I don't see him like he's alive. It's just his voice, that's all. I know it's not *him*.'

'Maybe whatever was in the case is just stopping you letting him go completely,' Skim said.

'Unlikely,' said Naddy. 'Why keep such an odd thing so carefully. Maybe this thing with Scheck is normal and you just need time. You'd need a psych exam and a brain scan, and they're out of the question. We've been exposed to you now, and so have others, and there's no epidemic. There could of course be an incubation period, we don't know. I think we have to rely on the lack of a hard and sharp danger warning on the case, and get on with the rest of it.'

Skim said, 'Scheck isn't acting in any way oddly, is he? Telling you to do things?'

'No. He's being himself.'

Naddy pointed and said, 'One more thing. In that pocket ...'

Quill brought out the small device he'd used to kill Java and Rheo.

'Interesting.' Naddy turned it over and showed it to Skim, who said, 'I haven't seen one of these before. Must be old tech. What is it?'

'A weapon. Broad beam device.'

'Not a patch on a molecular stream, then.' She put it down, uninterested, and Quill slipped it back into his pocket.

'Now, Quill, you need to find yourself somewhere to hide until Skim and I are done. You need to stay dead. As soon as you're not dead, you're in real trouble.'

Yeah, Quill, that's right, listen to the man. Look at me. I'm dead, and I'm just fine.

'Thanks, Scheck. That's very reassuring.' Quill caught Naddy staring at him. 'Don't worry.'

'Don't make me worry, then. Best place to be hidden is these coredors. Dock your coffin back of that storage niche. I know there are no cams within a hundred ems, so it's safe. If you need to be elsewhere, use the coffin, walk out of the wall somewhere else. I don't want you seen again anywhere near my approach coredors. Okay?'

CAP

My mind races, but I must set this down while it is fresh. I am rested again, though the present developments are beginning to trouble me.

Where was I? The election, yes.

Democracy, for my money, was the finest institution in the world, and I mean every word of that. It had its faults, Our Lord knows, but nothing in that world was perfect.

These, then, were my first thoughts as I woke up that day and stretched my arms out, and blinked and yawned and focused.

Here we were at last. On the very eve of an election in that greatest ever of democracies, The United Republics of Ameuropa.

Ameuropa. You could hardly say it, and hardly anyone did. The Americans amongst us called it the *You Are Ay*, since that sounded closer to the USA of old, and the Europeans called it *Yura*, which sounded closer to the Europe of old. And everybody else called it – well, I shan't confuse the issue. Whatever you called it, today was the eve of its very first truly democratic election.

And it was a perfect day. The weather was good in the regions most likely to vote for President Augustus Speke, and not quite so good in the regions of dubious intent, and downright inhospitable – true stay-at-home-and-close-the-shutters weather – in those regions likely to vote in a manner inhospitable to Gus. You might have called that climatic linkage symbolic, or an act of God, but I don't think I'd have been so mysterious about it. In a democracy, you used the elements at your disposal, and if those elements included *the* elements, well, that was what it was all about. This was a democracy, the rules were out there, and nowhere in the rules did it mention targeted tornadoes.

There in the Capital, the weather was just fine. A swirl of high cirrus away to the west, a creamy blue sky, a mild sun. Today, you could almost forget your skin-cancer barrier cream, your rebreather, your goggles. You could go out and vote, vote, vote for a better world under Augustus Speke.

I had a busy day ahead of me. And later I had meetings with Secretaries of State for Home Security, Foreign Compliance, all of the others, and later still, Gus himself.

At four a.m., over breakfast, I started to check my screens. First, the News Channels, simtransed where the language defeated me. Then I checked the weather predictions, just to be sure. All seemed okay. Rudy Cambi was up already and giving interviews, and he was being careful not to moan about our tactics. He knew what the consequences of that would be. Already he had a resigned look to him. His suit was crumpled and he looked like he hadn't slept for days, which I happened to know was the case. A man in his position should have been more careful what he ate.

After that, I checked my other screens. The Secretary of State for Home Affairs was not home last night, I saw. But no dalliance for EnvironAlliance, who had been a good girl. Speke was at home with a small party of a few dozen close friends. I was an absent invitee.

Then I checked my laboratories. First, I checked Astra, with its shiny walls and tables, its screens aswim with data and charts and maps, and Mike Altenberl, its crisp spokesperson, using his clipboard as usual to decline eye contact with me. But all was well there.

Then I checked Terra, which seemed appropriately more earthy, scruffier, rather more hands-on than Astra with its petri dishes and microbiospheres. All was well there too. Kath Grafe tried to engage me with fresh statistics on stimulated oxygen generation and seemed genuinely disappointed when I told her I really hadn't the time today.

And then I checked Terra's homophone, which was barely a laboratory at all from what I could see through the choke of cigarette smoke. But then they were quite, quite paranoid, and who could blame them? They were using me for their own ends, and I was using them for mine. It was all very democratic. But in the best traditions of their trade, I knew exactly who and where they were, and they thought they knew precisely who I was. They knew the face I showed them, and they had apparently successfully traced this comms line to its source close to Cambi's Central Office, and they were quite pathetically excited about that.

And finally, I checked my other and most important laboratory, which consisted of one man whom I dredged from a deep sleep, his head on his hands, at his desk. Jake didn't even know there was an election today.

I was very fond of Jake. I'd known him since he was identified as the brightest student by a long way in the best college in his – and in any – country in more than twenty years, and by an equally long way the craziest. They wouldn't continue to educate him. I would, and did. He never washed nor shaved, I don't think, but what he did do was quite astonishing. Not that I understood it. But I understood what he told me it could do, when it was done.

And it was nearly done, he told me.

'That's good, Jake,' I told him. 'I'm really proud of you.'

'Yeah, well.' He scratched himself, down out of camshot. The thought of it, and the look on his face as he did it, made me start to itch.

'You know, it's going to take a while to dismantle it all again. It's a shame, really.' He looked shyly at me.

'But you know you've made it, and proved the theory. That's enough, eh?' I've always understood the mentality of those curious freaks who sewed strings of hieroglyphs together to create computer viruses. Most of them were delighted merely to share the technical knowledge with their peers, but there were always some who just couldn't resist reeling their lines out into what passed for them as the world to see what happened, rather than being content simply to know what would. Luckily Jake wasn't one of them. He was safe. You wouldn't have wanted such things as he'd nearly made sitting in twitchy hands. Neither the programs nor the biological material. Jake was a true genius, a polymath, a lateral thinker of majestic proportions.

'Look, Jake, I'll tell you what. I've been thinking. I have a secure storage facility. We can transfer it there. How does that sound?'

Behind the moons of his glasses, his eyes brightened, and he wiped his greasy hair back. Was that a rat behind him, skittering away? It was. How could he live like that? And food cartons, plastic cutlery. There were forks on the table with chunks of food speared and then – I could imagine it – about to be eaten, maybe actually at his parted lips, and instantly forgotten for a new, shining thought, the fork and food let fall and not remembered again. How?

I was being supercilious. He was of Our Lord, as are we all. I understood his drive. He couldn't stop himself any more than I could, any more than the cigarette-smoking terrorists I had spoken to before him. Any more than my father. We were different, we few, but we were all very special, and because of this we were so much closer to Our Lord.

'Can we? That's great,' he said with real enthusiasm.

'But no one can know except us. It's too dangerous. If someone got to it—'

'Okay. I'm not stupid.'

He said it like he thought I thought he was. Like a resentful infant, his shiny lip pushed out at me.

'I know, Jake.' I waited. 'So, how long?'

He was utterly uncomprehending. How could someone like that have such a short attention span?

'Before it's ready. Jake. How long?'

He was back with me. 'Oh, maybe a week. I have a list of stuff I need. Is that okay?'

'Don't worry about it. Read it out to me.'

He vanished for a few moments. A small crash. I moved the cam to see him wiping noodles from a piece of paper with his hand and absently licking his palm. He put the paper down again and retrieved the food carton from the floor and started eating from it with his fingers. Black clots of sauce dropped on to his clothes.

I moved the cam away and waited for him to finish eating. Needing to take my mind from his mouth and the idea of him eating with the rats, I looked around the place.

Along with a few hundred dollars worth of mouldy cartons of take-out vegetarian noodles with black bean sauce, there was a couple of million dollars of investment in these few filthy rooms, of computing hardware and software (though he wrote most of his own software), of biomedical equipment and all the rest of it.

Occasionally at night it made me catch my breath and shiver to think of this tiny apartment somewhere in Texas where the security was so perfect that everyone else in the building, everyone else in the street, everyone else in the whole dustblown town was an employee of mine thinking they were the only plant in the whole place; each of them busily spying on each other and reporting back to me. It thrilled me to know that this little town was a perfectly tensioned web at whose hub was a remarkable, shambling genius who shared his food with rats. Jake. And the only one who was aware of his significance and who spied on him was me.

It sounded like he'd stopped eating. I moved the cam back to him.

'The thing that worries me,' he said, swallowing emphatically, 'is what I'm going to do after this. I mean, it's been all I've focused on, all this time. I mean, when it's done—' he shrugged and wiped his mouth, then licked his tongue around his lips. There was still food in his beard. I defocused the cam. It wasn't like him to think ahead. He really must be almost done.

'Don't worry about that, Jake. I'll think of something.' I waited, again. I could – I can – be quite extraordinarily patient.

'Okay, then,' he said vaguely, and started to move out of shot.

I followed him. 'Jake?'

'Mm?'

'The list. You haven't given me the list yet. In your hand.'

He started to read it out to me. The blobs of noodles in his beard bobbled as he talked. I wrote each item on a different piece of paper, and when the list was done and Jake was back in his own little world, I said goodbye to him and greyed the screen. And then I put each piece of paper into its own small envelope and put the fifteen envelopes into my wallet.

And then I sat down and had my breakfast of juice, toast, coffee.

I ate alone, which meant that I ate fairly well. I remember I was having trouble keeping food down at the time. There was nothing wrong with me, but the food would unpleasantly unswallow itself a short while after I had eaten, or else it would make me gag. Although, now that I think of it, the sensation of the food and acid rising up my throat and bursting out through my mouth and nose was extraordinarily cleansing. Like an absolution.

But it was mainly a nuisance. Eating in company made the situation worse, so I seldom ate in the presence of others. Once, Gus mock-joked to me that I was afraid of being poisoned. I wondered afterwards why that had come come to his mind.

After breakfast, I dressed soberly; white linen button-down shirt, Alabaman silk tie in presidential colours, grey jacket with narrow lapels and slightly flared cuffs, matching grey trousers, black socks and shoes. I always wore long socks, up to my knees, as the possibility that my calves might be exposed as I sat down made me uncomfortable. I remember once being told it was a fear of showing vulnerability, and I wasn't too big to accept that as a factor. It didn't do to dismiss these mental theorists to their faces. They were, after all, as emotionally fragile as everyone else.

I did my face, and then, although there was no need today, I put on my rebreather and goggles.

That was my vanity; conspicuous anonymity. You could clearly see me sitting in the back of the car that everyone knows is mine, you knew who I was, but you couldn't actually identify me. And it followed that those who did see under the shell were able to think themselves privileged, and that they were seeing the real me.

By now, it was five a.m. Voting here started in two hours' time. Where Cambi had his supporters, where he was strongest, where voting also started in two hours' time, night was just falling. It was a few days shy of the longest night of the year. There, voting stopped at around dawn. We offered him electronic voting from home, in compensation, but he declined that, citing a precedent of voting fraud and machine malfunction. But we offered. He knew he couldn't complain. And he had made the right choice. The tornadoes would be taking out most of the electricity.

I went to the door as my car came round the drive to collect me, long and black and quiet, its tyres spilling gravel. At the door, Jain slipped my coat over my shoulders and I walked down the steps to take my seat in the back of the car.

Bob pulled the car away and we started to make our way through the estate. At this time of the morning, even this morning, few people were up. It would have been nice if there had been a few birds, or at least birdsong, and I dictated a note regarding that.

From the broad, gently curving road, all the homes on the estate appeared similar in size. All the driveways were wide curls receding from black gates through green lawns to broad crescent driveways overlooked by Greek-style porticos with fluted columns, just like mine. Ionic, the architect called the columns. I liked that; cultured and scientific at the same time. Not that such an observation would ever have occurred to any of my neighbours here, whose only exposure to culture would have been the music they were subjected to while they were (very briefly) on hold at their brokers, and to science a vague appreciation of the suspension and acceleration of their cars.

But I was content to share external architectural fittings with them. I didn't like to be too conspicuous. Although I had my cams and their floorplans. There were no secrets behind their oak-hewn, brass-accessorised doors. They liked the solidity of marble, as if a hunk of rock could give any real comfort.

At the gate to the estate, Bob wound down his window and showed our ID to the guard. The gate closed behind us, and we were out.

Out here, the streets were well maintained. The roads were smooth and wide and well lit. The sky was lightening, and the orange streetlights were dimming. There was a smell of ozone. I wound the window down for a moment and the ozone faded into something that made me wince enough to wind the glass up again swiftly.

At the next gate, Bob presented our ID once more, and now we were fully out. Now the streets were pitted, the buildings cracked and most of the windows splintered, and there were fogs of steam, of smoke and of other things that might have been true emissions and might have been the interactions of emissions. As Gus used to say, environmental disaster and climate change are not straightforward diagnoses to make, and without a true diagnosis, what point is there in making changes?

So, the fogs swirled and competed. People took them for granted, by and large, but I didn't. I found them endlessly fascinating. The way people walked through it all, some with their faces drearily down, others heads up, some marching swiftly and some hobbling along. Some of them waved their hands through it as if the fog could have been dispersed. And the snorts of breath through rebreathers. Long streams here, short puffs there. A medic would have been in their element here, diagnosing this disease and that through breathing patterns alone. Huh huh huh huh huh. Hoooo, hoooo, hoooo. Asthma, heart failure, chronic lung disease. Fascinating.

Not today, though. It was too nice a day.

The car's suspension needed checking again, I thought. I could feel a faint judder of the ground coming through the upholstery.

Another gate, another few minutes, and we were in the Administration compound. The buildings here were imposing, and the sky was a blur of protective fields. The only thing that could penetrate that sky was sunlight, just about. It could filter out toxic chemicals and missiles with equal facility.

Bob got out of the car to open the door for me. I stepped out and walked up the stairs to the Department of Home Affairs.

This was my office for the day. I could have done what I needed to do today more easily and far more effectively from home, but Gus had no idea of that and had no need to know it either. *Mi casa es su casa*, he always told me. I'd chuckle and thank him.

Ah, democracy.

Coffee came; the opium of the administration. I settled with it before my screens and keyboards and comms equipment. The machinery was all quite clean, though I checked and rechecked. No inward cams, no bugs or slugs or hidden feeds. Gus's people had checked it, and my people had checked it. In that order.

I locked the door and stretched my cheeks and lips. It felt so good to be free.

Of course, everything went smoothly. The weather misbehaved itself punctiliously, the explosions outraged voters to a gratifying degree, and it was very swiftly clear that Gus Speke would be making a smooth transition from Vice President to President of the United Republics of Ameuropa.

HAZE

Marten stood beside Baraba and shivered. The sun had barely risen, and here they were in the arena. A low mist lay on the circle of packed earth below them. This was the first time the boys had been in the raised rings of seating.

Josefus stood in the centre of the arena, pale mist prowling around his feet. He surveyed the row of boys above him. When he breathed, the air curled like steam from his lips. 'Every morning,' he eventually said, 'I ask you for your confessions. And all you give me are your small mischiefs and disobediences. You still think this is a game.' He waited. 'Do you think this is a game?'

No one answered him. Marten wanted to look at Baraba, but didn't dare.

'Baraba! Is this a game?'

'No, Josefus.'

'No?' Josefus slid his empty gaze to Marten, who felt his head about to burst with the force of it, but then the lord moved it on to Emory, who was clutching Ghet's hand. 'Emory. I have waited for a confession from you.'

Ghet started to say something. 'I—'

Josefus raised his hand. 'Did I ask you to speak, my boy? Did you hear me ask you?'

'No, Josefus.'

'No. That's right. I didn't. The two of you, go down to Herad.'

Marten hadn't noticed Herad entering the arena. The old man moved so quietly. He pointed with his stick. 'You!'

Emory and Ghet stepped down through the wooden seats and into the misty arena. Herad led them away through the low stone doorway, and Marten let out a breath. They would be punished, and while this was a warning, life would go on.

'The rest of you,' Josefus said. 'Have you anything to say? It would be better to have said it already, but I warn you, if I have to ask you again

217

in a few minutes, your punishment will be a very great deal worse than what you're about to see.'

The arena took his words, and then Baraba said, in a shaky voice, 'I swim across the moat and back in the mornings. After I've done my chores in the fields.'

'Yes,' Josefus said gently. 'Why do you do that, my boy?'

Baraba shrugged, encouraged by Josefus's reaction. 'I like to swim.'

'And no one sees you?'

'I see him,' Marten heard himself say, as if in a dream. 'I see him swim.'

'Do you *watch* him? Or do you swim with him?'

'I . . . I've just seen him swim.'

'Good. Ley? Kash? No? Very well, that leaves Joridin and Hewl to speak up. Either of you? No? Maybe shortly, then. I believe Herad is ready. Aaah—'

Mist swirled around the doorway as Emory and Ghet came through. They were clutching real swords. Emory, the shorter of the pair, was dragging his on the ground, the sharp tip leaving a fine line in its wake. The arena's ringed seating carried the scratching of it clearly up to the rest of the boys, along with Emory's quiet sobbing. Ghet was holding his sword tightly, the tip pointed up into the air.

Herad followed the pair into the arena and took a skin pouch from his faded robe. He squeezed a ball of paste into the palm of his hand and went up to Emory, holding his hand to the boy's lips. Emory jerked away, but Herad put his other hand to the nape of Emory's neck and forced the paste into his mouth. Then he went to Ghet, who refused more vigorously until Herad whispered something into his ear. Ghet swallowed the paste. Herad wiped his hand on his robe and stepped over the low stone wall at its edge, to sit with Josefus.

'Well? Go on. Fight!' Herad hissed at the boys.

Emory rubbed his eyes and began to cry. He looked at Ghet and whispered his friend's name. Ghet swayed on the spot, then stood rigid. The mist was lifting away, and the light of the day was coming. Marten wasn't quite sure what was intended to happen. What was the paste Herad had made them swallow?

Ghet looked at Josefus and Herad and snorted. He put his head down and shook it, dizzily. Then he lurched abruptly to the side and grunted as if in pain, and raised his sword and yelled, 'Nooooo!'

Emory cried out and held up his sword barely in time to block Ghet's blow, and the two of them were suddenly attacking each other furiously.

Marten was unable to follow the fight, but Emory was first to fall, and he lay there crying and screaming as Ghet leaned back to scythe his sword down like an axe, two-handed, straight through Emory's raised forearm, the hand and wrist flipping away, to sever the top of his head at the bridge of his nose. Ghet stood over the body for a moment, his eyes closed, his body shaking, and sobbing, and then he stood back and came to the edge of the arena and squatted down, still shivering.

'Good, Ghet,' Herad said. 'You moved away. I thought you'd forgotten.'

Josefus stood up and turned round. 'Baraba, do you still think this is a game?'

'No, Josefus.'

'No. Do you, Marten?'

'No, Josefus.'

'Good.' Josefus paused, then said, as if in afterthought, 'Hewl, you haven't mentioned Joridin's theft of your food. You are aware that this is much more than a mischief. This is a crime, and for both of you. Come down here.'

Herad had his back to the arena and was watching the two of them falteringly descend to the arena. Behind him, Ghet stood suddenly straight and stared at the body of his friend, then pulled his sword up and covered the few steps between himself and the lords at a run, slashing the weapon at Herad's back.

Herad was unarmed. He twisted round and raised his arm as if to defend himself with it, but then dropped and swung his bare arm at Ghet's legs. The boy's sword slashed air and he fell, losing the sword as he hit the ground.

Herad picked the weapon up and gave it back to Ghet. He looked at Josefus, who nodded, and then he said, 'You! So you've learned nothing from me after all.' He gestured Joridin and Hewl into the arena and forced paste into their mouths, clamping their jaws as if they were beasts, and stepped from the arena again.

'It's up to the three of you. Finish it. If there's more than one of you left standing by breakfast time, I'll kill you all myself.'

Hewl and Joridin scrambled for Emory's sword as Ghet vacantly watched them, and Hewl won the struggle, shoving Joridin to the ground. Ghet made hardly any attempt to defend himself as Hewl hacked the blade into his chest. He opened his mouth as he fell, but said nothing. Joridin screamed and tried to grab Ghet's sword, ducking late as Hewl hacked at the top of his skull. Hewl caught him mostly with the blade's flat, but there was enough edge and force in the blow to open the side of Joridin's scalp. A curl of skullbone peeled high into the air and fell to the side of the arena.

Joridin dropped to his knees and toppled on his side. He tried to stand up again, but his left arm and leg were flapping uncontrollably. He was still holding the sword in his right hand, but there was no strength in it, and the tip scraped along the ground.

In sudden horror Hewl looked desperately from Joridin, who was burbling and spitting and trying to stand, although without control of his left side, to Herad. Herad shook his head, and Hewl began to sob as he hacked again and again at Joridin until he was still. Then, on all fours, he scrambled away.

Josefus said, 'We have lost three of our eight. I hope the lesson has been learnt. Hmm? I hope we are stronger now. Hewl?'

Hewl nodded.

'Good. Baraba?'

'Yes, Josefus.'

'And Marten. Have you learnt something this morning?'

'Yes, Josefus.'

'That's good. Because I'm sorry to say that you're leaving us, Marten. You won't be continuing here at the AngWat.'

Petey knew the life of the forest well, but now it was an enemy. She was jolted by the most ordinary of things. The cry of a bird and the crack of twigs sent her into a panic. The massacre in Semith's village would not leave her.

She ran for hours, crashing blindly through trees without any idea where she was going or where she was. When exhaustion eventually brought her to a stop, and she realised the forest was darkening around her, she found a sleep tree, pulled herself up it and lashed herself to a fork in the high branches and tried to rest.

Boars came in the night, a hunting pack growling and pacing round the base of the tree. They gnawed and charged at the crowded droproots and some of the thinner ones gave way, swinging free. Petey watched the animals, unafraid, uncaring, until they gave up and filtered away. After they had gone, the tree swayed more, but the rhythm of it in the night breeze comforted her, and she only woke up when the movement abruptly stopped and she opened her eyes to the flat blade of a machete arcing down between her eyes. She screamed and jerked, but the machete was a dream's blade, and it was just the sun cutting through the branches and into her eyes.

Still exhausted, she tried to sleep again, but as soon as her eyes closed, the soft rhythm of the tree and the hissing of the leaves became a machete and the song, 'Chop you, chop you, chop you.'

After that she didn't sleep at all. The massacre was a cocoon, preventing her from concentrating, from doing anything at all. The murder chant of the children blunted the forest's sounds, and whatever she looked at blurred and faded and she saw the blood and the mound of corpses and the wide wide eyes of that child staring at her.

Eventually, laboriously, she came down the tree and forced herself to construct a simple animal snare from branches and bark strips, the job normally of minutes taking her most of the morning. She had to rest frequently, finding herself exhausted without expending effort, and weeping almost constantly. Fleshflies came to the salty dampness of her cheeks, and she slapped them off, shuddering, thinking of the girl with the fly walking on her eye.

She climbed her tree again and shivered there although she wasn't cold. Night came, and the boars returned to her tree and pawed at it again, and growled and grunted, gnawing and clawing more of the droproots away and charging at the tree and shaking it. Even that didn't pierce Petey's cocoon, and then it was day again, and the dreams continued, and when she came down, she found a small tree squirrel wriggling in the snare, its leg broken. Her stomach was doubling her over with hunger, but she couldn't kill the squirrel. She might have released it if it hadn't been injured – not from pity, but because she wasn't sure she could kill it. Saliva was collecting in her mouth at the thought of eating, but suddenly she couldn't do what she would not normally even think about. She sat down beside the snare, drained of energy, and watched the squirrel try to free itself, wriggling and struggling as if Petey were not there. It kept at it remorselessly, as if escape were possible, as if there were hope. Petey stared at the small creature and was frozen. The snare bumped on the earth, shifting a little as the squirrel pulled at its trapped foreleg. The leg cracked away entirely, but the severed bone was firmly held by the spike and arm of the mechanism. Only the loosening sleeve of skin held the squirrel to its trapped leg.

Petey continued to watch. She felt nothing for the animal. She wondered why it didn't give up. The villagers had given up. They had stopped struggling. There was no part of what Petey had seen that she could understand, and yet at the same time it seemed obvious and inevitable, as though each moment had to lead to the next. It was like night or the wind. There was nothing that could stop it.

The squirrel was beginning to tire. Slowing down, it looked incuriously at Petey. The brief eye contact disturbed her and she made an inarticulate sound with her mouth, a small grunt, the first sound she had made for days. She looked at the squirrel and made the noise again, then gathered herself and forced the choking sound into a scream that curdled the air around her and cleared her head of everything, and while she was screaming she clenched her fist and hammered it onto the squirrel's tiny skull.

The squirrel was dead with the first blow but Petey couldn't stop herself screaming and pounding. When there was no breath left in her and she opened her eyes, the animal's head was spread all over the ground and Petey's hand was bleeding where she had impaled it again and again on the fragmented skull bones and the sharp wooden stave of the trap.

She made a fire and heated her knife to clean out her wounded hand, then she cleaned and cooked the animal, and when she had done that she realised she could hear the forest again, and could see clearly and think once more.

While she slowly ate the sweet flesh, she began almost unconsciously to sift the forest sounds in her head, separating them out and seeing them as colours and shades, and then setting them into a mental chart, just as she had learnt as a child. It was a special ability, and she was proud of it. Doing it now, she felt calm and light. Loren had been able to do a similar trick with the wind, knowing where it was coming from by its feel against his cheeks and on his opened hands, but Petey's hearing was her strength. Her heart thumped as she thought of the husband, and the fierceness of that memory was too much and too abrupt. The thought haunted her that if she had stayed awake long enough to weave the web that night, Loren would not have died.

She made the thought go, concentrating on the sounds outside of herself. Normally she would do it without conscious thought, but now she took pleasure in the interweaving of sounds and colours. The insects, the small animals, the breeze all became strands of a complex web that she held like a map in her head. Threads of coloured sound stretched to her left, to her right, strung away from her at ground level and stretching high above her. In her mind she coded the colours, finally holding herself at the brilliant heart. Insect sounds were shades of green, animal noises brown, the shifting foliage blue. Unrecognised sounds were red.

Once the chart was complete around her, she relaxed and let it take care of itself, quivering at the back of her mind. It shifted as the forest flexed itself. Reds and yellows flickered briefly, and when this happened, almost unconsciously she stopped and tipped her head, listening, until they clarified to safe colours.

Nearly herself again now, Petey sat by the fire and gnawed the thin squirrel bones while she tried to work out how much time had passed since she had fled the massacre. When the last of the bones were stripped white she picked her teeth clean with them, then climbed her tree and examined the broken twigs and crushed leaves. Two days and a half, she decided. She had been undisturbed that long. No one had followed her, or they would have certainly have caught her. She had been lucky. And the tree wouldn't hold another night against the boars.

On the ground again, she began methodically to destroy the fire, spreading the ashes and covering them with earth. Once this was done she'd have to move away from here quickly. Her luck wouldn't continue. She might not be far from a village, and her fire would have drawn attention. And that scream she'd made.

As she worked, the thrum and sizzle of the earth on the hot ashes dulled her sound web. The fire was an overload, a black core that rippled greys into the surrounding web. Concentrating on the fire, she didn't immediately register that at the far perimeter, directly behind her, the green was growing more vivid. Then she noticed a shrill alarm of insect noise and tilted her head, slowing her breathing to concentrate.

A sharp ripple of blue flared behind her and Petey's breath stopped. Now there was red, briefly, and it was gone – something, someone, had taken up position and was at ease there, calmly and quietly observing her. She fought the urge to freeze or to stand up and bolt, and made herself sit back on the ground. She let out an exhausted sigh. She set her hands on the earth at either side, palms down, and pressed them down hard on the warm earth to conceal her shaking.

They were still there. She could almost feel their eyes on her, and she had to fight away nausea, had to fight simply to keep still. Just stay there and watch me, she thought frantically. I'm oblivious to you. There's no hurry. Relax. Wait.

She concentrated on interpreting the sound chart, reading all she could. There was no brown where the blue slashes had been, but the green was intensifying at its edges, the insects warning each other, letting Petey know precisely where the newcomer stood.

A big man, or maybe two people standing side by side, maybe ten paces behind her. She tried to think. There had been two blue slashes, so yes, two of them.

Now there was a haze of red catching her attention somewhere away to her right, but it swiftly faded and she ignored it. A nervous animal sensing either her or the men behind her. It was irrelevant unless it drew their attention. There was no sign of their being distracted, though, and after a while the vivid green aura that defined their position paled and began to draw in towards their outlines.

She felt a sense of control returning. She could no longer hear her heart. She breathed out, slowly, and in again, and made a gentle rhythm of it.

They were patient and they were at ease in the forest. The insects were accepting their presence. Petey wondered who they were and how long they had been watching her. They were tall. Men, she guessed.

She shifted her legs as if the ground were uncomfortable, then yawned and laid herself down on her side, facing what little was left of the fire and with her hands pillowing her head. The firetube dug into her side, and she rolled fractionally to free it under her clothes. It was vital to leave her hands in their sight, for them to see she was unarmed. A few wisps of smoke rose from the flickering embers, pulling straight into the still air. A single birdcall sounded, long and mournful and far away. Petey tried to keep her breathing even.

After a while, she lifted her head and moved a hand to scratch her shoulder, replacing the hand under her head quickly at a swift red slash in the web where the men were. But they did nothing else and the web stilled again. She waited, then scratched herself once more. This time there was no reaction. She did the same thing again, moving her hand further, slipping it cautiously under her shirt, and at the end of the movement her firetube was in her palm and nestling comfortably against her cheek.

She counted in her head to a thousand, then made a loud sleep-groan and slowly, lethargically rolled over. She made the movement easy and smooth, letting them be comfortable with it, until through eye slits she saw them, two lords standing there in their orange robes, beside the buttress root of a tall tree. One had a firetube pointed at her while the other stood with his arms at his side.

Petey waited until the armed man started to mutter something to his companion, and then she turned the weapon in her hand to face him, firing it as her hand swung. The beam hissed through the foliage, struck the robe and glowed there brilliantly. She held the tube still, expecting the lord to drop, but the robe sparked like blown embers. Petey stirred it back over his chest. Nothing more happened. The lord stepped back, surprised but unhurt, then both lords lifted their hands and drew veils of the same colour down over their heads and stood calmly in the shade of the great tree. The armed one shook his head while his companion said to him, 'I didn't know she had that. Where did she get it?'

Petey fired at them again, but she had already realised the firetube wouldn't penetrate the lords' robes. She left it on the ground, drew her knife as she stood up, and ran at them, knowing she wouldn't get there, but not caring. With a flick of his hand, the lord with the firetube lanced a beam across her belly. She could see the thick beam in the air, crawling with motes and bright as fire. Petey didn't feel it strike her. She knew she was going to die. She was thinking of the husband, no, of *her* husband and *her* son. She flew at the lords, hoping the anger in her would drive her on and let her kill at least one of them before she died. She remembered the strength of dying animals protecting their young. She was avenging her family.

And she was there and the first lord dropped, his breath leaving him in surprise as much as anything else as her blade punched into his gut. But somehow the blade snapped instead of penetrating the robe and the lord was struggling furiously to push her off him. Petey used her fingers to rip the veil from his face and stabbed what was left of the blade into his throat and rolled away from him. His eyes were wide and abruptly empty. She was still feeling no pain at all.

The second lord was frantically pulling his firetube free of the folds of his robe as Petey hurled herself at him, but her arm was snagged in the folds of the dead man's robe. She couldn't get the knife hilt free so she drove her elbow into the lord's face with all the strength she had. His head snapped back and he was still.

Petey stood up unsteadily. There was little strength in her legs and she was panting for air. She put her hands on her knees and stared at the ground.

'Are you hurt?'

She spun round and nearly fell. Another man was there, standing just out of reach of her blade, glancing carefully from her face to the blade. He was dressed like a villager, though now that told her nothing at all. His face was smeared with mud. All she could clearly see of him were his eyes, but there was nothing to read in them.

The other alarm in the web, she thought. It hadn't been an animal at all. And now the web was in tatters, quivering with the shrill green of insects and the red of confusion and panic.

His eyes left her for an instant and she lifted the dagger, but as she did, a thick arm snaked under her armpit from behind her to drive her arm further up. Another arm came round from the other side, swinging over her shoulder, and the two arms locked, raising her chin and closing tight around her neck. She was lifted back and right off her feet, gasping for breath.

'Drop the knife and he'll let you go.'

The man said it in exactly the tone he'd used to ask if she'd been hurt. She couldn't say anything, the grip at her neck cutting off her air. She tried to kick her heels into the shins of the man behind her but he was wearing boots, and his hold around her neck prevented her from getting to his crotch with her free arm.

Petey dropped the knife.

HAVEN

Naddy Harke left the clearing and made his way alongside the river. The high sun played through the tall trees, lancing into the river and drawing sparks of brilliant light from the ruffled water. For the first few kils he encountered no one at all, but eventually the riverside path joined one of the busier tracks, and as he turned onto it, there were people to avoid. He never spoke to them. It was a good, clear day, and the clouds were high thin swirls.

He enjoyed the walk. He'd refined the program himself from the very few memories and descriptions available from the first generation, and added to them using environmental data from Haze that seemed to fit, and refined the whole thing with descriptions in *Rufus and the Jungle Trail.*

It took Naddy several hours to reach the hut he wanted in the distant village. He hadn't been here for a long time, and he knew that somewhere in Fact, his trip was being monitored and logged. But it shouldn't matter. He walked often, and Fact would have no reason to think that this walk and this visit were significant. A careful absence of pattern marked Naddy's wanderings and visitings.

He smiled as the door opened and she stood there. There was always a faint grainy clash at the borders of the opticked and the actual and for a moment, against the darkness behind her, it gave his old friend a ghostly aura.

'Naddy! Why didn't you say you were coming?' She threw the door wide and beckoned him in.

Zelda was looking older, he thought, if looking older were possible for her. 'You look well,' he said, all the same.

'Then maybe I should leave the lights off, and you'll know no better.' She put them on, though. She didn't need lights, with her eyes, but his opticks did, to see the real. 'Come into the kitchen and sit down, Naddy. I'm cooking.'

Naddy sat at the kitchen table and watched her fuss around her cook-top.

'So, Naddy. What hauls you down those long forest trails to me?'

The sudden noise of the cook unit made him raise his voice. 'I need some help. But I'll tell you first, people have already died getting hold of the questions I need answers to, so if you want me to go, I'll go. You might not be safe if I get caught here, even now.'

With a clatter of pans, Zelda turned round. Doing so, she was at the same time stiff and supple. The movement clearly pained her, but then she swivelled as far as was possible and kept on a few degrees, her chin finally nuzzling her shoulderblade. Naddy always wondered where she stopped and her tech started. But Zelda was still Zelda, that was for sure, whatever it might have been that made her so.

'The event,' she said, looking straight at him, her face slowly widening into a smile. 'Yes? It has to be. The way that was handled. Something big went wrong, didn't it? Hmm?'

'Just tell me and I'll go,' he said. 'I'm putting you at risk.'

'You're not going, Naddy. I felt the blow here.' She punched the unit with her hand, a dulled clang. 'They felt it as far out as Green. Citrine98. It was the first thing to *happen* here for years, Naddy. And you think you're going?'

She eyed him with those eyes of hers. Sometimes he could hear them struggling to focus, Zelda looking at him and away and back again, coaxing cooperation out of them. It made him chuckle, the idea of Zelda seeming embarrassed, the way she looked and looked away. And then when she'd got him sharp, she'd lock on him so tight she'd even sway in and out as he leaned back and forth, playing with her. When she was doing that, it was like she was looking through his skull and out the other side, checking every angle and plane, like she was giving him some kind of a psychological scan.

'You go, Naddy, and first thing I'll do is call Fact and tell them where you are and that you get your instructions from me. You know I'm safe. There's nothing they can do to me. I can nil pain, and I've lived long enough and more. If you've got something interesting, I want to know, and I want to help. So you just tell me the whole thing, Naddy.' She grinned at him. 'I know you're aching to tell me.'

'Who else can I ever tell, Zelda? There's just you and Skim.'

'So sit down and we'll eat, and then you'll tell me all about it and what I can do.'

She served it up and made him eat, swallowing her food along with him. No impatience, once she'd made her decision that he was going to tell her everything. Zelda was a good cook. She'd patted the myco into drumsticks, conjured the appearance of bird meat around seeming bones made from condensed myco. He finished it off, appreciating the variety of textures she managed to tease from the fungus.

'Good,' he told her, wiping his mouth. 'That was very good. I'm sure it tasted like the real thing.'

'I hope so. It was.'

Naddy nearly choked. 'You know I don't . . .'

'Of course it wasn't real. Helen Back, Naddy! Where's your sense of humour?'

He put down his fork, grinning. And then he told her all about Quill and what he had brought from the ship.

Zelda cracked her knuckles, the static standing up all the fine hairs along her forearm. 'So, one of the two dead heroes is still alive,' she said. 'He must be quite something of a man. What is it I can do here?'

'First, I need some data,' Naddy said. 'I want to do a facial reconstruction.'

'You think the corpse is significant?'

'Maybe not, but Fact went to a lot of trouble to destroy any trace of the ship. All we have are the skull and the case. I'm not sure about the case right now, but if I can get some tissue landmark charts, I can do a facial reconstruction from the skull. If we have that, we can look through Arrival records, and maybe identify our man.'

'A DNA search would be the quickest way. There should be DNA in the bone.'

'You do a DNA search through the Hub and you'd be lit up like a lump of jet in an opal field. If Fact know who the man was – and it's likely they do, the way they dealt with it – anyone who enters his DNA in an archive search will be picked up before the screen cleared. Right now, anyone looking at *any* Arrival data will be flagged. Even accessing up the landmark charts is a small risk, in the circumstances. But any other way, we'll draw guaranteed attention.'

Zelda considered it, then said, 'What about the blister case?'

He pulled a 3holo from a pocket and gave it to her. 'Quill's got the real thing. Frankly, I don't like handling it.'

'It's a container for pathological specimens,' she told him. 'I've seen something like it before.' She turned the sim over. 'Some years post-Arrival. This looks a little earlier in design, though.' She tapped her chin, thinking. 'There's a place I go for repair material, an old medical dump outdown of Red. There's mountains of them there. But this is in almost perfect condition, except for the dent. I wonder what was in it.'

'Any way of finding out?'

'Not now. If it's like the ones I know, it self-sterilises after discharge.

Standard safety measure. It would only have been unsafe for a few seconds.' She ran a finger over the marks on the shell. 'No specific indication of what it contained, effects, side-effects or toxicity.' She tapped the sim, its edge graining at the sharp contact. 'Just this graphic about the head or the brain.' Then she said, 'It wasn't a specimen for analysis in here, Naddy. This is a purpose-built container. No space for a label, no code-stamp to try and read. This is a onetime device, and whatever was in it would have been either self-evident or well enough documented that a label wouldn't be necessary.'

'You haven't any idea, then.'

She gave the sim back to him. 'No.'

He nilled the sim's small generator, voiding its image, and said, 'Which leaves the landmark data. Can you still get into the Vault?'

'They cut my privileges a long time ago. I might have another route, though. You ready for some caffé?'

Mexi dropped on to the long seat beside Zelda in the old woman's small leisure room. She looked fragile, more like a bird than ever.

'Thanks for coming to see me,' Zelda said. 'How is it in the Vault?' Behind her was a vista screen, set to a plain surface view of Haven. The sound was nilled and the view quivered with wind. Bundleweed blizzarded across the wall. A ragged mountain range lay pale blue in the far distance. Zelda would have nilled the screen altogether, Mexi knew, if it had been permissible. She never sat beneath the simviews of neat gardens or the grand views of the forests of Haze.

'It's fine. Interesting.' Mexi wondered what was going on. Zelda was never as polite as this. Inviting her to come for a meal, making smile-talk.

'Good. Three weeks, is it?'

'Yes, it's—'

'A pity you can't talk about it, but I understand that, no need to worry. Come into the kitchen and I'll make us some caffé. We can think what to cook, hmm?' She stood up and trotted off, her heels tapping on the floor, and Mexi followed her.

Zelda closed the door as Mexi said, 'What—?'

'I'll just put the water on. There.' The pan heater hissed to life, sizzling. 'Now.' Her voice became brisker. 'There are no cams in here, and the cook unit has an unfortunate malfunction that makes it interfere with any recording or transmission device. Those engineers from Maintenance come round all the time, but they can't seem to fix it. Here's your caffé.'

Mexi sipped at it. She wasn't sure which was oddest, Zelda's initial dithering or this new decisiveness.

The caffé was good, though, the same as ever.

'Now,' Zelda said. 'Tell me about Fact. Tell me what you really think of it. I'm not your guide. You can trust me, and it's important that you do. I have to trust you too.'

'I trust you, Zelda. What do you mean? Don't you trust me?'

'Oh, child. Mexi, I mean—' she smiled, and in it Mexi saw nervousness for the first time ever. 'You're in a new world, now. You must examine it. Tell me about Fact.'

Mexi swirled the dregs of the caffé around the warm cup's bowl. 'It's amazing. There's so much to find out, so much to know. They're constantly reviewing and researching the past. It's what I always wanted. And Haze. There's so much about Haze. I could get there, Zelda. Gild told me. In a few years—' she saw Zelda's face, and stopped. This was not what Zelda meant at all. She thought of Zelda, always questioning, teaching her always to question, never to accept. Suddenly and for the first time she thought about what she was doing in the Vault. It was researching, it was questioning, yes, but Zelda had meant more than that.

She said, 'No. We never see the original documents. They're too delicate to expose to the light, and it's for security, too. We see perfect copies. When we analyse something and the analysis is accepted, the document – one stage down from the perfect copy – is changed to reflect that analysis.'

'Yes?'

'It's fine to do that, because the original document and the perfect copy remain untouched.' She looked at Zelda. This was play, even if it was playing at the edges of unFact. It was like a game of Dare at kindlegarden, though kindlegarden seemed a long time back, now. 'But we never see the original document,' she added.

Zelda waited. 'Yes? And that means?'

'If we're wrong, we could be propagating unFact.'

'Take that further. Imagine. It's only me, Mexi.'

Mexi stumbled over the words. Zelda had brought out her troubled thoughts, and she realised that without someone to say them to, she would have accepted the situation. 'The past could be changed, got wrong.'

'You've said that. Next step.'

'If we're prevented from ever seeing the original documents, how do we know the copies aren't later adjustments? Even the perfect copy.'

Zelda nodded. 'Yes. On.'

'You mean, how do we know the past is not being changed deliberately? How can we trust Fact? But that's ridiculous.'

'Yes, it is. Let's say it is. Now, then. I trust you, Mexi. There is something inside you that's like me.' She looked rueful. 'That isn't a restful thing, not a good thing, necessarily, but it's there. In time you would have come to this point yourself, as I did, but there isn't time. The past is being changed, Mexi. I don't know why, but word by word and line by line, it's being changed.'

Mexi watched the old woman pottering at the cook unit. Zelda put a big pan on to heat and turned round again.

'I've always intended telling you about myself, and about what of the past I know, and what of the present. It seems the time for that has come a little sooner than I expected or imagined. And it may not be the right time, but we have no choice.' She turned away to taste from the pan, and said, 'I'm sorry to burden you with this. You have no one else, I know that. Just an old woman who lives in the house next to your parents' house. I wondered why you didn't move after they died, Mexi. It must be sad to live with their memory so close.'

'I like the memory. And you – you're my friend.' Mexi looked at her. The word 'friend' was not nearly enough, but she couldn't think of any other word. Instead, she stood up and went to Zelda and put her arms around her thin frame, hugging her close.

'Mexi,' Zelda whispered, squeezing her firmly. 'I'm here. I'm always here. You know that.'

There was hardly any flesh to Zelda, but it didn't matter. Zelda was as solid as Haven. Mexi couldn't imagine her not being there.

'Now then, girl. Don't cry.' The old woman squeezed her again, then held her at arm's length and stared at her. 'Oh, Mexi.'

She looked happy and sad together, and Mexi couldn't tell if the expression on her face was something complex that she didn't understand, or just the old woman's failing technology.

'I'm grown up,' Mexi said into the silence. 'Grown up and working.'

'Yes, and for Fact, and in the Vault. And your friend has a reputation which Fact are very aware of. You need a reason to be here with me. A friendship with me will make them suspicious. So I'm going to teach you how to cook. You came here after the bird was roasted on the fire, remember, curious about that. Everyone saw me showing you what to do with the lichens. We'll use that. They'll believe it, and you'll enjoy it. We'll both enjoy it, Mexi.'

Zelda took the pan off the heat, then reached up to start explaining to her the shelves of jars, the rows of lichens and dried, powdered termites.

There were bird bones and other things whose names Mexi didn't catch, or thought she'd misheard. She looked at the jars, then looked around further, not seeing what she expected to see. There was an oven hollowed out of the rock, a bath of cooking oil. 'Where's your myco?'

Zelda laughed, the rasp of breath surfacing sharply from deep in her chest. 'Yes, good idea. That's the lesson for today, then.' She bent herself at the knees and pulled at a ring in the floor, and a trap opened. Mexi leaned to see, beneath the floor, a small mycorium, the tank of dark nutrient palely speckled with myco. 'I grow my own myco. I've been doing it for years now, refining and adjusting. It tastes better than from the farms.' Zelda unhooked a rake from the trap's underface and skimmed some of the doughy crop into a long-handled pan, and lifted it out. She held it towards Mexi, who took it from her and smelt it cautiously as Zelda closed the trap again. She put the myco on the side, then took a tray from a ledge beneath the water basin. The tray was full of a thick slop with the colour and shine of scrubbed fingernails.

'I've been soaking this for a week,' she said. The slop settled in the tray, and Zelda nudged it with a spatula. Its surface moved in a single long ripple and was still again. 'I drain it, press it, dry it a week, then I slice it into thin sheets.' She judged Mexi with her eyes and said, 'You ever heard the word, "paster"? I thought not. You remember Saria? The story of Icarus?'

Mexi nodded.

'Saria's mother told her it reminded her of paster to look at. Everything I'm telling you comes from the little that Saria's mother told her of what she remembered of the Oath. She remembered food, that woman. She remembered more than she was supposed to, and she told more than the rules allowed.'

Mexi looked at Zelda, remembering and telling more than she was supposed to, Zelda with no daughter or son. Zelda's eyes were watering.

'Saria's mother was a cook, the colony's head cook. Everyone else, it was their job to make a viable world out of Haven; no remembering allowed, no looking back, only forward. Chemists, engineers, physicists, the rest of them. No wasting of time. No stories, no history for their children, just the passing on of the practical and technical skills the colony was desperate for. But as long as it concerned food, Saria's mother could do or tell anything. She had special dispensation.'

Zelda watched Mexi until the girl's face showed she realised how vital the head cook must have been, to be permitted to remember, and then she turned back to the cook unit, moving pans across the heating coils.

Mexi hadn't thought she was hungry, but the smells from Zelda's pans were making her swoon.

'She had to feed them all, make them want to eat. It was all they had between work and sleep, and it was her responsibility. She developed the myco, but she wanted more. She had to tell the geneticists what to aim for, even when they had nothing to work with but the fleet's insects and rats and a few birds. And the lichen we found here. But the Oath we came from – imagine it, Mexi. It was more full of life even than Haze. There were as many species of bird as Haven has lichens, and all response-evolved over billions of years. Imagine that.' She put a pan down and looked past Mexi, her fists working loosely, gripping air. 'Real-time evolution. There were crops on Oath, not like the modified grasses we failed to grow, but fruits and vegetables like on Haze, only more. Fragile things that needed an atmosphere of love. Ground animals the size of storm eagles and even bigger. Beefs and hamms. Maybe it was like Haze. It was glorious back on Oath, Mexi. It was everything you could wish for. And then it all went wrong.'

Zelda dropped something from a jar into the simmering pan, then dipped a fingertip into it and put it to her lips. 'I think we should eat.'

They ate in silence. The food that Zelda had cooked tasted unworldly to Mexi with its nose-flavour and texture on the back of her throat.

'Now,' Zelda said. She opened the hatch and removed the tank of myco, and took from behind it a tray of disks. 'There's a small, hidden catch.' She showed Mexi the tiny flush stub at the side of the tray, 'And if you fail to flick it as you take the tank out, it'll flood the disks with magnetic filings and wipe them clean.'

'Why are you telling me that?'

'No reason. In case.' She put the tray on the table between them. 'They only leave me alone because they don't want a fuss and they think I'll be dead soon and that'll be the end of it. They want to keep the past buried. That's a foolish attitude, and I don't know why they have it. It's an attitude that may destroy us, and it's why I'm showing you this, Mexi.'

She ranged a hand over the tray of recordings. 'I was with Fact. I was on the Watch Council.'

'I know. So were my parents.'

'Yes, there were a number of us. Only I'm left. The Watch Council liaised with Fact and with Contact. There was a brief time when the very first contacts with Haze, over a hundred years ago, were being re-evaluated.' Zelda pulled a disk from the pile. 'This is a perfect copy of a disk whose original no longer exists. The Watch Council voted to destroy it under instructions from General Factotem.'

'Destroy it? Nothing's ever destroyed.'

'We were told it held embarrassing scenes of negotiation, detrimental to the relationship with Haze. We weren't shown it, just required to authorise destruction.'

'What happened?'

'I was curious. Embarrassing scenes, I thought. I took it to the burnchamber, but first I copied it and removed the copy.' She slid the disk into a small machine on the table. 'What do you know of first contact, Mexi? How we discovered the existence of Haze.'

'I know about the Haze, the electromagnetic Haze that made it impossible to land there. A small scout ship discovered what lay beneath it by accident. It lost power in orbit, penetrated the electromagnetic Haze and crashed, disappeared. A rescue ship followed its course and by pure chance found a gap in the Haze, and that was it. After that, negotiations—' she shrugged. 'It was primitive. They were in awe of us.'

'Yes. They had no technology,' Zelda said. 'We gave them that, didn't we? In return they gave us wood, supplementary food, the rest of it.' She thumbed the screen to life and said, 'The accident was a lie. This is the truth, this disk. This is the real first contact.'

The screen suddenly shone, a stamped biscuit of light. On Zelda's arm, metal gleamed patchily.

Mexi waited for an image to appear, then looked at Zelda as she froze the screen, isolating the faintest shadow of an image.

'But this is Haven,' Mexi said, frowning.

'Yes.'

There were birds in the wind, and after a while a high bright dot that Mexi thought was a display fault, or a hovering bird. The dot swelled and caught fire.

'It's a ship coming down,' Mexi whispered, leaning forward into the small screen. She watched the ship shimmer down to the planet's surface on a heel of fire. It was a flame that even the winds of Haven could not diminish, though the small ship was shuddering and restabilising constantly, like an unstable holo.

'An old ship. Very old.' Mexi tried to imagine seeing it as it actually happened, scarcely believing it, and certainly unable to believe it could land in one piece.

But after an age spent quivering a metre above the surface, it landed. And as soon as the thrust subsided and the struts punched down to anchor the vessel, the winds started to rip at the hull and try to hurl it away. A ramp unfurled itself from the hull and was almost grounded when it sheared away and tumbled, gathering speed and falling apart, and shrank into the dust and distance.

Mexi's thoughts whirled. What must it have been like in that ship, at that moment? No operative comms above the ground, nothing. And what must it have been like for the Watch Councillor in her cupola staring through the wind at it? She said, 'What could they have thought?'

Zelda stopped the image. The ship stabilised. 'The report's at the end of the disk. They had no idea. Apparently there had been a message, barely decipherable, in anglish, saying they were establishing contact and arriving imminently, a week before. That was all. Fact had no idea who they were, except that they had once to have been from Oath. They were coming to find us, to bring us back, perhaps. Or to take over.' She held the frozen image there, letting Mexi start to feel a fraction of what it might have felt like to wait, not knowing. And then she released the ship again to the winds of Haven. It was firmly rooted. Zelda moved the image forward, shadows inching along.

'Six hours, they waited. And on the ship too, they waited.'

'Why didn't anyone go out to them?'

'No one was prepared to risk it. They had come to Haven, but no one knew why. Fact were getting themselves ready to send out a rec, but it never got to that.' She speeded the image on, the rocket's shadow in the rising sun circling it like a spring coiling tight. A black shape appeared above the rib of jagged metal where the ramp had ripped away – a doorway. And immediately a human shape oozed into sharpness, suited like in a kindlegarden cartoon, in silver, every bodily protrusion impact-buffered. Big claw-hands, bigger claw-feet. It looked like it could grip anything and never let go. A ladder crawled down the side of the ship and sank into the ground. Its feet drove down so hard that the cam shook.

'They thought they were prepared for Haven,' Mexi murmured.

'Yes,' Zelda said.

The figure turned laboriously in the doorway, never relinquishing more than one hold at a time, and started down the ladder. At the bottom it went to all fours, and started across the ground, head down. It moved lethargically, apparently lazily, each limb movement taking an age. Once it raised its head, and the wind took a grip and started to lift it clear despite the claws. Mexi could see the shuddering effort it took to drop that head again.

'You can see the claws have shock-thrusters. Seven digits, each penetrating a metre down, splayed.'

On the figure's back, a smooth hump, the oxygen. The air on Haven was fine to breathe, if you could drag any out of the wind. Face away from it and you'd suffocate; face into it and it would pop you like a bubble. Tanked oxygen was safer. Mexi remembered herself out there rescuing the little bird. She was in the open for maybe two minutes, though it had seemed more, and kept a low profile. She suddenly realized how stupid and lucky she had been.

Zelda moved it on. At thirty-speed the figure looked like a frantic insect. After a few minutes, Zelda dropped the speed again. Behind the figure, the ship was agitated. It seemed to shift against the ground, so subtly that Mexi almost failed to notice it, then the ship slipped its mooring. The wind slapped it sideways and flicked it away across the ground. It had disappeared in a few seconds.

The figure stopped and turned its head, and this time wasn't quick enough to hold firm against the wind. It stood sharply up, arms flung high by the onrushing wind, hand-claws still extended like great talons. For a moment it reared there, and then the feet were uprooted and the figure was hurled in the wake of the ship and gone.

Zelda stopped the image. 'That was how we found Haze. After that, we sent ships in search of the planet it must have come from. A scout ship did find Haze, and the rest of what you were taught, more or less, is true.'

'But Haze never was primitive, was it?'

'No, Mexi. And the Vault is not to be trusted.'

Quill told himself he took the coffin out to check its systems, but really it was because he felt soothed by its movement through rock. At full power in stable, well-mapped rock he could make twenty metres an hour. At that speed the engine was audible from a metre out, so he had to be careful where he docked.

He docked in a dead coredor and walked out of the rock to get some air and work his feet. The broader boulevards and avenues of the Primaries were more anonymous than the narrow coredors downbelow and outdown, and Quill was less likely to be noticed there. However, for five minutes of every hour, the street screens subscreened the Game and threw out images of Quill and Scheck, Heroes of Haven.

Just you and me, Quill, we're the heroes. Not Tanner. I always said he was useless. What is it they say? 'They also serve who only stand and wait'? It's crap.

'I never heard it. There was nothing he could do for us. They killed him, Scheck. They know he's dead. That's why he's not there.'

Anyway, that's thirty of me and twenty-eight of you we've seen today, Quill. I guess that makes me the bigger hero.

237

Quill didn't reply. It was more and more unnerving having Scheck inside him like this. But along the coredors the pictures of the two of them were still there, punctuating the Game.

He returned to the coffin. Waiting for Naddy Harke to come up with his answers, he lived in the coffin, shuttling it through rock, meeting Skim at different coredor coordinates every few days, so she wouldn't be seen too often walking into the cam-vacuum of Naddy Harke's coredors. She supplied him with food, fuel rods and the news that there was no news. After a week of it, he found he didn't like the coffin so much, alone with the creak and crack of rock as if the hull were failing. Tanner had been the dock engineer, holding the hull together, and Tanner was gone.

Okay, we miss him. Is that alright for you, Quill? I miss him too. He never would shut up, but now I miss his voice. It's all gone to Helen Back, hasn't it? All a bowl of tears.

And then Skim said, meeting him at the end of a single-aisle coredor, quartz dust picking out her hair, a disk in her hands, 'Let's go. I'm coming back with you to the coffin. There was a screencast yesterday and I think you should see it.'

She crawled into the coffin with him and laid herself down, giving him the disk. He took it from her, but what he was thinking was how easily she accommodated herself to the space.

'What is this?'

'Just put it in.'

The feed tray slid it from his hand and swallowed it. A man's face filled the screen. His cheeks were sucked in and shining with sweat. He was breathing rapidly and his lips and jaw were moving frantically, and his eyes flicked about. But his head didn't move at all. His head was as fixed and steady as stone. And he looked uncomfortably familiar.

'What is this, Skim?'

'Do you recognise him? This was screen-cast last night.'

The features lost definition as the cam peeled back, leaving the spectral head docked at the edge of the screen, and General Factotem faded into view to stare at Quill. Factotem's face was almost carved, his features sharply divided between flare and shadow. The screen seemed barely to contain him. Factotem was always the same, although he was re-elected from within Fact every decade. No one knew whether his face was sim or anima. Quill looked from his chiselled calm to the terrified face at the screen's edge.

General Factotem said, 'Under Haven, living in rock as we do, we live with uncertainty. We have no horizon, no sky. We can't see far, and what we can see is restricted and provisional.' A hand hooded his eyes, as if he were peering ahead. 'What's behind that wall? What's down the next coredor?' The hand dropped. 'Our entire world might crack apart tomorrow. In such a place we need as much certainty as we can get, and in this place, the security of Fact is vital.'

He drew closer, filling the screen with the solidity of his image. 'Fact is our only certainty. As soon as we doubt it, we lose our balance and our strength.' General Factotem faded gently away, his voice remaining to articulate the message as the terrified head drifted back to the centre of the screen and became more solid again, the cam drawing back this time to reveal his entire naked body.

In the background, Factotem's voice went on. 'This man was caught making unFact. He was talking about the Oath. He was saying things about the Oath for which there is no evidence in the Vault, and are therefore clear unFact.'

Quill couldn't comprehend the perspective of what he was seeing. The man seemed to be lying on a clear couch, or perhaps floating in water, the cam suspended above him. But his body wasn't moving at all, any more than his skull had moved. Only the agitated movement of his jaw and the fluttering of his eyes and eyelids, and some muscle movement of his cheeks, told Quill that the picture was not an instant image.

'His name is Tyler Hind, and he's of previously sound mental and social history. His past is solid, but recently his colleagues and family reported him for making claims about the Oath. He also began showing other signs of serious mental illness and amnesia. Shortly after being apprehended, his brain function deteriorated to the point where he recognised no one and nothing around him. Very shortly after that, he was judged clinically insane.'

Factotem returned to view as the man diminished to the side of the screen, his scalp brushing the upper edge and his toes, slightly pointed and clearly not supporting his weight, touched the lower edge. The cam closed towards Factotem's face again. His wide eyes glittered, their irises flecked with shards of brilliant jade. His voice hardened. 'If you know or have been in contact with Tyler Hind in the past two weeks and have not already been interviewed, you are ordered immediately to report yourself to Fact.'

Quill said, 'The name means nothing, but I know him. I just can't remember where from.' Quill also knew what he was watching, now. This was an unFact Caution. 'Why are you showing me this, Skim?'

'Watch. You have to remember the man.'

The cam was drawing smoothly away from Factotem. Quill remembered the pattern of unFact Cautions, though it was a long time since he'd watched one. To be trapped like that.

'Recognise him?'

'No. Crise, yes. Yes, I do.' Quill closed his eyes, remembering. It was him, no question. The last time he'd seen him, he'd been stumbling from the shuttlepod by the Canal, desperate to get away from Quill and his bag of illegal stones. Now he was in detention rock.

'Despite the fact that he remembers nothing else, this man says he simply *knows* the babble he claims as Fact—' the General made a small moue with his lips before continuing, '—and we must cut it off before it spreads through Haven.'

Now that Quill was aware of it, he could make out the translucent detention rock encasing the man, all but the mask of air at his terrified face, by its delicate reflections, the soft planes and marks where the synthetic rock had started unevenly to set as it had been poured. Looking more closely, Quill could see the faint passages of the fine nutrient and excrement tubes that entered Hind's nose and mouth and departed from his lower orifices. Quivering bubbles marked the movement of a thin golden trail of urine, and nearby was a pale, almost stagnant cord of faecal matter. It was as if the body of Tyler Hind were simply a stage in the passage of the tubes.

Quill shook the thought away and said, 'I saw him once, but I hardly talked to him. He seemed normal enough. I was concerned he'd remember me, so I scared him.'

'You scared him? How?'

'I told him I was a mineral trader, illegal. I said I dealt with senior factotems. He wouldn't confess to knowing that. It's the sort of knowledge it's best not to have. He'd be in big trouble if he admitted to it.'

'More trouble than this?'

'But this is nothing to do with me. He didn't recognise my face. I'm sure. Absolutely sure.'

Skim didn't say anything, and Quill stared at the screen. The cam came smoothly away from the man to reveal another prisoner in rock at his either side, similarly naked and intubated. And it continued to withdraw to show more people above and below him. And then there were four, eight, twenty tiers, and each tier was twenty, thirty, a hundred filled cavities wide. The detention chamber was immense.

At intervals of about twenty detainees, InOut tubes were bundled together and trailed away to service chambers at the rear of the cavern. Only their tubes connected the cavern's inhabitants together. The detainees were just nodes along the lines.

Quill had seen Survey charts of the region deepdeepdown of Indigo where the detention chamber was. The huge natural cavern stretched back almost a kilometre from the face of the detention wall. Quill wondered how many prisoners of Fact stood immured there. The even more vast toroid Game arena lay only a few hundred metres deeperdown. He wondered which was the worst punishment. Detention was for unFact, the Game for everything else.

Factotem was saying, 'Every one of these spreaders of unFact claimed to be announcing truth.' The cam moved close on a woman's face. Behind the still motes held in the rock she looked exhausted. Her eyes were heavy-lidded, but came abruptly wide with terror as the cam loomed tight on her. Quill wondered what else those tubes contained, what wiring, snaking where. She didn't look like Hind, though. None of them looked quite as crazy as Hind.

'This woman is a godsayer,' Factotem said. The cam moved, and another detainee blinked wide, jaw muscles tensing. 'This man said Haven is about to crack, this one that our myco is poisoned. Each has their own unFact.' He shrugged. 'They've had their time to recant, and they have not recanted.' He half-turned, and the cam shifted to confront him again. 'We will free them. They can keep their *truth*—' he mouthed the word more delicately than before, making it dirty. '—and we'll see if it supports them.'

'That's odd,' Quill whispered.

'What?'

'Don't they get at least a year to recant? Sometimes more, but never less.'

'Yes. They're putting Hind out very quickly.' She looked at Quill, expectantly.

On the screen, thickly braided coils and bundles of carrycables swung across the ceiling and caught one of the tiers of rock, and a cradle of cables brought it clear. The block held about twenty detainees. At its edges, bunches of InOut tubes gathered and stretched, quivering, and broke suddenly away, whipping brown and gold strings of liquid matter through the air as the block slipped away from the wall and swung free. The carrycables strained with the load. As their casing swilled heavily back and forth in the air, the motionlessness of the encased detainees hit Quill. An image of geodes came into his mind.

The cradle tracked towards the foreground and steadied before gently delivering the great casing on to the floor of the cavern. It juddered with the soft impact and creaked. Behind it, the detention wall was adjusting itself, tubes regathering and pulling tight, the matrix restabilising. The cam ranged over the new face of the wall for a moment, with its fresh rows of wide eyes, then returned to the block on the cavern floor.

Quill saw the fluttering of eyes and jaws. Nothing else could move and there was no sound. Tyler Hind was at the extreme left of the block, still babbling to himself.

With eerie precision and order, the entire row of heads began slowly and in perfect synchrony to droop forward – all but the head of a woman whose waist-long hair was held behind her, deep in rock.

Quill knew a little about detention rock. Its molecular structure permitted limited shrinkage and expansion. Detainees' nails and hair, as they continued to grow, grew directly into it. The only exception to this was facial hair, which was prevented from growth by additives to the mask of breathing gases, so that men couldn't swallow their beards and choke themselves to death. Quill wondered what it must be like to be in detention rock. He remembered why he had not watched one of these screencasts for so long.

The synthetic rock was being liquefied from the top down. Except for the woman with long hair, whose head had fallen back, all the detainees' foreheads were resting on the shelf of rock at their shoulders, and the liquefying rock was flowing more rapidly down the sides of the block.

Skim said, 'Why do you think they're letting Hind out now? He isn't the first to talk Oath-unFact. And he's obviously crazy. They don't put crazies into rock. No one's going to believe anything a crazy says. It isn't unFact. Hmm?'

Quill was concentrating on the screen, though. The cam drew back about a hundred metres to show General Factotem's sim standing at a long table, cavern-wide, set with beer, water, bread, savouries and sweets. There was food from Haze as well as myco-based food. There were plates and bowls, jugs and jars of it. It was about five metres from the casing of rock.

The cam glided forward again to show the rock containing the detainees melting more rapidly. It was at their waists, and they slumped forward as far as their trapped forearms would let them, though the long-haired woman was arched back to the full curve of her spine. There was a jerk of movement from them all as their hands were released, Tyler Hind the only one not to leave long curls of fingernail cracked away in the rock.

There were no cries of pain or relief. Only a faint hum muffled Tyler Hind's babble when the cam was on him. There was no sound at all from the other detainees, although the rock itself moaned softly and crackled with the redistribution of weight. The fractured twists of fingernail were freed moments later and slipped down the rock to the ground.

As it reached the lower thighs of the detainees, the remaining solid rock cracked and broke away to lie in scattered chunks that quickly dissolved. Quill watched the row of freed prisoners slump in exhaustion and relief to the ground, twitching as their InOut tubes pulled clear and slithered away over the floor to vanish. Tyler Hind lay with all the others, barely moving except for the jerking of his eyes and mouth.

'I don't want to watch this,' Quill said.

'I'm sorry,' Skim told him. 'But watch.'

He didn't have the energy to do otherwise, and felt unaccountably to blame for what he was seeing.

Factotem's voice was suddenly piercingly sharp, and his sim was standing beside the tables of food. 'Now they are all free.' He waved his arms, indicating this. 'Naked except for their unFact. Their truth.' He said the word like he had said 'Their Fact' before, and then he picked up a cake and took a bite and chewed it slowly, and swallowed. 'Their nutrient has been withdrawn for five days, their water for two. They will be hungry and thirsty. Let's see how their truth nourishes them. How their truth sets them free.'

He turned away from the cam, and it was as if he were simply watching just like Quill and the rest of Haven were watching. 'Come here,' he called. 'Eat. Drink.'

The sprawl of prisoners lay where they had been freed, too exhausted to move. Hind stood out from the rest by the twitching of his eyes, the constant movement of his lips.

Quill remembered the first time he had seen an unFact Caution, at school. It had been compulsory to watch the screencast, and he hadn't understood it fully, only taking in that it was a bad thing to happen, and that unFact was to be avoided. With forty other kids, he'd watched it for a few minutes before getting bored by the freed prisoners stupidly lying there. He'd glanced back now and then over the course of the day until it started to look odd, none of them really moving when they must be getting hungry. Then the next day they were still there, a couple of them twitching just enough to prove the picture hadn't frozen. And after that the school screen had been closed, though every day for the next weeks, walking to school and back past the doubleheight stores of green3, he'd looked up at the tall street screens. All the public service screens were bright either with the Game or with the freed prisoners of Fact. They were still unmoving. He remembered it vividly. The scene never changed, but the *realtime* logo was always flashing.

It had taken him a year, until the next Caution, to understand that the prisoners had been immobile so long that their muscles had wasted. Freed from the rock, they couldn't move. The tables could have been a universe away. The detainees lay a few metres from all that food and drink and died of thirst and hunger.

'Enough,' Quill said, and this time Skim pushed the screen on, hi-speeding the image until the caption read + TWO POINT THREE HOURS.

General Factotem was there again, kneeling in sim at Tyler Hind's side. The cam closed on the two of them. Tyler Hind's mouth was still moving, but the hum covered anything he might have been trying to say. Hind's eyes were darting about rapidly.

Factotem turned his stony eyes to the cam and said, 'Remember. If you've spoken to or seen this man . . .'

Skim closed the screen and said, 'They don't usually do that. You're right. And Hind hadn't been in rock long enough for that degree of muscle loss. They must have drugged him, a muscle relaxant or a neurotoxin.' She looked hard at Quill. 'And everywhere under Haven, images of you and Scheck. How you're heroes.'

'He doesn't look like the rest,' Quill said. 'They drugged him, yes, but only physically. They wouldn't have wanted him mentally dulled for interrogation. Look at him. You're right, he's really crazy. GenFac wasn't lying about that.' He shivered.

In the silence, she adjusted herself uncomfortably, her head bumping on the curved bulkhead, and said, 'How do you live like this, Quill?' And then went straight back to the screen and Tyler Hind. Quill liked the way she did that. Steady, matter of fact.

She was saying, 'They think you're still alive, both of you. Why do you think that is?'

'Tyler Hind gave me away. He must have done.'

'Yes. But not Scheck. He only saw you. They're putting equal emphasis on you both.'

'If I'm alive, they'll think he is.'

'True. But what about this – Tyler Hind goes crazy and starts saying rubbish about the Oath. If there's no Vault documentation, it has to be rubbish, doesn't it? So Tyler Hind's just the same as all the others. If that's so, why treat him differently? Why not give him a year, let his unFact just get forgotten? And on the other hand, if he's simply gone insane and babbling blueshit, why put him in rock at all? No one's going to take an obvious lunatic seriously.'

'If he said he's seen me, maybe he told them I told him about the Oath. They probably tortured him. He could have told them anything.'

'Exactly. He could have said anything to them. Especially if he's crazy. And your face is everywhere, Quill. Why would they think he didn't invent it about seeing you, just like he invented stories about the Oath. They aren't stupid. And why would he do that, anyway? GenFac said Hind was normal until you met him.'

'But I didn't *do* anythi—' he stopped.

'What, Quill?'

Quill saw himself pushing the open bag into Hind's face, and Hind drawing breath and then coughing. The bag with the skull and— 'The blister case,' he said. 'I cracked the bag against a bar in the pod as I thrust it at him. I thought I'd broken the skull, but I hadn't. It must have been the case. The second blister.'

Skim sat back as far as the coffin bulkhead would let her. She seemed to relax slightly. 'That's what Naddy and I thought. So, what was in it and what did it do to him? Did it just send him crazy? And what did it do to you, Quill? You're a little weird, but you're not crazy. Or if it didn't do anything to you, then why not?'

'Fact don't know about the case,' Quill said. 'And Hind couldn't have told them. He didn't look inside the bag. He closed his eyes rather than look. And anyway, why would they believe him about seeing me? Why would they believe anything he said? He's crazy. We still haven't answered that.'

She let silence fill the coffin. 'There's one answer to it,' she said. 'It explains why they're taking Tyler Hind so seriously. It's not just because he might have claimed to have seen you alive.'

'I'm not with you.'

'For one thing, it's the combination. Oath-saying *and* saying he's seen you. Maybe there's somehow a reason to believe the two things together much greater than believing either one in isolation.'

'We've just been through that.'

'There's another thing. Put that with this. What if, having been in contact with you, they think he's more likely to be right about the Oath?'

'That makes no sense. Why would they think that?'

'They know where you've been. They knew enough about that to want it concealed forever.'

'But he's still more likely to be just crazy.'

'Okay. Add this. What if his unFact is actually Fact?'

'How could it be? And how could they know if it is? That would mean that they know Fact about Oath.'

'Yes,' she said quietly.

Quill laughed, but the tension didn't break. 'That's as crazy as Hind,' he said. 'That's ridiculous. There's no Archive, nothing in the Vault. How could they possibly know that?'

'I don't know, Quill. But nothing else fits.'

CAP

You'll have to excuse me. I get tired. This business is not easy, and such a long time, so many years. Coming and going like this. Doing what I must do – I have to control what I think. I have to be rigorous. I have to compartmentalise. Mentalise in compartments. Here, I think what I need to think here, and no more. Other thoughts are dangerous. I've learnt that.

I stayed up to watch Rudi Cambi's campaign unravel completely, and then with a cup of coffee his assassination midway through his acceptance of defeat speech. No point in leaving loose ends to whip back and sting you later. After that I went home to bed, looking in on Mary before retiring, intending to tell her the good news.

Asleep, she looked beautiful and perfect. She was so tranquil there that I couldn't bring myself to wake her. I yearned for her. Standing there at her door, I vividly remembered my first heart-shuddering sight of her that day in the queue, when she had jerked her head and stared suddenly up at me as if physically feeling my gaze upon her. As if my sudden and total love had startled and electrified her as it had me.

Staring at her from that small distance, I was paralysed by love and yearning, and then without warning I was overwhelmed by stomach-cramping nausea. I gripped the handle of the door so hard that it cracked away in my fist and I cried out in pain.

She didn't wake, or pretended not to. Controlling myself quickly again, I remembered the past purity of our love, and felt immensely sad. She had destroyed that love, and now she had destroyed my mood. I was in turmoil. I wanted to embrace her, and I wanted to destroy her.

Not trusting myself, I closed the door quietly and left, and slept for a few hours.

And in the morning I was restored. Reflecting on another victory, the final one on this Earth, I rolled out of bed to go for a short run on my machine. Pulse steady, breathing easy. I felt good. I was no longer nauseous, and I had slept dreamlessly.

I spoke to John, who congratulated me. He knew nothing of what I had done for Gus beyond the speeches and the campaigning. I tried to read through his words, as by that time I always did, but as ever I couldn't tell what he was thinking, what he would have liked to have confessed to me. While he tapped away at his screens and gave me details of the movements and workings of my money, I wondered what he dreamed of. What he told me, the dates and figures and rates and routes, were so correct that I wondered whether he had discovered that he was shadowed everywhere he went, monitored and recorded.

He had deceived me, of course, telling me he had no feelings for her. I had realised that. Their love was making me so jealous now that I could hardly speak to him. They devoted themselves to the concealment of it. They would not even talk to each other without a code so complex that none of my agents could pierce it. They never met clandestinely, I was sure, which meant they knew I was aware of their betrayal. I watched vids of their meetings. All of their emotion was distilled into bland, controlled words, and I was angered beyond – almost beyond – my control. I wanted him tortured. I wanted her love again. But I knew I had to be above that. They even discussed me as if their interest went beyond a wish for me to die. As if their only mutual interest were my welfare.

I controlled myself. I thought of my father and I smiled at John and thanked him for his diligence.

After that, I shaved and dressed. I spent a while in mental exercise and then I had breakfast. I consumed a brioche, two eggs, waffles, honey, and I washed it down with orange juice and black coffee. All of it was quite tasteless to me, but I knew how important it was to give the illusion of appetite. For some reason, those who spied upon and suspected me relaxed their vigilance if I displayed a hearty appetite.

By this time, I was aware of them more and more, the paid men; their eyes upon me, their hidden hands and illusions of uninterest. But it was to be expected. The stakes were higher and they were cautious. I was still a step ahead of them, though. Or so I thought. I blew smoke at their mirrors. We stepped and dodged. We had our illusions, and we each had no illusions on the matter. We rubbed our eyes and squinted.

But they were accountants and lawyers, and their illusions masked only their claws and the drool that spilled from their mouths, while behind my illusions was something glorious, something beyond their comprehension. Behind mine was a vision.

So I ate my breakfast heartily, and when the last crumb was gone, I looked out the window.

It was a fine morning. The driveway was unusually thronged, but today was no ordinary day. Bob was driving me again. By then I was in an excellent mood and ready for the day ahead. He opened the door for me, and I made conversation.

'Thank you, Bob. No chance of missing a turning this morning, eh?'

He laughed.

'And how are you, this wonderful morning, Bob? You're well? That's good. And your wife, how is Stella?'

'Fine, sir,' he said, closing the car door and moving round the vehicle to the front. I'd taught him to look me in the eye when I was speaking to him. He needed to know he was the equal of any man in the world.

I leant forward and dropped the privacy panel to carry on speaking with him. 'And Troy and Jenna?'

'Both well, sir. May I ask after your wife?'

'She's radiant, thank you for asking, Bob. I left her in the chapel, giving thanks to Our Lord. Her head was bowed in prayer and and the sun was aglow in her hair.'

'Amen,' Bob said.

I closed the panel between us. Bob pulled the car away smoothly, and the outriders and the front and rear vehicles kept even pace with us like planets around their sun. The noise of their sirens and the wash of gravel barely penetrated the vehicle. I activated the wilderness screens to let the serenity flow through me for a few minutes.

For once, though, serenity would not come. In the moment of my success, driving to the Great House, flanked by sirens and lights and dark-windowed dark cars with their dark-glassed drivers, I found myself thinking about my father again. Perhaps it was the wilderness that lay before me that triggered it. I was thinking about my father's admonitions to me about the law, about lawyers and the way all money eventually trickles down into their pockets.

But he wasn't entirely correct to be so cynical. It struck me that the law was a vital, an equalising element in a democracy. A democracy trumpeted its law, and quite rightly, for the law was a fine and perfect thing. For a democracy to work, its law had to be all-embracing and immutable. The law was the ground a citizen walked on. For a man to thrive in a democracy, he had to understand the law. If he could also afford to use it, he was a member of the elite. Almost by definition. Ipso facto. Quod erat demonstrandum.

I wiped away the sudden acrid taste in my mouth, shut down the wilderness screens and briefly exchanged the pure and desolate plains for the crowds of cheering people who lined my route. They felt well served by the law, certainly.

The law was magnificently precise, I was thinking, and at the same time endlessly malleable. You could use it to secure your ground, and you could use it to delay. Like poker. It's a game. You could raise and raise until your opponent ran out of funds, and then you could spread your arms across the table, brush your enemy aside and take the entire pot.

In the car, I raised up the barren plains again. Our Lord's wildernesses always helped me to think. I reflected upon how the laws most immutable and most central to a democracy were the laws applying to the electoral process. With those laws you could in perfect conscience enfranchise and disenfranchise vast swathes of voters, you could adjust electoral boundaries to magnificent effect. Ah, democratic law at its most impartial was a glorious thing.

But my father was, in the end, wrong. Glorious though it was, the law was not the most perfect thing. Even in a democracy, Our Lord was more perfect than the law.

We arrived, and Bob opened the door for me. He looked me in the eye and said, 'Have a good day, Captain.' And then, shyly, at my gentle smile, 'Cap.'

'Thank you, Bob. I will. Our Lord is with me and I certainly will.'

The lawns stretched away into the far distance. I opened my arms wide, relishing the moment. The long curl of white marble stairs rose ahead of me, like a challenge to be met. Metaphor, I once told John, was the marker of the insincere, but this was a special moment and I felt I could indulge my thoughts.

'Captain, it's good to see you.'

'Hello, Pat.' I kept my voice even and shook his hand, then placed my arm around his shoulder before he could do that to me. I was six inches taller than him. Pat Calvert flushed and his composure was momentarily thrown sufficiently that I was able to turn him gently to face the photographers. Cameras flashed all around us, their flicker faintly degrading the cast image of smooth green lawns. Pat looked discomfited by the crowd of reporters. I knew Gus had tried to bar them, but I'd ensured they all had passes long before the formality of the election, and Gus knew he'd have looked a fool to rescind those passes.

So, he sent the Vice President out to greet me. I'd anticipated it. Gus never had any imagination. He was sending me a caution: your role is done, you've had the motorcade, but don't expect too much more. Pat had at least the grace to be mildly embarrassed at being such a message.

We posed briefly. Questions were called out at us. Rather, at me.

'Captain? Over here!'

'Captain? Are you honoured to be the new President's first visitor?'

'What will you be discussing with President Speke, Captain?'

'Do you feel you still have something to offer the President in his new role, Cap?'

Pat half-turned and waved, then moved on up the steps, obviously wanting to pull me into the building and out of sight. I speeded up, as if to go quickly with him, and as he relaxed I turned him round when we were still a few steps from the doors. I stood there with him, being pictured again, this time framed by the great doors behind and above us. His shoulders stiffened but he knew he couldn't do anything except stand there with me and smile and wait.

'It is not I who have something to offer the President,' I said quietly.

I waited for their silence. Then I said it again, with perfect humility. 'It is not I who have something to offer the President. No. I and he are mortal men, and what weight have we, balanced against the hopes and the fears of this world?'

I looked around, from face to face, taking my time, making sure their recording machinery was rolling. Gus's acceptance speech had been largely overshadowed by Cambi's assassination. *This* moment, the Captain and the Vice President standing together on the steps of the Administration building, my arm around his shoulders and these words ringing out; *this* moment would set the standard for Augustus Speke's Administration. In the months to come, this would be what the world remembered.

I made a slow, open-palmed gesture with my free hand, and I said, 'It is not I who have something to offer the President. With the help of Our Lord, it is this Administration that has something to offer the world.'

In the silence, a single, hushed question drifted up the marble stairs to me, from a reporter who happened to be from the national media of Rudi Cambi's nation. It was in the interests of reconciliation that he ask it. He had rehearsed it for days, and now he gave it perfectly. 'And what's that, Captain?'

The hand that I had been holding out, I now raised up.

'With the blessing of Our Lord, and with the help of the new President of the URA, it is a future.'

The reporters checked their monitors, and then, astonishingly, this crew of hardbitten cynics spontaneously began to yell out and cheer me wildly, all but the single vid-operator whose remit was to keep rolling and record them doing it.

'Mr Vice President,' one of them eventually calmed down enough to say, 'Do you have anything to add?'

Pat – and I admired him for this – managed a tight smile as he said, 'I think – I think we would all say amen to that! Thank you, ladies and gentlemen.'

I let him turn me round. He hissed at me, 'Jesus, Cap. Gus is going to kill me for that.'

I murmured back, 'Please don't swear, Pat. Gus'll thank you. Maybe not today, but he will. You have my word on it.'

Pat didn't say anything else as we continued up the last steps. My arm was still around his shoulder, but more companionably now. I said, 'What a night that was, eh? Cheer up! You're not by any chance hung over, are you?'

Behind us the cameras were still flashing, etching the stairs with our crooked shadows.

'I don't drink,' he said, coolly. He didn't even realise I was teasing him. I knew he didn't drink. I knew the precise date he'd had his last drink. I also knew he'd left last night's celebration rally shortly after two a.m. and gone directly to his mistress's apartment where they fucked twice, though he'd only released seed the first time. Though that was better than usual for Pat.

At the huge oak doors, the Guard came to attention and saluted us. Pat acknowledged them with a curt nod. I saluted them back and then said, 'Good morning, Jess, Samuel.' They smiled, held the salute that moment longer.

Details. I saw Pat taking in that lesson.

And then we were in the wide corridors with their thick carpets, and people in every doorway smiling at us. One girl I'd forgotten the name of, and I stopped and told her so, apologetically.

'Why, it's Margaret,' she said. 'It's an honour to meet you, Captain. I've seen—' Pat tried to usher me on, but I resisted long enough to kiss her hand. I was careful to let her observe the Vice President pulling me away. He hadn't learnt at all.

And we were at the State Office. Here the carpets were thicker, the pictures on the walls not merely older but real. The table, the round table that I'd only ever seen on surveillance screens, was a burnished, glowing brown. Around it were twelve men and women, each with their own agenda of business for the first day of the first term of, effectively, the world Presidency of Augustus Speke. And at the top of that agenda, though it wasn't written down, was Reiver Seraph. The Captain.

I. Have. Waited.

The words were so sudden and harsh and loud in my head that I looked around for reaction. I also looked, for some reason, for my father. But of course he wasn't there, and no one else heard the words.

It was true, nevertheless. I had waited so, so very long for this

252

moment. So had they, but not with the same passion or patience, though they would claim so. I had ached with it. I had yearned for it as I still yearned for Mary's love. I had dreamed, planned, prepared, so very long.

The President rose to his feet. He found it difficult to meet my eye. 'Reiver,' he said. Then, 'Captain.' He made a gesture – I saw how prepared it was, not in the least as spontaneous as I was intended to imagine – and they all rose together and applauded me very briefly. Most of them knew a fraction of the truth of the election, of Gus's total indebtedness to me. They knew something of how they had come to be there. I could see it in their eyes. Or the avoidance of their eyes. But that wasn't my problem.

Speke came around the table and took my hand in both of his and held it for a long moment, then dropped it and returned to his seat, gesturing me to take the vacant seat across the table from him. Not at his side. He sat before I did. The signals were as clumsy and tedious as Speke himself, but I made myself be patient.

'Congratulations, Mr President,' I said warmly.

'Thank you, Captain.' He cleared his throat. 'Reiver. Without you—'

I raised my hand to stop him. I didn't want him embarrassed. It was a complex situation facing him. He was not accustomed to working such things through by himself and in front of others.

I empathised strongly with him. It's one of my deepest talents. Someone once said something to the effect that evil is an inability to empathise. I empathise.

At that moment I was inside Speke's mind, thinking along with him at every step. The President, reminded by what his attention had just been drawn to on his media screens – he took his eye off me long enough to glare at Pat – was considering this: that there was only one person more powerful than the democratically elected leader of the Free World, and that was the person who fixed it for him. And he was thinking, if a little blurrily, what the hell do I do about that?

And he was also thinking, what is the Captain going to do about that?

So I needed to solve his dilemma for him.

You might be thinking, why was I worried about it? I was in a strong position.

But consider. If Speke were to have an accident, Pat would take over. The men and women around that table would still remain, or there would be others. It was the nature of a democracy – they had a somewhat undemocratic phrase for it, I recall; the king is dead, long live the king. So, regardless of its leader, the Administration, now it was in place, was set fast. It would have taken me months to correct it.

But if I were to have an accident – and I had no illusions there – there was no one else with my knowledge or vision. Mary and John between them – well, the thought of that, I shan't examine even now – they would have run my Foundation just fine, certainly, but it would not have retained its true purpose any longer. It would merely have calmed the world to oblivion. No. Of necessity, my plans were mine alone, my burden and responsibility. They would die with me, and I was not prepared to die.

Set down this. I am not prepared to die.

So we each had our own dilemma, Gus and I. My strength was that I was prepared to address his, while he had not even considered my own need to compromise.

His options, then. One of his options had to be to honour his debt to me. It was of course the option at the bottom of his list. Gus knew me well enough to imagine that that would be impossible. The amount of time, money, I'd invested in him. If it had been his money, he'd have expected . . . Well, he was a politician. He had a politician's expectations. You scratch my back, I'll scratch yours. An eye for an eye. That sort of thing.

So, now that he was in power and I was apparently redundant, the honourable option would not have been top of his list. But I knew him well enough to know that all his other options left me dead. In such an eventuality, they'd have been dead too, all of them sitting there, even if they didn't believe I could achieve that or might have planned for it, though Our Lord knows why they didn't. Sometimes I despaired at their ability to learn from me. But they thought that, deep down, I was simply a politician like them, with an eye to continuity and personal power. And on both counts they were so very, very wrong.

So I would cut the ground from under Gus's feet, as they used to say. I would ask for my reward, and it would be beyond his wildest dreams. I would leave them needing neither to destroy me nor to remain looking anxiously over their shoulders. Quite the reverse, in fact.

'Mister President,' I said, mildly. 'May I?'

'This is the State Office, Captain,' he said. 'You're among friends here.'

I could feel them tensing around the table. It was like a seance commencing, the room darkening, an apprehension of the unknown. A glorious feeling.

'I have a small request.'

Speke nodded, a little warily. Here it was, he was thinking. His Faustian deal about to be made plain, the fist clenching around his soul.

'I would like to have a few quiet words with you, in private, and then

I should like to return in a few days and be given an opportunity to address both the Houses of the Administration.'

'Both Houses?' He looked at Pat, anxiously.

'That's why I need to speak to you first, Gus. To reassure you that what I want to speak to the Houses about is in all our interests. I would summarise it now, but to do so would not be helpful. The matter is too complex. This is your first day of office, and I'm sure you have other matters to deal with. I would not presume.'

Gus stood up. He knew he had to be decisive, to say yes or no, and to have said no at that point was more of a risk. I let him put his arm around my shoulder and lead me away to his den. He closed the door, we sat, and I said, 'Thank you, Gus, for seeing me like this. I realise that things between us are different, now.'

'Nonsense, Cap,' he interrupted, but I stopped him.

'They are. Whatever is past, is past. But I still have something to say, and it addresses the future. I apologise for the incident with Pat on the steps outside, just before, but believe me, it will reflect well on you. Please hear me out.'

He sat back, a little soothed, and I began.

'I know that one of the subsidiary aims of your new Administration, Mister President, will be to send a colonising detail to another planet capable of sustaining life, should one be found. The Program is almost prepared, and all that remains is to locate such a planet. To that end, as you know, I am contributing in the form of my Eden Project.'

Speke pulled himself together sufficiently to joke, 'You have so many projects, Cap. I lose track.'

'I don't. I mean, I don't lose track.'

'I'm sorry.' He waved an arm vaguely. He was not yet interested. He had no vision, no imagination. He didn't see it. He said, 'Please go on.'

'I've been searching for a planet, too. A haven. Somewhere to make a fresh start for myself and any who want to come with me.'

'I never knew that, Cap.' Now he sensed something.

I held it back. 'No, Mister President.' I put on a mock-conspiratorial voice. 'There are some things that even the President of the URA doesn't know.'

He chuckled. 'Gus, please. We're still friends, aren't we? Call me Gus. You know, I thought your mission, your research was purely a genetic hunt.'

He caught me there, for a moment. I had nearly forgotten that. 'Not purely, Gus. Tracing our gene base back to Our Lord's Son is just one of our tasks.' Publicity. And it brought in a few million a year. 'But if we can't recreate the Original Genome, then we can try to rediscover the time of Genesis, recreate the innocence and beauty, and this time make it work.'

'Ah,' he said, half smiling, but half hooked. 'The Garden of Eden. Is that what you've found at the end of your telescope?'

Now it was my turn to nod. 'No, no, no. Not exactly. But my Foundation, thanks to our congregants and investment teams, is moderately wealthy, as you know, and the Paradise Project has finally been successful.'

'Well, well,' murmured the President of the Free World. 'Well, well.'

'Yes,' I told him. 'With your blessing, I shall present this, and in a great deal more detail, to the two Houses.'

'Nonsense. Unnecessary! You don't need Administration permission for this, Cap. But if it helps, you have my personal guarantee that we won't interfere.'

His eyes were bright. He was imagining that this was all I wanted. He was eager to help, now. I would get away without any checks or safeguards. My departure would be facilitated as much as possible. He wouldn't care if every ship blew up at orbital escape.

'How soon do you think—?' he said.

'There's a little more, Gus. My presentation will contain more than this. What I need from you, what I am requesting now, as a personal favour, is permission to access Environment Department databases.'

'Environment?' He sharpened. 'Why?'

I let him settle a little. 'Everyone is aware of the rumours, Gus. Irreversible climate changes, the world's end accelerating.'

'That's speculation. That's confidential information.'

Of course it was. The idiot. Otherwise I wouldn't have been asking. I could have got it anyway, but the situation was delicate. I wasn't prepared to risk my position being exposed now.

'Believe me, Gus. What I'm intending to propose to the Houses requires me to be fully aware of the situation in respect to the world's future.'

Gus nodded slowly. His eyes glazed over. What was in his mind? This: 'The Captain's located a planet. Well, well. Do I confiscate it, or do I let him keep it?' It was like watching a child count on its fingers. Speke was slowly working it out. Of course he had the answer, but he couldn't believe it was so easy.

I waited while he went over it and went over it again: 'If I confiscate it, I have an enemy greater than I want. If I let him have it, he disappears entirely and never returns. And if there's one planet, there will be others.'

'I want to start again, Mister President.'

'Gus,' he murmured distractedly.

'This is the opportunity I've dreamt of since I was a child. A new start. I shall be the Captain of the Mission. We shall leave the old world behind for a new, raw place. A blank slate. No baggage at all.'

His eyes came into focus again. 'You haven't said precisely why you need the environmental data. I won't have you driving your departure with fear.'

'I don't need fear, Gus. I have hope.'

'I'm not one of your congregants,' he said sharply.

'I'm sorry.'

When I'm excited, I can lack humility, I know. I'd underestimated Gus, and I had to backtrack. I made a contrite face and leaned forward earnestly. 'I can help, Gus. That's what I meant. If I wanted to create fear, I could do it. That's no threat. It's fact. But I have no desire to do that, and it's in no one's interest to do it. Fear will become panic. What we need is to control the situation.'

He tipped his head, agreeing with me reluctantly.

I went on. 'For twenty years the habitable Earth—' yes, that's what it was called, the Earth, '—has been shrinking. We're overheating. Tides and tornados. There are no longer hurricane seasons, just an occasional hurricane-free week. It's not a blip, it's not a natural oscillation and there won't be a natural correction in ten years or a thousand.'

He was nodding along with me, staring at his shoes.

'And it's accelerating, isn't it, Gus? None of EnvironAlliance's proposals will slow it a jot or make a damn of difference. It's too late for compulsory energy-based measures, even if you could pass them. It's too late. We could try to survive by clockwork and candlelight and the world would still end. I'm sure the Environment figures will contain a five per cent landmass habitability calculation, and I'd guess that would be about sixty years away. There has been no solution to the problem because there has been no acknowledgement of it. I won't go into the reasons. They're embarrassing.'

I stopped. Gus said nothing because there was nothing to say.

'But listen, Gus. Listen to me. I think I might be able to present you with a solution. Only to do so, I'll need the data.'

Gus thought a while longer, and then he nodded. 'I'll speak to Cori. Tell her to give you what you need. Don't let me down here, Cap.'

'I won't. Thank you, Mister President,' I said.

He walked me out of his den and back to the State Office. As we appeared, they began shuffling their papers and whispering. Gus quieted them.

'The Captain has good news for us all. But he will present it himself, in a week. Pat, you have some arrangements to make. Cori, walk with us, would you?'

Cori Shiel, frowning, rose to her feet and walked slowly around the table towards us. No one had wanted her job. Environment was, in every sense, a poisoned chalice. She dressed in perfectly tailored black suits, but no amount of power dressing could make her position look good. I was going to change that.

Gus watched her approach us. He murmured, 'Cap, I meant what I said. If you present anything I don't like, next week—'

'By Our Lord, Gus. I've been with you all the way. I'm not deserting you now.'

He held out both hands and smiled. 'Ah, Cori. Just the woman. Cori, I want you to give the Captain access to the Omega database.'

She started to say something, but he made a firm gesture. 'My authority. I believe the Captain will be liaising with you, once he's seen what he needs to see. You're to give him all the help he needs. Are you clear?'

'Ms Shiel,' I said, cutting Gus short, 'I'm here not to be helped, but to help you. I want to give your Department the high profile it needs at this time. The environment has been ignored too long. Gus has put you there because he knows what you are capable of, and he asked me to come onboard as a special adviser to assist you to fulfil your enormous task.' I gave her a complicitous smile and said, 'As you are possibly aware, I have modest resources of my own.' A gamble, but her face relaxed fractionally. 'You and I, we are honoured by the President's trust in us. We must strive to justify that trust.' I stopped in the corridor and shook her hand. She took a moment to realise she ought to turn and leave us, but as she smiled hugely and turned back, I said, 'The Earth awaits us.'

Gus and I walked on. When Cori was out of earshot, he chuckled and said, 'Cap, we shall sorely miss you.'

'Mister President, you flatter me. But I doubt it.'

He coloured a little at that.

'No, no,' I said, as if he'd misunderstood me. 'You'll move on. Greater things.'

Ah, how well I knew him. How little he knew me.

He came all the way out to stand beside me at the great doors, and we were pictured shaking hands and waving together to the reporters, to the world. So quickly did things change.

Bob was there for me at the bottom of the steps, holding the car door open.

'How did your meeting go, sir?'

258

'Very well indeed, thank you, Bob.'

He drove me home. I felt a strange mixture of excitement and apprehension for the next few days. I couldn't settle. When the Omega database terminal arrived, I took it to my secure room and opened it almost nervously. It came with a dedicated light source and instructions for the source to be set up as the only lighting in the room, and for it to be directed at the screen.

Once I had set it up, the screen came up like any screen would. It was quite ordinary, no different from any other CONFIDENTIAL – EYES ONLY Administration document. But then the terminal began carrying out its own security check, forcing me to shut down my own hardware. Only once I had done that would it allow itself to be opened.

As it opened, the light source changed colour, and it continued to flicker irritatingly at the screen so that the text and background, indeed everything on the screen, was constantly reversing. I couldn't accommodate myself to it at all, but I could just about read it. I tried switching the light source off to read by the screen's light alone, but the screen went grey when I tried that, except for an auditory message, 'THIS SCREEN IS AUDIO-VISUAL-CAPTURE-PROOF. PLEASE RESTORE THE DEDICATED ILLUMINATION IF YOU WISH TO CONTINUE.'

There was nothing of any surprise in Omega, as far as I could tell. Giving myself mild eye-strain, I scrolled through to the end and took in its conclusions, but of course there were no recommendations other than for radically increased powers of media censorship and military control of public unrest. Architecture was referred to in passing. The language seemed insufficient. In measured tones it spoke of riots and murder, looting and mass hysteria. It suggested percentage probabilities for these – temperature was the most significant factor, after actual hurricanes and earthquakes and tsunamis.

There were graphs and charts with captions like Wave Height (Pacific Coast) and Wind Strength/Structural Destruction. There were progressions of maps of various types, the earliest dated twenty years back, and carrying forward from there at five-yearly intervals. Temperature maps, relief maps, tremor distribution maps. There were coastal erosion measurements. Living underground was considered an untenable option (ironic, no?) and life undersea impossible.

At extrapolations beyond forty years the graphs and figures were all impossibly qualified, and after fifty-five years they stopped altogether. There were further figures, but that data was of no use to me, even though it was my primary reason for obtaining Omega.

A little depressed, I shut down the Omega terminal and let my thoughts wander. I thought of Mary, and I thought of John, and I thought of my Project. What I had just seen changed nothing.

I reasserted the security of my room and got through to Jake. He was busy on one of his own screens. I waited a few moments, but he was oblivious to the bleating of the call. I raised the volume until he turned round, his eyebrows raised, not in the least put out. I had learned that although his concentration was fierce and total, it was applied quite at random. He might be involved in a ten dollar screengame, or in divining the deepest secret of the universe. You could have no idea, and nor, perhaps, did he.

'Jake,' I said. 'I have the data you need for that program.'

'Hmm?'

'The program.'

'Not with you. Sorry.'

He had no idea what I meant. I couldn't say it, either. I couldn't risk it, even on this line. We didn't use a code because he was likely to forget it. The whole thing often led to these infuriating exchanges. Sometimes I imagined he was having fun with me.

'The program, Jake. Your main project for me. The program.'

'Oh, yes. Do you? Good. Go ahead. Send it.'

'Well, there's a problem. It's accessible via a terminal that won't permit connection to or even the presence of other hardware or software.'

'Other hardware, you mean. The software's irrelevant without the hardware.'

'Jake, just tell me what to do.'

'Okay. Give me a moment. It needs to think there's no hardware, obviously. Depends how it registers hardware. It got any sort of prismatic—'

'Jake.'

'Funny little light pointed at it, makes the screen work?'

'Yes.'

'They mean business. Where did you get this?'

'Someone I know.'

'Same someone who got me this apartment, huh?'

'There's a light. Do you want this data?'

'Right, the light's got the code, not the screen. The screen adjusts to it. That way, without the light, the screen's disabled. The point of the light's to prevent image capture via non-electronic and hence technically non-detectable means. So, we get the code, we can set up a clock-tech hence non-detectable camera with the right compensatory light-register-ing sequence to copy the whole thing.'

'Fine.'

'Except we haven't got the light's code.'

'Jake.'

'Calm, man. Put yourself through on vid and point the light at the screen you're watching me on. Let me see you.'

'Hold on.'

I slid my silicon mask on and checked there was nothing in the room behind me. 'Okay. Ready? Here's the light.'

It didn't go on.

'Don't worry. It'll be triggered from the screen. But the trigger'll be easy to break. Programmers don't do triggers.' He looked down, up, down again. 'I'm just running a little program here.' He went off for a few moments, returned and held up the dull, blank end of a fibreoptic cable. 'Nothing to see, it's infra-red ... and done.'

The light was flashing at the screen now. Happy with himself, Jake said, 'Hey, good thing I'm not fit-susceptible. They oughta warn you not to stare into these things.' He was holding the corded cable in front of his face, gawping at it. I did my best to conceal a momentary impatience with his sense of humour.

'Okay,' he said, 'That's fine. It's an interrupted repeat code. Two steps up from basic. I probably could have done it in my head. Okay. What time is it?'

'Just after eleven.'

'I'll go and see if they've got the right camera in the shop down the road. They probably do. They're pretty well supplied for a deadend town.' He started to stand up.

'At night, Jake. It's eleven at night.'

'Oh.' He frowned, irritated by the information. It was like a line of errant code to him. Someone else's mistake. He touched his lips, thinking what other mistake could also have been made. 'It's not Sunday tomorrow, is it?'

'No. Saturday. Shops will be open.'

'Noodle shop's closed Sunday. I have to remember to order double on Saturday.' He jotted a note for himself, hunched over the paper.

'The camera,' I said.

'I'll set it up for you so the screen triggers the light and the camera together, and that's it. All you do is point the camera in the right direction and run the program again. Okay? If you can get one of your friends to drop by tomorrow they can pick it up.'

'I'll see if anyone's in the area.'

'I'd send the camera back to me to unload, too. The data may not transmit—'

'Don't worry, Jake. I wasn't going to try.'

I disconnected him and peeled the mask away, rubbed my stiff cheeks and then freed my expression with a long, long smile.

It was all going very well.

HAZE

'Who are you?' Her voice was coarse from the arm around her neck. She rubbed her throat.

They said nothing. The man who had come from behind her stood and examined her. The other stooped to check the two lords, then stood up and said, 'Both dead. Now what?'

He looked at her, though Petey knew he wasn't expecting the answer to come from her. She stared straight back at him. He was unkempt, wiry, about her height. He had a dagger in his hand, a small weapon that he held idly. He was ready to use it, she saw. He was waiting to.

'You're not lords,' she said.

The other one smiled. He wasn't armed, though she sensed he was the more dangerous of the two of them.

He was tall and well-built, his shirt tight and creaseless around his shoulders. A thick, braided scar tracked across his left cheek from the bridge of his nose to his ear, and his left eye was cloudy. He didn't look like he could move as quickly or as quietly as he had. Her knife was on the earth between them, closer to her than to him, and he was waiting for her to go for it. The other one's knife was not a throwing blade, so it would be an even race.

Petey knew she was fast, and this man had seen that for himself. How fast was he?

'No,' the tall man said quietly, before she could start to move. He knelt down and picked her knife up by its handle and wiped the blade through a fist of grass before offering it to her. 'Take it,' he said. 'You might be quick enough, but where would it get you?'

As she took the knife, he held on to it a moment longer than necessary, not tightly, and somehow the brief shared grasp was a greeting. She looked into the quiet grey pool of his good eye and sheathed the weapon.

The unkempt man said, 'Well? They're dead, Reed. Now what?' He came forward across the small clear space, kicking the remains of the fire. 'This is not good.'

Petey noticed the firetube in his other hand. 'That's mine,' she said.

'It didn't do you much good, did it? It won't penetrate their robes.' The firetube disappeared under his shirt. 'You're lucky they missed you. Hmm?'

'Yes,' she said.

The tall man, Reed, said, 'He panicked and just grazed her. I saw. She moved well. She'd be good, Crique.'

Petey wondered why Reed had said that. She pulled her shirt to hide where the beam had burnt through it. Crique obviously hadn't noticed the robe beneath it. And what had Reed meant by the other thing – she'd be good for what? Petey was aware of a tension between them, an anxiety and urgency.

Crique said, 'If they'd just killed her—'

'They didn't.' Reed looked at Petey, glancing at her shirt, then at Crique again. 'Think about this. If they come and find the lords dead and her dead too, they'll work out that the lords couldn't have killed her before they died. It'll be worse if we do that.'

Petey felt faint. It *will* be worse. Not, it *would*. Crique wanted to kill her. He'd been actually hoping the lords would kill her. And whatever he was saying now, Reed had wanted that, too.

'It's a mess,' Reed went on. 'Not a disaster. We'll take her back with us. We just have to work out how.'

'We can't risk it.'

'We can't leave her. Think about it.'

Crique swore. 'We can't trust her, either.'

'Near here, the village,' Reed said. 'The villagers could have killed them. This one's killed a squirrel without authorisation. We'll have to make a trail to the village from here. It'll look like these two came across villagers illegally trapping, and the villagers killed them. That'll be enough. We can trust her, Crique. When she knows, she'll understand.'

'But, the village,' Petey whispered. 'They'll all be killed.'

'Be quiet,' Reed said flatly. 'You don't know what you're talking about. You don't know the alternative.'

Petey looked from one to the other. They were blaming her for this situation, and they were intending to let an entire innocent village be destroyed, their own village, to conceal their and Petey's presence. It made no sense. 'No,' she said, trying to keep her voice level. 'You can't do that. They'll kill everyone. Your families. Everyone there. Don't you realise that?' They were staring at her as if she had no idea what she was talking about.

Crique looked puzzled for a moment longer. Then his face cleared. 'Oh. You think that's our village! You think we live there. Hear that, Reed?'

'You don't understand,' Reed cut in. He spoke slowly, as if to a child. 'We can't be found. The two of us. Not under any circumstances.'

'But there might be a hundred people—'

'No.'

Crique said mildly, 'You still think we can trust her?'

Reed gave Petey a look that threw the question straight at her. There was no answer she could give him. Crique was the one she had to get to, and she said to him, 'What if they found the lords here, but killed by animals?'

Crique pretended not to have heard. Reed hesitated, then said, 'How?'

'A pack of boars come here at night. They scented me. I was sleeping up that tree, but it's been weakened by the boars' charging. With the weight of two lords in the tree, it could fall. They nearly had me down last night.'

Reed looked at the tree, then went over and put his hands to the trunk, leaned into it and pushed hard. Petey could see the muscles of his arms tensing under his shirt. Above him, branches swayed and high leaves crackled 'It'll go,' he said, straightening, and looked at Crique.

'We'd have to wait here a night,' Crique said.

'The AngWat won't start worrying yet. Lords don't use their comms this far away from the temple. I don't think they work.'

'You don't think.' Crique smirked so plainly that Petey wondered why it could be so funny for Reed to say that.

Ignoring Crique's expression, Reed said, 'I'm sure. We can wait a night here. Boars would leave nothing but bones and the robes. Her way works better, too. It looks natural. It makes an end to it right here. Nothing left to worry about.'

Petey tried to work out which of them was in charge. She couldn't tell if they were trying to assert themselves by arguing like this or simply bickering.

'That's not true.' Crique looked at Petey. 'It leaves her.'

Now Reed and Crique were both staring at her. 'You said you'd take me with you,' she said. She couldn't make any sense of this at all. Where had they come from, if the village nearby wasn't theirs? What were they doing here? 'I don't understand.' She tried to be calm. It seemed important to be calm, like Crique and Reed. They were thinking this situation through, and it was clear that they would only listen to her if she were thinking like them. Even though she didn't yet know why they were thinking like this.

265

Crique said, 'If the boars killed them all? What about that?'

Petey's heart thudded. He didn't care at all about her. What happened to her didn't matter. It was simply what was necessary to protect himself. It was what she would have done herself, when she was back in her own village. She knew she wanted to live, wanted it desperately. She thought of Marten and what she had seen since she had lost him, and lost her husband. She wanted to live and to do something about it all. But she couldn't speak.

'Maybe,' Reed said. 'It would look suspicious, though. A tableau. A neat scene, too perfect.'

What had he said? Tableau? Petey didn't understand the word. And the way he spoke was different from the way Crique talked, it struck her. Not greatly different, but even so, it was different. She noticed Crique had also reacted to Reed's odd word, and that Reed himself realised he'd said the wrong thing and corrected himself.

Reed, though, was trying to protect her, perhaps. Or perhaps just prepared to think further, to consider other options. Reed was her best chance, that was for sure. And she had to be calm. She had to show Crique that the best way to protect himself was to let her live. 'The boars,' she said. 'What if the lords were killed by boars just here, and there was evidence of my body being dragged away?'

No, that wouldn't do, and she could see Reed and Crique knew that. Why would boars eat them here but take her away? She said, 'What about my trail leaving here, and blood along the trail. Proof I'd been injured but escaped.'

Reed said, 'They'll follow the trail. Then what? There'd be nothing at the end of it. You couldn't just vanish.'

'There's the river nearby,' Crique said, to Petey's surprise. 'We'd need a lot of blood on the trail leading there, though. Enough to indicate she was near enough to death to drown. You want to do that, woman, to save your life? That's a lot of blood.' He brought up his knife. 'You want me to—?'

'There's a way round that. We've got the rest of the day,' Petey said. 'We can use one of the lords' bodies for blood.' She wasn't sure where this hardness inside her was coming from, but it didn't matter. She had a new determination and a new certainty, and she was thinking clearly. She made a gesture towards the corpses and said, 'If they're not going to find the bodies sooner than a day, we don't even need blood. We can drop a trail of flesh. Carrion eaters will leave nothing except their own traces, but that will be enough of a trail.'

Crique looked undecided, but Reed said, 'Yes.' He went to the nearest corpse and squatted at its side, then pulled up the robe's sleeve and used

266

his knife to slice a long strip of flesh from the forearm. He laid the strip on the grass, turned the arm and sliced again, and when the forearm was finished, he began on the upper arm.

It surprised Petey that she could watch Reed do such a thing. She noticed Crique looking at her, and met his gaze evenly. She said, 'We need the tree to come down. We have to pull it.'

Crique hesitated, and she wondered whether she had been too firm with him. She wasn't certain that Reed's acceptance had been enough. If she'd misread the relationship between them, it could have been the wrong thing altogether.

Crique looked at Reed, who had stripped both arms to the bone, and had a small pile of meat.

'That's enough,' Crique said. 'I'll leave the trail. You and the woman can pull the tree down. We'll have to wait for the boars, kill a few of them. The lords wouldn't die without taking a few of them.'

Reed said nothing. Crique came up to Petey and put a hand to her shoulder and held her, and brought up the knife in his other hand, holding it to her neck. Petey kept still, watching Reed straighten behind Crique.

Crique slit Petey's shirt and ripped the sleeve away. He sheathed the knife and turned away from Petey, who found herself breathing fast. Crique knotted the cuff of the sleeve and started to drop the cut flesh into the bag he'd made from the sleeve. When he was done, he looked at Petey. She cut away the other sleeve and threw it to Crique, who snatched it out of the air. Then she cut her trousers. Her knees were trembling. She said, 'You can leave rags—'

'I know how to leave a trail, woman,' Crique said. 'And I know how not to.'

'Petey. My name is Petey.' She looked at Reed the second time she said her name, and said it more softly.

As Crique walked away and disappeared into the trees, Reed murmured, 'Petey.' He went to the tree and walked around it, kicking at what was left of the droproots. 'Two nights,' he said. 'They'd have had you down tonight. They've done most of the work. You were lucky.'

'Not that lucky.'

Reed got his knife out and began to hack roughly at one of the remaining roots. 'If we break this one and those two there—' pointing with the knife, '—we should be able to push it over, that way. Don't cut them cleanly and roughen your blademarks. They won't check too closely, but they'll look.'

Petey knelt down and started working at a root. The tree shivered above her. It shivered above her and Reed together. For a while they worked in silence, half sawing, half rubbing through the wrist-thick droproots. Reed was first to break through, and he yanked down on the freed stem. The tree shuddered faintly, Petey feeling it through her own grip. He moved a few paces nearer her to start on the final root. It was within arm's reach of her, and she could hear him breathing at her side as he worked. She felt as if he were touching her through the tree. Her skin tingled.

Then she was through her root, and she stood up and stretched her shoulders and arms, watching him work. It didn't seem to bother Reed at all to have her standing behind him. The muscles of his neck rippled with movement and shone with sweat.

'Done,' he said, using the severed root to pull himself up. 'See how they work together, the boars,' he said, pointing. 'All of them on one side. They break all the roots this side, and they can charge the weakened central trunk and easily topple it the other way. Cooperation. Boars.'

'Yes,' she said. She set one of the thick roots swinging. 'Shall we work together, then?'

He leaned on the trunk. It swayed wildly, but didn't yield, and when Reed's legs buckled, the tree came back upright. 'I think so,' he said. 'But we can't push together. There isn't room. What do you suggest?'

Petey yanked on a root descending from a high branch. 'We could pull a couple of these over to the other side and haul on them from there. We'd get better leverage, and there'd be both of us. We could pull the tree down. As long as we draped the roots back carefully, no one would be able to tell the tree hadn't been pushed over by boars.'

He stood with her and they hauled together on the damaged tree, and it still drove the sweat out of them from just after midday until it was almost dusk. The tree groaned and complained, but it didn't buckle. And then it did, the droproots on their side of the trunk slackening and at last going limp as the tree tilted and fell. It only fell part of the way before coming to rest against other trees, but it was enough.

'They would have fallen out of the tree here,' Reed said, exhaustedly wiping his face with his sleeve.

'I think so,' said Crique.

Reed turned round and said, 'How long have you been standing there?'

'A while. I kept watch. You clearly weren't.' He yawned. 'I didn't want to interrupt your rhythm.' He swung a full drinking skin from his shoulder and threw it to Reed, who lifted it and drank hard. Petey watched his throat-knuckle bob as he swallowed, water leaking at his lips and soaking his shirt. He passed the skin to Petey, and she drank the rest of it quickly and tossed the limp skin back to Crique. 'Thanks,' she said shortly.

They waited until it was dark, and then the boars snuffled into sight, lumbering heavily towards the corpses of the lords. Reed and Crique killed a few of the pack with the lords' firetubes and then watched the remaining animals start to eat the lords' corpses. Even the boars' teeth couldn't tear the orange robes, but they pushed their snouts underneath to snuffle and chew inside effectively enough. It didn't matter, Petey knew. What they couldn't get to, the smaller animals would mostly finish off by morning. Crique and Reed tossed the firetubes at the boars, and they chewed a little at them before ignoring them.

The boars were gone by sunrise. They left behind them a pair of orange robes spattered with blood, but the blood sat in globules on the clean cloth, unabsorbed. There were scattered, gnawed bones and there were four dead boars, the bodies untouched by the rest of the pack, since there had been food available without the need for cannibalism.

Crique went and cut meat from one of the animals, wrapped it in a skin and tied it across his back, and Reed did the same. It bothered her for a moment to see the men doing this, until she realised her anxiety was because such scavenging was forbidden by the lords.

This was a new time for her. So much had changed. The lords were no longer the lords. Petey looked at the boar meat and said, 'I haven't anything to carry it in,' keeping her eyes from Reed as she said it. He didn't react, and again she wondered why he was protecting her stolen robe from Crique.

'Reed and I can carry enough for the three of us,' Crique said.

'Where are we going?' The idea of an actual destination hadn't crossed her mind. She knew they weren't from the village closest to here, but she hadn't considered that Reed and Crique had to come from somewhere, that they were, like everyone else, ultimately subject to the control of the lords.

But not completely subject, she reminded herself. Somehow they were able to leave their village without permission and roam without restriction.

'I can't go to any village,' she said.

Both men turned round. Reed said, 'This is the free village. We have no lords.'

Crique said, 'It's a long walk. We'd better get moving.'

They walked for the entire day, Crique in front of Petey and Reed behind her. It crossed her mind that they were constraining her as much as protecting her, but there was nowhere else for her to go. She did feel safe with them, and it was a relief not to be constantly on her guard. She kept Crique just in sight, stopping when he stopped, moving when he moved, and putting her feet in his footsteps where she saw them, although he moved as lightly as a bird. Once or twice they crossed paths, but otherwise they kept to areas of light forest, where they were well concealed, but it was still possible to move quickly and without leaving traces.

At dusk they stopped and Reed took charcoal from his pack and unfolded a metal brazier, Petey wondering how he'd got it, while Crique collected stones to rest it on, clear of the ground. Petey started to pick up dry strips of bark and twigs from the forest floor, but Reed told her to leave them. 'Bark makes smoke,' he said, and she felt stupid. She thought of the fire she'd made, that had brought the lords and Crique and Reed to her.

They ate quickly and in silence, and then looked for sleep trees. They found two easily, but neither looked strong enough to support more than one sleeper. Most of the trees in this part of the forest had great smooth buttress-roots and couldn't be climbed, and Crique finally found a third stilt-rooted sleep tree some way from the other two. Watching him climb it, Petey thought of Loren. Reed asked her why she was crying, but she just shook her head.

After the long day's walk and the previous night spent with the boars, she slid quickly into sleep. She woke twice in the night. The first time she imagined she heard a child singing and swinging a machete, the rhythm of the song and the beat of the thud of the blade through bone. The second time, there was no dream, and she looked through the branches to see Reed in his tree, sprawled awkwardly but tied safe and deep in sleep. It struck her that she could drop down from the tree now and leave them. It wasn't that she didn't trust them, but there was something very odd about the way they behaved with each other. At one moment they would be like friends, and at another like . . . not enemies, but strangers. She couldn't tell whether her presence was causing it.

She watched Reed for a while, deciding that she did trust him, at least, and slipped back to a dreamless sleep.

The next day they walked again. At about midday – she thought in terms of time now, not distance – the ground started to climb. Petey had never known the forest not to be almost completely level. Her feet began to ache, and her legs hurt. Today Reed was ahead of her, and he kept an even, swift pace. She forced herself to keep up with him.

There were fleshflies, and she heard the sound of water. This water was harsh to listen to, and she imagined it bursting down the slope. In the forest below, the forest she knew, rivers and streams whispered and gently meandered.

The flies clustered in swarms at her head and stung her cheeks and bare arms. When they came near her eyes, she flailed at them and wanted to yell and run. She couldn't control herself. It was the memory of the child, she knew, the fly crawling across its wide, unblinking eye, but knowing the cause didn't help. Crique caught her up and shook calmness back into her, then rubbed a yeasty paste on her face and arms, and after that the flies ignored her. She asked him if they could rest, but he said no. Hoping for sympathy, she looked ahead to Reed, who was waiting in the shade of a tree. He nodded briskly at Crique, then turned and went on.

The incline faded and reasserted itself. Her breath grew short, and she was gasping. It wasn't exhaustion. She was fit enough to go on for hours. The air felt thin and empty. The robe chafed her belly, but she couldn't do anything about it.

They were high, now, Petey knew, but still mountains rose at their sides and they were walking in shadow. Towards nightfall, there was a small cave in the hillside that Reed and Crique seemed to know, and they spent the night there, the two men taking turns on watch, with Petey sleeping soundly until dawn.

The next day, the path grew narrow and began to climb even more sharply. There were more birds to hear, birdsong she didn't recognise, and occasionally a croak or growl she'd never heard before, and unfamiliar bushes and trees. And there was an odd, musty tang to the air.

Towards late afternoon she trod on a sharp thorn that penetrated her leather boot. The pain was so sudden and intense that it took the air from her lungs in such a gasp that she couldn't make a sound. Heaving for breath, she sat down and shook her foot, but the pain was spreading up her leg. She sat down and tried to twist her boot off, but her hands were shaking too much. Tears were streaming from her eyes, and she couldn't see.

Crique had been behind her. She heard him running towards her, and he was pulling at her boot. She leaned back, bracing herself as the boot came off. She blinked and wiped her eyes dry. Although the pain was still there, she made the tears stop. It was one thing she could always do, stop the tears.

'Have you got it?' she asked Crique.

'You've been stung. Don't look. Let me—'

She pulled her foot out of his hands, though, bending her leg to see the thorn, wanting to pull it free herself. Except that she saw it wasn't a thorn. It was the head of an insect.

The body must have come away with her boot, but the sleek dark head with two wide green eyes was stuck to the ball of her foot. The head was the size of her thumb. It rocked slightly and seemed to be rippling. She wanted to rip it away, but the moment in which she might have done that, instinctively and without thought, was gone, and she couldn't bring herself to touch it. The eyes were gleaming at her.

Petey stared at it, a scream lodged solidly in her throat. The head wasn't rippling at all. It was pumping. The skin of her foot where the head squatted was turning purple.

She straightened her leg quickly, not to see any more, and the scream released itself. There was no strength in it, though. There was no air in her. Crique easily slapped her hands away and pushed her flat. He said, 'Keep still,' and then yelled, 'Reed! Here, quickly!'

Petey tried to lift her head, but it was too heavy. She heard Reed's feet pounding towards her, and then the pain and the forest closed in and swallowed her whole.

After that, consciousness came and went. She was floating, and she was as heavy as a mountain. There was a mountain on her chest, driving life from her, and the water on which she was floating was drowning her. When she could breathe, she wanted to stop breathing for ever. She woke up sharply and there was no pain at all from her foot, and she sat up and saw that it had been cut off above her knee. The stump was bandaged with cloth, and the cloth was red and clotted. She screamed, and then she noticed a man there in the room with her, frowning and coming out of a chair towards the bed. She tried to say, 'My leg's gone,' but before the words came, her body had drifted back under the mountain again, and her head had slid beneath the waves.

When she came up again, there was no pain. She sat up to look at her leg, but a tented blanket reached from her waist to the end of the bed, and everything beneath it was hidden. She had no sensation below her waist. She touched her abdomen, running her hand from the base of her ribs down past her navel. Below the navel there was no feeling at all. Panicking, struggling to pull herself up on an elbow, she reached down under the blanket as far as she could, but with no muscle control below her waist, she couldn't reach any further than the tops of her legs. Prodding her thigh was like pushing her fingers into a trunk of sodden wood. The deadness of it terrified her and she tried desperately to move, to pull it with her, but she was shackled to her lower body as if to cold, dead rock. The weight of it was astonishing. She fell back and stared helplessly at the slatted wooden roof of the hut, and then in her despair it hit her that she might have been dead, but wasn't.

With this thought she fell asleep again, and in her sleep the mountains sitting on her turned to hills and then to calm and empty plains, and the seas drowning her ebbed away, and she looked around.

'How do you feel?' said the man she'd seen in her dream. He was old, and she knew he was a healer by the way he held her wrist, his soft fingertip resting on her bloodbeat. His knuckles and the joints of his fingers were swollen by age, but his touch was still a child's. 'You were lucky,' he murmured, looking at her forehead, not into her eyes.

'But my leg,' she said.

'You were lucky,' he insisted calmly, and this time he held her eyes with his gaze. There was cloud in the white of his eyes, but the irises were bright blue and vibrant, and she felt comforted.

She was too tired to say any more. His palm, cold as night, was on her forehead now.

'You could well have died,' he said eventually. 'You're strong.'

The hut was large, and she felt it moving, creaking. She could even hear it moan. The roof was moving too, its slats parting and contracting. She felt dizzy. The angles of the walls were changing. There were animal noises below her, as if she were in a tree. She thought of the boars.

'It's all right. Stay there. Drink this.'

She drank. It tasted sweet on her tongue and bitter as she swallowed. She slept.

There was mist in the hut, faint tendrils of it entering through the shifting gaps in the walls. Petey couldn't tell if the mist was real or not. The tendrils held their shape for a long time before fading away.

There was still no feeling below her waist, and the hut was definitely moving faintly, and there were animals, pigs, underneath it. She knew that. By tilting at the waist, she found she could look down at the floor. She could see the wide flat boards grinding against each other, and here and there, there and gone, were cracks through which she could make out the pigs tethered to stakes. She straightened herself on the bed again, relieved that the movement wasn't from dream or fever. The hut was on stilts, and the wind was taking it like the canopy of a great tree.

The healer was there to feed her, but he wouldn't talk much. He prodded a sharp twig into her stomach and asked if she could feel it, and moved it down when she said she could.

'I can feel as far as my cleft,' she told him. 'You don't need to check.'

He took the twig away. 'If you don't trust me, I'll go.' He looked at her evenly.

She nodded. 'All right.'

'Good. As the numbness wears off, you'll have pain, but it should go. You'll be able to move, too, but you'll be weak.'

'My leg,' she said, remembering the stump.

'I think I told you, you were lucky.'

'I know. I'm grateful. I'm alive.'

He put his hands on the bed and said, 'What is it? We got to you in time to dig the eggs out. If we hadn't managed to do that, even taking your leg off would have made no difference. They—'

'I'm grateful.'

He shook his head and left. The hut trembled as the wooden door slammed behind him. The huff of air shivering through the hut was visible, and Petey noticed for the first time that there was a small fire in the corner, barely a pile of embers, and a chimney above it.

The healer came back and woke Petey up. She turned to see him and it wasn't the healer at all.

'Reed,' she said, and started to cry.

He took her hand and held it in one of his and stroked it with the other. She looked at him and there was something new in his face. There had been concern before, in his pale grey eye and the creasing of his forehead, but this was a concern for her that came from deep. She hardly noticed his scar and the clouded eye.

'My leg,' she said.

'What about it?'

'It's gone. They cut it off.'

He held her hand tightly. 'Haven't you seen?'

She shook her head.

He stood up and pulled away the blanket. 'There,' he said.

Petey spent a long time looking. Then she sighed, and whispered to Reed, 'It's still there.'

'Of course it's there. DeSa told you it was, didn't he?'

She put her head back and breathed out. 'Yes. Maybe he did.' She smiled. She smelt Reed's sweat as he bent to touch her cheek with his lips, and then he was gone. The hut shook, and she felt dizzy and happy.

DeSa, the healer, was there again. She asked him what had happened to her legs, why they were dead.

'The insect that laid its eggs in your foot was a parasite. You were lucky it got caught in your shoe and decapitated. Otherwise you would have known nothing until the eggs under your skin, all over your body, started to swell. By then, there's nothing to do. You'd lose weight as the insects sucked you out, and then they'd be ready to hatch.' He looked speculatively at Petey. 'The pain of that's like fire. At that point, animals throw themselves into rivers and drown, and the insects swim away to breed. But we'd have had to kill you. The pain's beyond bearing. Men and women die or go insane. So you were very lucky.'

'But why are my legs dead?'

'I removed the proboscis intact from your foot. It's a fine needle, and since the insect started to inject the eggs without numbing you, I was able to use the sac of anaesthetic from its thorax. I injected it into your spine. I told you, "This will hurt a lot, but then it will be easier." Do you remember that?' He examined her with interest.

'No.' Then she said, 'Yes. I do,' the memory rising with DeSa's question, and she shivered. There must have been several of them holding her down as she screamed in pain, forcing her to be still as someone – DeSa – plunged something into her back. She remembered the astonishing pain arching her body, and DeSa's voice swearing. And then a warm thick river of numbness running down and flooding her legs, and then nothing but the dreams.

'The memory of pain is a strange thing,' DeSa said. 'It will go, but it will change you. It takes us all differently.'

She looked at her legs. She felt oddly exhilarated as DeSa began to poke the skin of her thighs. He reached her knee before deadness blunted the feeling.

'Another few days and you'll be walking again. Your foot will be sore for a long time, though. We had to dig around to catch the eggs. They'd started to move already. You'll hobble for some time.'

His tone had changed a little, and Petey watched him as he packed away his bag of medicines.

'DeSa,' she said, bringing herself up on her elbows. 'What was your pain?'

He almost smiled. 'Not physical, though there was that, too. You'll find a lot of people here like me, Petey.' He fell quiet, and for a moment his eyes lost their focus.

Petey realised this was the first time he'd called her by her name. She waited a moment, until DeSa made a small tutting sound with his teeth, and blinked, and then she said, 'Tell me about here, will you? Where are we?'

'This is Nepenth. We're hidden away, safe from the lords.' In exhaustion he rubbed a bony shoulder and smiled gently at her and then he moved to the door. She thought he was leaving, but he opened the door wide and held it so that she could see outside.

'Look,' he said.

There was nothing outside but whiteness, and then faintly, through it, the pale shadows of trees fading and shifting. She thought it must be a curtain of thin cloth, perhaps to block insects, but DeSa put his hand into it and it vanished utterly. Petey gasped, thinking of her leg, until DeSa pulled his arm back and retrieved his hand from the whiteness.

'The Haze,' he said. 'Its strength comes and goes, but it's always here

275

with us. The lords' communicators – I expect you call them beetles – don't work in the Haze. They don't know we exist. They don't ever come up here. As you see, it's thick today.'

The Haze was solidly entering the hut now, and DeSa closed the door on it. The cloud that had come inside moved into the room and hung there, congealing. DeSa went to the fire and fanned the warmth and smoke towards the small cloud with his arms. The Haze gradually vanished.

'Dry heat,' DeSa said. 'That disperses it for a while. Nothing else.' He sat down beside Petey. 'Nepenth is fertile, though. Things grow here. Plants, trees, animals all thrive up in the Haze. Parasites too, of course.' He smiled tentatively, and she smiled with him.

'Everyone knows you're here, and that you're from the forest below. Some will talk to you, some won't. You'll remind them of where they came from, of what they've lost. You'll give them good memories and bad. You'll have to be prepared for that.'

'How many people live here?'

'A few hundred. Nepenth is a sprawl. When the Haze is thick, you can get lost easily. When you leave the hut the first time, make sure you know your way back with your eyes closed before you head out further. It takes most firstcomers months to get accustomed to the place.' He looked around the hut. 'This will be yours. The woman who lived here died a week ago.'

It suddenly dawned on Petey that she'd be living here for good, now. That she wouldn't be returning to the forest at all. The thought made her uncomfortable. Now, the possibility of ever seeing Marten again was really gone.

She forced herself away from that. 'What happened to her?'

'An animal took her. She was dragged away in the middle of the village, in the middle of the day. Most of us heard it, but it was quick and no one saw anything. Animals use the Haze like a cloak. They understand it. They sense its borders. As I told you, everything thrives here. We found her bones a day later. Carry a knife and listen always.'

She asked him about Crique and Reed.

'They're our scouts. They keep us safe.'

'Are they friends?'

'Friends?' He seemed about to say something, but stopped himself. 'You'll have to ask them.'

And DeSa left her. With the opening and closing of the door, a small cloud of Haze came into the hut to lie in the air where he had been, like an unclear memory, fading slowly in the hut's warmth.

The next day, Crique came to see her. Petey wondered whether DeSa had said something to him. Just as Reed had looked at her differently here in Nepenth, Crique did too, though his expression was harder to understand.

'We'll take a walk,' he said. 'DeSa says you're well enough.' He helped her from her bed, his arm firm. He turned his back while she dressed. The unfamiliar clothes hung well on her. A dead woman's clothes, she thought.

'He was worried about you, for a while,' Crique said while she finished dressing, speaking in a way that made Petey wonder if it was Crique's worry too. 'Are you ready? I'll show you Nepenth.'

She stood with him at the door and stared down at the ground, at the thick scrub, the trees and the confusion of tracks and muddy paths leading past the hut and away. Her foot wouldn't bear her weight.

Hesitating at the door, she said, 'The Haze isn't as dense today.'

'No. It comes and goes. It could close in and separate us in a moment. You can't ever relax here. Appreciate this while you can. Come on.'

He went in front of her down the ladder, bracing her waist as she descended. On the ground, he gave her a stick to take the weight of her bad foot. The pigs squealed at her and pulled at their ropes. She hobbled awkwardly after Crique.

He pointed to a hut and said, 'This is mine.' And switched his arm across the path to indicate another facing it directly. 'And here's Reed's. I live with my wife, Yameen. Reed's alone.'

That was almost all Crique said. Petey asked him if he had children and he said, 'Concentrate on remembering the paths underfoot, the distances in paces between their forks and twists. When they rise and tilt. Which paths are earth and which cobble. That's more important here than anything else. Once you know that, you can start to look around yourself properly.'

Only later, alone in her hut, did Petey start thinking about Crique with a wife and Reed without anyone, and why that might be, and about Crique and Reed looking out of their huts at each other through the Haze.

Over the next weeks Crique walked with Petey almost every day. It was only when she discarded the stick that Crique smiled for the first time. He never started a conversation, and wasn't good at maintaining one if she did.

'Have I done something to upset you?' she once asked him.

'No. Why?'

'You hardly say a word.'

The Haze came and went around them.

'What is there to say?'

Her breath came more easily as she grew fitter and stronger, and her foot healed. When, occasionally, the Haze almost fully lifted, the height of the mountains around her took her breath away.

As her confidence grew, she started to explore the village alone. Nepenth was ghostly and vague, its houses and streets and people looming and fading, and Petey found she had a constant low headache. She never saw Crique or Reed in the winding streets, and no one talked to her, although they all stared.

She met Yameen, the woman abruptly appearing in the doorway of her hut as Petey was walking past. Petey stopped and waved up at her and said, 'Are you Crique's wife? I'm Petey.'

Yameen peered down at her. She was tall and slender with thin features but astonishingly wide eyes. Brushing a hank of black hair behind her ear, she said, 'Yes. I've seen you.'

'I don't know anyone here except Crique and Reed,' Petey said.

'You know DeSa.' The woman didn't move. Petey nodded, wondering whether Yameen distrusted her or was simply as taciturn as her husband, or whether this was the way of Nepenth, and that everyone here lived cocooned. She was about to move on when Yameen said, 'Come up.' And the woman turned and let the door close, leaving Petey to climb the ladder and follow her inside.

There were skins on the walls, and it was warm inside. The fire was stronger than the fire in Petey's hut could ever be made, and the air inside was extraordinarily clear.

'Sit down,' Yameen said, but Petey was already moving to the small cot beside the fire.

'You have a baby,' Petey said in surprise. 'Oh, he's beautiful.' She looked at Yameen, who was at her side, and added, 'Crique never told me.'

Yameen was bringing the infant out of the cot in its warm stitchings, and humming to it as if Petey wasn't there. Petey wasn't sure what to do. She said, 'How old is he?'

'Two months,' she murmured. 'His name's Artis.'

'Does anyone help you with him?'

Yameen was keening gently to her son, rocking him in her arms, and Petey felt she wouldn't notice if Petey walked out of the hut.

'I don't understand Nepenth,' she said.

Yameen didn't look away from the child. 'It takes time.'

'Crique doesn't say much.'

'There's nothing he can do.'

She stopped, and Petey waited, seeing her struggling to say something more.

'Artis is the youngest child here.' She looked up at Petey with her great eyes, in the clarity of the hut, and said, 'The oldest is just eight years.'

Petey looked at Artis, then at Yameen, and said, 'Nepenth has been here a long time, hasn't it? I'd have thought there would be more children.'

'DeSa says it's their lungs. All the children born here die here.' She made a vague gesture. 'I keep the fire going against the Haze, but I can't keep Artis in the hut forever. What life would that be? What would he learn?'

Petey looked at the child cradled in Yameen's arms, and had nothing to say. She stood up and went across to the woman and touched her cheek, and then the baby's, and then she left.

HAVEN

Marten opened his eyes and gave up trying to sleep. He hadn't slept properly since arriving on this dark cavern of a planet. Every night was the same. He dreamt unpleasantly and woke up tired.

He pulled the thin pillow over his head, but that didn't help, and eventually he sat up and looked along the dormitory. The nitelites gave it a ghostly glow. Everyone else was sleeping peacefully, but he couldn't. Sometimes he wished he wasn't allergic to any of the drugs. He listened to the subdued roar of the rockets through the rock and imagined their long shadows as they rose away into the night between the worlds.

This time, it was the girl invading his thoughts. He turned over and squeezed his eyes closed, but she wouldn't leave him.

He'd first seen her walking down blue5 with the huge bird draped over her shoulders, and the sight of it had taken him instantly back home. Without thinking, he'd switched direction to follow her, and watched them cook the bird over Zelda's illegal fire. Zelda had already been pointed out to him by Corven, and Marten was curious that the girl was friendly with her.

He couldn't work out why the girl had offered him meat from the bird. He shouldn't have taken it, and he certainly should have told Corven about it later.

The dormitory was cold, and he felt stiff. He still couldn't sleep. A few people were snoring. It sounded like the cries of animals in a field. Usually it was soothing, the comfort of the presence of others, but not now. The night made him anxious. Corven made him anxious, too.

Marten sat up and sipped at the glass of water by the bed. His bed. It sounded odd, the possessive used like that.

That evening had been the real start of it. Reporting it to Corven. He ran through it again in his head, searching the conversation for the start of the trouble. It still might be a test. Marten had to be careful. Trust was dangerous. Maybe he should report it to Corven's superior.

'Zelda,' Corven had said. 'Did you say she was there, when the girl tried to talk to you? Was she?'

'Yes.'

'Zelda, Zelda, yes. She's close to this girl?'

'It seemed so.'

'Good. And, maybe . . .' He opened his mouth, hesitated, and said, 'That was quite an event last night, eh?'

That had been it. Marten thought Corven had been about to say something altogether different, but he'd shifted tone. He was asking Marten's opinion. He was confiding in him.

The clock high on the wall read four-thirty. Marten felt awake and tired at the same time.

Corven's face had been suddenly alert. Marten had seen him as someone isolated, eager to talk openly. An instant had passed, like a chasm opening. Marten could have closed himself away as usual, but for some reason he hadn't.

'It was incredible. I watched it from a turret. The girl was up there too, and Zelda.'

'Were they?' Corven smiled. 'Anything else, Marten?'

'No.'

Instinct had stopped him there. He didn't tell Corven that he'd sat for hours in the shadows of the dying fire in the long, hollow coredor, thinking of village nights and the shadows of trees, and a father and a mother. He didn't say that seeing them in the turret wasn't a coincidence. He'd probably already said too much.

'Nothing could have survived that, eh?'

Marten had shaken his head, but been curious. The idea of nothing surviving obviously concerned Corven.

'No,' Corven said. 'It's all over, anyway. The *khuks* have cleaned the slate. No loose friends, as the *khuks* say.'

'Yes,' Marten said, not understanding. *Khuks*, he thought, troubled by the word.

It was nearly five, now. Marten yawned. It was always the same. He was ready for sleep when it was too late.

A few people were starting to stir and roll out of bed. The showers were starting to hiss.

Marten knew Corven approved of him. He'd told Marten on his first day that he was considered a risk. He clearly liked the idea of that. Why?

'Watch the girl, then. Watch Zelda too. You're doing well, Marten.' He worked his lower lip with his teeth. 'She suspects Fact, and that's fine. It might even be helpful.' He clapped a hand on Marten's shoulder.

'I knew you'd be an asset here. No one else here would have done what you've done, standing so close, almost touching the *khuks*.'

It was that. It was the way Corven said *khuks*. It shot him back to the AngWat.

'Marten?'

'I'm all right.' But he was holding the hem of a lord's robe and seeing the mother recede as he was dragged down the causeway towards the AngWat.

He shivered. It was almost time for him to get up. He had an allocation of eight minutes for a shower at five twenty-three. He closed his eyes again, remembering, wondering if he was misjudging Corven.

'The girl will be taken into Fact. At some point, Zelda will try to use her. Gild knows about Mexi already. He'll be her guide. You'll work with him. One more thing, Marten.'

'Yes?'

This was it. This was where it had become really dangerous. Had Corven been testing him all along, or was Corven the one taking the risk. If Marten guessed wrong, one of them would be dead. Maybe both of them. Confession had to be swift.

Corven had said, 'I was told you're sometimes uncomfortable with what needs to be done.'

Marten had heard this before, always followed by warnings and threats. He didn't react.

Corven's voice dropped. 'So was I. Look at me, Marten.'

There was a new expression on Corven's face. Marten was sure of it. It was real. It had to be real. He was suddenly open, the creases at his eyes less deep. It was as if something hard for him was over. But what? Marten had been sure of him at the time, but now he was less sure. Would Corven have taken such a risk?

Marten balled the sheet and threw it on the bed, and rolled to his feet, rubbing his eyes, remembering, running the conversation's end through his mind again, for the hundredth time.

'I've seen how uncomfortable you are when I use certain words, Marten. And there have been small disobediences.'

'Corven—' He'd tailed off, waiting for Corven. Should he have confessed immediately? Had he betrayed himself?

But Corven had said, 'I was uncomfortable, like you. I still am. We have something in common, and in common with a few others.' He waved a hand. 'That's all for now. This is between you and me. You understand? We'll talk again.'

Marten stood beneath the jets of the shower and let the lukewarm water sluice over him. Under this world of rock the water rose hot and

282

stank of sulphur. It never cooled enough to jar him properly awake. He longed for the bright freezing water of Haze.

He didn't know what to do.

The flask at Mexi's elbow was almost cold and the Vault's good caffé separating to water and spore, but she still sipped from it, absently pressing the tiny gel spheres with her lips until they burst. The lightlance was an extension of her hand, and her fingers rippled down the control ribs as rapidly as thought.

The Robe was still standing quietly beside her. It was a man, she was sure. He'd come in after her and stood without making a sound all day, staring at the screen with fascination.

It was odd, Mexi thought, the effect they had under Haven. Children who couldn't speak yet, factotems, everyone was silenced by the silent Robes. They came to Haven with sunbrowned faces, and here the colour was leached out of them. As a child Mexi had thought they returned to Haze when all their colour was gone, all except the orange of their robes.

Once, when she had been birdfishing, a Robe had come to join her. In the closeness of the turret and the howl of the wind she had had a strange sense of companionship. Mexi had been concentrating on the line and her bird, and hadn't been able to tell whether the Robe was a man or a woman. It almost didn't matter that it was a Robe beside her. But she was aware after a while that the Robe was staring away to the south, towards the brilliant flickering of the evening's advancing aurora. And by the fall of the cloth that it was a woman, and by her pallor that she'd been on Haven for at least six months.

Haze, Mexi had thought. She's looking towards Haze. She's homesick. Mexi had reeled the small bird back in, and the kite, without a catch, and then turned to the woman with a smile, but she had gone.

Mexi leant back against the chair and stretched. She'd done her work for the day. Now she was free.

Concentrating again, she wondered if it was safe. But the Robe seemed more interested in the changing colours of the screen than in trying to make sense of the words and images. Gild had told her that in any free time at the end of her tasks, she was free to explore the Vault.

The Robe showed no sign of leaving. There was no risk, she was sure. She lightlanced a datascan request in human anatomy, and accessed the database Zelda had asked for. She punched out a hard print and held it carefully while the paper cooled, the shine seeping away to leave it matt and smooth.

She looked at the tables. The column titles meant no more to her than the names of minerals. Gnathion, philtrum, malar. The words brought nothing to her mind, and the racks of numbers aligned by them were meaningless.

She closed the screen and went to the door, ignoring the Robe. The door should have opened at a touch, but didn't. She touched it again, more firmly. Nothing happened. Behind her the screen made a small sound, and she turned to see a gleaming line of script.

WAIT AT SCREEN

Mexi felt instantly cold. She looked at her hand, which was shaking, and then at the Robe. Sweat grained her back.

Robes could go anywhere. No doors were ever closed to them. 'Please,' she said, touching the door again. 'Can you open it?'

The Robe looked at her, and she suddenly realised she knew who it was. From his face, she couldn't tell if he had even heard her, but he must understand what she wanted. 'I gave you the meat from the bird,' she said. 'Remember? Don't you have a tradition of exchange? Please help me. It's important.'

His shoulders moved slightly, the orange cloth billowing gently. Maybe the door was locked against him, too. Maybe he didn't want to do something for her. Maybe he simply couldn't.

'What's your name?' she said. 'My name's Mexi.'

'I know,' he said.

She stopped, realising she hadn't expected an answer. She gathered herself to say, 'And you? I know you have names. They're like our names. You're like us.' She made a gesture, head to foot, meaning human, but immediately felt stupid to be treating him stupidly. He wasn't primitive at all.

He stood back against the side wall, and by moving away from the door, she felt he was against her. He was just waiting to see what would happen to her. Then he said, 'Marten.'

The door hissed open, and Gild came in. He glanced briefly at the Robe, then said, 'That's an unusual search, Mexi. I wonder why you made it.'

She looked across at the Robe, making herself concentrate, and said, 'You know I'm interested in Haze. I was thinking about any anatomical differences there may be between us. The gene pools have never mixed since Contact. How have we evolved differently, if we have at all?'

Gild nodded, but there was no sign of interest in his face. 'How were you going to make comparisons, Mexi? I don't think we have any data on Haze crania. We aren't permitted. Your companion, here—' he dipped his head courteously at the Robe, and Mexi was sure there was mutual recognition, '—Were you about to dissect him?'

Mexi dropped her head. 'I'm sorry.'

Gild smiled. 'But it was a good thought. Security here is sometimes harsh. It's an active system. It looks for patterns. You haven't been here long, so you haven't established your own patterns. It'll catch you again, I'm sure, but once the system understands your interests, it'll monitor you less severely.' He reached out for Mexi to put the sheet of paper into his hand. He tossed it into the reconstitution bin, and left the room.

Mexi stood facing the closed door for a moment, then twisted round at a small noise. Marten was unbending from the bin, holding a limp rag. He held it out to Mexi, who took it and stretched it flat. It dried quickly in her hand, the shine swiftly dulling again.

It was thin, already half returned to myco, but the full-thickness script was legible. Mexi started to say thank you, but the Robe had gone.

The head looked new-born, barely squeezed out into the world. It was brown and smooth and quite hairless. The eyes were its most disconcerting features, and Naddy seemed to know it, saying, 'The pupils are obsidian marbles, and I used jade for the irises.' He walked round the table, looking from the head to Skim and Quill. 'There's no way of knowing what colour his eyes actually were. The whites are rock crystal. Everything else is clay.'

Quill squinted at the reconstruction as Naddy turned it on its little roundel.

'Does he look like you could put a name to him?' Skim said.

Its face looked faintly familiar to Quill, but after Tyler Hind, Quill wasn't going to jump to identify him.

Naddy said, 'Yes. It's at the edge of my thoughts, but I can't quite touch it. That could be my fault, though.'

'What do you mean?'

Naddy sighed unhappily. 'Well, I left him hairless. Hair colour and style, possible baldness, I didn't want to guess at. But there are other variables, and I wanted to avoid unFact as much as I could. Like the shape of the nose, ears, soft tissue variation, scars—'

'Okay, Naddy. We know you're good.'

'No, it's important. There's about a sixty per cent chance of getting the shape of the nose right, forty per cent of getting the tip right, less still of getting the mouth right.' Almost tenderly, he rolled his hand across the face, his palm not quite touching it. 'I measured tangents from his nasal cavity, so I'm confident of the nose length, at least. He's got short teeth, so his lips were probably thin, and there were clues on the skull to his earlobes. But all the same...'

'You've got the skull, Naddy. You must have got something right.'

'I hope so. It just worries me, what I've done unconsciously.' He sighed. 'But the general facial dimensions are right. How wide apart the eyes are. Chin to eye distances, the general anatomy.'

'He looks familiar to me, too,' said Skim.

Of course he does.

Be quiet, Scheck, Quill thought. Not now.

Naddy was irritated. 'Yes. That's the thing. While I was doing it, I was thinking, why are we doing this? I mean, how could he look familiar? His genes will have dissolved over generations.' He slapped the palm of his hand theatrically on the crown of the skull. It sounded dull and dense. 'It means I was probably thinking of someone at some point. The general dimensions must have reminded me of someone, and unconsciously I skewed the variables towards them.' He pushed a finger down into the top of the clay head, leaving a small impression behind. 'But I can't think who it is.'

They all stared at the skull. Naddy turned it slowly, and now it looked like something exhumed, reconstituted from the earth.

Alas, poor Yorick.

'Who's that?'

A joke. I knew him, Quill. Look at him. You know who he is.

'Hallo, Mexi,' Gild said, unsurprised that Mexi should be opening Zelda's door. 'Visiting Zelda?' The question was casual, but there was stone hardness in his eyes, and Mexi felt her heart react, thumping. The street behind him was empty of sound. A few minutes ago it had been busy with the day's end.

'I live next to her. I—'

'I know where you live,' Gild said easily. 'No need to defend yourself. I was going to call on you after I'd done with Zelda, but it doesn't matter at all.' He glanced to his left and said, 'Two dogs with one bone, eh?'

Gild pushed past Mexi and more men appeared, one from either side of the doorway, following Gild into Zelda's house. They went through towards the kitchen as if they knew the way and that Zelda was there. Mexi followed, calling out to Zelda, but was stopped from going through by the men who stood shoulder to shoulder at the kitchen door.

'Zelda,' Gild said warmly. 'It's been a long time.' He glanced back at Mexi, making a casual gesture for the men to let her through into the kitchen, and said, 'Zelda was my guide, once. Did she tell you? She took me on my first tour of the Vault. It seems she still can't stay out of it. And as for you, Mexi, I'm disappointed.'

He nodded, and the two men took Zelda by the arms. Her arms

whined and started to straighten, pushing the men away, but then her whole body fell limp.

'I think you've just had a power failure, Zelda,' Gild said. 'Now, where are they?' The men pulled Zelda to the table and stretched her out, sweeping plates and pans clattering to the floor. On the cook unit, a pan was starting to boil, steam rising in wisps. Mexi stood in the doorway, not knowing what to do, sure only that trying to intervene wouldn't help.

With an effort, Zelda lifted her head. 'Who?'

Gild put the tube of a weapon to her hand, pressing it so deep into the palm that her fingers curled. Mexi watched a bright aura of light bloom at its circumference, and when Gild removed the tube, Zelda's palm was black and smoking. One of the men adjusted his grip on her arm, wrinkled his nose and coughed. Gild said, 'This is a kitchen, Dewli. You have to expect kitchen aromas. And we're in the presence of a fine cook, here. Aren't we, Zelda? You spend so much time in here. What's Quill's favourite dish, hmm? What does Scheck like to eat?'

'I still don't know who you're talking about,' Zelda said steadily. Her calm told Mexi that she was right to keep clear of this, though her heart was still thudding. Zelda knew what she was doing. 'And nor does she,' Zelda added.

'Maybe she doesn't.' Almost idly, Gild started opening cupboards and pulling out drawers. He sniffed at jars of lichens, pouring the powder onto the floor. The boiling pan was throwing up clouds of steam, bubbling hard enough to start the pan clattering on the hot ring. Gild picked the pan up and held his palm over it for a moment, then took it quickly away, whistling at the heat. He held the pan above Zelda's face and tilted it fractionally. Mexi heard the slop of liquid and couldn't stay quiet. 'Leave her alone, Gild!' she yelled.

'I shouldn't worry about her, Mexi. She can adjust her pain thresholds.' He hadn't taken his eyes from Zelda. Changing the tone of his voice, he said, 'We could refine them in the other direction, Zelda, but you'd probably find a way to kill yourself.' He put the pan back on the cook unit, then took Mexi by her wrist, twisting it viciously so that she was cracked down and on her knees, head to the floor, her arm torsioned straight behind her and the weapon's barrel pressing into her palm. Pain lanced through her shoulder.

'She just did me a favour,' Zelda said. Her voice was slightly less than even. 'She doesn't know what it was for.'

'Really?' Gild relaxed his grip just enough for Mexi to straighten her back.

It was the Robe, Mexi thought through the pain. The Robe had given her back the table of figures. He must have told Gild.

'I'm not wasting time. Quill and Scheck – where are they? We know you've been seeing Naddy Harke here in this noisy little kitchen of yours. We're fairly sure Naddy's seen Quill. We've caught glances of him in coredors here and there, but not Scheck, yet. Is he dead?' He waited. The pan began to hiss again. 'We'd have liked to pick them both up together, but we're not waiting any longer.' He twisted Mexi's wrist again, hard, turning her shoulder to crack her head on the floor, and said, 'Last chance, Zelda. Or I'll kill Mexi.'

Zelda said, 'Naddy wanted some data. Anatomical base data.'

'Good.' Gild let Mexi straighten to her knees again and told one of the men holding Zelda on the table to release her burnt hand. She examined it, turning it over. She closed her fingers, but couldn't quite make a fist, and the hand wouldn't open again for her. The fingers pumped slightly, in and out.

Zelda said, 'I didn't ask him why he wanted the data. I asked Mexi to access it from the Vault. That's all. Anything else, you'll have to ask Naddy.' She pumped her free hand again and added, 'Scheck and Quill, weren't they the dead men from Survey?'

On the cook unit the pan was bumping and rattling, clouded with steam, and Zelda had to raise her voice. 'I saw the event with Mexi from a turret. No one could have survived that.' Then she twisted her head and said, loudly and sharply, 'The pan!'

As the men started to turn towards the cook unit, Zelda ripped her other hand loose and tried to roll from the table. Mexi managed to pull herself away from Gild, her wrist sending a stab of agony up her arm, and started to her feet. Gild's arm came round, a beam of light spinning towards Mexi. Beyond Gild, Mexi saw a flash of colour, someone running hard from the outer door towards the kitchen. The lance of Gild's beam missed Mexi, but she realised it hadn't been meant for her. It almost caught Zelda as the old woman hit the ground, instead scarring the kitchen wall.

Zelda hauled herself halfway up the cook unit and fumbled for the pan. As the two men grabbed her, she pulled the pan down. The thick liquid poured over all three of them. The men fell back screaming, their faces hissing. Sprawled on the floor, Zelda blinked and shook her head.

Gild was standing against the wall, legs braced and steady. He fired at Zelda again and hit her squarely. Her chest bloomed red and then silver and she fell, quiet and still. Mexi screamed and grabbed at Gild's arm, falling with him to the ground. She heard the screech of another weapon, but this one quieter than Gild's, and recognised the Robe, Marten, as he fired light at Gild's men.

As Gild stared at Marten, Mexi pulled the factotem's weapon from him. He stumbled back and fell, and she came down with her knees on his chest, jamming the breath from him. She smashed the weapon across his face, then opened the beam and hammered the barrel into his chest at the same time. The gun whined in protest as she killed him with it, her eyes closed with tears and fury at Zelda's death.

Mexi stayed there, crying, the gun whining and heating up in her hand, until Marten's hand on her shoulder shocked her back to consciousness.

She opened her eyes. She could see the floor beneath Gild's spine, and smell his flesh. She let the weapon go and sat up, breathing hard, her eyes going to Zelda.

'I'm sorry,' Marten said.

She looked at him. Gild's factotems were dead at Marten's feet, and he was holding a weapon like Gild's but smaller.

'I wish I'd been swifter,' he said.

'Well, you weren't.' She tried to stop crying. Zelda was dead. There was nothing Mexi could do.

Marten pulled her to her feet, holding her by the shoulders with firm hands, and said, 'You have to go. You can't stay here.' He lodged his weapon carefully in the folds of his Robe and looked straight at her, and said, 'This isn't good, but it's done. Now, you have to hit me, then leave.'

She took a shuddering breath. 'Where do I go?'

'Turquoise. Wait for me by the drop-pods to Azure, but don't go there directly. I'll be with you as soon as I can. I have to find out if there's someone I can trust.'

She steadied her breathing as much as she could, putting Zelda from her mind, and said, 'I thought you must have told Gild about me.'

'No. They were watching Zelda. You have to hit me hard.'

'Do you trust me?'

He gave her a thin, empty smile. 'You won't hurt me more than I've had before.'

'I didn't mean that.'

Marten shrugged. 'We have no choice. We're bound together.' He pulled back his cowl and she saw the soft burr of his shaved head. He was suddenly human. He said, 'On the cheek, below the eye. Hard as you can, but glancing, so you don't fracture the bone. I'll get to you as quickly as possible. Now.'

289

Mexi made a fist, and used the anger inside her. Marten fell like a stone.

A bleep sounded and repeated more insistently, and Naddy stood up and went to a screen. 'We may be receiving guests,' he said. Then his voice dropped slightly and he said, 'Ah, guests with guns. Factotems. Quill, I don't know what they want, but they mustn't find you here.' He picked up the head and shoved it into Quill's arms. 'Take this, too. Skim, go with him. What are you waiting for? Quickly.'

'I can't go,' Skim said. 'They must have been set up for this. They'll have seen me walk in, but they won't have seen Quill. If I'm not here, they'll turn this place upside down and find the coffin's trail.'

Quill knew she was right. If they got to the trail quickly enough, they could track him, send a fast pulser down his vitrified trail. As long as his wake was hot, he wouldn't be able to shake or outrun it.

'Go,' she said. 'You have to go, Quill.'

Turning away, Naddy said, 'We'll hold them off as long as we can. If we're still alive, Horvath will know.'

Quill gathered the head and slipped through the door at the rear of Naddy's workshop to the concealed niche. Naddy yelled again, 'Remember – Horvath.'

A door of two-metre granite shielded the niche. Quill shut himself inside, crawled into the coffin, closed the door and went into the rock, hard and fast.

He set the clay head on Scheck's bunk. It would take the trail two hours to cool enough to be untraceable. Skim and Naddy had to stall Fact that long. After that, even if they discovered the niche with its vitrified back wall, there wouldn't be anything to follow him down. He thought of Skim and Naddy, and found he had no doubt about them holding Fact off. For now, they would be fine. Later, he didn't want to think of.

So, here we are, the three of us. You, me and . . . and who, Quill?

'You tell me.' Quill was looking at the screen. The motor was smooth and quiet, and he was making good speed. He checked the charts and changed course, heading deep, towards the dark shades.

I'm not sure I can do that. It comes and goes, Quill. I'm not sure I'm myself any more.

'Well, you're right, there.' He stopped the chart and swivelled round. He was suddenly thinking of General Factotem on the screen, the smoothed, recontoured, firm features of his face. 'Scheck, you know something?'

Yes. We know who it is.

It wasn't just Naddy's errors and unconscious assumptions in building the head that needed allowance. It was the portrait too. The image that had been adjusted to make him the hero that he'd been and remained, then and now and forever. It was recontoured, restyled, just like General Factotum was restyled.

That's right, Quill. You're looking at the Captain.

The head stared at him. Quill imagined the Captain's hair set on the glistening scalp. Naddy had the set of his lips slightly wrong, but once you'd allowed for the stylising over all those years, it was the Captain staring at him from Scheck's bunk.

Quill thought back to the ship, the small escape pod that had crashed into the planet and buried itself for centuries. The scrawl on the ship's walls. *I was betrayed.* He must have been cast out in the pod.

And Fact knew it. They knew where the ship had landed and must be, and they knew it would be found, one day.

More than that. They knew exactly what was in it, and needed it destroyed. And as a direct consequence of Tyler Hind's unFact-saying, they knew Scheck and Quill were probably alive.

They had known about the blister case. Skim had been right. It was the pure extent of their knowledge that was astonishing.

He made a face at the Captain, then brought out the small case from his pocket and looked at it for a long time, at the single unbroken blister that was all that remained intact of the lost Archive. And all else that was left of it was in Quill's head.

It had driven Tyler Hind insane. But why couldn't Quill get to it? Why didn't he just *know* it? And why did Fact want it destroyed?

CAP

I was distracted for most of that week, waiting for Jake to do what he needed to with his program and the Omega files.

It wasn't just the Omega data that this last project of his required. Because of the truth, for fear of it getting out, most Earth Science research was forbidden or embargoed, escaping in headline and rumour to be reflexively denied by Administration scientists. What there was I obtained, naturally. The fiercely protected Omega data were the final figures Jake needed.

While I waited, I fussed about my own preparations, and I saw Mary and John.

I found that while I was quite certain of the future, of my plans, my thoughts of John and Mary were still in turmoil. At times I imagined I was reconciled to John, and I could almost believe again that he had no feelings for her. But it puzzled me that nevertheless I still could not fully trust him with her. I was certain that she loved him, though. And while she did, while he was around, I knew that she would not love me again.

And yet I could not deal with John on such a basis. Nor would I allow Mary to drive me to this situation.

My dreams were confused. I woke sweating or screaming. My father was mostly in the dreams, and when he was not, there was the swirling blackness of space and I had no purchase there, my arms flailing and the breath leaving me and leaving me in a long, unheard cry. I was like Our Lord in the wilderness.

But this dream was a message from Him, of course. It warned me of the suffering to come, both mine and the suffering of others that I would also be taking upon myself.

I was sick and feverish. I spent that week in my room, alone, much of the time staring at Jake as he sat at his screens and tapped and waved his hands and drank Texicola and ate noodles.

His presence was comforting to me. Whenever I woke up gasping or retching, he was reassuringly there on that glimmering screen, tunelessly moaning to himself, endlessly stringing together signs and numbers. Delirious, I imagined his screens were petri dishes and the proliferating symbols were what they called the building blocks of life. Which, when I considered it, was as true as it was false.

I communicated with Gus too, by screen, reassuring him constantly that he could trust me, that I would be prepared for my presentation to the Houses.

Gus had his own problems, though, which relieved me of some pressure at that time. With the exception of the waste continents, democracy had been proclaimed worldwide, but it had its limitations. By evangelising it so forcefully, they made it fail. Democracy could only ever function by compromise, and there would always be those unprepared to compromise. Nations exempted themselves on this issue and that by veto and vote, and factions exempted their nations by bomb and gas.

It was what I had foreseen, and what I would address. What I am addressing.

This was the problem: Gus, and the people around him, were working towards a definitive world. A world where their own personal wealth and power could coexist in a stable relationship with universal justice and fairness to all. World without end.

It could not be. My father could have told him that. There would always be fresh unaddressed squalor, and there would always be men and women wanting their own wealth and power at the expense of that of Gus and the members of his Administration.

And there was no way around it. You couldn't educate the world. You couldn't take into account the vagaries and hard effects of experience, of cancer and abuse, or the lottery of the gene in each new generation.

And yet I was the product of democracy. Oh, my father! Were we coincidence or design? Were we tragic or were we simply laughable?

I sat in that room, alone, and wept for the world. Above me on a wall, Jake tapped away at the future.

John, on a screen, told me he was worried about me, that he and Mary were both extremely concerned, and he insisted he see me. I did not have the strength to say no.

I left my office. Bob drove me. He sensed that I was in no mood to talk. I don't know whether it was the Omega data that I had read, but I was more keenly aware of the state of the streets, of the gritty air, of the few masked walkers striding quickly.

I met John in the small office of the Heart Suite in the Foundation's Core Block. The Foundation was by now the size of a large town. Much of the land had been donated to me, the rest I had bought. Structurally,

I'd modelled it on the old Pentagon, but it was more efficient than that. By internal pipe rail from the Core, you could travel west to reach the organised sprawl of Mary's medical research facilities in twenty minutes, and if you went east you could be at Our Lord's Central Cathedral in the same time. To the north was the Stadium of Life, and to the south, the Media Centre and Hub of All Hope.

Thinking of it now, I have some small nostalgia.

The Heart Suite was by then my true centre of operations. If I describe it, it will be familiar to you. It was a small glass-walled building in the middle of a grassed courtyard. There was room for a few offices, and bedrooms for Mary and me when I was working late. I thought of the Heart Suite as an oasis of peace and an emblem of openness. Nothing there could be concealed, though the walls could, when necessary, be opaqued. At night, for instance.

I watched John cross the grass towards me, and let him in. He strode directly up to me and hugged me warmly. He held me in his arms, and when I pushed him gently away I was crying.

'Cap?'

'I'm sorry, John,' I said, not knowing why. At that moment, if he had asked me what I was doing, I think I would have told him everything. But he didn't ask me.

He said, 'When did you last eat? You look terrible. Let me get someone to—'

'I'm fine, John. I'll eat later. There's too much to do. Time. There's so little time.'

'Let someone else do it. Let me. Please. You need to look after yourself. What good are you to the world if you're sick?'

'I'm not sick.'

'Sit down. Sit down, Cap, please.'

Despite my instructions, he called for something to eat, and when it came, he made me swallow it. I hadn't realised there was so much hunger in me. I devoured everything. There was no nausea.

I can't remember what I ate then, but I remember what it was like to be hungry. Of course, there's no hunger now, and I don't need to eat, though I still have dreams of vomiting and retching. Even now, so far away in time and distance, my father has not left me.

But I recall that sudden acknowledgement of ravenous hunger. I know that I can be so consumed by something that in the fever of it, I forget everything else. I had it in common with Jake, although he didn't share my vision. I occasionally wonder if he ever appreciated what he had done. I hope so, for at least that last split second.

'Tell me how we're doing, John,' I said at last.

'You don't need to worry, Cap. But Mary—'

'She's fine.'

'I couldn't get through to her this morning. They said she was staying home again.'

'That's right. She's a little weak. A reaction to the new auto-immune medication. Why did you need her?'

'No reason. I couldn't get you at first, so I tried her. Peter was concerned about her too.'

'He's no longer her physician.'

'No, but he knows—'

'Mary needs to rest. Talking is the worst thing for her at the moment.'

'Are you sure? Maybe someone else could look in on her.'

'John,' I said, firmly. 'Do you trust me?'

'Yes, Cap. Of course I do.'

'Mary is my love. She has everything she needs, and she always will, no matter what happens. Do you understand me?'

He understood me. I could see it in his eyes. We discussed business for a while, and then he left.

I returned home and went in to see Mary in her room. She was awake, but drowsy. She lifted her head towards me as far as she could, listening.

'Nurse? Is that you?'

I watched her with love.

'Cap? Nurse? Who is it?'

This voice was thin, and each word was preceded by a watery, hollow gulp, the sound of a stone in a pool in a cavern. Her synthesiser had been removed.

'Hush, my darling. Don't try to move. Don't tire yourself. Rest.'

'I can't—'

'I know. You've had a fever. The doctor doesn't want to risk you falling out of bed and hurting yourself, and the light would damage your eyes. We have to wait until you're strong again. Are you uncomfortable?'

'Yes. It's too tight.' She struggled a little.

'I'll get the nurse to adjust it. Poor darling.' I stroked her throat, quieting her. The contact made her gasp. It was an odd sensation. She struggled a little, but there was no strength in her.

'John tried to get through to you earlier.'

'Did he? That's kind.'

'Yes. Do you know what he wanted?'

'What?'

'I don't know. I thought you might.' There was nothing to read in her face, with her eyes covered as they were.

'Ask him,' she said.

Every restriction she used against me. She was cunning. There was nothing to betray her thoughts in that impassive voice.

'Mm.' I kissed her softly on the lips. Maybe it was the tracheotomy, the redundancy of her mouth and nose, but I didn't think so. There was no emotion in her kiss, and I left her.

The remainder of the week passed. John didn't trouble me again. Jake completed his work with a day to spare, and I had it picked up. I had each courier watched, and I had the watchers watched. I had never taken such care. When the package arrived at the Heart Suite, I sat for a minute before I opened it, and then I sat holding the two white cubes, one in each hand. They were the size of casino dice.

As usual, Bob drove me, and I was in a fine frame of mind. He and I chatted all the way to the House. There were no reporters today.

'Cap,' Gus said, walking me in. 'Are you ready?'

'I am. Don't worry, Gus. It's going to be fine.'

And then the tall doors opened, and I was standing at a podium, about to give the most important speech of my life.

'President Speke,' I began. 'Ministers of the Two Houses. Good afternoon.' They didn't respond. I hadn't expected them to.

'I would like to show you a future.' I smiled. 'Maybe more than one.'

Still no reaction. It didn't matter.

I looked them over, taking my time. I controlled my breathing. There they all were. The room was full of them, the best and the brightest of the Administration of the world. Their suits fitted them better than their skins. They had never had to breathe the bad air of the streets, though they were responsible for it. I smiled my best and most relaxed smile at them. These men and women wielded between them as much financial and political power as all of my organisations combined. Of course, they were a political organisation, and so each man and woman also had their own personal interest to defend, while I was not so divided.

It was hard for me to hit quite the right tone with them. I was not as nerveless as I seemed. I was good at silence and rousing and cajoling and goading. But I was not so sure how good I could be at speaking to those who considered me an equal or less than that. Their silence did not reassure me, but there was no muttering.

I began. 'The Paradise Device, as you all know, has been raining – indeed deluging – its data down on us for some time, now. I have news for you, and some very interesting results, but before I discuss them with you, I should like to brief you on another of my projects.'

I paused. Despite everything, politicians were very like the rest of us. In fact they were more so, as I'm sure someone said. They had a very short attention span. You could tell them the most astonishing thing in the world, but if you told it to them for more than a few minutes, they lost interest. So you needed a lot of carrots to dangle. But I had a whole bunch of them. And now I had the tone right.

'As I don't need to tell you, the Earth has been subjected to increasing wear over the past decades and more. Atmospheric events, earth events, whatever you want to call them, have taken their toll. We are not as comfortable in our own back yard as we should be.'

Some of them looked faintly irritated, and some a little more than that. I was talking about pollution, about planetary self-harm. I was also talking about their company profits. I soothed them. 'This is unfortunate, but it is entirely reversible,' I said. 'What we have done, we can undo.'

I threw some scenes onto the vidwall behind me, and talked over them. Deforestation, coastal erosion, all graphically smoothed away, reversed, the passing of centuries in seconds. There was music, soothing colours.

The images rolled on, fairytale images for these secretly yearning, jaundiced adults. I was showing them not just their world, but their youth restored. I was offering them absolution. I had spent my life in the telling of such things, and I could do it to this audience. How proud my father would have been of me.

'We can fix it all,' I told them. 'We can patch ozone holes, stabilise ocean currents, we can return to the pre-industrial age. All it will take is time and determination.'

I stopped there. I was under no illusions. I knew I was at the edge of what they would accept. 'Keep that in your minds for a moment. Bear with me.'

They were silent. Their little eyes shone.

I slipped the other, bigger carrot before their eyes and waved it. I brought it up as a pixel in the high corner of the great chamber and let it gradually swell and drift down to sit above my head, a holo that swayed in the air, big and round and swirling with blue and white. They gasped, though why they should have done so, heaven knows. They simply knew it was expected of them. They were politicians, but they knew how to be an audience.

'Here is a planet,' I said, leaning far enough from the podium's voice projector to make them strain a little to catch my words. 'A Paradise image, of a planet in a solar system far, far away.'

They didn't know how perfectly-sized this discovered world was, how almost unimprovable it was in terms of the requirements of human life. I told them.

I tapped the air beside the holo. 'It needs a few environmental tweaks, that's all. Its gravity is perfect. There's water, plant life and rudimentary animal life. Mainly it's forested. There are oceans. Think of Earth at the time of the dinosaurs, only without the dinosaurs. The Cretaceous Period, sixty five million years ago.' Some of them frowned, as if I'd confounded their understanding of me. They expected me to talk of Intelligent Design, naturally. I believed passionately in that, of course, but not in a way that any of them could possibly imagine.

I showed them some images, then. It made the heart ache to see those images. They reeked of innocence and hope. Clear skies, clean seas. 'We could send ships, a colony . . .' I trailed off, letting them stumble on with their own imaginations.

Someone said, 'How much?'

'Wait. Let me go on,' I said.

'How much?' the voice repeated. And someone else said, 'Good question.'

'Here is another planet,' I said. 'Please, let me finish. Your question will be answered.'

And I showed them *my* planet. It was grey and brown.

Air screamed and whistled around it. I felt cold standing below the holo of it. It could have been a ball of tumbleweed there at my shoulder. It was the planet that had brought everything into focus for me.

'Here are some close-up images of this one.'

They stared at the hardly varying pictures, at the wind-whipped, raw surface of it. Barren, an empty slate obsessively scrubbing itself clean.

'I call it Haven,' I said, quietly.

I let the images continue. Close-up smears of lichen, vast horizons of tumbling rock. There was no sound, but you could simply see that it was deafening on that surface. I whispered into that bursting silence, 'Haven can be made habitable. It has the essentials – the bare essentials—'

They smiled, and I knew I had them. They were in the fist of my hand. Haven had hooked them as the other planet had not. Haven had shown them just how desirable the other world was.

'Haven has the essentials for terraforming to work on. Believe it or not, the same techniques that will save the Earth and fine-tune the other planet you just saw can be used to terraform Haven.'

The desperate images of Haven rolled on. I looked up and savoured them with my audience for a few moments. 'Everything necessary to the task can be transferred and put into place via the Paradise Device. Once in orbit and activated, the terraforming machinery will be self-govern-ing. A colony can set out now, in cryo, and by the time it reaches Haven, the planet will be habitable. It will not be like the other world, of course, we aren't gods—' I let them chuckle, '—but there's plentiful water under the surface, and a form of fungus underground that we can cultivate for food. Ministers, it can work.'

'Why *two* planets, Captain? Isn't one enough?'

That was Speke.

I grinned at him. 'One for you, Mister President, and one for me.' There was general laughter. Someone suggested we toss a coin for them, as long as it was *his* coin.

'Seriously, Ministers. I foresee the Earth, despite our best efforts, becoming an intolerable burden to us. My Foundation – and I have seen the Omega file – suggests that to carry out the degree of atmospheric correction required here would be possible. Indeed—' I made a show of bringing one of Jake's dice from my pocket and holding it up, '—my team have come up with a program to that end.'

They made little noises, and I was gratified to hear that the sounds were of astonishment rather than disbelief.

'Unfortunately it would be, temporarily, somewhat disruptive.' I smiled, ruefully. 'It is not a rabbit from a hat. It would necessitate most of the world's population being put into orbital cryosuspension while the work was completed.'

Someone whistled.

'Yes. Cryo is already viable, after all. It's routinely used in surgery for periods of several hours. We'd just extend the period. The work on Earth would take, at a conservative estimate, several hundred years.' I made another mournful face for them. 'Though we all know how accurate builders' estimates are.'

I had made them happy. I had heard their Confession without them having to open their mouths, and I had absolved them with no penance. They could accept the inevitable, and I had given them not merely a way out, but also a choice for them to present to the world.

They waited for me to go on. I was one of them, now. I caught Gus's eye. He winked at me.

'So, if we are to go into the freeze-box, why not do so for a little longer and wake up at a new home? Why refurbish when you can move house and start again? Hmm?'

I left that carrot dangling. The planets were still up there above me.

'Let's talk about me, then,' I said, and chuckled with them. Oh yes, I had them. They so very much wanted to be had. 'I want a new start. I won't deny it. But I want a challenge. I want Haven for myself. I want to take my own people, my volunteers, and create with them a new world of freedom. I'll be honest—' We all chuckled again. 'I want Our Lord to be with me, and my people, and that is all. Much as I have enjoyed working with this Administration, with all of you, I don't want to share my world.'

I closed my mouth and waited a moment for the atmosphere in there to change. It took them a moment to adjust, to realise I was being quite serious.

'I don't want to compromise,' I said soberly. 'But I can't afford to do this huge thing alone. Ladies and gentlemen, I need your help.'

I let them see the solution in front of them. I let the holos of the planets wobble in the air like balloons.

'These two planets are close by each other, in the same system. To reach them, we can help each other, your Administration and my Foundation. I shall be responsible for the majority of the terraforming costs, since most of them relate to my planet. I propose that we share most of the cost of the fleets of ships, in proportion to their number.'

I stopped talking and stood there for just enough time to get their full attention in silence, and then I tossed the tiny white die in my right hand high in the air. It rose, tumbling over and over, between the two planets and fell back into my fist. I walked across the chamber to Gus and I placed the die in the palm of his hand.

'Cori,' I said, making sure we were being noted, the two of us together, 'Thank you for letting me help you.'

She came up and shook my hand, and then someone else came up too, and for the next twenty minutes I was shaking the hands of every member of the Two Houses of the Administration of the United Republics of Ameuropa.

And when that was done, Gus was standing at the podium, waving the room to be seated again. I sat with the rest of them, beside Cori Shiel. This was Gus's moment.

Gus said, 'I'll confess, Captain, I had no idea what the outcome of this meeting would be. You were so unquestioningly supportive of our policies that we almost wondered whether you had an agenda at all. We wondered what you might ask of us, in reward for such extensive assistance during the campaign.' He glanced around the room and smiled. 'Some of us thought you might expect something we would have had to refuse.'

When they had finished chuckling, I said, 'A lesson in politics, Gus. When they expect you to ask the impossible, ask nothing at all. Instead, offer them a gift.'

'Well,' Gus said, 'I'm sure we can accept your gift, Captain.' He held up the little die.

'Mister President—'

'No, Cap. Listen to me. Once the Houses have endorsed my decision, we shall ensure that any bureaucracy is minimised. You can commence your preparations.' He signalled me to stand up again. 'You have the President's promise, Captain.' He smiled at me, and around the room, the Administration of the URA began to cheer like children before a conjuror in a sequinned suit. Gus let them applaud for a minute, and then hushed them, and said, 'And you have my word too, Reiver.'

He handled them well. I had forgotten how good he could be. He was smooth again, confident, convincing and false; this was the man I had elected. I was proud of him.

And naturally, they agreed.

The first thing for Speke to do was to announce that the thoughtlessness of previous unfederated Administrations and the stupidity of the remaining non-Ameuropean regimes had resulted in this impending environmental catastrophe. The announcement surprised no one.

Cori Shiel was put in charge of the Earth Project. Jake's little white die – the second of them was my secret – was pored over by Administration scientists and declared both practical and remarkable. They asked me who exactly was in the extraordinary team that had produced it, and I told them that their strict religious observances forbade any personal acknowledgement or outside contact. I expected a harder struggle to protect the true source, but this explanation was not merely accepted but considered to validate the team's genius.

Cori became an enthusiastic ambassador for the Earth. I myself was busy speaking again. I announced my intentions for Haven, being careful to claim nothing impossible. I had John coach Cori personally. She released the Omega files, firmly linking them with Jake's program of reversal. There were very few riots.

The tiny datacube became a symbol of hope and choice. A small dice-rolling flick of the hand became a universal gesture. The Moon became a manufacturing site and storage facility, and rockets roared away there in a fierce procession interrupted only by hurricane and tornado.

Slowly, the fleet began to take shape. Terraforming machines were sent through their hoops and guided into position around Haven and the other planet.

The other planet, the green planet, needed a name. There was a competition whose prize was the choice of where to be assigned to live on the new planet. Most suggestions were suitable for naming a pet or a sanitary towel.

It took time for all this to be carefully rolled out. I was otherwise involved. My preparations were complex. In fact, I relaxed my attention too much.

I tried to interest Mary in John's work with Cori, but she feigned exhaustion or made out that she didn't care. I still loved her – I always will, no matter how she tests me – but I was not prepared to let this behaviour continue indefinitely. She would have to make her choice, or I would force it.

My relationship with Gus was suffering. Because of Mary's continued indisposition, we were not meeting on Friday evenings, and Gus and I seldom talked privately. Once Gus mentioned, as if idly, that he'd had blood tests. I knew he was telling me he was aware of certain actions of mine.

And then there was an invitation to what Cori described as an environmental status meeting.

I couldn't keep track of everything, and that is what they had banked on. There was so much to do, and very little that I could delegate.

When I asked John what was going on, he acted as if he didn't know what I meant.

'Cori didn't say.'

'She didn't mention the meeting?'

'I'm her voice coach. I look at her speeches.'

As usual, now, he was brusque and defensive. He had discarded his veneer of any bond between us. There were no more platitudes on his part. I was close to admiring him for it. The situation between us was almost out in the open.

'She must be speaking at the meeting. Why wouldn't she tell you?'

He looked down, opened and closed his mouth, and blurted out, 'You can't be jealous of this.'

'What! What!' I tried to utter something, but my throat was clogged with bile and I had to choke it down.

'Captain. I meant—'

'Do you think ... Do you actually think ... ?'

I waved him down. I had to leave the room. He was paranoid. Did he imagine I thought—? What? That I was jealous of him and Cori? When all I wanted was for the two of them to fall in love and be happy, so that I could show them in all their glory to Mary? So that all of us could be happy again?

I had simply meant, of course, that Cori and Gus must be plotting something against me. But that was far too simple a conclusion for a mind as perverted as John's.

So we met, for this status report. Gus was there, Cori of course, and a number of others. Some I recognised, some I didn't. I know that there were too many people now for me to have monitored, and this was their strength and intention, to confuse and distract me. There had been a time when I had known the names of the cleaners.

Gus introduced me to them all. We shook hands. One of them made the dice-rolling gesture and chuckled. I wondered what he knew, why exactly he had done that, and how he expected me to react. It was a mistake on his part, though.

'I didn't catch your name,' I said.

'Maine, sir. Maine Abreha. Primary Restoration Committee. Truly honoured to meet you, Captain.'

He reminded me a little of John as he used to be, with his panting tongue and his false eagerness.

'Shall we sit?' Gus said.

Maine ushered me to a chair, and took his own at my side.

Cori stood before a makeshift screen and said, 'I'll make this brief. I think everyone here is aware of the state of the fleets and the hibernation orbiters. It's going almost according to schedule. Launch failures are growing fewer.' She pointed to someone sitting behind me. 'I know this is your field, Dell, and not this afternoon's business. I'd just like to take the opportunity to acknowledge the immense achievements of your Department and your company's resources.'

We applauded. I twisted round and nodded to Dell, who briefly thanked Cori on behalf of his Department and shareholders.

Cori went on. 'We're on target for Restoration Initiation – that's stage one of Tide and Burn, which according to the program can be commenced simultaneously – in thirty-four months. We all know what we have to achieve in that time. I won't take up too much more of that time now. What I'd like to show you is some vid of the state of various parts of the world now, just to emphasise what it is we're facing in human terms. This is to be made available for marketing use by Administration Departments and all accredited companies. And of course—'

I nodded back at her.

She sat down.

My chair was tight at the seat, and had low, wide arms. The room was warm, and like everyone else I had taken my jacket off and hitched up the cuffs of my sleeves. The only comfortable way for me to sit was to rest my forearms on the thick, moulded arms of the chair.

I hardly noticed this at first. But then, as the images began to play themselves out on the screen, I started to consider it.

Scenes from orbit, objective and impersonal, began the show. I wasn't interested. After that came indeterminate flurries of dust and water, and after that a clapboard house seemingly struggling with itself, and then a bridge flexing, whipping cars off itself like you might have dislodged a mosquito from the back of your hand. These images were fascinating, though not fresh.

And then there began to be people. In a hurricane, slowed down to a curdle, a naked woman, digitally enhanced, tumbled gracelessly across the screen. In all likelihood she was dead, but the image was nevertheless effective.

I tried to catch Gus's or Cori's eye to indicate my approval, but they wouldn't look at me. It was odd, but I didn't immediately think much of it. The next images were more graphic. A boy taken by a sudden huge wave – from the Malecon in Havana, I thought – and dashed back against the sea wall, and then dragged by the water to and fro, again and again, scraped and whittled away by the waves on the rocks. It reminded me of primitives washing their clothes by slapping them on rocks at the river side. As a child I had tried to copy them, squatting down in the thin stream of a sewer drain, but I'd only succeeded in cracking off all the buttons and imbuing my shirt with a stench. My father had punished me vigorously for it.

On the screen, the water crashed and crashed again, shredding the body to nothing. I looked to my left and whispered, 'Is that Havana, do you think?'

I didn't get an answer. There were more images of such scenes, beautifully judged for colour, composition and effectiveness, although the message was crude. I realised early on how they were refining down from the distant to the close, from the vague to the definite.

At several points in the show I turned round to gauge the general reaction, but whenever I did, I received a quick glance of guilt or clear accusation, or else the person I examined refused to meet my eye.

The only one of them who would look at me directly was Maine Abreha, who smiled enthusiastically and did the dice roll gesture again. I grinned back at him and set my arms more securely on the arm rests again.

The final caption of Cori's sequence, below the frozen image of a baby's swollen corpse in the centre of a flooded field, was, THIS NEED NOT BE THE END.

No one said anything. No one looked at me. I was thinking, Why did they show me these images? Why was the room so warm? Why weren't the metal arms of the chairs upholstered?

They suspected something. The sudden realisation drew sweat from me, and I had to struggle momentarily to control my breathing. It came to me in a rush – it was almost a vision, even an epiphany – that the entire event was designed around my presence. The rest of it was a charade. They had brought me there in order to examine me, to carry out electrical skin conductivity tests. They had shown me images that were calculated to be distressing, and they were investigating my response to them, to see whether I displayed psychopathic tendencies.

As I took this in, I began to feel calm again. These were tests we routinely carried out on some of my congregants, and I had taken those tests. I knew that I could empathise. My empathy could be titrated and plotted. I knew its curve.

The episode shook me, though. It brought home to me that the more responsibility I took on myself, the less I could trust those around me. I was burdened, and I was alone. I longed for someone to rely on. I longed so very much for Mary's company. But she was weaker and weaker.

I had imagined Gus to be reliable, but now I doubted it. I had given him every reason to continue to value me, and yet he was planning to throw me aside.

Of course I was angry. I didn't deserve this. To have such a situation to deal with now, so close to the realisation of my plans, was insufferable, and I was not prepared to accept it.

Even so, I had to rein in my impulse to deal summarily with the situation. I didn't know how much Gus knew, and I had no idea where where to start, in order to find that out.

My first move was to contact a few of my most trusted congregants. It pleased me that they were those who had also endured the skin conductivity tests, although their curves were shallower, a lot shallower, than mine.

They retrieved Maine Abreha from the streets.

HAZE

One morning when the Haze was thin, Crique took Petey to the small market. He had to explain the principle of it to her, that in Nepenth people could freely barter animals, food, cloth. She walked through it, fascinated, and down a small alley she found a woman with river ducks and chickens clucking in broad, low woven baskets. A customer came up, pushing Petey aside, and the woman reached into the wide neck of her basket and pulled a chicken out. She held it firmly in one hand, its body flexed over her forearm, and drew a blade across the bird's throat, letting the blood out in a thin black string that coiled to fill a white stone bowl. When the blood stopped, she tossed the bird back into the same basket, where its body flapped and its wings flailed and its head hung down like a weight, slackly flung about by the gradually subsiding body.

Petey stared. The other birds in the basket clucked agitatedly, as if trying to ignore it all. Once the dead chicken had stopped moving, the woman retrieved it and held it by its feet to plunge it quickly into a wide bowl of water over a fire. Then she started to pluck it.

Petey had seen all this before, but she felt abruptly insecure, the unexpected shock of bloodletting leaving her somehow open and vulnerable. She wanted Crique to be there with her, but he had gone. She turned around wildly and saw him, and almost fell into his arms, crying.

'Well,' he said. 'Well.' But he held her until she pushed herself upright again.

After that, he stayed with her, guiding her through the stalls. She made herself watch the next killing of a chicken, this time the bird releasing a white jet of shit over the woman's apron as the blood came. And then Crique showed her basins of river fish she'd never seen before, and crabs with their claws wrapped in braids of waterweed. And there were plump grubs, and seething bowls of tiny, translucent shrimps. There were piles of fat bright fruits and earthy vegetables, and skins and cloths and leather boots. There were clothes for barter, but none for children, and in the quiet hubble of the market there was no sound, as there was never a sound anywhere in Nepenth, of children.

Crique started to walk her back to her hut. 'You've been here more than a month, now. We've fed and clothed you,' he said, 'And until your foot—'

'I can hunt, and I can trap,' she said quickly.

'I know,' he said, his voice sharp. 'I know what you can do, Petey.'

'You don't need to worry about me.'

'Have you seen Reed?'

Her heart thumped at his name. 'Yes.'

Crique glanced at her, but he said nothing.

'A few times,' she added, feeling awkward and for some reason slightly guilty. Reed had come to see her as often as Crique had, but they had stayed in the hut and talked. He'd asked her about her past, and she had told him everything. He had understood it all, and told her nothing about himself. He'd tell her later, he always said. Now the importance was for her to remember her past, while it was still clear. His own past was already distant and cloudy, and wouldn't change further. She felt the evasion in his voice, and it troubled her. In the forest below, everything had been clear, and now it wasn't.

Walking in the Haze with Crique, the Haze holding them together, she wanted to ask him about himself, about himself and Reed. But she didn't. She thought of Yameen and her child, and it crossed her mind that perhaps there were more things here that she feared the truth of. Around them, invisibly, people talked, birds screeched, and the wind rattled the trees. Crique said goodbye tersely and left her before they reached her hut, and she walked the last of the way alone.

It was cold and constantly damp. Fires were always going in the huts, the rising smoke indistinguishable from the steam from drying clothes. On the clearest days, white clouds rose from the huts' mud chimneys to merge with the faint and slowly swirling Haze. She always wondered how many of those huts held doomed children.

Petey knew her way around the village by now. When the Haze came down like a white blindfold and disorientated her, she would move until she could touch something she recognised, and walk on from there. In the worst of it, people would call out and be answered. They talked more when they could not be seen. And Petey drew her knife and kept it ready, remembering what DeSa had told her about animals in the Haze.

Whenever Reed came to see her, her heart beat faster. The more she saw him, the less she could control it.

He sat down on a chair in the shifting shadows of the hut. 'Now,' he said. 'Ask me.'

She stared at him. *Do you want me?*

But she didn't say that. Wanting him was the truth of it, but it wasn't how she wanted to be. And there were other questions too. So what she asked him was, 'What happened to the robe?'

'It's safe. I'll show you later where it is.'

'Crique?'

'He doesn't know about it. He doesn't need to.'

She wasn't sure about that, the way Reed made it not just something between the two of them, but something to distance them from Crique. Crique was impenetrable, but Petey felt he was honest. Reed, though – she knew how her heart felt about him, but her head wasn't so sure.

'Why not?' she said. 'Why not tell him?'

'You'd never see it again. Like your firetube.'

She sat up. There was something that had to be dealt with. 'You wanted to kill me, down there in the forest.'

'No,' he said.

'You did. Don't lie to me. When the lords were dead, you and Crique were talking about killing me.'

Reed pulled the chair towards her. 'We didn't want to kill you. The lords follow everything that happens down there. They have to have an explanation for everything out of the ordinary, Petey.'

He stared at his hands for a moment, and she wondered what he was thinking.

'You can't kill a lord and get away with it. If they suspect a lord's been murdered, they won't rest. If we didn't leave them a clear explanation for the deaths of those lords, they'd keep on searching, and eventually they'd find us. They have no idea Nepenth exists, Petey. There are over five hundred of us here. We can't risk being found. You know what the lords would do.'

'But to kill me in cold blood?' She tried to read something, anything, in his face, but she couldn't.

'We didn't want to do that. We didn't want to kill you,' he said.

Petey didn't know what to say, and as she was thinking, the ladder outside trembled, and Crique came in. He looked from Petey to Reed. 'We didn't want to do what, Reed? Eh?'

Reed shrugged.

'You were listening to us?' Petey said, into the extending silence.

'I was underneath you, yes. I was listening.'

'That's—' But Petey hadn't the words for what she felt, the outrage, what she wanted to say to Crique. She stared at Reed, expecting him at least to react, but he didn't. He didn't seem surprised at all.

Crique repeated, 'We didn't want to do what, Reed?'

'Kill her,' Reed said softly.

Petey had the sudden feeling that she was the eavesdropper, and not Crique at all.

Crique smiled at Reed. '*You* didn't want to kill her?'

He looked at Petey. 'Is that what he told you? You need to watch out for Reed. He's a careful man. You need to be careful what you ask him.'

'He said you both didn't want to kill me,' Petey said, feeling lost. 'Not just him. Is that a lie, then?'

Crique shrugged and said, 'It's the truth. But Reed's full of the truth. Aren't you, Reed.'

And Crique left.

Petey looked at the hut's floor, peering through the cracks.

'He's gone,' Reed said, without moving.

'But he was listening to us. Don't you care? Don't you care about that?' She was almost shouting at him.

And she was thinking, *Don't you care about me?*

He stood up, and he came over to her and kissed her full on the lips. 'He can't see us, though.' He took her to the bed, and for a moment she thought of Loren and felt guilty. She felt guilty about being with Reed so soon after Loren, and guilty about thinking of Loren when she was with Reed. But this felt good, to touch someone so intimately, the long, warm touch of love. It had been so very long since she had had this. It was comforting, and giving pleasure was good, too.

After a while, she stopped Reed and held his face in her palms, and stared at him. He looked curiously at her with that grey pool of an eye and began to pull away, but she wouldn't let him, and he looked at her again, and his lips opened in a wide grin, and he took her cheeks in his great warm hands and kissed her hard, and murmured, slowly, 'Oh, Petey.'

And then, as she felt Reed's body relax, and then fiercely stiffen, and thud and flood into her, she found herself, all of herself, growing warm and joining him in a long, gently pounding release that left her crying.

Afterwards, she stared up at the roof. It seemed sharper, as if her vision were suddenly clearer. She told Reed so.

'Our warmth,' he smiled. 'It's cleared the Haze. It does that.'

She wasn't sure if he were joking. 'It really doesn't bother you that Crique was listening to us? I don't understand the two of you. You work together. If you hate each other like this, why do you do that?'

He sifted his fingers through her hair. 'Who said we hate each other? First of all, Petey, there's no real privacy in Nepenth. Or rather, there's as much in the streets as anywhere else. We all accept that, here. You must, too.' He pushed himself off the bed and started to pull his clothes on again. 'Talk to Crique. There's more, but let him tell you. Then come back and talk to me, if you still want to.'

Petey felt suddenly frightened. The bed felt cold. 'What is this, Reed? What do you mean, if I want to?

He was at the door now. 'Crique and I were friends. He doesn't hate me, but he doesn't trust me. That's why he works with me, so he can watch me. I don't want you to come between us as well. Talk to him, Petey.'

And he was gone, replaced by a faintness of Haze that the warmth of their lovemaking couldn't dissipate. Petey lay in the bed for a while, feeling empty, and then she searched Crique out and walked with him.

The first thing he said, speaking before she could say anything, was, 'I wasn't intending to eavesdrop. I came to feed your pigs. I didn't know Reed was with you.'

She nodded, but couldn't tell him it didn't matter. 'What did you mean about Reed being full of the truth?' she asked him.

Crique was quiet again, and Petey thought this would be another of their conversations that withered away, but then he said, 'We didn't just come across you at the end, there, with the lords. We'd been following you for a long time before that. We followed you from the village where you saw the massacre. We were watching you all the time. We watched the lords come across you.'

He stopped in the street and faced her. They were both wreathed in Haze. 'This is the truth, Petey,' he told her. 'No, we didn't want to kill you. We wanted the lords to do it. Like Reed told you, once they were aware of you, you couldn't be allowed to live. It was a calculation we had to make. It was you or us.'

'But there was a way round it,' she said, her voice cracking. She wouldn't believe him. Mist coiled between herself and Crique, thickening.

He shook his head. 'We couldn't be sure there would be. When we suggested sacrificing that village to save you, you came up with an alternative. But suppose there had been no alternative, and it had been either you or the village. Would you have accepted death?'

'There was an alternative. There's always an alternative.'

'Is there?' He looked straight at her, then jerked his head in sudden disdain. 'You've lived your life in a village down there. You've suffered punishments and you've seen them carried out. Did you try to prevent them? Did you always look for an alternative? Did you *ever* look for one?' He walked away, and the Haze came down around her like a shroud. In the emptiness Petey didn't move. She felt insecure and threatened. She drew her knife and stood there, shivering with harsh thought.

How had they known she was there, watching the massacre, unless they'd been watching it too? But that would have been too much of a coincidence, she knew, and the answer struck her at the same time as that thought.

Even before the massacre, they had been following her.

In the Haze around her, voices came and went, but she didn't move. When it finally lifted, she went to Reed's hut and demanded, 'Why were you following me? When did you start following me?'

He didn't hesitate, but his voice was subdued. 'Crique and I keep watch on the road behind the AngWat. That's where we first saw you.'

Her first thought was shock that they'd been watching her for so long, but then she said, 'Why do you keep watch on the road?'

'There's a great deal you don't know, Petey.'

'Tell me, then.' She sat down on a thin floor cushion and waited. The cold of the wooden floor sank into her bones.

'The AngWat isn't the centre. It's just the mouthpiece of it all. The road connects it with the city that controls everything. We look for raised levels of activity along the road. If there's a threat to Nepenth, that's where it will originate. Not the AngWat.'

Petey tried to take this in. She'd always assumed that the AngWat was the lords' centre of power, and the road just led somewhere else in the forest, far away. But this was almost unimaginable. She told him to carry on.

'You know the village lords are not the most powerful ones, but nor are the lords in the AngWat. There's a place in the city at the end of that road where children are prepared . . .' he trailed away, breathed hard, and said, 'There are things you wouldn't believe. There's another place, Petey. Another world.'

'How do you know all that?'

He seemed to wilt in front of her. He went to stoke the poor fire. The Haze was creeping through the walls.

She was almost shouting. 'How do you know it, Reed?'

But she didn't need him to tell her. Reed had known the robes were impervious to firetubes. And he must have known it because he was a lord.

'Petey?'

She could hear his desperation. She stood up and ran to the door and clattered down the ladder, and ran blindly. But the Haze swirled and couldn't hide her. He was chasing her and grabbing her by the shoulders, holding her.

She shook him away and said, 'This time, tell me everything, Reed.' The market was somewhere behind them with its chatter and the cluck and bark of animals.

'I was taken to the AngWat as a child. I was six years old.'

She thought of Marten, and of how Reed had calmly listened to her telling him about her son. How could he have done that? She wondered how much of her son's future she was about to hear now, from Reed.

'After a few months at the AngWat, I was taken to the city. They use the AngWat to separate the children from their parents, and then from each other. They teach them a little, and then they divide them into the ones to be educated further, and the ones to enforce—'

'Some are killed, aren't they?'

'Yes. You're thinking about your daughter. I'm sorry, Petey.'

'Perhaps Marten, too.'

'It's possible.'

She rubbed her cheeks hard with her hands. 'Go on.'

But he looked away from her, and for the first time since she'd known him, it was plain that he didn't know what to say.

Eventually she said, 'What happened?'

'After my education, I was sent to a village for a while, to observe how the villages are controlled.'

'Wars between villages,' she started to say. Then she realised she didn't know how it worked at all. It was a masquerade. 'Tell me.'

'Violence and distrust are deliberately cultivated by the AngWat.'

'Yes, but why?'

'We're social animals, Petey. We're evolved – it means bred, like we breed animals to make better meat, only this is nature breeding us to survive – we've evolved to cooperate with each other, except in extreme situations where cooperation won't help. Villages are put into extreme situations. That's how they're controlled.' He made a thin smile and said, 'People are as predictable under extremes as they are under stable conditions.' He stopped. 'Do you know how we came to be here, Petey? In the first place?'

'There's a story,' she said, making it plain she didn't believe the forest myth of ghosts and dust.

'There are lots of stories. In a way, the AngWat is a story. But the truth, Petey. We began on another world, where there were tools that gave one man the strength of more than many thousands. One person could destroy everything. With those tools, Petey, one person might destroy the whole of Haze.'

She looked around at the fog and tried to imagine it all gone, the world beyond it destroyed. It was impossible. The sounds, the smells, even in the Haze, it was so solid.

'But we escaped. We fled here, through the stars. Even so, we were pursued, and we used the forbidden tools for the last time to protect ourselves. When we got here, the fire of the stars had destroyed our memory, so we could start again.'

'If they had destroyed our memory, how do you know it?'

'The Great Lord knows.'

'The lords have tools,' Petey said. 'Why, if tools are so bad?'

'There are rules. The lords are punished when they break the rules, just like you.' He smiled thinly. 'The village lords are as scared as you.'

'Who makes the rules?'

'There's a special place in the city, barred to almost everyone, called the Heart. The Great Lord lives there. I've seen it. Seen him.' His voice seemed to fade briefly, and she could see the memory in his eyes. 'Everyone taken to the AngWat is taken there as a child.'

'But why destroy villages? I still don't understand?'

'It's necessary. I told you how in the past, an entire world was destroyed, everything turned to nothing. This way, it can't happen again.'

It sounded to Petey as if Reed were justifying it to her, using the word *necessary*, and she felt uncomfortable. She thought of Crique, who knew him better than anyone and still distrusted him. And the way he talked, the words she half-understood. She repeated, 'The lords have tools, Reed.'

'I told you, the lords are controlled, the same as you.'

'But it's their rules.'

'Not created by men. For time beyond time, the Great Lord has kept the rules. Every week, the high lords go to receive the next week's instructions. In all that time, Haze hasn't changed.

'It stays the same,' she said, giving up on the idea of time. 'All this death.'

'The forest is conserved. People would die anyway. In the previous world, people destroyed the forests and killed each other. This way, fewer people die. The massacre you saw, such things are hardly ever necessary.'

Necessary. She stared at him. The Haze blurred his face.

'Villages destroy each other regardless. The lords' culls are planned.' He registered her expression. 'This is what I was taught,' he added quickly. 'But I'm here, Petey. Not there. It's not what I believe now. Just as you and I can't easily trust each other, nor can the lords.'

'You killed other children, Reed.'

'We were fed pastes that made it easy. Drugs. You saw the children at that village. And then I was taken to the city and taught more. In the end, all I believed in was the importance of keeping the world the same.'

She said, 'How did you escape?' But that wasn't the question in her mind. Not the way he was talking, the light in his eyes. She said, '*Why* did you escape?'

'The village lords . . .' He stopped, then started again, and she wondered why. 'In the AngWat,' he said, 'They think cruelty doesn't matter. Life in the forest is random but stable. It's a steady state of disaster and tragedy. With people, it's different. There are feuds and massacres over food and territory. That's why there are quotas and the need for control. Without control, there would be constant war. That's *khuk* nature.' He reddened. 'I'm sorry, Petey. I was a long time in the AngWat.'

He waited. Petey had nothing to say. He took a shivering breath and went on. 'But village lords are used to violence. They haven't been taught anything more. At the AngWat, they think it's right to make the villagers behave like animals. They think only a few villagers are able to become lords, the rest worthless. *Khuks.*'

He looked at the ground, then uncertainly at Petey. She wondered whether he was looking at a worthless *khuk* woman. She remembered Jemus looking at her. Reed was not like Jemus, though. She was sure of that. She trusted herself. She trusted the beating of her heart for Reed.

'I asked you why you escaped.'

'After my education in the city, I was sent back to my village, to observe. I stayed with the lord. He didn't realise it had been where I was born. He tried to impress me by killing a man for a small crime.' His voice seemed to crack away. 'It was a man I knew. It was the father.'

And that was it for Petey. She knew Reed was not lying. He couldn't even say it, even now. *My* father.

'I argued with the lord. I fought with him, in front of the whole village. I beat him unconscious, and even then, I couldn't stop. I killed him with my fists. And then I took the father's body and carried it out of the village. He was light.' Reed was almost choking. 'So very light. I put on the father's clothes, and then I dressed the lord in my robe and left him for the animals to eat. And I ran.' He wiped his eyes, although they were dry. Petey could see him remembering. She felt the rawness of her own remembering.

'The lord was the same size as me. They would have thought he'd killed me and fled. The villagers would have said so. It would have put them in more danger if they'd said otherwise, anyway. In their eyes it was his right to kill anyone. Lords go berserk occasionally. The AngWat knows that.' Reed took a shivering breath. 'I ran and I concealed my tracks. I threw away the robe. I ran until I was sure they would give him up for crazy, dead and eaten.'

'And then?'

'I came across Crique by chance. Or he found me. We were both about the same age. Eighteen. He was hunting illegally, emptying a trap when I came across him. I was almost naked. He didn't know I was a lord, or what village I might be from. I was desperate. I was watching him from behind a tree when he saw me. He had a knife and I had nothing. There was a moment when he could have killed me and nothing would have changed for him. He could have just gone back to his village as if nothing had happened. It would have been natural for him to kill me. I was just a mouth.'

Petey understood what Reed meant. A mouth needed feeding, and a mouth could betray you. 'He didn't kill you,' she said.

'No. I told him I'd run from my village, and he decided to leave his. He'd never been able to talk to anyone before. I told him I'd killed a lord, and that was enough. We hunted together, avoiding villages and trails, moving steadily away from the AngWat. We became friends. Then we stumbled upon Nepenth, as people still sometimes do, and we settled here. We returned regularly to the forest below to see how life was, whether it had become any easier. That first time back, we found a woman outcast in the forest, and brought her back. Over time, we found others. The village grew. Now it's as you see it.'

'You and Crique,' she said. 'What happened between you? Was it the woman?'

'No, it wasn't that. For a long time I still didn't tell him I'd been a lord. At first, I was ashamed of standing there and letting the father be killed. Then there was never a time. By the time he found out, we were such close friends that it ruined everything.'

'How did he find out?'

'Someone joined us who had lived in my village. They remembered me killing the lord.'

'Surely that proved you were no longer one of them.'

Reed made a face. 'I'd lied to Crique. Or rather, I hadn't told him the whole truth. It shouldn't have altered who I was to him, but it did. Since then, he hasn't trusted me. When I leave the village, he goes with me.'

Hearing him speak about not speaking and the effects of it on himself and his closest friend made Petey want to say all the things to Loren that she'd never said. She suddenly ached for him. It hadn't been distrust between them, but the blurring of uncertainty, like the Haze that came and went here in Nepenth. And with Marten and her daughter, not being able to trust a child for its innocence, and then, by the time the child knew what it was safe to say, it was too late to teach trust.

'Too late,' Petey murmured. She licked her lips. Salt. 'Too late.'

'No. It's not too late, Petey. We escaped. It's not too late.'

But she was thinking of Marten, and saying his name into the air.

'Forget about him. The lords never let go. That's what was. We've escaped, Petey. You and I.' He moved forward, awkwardly, and was hugging her, holding her gently as she cried. She remembered his close smell from the first time, his arms around her neck from behind, starting to choke her. She pushed him away.

'You escaped, Reed? You said the lords never let go.'

He slumped down on the ground and squatted there, head down. 'What they did to me will never leave me. What I did, what I do, it's all to safeguard the future.' He lifted his head. 'Yes, I would have killed you, Petey. You cry, I never do. I look at you now, and I see . . . I see what I haven't seen for a long time. Most of the people we bring here are full of fear. They cry. They cry because they're afraid we'll kill them, and then they cry with gratitude, or relief. When I was at the AngWat——' He took a long breath. 'What I saw there never goes. When I was at the AngWat, I was trained. When I saw fear in a *khuk*'s eyes, it made me strong. When I saw gratitude, it made me contemptuous. Those things still do that to me. I can't help it.' He stared at her, long and evenly, and said, 'But you, Petey. You cry for another reason, and you make me feel different. That's all.' He breathed as if surfacing from deep water. 'But I'm not changed, Petey. And Marten is not your child any more.'

No. Nothing is ours, Petey thought dully. For a moment she was back in her village, in the doorway of the children's dormitory, Loren beside her, the two of them looking at Marten asleep.

'Nepenth is a dead place, Reed. It has no children, no future. What use is it?'

'Something will change. The AngWat can't last forever. New people arrive in Nepenth, as you did. Let me show you.'

He walked with her. They went through the village and out again, to a place through a narrowing of tall rocks that she hadn't seen before. He made her wait patiently until, for a brief moment, there was a view through the Haze.

She felt dizzy and braced herself against Reed, and stared at the seemingly endless blue beneath them, with its flecks of white, and squalls of birds wheeling above it like fragments of cloud, the sudden synchronised show of underwings as they turned making them shine like glass.

'That's the sea. One day it will be safe to go there. The children who are born there, Petey, they will be a little better than us. Their children will be better. In time, everything will be different.'

'In time? But what about *now*? We're not so far away from the AngWat. They'll find us. We have to do something.'

'Forget that, Petey. Forget your son. They won't find us here. The Haze protects us. Until we go beyond the mountain, we're safe.'

'They'll find us.'

There was silence between them. The sea went and came again. She wanted him to say, *No*, but he didn't.

'They have their world,' he said. 'They want to keep it the same. It's all they want. I know, Petey.'

'You don't know. You *don't*.' She was crying again, staring at the beauty and thinking of Marten.

'They have no hope, Petey. They don't care. We have hope. We have this vision.' He took his arm across the blinding vista. 'What's our alternative? We can't attack the AngWat. It's impregnable. The lords can bring down the causeways. They can pour poison into the moat. The firetubes aren't their only weapons. And there's the city.'

'In the end they'll find us and kill us.'

'In the end we'll all die.'

She made a sound of despair. 'You talk about hope, and then you say that?'

'Maybe there will be a time, but it isn't now. We aren't ready.'

'We aren't trying to be ready.'

'No. We aren't ready to try. Petey, you're thinking about your son. You have to accept he's gone.'

He stood and turned away from the distant, shimmering sea, and she followed him back through the village.

'Now you know almost everything about me, Petey.'

'Almost? What else is there?'

'It's a small thing. It troubles Crique. The nights are bad for me, sometimes. I need to be by myself, and I go walking. Occasionally I spend a night alone, to think in peace. It's nothing more than that.' He seemed to hesitate. 'Would that worry you?'

It was an odd way to say it, Petey thought. But as Reed said, it was a small thing. She said, 'Why should it worry me?'

'If I wake you up. Or if I don't wake you up, or if you wake up alone and I'm not there.'

She realised he was asking her to live with him. She laughed aloud. 'No,' she said. 'It wouldn't worry me.'

He put his arm around her, and for a while they said nothing, moving together on the rickety bed, rising and falling in gasps until they were both done and breathing soft again.

Then he said, 'Good. Because Crique tries to follow me. Sometimes he stays behind me all night, and sometimes he loses me. When he manages to keep up with me, he imagines he's prevented something, and when he loses me, he thinks . . . well, you'll have to ask him what he thinks.'

In bed again that night, Petey said, 'Crique and Yameen have a child.'

Reed held her. 'You know what happens to children here.'

'Is that why you haven't had a woman in Nepenth?'

'There hasn't been a woman I wanted until now.'

Staring at the roof, feeling unaccountably anxious, she fell asleep, but woke in the night with the fire low, and Haze enclosing the bed. The hut creaked around her. She felt for Reed, but he was gone. After a long time, she went back to sleep.

'Reed told me he was a lord,' Petey said. 'He told me everything. He told me what happens in the city behind the AngWat.'

Crique walked on and she raised her pace to keep up. The Haze was thick, but Petey knew where she was now. She knew how many steps she'd need to reach the edge of the market, and from there to her hut again.

'That makes him trustworthy, telling you that? He's one of them. He knew Nepenth was here, Petey. We didn't find it by chance. He led me here. I just didn't realise it at the time. He was very clever, but then he was trained to be. And you know about his night-walking?'

'Yes,' she said, but she was unsettled. 'He hardly wakes me.'

'Does he tell you where he goes?'

'No. He walks.'

'Aren't you curious?'

'He's restless. He needs to be alone sometimes. I trust him.'

'Everyone's alone in Nepenth, Petey. Don't you know that, yet?'

'You're alone, Crique. That's all. You may have Yameen and Artis, but you're alone.'

She was immediately sorry for saying that, but it didn't seem to bother him. He said, 'Reed's up to something. I know he is.'

'He says you follow him everywhere. You should know.'

Crique shook his head and walked away.

Later, she lay with Reed, his arm around her, warm and comforting. She stared at the roof of the hut, still troubled. She thought of the glittering sea. There had been a faint smell of salt.

Reed said, 'What would you expect him to think, Petey? I'd be thinking the same thing. Wouldn't it make sense for the AngWat to keep an eye on free people? To monitor them? Then we could know when there was a need to destroy them.'

'We? Them? Who are you, Reed? Which side are you on?'

'I was looking through his eyes, Petey. I know what side I'm on. I can't convince you with words, Petey. I know that. It's a matter of trust. You believe me or you don't. Crique never will.'

HAVEN

After leaving Naddy and Skim, it took Quill a week to reach the coredor he needed. On the way he left false trails and drove the coffin through a field of obsidian that would perfectly conceal the vitrification of his passage to any tracking technology he could think of. He crossed his routes and left false exits at a series of niches and dead coredors. It wasn't perfect, but it was probably enough.

He spoke to Scheck a lot, and when he finally came out, deepdeepdown and in the outer reaches of Green, he was thinking of Skim. And then it was time to find Horvath.

Quill had heard of the man, but talk of him was like whisperings of unFact. Quill found him where the rumours said he was to be found, in the recesses of an old magnetic ore excavation, where the faintest colour had faded away from the names of coredors. He walked through the quarry until his eyes started to accustom themselves to the mine-dark space, and waited until a shape began to separate from the shadows.

'Horvath?'

'I'm awake. I can see you. Take your time.'

'I was afraid you were dead. Nothing left of you but rumours.' But there he was, like some monster, sitting there in the darkness. Quill stared at him, and the chamber was suddenly flooded with daylites. Quill squeezed his eyes closed.

'I'm alive. Is that uncomfortable for you?'

Quill squinted. 'Yes. I wasn't expecting—'

'I tolerate light for short periods.'

Horvath moved his head. The translucent crystal that had made him legend had pierced his skull above the temple, burying itself like a dagger. It was deep, but how deep was impossible to tell. Light shot down its length and became confused, so that for a moment the inside of Horvath's skull looked entirely empty, a magician's trick, and the next moment it seemed more full of brain and deeper than his skull could allow. Even in the brightness of the daylites, Quill couldn't make it out.

Now the blaze of the crystal was blinding, and now it was darker than obsidian.

Quill took a seat across the chamber from the man. It was whispered that he could receive radio signals and speak with the dead, that he could dowse for magma and raise pebbles from a table and bring them into his hands. It was said that he was crazy, and it was said that he was sane, but all of it was probably unFact.

The only thing Quill knew for sure was that he wasn't Horvath any more. He didn't know what had happened to Horvath, because the man clearly hadn't died, but just as surely he wasn't there any longer, even though the only thing different about him was the lance of crystal that jutted like a horn from his right temple.

Horvath couldn't see it. He couldn't see anything on his right hand side, so his brain had constructed for his eyes a mirror of his left side. The only thing Horvath thought odd about that was that he could close his left eye, look at himself in the mirror and see himself with both eyes closed. Which was very odd indeed. Though not as odd as seeing himself in the mirror with a crystal horn would have been.

But this horned creature was like a screen with all of Horvath's data and nothing else. It had his voice but not quite its tone. The horn was a tube through which Horvath had been sucked, clumsily copied and the copy installed in its place.

'How are you, Horvath,' Quill said.

The great head turned, and as it did Quill had a sense of something else, another hornheaded monster from another time and place, and in his head Scheck was whispering of myth and legend, of unFact. Minotaur, unicorn.

'Well?'

'I need help,' Quill said. 'Naddy Harke told me you'd help me. He was taken by Fact.'

Horvath's head tipped and jerked, taken by something Quill couldn't see. 'Ah, Naddy. When did he tell you this?'

'A week ago.'

'It's too late for help now. He's playing the Game, now. I'm sorry. He was dropped into the arena two days ago. Not that I could have helped you even before that.'

Quill said, 'There was someone else with him.'

'A woman. Do you want to see?' Horvath moved his head again, and a lance of light shot from the tip of his horn to the excavated face of the wall, and Quill was seeing the Game.

'A good advance made here, Dan, wouldn't you say? Five point two metres over the twenty-four period?'

'Blue seem to be on the roll,' Jan agreed.

Their voices boomed in the small cavern. Quill made out Naddy first, his unmistakable gut bulging against the blue tunic. He was scouting for the ball-pushers, looking at the stalagmites and tapping them with his knuckles.

'See that, Jan? He's sharp. He's instructing them how to most easily crack them away. Looking for their weak spots. He's a find, that one. Red will want to target him, get him out of the game as soon as possible. He's been lucky to survive this long.'

Quill couldn't make Skim out. 'Keep still, Horvath. You're moving.'

'You want me to stop breathing?'

'No. Sorry.' There were five others pushing, and one scouting ahead with Horvath. Quill couldn't tell if it was a man or a woman.

Jan said, 'Red have been very quiet for a few hours, Dan. You think they're building up to something?'

'Well, if I were wagering on Red, I'd be wanting blood by now, that's for sure. If they don't do something about this very soon, they'll be penalised. One way or the other, there will be blood, Jan.'

Keeping to its side, Quill went closer to the quivering projection. A blur of crimson crashed into view from the left of the screen. There were five of them, Quill saw, jumping from the cover of a quartz outcrop and leaping over the rough ground of the arena towards Naddy and the other scout. They were armed with axes and jags of rock.

Naddy shrieked as the other Blues ran forward to defend him. Two of the Reds split away from the others and slashed at the main body of Blues, keeping them clear of Naddy and the scout, while the other three went directly for Naddy.

Naddy stumbled backwards and sat down. His companion picked up a rock and swung her arm – it was a woman, Quill was sure – at the nearest Red, who tried to dodge but lost his footing and fell into another Red. They both fell, and the woman brought her loaded fist down on the forehead of the nearest Red, finishing it for him. She was turning quickly to the other when he backhanded her to the ground. She fell awkwardly, face down, and didn't move again. The screen moved to follow another Red as he went for Naddy, who was on his feet again. Naddy swiped a rock across the Red's face, and the man fell. Only one Red was left standing. He looked at Naddy, then turned and fled.

'Today's definitely a Blue day, Jan. Red will be applying for replacements.'

The cam went back to Naddy, who was grunting as he struggled to push the Red corpse off the Blue woman scout. He succeeded just as another Blue reached him, pulling the scout's body over. Quill registered at the same time that she was dead and that she wasn't Skim. The cam went to Naddy's blood-streaked face. The Blue at his side was Skim.

Quill breathed out, and realised he'd been holding his breath. 'I have to get them, Horvath,' he said.

The screen died on the wall. The mine dimmed. 'And how are you going to do that?'

'Naddy knew he'd be put into the Game. He sent me to you. I can get to the arena, but I won't know what to do from there. I don't know what part of the arena they're in.'

'It's immense,' Horvath murmured. 'What would Naddy think I knew that could help?'

'Can you access Fact screens?'

'No. I can only receive and observe what's faintly there in rock and coredor. Fact screens are shielded.'

Quill said, 'How many cams are there in the arena?'

'Thousands. The arena's a torus. It has a median circumference of more than a hundred kils.'

'Can you only receive from the cam they're actually screening?'

'That's the only one I can get clearly. The others are always operating, even if they're not upscreened. I can get them.'

'Could you find a cam by the drop tube?'

'Why?'

'My coffin charts show the top point of the drop tube. If we can use your access to the cams, we can use their overlap to fix Naddy and Skim's exact location within the arena. If I link that with my charts, we'll know exactly where they are.'

Horvath shrugged, his skull spike seeming to fracture the cavern, and then he filled the wall with a cam view. In the centre was the black and white circle of the drop point. The image cut to a quarter of its size, and three more images appeared. There was no connection. Ice in one, jagged fields of quartz, then slate, and the shine of mica.

Horvath murmured, 'There are thousands of these.'

Quill stared at the wall as Horvath quartered the block of images and put up three new ones in the free space. There was no link between them. He shuffled them about, then abruptly filled the entire wall with fingernail images. Quill couldn't even see the Reds and Blues.

'This is what you need to sift and sort, Quill. I can't help you with it. I can just put them here for you.'

'Crise.' It looked hopeless. 'Can you give me a copy of this?'

Horvath spread his arms sorrowfully. 'There's just me, Quill. That's all there is. That's why they leave me alone.'

'Hold on.' Quill went back to the coffin. When he returned, he set a small square device down on the floor and said, 'This is an optical mineral sorter. If I correct it for lighting, it can give us a precise reading of rock and mineral type. The images are full of rock. It can correlate them.' The machine hummed and shot a faint beam at the wall of images. Quill said, 'This is going to take a long time.'

'Time's what I have. Whatever I do, it goes.'

There was almost silence. The optical sorter clicked and tracked at random from image to image, then hummed again as the thin beam flicked steadily between two tiny images. Quill smiled. 'Now, Horvath. Put them together ...'

It took three hours to sequence the cams, but at the end of it Quill and Horvath were looking at the arena laid out on the wall like a ring of colour and gleam. It swallowed itself, glittering and gloomy, and like an eye, there was black at its heart. The drop tube was arbitrarily centred at the top, a silver slash arrested in mid air.

At the moment the Game was taking place about ten kils from the drop tube. There was a small cluster of transport carts by the tube.

Horvath brought up the view of Naddy and Skim.

'Tie your hair back and take off your clothes,' Marten said.

In the small niche with its single proximity light, Mexi looked at him warily.

'It's all right, there are no cams here.' He started to untie his robe.

'What are you doing? If you think—'

He pulled another orange robe from inside his own and held it out to her. 'I like you and I'd like to,' he said, 'But not now. Put this on. You'll be safer.'

She took her clothes off. He didn't turn round. He looked at her as she pulled the robe around herself and gathered her clothes together into a bundle.

'I like the way you move,' he said. 'You move easily. We don't tie the waist cord like that, though. Let me—'

He started to work the knot, but stopped and shook his head. 'I'm not used to doing it from the front. Turn round.'

She held her arms up for him and he went behind her, his chin brushing her neck as he made the knot.

'Now you do it. You have to be able to do it.'

'Why?'

'Factotems will notice clumsiness. It could give you away.'

She did it twice for him. Then he took her clothes and put them inside his robe. He did it carefully, and she thought of his hands on hers. She thought of him saying, 'I'd like to.'

'Let's go,' he said. 'We may be too late already.' He let them out of the niche and into the narrow coredor. They began to walk.

It felt strange to move in the robe. The material was lighter than she'd imagined. And the way he talked, his language. He wasn't a primitive at all. 'I don't understand this,' she said.

'What don't you understand?'

'Anything. I thought you were all uneducated, but you can't be. So why do you wander around and watch us? What does it prove? It's pointless.'

Without slowing, he turned his head towards her. 'We don't just watch you. Didn't you realise that?'

The rock took them down. Mexi knew where she was, but she felt more lost than she had ever been. Zelda was dead and here was a Robe telling her that everything she knew was wrong.

'Here we are,' Marten said eventually. 'Naddy—' he stopped.

Mexi heard it too, the sound of voices beyond the curl of the coredor. 'Wait,' Marten said.

He returned from the curve of the coredor and said, 'We're too late.'

'I'm going to see for myself,' she began, but he put his hand on her arm and pulled her back.

'No. They ignored me, but they might not ignore another Robe appearing so soon. You wouldn't be able to conceal your interest. As far as they know, you murdered their factotems. They're after you.'

'Why did you help me?'

He hesitated, then said, 'I wanted to.'

She sensed that he meant it, though it was clear there was more than that. 'We can't stand here, then,' she said. 'What shall we do?'

'I have to go back. To report. I'll say I was dizzy and went wandering. I have . . . a friend. He'll help me.'

She could see how hard it was for him to say that. A friend. 'And me?'

'Stay deep. Avoid the Primaries and keep to the smaller coredors. If you see another Robe and can't avoid them, keep your head down. I'll find out what's happening.'

CAP

It is of huge evolutionary advantage to lie convincingly. We have our opposable thumbs and we use tools, but more importantly, we're social creatures, and one can only succeed as a social animal if one can deceive the social animals around oneself.

There are exceptions, like Jake, of course, although his evolutionary disadvantage was temporarily outweighed by other factors. He set off his personal evolutionary disadvantage by contributing to my advantage. It didn't help his genes any, but when you stop to consider how little anyone else's social skills helped them in the end, back on Earth, none of it mattered a damn.

And sniffing out a lie, or a liar, isn't always possible. You can only tell a charlatan face to face, if you can tell them at all. And there are tools to help liars. Put a liar on a screen, and if they are any good and surrounded by anyone any good, you haven't a snowball's chance in hell of picking them out. Assuming you believe in hell.

Politicians are alpha charlatans. And they have access to the tools for the job.

I was talking about lying, though. It's been shown that the most successful liars are able to temporarily believe in their lie. Brain scans show them to be using a different part of the brain. It's an evolutionary thing. We have evolved to be able to identify liars by their self-conscious gaze, the sweat on their upper lips, and in response liars evolved the means of concealing that. As we developed better ways of picking the lie, they actually developed the ability to believe what they were saying. It's unbeatable, you'd think – how can you pick a liar who actually believes for that moment that they aren't lying?

But of course, it isn't unbeatable. I'll get to that.

We took Maine Abreha, then. He was good. I expected that, of course. Gus would not have used fools. He always chose carefully. After all, he had chosen me. So it didn't surprise me that Maine was able to fool the lie detectors. Skin conductivity, temperature, he passed all those tests and more. Ironically these were, in part, more or less the same reactive tests they had been using on me, to discover whether I had psychopathic tendencies. By his behaviour Maine himself had alerted me to this – again, ironically, in view of its imminent consequences upon him – and I was aware how easily one could train oneself to make the tests misread.

Maine Abreha, then, was highly evolved. He remained dry when he needed to, and he sweated appropriately. Profusely, even. He stared wide-eyed, he looked away. Under mild stress he reacted as he had been trained to. He was confused, indignant, angry. The smooth perfection with which he went from one phase to the next reminded me of the cancer acknowledgement sequence, its mental aspect. Disbelief, anger, acceptance.

Oh, denial. I forgot denial. Maine denied consistently. With cancer, they say, you eventually accept.

My father, of course, never accepted the truth. Like me, he was strong. For one inexplicable moment I looked at Maine Abreha and I saw my father sitting there, straining and sobbing, and I had to stop briefly and leave the room.

And like my father, Maine Abreha never accepted it; neither that he had been given the task of spying on me, nor that the President had guessed I didn't trust him. He could have admitted these without dishonour, but left it too late, and by the time he realised it was too late to backtrack, he knew it must be clear to me that he was so good that I could believe nothing he told me. So I never asked Maine what the President intended doing about me. It would have insulted Maine, and by the time we got to that point, Maine and I had developed an unspoken empathy.

As the days went by, Maine just got better. His training astounded me. He was a natural. He followed the exact reaction curve of a naive respondent. He seemed to break down. He denied, then invented, then contradicted himself. He sobbed. He screamed.

It was a perfect interrogation, ending with his death. I was honest. With someone as full of integrity as Maine Abreha was, it was important not to lie. At one point I said to him, 'You're thinking that I'm going to have to kill you anyway, and that what I'm offering you is an easy death. But I'm not. It will be hard. I'm being honest with you, Maine. The voltage will go up. We can hold your head under for longer. There are finer wires, longer needles. There is your sight.'

Nevertheless, he maintained his integrity to the end. I closed his eyelids, as far as it was possible, with my own fingers, and I said a few words. I felt the gesture to be important. We must always maintain our humanity, even under the most strenuous vexation.

I said that I would get back to how one can know a lie for what it is, despite the teller's own belief in it. That's the highest evolutionary marker, socially speaking, that ability. It comes down to an equal knowledge with the liar, in the lie as a lie. It comes down to the schoolyard words *I know you know.*

All along, throughout the entire process, I had known Maine Abreha was lying. I had known he would lie.

You're thinking, why did I interrogate him?

I interrogated him to discover the depth of the plot against me. And what I learnt from the process was that the plot was deep, and that I had everything to fear from Gus. He suspected me, and a man like him was not going to sit back and let the world go by. I reminded myself again that he had chosen me when he had needed awkward work done, as he had chosen Maine Abreha. There would be others. Gus was an untethered man of brutal ambition.

But nor was I going to give up. I had my plans.

I retreated to the Foundation for a few days, and I took stock. There was much to do, but there was always much to do. I relied on John for a great deal of it. He knew nothing of Maine Abreha, nor of Jake, nor of any of my core plans. From that point of view, he was perfectly trustworthy. And he had enough work to do that he was left no time to spend with Mary.

Now that I was quite certain I was being monitored, I knew to take precautions. I was careful not to search for bugs or in any further active way investigate how it was being carried out. I was sure they had no knowledge of Jake, or of the second cube, or of certain other embedded devices. As for the rest of it, it was still in my head and there alone, and would remain there until the last minute.

Jake provided me with security of communication, and the tasks I needed performed were carried out by a small group of dedicated men and women who knew it was Our Lord's secret work. If they were to be caught, there could be no connection with me, but they were safe enough. There was sufficient civil unrest for much crime to go uninvestigated, although the brutal abduction for ransom of Maine Abreha and his subsequent torture and murder when the Administration refused to pay for his release were headline news. When his corpse was recovered there were even vows that the perpetrators would be brought to justice. The state of the body provoked considerable comment. Gus had the gall to call me and ask if I had sufficient protection, and I wondered for a moment if he knew.

But of course he didn't. The apparently random burglaries, murders and firebombings worked well, and if targets could not be addressed in this manner, there were still enough terrorists and conspiracy theorists mumbling away to themselves as they armed their bombs and scratched away at what they saw as their truth, eager to incorporate fresh plot strands into their end-of-the-world-views.

Amid such uncertainty I found it an oddly comforting time. I was sleeping well and growing eager for the time of departure. I knew there was a plot against me, and I had made my plans. I hoped they would be enough.

And what of the world?

People were making their choices. The figures were quite fascinating. An astonishing ninety-three per cent opted to remain on the planet during the Restoration procedures, despite being told there would be fires, storms, floods, all that Old Testament stuff. The various stances taken by religious leaders helped. Many of them had a response similar to mine, seeing a potential for human rebirth, but unlike me they focused on the rebirth of the Earth itself, preaching that it was a matter of observance to remain, or else that it was a trial set by Our Lord, or that it would be a sin to leave. Whichever argument they chose, they were persuasive.

The conspiracy theorists believed that this was still an environmental blip, or that this was an Administration plot to reduce the Earth's population and that the ships were orbiting abattoirs, or that the process of Restoration would actually take no more than a few weeks, or that aliens were playing with their brains.

All views were encouraged by the Administration. In such delicate times there was no preferential treatment. Media and internet exposure was available to all. Environmentalists shared screen time with fundamentalists, survivalists with New Middle-Earthers. An organisation calling itself Vole Pogrom firebombed rocket sites and was rewarded with an hour of airtime on a minor channel.

Clearly, there were not going to be enough ships to take more than a tiny number of people off the planet. Any who remained voluntarily were given tax breaks. Terrorist groups registered eagerly for these.

I learnt that in irrational circumstances, people would provide their own rationality even if it were crazy, and that if you imposed a rationality upon them they would mould themselves to it. People can be like goats, of their own minds, and yet they can be like sheep, blindly eager to be herded. And in the latter condition, they will actually refuse to revert their state.

The figures broke down interestingly. The ninety-three per cent stayers included the Don't Knows who didn't return their papers in time. (That was not the Administration's fault. They air-dropped at least three times the number they estimated were required, over even the waste continents.)

Four per cent decided to go into cryo-orbit during Restoration. The Administration expected more demand for this, but found that many of the ninety-three per cent stayers had rejected the hibernation option on the basis that they would return to their homes after several hundred years to find them looted.

Almost five per cent decided to go with the Administration fleet to Haze, as they called it. Mainly because Gus had such a fine and comforting voice.

And a thousandth of one per cent of the world's population opted to join me in the great adventure.

In the middle of this storm of betrayal, I was most heartened by that.

There was a small problem, in that several thousand million souls in excess of capacity chose to leave. After all, fifty million souls wanted to go with me. I had capacity for a few thousand, the Administration for a few hundred thousand.

A second wave was announced for a year following the first, and a program of more while the Restoration built momentum. There was no intention of a second wave. It was impossible, but the reassurance was important.

Shipbuilding figures were exaggerated. Some of the conspiracy theorists guessed at much of this, even suggesting that there was never an intention that more than a chosen few would leave, and that the whole thing had always been a device to facilitate this, but their voices were drowned in the general conspiracy babble.

Democracy, such as it was, triumphed. This was its last and greatest shout. More than six billion people lived on the planet, and every one of them was given the opportunity to make their personal choice. They spoke to their neighbours. They opened their screens. They hooked into the infosphere, that electronic layer of unsifted information and junk that by then circulated invisibly all around the planet in just as polluted a state as the atmosphere and the stratosphere. They threw dice, coins, yarrow sticks. They informed themselves, they decided, they selected. The Administration, and I, took every single person's choice into account, by means of a sophisticated lottery-based computer program.

I knew what I was going to do about John and Mary, and the rest of my congregation, but I was in two minds about Jake. He had no interest in the outside world – he actively cut himself off from it, concerned only with its capacity to supply him with noodles and Texicola – and I was not going to disturb his peace of mind or concentration. He was still a help to me. I knew that when I left, he would be a lost soul.

Some time before the two fleets were scheduled to depart, the question arose of what heritage would be taken. History was important to Gus. He wanted to maintain a connection with the past. I, on the other hand, needed nothing at all for my own fleet. I wanted a world unshadowed by the past. For me and my people, it would be a new time and a new ground to build on. We cast around for catchphrases, but of course the two obvious ones – Year Zero and Ground Zero – had already been appropriated.

There was of course a third fleet, a fleet of ships that would circle the Earth with a cargo of sleepers, a convoy of vessels chasing its own tail as its planet was renovated beneath it. These ships also carried an Ark of eggs, cells and embryos, and the more fragile objects of human history. What could easily be removed was transferred to space for safety until the terra-reforming of the Earth was complete. Museums were relieved of their stores.

Sites of cultural importance were protected from the renewal process as well as they could be. They were covered first by vast shrouds of silicon and then blanketed thickly in a chemically reversible rock gel for protection. No one had the slightest idea whether it would be sufficient to resist the forces of planetary change. You would have imagined that the people choosing to remain on the surface would have been nudged into reconsideration by seeing these measures; The Great Wall of China (a few token kilometres of it), Angkor Wat, the Taj Mahal, Persepolis, the pyramids, others I forget, all were buried under hundreds of metres of what was effectively volcanic lava. And people in their millions stared and marvelled and then closed their doors and expected to survive the forces that we had designed these immense sarcophagi to withstand.

Such faith. Where can it come from, such a thing? To believe so strongly in something so crazy? Even now, I marvel.

Look where it got them. But then, if you had the choice, what would you go for? To die desperately on Earth as the seas boiled and the mountains melted, or else to drift into a cocooned, icy sleep and wake up briefly, adrift in space, alone and trapped in a dark metal coffin, and then to slowly starve or suffocate to death (I forget the finer details of Jake's blueprints) a century or two later. Not, of course, that they were aware of that.

There was much discussion about the archive to be taken by Gus. There was no room for the inessential. There was hardly space for the essential. If you have to choose between books and people, artefacts and humans, what do you take? Gus decided his answer was people. Stuff the ships with people. As with the orbiting fleet, the animals could be fertilised eggs or embryos or whatever else was small enough to freeze, so that wasn't an issue.

Knowledge was an issue. The sum of human knowledge – I say again, look where it had got us – was immense. Page after page, library after library. One ship took the main copy, on disks, but, in case of catastrophe, there was also a backup memory.

The backup memory. Aaah. The banana skin I seem to be slipping on, sprawling momentarily. Such a tiny thing, so long ago.

It was well known that you could make a code for language using the four bases of DNA, cytosine, guanine, adenine and thymine. The trick was initially illustrated using the genome of a bacterium that I believe causes stomach ache. The information was retrieved imperfectly, but it was a start. After that, retroviruses were more successfully used. With them, vast quantities of information could be encoded in a storage device smaller than the head of a pin. Not only language, but physical information too, such as movement, and all carefully located on chromosomes in what was laughably called junk DNA.

It was fascinating. The retrovirus was manipulated to be infectious so that it could be caught, just like a cold. Only if you caught this, it wouldn't prompt you to sneeze. It would prompt your brain to decode and store the information as a form of accessible memory. The archived memory was naturally incomplete, even though it was vast. The Archivirus was divided into three parts, and wasn't intended to be caught directly by a human subject. The parts were to be cultured primarily in vitro and only then, secondarily, transmitted to humans. Primary – total – transfer of the Archivirus from its case was made to be possible only once for each blister, for safety, as any human accidentally exposed would be driven insane by the flood of unblocked information. Secondary infection or transfer was the intended route of Archive release. Those exposed to it obtained different parts of the Archive and to different degrees. This was unpredictable. Due to retroviral mutation and the interaction between the individual's pre-existing memories and the retroviral memory, there would be omissions and errors. The Archivirus wasn't perfect.

As another safety measure, only the primary source could transfer the Archive onward. Subsequently, it was like an attenuated vaccine. In order to prevent progressive data corruption, secondary recipients were not infectious.

Data corruption, yes. It has the sound of a cold, machine malfunction.

332

I think of my past, the lies of my memory. Memory is an uncertain thing. It's unstable. It can swamp you and it can as easily disappear. It can change subtly or utterly. It can lie. It can torture you and it can save you.

I must concentrate. Set down these memories, these data.

This, then, was the Archivirus. Oddly enough, it was Mary, my Mary, who launched herself into this particular project. After the neverending setbacks of her personal struggle, she had given up, and in its place the Archive had taken her fancy.

I wasn't especially interested in it, but Gus . . . Gus saw the Archivirus as Salvation alone. Each ship of his fleet carried a case of the Archivirus. On arrival – should the main Archive have somehow been damaged en route – it could be cultured and selected colonists infected with it. He thought that although each carrier would have faulty memories, the number of correct memories would counter the errors, and a consensus of fact could be made. The Archive could simply be remembered, agreed and transferred back into a hard form.

Fact is not like this. It is not a thing that can be held in the hand and examined like a piece of rock. It can't be relied on. I knew that then, and I know it now.

Gus and I agreed that we should each carry the lieutenant of the other, as a testament to our faith in each other. It was my idea. John went with him, and Cori came with me.

And finally, the day came.

The skies blazed as the fleets set off. It was like the most glorious sunset you would ever see, and it was so very, very poignant. It took two months for the ships to leave. Two months of sunset. By the end, apparently, people were moaning about it, about the brightness, the coarse colours, the impossibility of sleep. If they had only known what sleep was coming.

And the noise, too. My father used to tell me of freight trains rumbling endlessly down the lines, and this is how I thought of the fleets – freight trains through the eternal night.

Gus and I spoke one last time. He talked of his planet, Haze, and so did I.

His plans were ridiculous. If I had had any doubts, our final conversation dispelled them. He was full of great words, but he had no awareness of the lessons of the past. He talked of democracy, of the end of strife, of glory. I, on the other hand, knew more firmly than ever – and not without a certain sadness, knowing the sacrifice I was to make – what had to be done.

He saw how sad I was. In the shadow of the ships, he clasped me to him and hugged me. I thought of my father holding me tight, but managed not to hurl Gus from me. I think I even squeezed him. He looked me in the eye and said, in his best voice, 'I shall never forget this moment, Cap.'

Never? What was he to know of eternity?

And so the long parade departed. We left the Earth behind us, with its own carousel of silently orbiting ships.

The terraforming machinery would have worked perfectly there, I'm certain. It would have been such a magnificent sight. Cameras were set to record it all from a thousand distances, in tens of thousands of perspectives. Such an awesome procedure. What we did to Haven and Haze shrinks to the mundane in comparison with that. I have watched it so many times. In my moments of self-doubt I have sat by Mary's side and held her limp hand and watched it. The cleansing storms, the swirls of gas, the fires of centuries, and in the end, the revelation of the new Earth. It moves me to tears.

And it made me realise I am, after all, not immortal. It pricked me to begin this record of my time, to set down this.

To set down this. Yes. One day even I shall be gone and judged, and though those who will judge me are unfit to do so, they should have the facts. They should understand what I have done for them.

The fleets, then, travelled serenely through space. We were a pair of umbilical cords, severed from our mother. Not foetuses even, but hoards of stem cells able to become ... to become anything at all.

We hibernated for centuries, our arteries and veins flooded with gel and cooled beyond death. I was a living mummy. A few of us were roused occasionally to carry out essential procedures, the adjustments of temperature and course. No one suffered more than was unavoidable.

The landings went almost perfectly, but not quite. John came out a little early from his sleep – I'm sure he somehow arranged it. As ever, he lacked trust. He also, somehow, had a copy of the Archivirus.

His sabotage failed, of course, but I was unable to prevent his departure from the fleet. His escape pod crashlanded on Haven. What he took for a sea turned out to be rather hotter. I noted the site, which was well away from where the colony subsequently landed.

Gus's fleet was rerouted by, let's say, faulty navigation devices (I could blame John, but I shan't) and came down on Haven instead of Haze, where I myself landed as planned. The fleets, of course, were decimated by the landings, instrument failures, hibernation failures, and in the end we were a few thousand who survived. Gus, and the entire Administration, perished. On my ship, Cori failed to survive.

Here on Haze, I set my plan in motion. I divided my people, sending some into the forest where I had my AngWat built, a reasonably faithful copy of Angkor Wat in Earth's Cambodia. It was to be a reminder to me of the dangers of both godhead and godlessness. Far from my AngWat, I built this city, and a hierarchy of lords and a cadre of scientists. I had my regime and my routine. I separated everyone from their past, and I ensured a constant present.

This constancy of the present was vital. I was to be immortal, but not quite ever-present. That is not possible. The techniques that allowed me to hibernate during the journey and wake my aides when necessary to carry out navigational and other adjustments were to give me all these hundreds of years of life now. But if I were to be awake and active for an hour or two each week, and cerebrally conscious for some of the remainder of the time, it was vital to prevent the world from moving away from me in language and comprehension.

That was Haze. I'll come back to it. There is so much.

Haven was a different matter. Frankly, I didn't expect them to survive more than a couple of generations, but they did. When the first of my ships landed a century or so later, simply to confirm their extinction, it was a shock.

But I have always seen adversity as opportunity. They had lost much of their past in the struggle for survival in the present, and belatedly set up a rudimentary archive of memories. That first ship gave nothing away, and when they were stable enough to begin travelling, we let them discover us – not my city, of course, and never my Heart – and then we traded. Gradually, we exerted our influence. We observed as they blindly wormed their 'coredors' towards where John's ship had to be, and I prepared – insufficiently, it turns out – to deal with that. We aided their leading cadre, Fact, rewarding them with skins and timber in return for freedom for my people to roam their Vault.

Over the years, we gently changed the Vault data. The more Fact delved into its own history, the less it reflected the truth of that history. My – the Captain's – image even slowly became John's. It amused me to allow him in death to supplant me.

Mary stayed with me, though. She's faithful to me now. I have her sleep most of the time, as I do. I'm active for those two hours every week. Sometimes there's more to do, sometimes less. Two hours is an average. The lords I can trust carry out my orders. After all, I'm a god to them, though I've never permitted them the concept. As far as they're concerned, I'm immortal. Ageing two hours a week, or less than one week every year, in two thousand years I'll barely be eighty years old. It should be long enough to establish a stability here, once I've regained my balance after this little business of the Archivirus.

Mary has her few hours of consciousness too. I want her to age with me, even though her consciousness has to be staggered with mine – I have no time for her when I'm awake. There are things to be done, so many things. But even when she's awake, Mary is confined to her bed. I'm more able to trust her like that.

HAZE

The seasons passed in Nepenth, marked by warm summer rains that turned the streets and alleys to mud, and by cold, dry winters of frost and ice. The only constant was the Haze – the rains battered it down, curdling it thickly on the ground and around everyone's feet, while the winter cold pushed it through the walls and into the huts, and even the fiercest fires couldn't hold it out.

Through the years, through everything, Petey still thought of Marten. She thought occasionally of Loren too, and of her daughter. Most of the time, if she let herself think of anything at all, she thought anxiously of the future, and what it might hold for her new son.

Now, she tried to rub away the exhaustion in her eyes as she looked at him, peacefully sleeping in the bed Reed had cut and carved. He stirred under the sheets, and she stroked his hot forehead. He'd started to cough a few weeks back, and she was worried.

The love she had for Duneld troubled her more and more, as he grew. The boy was a reminder of the long past, and in the past love had never done her, or those she loved, any good. Duneld was as old now as Marten had been when, so long ago, he had been marched away down the causeway to the AngWat.

'How are you, Petey? And how's Duneld?'

She looked up and turned, startled at the voice, and Yameen took her hand and held it a moment.

'I didn't hear you come in,' Petey said. 'We're well. You?'

Yameen gave her the smile that meant nothing, and sat down beside her. Artis had finally stopped coughing when Duneld had been two years old. His death had strengthened the bond between Petey and Yameen that had begun with Duneld's birth. That had also been the time Petey had begun to be accepted in Nepenth. With his arrival, she'd become a part of that doom, realising just how many women had borne children and helplessly watched them die in the village.

'I'm well,' Yameen said quietly.

The women said nothing else until Duneld woke up, rubbing his eyes. There was something of Marten in his looks, though Petey knew it was just part of herself handed down to both of them. Duneld was Reed's son, and she was constantly trying to understand Reed through the boy.

Sitting up, Duneld looked eagerly around the hut. 'Is he back?'

She stroked his soft hair. 'Three days, they said, Du. This is the third day, so they'll be back by nightfall.'

The boy coughed, then cleared his throat. 'Can I stay up to see him and Crique?'

'Of course.'

It still surprised her that Crique stayed close to herself and Reed. She couldn't work the two men out. Occasionally they flared up at each other, but most of the time they worked together well. Her arrival, those years ago, had caused the worst of it, but since then it had calmed down again.

And despite Crique's suspicion, nothing had happened to Nepenth. It was still there, its sprawl slowly spreading through the rocks and the Haze. The AngWat hadn't attacked. Crique was still convinced Reed was a spy, but there was no proof. Reed, when he and Crique weren't away together, would still disappear in the middle of the night every week or so, and return a few hours before dawn. Yameen told Petey that Crique often sat by the window all through the night, and if he saw Reed leave, he'd slip out after him. Yameen and Petey laughed awkwardly, embarrassed at the men's behaviour. Sometimes Petey thought the whole thing was a joke between them, a pointless game between men.

At Reed's touch on her forehead, Petey woke up. She yawned and would have gone back to sleep as she normally did if he woke her as he was leaving, but this time he went to Duneld's bed and whispered something into the sleeping child's ear before leaving. This wasn't normal at all. He'd been out the night before, too, and hadn't returned until just before dawn, and then been anxious and withdrawn the whole day.

With a sense of foreboding, Petey quickly dressed herself and went quietly down the ladder after him.

It was easy to follow Reed. The Haze tonight was a thin mist, little more than a blurring of vision, and although she'd never left Nepenth since arriving there, Petey knew the local woods well. Reed wasn't trying to hide his tracks, anyway. He never went out twice on consecutive nights, and Crique would be confidently sleeping. Tonight Reed wasn't taking precautions against being followed.

She moved quietly after him. He was going in a straight line, and his

338

carelessness worried her. Something had to be seriously wrong. His trail was so clear that she followed it too rapidly, and almost fell over him, crouched down with his back to her. He stood up, startled.

'What are you doing, Reed?'

He looked at her, and in his eyes was something entirely unfamiliar. It reminded her of the look in his eyes when she'd first seen him down in the forest, all that time ago. He was holding a communicator. At his feet was a folded orange robe.

'I said, what are you doing?'

He whispered something into the device, then closed it in his hand. He steadied his voice. 'It's not what you're thinking, Petey. What are you doing here?'

'What is it, then? You've always said those things don't work up here.'

He didn't answer her.

She said, 'All along, Crique was right. I never believed him.'

'Keep your voice down, Petey.' He started towards her, and she stepped back.

'Don't come near me. You are a spy. You're still a lord.' She felt nauseous. 'I had your child, and all I am to you is a *khuk*. Is Duneld a *khuk*, too? When were you going to take him?' She put her hand to her mouth. 'You're arranging it now, aren't you? Arranging to take him away to your city. Is that it?'

'No. Petey, listen to me.'

'You betrayed me. All along, you were lying.'

'It isn't what you think. I swear it, Petey. You know I love you.'

'Then what is it?'

'Yes. What is it, Reed?'

Petey turned towards Crique.

'Tell us some more of your truth, Reed. But you'd better be fast. And drop that thing. It was only ever you who told us the Haze wouldn't let them work.' He waved his hand through the mist.

'Don't, Crique,' Reed said.

'What else have you got here? Firetubes? And what more? Are they coming, your friends? What's your job, to prepare the way?'

'I do have this,' Reed said, and showed them a firetube, though he pointed it at the ground.

Crique took a step towards Petey.

'This is nothing to do with you, Crique.' Reed started to raise the weapon.

Crique stepped forward again and quickly took Petey's arm. 'You betrayed her. Will you kill her?'

Reed held the firetube steady, its mouth towards Crique. Petey felt Crique's dagger at her throat, cold and firm.

'You told her you love her,' Crique said. 'Drop that, or I'll kill her.'

Petey smashed her elbow into Crique's chest and pushed him away. 'Reed!' she cried out.

'I'm sorry, Petey,' Reed said, and he stooped to pick up the robe, and stepped back and vanished into the trees. The Haze swirled, and he was gone.

Crique swore. 'That was stupid. Now he's away.'

She went to where Reed had been standing and picked up the communicator from the ground. She opened it and heard a voice saying, 'Reed? What's happened? We—'

Crique smashed it from her hand and cracked the back of the case with his heel.

'That was stupid too,' she said. 'We could have found out what was going on.'

'We?' He shook his head at her. 'How do I know you weren't with him in this?'

'You heard us,' she told him. 'You saw what happened. He lied to me as much as he lied to you.'

Crique had trotted over to the trees where Reed had disappeared. He was squatting to peer at the earth. 'Maybe,' he muttered. 'Come here.' He stretched out an arm to her. 'We'll go after him. We'll catch him.'

'Duneld,' she said, shaking her head. 'I can't leave him.'

He straightened. 'Yameen will look after him until we get back. But you'll help me, Petey, or I swear I'll kill you here.'

'Crique—'

'Listen. I'm not waiting for you, and you're not going back. I won't have you both out of my sight.' He raised his dagger and Petey saw the craziness in his eyes. He said, 'We'll go fast. While he's running, he isn't hiding his trail. You'll do what I tell you or I'll open your throat right here. I swear it on my son's ashes.'

Not knowing what else to do, she let him drag her into the trees. Breaking into a trot, Crique hissed, 'And you'd better keep up. If you hold me back, I'll know you're his accomplice.'

Petey tried to keep in her mind the route they took, but all she could take in was that they were heading downhill. After an initial burst of speed, Crique settled down to a steady pace. Even to Petey, Reed's trail was clear. It was obvious he was expecting pure speed to save him. She looked back from time to time, but there was nothing to stick in her mind, nothing but trees and rocks. Once, regaining her footing after a root had tripped her, she tried to scratch a mark into the bark of a tree, but Crique saw her and said, 'You'll never remember. Nepenth's well hidden. You'll never find it again without me.' He was moving on swiftly. 'Unless you return with Reed and his friends, of course. You'd better hope he didn't summon them. If he did, Duneld will die with everyone else.'

'If he did, what's the point of following him now?'

'He'll pay for what he's done. There's nowhere for him to go, except the AngWat.' He glanced at her, a long look that slowed him a moment. 'And there's nowhere for us, either. All that's left is to kill him.'

'It's crazy. I can't believe he'd do this.'

'You think everyone's fine and good, Petey.' Pushing through trees, Crique let a branch whip back at her face.

'I believe in him.'

'Then you're a fool. I told him I'd kill you if he ran, and he ran. And you have faith in him?'

She wiped blood from her cheeks. 'He knew you wouldn't kill me. He believes in you, Crique. You're his friend. And mine.'

'You've been with him too long. You're as slippery as he is. Faith and trust are nothing. There's only what you can prove.'

On they went. They travelled through the rest of the night without slowing down, Crique tracking Reed confidently, keeping the pace constant. Even so, they were still high in the mountains when the dawn came. The Haze was thickening above them, glowing brilliantly in the creases of the high peaks as the rays of the rising sun fell on it.

As they began to enter the low forest, Petey felt at home again. There were trees and plants she remembered, and the cries of animals from the old days. The familiarity washed away her exhaustion. At a stream where Reed had stopped to drink, Crique let Petey rest briefly. They picked leaves from the same wake-up bush Reed had ripped at as he passed. Chewing the bitter leaves, Crique said, 'I've waited a long time for this, Petey, and I can still wait.' He spat and wiped his mouth. 'He still isn't trying to hide his trail. I can track better than he can hide, and he knows it. He'll only lose me in death.' Crique stood up and stretched. 'He's still going for speed, hoping I'll be slowed by you and he'll reach his friends before I reach him. He won't.'

'He doesn't know I'm with you.'

'He does. He knows me. Let's go.'

The wake-up leaves had stung her awake again and reinvigorated her tired muscles. Petey said nothing else, trotting steadily after Crique. She no longer knew what to think about Reed. He'd lied all along, there was no doubt. She'd been too desperate to believe in him. Perhaps, if it hadn't been for Crique's distrust of him, she would have realised it sooner. Crique was right. Reed had betrayed them all.

After a few more hours, Crique stopped and knelt at the foot of a tree, then stood up and squinted at the high branches. 'He rested here. Wait for me.'

He climbed the tree and came down again after a short time. 'He slept an hour or two up there. He's tired. Running alone is hard. We're getting close.'

'I need to rest,' Petey said. 'Really.'

Crique looked hard at her, then said, 'All right. One hour. Stay up there, though. I'll be here.'

She slept solidly in the tree until a distant sound woke her up. It was like leaves crackling, but far away. There was a yellow light in the distance, too, and a faint scent of smoke. Fire, she guessed. Forest fire. It would be controlled and put out soon. That was one thing the lords were good for. She descended the tree and found Crique gone. She waited until he came back. He had a fish under his arm, its silver scales glittering through the leaves he carried it in.

'You're here,' he said shortly. 'Well.'

They both knew what he meant. She'd accepted that Reed was a traitor. That he was still a lord.

Crique opened the fish and stripped out its guts and spine, and they ate the glistening flesh raw. There was smoke on the breeze.

'We're less than a day from the AngWat,' Petey said. 'But Reed's not heading there, is he?'

'He's making for the road. It's closer.' Crique sniffed the air and made a gesture. 'I was near a village and I spoke to someone.' He picked a bone from his teeth. 'The fire's coming from the AngWat.'

'The AngWat's on fire?'

'Unlikely. They have the moat, remember. They set the fire. They're spreading it outwards, into the forest.'

'Why would they do that?'

Crique didn't answer. He wiped his hands and mouth on the grass and stood up. 'Let's go.'

A boar shot past them, and shortly afterwards a pair of deer, running shoulder to shoulder. Petey said, 'The smallnose deer, they're night animals.'

'Yes,' Crique said. 'It's a big fire, and it won't stop unless the lords stop it.'

'Do you think Reed—?'

'I don't know. You can ask him.'

342

A wind was blowing at them as they moved on, pushing squalls of smoke through the trees, and the air was becoming acrid.

'He hasn't changed his course,' Crique panted. He stopped and bent over, struggling for breath, and took stock. 'He's still heading west of the AngWat. Either he knew this was going to happen or he has instructions. The fire's heading that way too. If the wind doesn't change, he'll take us right into it.'

Clouds of birds filled the air above the trees, darkening the forest, and all around them was the crash and rumble of animals in flight.

'What do we do, then?' Petey said.

'As long as there's a trail, we follow him.' And Crique moved on, into the hot wind.

It was impossible to be alert against attack any longer, just a matter of reacting in time. They ducked away from bands of armed villagers. Sometimes villagers saw them but let them be. Then there was a lone man armed with a spear, a red-stained sack over his shoulder. Crique wanted to go on, but Petey stopped the man. 'What's happening?' she said.

He put the sack down but clutched its neck as if she'd tried to take it from him. She thought it was filled with large rocks, or blocks of wood, but then she realised the seeping colour was blood. He'd been taking advantage of the panicking animals. She smiled at him, trying to calm him. His eyes were wide and gleaming. With so much meat, no wonder the villagers were going crazy.

'We've eaten,' she said. 'Keep it. Do you know anything about the fire?'

He wiped his forehead. His eyes darted. 'All the village lords left without saying a word to us, and then the fire started. Everything around the AngWat is burning. All the lords running back there, such a sight. Some of them didn't get back in time.' He grinned at Petey. 'The lords are killing everyone, but we're killing them too. The firetubes run cold in the end. The lords aren't so hard under their robes.' He swung the bag back over his shoulder, its awkward weight making him stagger. 'Some of them,' he mock-whispered to Crique, 'Some of them say they're with us, not against us.' He hefted the bag. 'With the knife at their throat, that is.'

'What's in the bag?' Petey asked, suddenly nauseous.

'They're mine, these are.' He caught himself, then set a smile in place and firmly repeated the possessive. 'My heads. Collect your own.' He turned and limped away, chased through the trees by tongues of smoke.

'I wonder if Reed was one of his trophies,' Crique said, watching Petey for reaction. 'Maybe we should have checked.'

Petey just said, 'Come on.'

'I wonder why they started the fire? It seems a crazy thing to do.'

'Whatever it was, the city at the end of the road must be where Reed's going. Perhaps they were summoning him back.'

'Maybe,' Crique said. 'But if I were heading there, I'd give the fire a wider berth than he is.' He ran on at Petey's side in silence for a while. They came out into a clearing and saw dark clouds streaming above them. The wind screamed and pushed the grass flat, and in thickets the bent branches showed the pale undersides of their leaves. It was like night.

Crique fretted over the trail out of the clearing. He turned to Petey, raising his voice for her to hear. 'He's panicking, or he would have lost us by now. This way.' Then, in the relative silence of a lull in the wind, he added, 'I don't know what could have happened. We were here two weeks ago, and there was no hint of anything. The forest was calm, and traffic along the road was no different.'

'And Reed?'

'No different.'

They went on, hardly talking any more. The fire was closer, smoke drifting through the trees in huge clouds, a pale orange light beginning to be visible further ahead. The clouds carried shreds of burnt leaf and bark, and a foul smell. The heat had suddenly grown intense.

Crique motioned Petey to stop. She crouched beside him, and through a swirl of leaves, at the edge of a broad river, she saw Reed talking to another lord. Her breath caught at the sudden sight of him. Both men had their hoods down, but the wind was whipping the orange cloth at their necks.

Somehow alerted, the other lord tipped his head and turned in Petey's direction, but before she could react, Crique's dagger was spinning towards him. She watched it turn in the smoke-wisped air to bury itself in his throat. His head jerked back and he dropped to the ground.

Crique was drawing another blade as he ran towards Reed, who tried to pull away but tripped over the arm of the dead lord, and sprawled to the ground. His head hit a rock with a thud that pierced the crackle of the fire, and he didn't move again.

From the trees to Crique's left, another lord appeared. Petey screamed a warning, but too late as the lord's firetube beam leapt at him. Beyond Crique, the beam dropped branches from their trees. Crique opened his mouth but no sound came out, and he spun back into the water with a loud splash, a thick cord of blood whipping and falling around him, and Petey knew he was dead.

There was only the sound of the approaching fire. The lord was bringing his firetube to bear on Petey when Reed made a faint movement.

The lord turned sharply. Reed raised his head and squinted at him before falling back again. The lord frowned, then turned back towards Petey and took aim. Petey tried to move but couldn't.

Weakly, Reed lifted his firetube. The beam drew sparks from the lord's robe, distracting him again. He pulled his hood down over his face and moved towards Reed, and as he did so a boar ran out of the trees, squealing in terror, and bowled him over. As he tried to gather himself, Petey hurled herself at him, ripped his hood back and slit his throat. Then she lay on the earth and stared at the smoke-blown sky through the canopy of trees.

'Petey.'

She sat up and looked at Reed, who was getting groggily to his knees. He was blinking but concentrating on maintaining his aim.

'Now kill me,' she said emptily.

The barrel of his firetube was trembling. 'I'm not one of them. Not in my heart and not in my head. That's the truth, Petey. I swear it.' He wiped blood away from his good eye, but it welled again from a long cut on his forehead. 'Do you believe me?'

'I don't know.'

He wiped his eye clear again and said, 'I'm not sure I can hold this still. If I put it down, will you kill me?'

She shrugged and then shook her head, and he tried to smile. 'You always give me another chance, Petey. What is it about you? You've lost everything, and there's still trust and hope inside you.'

'Tell me what's going on.'

He shook his head, and the firetube wavered. Petey moved a fraction closer to him, but he gestured her sharply away. 'I don't know. It could be the end of all this, or it could be this carrying on forever. Go back, Petey. You can't stay here.'

Not knowing what to say, what to believe, she turned her back on him. She could almost feel the beam cutting at her, but there was nothing. She knelt at the edge of the river and stared hopelessly at the slow water. Crique's blood stained the lank weeds drifting in the slow current. His body had vanished, carried away by the water or held down by the deep weeds. The forest was cleaning itself.

Reed was standing next to her. He looked at the water and said, 'Go back to Nepenth. It isn't safe there, but at least it's a long way from here. Look after Duneld.'

She thought of how she'd watched Marten disappear down the

causeway, and she thought of Duneld dying in Nepenth. Smoke swirled around her, and the light towards the fire was thick and yellow. She said, with a force that surprised her, 'No. I'm not going back. Not yet. He's safe with Yameen. If there might be a chance to bring him safely out of Nepenth, I'll fight for it. I won't go back just to watch him die. I chose to live with you, Reed, even though I wasn't sure it was the right thing. I'll die with you or live with you.' She took his hand. 'What do we do, then?'

He slipped the firetube back inside his robe. 'There's a small group of people planning to overthrow the lords, but I don't know much more than that. They call themselves the True.'

Petey rubbed smoke from her eyes. Grit came away on her finger. 'We can't stay here,' she said. 'And you have to take your robe off. The villagers will kill you.' She knelt and stared at the water while he removed his robe.

'Don't drink from it,' he told her. 'It'll be poisoned. I've got water, and you can take Eduar's. And we'll take this one's.' With a foot he nudged the lord Petey had killed.

The river was moving more swiftly. Petey saw a body float by and her breath caught, but the body wasn't Crique's. His would be well gone, and downstream. This was a woman's corpse, face up, open-eyed, shiny-skinned and starting to bloat. There was no blood, no sign of how she'd died. Not too far beyond the river was the fire, and she knew it would cross the water easily. The air was drifting with sparks as well as burnt material.

Reed tied his robe under his shirt, and gave her the other lord's to wear under her clothes. 'Ready? Let's move,' he said.

In her mind, it was as if Crique were saying it, and Petey thought she would have cried a little if there were water in her to spare. But there was none. In the hot wind her throat scorched more at each breath. 'Tell me about the True,' Petey said, to clear her head of Crique. They were travelling alongside the bow wave of the fire, keeping as close to it as they could bear, hoping to reach the road before it cut them off.

'I only ever had one contact with them, and Crique killed him before I found out any more. I don't know why they started this, but something must have happened. All we can do is try to get to the city.' By keeping so close to the fire, Petey and Reed stayed mainly clear of villagers, and they saw no more lords. They managed to conceal themselves from a band of children armed with firetubes and machetes who were slaughtering everything they saw. They never stopped moving and slowed down only to drink from their waterbags. The water was warm and tasteless.

There were villages all but deserted, and disorientated men and women wandering at the edge of the fire and even into it. Once, tired, they were surprised by a dazed band of men who attacked them half-heartedly before fleeing when Reed used the firetube at the ground around them.

At last, after hours, the smoke and heat receded from their route. Reed said, 'The wind's starting to take it the other way.'

'Some good luck, at last,' Petey said.

'Not luck. Nothing is luck. They're steering the fire where they need it. They don't want it anywhere near the city.' He hesitated, then said, 'They can control the wind for a while, but not for long. Maybe they'll lose control.'

Night fell without them noticing, the yellow glare of the fire overwhelming the sinking sun, lighting everything exaggeratedly, and the forest full of desperate, streaming life. The noise of the burning forest and the tormented animals and birds became a strange emptiness in Petey's head.

Reed kept up the pace. She seemed to be walking with her eyes closed, as if in a dream. She woke up with her face in the hot earth, Reed pulling her to her feet, pushing wake-up leaves into her mouth and making her chew them. After that, everything was uncomfortably sharp.

Reed went for long periods of saying nothing, and then suddenly he started talking, ignoring any questions she asked. It was as if the fire had burnt everything away.

'After I was taken from the AngWat to the city, it was worse than I've told you. And there's more, that I haven't said. The communicators do usually work in the Haze, though not always. The lords know all about Nepenth. The Great Lord lets it exist because it's no threat as long as its children die. It draws all the escapers of the forest.' He corrected himself, and Petey thought she understood what it was taking him to tell her this. It was like the admission of a dying man. The closeness of death back in the clearing had drawn this from him. 'I mean, my job was to draw them there. Without Nepenth, they might find somewhere else. I monitored it. Crique was almost right, but how could I have told him, or you, any of that?' He looked anxiously at her, then said, 'I always made sure Nepenth was safe. I did my best.' He stopped talking for a long time, the hot wind seething around and between them, and then he began again. 'I—' But he stopped himself there.

Dully, Petey took it in, not questioning him or even wondering what he'd been about to say. She was incapable of reaction any longer. She had left Marten to the AngWat — how could she judge anyone else? She trusted Reed now, more than trusted him, and that was all she could do.

347

By the time they reached the road and started to walk by its side, the sun was rising behind them out of the fire's flat glare. There was no traffic on the road. Before them, stretching away, it was a black strip, dark as a trench. To their rear it gleamed like a frozen river. Reed stopped and shrugged his robe back on. 'We're safer here if I'm like this,' he said. Petey said nothing. In the open she was nervous and kept turning round, imagining sounds behind them and movement across the road.

Reed resumed talking. 'I did kill the village lord, like I told you, but I didn't escape. I was caught and taken back to the AngWat, and I was punished.' He touched his scar, blanching it with a finger. 'They gave me the story I told you, and my instructions. But the man who gave me those instructions belonged to the True. My killing that lord made Eduar risk trusting me. He told me there would be an uprising one day.'

The sun rose. There was no end to the road. 'Eduar said we'd only have one chance, and that if we didn't take it, there could never be another.'

That seemed odd to Petey. For her, there was always hope. 'That's crazy. If you fail, you don't give up.'

'He was sure of it. I don't think he knew why. Whoever recruited him told him. He didn't even know how many of us there were, whether it was ten or a thousand.' Reed sighed. 'I never met anyone else, and now Eduar's dead. All I know is we have to get to the city.'

The orange sun was now so high that they had to hood their eyes with their hands to look at the fire behind. 'I think it's getting closer again,' Petey said.

'It can't be. It's just the sun.'

'No. The noise is growing again. The wind's behind us.'

Reed stopped a moment to listen. 'Maybe they can't control the wind entirely. And if the forest isn't safe for them to be in, they can't set fire breaks.'

Petey wasn't listening. Uprising, she was thinking. Is this an uprising?

The horizon ahead seemed unnaturally sharp and ridged. Not a silhouette of trees or mountains at all, and they couldn't possibly be houses, so far away that they shimmered in the dust.

'The city,' Reed said. 'But Eduar's dead and I don't know what to do when we get there.'

'Crique thought he was doing the right thing.'

The horizon was rising like a wall of thorns when a sound rose behind them, and Reed pulled her to the side of the road. He flashed the firetube three times, two short flashes and a long one.

She said, 'What are you doing?'

'It's a car. I'm hoping for a ride. It's a signal I was given. I'm hoping we're not alone.'

As it drew closer, the vehicle slowed, and a pair of lights set low in its muzzle flashed, two long and one short. It growled and stopped.

Reed sighed and gave her a small, quick smile. 'They're with us. They must have escaped the AngWat. Now we might find out some more.' He went towards the vehicle, with Petey a few steps behind.

A tall, thin lord got out, smiling at Reed, who held out his hand. The lord brought his hand up, too, but there was a firetube in his palm.

'Don't get any ideas. This has been adjusted to penetrate your robes.' The lord grinned. 'You're our fifth rebel today. And with a little *khuk*, too. A flourishing little cancer in our heart, aren't you, eh? Quite a surprise, at first.' His voice was relaxed and easy. 'But the trouble with such a protected network is that you can't tell when your codes have been betrayed.'

Reed started to turn to Petey, but the lord flicked a sharp lance from the firetube at the sleeve of Reed's robe. There was no spark. The earth hissed behind him.

Reed lifted his arm and looked in surprise at the neat hole in his orange robe. He dropped his arm again and stood quietly.

The lord's voice sharpened. 'Your name, and who were your contacts? Just for my records. Then I'll kill you reasonably cleanly. Otherwise it'll be rather long and very messy.'

Across the road, Petey thought she saw a small movement, but there was nothing. There was someone else in the vehicle, though, and she saw his head turn to the side, briefly distracted by whatever had caught Petey's attention, and then relax again.

'I had one contact, and he's dead,' said Reed, staring into the muzzle of the firetube.

'The *khuk* first, then. One hand at a time. I'm very neat. The beam cauterises as it goes. She'll probably pass out, but she won't die, and when she comes round, I'll ask you again.'

'My name's Reed. My contact was called Eduar, but he's dead, and that's all I can tell you. Let her go.'

The lord smiled broadly and leaned against the side of the vehicle, keeping the weapon steady while he brought another from beneath the robe. 'Where do you imagine this small revolt will get you? We'll get the AngWat back, and you won't hold those few sections of the city much longer. You only keep them for now so we can gather you up there.' His eyes wrinkled in an easy smile. 'Now, let's get on.' He jerked both weapons in unison. 'I promise you I'm perfectly ambidextrous.'

One firetube was covering each of them. 'These really are remarkable devices,' he said. 'Yesterday I carved both hands and feet from a man, then both legs to above the knee, one arm to the elbow and the other almost to the shoulder before he died. I know where I made my mistake, though.'

This time Petey definitely saw something at the edge of her vision. A man was crouched at the rear of the vehicle. She couldn't make out more without turning her head.

'You don't seem to be listening to me, *khuk*.' The lord's hand moved fractionally. Petey hardly registered the brief shaft of light connecting the weapon to her hand, and for an instant there was nothing but a cool sting, but then the jet of pain was worse than anything she had ever known. For a moment she couldn't even breathe, and it was all she could do to keep on her feet. She looked at her hand, and for a moment, as her vision cleared, she thought that somehow nothing at all had happened except the pain. Then she saw her little finger had gone.

'Are you listening now, Reed? Good. You see, the man dehydrated. You're thirsty, aren't you, *khuk*? I've got water today, and I'm sure I can get considerably further.' He raised his voice. 'Marek, get me the water bag.'

He waited, but there was no movement from the vehicle, and without taking his attention from Reed and Petey, he kicked the door. 'Marek. Are you asleep in there? Marek!'

Marek still failed to answer, and the lord irritatedly told Reed to lie face down on the ground, and Petey to lie on top of him, making her tuck her arms beneath him. She almost passed out from the pain in her hand. She felt Reed trying to raise himself enough to relieve the pressure on it, but they were both immobilised.

'Stay quite still. I'll kill you both if you move.'

Out of the corner of her eye, Petey could see the lord bending to look inside the vehicle. He opened the door and reached an arm inside to shake his companion's shoulder. Then he swore and started quickly to back out again.

He was still straightening as the man behind the vehicle hurled himself into the small of his back. The two men sprawled in the road, and Petey couldn't make out the flurry of movement until it suddenly stopped altogether. The lord was kneeling tautly and staring directly at her, his mouth stretched wide. There was a thick forearm around his neck, and a hand across his forehead. He started to say something, and then his head snapped back and cracked, and the arms let his corpse slump.

With a grunt of pain, Petey managed to pull herself free and rolled away from Reed, who stood up and wrapped her in his arms. They both stared at the man who was coming to his feet, holding the lord's firetubes.

'Crique?' Petey said. 'But you're dead.'

Reed put his hand out. 'Wait, Crique. Please.'

'It's all right, Reed. I heard what he said.' He went to the other side of the vehicle and hauled Marek's corpse from it.

Relaxing a little, Reed said, 'How long have you been behind us?'

'Since I came out of the water. I nearly drowned, but the shock of the water kept me from passing out. The wound wasn't as bad as it felt.'

'Or looked,' Petey said. There was crusted blood at his shoulder.

'I managed to pull myself to the bank and saw you save Petey,' Crique told Reed. 'I decided to hold back, just to be sure. I'm sure now.'

'You nearly held back too long.' Reed put a hand on Crique's shoulder, and said, 'I'll tell you everything I know—' unable to hold back a small grin, '—once we get moving again. But we need to do something for Petey first.'

The shock of being saved had taken her mind from the pain, but now it was coming back in dizzying waves. She clenched her fist against it, and felt her absent finger curl with the others. She opened her fist and it straightened. The finger was gone, though. She could feel it throb with pain, feel it move, and yet it had been cut away. She was faint and nauseous.

Reed came from the car with a pack marked with a red cross. He took a white pad from it, took Petey's hand and bandaged the stump of her finger. 'This will help. It has an analgesic.'

Her pain started slowly to seep away, and she felt suddenly so tired that she could barely keep her eyes open. Reed helped her into the back of the vehicle and said, 'You can sleep now, Petey.' Then she heard him say, 'Let's go. I can drive the car. Put on the lord's robe and I'll tell you what's going on as we drive.'

Hugging her throbbing hand to her stomach, Petey curled herself up on the seat as Reed and Crique sat themselves in front of her, and the vehicle hummed. Crique said something sharply as the vehicle began to move, and laughed.

The seat was smooth and evenly cushioned, and Petey made herself as comfortable as she could. The bandage wasn't enough to block the pain altogether. Her remaining pain developed a rhythm, and she began to bring it under control, as she had learnt to as a village child.

Odd, she thought, to be reminded of her childhood by pain. As she drifted towards sleep, a sudden flood of memory woke and over-whelmed her. She remembered her back being whipped raw as a small girl in the village by the lord then, and staring at the mother who was silently holding her still as the lord grunted and swung, over and over.

She squeezed her eyes shut and abruptly saw the mother's eyes locked with her own, the unbearable pain in the mother's. The memory made her curl up tighter and knot her throbbing hand. She could smell the sweat of the lord. She remembered the feeling of being linked to the mother by pain, and forever separated from her. And she knew that the mother had recognised it too.

She squeezed her eyes tighter, but couldn't stop the tears, even though she had forced away the pain. After a while, she began fading to sleep on the waves of the men's conversation. She heard them chuckle together, and felt the beginning of a sense of ease. On the edge of sleep, she heard Reed say, 'Are we really back where we started, Crique? All those years ago?'

'No, we're better than that. Now we understand each other.'

Petey slept.

HAVEN

Marten pushed a plate of food across the table to Mexi. She ate greedily. 'Slow down,' he whispered. 'You'll draw attention.'

She looked round at the great canteen full of Robes, and rubbed the palm of a hand across her head. The smoothness of her skull still felt odd. 'I'm sorry. But this food—'

He smiled. She liked his smile. 'We might have to live here, but we don't have to eat your fungus.'

She chewed the mouthful of tender meat and swallowed it, thinking of Zelda and her recipes. Her eyes began to water, and she made herself stop thinking of Zelda. There wasn't time for it.

'Did you speak to anyone, Mexi?'

'I did what you said. I slept rough. Not that I slept much. These robes aren't very thick.'

Marten's eyes darted. Someone passed the end of the table, and Marten waited a minute before going on. 'Did you see anyone who might have recognised you?'

'I had to go through a couple of checkpoints, but they didn't ask anyone their name or for identification, just a few ridiculous questions. I didn't even understand the questions. Why are you so nervous?'

'Because you aren't, and you should be. Do you know what's been happening?'

'How could I?' But the truth was, she'd been thinking of Zelda, trying to imagine life without her.

Marten said, 'There's an epidemic of unFact. They told us the sayers have some sort of virus, a neurological disease and no cure. Everyone affected is being quarantined. Sections are being sealed and they're setting up the checkpoints you saw. They're saying it started in Survey. Survey's closed down, all its operatives quarantined.' Marten stopped, then dropped his voice further and said, 'That's the surface story.'

'What do you mean, the surface story?'

'Corven told me there's more.'

Mexi was quiet. She had a sudden, dizzying sense of being involved in something that extended beyond Haven, something beyond her imagination. 'What's going on, Marten?' she said in a voice that came out small and scared. She took a sharp breath, thinking again of Zelda, and hardened her thoughts. She had to be strong. 'How does he know? Who told him?'

'He wouldn't tell me much more.'

She looked straight at Marten, his clear eyes and broad cheeks, and she said, 'Do you trust him?'

'I believe him. Right now, that's enough. He opened up to it without expecting anything back from me.'

'Did you tell him anything?'

Marten hesitated. 'I told him I might be able to find you.'

'Crise, Marten.' She looked around, lowered her voice. 'What else did he tell you?'

'There's an uprising started on Haze. We can do something, Mexi. There's confusion here, and that helps us.'

'We're more confused than everyone else. How do we know what to do?'

'We need Quill. Fact think he's the source of the virus, and Corven thinks so too. He has information we need. We have to get him away from here. We have to take him to Haze.'

Following Marten's gaze, she looked down the length of the canteen, at the great arch that led to the rocket pits. She was almost used to the regular heavy rumble of the closing terralocks and then the grinding roar of the engines as the rockets rose away. She'd had no idea there was so much traffic between the planets until now.

'We'll catch it from him,' she said. 'That man, Tyler Hind, went crazy.'

'Corven says the virus is Oath's memory. I don't understand, but no one apart from Tyler Hind seems to have gone crazy. The unFact-sayers aren't insane. Quill isn't. To catch the virus is to know the Archive.'

She tried to take that in, then shook her head decisively. 'I don't believe that. Why are Fact after Quill? If it's safe, what's the point? Why would Fact want to suppress the Archive?'

He leant forward. 'It isn't anything to do with Fact. It's Haze. Fact is controlled from Haze. General Factotem gets his instructions from Haze, from the Great Lord. In effect, Haze runs Haven. If we can get Quill away to Haze, safeguard the Archive, there's a chance we could free Haven and Haze.' He paused. 'Mexi?'

She examined his face, but he was open and serious, and somehow she believed him. Maybe Haze was in control of everything. It would explain so much, and made more sense than what she'd always been told. The freedom of the Robes to wander. Even this canteen with its variety of food. She said, 'If Fact haven't found him, how can we?'

'Fact have their hands full with the unFact-sayers. The lords – the Robes – are mostly assisting, but there are a few of us sabotaging it. We can concentrate on finding Quill.'

'Where do we start?'

'His only contact was a renegade tech called Naddy Harke, and he's down in the Game. Fact are keeping him alive as bait for Quill. It seems Quill has a history of loyalty and foolhardiness.'

Mexi remembered the Survey presentation at her choicemaking, the sobbing boy destined for Survey. She said, 'We can't get to the arena, and even if we could – do you have any idea how vast it is?'

'There has to be a way.'

'Quill's that important?'

'Corven says the virus is.'

Mexi glanced up at the Game. Even in here, the screens threw it out every minute of the day and night. 'If Fact are waiting in the arena for him, I don't see where they could be. There's nowhere to hide. Just rocks. The cams are never off. No one could get down there without being spotted. That goes for Fact as well as Quill.' They watched for a while, then Mexi said, 'Are you sure Naddy's even still alive?'

Marten waited, then pointed him out. 'Blue team, there. The one next to him's called Skim. They were taken together. They've survived well, but Fact are manipulating the Game around them to keep them alive. They want their bait fresh. Almost everyone else has been killed and replaced since they were taken down, but not these two.' Marten smiled thinly. 'You could make money betting on them staying alive, as long as you draw your bet as soon as Quill turns up.'

'But how will they get him? There's nowhere to hide. The whole area's seeded with cams. That's the whole point of the Game – there's no escape. Fact can't set an ambush. The only way in's the drop point. And how do *we* get to him?'

'I don't know.'

The tall, far doors opened, and a new troop of Robes came in from the launch area, smoke billowing around them. Mexi abruptly pushed her empty plate away and said, 'I might know a way. You have to get me to Nutrition, though. Can you do that?'

Rainer sat back. 'No way. No chance. No. Those drones might be small, but they're not invisible, not at any speed. And you wing a coredor wall, you're finished before you've started. *I* could do it, a milliem either side, but you, girl?' She shook her head. 'And as soon as you get anywhere near the drop tube, Fact'll have plotted your route and guessed your destination. No. Won't work. Sorry.' She jerked her head at Marten. 'Does that say anything?'

Mexi said, 'He. I have to take the risk, Rainer. Maybe I can—'

'Forget it. Not with me.' She grinned. 'Of course, there is another way. Same danger but less risk, maybe. You want to know?'

Marten raised his head slightly, and Rainer ducked hers, trying to peer under the edge of the hood. 'He understands, then,' she said. 'Boyfriend, is he? Is this some kind of a dare? Like your headshave? Which doesn't look good, by the way.'

'No.' Mexi felt herself colouring. 'What other way?'

'The myco caverns are deep. They're linked in places to the arena. Small, natural tunnels, unmarked and unmapped. The caverns are totally toxic, so there's no security risk, but I've been bored and flown drones to the edge of the arena. I can get you there.'

'Where do you come out in the arena?'

'No idea at all. But the drones are fast. Once I'm in, I guess I could do a complete circuit inside an hour. We could find them easy. How much time we got?'

'Not an hour,' Mexi muttered, looking at Marten. He shook his head in agreement.

Rainer looked from Mexi to Marten. 'You sure you don't want to tell me any more about it?'

'I don't know much more.'

'Your boyfriend does.'

Marten didn't react. Mexi said to him, 'It's our only hope.'

'Then let's do it,' Rainer said. 'I've never been down in the arena before. Make a change from harvesting myco.'

'One thing. If we do it,' Mexi said, 'Can they trace you?'

'Their cams will tell them the drones came from Nutrition, but Voice doesn't keep track of individual machines. No one does. We crash and lose them all the time in the caverns.' She smiled. 'Well, not me. We'll leave the drones down there. Voice'll be in trouble before me. Don't worry, he won't spill the dreams on me. Anyway, Fact are overstretched at the moment trying to lock down the unFact. Every avenue's gated and guarded from the Primaries down to the deepest shades, pretty much. They're asking everyone stupid questions. Even the Robes.' She looked at Marten again. 'Robes asking Robes, can you believe that? Meaningless questions with no answers, but if you answer any of them, they take you away.'

She waited, but no one said anything. She tried again. 'What's going on, Mexi? You're a factotem. So how do Fact come up with the stupid questions?'

'That's a good question. But I'm not a factotem. I don't know what I am.'

Marten stood up. He said, 'Thank you. We have to go.' Then he said to Mexi, 'He'll be at least two days getting there. We'll be back here in forty hours to stand watch. Either they'll screen Quill as part of the Game, or they'll pull the cams and call it interference. Either way, we'll know.'

Rainer pushed herself back in mock astonishment. 'He talks! A Robe talks! These are mysterious times.'

'These are new times,' Marten said. 'At least, they may be.'

The coffin seemed spacious. Quill had stripped out everything but the screen and controls, and stocked up with food and water. He had never been as far deepdown as this before, and he felt fragile. For the first time in his life, he was unsure how much he could trust the charts. Even these charts. Nothing was certain any longer.

I'm here, aren't I? You can trust me, Quill.

'You're not here, Scheck. You aren't anywhere.'

So who are you talking to?

'I'm talking to myself.'

You want me to be quiet, then?

Quill closed his eyes. 'No. I like the memory of you.'

He adjusted his course according to the screen, thinking of Horvath. He couldn't quite remember what he had looked like, except the spike through his skull and the light spearing from its tip. Quill wondered about himself. Perhaps Scheck was an invisible spike in his skull, confusing his thoughts. Had he been different before? Had the virus changed him? Had the event on the escape pod changed him?

Something had changed him. He was different now, that was for sure.

He shook away the thoughts. Even to have them, to be wondering like this, was new. Until recently, Survey had been his life. He'd been hiding away in the rock, he realised. Whenever reality had attempted to intrude, he'd run for the safety of rock.

And now it was time to come out.

The charts gave him their message in colours and numbers. He skipped between Horvath's mosaic of the Arena and the coffin's readout. The game was unlikely to have moved further than a few hundred metres while he'd been in rock. They might even be in plain sight of his entrance into the arena.

He slowed, checking and rechecking his readings. The rock at the wall's edge was choked with amethyst, and he spent time carefully laying the coffin up against the fragile edge of a brittle cluster until barely an eggshell of crystal remained between the coffin door and the great void of the arena. He closed down the screen and carefully slid the door open.

The crust of amethyst grated against the metal, but held. The veil between Quill and the arena was intact.

This was perfect. He hadn't even needed the probe. The crystal glowed with the light beyond, its prismatic tracery sharp and bright.

He chipped a tiny window in the wall, pulling the fragments of crystal back into the coffin as far as possible. The air was faintly soured by sulphur, but still better than the filtered coffin air, and he sucked greedily at it for a moment. Then he put his eye to the window.

At first he couldn't focus. His eyes weren't used to such distance. He caught a blur of colour, of green and yellow. He blinked and drew back, then tried again, this time holding himself still, trying to focus on a single point.

It came sharp. There was distant detail, a cluster of brilliant opal surrounded by fluorspar, perhaps. He ranged his gaze carefully across, as if he were in the probe and the scale was microscopic. But then, without meaning to, he looked down, and his eyes swept him nauseatingly across a vast mineral-strewn floor towards the far, far side.

His stomach heaved and his forehead crashed against the thin wall, knocking it away and opening him up to a greater unprotected panorama. He retched again and spewed violently down the wall, then reeled back into the tiny space and sat down on the narrow bunk, staring at the coffin wall, sweating.

It was too much. He was used to measurements in millimetres. In rock, time extended and distance contracted. Until now, his only sight of the arena had been on screens. There had been no real scale to them. He couldn't remember the last time he'd been uptop. It had been before he'd joined Survey. Surely even uptop hadn't been as vast as this.

He pulled his breathing into a steady rhythm and waited until he had it under control again, and made himself contemplate the distance as calmly as possible. He thought of Walker's Sea. For a minute his breathing remained even, and then he lost it again. Walker's Sea was endless, but at least the mists concealed it. Here, there was no protection at all from the sheer, raw space.

Quill closed his eyes and shivered, then forced himself to his feet and walked the single pace to the amethyst window, and squinted straight down. Breathe in, breathe out. Slow. Slower, slower still.

Good. Better.

'Thank you, Scheck.'

He was about three metres from the ground, and the climb down looked simple. There was no movement to catch his eye, no sign of the Game. But nor was there any sign he'd been spotted.

He was ready. He took a long breath and looked straight out again, trying to see the arena as if it were screened rather than actual. There was a faint sound of air rushing by, a delicate wind tainted by sulphur and ammonia. Quill gathered himself and assessed the situation. He was standing in a pinprick of an opening in the outer circumference of the cavern of the arena. Across the vast space from him was the inner wall, the centre of the natural torus curving away to left and right, the roof soaring up and rushing towards him—

He looked down, paused, continued. To his left and right, he could just about make out the curving away of the inner wall before it lost itself in the faraway steamy haze.

Sweat was dripping from his clothes. It was desperately hot down here.

He went back into the coffin and brought out a heat sensor, and ranged it from left to right. He had hoped for a reading of human core temperatures to locate play by, but the sensor was in shock. It was too finely tuned, and the arena with its hot sulphur baths and pores of steaming rock confused it beyond use. Quill discarded the sensor, rapidly cracked away enough amethyst to give him space to crawl through and scrambled down the rough rock face to the ground.

He felt dizzy again, but this time he controlled it quickly. The roof was glittering like a slick of stars, and far away to his right was a great lake of sulphur, gleaming brightly. The ground was rough with crystal outcrops, stalagmites, boulders and bars of stone and scree.

His ears were starting to attune to the arena, and he thought he heard voices. The air was studded with pixels of light, making him squint. Then, at his vision's edge, he registered distant movement. Blue shapes. He pulled the weapon from his jacket, charged it and moved off, keeping to the wall.

There was the Blue team. He held back, looking for Red, but couldn't see them at first. He stopped and concealed himself to work out the positions of everyone visible.

Beyond Blue were Red, and they had the ball. They were moving it along the edge of the arena, taking advantage of a sulphurous stream running briefly along the wall. The ball tumbled awkwardly along the bed of the stream, pushed by a pair of Red players, one keeping to each side of the sulphur. They were making a slow but steady pace. Six other Reds stood keeping watch on Blue.

There was Naddy in blue. Skim was harder to locate, but he saw her too, recognised her profile behind the grime and glitter of the arena. His heart thumped at seeing her, and it was all he could do not to yell out and run straight for her.

He looked back. The opening in the rock was just visible. It would take him about two minutes to make it from here, running hard. Naddy would take longer. Fact would be somewhere here, too. That was for sure. But not in the walls anywhere nearby, Quill was certain. The walls were true. He could tell doors and hides by their telltale angles and giveaway false reflections. Where were Fact, then?

Don't think, Quill. Do. Wasting time.

He took a breath and yelled, 'Naddy, Skim! Over here, run!' He was standing up, waving his arms, and they were looking round, not seeing him.

'Here! Over here.' He was waving his arms, and now they were turning towards him. Skim was tugging Naddy into a run, and Quill's heart was pounding at the speed of it all. There was no sign of Fact. Quill looked at the wall, expecting it somehow to erupt with factotems, but there were only the other players stopping everything in astonishment at Quill, who had come from nowhere, out of the rock, dressed like no one else, in dark grey.

A voice boomed down, filling the air. 'Now we have some added excitement, Jan! Look. An extra player.'

Naddy and Skim were half way to him and still coming. We've done it, Quill was thinking.

'Will you say something, Quill? Talk to us. You're upscreened all under Haven. We've all been looking for you, Quill.'

The Blue players were starting to react, glancing at him, at Skim and Naddy, and then at each other. Time seemed to be slowing down, and Quill knew something was wrong. Dan and Jan weren't surprised or panicking.

'You haven't much time, Quill. You're in the Game and out again. This could be a record, what do you think, Dan?'

Beyond the Blue team, the Reds were gathering. The ball-pushers had joined the rest of their team, leaving the ball sitting in the stream. That was definitely not right. They should be taking advantage of the distraction to make ground.

This was a trap. The Reds were factotems. The entire Red team was Fact, waiting for him. They were drawing weapons from within their tunics. They shouldn't have weapons.

'That's right, Quill. It's hallo and goodbye.'

Quill sighted the beam and sprayed it. A Red dropped into the yellow stream, the sulphurous water hissing and bubbling. The other Reds scattered into the rocks.

Skim was at his side, crouching, and Naddy collapsed beside her. A low outcrop of jade slanted up from the ground a few metres back, and Quill crawled behind it after Naddy and Skim. He glanced out and saw Blue and Red players linking up to outflank them. Blue and Red together. The entire Game was set up for Quill, and he'd walked right into it.

Pushing Skim and Naddy on, he started retreating towards the coffin. A pair of Blues were running fast and wide, outflanking them, heading for the coffin doorway. Quill aimed carefully and dropped them both. A spike of crystal by his head sparked and he ducked, and a Red was climbing the wall and almost at the coffin before Quill's weapon recharged. He fired and the beam clipped the man's leg. He fell and lay groaning. Quill moved to crouch with Naddy and Skim beside a broad, ridged bar of banded rhyolite. It was the only cover for about ten metres. Reds and Blues fanned out around them and waited.

'We can't move from here,' Skim said. 'We're stuck. This was a really stupid thing you did for us, Quill.' She leaned over and kissed his cheek, grit on her soft lips, the unexpected touch startling him. 'Thank you.'

'How very touching, Jan. Don't you think?'

Quill looked up at the roof and saw the small flashing light of the cam, and sent a beam to nil it, and there was silence.

What we need right now is the cavalry.

'What's cavalry, Scheck?' Quill said aloud.

'Cavalry's what saves you when all hope is gone,' Naddy answered. 'They come on horses. How do I know that?'

'I think you've got the virus,' Quill said.

'I think I do, too,' Skim said. 'Only I'm not sure they save you. They all die hopelessly, tragic heroes.' She looked round, her eyes wide, murmuring, ' "Cannon to right of them, Cannon to left of them, Cannon in front of them, Volley'd and thunder'd." '

'I've got it!'

Quill looked at Naddy, who was grinning, his eyes bright as phosphor. 'Good,' Quill said. 'What do we do?'

'The virus. It isn't stable,' Naddy said. 'It accommodates itself to host memory.'

'Crise, Naddy,' Skim said. 'We're about to die and you're thinking how the virus works.'

'It's important. This is how it started. This is *why* it did.'

'I'm not dying like this,' Quill said. 'Not with the two of you bickering.' He put his head up to see what was happening, and the rock sang at his ear. He pulled back quickly. 'Maybe you could think of some way out of here. That's quite important too.'

'This is not bickering. Listen to me. Remember this. The virus contains too much information for any one person's brain to process and remember. People take in what they can and discard the rest.' He stopped, nodding excitedly to himself. 'Some information will be corrupted—'

'We're about to die, Naddy,' Quill said. There was movement around the edge of rock, and he fired quickly and heard a short scream. The movement stopped. 'This is not the time.'

'It's the only time. It's the last time. Quill, listen to me. They don't care about us, just you, because as far as they know, Scheck might be alive too. If they wanted us all dead, we'd have been killed the moment you stood up and shouted your head off. So are you listening?'

'We all die together, or none of us dies,' Quill said.

'Then it doesn't matter, and I'm telling you anyway. Everyone exposed to it reacts differently. There will be gaps and overlaps and errors. But every individual is important to the whole. It's a mosaic of memory and knowledge. In the end it still won't be entirely clear, but it will be enough to work on. We are all the Archive, now. Someone knew that would happen. That's what this is all about. But only *you* can pass it on. Only the first one to get it from the case. Now Tyler Hind's dead, only you have it all. After you, it's attenuated, a mild, non-infectious form, like a vaccination. That's why they're so desperate to get the case.'

A yell came from behind Quill, and he turned sharply round. Colour drew his eye, the scarlet centred in the expanse of green crystal. The injured Red player had somehow made it up to the coffin and was standing in the opening.

'Put down the gun, Quill,' he yelled. 'Give us the case and the others can stay in the Game.'

Skim said, 'It was good to know you, Quill. There's no hope now, but—' She shrugged. '—you know something?'

'What?'

'Right now, I feel alive. I feel part of something, and I never felt that before. It's not the virus. It's you, Quill.'

Red and Blue players were steadily redistributing themselves around the outcrop, closing in, firing occasionally to keep Quill's head down. The rhyolite shield screeched and sparked, cracking away.

'It's not finished,' Quill said.

'Don't be silly. I want to kiss you and then I want you to shoot me quickly. Naddy, goodbye.' She kissed Naddy on the cheek, then turned to Quill.

'Before you kiss him,' Naddy said, 'And not to spoil your moment, you can just tell me what that is, over there in the distance.' He pointed.

Quill saw the dots as their tiny wings became visible. They were either huge and far away, or tiny and close. In the haze of the Arena it was impossible to tell.

'Drones,' Skim said. 'They'll be Fact drones coming to resolve the standoff.'

They were about the length of a man, Quill saw. Two of them, descending at extraordinary speed towards the rocky outcrop, one of them dipping so low that Quill, ducking, felt the rush and suck of air. The drones rose again and slowed to range above the ring of players, who looked up at them in apparent surprise. The drones hummed to a dead stop, the air around them quivering.

In the brief pause, Skim kissed Quill on his lips, probing them open with her tongue. He liked the taste of her, and something inside him felt empty and full at the same time. After a long moment she pulled gently away, and closed her eyes.

'Now, Quill,' she whispered. 'Please.'

'I'm not sure,' Naddy said slowly, 'But they don't look like horses to me.'

'Now, Quill!' Then, more softly, 'I love you. Goodbye.' Taking his hand, she put the barrel to her temple. Quill was frozen between her and the expression on Naddy's face.

Skim's fingers found the fire button.

The drones started to release arcs of brown rain over the players, who opened their mouths and then slowed, gasping for air, and dropped to their knees before collapsing.

Skim's grip set hard as she pushed the button, and the weapon keened shrilly. Quill jerked it from her loose hand and stared at it.

Nevertheless, I think Naddy's right. I think they're the cavalry.

Quill pulled Skim to him, his heart pounding, and hugged her. 'It wasn't charged,' he yelled at her. 'It wasn't charged. Don't ever do that again.'

Naddy stood up and pointed at the opening in the wall where the remaining player was standing as if frozen there, staring at the fallen men in the field of the arena. 'If he destroys the coffin—'

The drones seemed to register Naddy's gesture. One of them swung hard round and whipped along the wall, its wingtip scratching a falling arc of brilliant sparks from the amethyst. The factotem started to withdraw into the coffin but too slowly, and the drone's razor-edged wing opened the chest of his tunic like a bookpage. He toppled down the wall, screaming, the jagged wall flaying him as he fell, his blood slaking the crystal, bright red on the brilliant green.

The other drone circled the rhyolite bar. Quill stared up at the blank metal underbelly. The inset cams turned on him and locked there, their irises opening and closing, and he wondered who was examining him.

After a moment, the machine rocked its wings in what looked like some kind of salute, then flicked sharply away towards the opening in the wall where the Red player had stood a moment before. Quill thought it had to crash, but at the last instant it veered away in a harsh whine of acceleration, and he thought it shed something as it turned out again towards the arena.

Together in the high cavern, the drones circled a few times, then straightened and flew in perfect alignment, their wingtips almost touching, as if readying for a race.

Skim said, 'What are they doing?'

The drones began to accelerate, then gradually parted into great mirror curves until Quill couldn't hold them both in sight at the same time.

'I don't know,' Quill said. One was scything back in the direction they had come from, while the other was heading away.

'Wait,' Naddy said. 'Look.'

Still mirroring, they were changing courses, turning back again simultaneously in huge, beautiful arcs.

'They're destroying the evidence of themselves,' Naddy murmured. 'I wonder who they are.'

Quill had both drones in sight again as they began to close on each other, far across the arena. He could hear their engines whine in the distance. Scheck whispered something to him, and without consideration he thought, yes, they sound like mosquitoes. His eyes went to the empty point in space where they had to meet, and when they did, in an explosion that took a second more to reach his ears, he felt as if his eyes had drawn them to their destruction.

The detritus hung motionless in the far air for a few moments before beginning to drift down, and the oddly disjointed explosion echoed and faded.

'Let's go,' Quill said finally. 'We won't have long.'

'I'm not coming with you.'

'There's room for us all, Naddy,' Quill said. 'It'll be tight, but there's room.'

'No. I can't take the restriction. I haven't got my program. I'm not coming.'

Skim said, 'Naddy—'

'We talked about this, Skim. I'm not changing my mind.'

Quill looked from Naddy to Skim, not understanding. He said to Naddy, 'You can just keep still and imagine you're elsewhere. You'll make it.'

Skim's eyes were bright and wet. She wouldn't look at Quill.

'No, Quill,' Naddy said quietly. 'I can't do that. I'll take a gun from one of the players and go for a walk. I'll enjoy it. Here, in the open. I've never seen such space. Real space.' He touched Quill's arm, and took Skim's too, holding them both, the three of them solidly connected. 'I'm as sure as I've ever been. Go.'

Skim wiped her eyes, then said, 'Goodbye, Naddy. I won't forget you.'

'I hope not. Quill, you take care of her like she will of you.'

Skim wouldn't look back as she walked to the wall with Quill, but Quill glanced over his shoulder once as he climbed the rock. The player's blood was already dry and brown in the heat, flaking and drifting down to the floor of the arena. Naddy was standing up from one of the corpses, a gun in his hand. He turned and caught Quill's eye, and raised his free hand in a brief wave, then turned away again and walked on into the distant mists of the endless arena.

In the coffin, Quill picked up a disk from the floor. 'The drone must have dropped it,' he said. He slid the disk into the screen and watched the words fade up, sulphur yellow on the grey background.

JUNCTION CRIMSON44 AND SCARLET56 8PM 3 DAYS STAY IN ROCK UNTIL THEN FOLLOW TWO ROBES BE VERY CAUTIOUS CHECKPOINTS

'Three days. Can we make it?' Skim said.

He set the course and sat back. 'Just.' He could see her struggling to control her face, to keep it from collapsing into tears. He said, 'I'm sorry about Naddy. I didn't think—'

'We talked in the arena. He said he wanted to die there, but I wasn't really listening to him. I didn't think we'd get out of there anyway. I was just trying to stay alive as long as possible. I thought he was just trying to keep me going, talking about you, martyring himself.' Her head dropped, and he put his arms around her. The coffin hummed around them, transporting them through the rock.

She said, 'He knew you'd come, even though it was the wrong thing to do. He called you a stupid hero.'

'Is that what you think?'

'Yes.' She looked up and kissed him. The thrum of the coffin became her, in the kiss, as they sat together.

'I'm sorry,' Skim murmured. 'I'm so tired. I haven't slept—' And she was asleep.

Quill put a sheet over her and rolled carefully to his feet, and sat at the screen. He thought of Naddy. He thought of Naddy, the claustrophobe, and of . . .

Not forgotten about me, then.

Jealous, are you, Scheck? Jealous of Naddy? Of Skim?

Of course not. I'm dead.

You're dead, and you're there, and you know so much.

Oh, I could tell you things, Quill! I could fill your head until it cracked. I—

'NO!'

Quill felt himself on the edge of something, teetering. His breath caught, and he looked at Skim, wanting to wake her up and hold her in his sudden terror, but the terror slowly faded. It was enough to see her there, asleep, and to remember her in the Arena saying, 'I love you.'

Naddy turned and watched the coffin go, the hole in the wall cracking further, swelling and darkening before collapsing back in on itself. The crystal wall shimmered and melted in brilliant heat, great glassy tears sliding down the amethyst wall. Soon the wall hardened and dulled into a smooth, vitrified scar, and Naddy was alone.

He carried on walking over the rough ground, settling into a steady pace and a rhythm of thought. 'Australia,' he said aloud, relishing the word. 'Aborigine.' There was a picture in his mind. 'Walkabout.' Another picture came, and he said the words that went with it. 'Rift Valley. Masai.' The glorious space, the light, the searing heat. An animal bounding through grass like a brilliant low sine wave. Cheetah.

He continued to walk, feeling faint now. The rocks beneath his feet were changing, and he was walking on grass. He could smell the grass. It was a glorious smell that almost made him cry. Like childhood, but untainted. He thought of memory linking times, linking people. It was such a powerful thing, the memory of a smell that could do this.

He was summoning images effortlessly. There was a desert, and he was making for a caravan moving along the burning horizon. The gently lurching animals, it came to him, were called camels. The words were exotic. Dromedary, bactrian.

Naddy understood why memory was a thing to kill for. It was power, and its absence was hopelessness. Without memory, people couldn't join together, and without society there was no resistance.

Memories flooded through him – Earth! But others would know that too. He didn't matter.

There was so much knowledge, so much space. This was perfect, and he could take it all with him.

It was hot now, and there was the smell of sulphur. He was so tired. He couldn't go on, but he didn't want or need to any more. He sat down against an ash-grey boulder studded with black neptunite, put the gun barrel into his mouth and touched the warm zero to his palate. In his head he could see it like a diagram, the floor of his brain and angle of penetration.

He sat there for a while, thinking of the perfection of it all, the endlessness of death that was like space.

There were drones approaching, now, a squadron of them. Squadron, he thought, amazed. Where had the word come from, opening his mind like this? Screaming planes, terror, bravery and death. And hope, and freedom. But there was no hope in these. These were Fact drones.

He squinted at the distant, humming swarm, then took the gun out of his mouth and laughed to himself, put it back, closed his eyes, reconfirmed the angle, and fired.

Through Azure and Ultramarine the coffin travelled, rising from deepdeepdown to deep, and Quill and Skim moved too, quickly the first time, then almost as slowly as the coffin; exploring, touching, making love in their own time.

'No hurry,' Skim said, nestling close to him. 'It seems there's all the time in the world, in here.'

'It's like that, in rock. It isn't real.'

Skim sat on the edge of the bunk. 'It's odd. I keep thinking of things, then realise I can't place them. This reminds me of an iron lung, but I don't know what an iron lung is.'

'Scheck says maybe you mean an iron maiden.'

Skim chuckled. 'We're a tiny bit of the mosaic, just like Naddy said. Imagine it. All those people connected. All those people touched by you.' She stroked his cheek.

'I wonder how many it takes to hold the entire memory.' He took out the small case with its remaining blister, and turned it over carefully.

'Hundreds? Thousands?'

'Would they kill that many people to keep it hidden? Is it really that important?'

'I'm not sure that's the question. Maybe we should be wondering who it could be that important to?'

'Perhaps we'll find out in a few days.'

Skim said, 'One of the things I don't understand. Tyler Hind went crazy. Why didn't you?'

'I don't know. Maybe it has something to do with the shock I'd just had, seeing Scheck dead.'

That's it. Blame me.

'Why are you smiling, Quill?'

'Am I?' He smiled and kissed her.

Skim kissed him and said, 'You were talking to Scheck, weren't you?' She pushed him back. 'Let's see what he thinks about this.'

'What is the capital of France?'

'Paris.' The woman frowned at what she'd said. She looked faintly dazed.

The factotem looked up, his eyes magnified by the breathing mask. He made a gesture, and one of the guards took the woman's arm and pulled her away. She was screaming, 'What have I done? I haven't done anything. What's France? I don't even know what France is.'

When she was gone, the factotem said, 'Next,' and Quill walked forward.

'You look familiar,' the factotem said.

'Probably. This is my second time today through this checkpoint. Can you pass me straight through?'

'No. You might have been infected in the meantime. You know the routine, then. Answer every question immediately, without thought. Give an answer or say, "I don't know." No other response is allowed. Do you understand?'

'Yes.'

'What's your name?'

'Vais Chalker.'

'What Primary is directly west of Blue?'

'Red.'

'Name two districts immediately deep of Blue.'

'Azure and Cyan.'

'What colour are polar bears?'

White.

'Quickly!'

'Wh ... what? I don't know. Look, I'm late, and you just saw me a few minutes ago.'

The factotem hesitated, then glanced beyond Quill at the line of people extending back along the coredor, and said, 'All right. Go.'

'This woman was with me. Remember?' Skim didn't have Scheck to filter the questions for her. She'd be caught.

The factotem rubbed the glass of his mask, and said, 'I'm not sure.'

'Why would I lie? She was with me all the time. If I'm safe, she must be, mustn't she? Doesn't that make sense?'

'All right. Go.'

Quill pulled Skim through the barrier. There were no more checkpoints before they reached the meeting place in Crimson. They saw two Robes and followed them to a small coredor.

'Quill,' said the taller of the two. He looked young, barely more than a boy, but he spoke firmly and with confidence. He pulled a pair of robes from under his own and shook them out. 'Put these on. Cover your hair. You're Skim?'

'Yes. Who are you?'

'I'm Marten, and this is Mexi. Mexi was one of the drones.'

'Then thank you for saving us. Why did you?'

'I was expecting you'd know that.'

Quill laughed at the absurdity as he stood in the orange robe. He looked at Skim standing uncomfortably in hers, and at Marten and the girl, Mexi. A boy and a girl, that's all they were. The girl didn't look like a Robe, somehow.

'You started this,' Marten said. 'All this confusion, all this knowledge. There were two of you, weren't there?'

'They killed the other one. Scheck.'

'I'm sorry. That's a pity.'

Yes. It was.

'The case with the virus, you've got it?'

Quill nodded, patting his pocket.

'We have to get you to Haze with it. There's a cargo ship about to leave. We have a friend who'll get us aboard, and another friend piloting. Are you ready?'

Haze. Quill wondered how he was supposed to cope with that. Haze would be even bigger than the arena. But Skim took his hand, and he knew it would be all right.

From the hatchway of the ship, Mexi watched Corven embrace Marten then push him away to slip through the great doors as they were closing. Marten ran up the ramp. They were strapped in their seats by the time the terradome opened. The ship juddered.

'That's not the engines,' Marten said. 'That's your winds.' And then the ship roared and began to shake.

'Those are the engines. And—'

And then the acceleration took everything away until she woke up to look through the tiny window and see it was black outside and peaceful, lanced with stars. Marten was asleep beside her. Mexi whispered to herself, 'Haze.'

And she slept again too, dreamlessly, waking a second time to a brilliance that made her wince as the ship flattened its flightpath and pushed out its wings in a perfect blue sky, as blue as endless lazurite.

Mexi looked down and saw Haze below her.

Haze was all there was – a white cocoon of it, a creaseless shroud. She looked momentarily across at Marten, wondering how such a planet could be. He was staring almost hungrily out of the porthole, his nose pressed to the glass. Quill and Skim were sleeping across the narrow aisle, her head in the crook of his neck, their hands clasped on her lap. To sleep at such a time, she thought. She wondered what Quill had been through, what had happened or was happening inside his head. All the time he muttered to himself. Even in his sleep, he was probably muttering. It didn't seem to bother Skim, though. Mexi decided she liked Skim. There was a stillness to her. And she'd lost someone close, the tech, Naddy Harke. Mexi thought she'd talk to her about Naddy when there was time, and tell her about Zelda. She thought Skim would understand about Zelda in a way Marten couldn't. She didn't feel she knew Marten properly yet.

She looked out again. The ship had dropped closer to the endless whiteness. Its wings were fully extended and juddering. This was what she'd always dreamt of. Contact. And as she thought of it, her heart thumped painfully. She wanted so much to tell Zelda about it.

Marten murmured, 'I've never seen this before.'

'What do you mean?'

'They always keep us asleep, taking off and landing.'

She waited for him to go on, but that was all he said.

It was a sea of cloud, but stagnant and lifeless. So different from Haven with its tornadoes and whirlwinds, its thunderous, thundercracking skies. Haven had a theatre of physics in place of a climate. This was different. This was a suffocating blanket.

The ship continued to drop. The clouds were smooth here, pitted and hollowed there, like the hint of a dream. Distantly there seemed to be dark mountains, but they were just roughnesses in the Haze. The ship fell further and was abruptly smothered, the shuddering wings swallowed by the mists almost to the fuselage. For a moment the swallowing white was brilliant, but as they fell below the penetration of the sun, the Haze darkened from white to grey and became dull and stifling. The wings disappeared altogether. The mists continued to flicker, greys darkening and growing pale again, and the ship bumped and thumped in the hard wind.

'Is it all like this?' she said eventually. 'The Haze? Is it everywhere?'

'It covers almost the entire planet. There's just a tiny, clear habitable region. Part of that is forest. People live there in villages. I was born there. At the edge of the forest is the AngWat. I was taken there.' His voice cracked, and he was quiet.

'Go on,' she said, putting her hand to his shoulder. The tension in him barely relaxed.

'The other part's a city. That's—' He jerked back suddenly and said, 'There!' He pointed. The Haze was dissolving around the ship. 'That's the forest. And there's the AngWat.'

Mexi saw a grid of stone buildings, and as she stared at it, pictures came into her head, pictures like memories, and she knew she had Quill's virus. She stared and stared, and then glanced at Marten. He looked at her, and she knew he had it too. She whispered, 'Angkor Wat.'

He looked again, frowning, tense, and said, 'Down there, that's not the Haze. It's on fire. The forest, all of it. I don't understand.'

She could still see only the white Haze, but it seemed different. The crawling smoke was greyer and flecked with yellow and orange.

As Marten started to say something, the pilot's voice cut in. 'I'm getting a message. The port isn't secured. I can't land there.' The speaker crackled, then the voice carried on. 'We have incoming missiles. I'll try to put us down on the road. Buckle up, please. Landing in about one minute. It may be rough.' The speaker cut crisply off. Mexi was conscious of wind noise and the cabin jumping.

Ahead, Quill and Skim were sitting up, staring out the window. Skim started to turn round, but didn't make it as the engines roared and the ship threw itself back, banking hard. Mexi looked through the porthole, trying to see where the ground was, but all she could see through the blur of vapour was the wing deconstructing itself into shuddering flaps. The engine noise rose to a scream and kept rising.

The pilot's voice rose above it all, in sudden and extraordinary calm. 'I'm sorry. This is going to be a little untidy. I'm jettisoning you. Hold on—'

Mexi yelled, 'Marten—' and the ship seemed to strike something or be struck, bucking hard. Marten's mouth opened, but across the cabin Skim's scream drowned whatever he might have been about to say.

HAZE

Reed was shaking her shoulder. 'Wake up, Petey.'

The pain was there the moment she opened her eyes, and she couldn't stifle a gasp. She sat up for Reed to redress the stump of her finger, and the agony eased fractionally. She could still feel the finger there, invisibly blazing with pain.

'That's the last of the analgesic,' Reed told her. 'There'll be more in the city.'

She looked around, forcing the pain away. 'Where are we?'

'Nearly there. We walk from here. If that lord was right and the True hold the entrance to the city, we can't risk arriving in a car.'

Crique helped her out. The smell of the fire was immediate and sharp, and the air was speckled with burnt matter.

'It's coming this way,' she told Crique, and he nodded. Reed was in front, striding quickly ahead. Petey could sense his anxiety.

They walked for an hour. Although it was advancing, the fire was still a long way back, visible as a long weal of orange lying beneath the sun. The wind blew at them and the stink of the fire was constant. Petey's throat was raw and her face felt hard and dry. Her eyes prickled. A small high sound made her look up, and Reed and Crique stopped to look with her. From the horizon ahead of them, the heart of the city, a small, dark dart was arrowing up into the sky.

A gust of smoke stung her eyes and she lost the dart. She wiped her eyes and squinted again. A whine and grinding squeal filled the sky, but there was no sign of the dart. And then suddenly, behind them, a boom rolled down, harder than thunder, and she turned to see a white flash hanging in the sky. A thin trail of cloud bloomed from the flash in a tightening curve and straightened out, descending towards the road behind them. It merged with the road in a silent flare of light, then a soft white bush of smoke rose and the ground under her feet shuddered. As it began to settle, a hollowed rumble and screech filled the air and continued for several minutes before trembling to nothing. The bush of smoke began to whirl away in the general wind.

'What was that?' Crique said.

'I think we just saw a ship shot down with a missile.' Reed looked at Crique, but Crique didn't ask anything else.

'We have to help them,' Petey said, understanding that someone must be hurt.

'No. We don't know what it means. We go on.' He started walking again.

Ahead, there was no forest at all now. Petey felt uncomfortable, and she could see Crique did too, though he wasn't going to let Reed know it. This had to be the city. The horizon was toothed and crowded with dim, shadowed buildings. As they continued, the forest at their sides shrank away. The trees became bushes and weeds, and as they walked, these withered away. Small houses of brick and metal spread away from the road. There were no people.

The place they were entering was leafless and lifeless. There was nothing here that had ever been alive, ever grown from seed or egg. One house was the same as the next, and Petey knew they would be all the same inside, too. Reed had described the city to her, but this had not been the picture that he had conjured for her. This was like a grave-field, full of the markers of past lives.

Crique was saying nothing, staring at it all as they walked on. Buildings were piled seamlessly above each other, without joint or clue at all to how they were made. They were high without stilts, and they blocked the sky more perfectly than the densest forest. And still it was deserted. There were no people, no animals, no birds.

'This is a place of the dead,' Crique said sourly.

'This is where I was educated and trained,' Reed said. 'This was—' and he shook his head and was quiet.

On they went and further. The only sound was the sound of their feet on the road, and it terrified Petey.

'The lord told you the rebellion was small and failing,' Crique eventually said.

'He lied. The lords have withdrawn from here.' Reed stopped abruptly, cupped his hands at his mouth and yelled, 'Hallo! The True! We're True!' He paused, and tried again. 'Can you hear us?'

Petey couldn't see anyone. Reed's call echoed a few times and died.

They went on. The road divided into several narrower tracks that Reed called streets. They kept to the broadest. There were holes in the road, and debris that they stepped over or walked around, and many of the walls were scored deeply and pitted. Some of the buildings were blackened and gouged away. There had been fighting here.

'Stop! Stop there, all of you.'

Petey froze. The sudden voice echoed round the small square they were passing through.

'Lift your hands up high. Good. Don't move.'

Petey could see no one in any of the buildings. There was a smell of smoke, but this was not like the burning forest.

Crique whispered, 'Up there, window on the right, third level.' He chuckled to himself and murmured, 'Three levels, and two more above that. And we live in windy huts.'

Another thin voice floated down. 'Give me a name, if you're True.'

'I'm Reed. I was with Eduar. These two are with me. They're *kh*— they're villagers.' He glanced at Petey and Crique, but neither reacted.

The voice came again. 'Wait there.'

Petey's knees were trembling uncontrollably. She sat down on the hard ground. Crique sat with her. Reed tapped his fingers impatiently.

The voice drifted down again. 'Your name's here. Take this.'

A small flat stone fell from the window and Reed caught it – not a stone, Petey saw, but one of their devices. She watched him open it and put his wide eye close to it, then lick his finger and put it to a pad there. He closed the device and threw it up to be caught again. The window dulled. Reed sat with Crique and Petey.

Crique said, 'They can check you, but we can't check them. Hmm?'

Reed didn't answer.

And suddenly there was a man in the doorway of the tall building, beckoning them. 'Quickly, Reed. Just you.'

Reed told Petey and Crique to wait, reappearing in the doorway after a while and calling them inside. His face seemed quite different, the lines faded and his eyes brighter.

Petey couldn't understand how so many people could be unheard from the street. Inside, people were running around, shouting to each other. They were ferrying machinery that had the focused look of weapons, and there was nothing at all to be read from their faces. They were preparing themselves for something, though. That was clear. There would be fighting. Reed grabbed a man by the arm and said, 'This woman's hurt. Her name's Petey and she needs help.'

The man looked at Petey without curiosity. She showed him the stump of her finger and he nodded. Reed said, 'Crique, go with them while I find out what's happening.'

The man took Crique and Petey through a maze of corridors without a single window. It was like being underground. She was aware of

Crique softly counting doors and registering turns. She knew she ought to do the same, but she didn't have the energy for caution.

And then, in a smooth, pale room, her finger was pricked and bandaged by another man whose tired smile was as comforting as the relief from her pain. She thought of DeSa, back in Nepenth, and of Duneld. Should she be there with him, instead of here? She didn't know, and tried not to think of it. Through an open door across the corridor she could see a long room full of occupied beds. A tide of moans and awful cries rolled from the room and Petey tensed at the sound. The man working on her finger glanced up at her and said quietly, 'It's hard when we see that. But we have to remember the future we want.'

Petey and Crique were eating in a huge dining chamber when Reed found them. Another man was with him, who didn't say a word, pulling up a chair and sitting at the table. He didn't eat. Petey felt awkward in his presence. She couldn't hold her fork properly. There was no more pain, but her finger was still there when she closed her eyes. It felt swollen and heavy.

'This is Commander Nagawa,' Reed said.

The man nodded tersely. He had thin lips and his eyes were cloudy blue. His fingernails were chewed down and his hair was shaved to the scalp. People at nearby tables glanced across at him.

'What we saw on the road,' Reed said. 'A ship's come down from Haven. The lords tried to destroy it. There may be True on board.'

Petey said, 'I told you we should have gone to help them.'

'We didn't know,' Crique said quietly. 'Reed was right.'

'Now it's different,' Reed said. 'It may be important. There may still be survivors.'

Petey realised Crique had absorbed all this strangeness. He had accepted the city. He said to Reed, but glancing at Nagawa, 'What about the uprising?'

The commander touched Reed's arm as he answered Crique. His voice was low and Petey had to lean forward to hear him. 'We aren't strong enough to win an open battle. We've taken the AngWat, but it's almost completely destroyed. The True there aren't any use to us. Whoever survived won't reach us in time. The lords destroyed all the vehicles they didn't escape in.'

Petey said, 'If we lose here, they'll have no hope at the AngWat.'

Nagawa said, 'That's right.'

'And here?' Crique asked.

'About five hundred men and women. We're barely holding our perimeter. The rest of the True, about a thousand, have been forced out of the city. They're regrouping for a final major attack to the east. When they launch that, we'll try to break out and engage the lords' other flank. With surprise—'

Crique gave him a look of disbelief, and the man shrugged. 'It's the best we can do.'

A man came up to Nagawa and said, 'Sir?' There was exhaustion in his eyes.

'Yes, Jerza?'

'I think you need to come to the comms room. We have something odd.'

Nagawa stood and excused himself. Petey watched them go, then looked at Crique and Reed. 'You act as if it's hopeless. It's never hopeless.'

'Oh, to have your faith,' Reed said softly. 'There are fifteen hundred of us, and several thousand of them. They have the Great Lord to marshal them.'

'We have surprise, surely.'

Nagawa strode back to the table, Jerza half a pace behind him. The commander said to Reed. 'We're getting a voice calling for help from somewhere very close to the Great Lord's Compound. Jerza thinks it's a woman, but the call's faint. She knows the frequencies and codes, though. She asked my name, and said she knows me.'

Reed said, 'You know her?'

'She says I don't, and won't give her name.'

'It could be a trick. They could have broken our codes.'

The commander shrugged. 'Maybe. But she gave me other names, all of them the True. The names match the list I've compiled since the revolt, and she has more. I don't know how anyone could have such a list.'

'That lord on the road?' Petey suggested.

'His list would be mainly of the dead. Ours and hers are of the living.'

Crique said, 'What is there to lose? Maybe she can help us.'

'It sounds like the other way round,' said Nagawa. Then he said, 'One of the names she volunteered was yours, Reed.'

Reed shrugged. 'What does that prove?'

'Nothing. But I can't make sense of it, and I don't want anyone else here talking to her. Everyone's unsettled enough. I don't want distractions. If it is a trick, I don't want anything accidentally given away.'

'You want me to talk to her?'

Petey stood up with Reed and Crique to follow Nagawa and Jerza through corridors again and down stairs to a long, low-ceilinged room stacked with glowing boards and flashing lights, where rows of people sat talking to machines, or perhaps themselves. There were desks and shelves overflowing with papers, wires across the floor like tangled roots.

'Through here,' Jerza said, gesturing, and they went through to a smaller chamber with a single small black bulb to speak into and a grille that leaked the sound of wind. At the commander's nod, Jerza leant over a table of dials and buttons, and a voice trickled into the air around them.

'Are you still there?'

Petey immediately knew it was a woman's voice.

'Who are you?' Reed said into the bulb.

'You don't know me, but I'm ... I am True. I am the True.' There was a break, then the voice resumed weakly. 'I haven't spoken to you before. I need your name.'

Reed hesitated, then said his name.

The voice repeated it. 'Reed. Nagawa didn't tell me you were there.' A pause into which a faint wind whistled. Then, 'I haven't heard from Eduar for some days.'

'He was killed.' Reed looked at Petey, who whispered, 'That means nothing. She could be guessing.'

Reed said, 'How do you know me?'

There was a sigh, or perhaps the wind again. 'I know you all, every one of you, your fathers and mothers, your lives and your deaths.' The voice seemed to be fading, but took strength again. 'I'm glad you're alive. You had a hard task. You were with the woman called Petey. She's in Nepenth with your child?'

Involuntarily, Petey said, 'No!' And more softly, to herself, 'I left him there.'

'She's with you?' The voice sharpened. 'Reed? I heard someone, is it her? Why is she there?'

Reed said, 'Stop this. Who are you? What is this?'

The voice faded. 'Help me, please. I am the True. I am your only chance. You have to take it.'

'Your only chance,' Petey murmured to Reed. 'That's what you said, isn't it? What Eduar told you?'

Reed nodded.

The voice came back. 'Petey, can you hear me? I'm sorry about Loren. There was nothing—'

Petey pushed Reed away and yelled, 'What do you mean? How do you know about Loren? Who are you?'

The voice seemed to lose attention. 'He listens to you, but I listen to him. I've listened for so long ... he can't hear this, though. I don't think he can. Not yet.' The voice faltered. 'Your attack will fail. He knows. He listens. You had surprise, but it's used up. I can't—'

'Who? The Great Lord? Who are you?'

The wind through the grille died. And then, in silence, the woman's voice whispered, 'The ship that crashed. Go to the ship.' A long, tired breath came into the room. 'Listen to me, Petey. Your son was on the ship. Marten.'

All the air left Petey.

'He should have the Archive. You must keep them all safe.'

Petey sagged, whispering, 'I don't understand.' She gave the bulb back to Reed, her hand shaking. Marten was alive?

'Then what?' Reed said into the bulb. 'What archive?'

'Then come to me.'

The wind came up and died again, and the room felt impossibly hot. Reed yelled into the bulb, 'Who are you?'

'It's down,' Jerza said, sitting back in his chair. 'It was cut at that end.'

Petey said, 'We have to go quickly. We have to find Marten. He's alive!' She was seeing a child walking away from her down the long stone causeway of the AngWat. She had woken in tears from that dream vision, year after year. But now he was turning back towards her. She couldn't see his face, but he was turning.

'It may be a trap,' Crique said quietly.

'Why? Why would it be a trap? We're worth nothing. We have to trust it.'

Reed said, 'We don't know who she is. We don't even know where she is, except that she's close to the Compound.'

Jerza looked up from his dials. 'Oh, no. She isn't somewhere close to the Compound. She's in the Compound.'

The commander sat down. 'Well,' he said, uneasily, as if to himself. Then, 'Thank you, Jerza. This is not to be discussed with anyone, understand. Leave us now.'

Crique said, 'It's straightforward enough. She says we have to go to the ship, then to the Compound to help her.'

'And she said the attack will fail,' Reed said.

'How do we know that?'

Petey said, 'We have to believe her.'

'I can't spare anyone to help you,' the commander said. 'Everything here's committed. Why didn't she tell us sooner?'

'She couldn't risk it. She said he listens,' Reed said. 'Why wouldn't she give her name?'

'She said it would mean nothing to us,' Nagawa said.

'Or maybe it would be too much of a risk,' Crique said. 'Although she's risked a lot even to contact us now. Especially if she is in the Compound.'

Reed said, 'A rebel in the heart. She must be brave.'

'She said Marten's alive,' Petey murmured.

Crique said, 'Just give us a car. We'll go to the ship.'

Reed said, 'When's your attack due to start?'

The commander shook his head. 'If you're leaving, I can't tell you that. You might be captured.'

'All right,' Crique said. 'We'll go to the ship, then to the Compound. If we take the car, we'll be able to get through the city to the Compound. Isn't that right, Reed?'

Reed nodded and looked at the commander. 'If it's true that everything you transmit is being heard, they won't expect anything like this.'

Nagawa hesitated, then said, 'Okay. You'll need two cars. You can get the one you brought here, and I have another you can take.'

Crique said, 'You're the only one who can steer one of those things, Reed.'

'It's easy. You just need to keep awake in case of an emergency. On that straight road, it'll do everything else.'

'And if there's an emergency?'

'Just keep awake.' Reed stood up. 'Now, let's go and see what we can load the cars up with.'

'There!' Petey almost hit the screen with her hand, leaning forward in the seat.

What was left of the ship crawled with smoke. Patches of raw metal glowed like white fire. It was ripped and crumpled. She thought of Marten in there, but refused to continue the thought. He would not be dead. Not now.

Reed slowed the car, and Crique's vehicle slowed behind them. They approached the wreck at a walking pace, wheels rumbling on the cracked road.

It seemed small in comparison to the fire and thunder of its landing, Petey thought. But the land around them was in thunderous turmoil. Beyond the ship, the sky was livid and the horizon grey and blurred. The forest fire was advancing. At the sides of the road, trees shook crazily and the air was full of charred leaves and cinders.

Some way from the ship in its shallow crater, Reed drew the car to a halt. Maintaining its distance perfectly, Crique's car stopped behind it. Even at rest, the vehicles shuddered in the immense wind.

Crique stepped out and slammed the door. Glancing at Petey, Reed forced a grin. 'I don't think he enjoyed that,' he told her.

Although the fire was closer than it had been, the ship still generated its own, greater heat. They walked around it. The fractured metal glared and creaked.

'No one could have survived that,' Crique murmured at last.

'No,' Reed said. He continued round the ship. 'But they might have ejected in the pod. See?' He pointed to a sharp-edged oval breach partly visible in the upper part of the fuselage.

'Then they could be anywhere.'

'If they landed in the forest, they might yet be dead. We'll never find them. There's no trail from here.'

'If it were me,' Crique said, 'And I thought there was any chance of help, I'd come back here and lie low, watching to see who comes along.' Turning his back on the ship, he drew breath and yelled, 'We're here to rescue you. Can you hear me?'

The sound dissolved in the wind and trees.

'We're True,' Reed yelled. 'Come out! It's safe. You're safe!'

Petey stared at the trees to the side of the road.

'Marten,' she whispered. She said it aloud, 'Marten,' and then the name welled up again inside her and she released it in a desperate yell, 'Marten!'

There was no answer at all. There was nothing but the wind and the thunderous forest. They went round the other side of the crashed ship and tried again. And then, as they went round once more, there was a woman standing at the edge of the trees. She was pale and emaciated, and her hair was the colour of dead leaves. She looked more sleepless than any of them, but her eyes were bright. She pulled herself upright.

'I'm Skim. Who are you?'

Reed started to speak, but Petey was quicker. She said, 'Marten – where is he? Is he alive?'

She shook her head. 'I need to know about you first.'

'We're True,' Reed said. 'My name's Reed. Are there more of you?'

Skim gestured towards Petey, who was running along the edge of the road, staring into the trees, yelling Marten's name. 'Who's she?'

'Her name's Petey. Marten's the son. Is he alive? And we were told you have some kind of archive. Do you?'

'What do you know about that?' she said. Then she half turned, cupped her hands into the wind and yelled, 'Quill, it's okay! You can get the others.' And then said to Reed, 'Quill's got the Archive. He sort of is the Archive, too.' She wiped her hair from her eyes. 'We all are, a bit. Marten and Mexi are back there in the trees. We thought it would be

380

safer like that, in case you weren't the cavalry.' Skim grinned at Reed's incomprehension. She seemed to be filling with energy now. 'Don't worry. Quill's going off to bring them back.'

Petey was with them again now, panting, flushed.

'You look like Marten,' Skim told her.

'She would. She's the mother,' Crique said.

'What do you mean?' And then, incredulously, 'You mean *his* mother? She's *Marten's* mother?' Skim laughed. 'That's crazy. We come down here in the centre of nowhere, and his mother's here to meet him?'

Petey said, 'Where are they? I have to see him.'

'It'll take Quill ten minutes to get to them.'

'How many of you are there?' Crique said.

'Me, Marten, Quill and a woman called Mexi. There was a pilot but he stayed with the ship. I had a look, but it was too hot to get close. He was a brave man.' She watched Petey dancing anxiously from foot to foot, peering into the trees, and then she waved her hand at the forest and said to Reed, 'This takes some getting used to.'

'She hasn't seen him for about fifteen years.'

'I meant this place. It's—' she made a face. 'It's so still. So quiet. Even with the volcano way over there.'

'That's a forest fire. You think this is quiet? The forest is burning.'

Skim shrugged. 'We don't even have forests. I'd just heard about them.' Her tone changed. 'Marten didn't know what we were going to do once we got here.'

'We go to the Compound, where all the orders come from. It's the heart of all this. We have to get there and try to destroy it.'

'Just us? You three and us?'

Reed nodded. 'We think there's someone there who may be able to help us.'

'Won't it be protected?'

'It's sure to be. But if our information's right, we have a better chance than a few thousand others about to fight.'

Skim raised her eyebrows. 'That's good, then.'

Petey screamed, and everyone turned.

Two men and a woman had appeared at the edge of the trees. They all had the pallor of Haven. The woman was slim and had a stubble of fine, white hair, and one of the men was short and wiry and looked about as old as Reed. The other was Marten.

Petey ran to Marten, then stopped just paces from him as if at a chasm. She could hardly speak. She whispered, 'Do you remember me,

Marten? I'm the . . . your mother.' She barely heard the words herself in the screaming wind, but she could see he'd heard them.

For a moment he didn't move. Then he reached out his hand towards the white-haired woman, who held it tightly. He said nothing.

'Marten?' Petey said. 'Don't you recognise me?'

He opened his mouth, swallowed the wind, tried again. He said, 'No. The mother left me.'

For long seconds, there was only the cracking of the wind. Then Reed took Petey's hand and said, 'There isn't time for this. You can talk on the way. We don't know when the True attack is scheduled to begin.'

Crique gently pulled Petey away. Reed turned to Quill and said, 'The Archive?'

Quill nodded.

'Good. Let's go.'

Quill touched his elbow, holding him back, and showed Reed the small case. 'It's in here, too,' he said. 'But it's me. And in part, I pass it to whoever comes near me.'

'So I'll get it,' Reed said.

'You're getting it now, all of you. How much of it, and how long before you realise it—' he shrugged, '—seems to differ from person to person.'

Mexi came over to Reed. Glancing across at Petey, she said, 'Marten wasn't expecting this. I think his mother should go in the other car. I'll talk to him.'

Reed said, 'Marten will be able to drive one of these. I don't think Crique will mind him taking over. And I want to talk to Quill. So how about if you and Marten go with Crique, and Quill and Skim come with me and Petey.'

Mexi nodded. 'That gives us a Robe in each car. Can we talk between cars?'

Reed couldn't make out how old this girl was. She wasn't a lord, but there was an extraordinary sharpness to her. He said, 'No. We assume all comms are intercepted. I'll lead. I have maps to get us to the Compound. We'll drive fast round the edge of the area we hold, and Nagawa's men will open fire on us as we leave. It'll look like we've broken through. We'll keep going. We'll tell them our comms are disabled, which is true, and that we have urgent information from the AngWat for the Compound.' He hesitated. 'Is Marten going to be all right? This was a shock.'

'He's strong.' Mexi smiled at Reed. 'He saved my life and got us here. Don't worry. What about her?' Nodding at Petey, who was standing as if in a trance.

'She'll be all right. She's his mother.'

Petey didn't protest as Marten got into the other car. She said nothing, sitting next to Skim at the back, while Quill sat with Reed in the front. They all wore robes now.

The road rumbled beneath them, and when Reed stopped talking, Quill took over, or sometimes Skim. But Petey said nothing, lost in her own thoughts. Reed wondered if she'd be all right. In the rear mirror he saw Skim murmuring to her from time to time.

After that, he kept silent and just drove, taking roads through the city at speed. At first he had to slow for Marten to keep up, but then the boy – not a boy, but he thought of Petey's son that way – was on his tail, and it became almost a game, Reed trying to lose him and failing. And abruptly there were huge bursts of fire across the road and he swerved and nearly lost control. Quill yelled and grabbed at the screen fascia, and Skim swore.

And they were through the rebel zone, and stopped dead at a roadblock.

Marten's car was stopped just behind them. Reed saw Marten gesticulating furiously, and then Reed's door was jerked open from the outside. Reed reached out and slammed it shut, and slid the window down. Then he yelled at the lord standing there, 'Crise, man! Was that you trying to kill us?'

'Not us. You didn't look like you'd make it. Where did you come from?'

Reed wiped his forehead. 'The AngWat. We're in a hurry.'

'We noticed.' The man relaxed slightly. 'Going where?'

'To the Compound.'

'Wait here. I'll have to check that. Who are you?'

'I was on the road with Marek. We were nearly hijacked. The others—' Reed gestured at the car behind, '—I don't know all their names, there wasn't time.'

The man wasn't moving, and Reed sharpened his tone. 'There's a fire, you may have noticed.'

The man shook his head. 'There are rebels, you may have noticed. Wait.' He started to move away. Reed glanced at Skim in the rear mirror. She shook her head tightly.

Reed put his head out of the window and called the man back. 'I said I was with Marek. Check our file. Then say I have fresh information about the rebel attack. Tell your commander I said the main attack will come from the east, with a flanking attack right here.'

The man held his ground. Reed opened the door and got out, leaving the door wide. He prodded the man's chest and said, 'That means they'll be overrunning your post. Did they tell you that, or is the real line of defence behind you? Did they tell you you're just bait?'

The man blanched and finally turned. 'Wait.' And then said, 'Your partner was Marek. Your name . . .?'

'Just check Marek. That'll be enough. Don't waste time.'

The man disappeared into a low guardhouse, then reappeared in its doorway, waving the cars urgently through the rising barriers.

'They're expecting us now,' Quill said as the barriers closed behind Marten's car.

'And if they didn't know the True plan, they do now,' Petey said.

Reed said, 'We just confirmed they know it, that's all. That's why we got through. And anyway, by the time we got anywhere near the Compound, they'd be expecting us.'

'This could still be a trap. We're bringing them the Archive. Did you think of that?'

Reed didn't answer. The roads were better now. There were soldiers gathering, but they were concentrating on fortifying the buildings and readying heavy weaponry. Every few hundred metres, barriers were raised ahead of the two cars and dropped behind them. The two cars hardly needed to reduce speed. They were being monitored all the way.

'There's no way through this,' Quill muttered. 'If they're this prepared for the flanking manouevre, I wonder what they've set up for the main thrust.'

'Can't we tell Nagawa?' Skim said.

'No.'

Eventually the roads cleared, and they were behind the fortifications. Here the city looked deserted but otherwise normal. Reed glanced back at Marten, who was keeping a steady distance from him, and wondered how the boy was feeling about being here again. It made Reed anxious to be in the heart of the city.

It wasn't perfectly deserted, though. There were still barriers rising and falling for them. 'The Robe at the checkpoint,' Quill said suddenly. 'If he got the virus from me and it takes him quickly . . .'

'Let's hope it doesn't. I'm—' Reed let his mind float, but he didn't know what to expect, what it might be like. There seemed to be nothing unusual. 'I'm still okay. Petey?'

'I'm okay,' she said. 'Hunkydory.'

She was quiet, registering Reed's expression. She murmured, 'It means okay.'

Quill looked at Reed. Reed increased his speed. 'They're still letting us through. He wouldn't understand what's happening to him. Nor would people around him. You expect craziness in times of war. There's always been—' Shellshock, he thought. Soldiers driven crazy and shot for cowardice. Reed saw trenches filled with mud and corpses. The First World War. He clenched his mind against the unwanted unmemory. How much of this was there? He glanced at Quill, wondering how the man held it all.

And then he slowed the car, raised a hand in a signal for Crique behind, and said, 'We're about there. Skim, Petey, there's a hatch through to the back of the car. The catch is—'

'I've got it,' Skim said. She ducked her head and whistled. 'You have guns.'

'You can work out how to use them?'

'I seem to know the principle,' she said dryly.

'Can you show Petey? And pass a couple forward for me and Quill.'

Reed watched the movement in the car behind and waited for them to settle. Crique made a hand signal, and Reed speeded up again.

They joined a broad avenue lined with trees. These were the first trees they had seen in over an hour of driving, and Skim murmured, 'It's just like the Champs-Elysées.'

They drove down the long, straight avenue. Wind was taking the trees, throwing the branches around, filling the air with leaves. 'There's never a wind here,' Reed said. 'There's never sun nor rain. Just stillness and the Haze above.'

Reed thought about the Haze, about the final secret he had kept from Petey. He thought of her, and of Duneld, and all that he had done. It had to come out eventually, but not now. Not yet. His head roared. It was this virus Quill had infected him with, sending him crazy. Shellshock. He was going into his shell, but that couldn't be it. That wasn't why it was called shellshock. The memory was faulty, like Reed himself.

He had to hold himself together for a little longer, for Petey, if not for Duneld. It was painful to think of their son.

'It's the Pentagon,' Skim whispered a little uncertainly, and Petey murmured, 'Yes.'

'No,' Reed said, though the word was vaguely familiar. 'It's the Compound.'

Quill said, 'It's much smaller than the Pentagon.' Then he said, 'There's no one outside. No guards. Reed, is that right?'

Without considering it, Reed pulled the car down a small side street and stopped. The other car pulled to a halt behind him. He sat back and controlled his breathing, still having trouble thinking straight. He said, 'Everyone who becomes a lord is brought here once. When my class was brought to the Compound, we were told that the heart is always open.

Strength is outside, openness within. But it isn't a real openness. It's just a readiness to betray.'

He noticed Quill's head tilting as if he were listening to something. His lips moved, and he nodded and murmured, 'Yes!'

'What?' Skim said to Quill.

'The heart is always open. It's what he used to say.'

'Who?'

'The Captain. The heart is always open.'

Skim said, 'The Captain? On Haven? But he's dead. What do you mean?'

'Not Haven. Earth.' Quill made a gesture towards the Compound. 'He built it to resemble the Pentagon, an old building there. This is a small-scale model of his Foundation on Earth.' He was talking fast, but suddenly he slowed down. 'In . . . . In . . .' He swallowed, and then shuddered heavily and struggled to carry on. 'Inside it we'll fi . . . we'll find the Heart Suite.' He stopped. His mouth moved a few times, then his lips gently closed and he was still.

'Quill?' Skim was shaking him. 'Quill!'

Quill blinked, but he didn't move. His eyes stared straight ahead.

'What's happened to him?' Petey said.

'Scheck filters the information for him. That's what protects him. I think Scheck just disappeared.' Skim seemed to lose energy. 'Maybe there was suddenly too much for the Scheck mechanism to cope with.'

Reed shivered. Petey leaned forward and held his shoulder. 'Not you too, Reed. Please. I need you. We need you.'

The door opened, and Reed jerked suddenly. Marten was standing there, holding a gun, and Crique and Mexi were with him.

'What are you waiting for?' Crique said. 'We're wasting time.'

Reed pushed himself out of the car, and the others followed, except for Quill who still wasn't moving at all. Petey looked at Marten, but he ignored her. Marten said, 'Come on, Quill.'

'He can't,' Skim said. 'He—' She caught on the word and stopped. 'We'll have to leave him here.'

'Someone has to stay with him.'

'No,' Crique said. 'We need everyone.'

'We can secure the car,' Marten said. 'There are no guards. There are no weapons here except ours.' He made a small grin, and Reed could see the effort it cost him. 'The heart is always open.'

'Even now?' Petey said.

Marten looked at her. Reed could see him fighting to speak to her, but he couldn't make it. He had hardened himself too much. He was closed away. He responded to Reed instead of Petey. 'It's safe here, isn't it? There's nowhere to station guards without them being exposed. That's the whole point.'

Reed said, 'Yes.' He put his arm around Petey, who sobbed once and was steady again. 'Quill should be safe here.'

It was eerie, though. There was the wind blowing, and the air was starting to fill with ash and burnt material. Standing here, it was hard to think of fighting. The battle seemed already abandoned. Reed felt lost and lethargic.

'Reed? Reed!'

Crique was gripping his arm, shaking him. 'Time, Reed. We have to move. The woman, remember?'

Marten said, 'Do you remember the way to the Heart Suite, Reed?'

'I think so. You?'

Marten said, 'I have two memories. One's my own, and one's—' He tapped his head. 'Back on Earth.'

'I just have one,' Reed said. 'That's enough.'

Mexi picked up a gun. 'Let's go.'

As she said it, Crique yelled and threw himself at Petey, and Reed turned and fired the gun before he'd even see the lord shooting at them. The man fell, his weapon clattering on the ground.

Reed dropped flat and rolled to the side of the car.

'Reed! Move!'

He stood up and ran, obeying Crique instinctively. Out of the corner of his eye he saw a man standing at the street corner, lobbing something towards him. Crique was firing at him and the man screamed, twisted and began to fall, and Reed's attention as he was still running was taken by another lord coming up behind Crique. He yelled a warning, but the car behind him boomed and everything was bright and he was lifted into the air and thrown towards Crique, who was taken an instant later by the same blast and hurled into the lord behind him.

Stupid, he thought. It was all a trap. He rolled again and kept rolling until he came up against a wall, and pulled the gunsight to his eye. He had to keep going.

The street was empty. The car was in flames. He yelled, 'Crique!'

There was a faint glare and a white dot moving along the ground towards him. He rolled away and stabilised himself quickly, and made out the grain of the backbeam, and fired a burst approximately along it, moving the gun wildly. The dot moved sharply towards him and then was gone. Reed squinted up and saw the glint of the gun again, and this time fired more carefully. He heard a grunt and saw a shadow fall and be still. He sat back against the wall, listening, steadying the rasp of his breath.

'I think that's all of them,' he heard. Mexi's voice. He struggled to his feet. The car was still blazing. Skim was crouched down, sobbing, and Mexi was with her. Quill was dead, then. Reed wondered if the Archive case had been in the car with him. Stupid. He looked round, searching for Petey, and his heart thumped and then quietened as he saw her with Crique. Crique's face was black and scorched, but he was all right.

'Reed. Are you okay?'

Marten's hand was on his shoulder.

'We should have expected this.'

'It might work for us. They'll think we're dead.'

Marten straightened himself, pulled Reed to his feet. 'You saved us, Reed.'

'Me? Don't try to be kind.'

'You came off the avenue before we reached the Compound. I would have driven straight up to the gate. The heart is always open, huh?'

'I panicked, that's all. Memories. I didn't think. We lost Quill, the Archive.'

'Lost Quill? That's what Skim thought. No, he's in the other car. I don't think he knew any of this was going on.' Marten walked Reed round to see Quill sitting safe in the car. 'He's just lost in the past, that's all. He might never come back, but he isn't dead.'

Petey came over, and Marten stiffened. She looked at him, her eyes pleading with him to speak, but he didn't. She said, 'Reed? Are you all right?'

He touched her arm. 'Yes. You?'

She nodded, then quietly said, 'Marten?'

'I'm fine. Get yourself ready.'

She went off, and Reed said, 'She never believed you were dead, Marten. She's waited for you all these years.'

'She gave me away. I was a child. I turned round and saw her watching them take me.'

'You know that isn't true. That's one of the lies they use.'

'Mexi!' Marten beckoned her over, dismissing the conversation with Reed. The white-haired girl glanced from Marten to Reed, raised the gun in her hand and said, 'Now?'

'Wait. How many of them were there?' Reed said.

'We got five.'

'Was that all of them?'

'I don't know.'

'Did they have comms?'

'Yes.'

'Can you get one that's still working?'

388

She went off.

'What are you thinking?' Marten said.

'We can't pretend to be them. When they don't return, the Compound will know at least some of us survived, and they'll be waiting for us. We've got nothing to lose by talking to them.'

Mexi came back, rubbing blood from the unit she was holding.

Reed thumbed the machine to active. There was silence. He shifted frequencies, getting nothing until suddenly he heard coarse breathing. He said, 'Can you hear me?'

'Who's that?' The voice was muffled, and there was a cough at the end of it.

Reed glanced at Mexi. She shook her head.

The voice repeated the question uncertainly, still coughing. Then it said, trembling, 'Are you the True?'

Reed still didn't answer. He looked at Marten, who shrugged.

Hesitantly the voice tried, 'Please. Is that Reed?'

Reed put the unit to his mouth and said, 'There was someone else. I spoke to a woman. What's happening?'

A small sob came from the unit, then another bout of coughs. The breathing was harsher. 'You need to come in. I can't get to her. The Heart's sealed. I don't know what's going to happen.'

'Who are you?'

'Techmedic. Mamoud.' Coughing again, and now spitting too. 'When they sent the team out to kill you, I took my chance and flooded the vents with gas. Last resort. It was all I could do. I think they're all dead.'

'What about you?'

'Not long. No masks here. Just a makeshift . . .' A muffled sound like vomiting. 'Ten minutes to purge and clear, then safe for you.' And a machine whine, and nothing more.

'Are you there? Hello?'

Nothing. Reed threw the unit down.

Marten said, 'Well?'

'Too elaborate to be a trick,' Reed said.

'Is the woman dead too?' Skim asked.

'Maybe. He said he couldn't get to her. And we don't know about the Great Lord.'

'If he's still alive, he's isolated. Sealed safe, but trapped. He'll have called for help. We can't waste time.'

'Let's move, then. By the time we get there, the ten minutes will be up.' They started walking down the long, wide avenue. Reed found himself shaking as they approached the doors of the Compound. He saw himself as a child walking down the endless causeway towards the

AngWat, and then as a fourteen-year-old here, seared almost beyond hope, queuing to file past the sleeping Great Lord of Haven in his heart of glass. He had felt so isolated. If it hadn't been for Eduar . . . He looked at Marten and saw the boy flinching as they were almost at the gates.

'Come on,' Reed said to the boy. 'Take my hand.'

Marten shook his head. 'No. Mexi,' he whispered. He held his hand out to her.

Crique said, 'Are you sure it's safe, Reed?'

'It's quiet. They would have fired at us by now.'

Petey tried to take Reed's hand, but he shook her away. They were in the shadow of the doorway now. The Compound's wall was metres thick, the approach to the doorway a short, arched passage. The lighting in the passage was pale and made ghosts of them all. Marten was still outside.

Reed pushed the great doors. They moved silently on their hinges, all the way back. 'The Heart is open,' he murmured.

Petey said, 'Reed?' and touched his hand again.

Reed couldn't do it. He couldn't fight off the thought of Duneld up in the Haze. He was overwhelmed by the thought of what he'd done, the lies to Petey. So many lies. Again he shook off her hand, and walked straight ahead and into the Compound. He knew the way. He could hear Petey behind him, weeping gently, alone.

Behind him, Mexi said, 'No, Marten. You take your mother's hand. If you can't take her hand, I'm not ready for you.' And she followed Reed through the doorway into the Compound. Skim followed her, and then Crique. Only Petey and Marten were left outside. Reed looked back towards the ashen daylight.

Petey was holding her hand out to her son. Marten didn't move for a moment. Then he turned towards the Compound and started to walk in, leaving her behind.

Reed stared at the two of them, his heart hollow. He looked round. There were rows of passages leading away to either side of him, and up ahead, across the broad, open central courtyard, was the glass wall of the Heart Suite.

Reed looked back at Marten again. The boy's eyes were clear and empty. Reed shook his head tightly. Marten stopped abruptly, then turned and ran to his mother across the great causeway of time that lay between them, and brought her inside.

Watching Petey holding her son, tight as swaddling, Reed felt emptier than ever. 'This way,' he said.

Behind them all, the doors of the Compound slowly closed, and the air fell quiet and still.

There was an odd smell in the air that made Petey feel faint, but Marten was with her, and the joy of that was enough to make her forget almost everything else.

Reed led the way at a steady pace. He paused to check no one was falling behind, but wouldn't let anyone keep him company. Petey thought it odd, but she thought Reed was probably jealous in the stupid way men could be.

And then the passage abruptly opened out into a single, vast courtyard. At its heart was a broad circular stone plinth with a network of dark internal walls. All it lacked was an outer wall. Furniture was carefully laid out in the room facing them. It was a bedroom.

'The Heart Suite,' Marten said, releasing Petey's hand.

'There's no wall,' she said.

'Glass,' Reed said.

Now she saw the faint lines and blocks of reflection in the curved wall socketed in the perimeter of the plinth. The glass was touched with pink. She looked up and saw that the courtyard wasn't actually open at all. It was a dome of the same glass, glittering in the fiery sky. Above the dome, ash and specks of burnt material swirled. Down in the courtyard, everything was still.

'There's his bed,' Reed murmured.

Marten whispered, 'He must be awake. Only the High Lords ever see him awake.'

The empty bed was like no bed Petey had ever seen, with its tubes and wires and screens. The bed looked so comfortable, though, and she was so very tired. She felt she could just walk across to it, step up onto the plinth, smooth back the sheets and go to sleep.

Like Goldilocks.

Goldilocks?

Glass? How did she know about glass? In the city, she'd accepted it without understanding. Now, suddenly, she knew what it was. And she could concentrate and know about plate glass, frosted glass, laminated glass, stained glass . . . and stained glass made her think of cathedrals, mosques, synagogues, and of god . . . the idea of god was elusive, though. It meant nothing to her, and led nowhere in this maze of knowledge except back on itself.

Crique was saying, 'How do we get in? There's no door.'

'There must be one.' Reed and Marten walked out of the shadow of the walls and into the open courtyard. They began to walk along the glass wall, passed the first internal wall and stopped dead. Marten murmured, 'There. That's him. The Great Lord of Haven.'

As the two men stood and stared, Mexi and Petey joined them. Reed was shaking.

Mexi said, 'He looks old and harmless.'

The man was sitting in a chair, talking to himself, making gestures. He hadn't noticed them watching him.

And then he looked up and across, and smiled at them.

Petey stared. His eyes were palest blue, and his hair was fine and blond, a colour warm as sunshine. She sensed kindness there. He stood up slowly and steadied himself. He was stooped, but she could see the life still bright in him. He was glorious.

Reed put out his palm and touched the glass, and fell back screaming and holding his hand.

'Get back,' Marten yelled, pulling Reed away. Petey wasn't ready to move, but Mexi dragged her towards the shelter of the outer passageway.

The man raised an arm. 'Wait there,' he said, taking a small box from his pocket. The voice boomed all around them, filling the courtyard. He moved slowly, and his calm, encouraging voice trembled faintly with age. The box caught in the folds of his robe and he fumbled with it, staring at Petey with his rheumy eyes. There was an odd look, almost of longing, in them. For a moment as they ran, the inner screen shielded them from him, but then he was through a door in the screen and gazing at them again, clutching the box in both hands.

'Run!' Reed said, pushing at Skim, who was still in the courtyard, and in sudden panic they all made it to the shelter of the arch. Nothing had happened.

'He's calling us back,' Mexi said. 'Look.'

He was beckoning to them, nodding and calling them. The voice came again. 'There's nothing to fear. You're wrong, you know. Whatever you think, it's wrong. Please come closer. I can't see you from here. My eyesight isn't good. Where are you?'

'Look,' Skim said, pointing. 'Beamguides up there on the framework, trained on us.' She lifted her gun and fired it. The beamguide flashed as she fired, and she dropped the gun.

'No! Don't do that. You'll be hurt. I'm sorry, it's automatic.' The Great Lord brandished the small box. 'I'll turn it off. But you're safe as long as you don't shoot. Please, please come out again. I want to see you.'

CAP

But they won't come out again. Rats in mazes, Pavlov's dogs, humans – they all learn in the end, if you condition them well enough.

Let them wait. They won't get in here. The technology to get in here doesn't exist on Haze. They have it on Haven, but Fact have dutifully prohibited it from transportation here. So I can wait for my people to obliterate this nuisance of a rebellion and come to restore normality.

The True? Where did that come from? Where did *they* come from? An odd coincidence, the uprising at the same time as the Archivirus escaping. By itself, neither would have been any threat, but together, each was a small distraction from the other.

I feel I'm missing something. Perhaps it's age. All the responsibility for two worlds.

It should of course only have been one world.

So. To go on.

I think back to the Earth, still. I think fondly of Bob and his family, who passed away peacefully or otherwise in the ships, and of Jake, who died in his apartment. Jake might have liked to see the film of the Earth's Restoration, though I think he had enough self-confidence for the actuality to be unnecessary. Maybe the theory was enough for him. He never had much imagination. I feel he died as he would have wished, eating a last meal of noodles washed down with Texicola. I doubt he even noticed the taste, and it wouldn't have been the first time he'd fallen asleep over the carton.

And I still think of my father. The dreams have not left me, even after these centuries. I am still nauseous.

But I don't have to eat any more, which is a help. I am nutrified while I sleep.

The Earth. I sometimes dream of it. A new Eden and more perfect. A silent Earth, green and calm and eternally quite empty of man, thanks to Jake's tiny virus in the terraforming program. Psalm 103 comes to me. *They are like the flowers in the field. The wind blows and they are gone, and the place that knew them knows them not.* Such peaceful, reassuring words.

Another interruption. A noise. Something moving.

Nothing can get in here.

How did Mamoud gas them? Why did he? He must have been insane, killing himself too. And my comms aren't working as they should, and no one to fix them. Scratching. What is it?

A distraction, that's all.

I have to finish. The Haze that gave the planet its name also gave me the idea that makes it secure. I knew I couldn't control an entire world. It simply isn't possible for one man to do that. So I simply didn't allow a world to be. The planet is vast and was almost entirely inhabitable, once the small terraforming procedures had banished the Haze, replaced it with Earth-like cloud and allowed the sun through.

I decided on the extent of the city, keeping it small and manageable. I left the forest with its carefully marshalled life of animals and *khuks*. *Khuks*, yes. It was a carefully researched word, without meaning or association, a pure snarl word. *Khuk.* Language is so important. Now that I think of it, it sounds like that croak of my father as he spewed and spewed. *Khuk. Khuk.*

My father. Always my father.

The Haze. I must concentrate. What *is* that scratching?

In a ring beyond the whole region I had electromagnetic attractors and generators seeded in tight formation, embedded deep in the ground. The chemical Haze controlled by these attractors is multifunc-tional, secluding the city from Haven's ships, and keeping the *khuks* from proliferating and spreading. I set up Nepenth as a small safety valve, more loosely set with attractors so that while they can survive there, their children will safely perish from lung diseases.

In the city, they're not allowed to have children. They are warehoused in dormitories. Children are brought in to be educated, so no attachments are made. Attachments are forbidden except in the forest, where they can be used as part of the control. It's a perfect, stable system.

So how has it gone wrong? Where did the True come from? Someone must have started it. Not in the forest, surely. It would have started and been ended there. In the city? Impossible. They sleep in dormitories, they hardly meet except in groups, and they inform on each other. In the AngWat? Those are my most trusted, my most certain men and women. On Haven?

Did it start on Haven? It can't have. How would anyone have known about the Archivirus?

Haven was a mistake. I should have destroyed it as soon as I realised the colony had survived. I shall not make that mistake again.

Scratching again. They're still out there. It isn't them. Where's it coming from?

The uprising will be suppressed shortly. I shall destroy Haven. In the meantime, what's causing this irritating noise? It seems to be coming from Mary's quarters.

The door's catching. No, it's malfunctioning.

Mary? Mary!

The scratching's coming from behind it. I'll stop the record a moment and call to her. Note to delete from here.

Mary? Are you awake? Are you trying to get out? Can you hear me?

She isn't answering. The scratching stops, then starts again.

I— Cancel the delete.

Mary Trulove. My own Mary. I feel hollowed out, nauseous . . .

I just vomited. Nothing rose, but my ribs ache. I'm weak, and I need strength. How did this happen? She's the one person I trust.

MARY! MARY! ANSWER ME!

I can hear her whispering now.

The True? Has *she* betrayed me?

MARY TRULOVE

He'll open the door. There isn't much I can do about it. Mamoud's device to freeze the mechanism is only makeshift. I can just be as ready as possible.

I've heard his so-called record. I couldn't risk setting down mine, the truth, but I have to say something now. Maybe he'll erase it. Either way, I'll be dead. I'm tired, though. I'm almost ready for death.

All this time I've waited, through the murmur of machines, the cool, lethargic flow of the hibernation gel.

I'm not patient. You may think I must have been, but I had no idea of the passage of time until recently. Recently? A hundred years ago, maybe. I wake up, I sleep. I can't move, but I can think. Sometimes I'm wet when I wake up, and I know Cap was awake recently – within an hour or two – and he raped me. I have no idea how often he's done it and it dried before I woke.

Once someone else raped me, apparently – not that I'd have felt it, though that isn't the point. Cap had them disembowelled. I was asleep for both events. I only know because he left notes for me. At least I don't have to see him, though he still fills my dreams.

You have dreams in this state of sluggish cold. I've wished him dreams to wake him screaming, but now, after what I've heard, I hope he sleeps calmly.

I hear a lot. The systems that maintain me are the same systems that maintain him, and they feed his sleeping skull with what's happening. They aren't supposed to input into my head, but all those years back, they began to. It was a misunderstanding by one of the techmedics, one of Mamoud's predecessors. He was too terrified to tell anyone what he'd done, and he told me. I asked him if there was someone else he thought he could trust, beyond me. It turned out there was. One single person.

He's still ranting and screaming out there. I can move my hands and arms, but the muscles are weak. My legs feel soft and swollen to the prod of my fingers. Ah, I can move them, though it's slow and hard.

Bring the knees up. Pull the bedclothes back. Even to do that exhausts me. Look at my legs, not swollen at all. They're twigs. My knees and ankles are swollen knots.

That's how the True started, with one single person and then another. From that terror replaced by trust, it grew over the decades to become a group that extends beyond the AngWat, beyond Haze, even.

I chose carefully, and the people I chose, chose carefully. It's always a combination of factors. There's surely a genetic element to it, but it's more than that. Acts of opportunistic kindness are a guide. Selfless kindness. Cap's systems weed them out, while I cultivate them and protect them. I protected Petey as best I could, and I protected Marten. I protected many others, of course, Loren amongst them. It was luck that Petey and Marten survived. There was a lot of luck involved.

There's always luck, but of course there are two types of luck – not good and bad luck. Good and bad are words without meaning, here on Haze. There's just brute luck and option luck.

Brute luck is the bolt from the blue, the event you can't predict or do a thing about. What led to Loren's death was brute luck. My dad shooting me was my own brute luck, but his getting fired was option luck. He should have seen it coming.

What Cap did to the Earth wasn't brute luck – they should have seen it coming. But there was oil, and land, and the opportunity for wealth accumulation to confuse those who should have seen it. And after all no one saw any of the other great dictators coming, back on Earth, did they? Or did they just think it would happen to someone else?

Quill recovering the Archivirus from John's ship was pure, wonderful brute luck. There was nothing I could do about that. Without that, it could have been years, maybe centuries before I had an opportunity to launch my True.

I would have liked children. I regret that. But I feel I have a family.

He's still screaming. I'm amazed he has such energy. Can I raise my arms? Yes, look. It's tiring, though.

Mamoud used the gas, then. All those years, secretly preparing it, storing it up, waiting. I wondered if he could do it, and he did. He was so faithful to me. Killed them all and cut Cap off, but cut me off as well. There'll be panic among his lords, though. They aren't used to independent thought. That helps.

I'm frail, but we both are. It's against nature to live so long, though I'm not sure I even remember what nature is, I'm so removed from existence. This sleep we have – how does he endure it? But I know, of course. It's what's always driven him on. His father.

I remember my dad, too. I remember what he did to me, in his despair and anguish. I never blamed him, not for a moment. I hated him for a long time, but I never blamed him.

Not like Cap. So long ago, so very long ago, and so very far away, but he still can't forgive.

My family. I hold them all in my head, like a map of a place I've never seen. Some are distant relations, others close. Some are achingly close now. I even know their names. I wish I could see them, just once.

I have senses for them, and textures. Reed is rough like the teeth of a zip, Petey is soft and strong at the same time, like worn leather. Loren was a good man, deserving to live through this, but there were so many more who also deserved that. Their parents, and others, the parents of others. So many genes I secretly harvested over the years, so much mercy and kindness I saved against Cap's hatred and destruction. I hope they survive, these last men and women. This is the final chance I have for them.

Reed and Petey and Marten. All the time I was with them and all those others, trying to imagine their lives from the crumbs I was given. I have to forget about Zelda. She was one of my best.

It's hard to concentrate with him screaming at the door, but let him scream. When he calms down, he'll start to think, and then he'll get the door open. My legs, now. Swing them to the floor, yes. The floor's warm on the soles of my feet, or am I imagining I can feel that?

Ironically, it was his obsession with documentation that made it possible. When you trust no one, everything has to be proved to you. What I know, I know because of Cap. Everything I've done was possible because of him; his record-keeping, his long sleeps, his agents with no authority but the machete and the firetube. Their actions often cut my plans away, but I had good people, and I trusted their reactions. I watched over them, but I couldn't do everything. I let people die because to do otherwise would have revealed myself and then there would have been no hope or help at all for anyone.

I don't know if I can move from the bed, although the neural networks of my limbs are intact. But it's good to know I'm not in the state imagined by him, and that Haze and Haven aren't, either.

There wasn't much I could do. Occasionally I manipulated data so Cap might decide what I wanted him to. But I did too much once, and he suspected one of his most trusted thugs and had him killed as a result.

He's stopped screaming. I have to get ready for him. The cameras are blinking, seeing it all. At least they'll have this record as well as his.

Sometimes I remember the Earth clearly. I remember people. My dad, my mom. I even at times recall a kind and hopeful man, a haunted one, who loved me, and when I'm remembering that man, it's a jolt to think of him as Cap.

And I remember John, which always makes me sad. He so loved Cap. Such betrayal. And Cori, who looked at me with such pity. It was so obvious she thought he'd have her when I was dead. But he betrayed her too, and everyone around him. He destroyed the Earth, killed billions of people, and I never saw it, never guessed. How could I have failed to see it? How?

No, I can't stand. Can't risk falling to the floor. He'd stamp me out like a beetle.

I remember him once telling me there was no difference between the killer of one man and the killer of a million. Indeed, he told me that to kill one man was harder than to kill a million, as you could look into his eyes, like his own father had looked into his mother's as he had raped her. He was talking to me about forgiveness at the time, and I never saw the truth. He was so very convincing.

Unravelling the lies. Is it harder to fool an entire world than to fool a single person? Cap did it all. He killed his own father, of course, and got away with it, and then a world, and still he hasn't stopped.

Did it start with his father, or before that? Genes or events? I'm haunted by my part in it. I must be part of it. I should have seen it. No one else did, but I should have. I was closer than anyone.

Standing up. Maybe if I hold the framework of the gel-driver. Steady. Sit down again. That won't work.

Milton Parker. That was his real name. I was the only one who knew that. He told me in the dressing room that first night. When he became a preacher he changed his name to Reiver Seraph, and later he called himself The Captain. Now he's the Great Lord of Haven. But he started off as Milton Parker.

He's at the door again. Tapping – no, hammering – at it.

I remember how small the dressing room was. Peeling paint the colour of cheese mould, a dead bulb in the ceiling, the whine of the airconditioning. A half-eaten sandwich among his bottles of make-up. I could smell his sweat. I had olfactory nerves – the glial cells we used for my recovery. Why didn't I guess its failure was Cap's doing, pushing me back down as I pulled myself up? I guessed nothing.

But in the dressing room, smelling his sweat. 'Milton,' I said through my voicebox. 'He was a poet, wasn't he? *Paradise Lost.*'

'And *Regained*,' Cap said. 'They forget that.'

'So why change it?'

He had such a smile. I remember his smile, and that first kiss. It was soft, like a woman's kiss. He was gentle . . . I'm crying. Even now, he can do that to me. I love . . . I loved him.

He said, 'It was my father's idea to call me Milton. He thought it sounded grand, the bottle sitting there on the kitchen table. Milton's. He was English, my father. In England, Milton's was a sterilising solution for babies' bottles.'

He'd put on a sad, soulful expression. It was part of his repertoire, but even later, when I was aware of that, it still worked on me. It always worked. You knew that no matter what, *you* were the only one who mattered to him. I don't know how he did it. I'd catch him on the screen, a worldcast to billions, and he'd be talking to me alone, and everyone else was just eavesdropping.

This time, though, for the first and last time, it didn't quite work for him. The strange thing is that if it had, everything might have been different. I'd probably have left the dressing room, or he'd have found me dull. But he went on talking as if it had worked. He said, 'When my father told me that's how he'd named me—'

And Cap stopped. He stopped talking and stared at me.

I was laughing, I couldn't help myself, and the sound of it, my body unmoving and this ridiculous gurgling noise pouring from my mouth, startled him. He'd thought to make me sorry for him, and instead this was happening.

And then, probably in surprise, he began to laugh too. He wasn't used to laughing, and it sounded as odd as I did. And there we were, these two wounded people in that tiny room making stupid noises at each other. Momentarily we were, in a most peculiar way, a pair of entirely normal people. John came in and asked if everything was all right. Neither of us could draw breath to answer him. He couldn't work it out. He stared at the two of us croaking and clucking for a few seconds, then quietly closed the door and left us to it.

That was it. Milton Parker. He never mentioned it again. He said it was too painful. From then on, I called him Cap. I could never call him Reiver.

And here you are, now. Hello, Cap.

HAZE

Reed said, 'We'll search the rest of the Compound.'

Petey seemed to hear him from a distance, his voice bubbling away. Her head swirled. She tried to concentrate on him.

'We can't risk going back into the courtyard. Marten, go with Mexi and Skim. Go clockwise. Check everywhere. I'll go the other way with Crique and Petey. Petey? Are you all right?'

'Yes. I think so.' She was so full, her head bursting. She felt like singing, and there were songs inside her, such music. There were stories. They weren't quite memories, but they were there if she started to wonder or drift. She'd look at this wall and know how it was built; she'd recognise metal but not know what type of metal or how it was made.

Marten said, 'There must be comms equipment somewhere here. Maybe we can contact the woman.'

'She might be dead. Gassed along with everyone else. Petey, are you sure you're all right?'

'I'm fine, Reed.' It was true. She felt wonderful.

At first they kept looking back for her, but after they'd been through the first rooms with their sprawled corpses, they forgot about her entirely.

It was plain to Petey that everyone here was going to be dead. She stared at the dead without curiosity. She'd seen death before, and more than this and worse. What was going on in her head, the reorganisation of her thoughts, was far more involving. The men muttered to each other and checked the dead and moved on.

Many of the rooms were communications suites, and all the comms equipment was open-channelled, the still rooms filled with whistlings and blowings and clicks. Urgent or despairing voices called down the wires now and then, but whoever was out there had mostly given up on any response. Reed and Crique flicked the power off as they went. The gathering silence was stranger than the noise.

There were observation centres too, room after room with walls of screens and rows of chairs, and corpses in the chairs. Just like in the communications rooms, these corpses were randomly slumped forward, pitched back, slid to the floor. Most of the screens were dead, reflecting Petey and Reed and Crique, but some flickered with life. One showed the road blowing with ash, another a view of the AngWat burning. Angkor Wat, she knew, which was confusing. This wasn't Earth, was it? No, they'd left Earth. That was the last she seemed to know. This was called Haze, and one of the fleets had been set for Haze. But the glass building – she knew what it was. It was the Captain's Heart Suite, the very centre of his Foundation.

'I knew they watched everything,' Reed was telling Crique. 'But not to this degree.' He shook his head at the scale of it.

'Who do you think killed them? You think he could be one of these?'

'No. He'll be alone somewhere. He said they were already dead. He's isolated from this.'

Petey looked at their faces, the dead. They had died in pain, eyes wide. She knew how the eyes close against the thought of pain, but open wide at the fact of it – that was her own knowledge and not part of the thing planted in her head. There hadn't been time to try to run, or maybe they'd been paralysed. 'Cyanide?' she murmured. But she couldn't draw up more than that. So much she knew, and so much more she didn't.

Crique glanced at her. 'Maybe,' he answered shortly. Petey could see he knew something of what she did, but he was better able to hold it down.

Reed shrugged. 'What about the woman?' He touched a seated body with his boot, the chair twisting and the body slumping heavily to the floor.

'It sounded like they were both True. She should be alive, somewhere.'

They moved on, through room beyond room. After the corridors of communications and observation rooms, there were dormitories and conference chambers, canteens, washrooms, laboratories, all adrift with the dead.

And then there was a thick double door with a pair of small windows set in it, and through the thick glass Petey saw a row of naked men and women suspended along a girder whose ends were out of sight from the doors. They were hanging by their wrists, which were tied behind them. Their arms were straight, shoulders mostly disjointed, and Petey was glad their heads were down so she couldn't see their faces. Other bodies were strewn in shackles on the floor. Some had clearly died before the gas had been released. Black flecks bristled the floor, which puzzled her until she realised they were dead flies. There was a long tub of water with a plank sloped into it, and a neat row of batteries with wires and clamps. Petey knew what they were for, and she could see Crique did too, and Reed, as they turned away.

They moved on. There were store rooms of weapons. There were dead in corridors and doorways.

And still there was no sign of the man who had done all this.

At a junction in the main corridor, Petey turned left, heading back towards the courtyard. Crique and Reed were talking and went on, not noticing her leave them. She headed towards the light of the archway, and there was the glass-walled Heart again.

From this viewpoint she was looking into another bedroom. She stared at the woman in there, trying to get out of her bed, muttering to herself. Petey could see there was something very wrong with her. She was skinny and weak, her elbows and knees swollen.

Slowly and effortfully, the woman picked up a comms unit and brought it to her lips, and spoke into it for a few moments. A beetle, Petey thought to herself, and the memory brought Duneld so heartwrenchingly to her mind that she gasped aloud. She wondered if she'd ever see him again. She remembered his face, seeing herself in his features, and seeing Reed there, and Marten too. She remembered the lightness of his voice and wanted to hold him, hold him. To tell him she loved him, and how much she did. She didn't think she'd ever said that to Marten, and that thought emptied her.

Exhaustedly, the woman in the bedroom put the unit down again at the side of the bed. It was a hospital bed, surrounded by readouts and screens and drips and drivers. The woman had pulled out all her tubes. Liquid was pooling on the floor.

In the courtyard between Petey and the Heart, a breeze was stirring. From somewhere behind her, from one of the comms rooms, a crumpled ball of white paper tumbled across the green grass of the yard. Petey looked up at the dome, but it was quite intact. The breeze was coming from behind her. The doors to the Compound must have been opened.

The breeze stopped again, and the paper was still.

The woman in the bedroom looked sad and tired. Petey stepped out into the courtyard and went up to the glass, but the woman obviously couldn't see her. One-way glass. Petey couldn't remember exactly how it worked, though. She didn't have everything. She walked around the Heart until she came to the man's room, where she stopped.

He could see her. He was talking, pacing his room, picking things up and replacing them urgently, then going across to the door that led through to the woman's room and pulling at it. It was clearly stuck. All the time he was talking, even though there was no one else there with him. He was old, as old as the woman. Every now and then, when he'd turn and be momentarily facing her, his screwed-up face cleared entirely, and he gave her such a smile.

Petey stood at the glass and stared at the Great Lord. She knew who he was. He was Reiver Seraph, the Captain, the saviour of the world, and the woman was Mary Trulove, the love of all his life.

Petey smiled back at the Captain. Whatever had happened, it would all be all right now. Mary Trulove had called for help, and now she and the Captain would be saved.

In the first room, Mexi arched over, opened her mouth and vomited. There was no blood to be seen, but one of the corpses had fallen back onto the ground and the neck was broken so awkwardly, and the eyes staring straight at her . . .

She saw Marten wasn't bothered by it in the least. He asked if she was all right, but in an odd way, as if he were simply being polite.

Skim gave her a hug, and Mexi realised the comfort was for her too. 'He'll be okay,' Mexi told her. 'Don't worry. Quill's strong.'

But Mexi had seen what had happened to Tyler Hind, driven insane with all the knowledge of the Earth. And Quill had been in Survey, living his life in rock. Even without the Archivirus gnawing away inside him, it had been crazy for him to come to this world of still skies and burning forests. 'He's strong,' she repeated, trying to make it true.

'Maybe. Anyway, it doesn't matter. It looks like we'll all die here. What sort of place is this?'

Mexi didn't know if Skim meant the Compound or the world. She wasn't sure there was much difference. They went on, and after the fourth doorway Mexi found she could look at the dead without retching. They stopped talking, simply moving from room to room, until without warning the lights cut out and everything was dark and silent.

'It's all right,' Marten said, his voice taut. 'Wait.'

Mexi swallowed and waved an arm towards where she thought Skim or Marten might be. Her hand caught a sleeve, and she worked her way to the wrist before realising she was clutching a dead man's hand. She threw the cold limb away and felt a scream of fear rising in her throat.

The light came on again, but more dimly, and the whistling in the wires began again. Skim was white and shaking.

'Look for torches,' Marten said. 'Are you two all right?'

Mexi nodded, not trusting herself to speak. Skim showed a thin smile.

Marten said, 'This is emergency power. Reed must have found the main generator and disabled it. He'll cut the secondary in a moment. There'll be torches here, somewhere. Look for them.'

'Got one,' Skim said, pulling a thick tube from a drawer and thumbing the light to life. The beam shivered, then gradually steadied. And there was darkness again as the emergency power went down, Skim's beam ranging across the chamber.

Marten located a torch and threw it to Mexi, and she held it to help him find another. Her heart was thudding. They moved on. There was no noise but the squeak and tap of their feet.

'Here,' Marten hissed, beckoning them down a short corridor. 'This door's sealed. Nothing else in here even has a lock.'

Skim threw Mexi a brief, empty look, and followed Marten. Mexi stayed back a moment more, thinking of Quill, and of Zelda too. Zelda would have known what to do. Then she went after them.

Marten seared the upper hinge away with a firetube, and Skim dealt with the lower. The door creaked, and Marten kicked it down.

'Here's our man,' he whispered. He shone his torch full on the man's face. The corpse looked up at them, green eyes wide and full of pain and death. There was a makeshift mask over his nose and mouth. On the floor beside his straightbacked wooden chair was a pair of small, empty buckets. One had a grey powdery deposit at its base. Streaks of dark liquid ran down a wall beneath a high air vent which had been blocked off and sealed with wide strips of blue tape. The tape had run off course, been creased back, torn and restarted, layer on layer. Mexi could almost see the man pouring the chemicals into the vent before sealing the duct, fighting off panic as he worked.

Marten picked the mask from him, with its ragged cloth filter, and sniffed at it. 'Charcoal and something. Doesn't look like it gave him long, or made it any easier.'

Skim looked at him, slumped there in death. 'He must have been holding on, hoping we'd be there, waiting for us to pick up a unit and talk to him. What gave him such faith?'

'Someone did,' Mexi said. 'Someone kept us all going.' She had an odd, fleeting sense of companionship with the dead man, and with this woman she'd never seen.

Skim knelt down by the buckets. 'He poured the two constituents into the vent and sealed it before the gas could form and gust back,' she said. 'Efficient aircon. Must have killed everyone else in the Compound through the vents, then finally got to him through the door cracks.' She touched the used rolls of tape with her foot. 'He sealed the vent all right, but he didn't have enough time to seal the whole door frame.'

Mexi could see where he'd run dry of time, the final roll on the floor ribboning to the door frame. He'd almost made it. 'He should have sealed the door first,' she said.

'Couldn't risk it. Might have drawn attention.' Marten ripped at the roll of tape, pulled a length out, the plastic screeching as it came. 'See? Too noisy. He was a brave man.' He touched the dead man's shoulder, then slipped the comms unit off the slack head and put it to his own ear. 'No one there,' he murmured, and dropped it. Skim wandered out of the room.

Watching her go, Mexi said to Marten, 'What's happening here? Do you understand it?'

'No. It's just death and more death.'

'I'm not used to it. You are, aren't you?'

'I—' He paused. 'Yes. Not on this scale, but yes.'

His eyes were wet. Mexi was going to say something, moving towards him, when Skim's voice carried to them from outside.

'Here, quickly. Look.'

Mexi put the comms unit into her pocket, then followed Marten out to the passage, following Skim's voice to where an archway opened out into the bright courtyard. To their right, in the opening of the next archway, Reed was standing with Crique. Both of them were staring at the Heart.

Skim pointed and whispered, 'Look.'

Petey was in the courtyard, up close to the glass, close to the Great Lord, who was apparently talking to her, though the courtyard's outspeakers weren't active, and there was nothing to be heard.

Mexi said, 'What's she doing out there? Doesn't she realise it's dangerous?'

'Out there?' Marten said, looking at Mexi. 'She isn't out there. Don't you see?'

And Mexi saw it. Marten was right. Petey wasn't in the courtyard at all. She was standing with the Captain, inside the Heart.

'She's a little crazy, Petey,' Cap said, his voice full of sorrow. He had a voice like honey, Petey thought. Warm and golden and runny and sweet. 'I love her – you know how I love her – but sometimes she's like this. I've let my grip falter because of Mary, though I'd never blame her for any of it. I let a few others take control, over the years, and only now I've found out what's been going on in my name. Killings . . .'

He sighed, and Petey wanted to comfort him. He was old, but like a child, astonished at the nature of the world.

'If I can only get to her, I know she has a communication device. I know it. She must have been—' He had to fight to control the trembling in his voice. Petey could see the emotion there.

'—She must have been talking to someone. There's been an error. She's been talking, and I'm cut off.'

'Why don't we just go outside?' Petey said. 'Open the door again. I'll tell them what's happened.'

'I feel safer in here. You understand me, but some of your friends might not. There isn't time to explain it to them. This way will be quicker. I can call—'

He was rummaging through drawers, frustrated. 'No weapons in here, that's the trouble. Nothing to cut through the lock.'

'I have a weapon,' Petey said. She held out the firetube towards him.

He was radiant, accepting it. 'Thank you, Petey.' He kissed her hand. His lips, his touch, were soft and gentle. 'Now, once we get to Mary, we can get through to the lords and tell them to lay down their weapons. We can start again, Petey.' He stood by the door, ready with the firetube. 'Are you ready?'

She nodded.

'I'll open the door, and I want you to go through first. I want you to sit with her. When she's like this, I don't know what she might do. We have to sit her down and talk to her. If I can only talk to her. Only talk, Petey. Anything in the world can be resolved by talking it through. Fighting resolves nothing. You, Petey, say nothing. Leave the talking to me. I may have to speak to her in a way you don't expect, just to shock her out of her state. You won't worry, will you?'

'No.'

'Good. From the moment I saw you, I knew I could rely on you. Now. Here we go.' He sent a small stream of light at the door, and pushed it open.

The woman on the bed said, 'Hello, Cap,' and then, seeing Petey, 'Who are you? I haven't seen you before.'

Petey said nothing. Mary looked sad and drained. Petey wanted to put her arm around her.

'Now, Mary,' Cap said. 'Let's all sit down on the bed together.'

'Cap—' Mary tried to get up, but Petey gently helped her back down again. She wanted to tell her it was all going to be all right now, but remembered what Cap had said.

'That's right. Now, Mary. Where is that comms unit? Ah, here it is, under your pillow. That's good.'

Mary said, 'No use to you. It won't transmit beyond the Compound.'

'You evidently transmitted beyond it, my darling.'

'Not with this. Mamoud took that unit.'

'Ah. I should have known, shouldn't I? He'd never meet my eye, that one. But never mind. Water over the parapet.' He closed his hand round the device, smiling warmly. 'Firetube and comms unit, and Mary and Petey. I think I have everything I need. Why don't the two of you just sit here quietly together while I go and sort it all out?'

He closed the door behind him.

His voice wasn't quite the same, just then, it struck Petey. She looked at Mary. Mary Trulove was staring at her with the most curious expression.

Something here was not right, Petey thought.

Mary Trulove said, though her voice was barely a whisper, 'Petey?'

'I've deactivated the defensive system. You can see that. You know I wasn't lying to you.'

The voice of the Great Lord booming across the courtyard from the Heart was slightly dissociated from the movement of his lips, Marten noticed. Petey hadn't returned from the other room. He assumed the Great Lord had locked her in there, but why had she given him the firetube? Why had she walked in there? Mexi flexed her hand in his grip, and he realised how tightly he was clutching it. Had Petey deserted him all over again?

No. No, she hadn't. He made himself remember the first time he had seen the Great Lord of Haven. He had sat with all those other half-children in the great auditorium, after the beatings and the deaths of his education, to be told by this gentle man how privileged he was to have been chosen for a lord. He had sat there and wanted to believe it. He had looked around and seen all the others believing every word of it, hearing how their lives past and yet to be were justified in a few words by this man, the Great Lord.

Marten was here now because he and a few others hadn't believed it, and also because of Petey. She had never deserted him. Not then and not now. In his heart Marten knew that.

'You deactivated it to draw her in,' Reed yelled back across the courtyard.

'Maybe someone else could speak,' the Great Lord said gently.

'No. Just me.' Reed looked around, checked everyone. He looked at Marten for a fraction longer than the others, and Marten nodded. Reed was acknowledging his closeness to Petey. Reed yelled, 'Talk to me.'

The Captain hesitated. Marten found it confusing, thinking of him as the Captain when he was the Great Lord of Haven. Memory and knowledge were different things, he realised, and neither was necessarily the truth.

'Okay, stay out there, then.' The Captain took breath. 'I need to talk to my lords. You have to patch me in to the Compound's main comms lines.'

'Send Petey out, Reiver.'

There was a moment of silence, and the Captain nodded.

His voice came back as a whisper. 'Reiver. Well, well. Reiver Seraph. I haven't heard that name in a very long time.' His face emptied briefly, and he looked truly old. But his gaze sharpened swiftly, and he said, 'The Archivirus, hmm? It's been brought here to Haze?'

Marten looked at Reed, and saw they were all looking at him, Mexi and Skim and Crique too. Reed was right. The Great Lord was just a man, and they had to see him as no more than that.

Reiver Seraph gathered himself. 'Very well. All I need to do is tell the lords to hold off. Once I've done that, we can all calm down.'

'Send Petey out and we'll calm down.'

Seraph nodded. 'All right,' he said. 'How about this? Patch me through or I'll kill her.'

'Kill her and that's the end of it.' Reed rubbed sweat from the palm of a hand against his leg. No one else moved.

'I don't think so. You'll lose this in a few hours anyway. My lords will arrive and you'll be overrun. You think the Archivirus will save you? No matter how quickly it spreads, the memories won't be enough. History proves I'm a saviour.'

'Then why don't you simply kill her, and sit there and wait.'

'Fine. I have always done what I promised to do. I shall do that.'

Reed didn't answer. Then, his voice a fraction lower, he said, 'I can't patch you through. The power's down in the Compound. I shut down the generators.'

'Then you can reactivate them.'

'Not the way I shut them down.' Reed shot a beam of light from the firetube at the Heart's glass, which sprayed sparks out into the courtyard.

'All right. There's a generator here in the Heart. You can bring me a power cable from the central transmitter and a communicator. I'll send my message, and when I'm done, you can have the woman. You have five minutes.' Seraph sat down and lowered the comms device, making a show of not waiting for an answer.

Reed turned his back on the courtyard and said, 'He'll have to open the Heart's door to get the communicator and cable.'

'Power cable's thick,' Skim said. 'He's old. He won't be able to lift it himself.'

Mexi said, 'No chance of us doing anything, though. Whoever's

409

holding the cable, they'll need two hands. He won't stand in any line of fire.'

'But once the cable's in, the door will be propped open,' Reed said. 'He won't be able to close it again.'

'Not wide open,' Marten said. 'A handspan. What are you thinking, Reed?'

'I'm not sure yet.' Reed switched the torch on and started walking down the corridor, following the beam into the darkness. 'Mexi, stay here and watch him. If anything happens, yell. The rest of you, come with me.'

Marten caught up with him. 'What are you planning to do, Reed?'

'I said, I'm not sure.'

'Yes, you are. Tell me. Petey's my mother.'

'And she's in my heart too. But Reiver intends to kill her. Can you think of a way to stop him?'

'No,' Marten said in the darkness.

'Then leave me to do my best.'

And back in the heart of the Compound, in darkness spotted with beams and circles of light, Marten pulled cables from a central transmitter until he found one as thick as a thigh. The shadows of corpses crawled all over him as he unsocketed it and hauled it clear. 'Here,' he said, holding up the fat tube by its insulated ribbing. It was heavy. Reed had already picked up a communicator.

Reed said, 'Good. Crique, Skim, feed this out to us. When it runs out, take another cable—'

'I know what to do, Reed,' Skim said shortly. 'I know what connectors look like. I could do your end better than you. It's crazy me being back here in the dark.' She stood up. 'I know comms equipment a lot better than you, Reed. I could rig the communicator, give him a shock—'

'I'm doing this, Skim,' Reed said sharply. 'Thanks, but I'm doing it myself.'

'You're not under control. I'm the logical one. You're too close to it. He's got Petey. Marten's got Mexi to think of, too, and Crique's got a wife. You know what's going to happen, don't you? I'm the only free one. It should be me.'

Marten listened to her and thought of Quill. Skim showed nothing of her feelings, but in the darkness it came through in her voice. Skim had lost Quill and she was empty.

'I don't know where I am any more,' she said. 'My head's full of a vanished world, and I'll never see my own again. Let me do something. Let me do this.'

'No,' Reed told her. 'I'm doing it.'

Crique started to say something, but Reed cut him off. 'You still don't trust me, do you? This has to be me. Seraph thinks I'm crazy, I'll do something stupid. That's fine, it's what he has to think. Anyone else goes up to the glass, it won't be the same.' As he talked, he was hauling on the cable, Marten pulling with him, and they were through the door and round the corner, out of the others' sight, and tugging the cable was taking all their energy. They pulled it in silence, until the light of the archway was in view, Mexi's silhouette stamped there.

Before they reached her, Reed stopped and set the cable down. Marten thought he was just taking breath, but then he said, 'Marten, whatever happens, I don't want her crying for me. No one to cry for me.'

Marten frowned.

'Listen. Tell her I knew about the Haze. It was the Haze killing the children in Nepenth. Part of my job was to make sure the machines worked properly. I couldn't risk exposing myself by sabotaging them. It was only when Duneld was born that it hit me that I'd been wrong. I should have done something. Crique's son. All the others. I killed them.'

'They would have sent someone else. It doesn't matter now,' Marten said uncomfortably.

'It will do, Marten.'

'Nothing's going to happen to you, Reed. We'll be behind you. You can tell Petey yourself. She'll understand. She left me, remember? She knows what it's like to—'

But Reed was lifting the cable again. 'Tell Crique, too. Tell him he was right all along not to trust me. Tell them I'm sorry.'

In the darkness, Skim said to Crique, 'We could disconnect it now. Be sure Seraph can't transmit.'

'No. Reed knows what he's doing.'

'You really trust him?'

'Yes.'

They fed the cable out, its stiff weight dragging noisily on the floor. It snaked and twisted, catching on the feet and arms and heads of the dead, so that they had to pull the dead flesh clear. The bodies were lighter than the cable. They laboured without speaking, finding it more comfortable to work in the dark than in the patchwork of brilliance and total black that the torches provided. Skim found herself thinking about Naddy Harke, how he would have complained at such labour. In a moment of silence between hauls, while she was connecting a new length of cable, a sound made her pause. 'Someone's there,' she said sharply, and raised her voice. 'Who's that?'

Crique shot his torch around the room. They both squinted, but the torchlight was too sudden, blinding them. When at last they could see, there was nothing. Crique switched the torch off.

'I did hear it,' Skim said, as her eyes readjusted, and the darkness slowly shook out the room's detail again.

'So did I,' murmured Crique, feeding out the cable steadily. 'Whatever it was, it's gone now.'

'Drop it there, Petey, just there on the floor.'

Inside the Heart, Petey let the heavy cable fall where the Captain told her, against the edge of the glass, then stood up. He put his arm around her, like a father.

Outside, Reed and Marten laid their final loop of matching cable down on the grass. She wanted to say something to them, but the firetube was digging hard into her side.

The cable lay in a coil on the grass out there, its free end resting against the glass. Marten touched Reed's arm before walking back to the shelter of the archway, and turned to face Petey from there. She looked at her son and saw the sadness in his face, and realised with a shock that he was not a boy any longer, but a man, and that he knew she was about to die. She wanted to tell him how sorry she was for everything.

'Reed, stay where you are,' the Captain said. 'One of you, fetch the others. I want to be able to see all of you.'

He was completely without tension, Petey realised. He waited patiently, and then, when all of them were standing in plain sight, he asked her, 'Is that it, Petey? Don't lie to me. I'll know.'

She nodded. Mexi, Marten, Skim, Crique and Reed. She'd failed them all.

'Now. No one moves, or she's dead. Understand? Reed, pull all your pockets out and let me see you're unarmed. Good. Now show me the communicator, and keep your other hand palm out, show me it's empty.'

Petey looked at Reed's strong, empty hand with its calluses and lines, and yearned to fill it again with hers. She wanted to hold him again. That time had passed, though. The glass shivered and a long crack opened in it, the crack through which Petey had stepped.

The Captain said, 'Throw in the communicator first. Keep both your hands outside.'

Reed tossed the unit inside. It fell to the floor, the Captain making no move towards it, his gaze remaining on Reed. 'Now bring the main cable in and connect it for me. Move very slowly and keep your hands in sight.'

Reed stepped up to the glass. He picked up the cable by the socket, and reached a hand inside the Heart.

Petey gasped at the suddenly increased pressure of the firetube at her side. Reed looked up.

'Concentrate on what you're doing, Reed.'

Away behind Petey, something moved. She turned her head fractionally, and out of the corner of her eye, she saw the door of Mary's room opening.

Reed's eyes shifted. The cables joined each other in a faint click, and a small yellow light illuminated on the socket of the Heartside line. The small communicator hummed and its active light flared on.

The Captain smiled. 'Now, Reed. Step slowly back.'

In the doorway, Reed started to rise.

With sudden strength, the Captain swung Petey towards Reed, pulling the firetube up as he shot, its beam sweeping in an arc to take them both down together.

Petey saw Mary Trulove propped in the doorway. Her mouth opened and she yelled, her voice loud with fury, 'Milton! Hey, Milton Parker!'

The Captain stopped as if lightning-struck. The firetube beam screeched against the glass by Petey's ear.

'Milton! You hear me, Milton?'

The Captain jerked and dropped to a squat to dry-retch, over and again. The firetube beam died.

Petey ducked and ran to the corner of the room.

Behind the Captain, Mary Trulove gasped and fell awkwardly, the effort of getting there and then the cry costing all the strength she had in her. Her arms and legs crumpled almost weightlessly and her head struck the doorframe with an egg-cracking sound. She blinked and her eyes dimmed. The Captain glanced back at her, then shuddered and stood up, holding the firetube firmly again.

'Reed!' Petey yelled. 'Get back.'

Reed wasn't moving, though, neither forward nor back. He simply held himself rigid in the glass doorway, gripping the glass tightly as the Captain shot him. His chest opened with blood, and he gasped away all the air there was in him in one long breath, and slid down into the blood. The glass tried to close on him, but his slumped body held it wide. The glass opened and closed, opened and closed. Reed's dead, Petey thought. And she thought of elevator doors.

'Stay there,' the Captain shrieked at Petey, and through the glass door at the others too. He knelt and picked up the small communicator, and backed to the far end of the room, and opened a door where Petey hadn't seen a door at all. The glass doors were still opening and closing on Reed's body. His knuckles were white, holding him there even though he was dead.

'Petey, stay here.' The Captain was composed again, but he looked ill, wiping bile from his mouth with the back of a hand. Petey could smell the acid. 'Sit. Face the glass. Don't move, don't look back, and I won't kill you too. You know you can believe me, don't you?'

She nodded.

'I'll be watching you through the doorway. I'm going to talk for just a few minutes, and I'll be back.'

And he was gone.

Petey looked at Reed's body. Beyond it, Crique and Marten were starting to move across the courtyard towards the open door of the Heart, Crique wide-mouthed and screaming. Mexi and Skim were moving to right and left.

Petey whispered, 'Mary?' She could just turn her head enough to see that Mary Trulove's neck was broken.

Marten was on the grass, ripping the sockets of the power cables apart. Petey waited for the pain of the firetube, but nothing came. Crique was behind her at the concealed door, cursing.

'Round the back. There's another way out into the courtyard. That's why he wanted us all in sight here. He's gone.'

Mary Trulove's mouth dropped open and a long, deep, rasping breath began coming out of her. Petey crawled across the room and took her hand, and stared at Reed and began to cry.

It's almost over. Have I done enough? Have I done anything?

I'm glad I met Petey. They say the worst thing for a parent is to outlive their children. My father ... odd to think of him now, at my very end. I used to wonder what he was thinking when he killed us all, or thought he did. Fathers and mothers and children. In the end, that's all we have and all we are, but still, it's so, so very much.

I miss him so hard. I saw how very much he loved us all, as he killed us. He was crying. I wish I could cry again.

Hold my hand, please. Tightly.

Quill blinked and clutched at the seat.

Are you all right?

'Crise, I thought you'd gone, Scheck.'

And leave you? Anyway, where is there for me to go? And where's everybody else?

Quill pushed the car door open and sat staring at the street, trying to make it make sense, to remember.

The crash, he remembered that. It hadn't been too bad in the forest, after that. The thick canopy of trees had lowered enough to make him feel secure, and along with the heat, he'd been able to think of the smoke and fire as molten rock. But then they'd left the fire behind, and the endless roads of the city had unnerved him. And then—

'What happened, Scheck? Where are the others? Skim. Is she all right? I don't remember.'

If you don't, I don't. Sorry.

Quill stood up, forcing himself to look at the sky. He gripped the metal skin of the vehicle, comforted by its curve and a small detail of the window frame that was like a weld in a coffin. Something dropped from his pocket, but it didn't matter.

Like I said, Quill, I'm sorry. I'm dead. I'm a passenger. You're my coffin. You're the one in charge.

'Well, don't leave me again. Scheck? Scheck?'

Okay, I'm here. I'm just a little sleepy.

'Stay awake, will you?'

I'll try.

Quill started to walk back towards the main avenue.

'Which way now, do you think?'

That looks like the outer part of the Heart Suite. Reiver Seraph, the Captain. Evangelical politician back on Earth. The epicentre of his operation was the Heart Suite. He and President Speke masterminded the fleets to Haze and Haven, and the Restoration of Earth. Reiver Seraph was a great man. He—

'Okay, Scheck. Let's assume that's where they went.'

Quill speeded up, trying to keep himself under control. He thought of the trees as dendritic pyrolusite, the stretches of grass as Pelée's hair. The buildings were vast crystals of tourmaline and barite, and that was not the sky above him. He chanted rocks and minerals to himself, but couldn't concentrate. It wasn't the scale of things, and it wasn't the space all around him. The emptiness he was aware of was Skim's absence. He was thinking of Skim. Where was she?

Around him, a wind was growing. More than a wind – the fire was approaching. He could smell it like the fumes of crusting lava. Roadside trees were flailing their branches, and birds gusted in the air, whirls of dark almandine held in mica. He staggered on, slapped by the wind. He wanted it to be still, but it surged and threw him face down to the ground.

Hugging the earth tight, he thought of Naddy. Naddy would have loved this wild openness. Skim had lost Naddy to rock, and now she was losing Quill to the sky.

415

He held his cheek to the ground and closed his eyes, unable to move, and pulled his arms and legs in to his chest, making himself a pebble. 'Scheck,' he said out loud. 'Help me.'

I can't help you with this. You know I can't.

Quill stayed there, then raised his head and forced himself to open his eyes. The wind thumped at him, and the hardness of it helped. He pushed himself to his hands and knees, trembling, and then, slowly, got to his feet and stood there while the wind pummelled him.

'Skim,' he whispered. 'I'm not losing you. I'm coming.' He took a step against the wind, and the next, and kept on walking. The building ahead was a crystal of aragonite.

I don't think so. It has five sides, Quill. Aragonite is pseudo-hexagonal.

'Thank you, Scheck. You think of a pentagonal crystal, you tell me. Anything else?'

Yes. Let's assume this block of aragonite is not a good place. This is Haze, remember. Reiver Seraph was headed for Haven. The Heart Suite ought not to be here at all.

Quill pushed the doors open. The wind rushed briefly in behind him and then the doors closed it away.

After the streets with their roar of wind and crackle of approaching fire, it was silent inside, and it was dark too, which eased him. Walking into the heart of the darkness, he started to feel whole again. The bodies didn't surprise him. He'd seen the gassed before, the sudden dead in cracked rock pockets of methane and carbon monoxide.

When he saw Skim there, hauling on cables, he watched her for a few minutes, not needing to say anything. For now, it was enough to know she was alive. He wasn't ready to talk to anyone except Scheck yet. He knew what he wanted to say to her, but not how to say it. She was alive and safe, and that made him stronger. He carried on walking. There were archways of light, but he avoided them. He walked on among the dead, feeling calm and increasingly steady. He felt himself rising as if through water, holding his breath, waiting for the light of the sun to appear and the surface to break warm above him.

And then in the gloom he saw a living man, throwing down a comms unit, hurrying towards him.

That's the Captain, Quill. That's Reiver Seraph.

'How can it be? He was hundreds of years ago.'

You'll have to ask him, Quill. Though maybe that's not a good idea.

Quill started towards a side corridor, but Seraph had seen him.

'Who are you?' Seraph said. 'You're not one of mine.'

He took a firetube from a pocket, Quill searching his own pockets before remembering the sound of something falling to the ground out on the streets. The weapon. He held the other thing in his hand.

'Put that down, whatever it is,' Seraph told him sharply.

Quill held up the case, though, and Seraph laughed. His laugh echoed among the dead. 'You're Quill! Perfect. You've brought me the Archivirus.' He held out his hand. 'Give it to me. Quickly, or I'll kill you and take it anyway.'

Carefully, Quill held it out in the palm of his hand. He felt himself rising, rising, the sun's brightness billowing down towards him. Seraph came cautiously forward, the firetube pointed at him.

Quill moved his thumb to cover the last blister.

'No—' Seraph began.

Quill squeezed his thumb down, hard. The glass cracked, barely audibly.

Seraph reared back, dropping his weapon, and in the darkness Quill watched a silvery spray of dust blossom from the case, swelling into the air. It filled the passage, glittering brilliantly, engulfing the two of them in motes of silver and chrome, and Quill knew that everything was going to be all right. He took a long breath in the bright, bright sun.

The gleaming dust began to fall and disappear. Reiver Seraph sat on the ground, gasping, and looked up at Quill.

'You—' he murmured, breathlessly.

'I'm crazy already. It can't make any difference to me.' Quill took the old man's arm and pulled him to his feet.

'They're coming,' Reiver Seraph whispered. 'My lords are coming.'

But it will be too late.

At the end of the day, they used to say. And at the end of this day, this long day, what have I done? I have done my best. I have created a world that is, or was, fair. There was no preferential treatment. Everyone laboured under the same conditions, more or less. No one suffered – as I did so very much – for the sins of their fathers.

I had my day. Our Lord had more than that, and what did He achieve that I have not? I never deserted my people. I was always there, as best I could be. The flaws I may have had were not of my doing. They were Our Lord's. What I achieved, I achieved despite those flaws.

I can feel it coming. To know all that was known. To know, like Our Lord, everything that was known by man . . .

What was my downfall? It was love, no more than that. It was the desire to share my quiet times with another. In the end, the story was the same. It was the end of the Garden. But it was not my fault.

Here it is, rising like vomit. As I think, it comes. I have to block it.

Look at the floor. It's just stone, a stone floor, just granite, a simple, coarse-grained igneous rock, and I can see a xenolith in it, and there may be sphene there, and magnetite and apatite . . .

Block it. My father. My father. All the dead. My father, and John, Jake, my mother . . . I had no choice. I was the martyr, not them. What did any of them suffer, compared to me? What was their pain, compared to mine?

The sky, then. Think of the pure, empty sky, with nothing but clouds, cumulus, cirrocumulus, cirrostratus, altocumulus, altostratus, stratocumulus, nimbostratus . . .

Block it. I can do it. I can hold it all at bay, like I always have done. I held my father at bay, and after he was gone, nothing could come near me. I am Reiver Seraph. I am the Captain, the Great Lord of Haven, and I can . . . do . . .

HAZE

Quill blinked at the sudden light that was everywhere.

He let Reiver Seraph fall and sat down on the stone floor facing him. Seraph was kneeling and muttering to himself.

At a noise, Quill looked up to see Skim running along the passage towards him. She stopped dead, glanced at Reiver Seraph, then grinned for a long time before saying, 'Power's back, Quill. It's good to see you.' She wiped her cheeks with the back of a hand. 'I'm crying. Look what you've done to me. I thought—' She took a breath. 'And you've been busy. Are you all right?'

'I think so.'

'I thought I'd lost you.'

'Scheck came back.' With an effort, Quill stood up and rubbed his eyes. 'I thought I'd lost you, Skim. Found everything but lost you.' He took her hand. It felt hot as fire, full of life. 'This may be a ridiculous question, but do you think you could live with Scheck? Not that he exists. I know that.'

Hell of a proposal there, Quill. And you're the one of us with social skills.

'You can't live without him,' she said gently. 'I don't think I have a choice.'

'You have a choice.' And looking at her face, Quill knew that her smile was the sun he'd been rising to, bright and glorious.

'And I've made it,' she said. 'I want you, Quill.'

Marten pushed the glass door wide until it locked open, and saw Petey crouched beside Reed's body.

'It was my fault,' she said emptily. She touched Reed's hand, folded it in hers. Marten watched her trying to make the dead hand grip her own.

Marten looked around the small room. The empty bed looked odd with its crumpled sheets and tubes and wires. The room smelt dank and of sweat. It struck him that there were no pictures here, no papers or books, no clues at all to the existence of a person. He remembered as a child being shown the Great Lord at rest here in the Heart, through the glass. He remembered the man's sleeping profile. He had seemed like a perfect father, a man you wanted to be proud of you. And what he had been was a monster.

Mexi interrupted his thoughts, murmuring, 'I heard Reed saying something to you, Marten.'

'It was nothing,' Marten said shortly.

Petey looked up at him. From her face, it was clear that she had caught his tone. Seeing her anxiety and doubt, Marten felt even more jealous of Reed.

Petey said, 'If he told you something before he died, I want to know.'

'He said he was sorry. That's all.'

'What for?'

His mother was still hopelessly clutching Reed's cold hand. Marten felt betrayed, that everyone he had trusted had deserted him. He looked away. The power was on again. Against the light, the courtyard seemed dark and shadowy. The sky above the dome was blazing orange. Marten closed his eyes and took a long breath, and his head seemed to clear. When he opened his eyes, his mother had her head down, sobbing.

He knelt and touched her shoulder. He said, 'Petey?' and she raised her head.

'He didn't say why. I don't think it matters. In the end, we know he did his best. We all did our best.'

He glanced at Mexi and thought he'd never seen such a smile as hers. She said, 'Yes. Let's lay him out here on the grass, Petey. Not half in, half out. He should be dignified.'

Marten helped them move Reed, then saw Crique coming across the courtyard, holding Reiver Seraph by the arm. The Great Lord was stumbling, his eyes screwed tightly closed, singing rhythmically but barely audibly to himself.

Marten asked Crique, 'What's he saying?'

'I think it's called praying,' Crique said. He released Seraph's arm and the old man crumpled to the ground, hunched in and curled small as a child. Marten could just about make out the words of the unceasing chant. His eyes screwed tightly closed, hands over his ears, Reiver Seraph was muttering, 'Myfathermyfathermyfathermyfather . . .'

Mexi looked at Quill, a thought blooming in her head. 'There's something I want to ask you,' she said. 'The Archivirus . . .'

Marten shook his head. 'Don't you have enough of the past inside you?'

Quill said, 'The last blister's gone. Is that what you mean? There's just me, and what passes from me to others.'

'No, not that,' Mexi said. 'There's a word.' In her mind it sounded alien and exotic. She wondered if she had it right. She tried to remember how Zelda had said it, but all she could recall were Zelda's face and the gentleness in her voice. 'Icarus,' she said carefully. 'It means nothing to me. Does it mean anything?' She thought of Zelda, of the storyless story the old woman had carried all those years and finally passed on to her. That too was part of the past, and as she watched Quill waiting for Scheck to answer him, she realised she didn't want her own memories overridden and lost. Icarus did mean something to her. What else it meant would come back, of course, as everything inside Quill eventually would. But not yet, and not to her.

Above them all, the flaming sky streamed with ash and the clouds scudded past. Mexi felt dizzy and unbalanced. She took Marten's hand and gripped it tightly, and the moment seemed to freeze with his sudden smile and Quill's mouth half opening. She looked up through the glass of the Heart. The sky fizzed away, out of reach and faster, it seemed, than time.

'No,' she said to Quill, quickly, looking back down to the ground at her feet. 'Don't tell me. I don't want to know.'

ACKNOWLEDGEMENTS

These things at the ends of books often sound pretentious and deliberately opaque and probably irritate you as much as they irritate me, so I apologise to the irritated. I haven't the room here to explain.

This book took even longer than usual to get completed, and nearly didn't, for reasons beyond the normal excuses.

There are two sets of thanks I'd like to make, some of the recipients having little or nothing directly to do with the book, although there is much crossover. Without the first acknowledgees, the book might not have had the chance to exist.

Because he was there before anyone else, and simply wonderful, Kim Speed. Simon Wooden and Karen Garvin for their unquestioning and instant reactions. The emergency surgical team at North Middlesex Hospital and the nurses of Nightingale West ward. Tony Taylor for being exactly what I needed. Michael Howlett of the Zito Trust for advice and valued support. Jeffrey Arthur, David Symes and Vicky Cann. I'd like to acknowledge Ernest Meads, though I never had the privilege of meeting him.

Terri Brown for dealing with everything in her usual magnificent way while I was unavailable. Lucinda Cooper and Ella Colley and all the people at Tetherdown school and elsewhere who pulled together for us. Debbie and Peter Garvin for their love and help, and Graeme and Sarah Levy too.

Dr Mike Zybutz for special kindness out of the blue. Michael Brodtman and Naomi Fine for a week of tranquillity in which to write, prior to all of this.

Also, equally immensely – and here's the blurred crossover – Elise Valmorbida, Steve Mullins, Anne Aylor, Annemarie Neary, Sally Ratcliffe, Aimee Hansen, Sue Edwards, Adam Roberts, James and Lou Lovegrove, Simon Spanton, Antony Harwood, Tony Cullen.

Above all, Tina.

The Archivirus had its genesis in an experiment by the artist Eduardo Kac, reported in *The Body Electric* by James Geary.

One of the catalysts for this book was Cambodia's tragic history. My reading included, most significantly, *The Gate* by Francois Bizot and *Children of Cambodia's Killing Fields* compiled by Dith Pran.

The quote on page 361 is from *The Charge of the Light Brigade* by Alfred, Lord Tennyson.